THE
Second Chance
BRIDES
COLLECTION

Nine Historical Romances Offer New Hope for Love

THE
Second Chance
BRIDES
COLLECTION

Lauralee Bliss, Angela Breidenbach,
Ramona K. Cecil, Pamela Griffin, Pam Hillman,
Laura V. Hilton, Grace Hitchcock,
Amber Stockton, Liz Tolsma

BARBOUR BOOKS
An Imprint of Barbour Publishing, Inc.

Print ISBN 978-1-68322-246-0

eBook Editions:
Adobe Digital Edition (.epub) 978-1-68322-248-4
Kindle and MobiPocket Edition (.prc) 978-1-68322-247-7

Published by Barbour Books, an imprint of Barbour Publishing, Inc., P.O. Box 719, Uhrichsville, Ohio 44683, www.barbourbooks.com

Our mission is to publish and distribute inspirational products offering exceptional value and biblical encouragement to the masses.

 Member of the
Evangelical Christian
Publishers Association

Printed in Canada.

Contents

Love in the Crossfire

by Lauralee Bliss

Acknowledgments

To all our veterans, past and present, you are true heroes and patriots.
Thank you for the freedom you preserve.
With thanks to Tamela Hancock Murray and Grace Hitchcock
for allowing me to be a part of this collection.

Where the Spirit of the Lord is, there is liberty.
2 CORINTHIANS 3:17

Chapter 1

hy must you leave?"

She waited what seemed like a lifetime for the answer, even as she watched him clean his musket, check his cartridge box, and fill a haversack with biscuits, still warm from the morning's baking. Finally he turned, his stark blue eyes she once found so engaging narrowed by fierce determination, reflecting the orange flame of the candle resting on the table. His lips she once felt on her own let out a sigh of resignation. His crop of blond hair stood on end. His hand reached out to caress her cheek as he murmured, "You know why, Gretchen. It is my duty."

Gretchen shook her head at the words uttered from the lips of her fiancé, Rolf Braun, before he left to join up with the Hessian troops in pursuit of the colonists near Brooklyn. Now she gazed at the parchment reporting his death in battle some weeks ago. Instead of grief, anger burst forth from her soul. All his words of duty, of bravery, of fighting for a cause she now questioned. What had it brought but his death at the hand of those whose cause she now contemplated?

"Ach, very sad," her papa murmured, pointing to the parchment on the table. "You must be so grieved, *liebste Tochter.*"

Gretchen liked hearing his endearment of her. "Thank you, Papa. I will leave my sadness in *Gott's* hands." She would do as she did every day—immerse herself in the daily chores and try not think of Rolf or the war ravaging the countryside. Yet the scars of war were everywhere. It was seen in the faces of people, in the news whispered about, in the weary men marching off to battle, many of whom never returned. Fear lay thick in the air, as did the uncertainty. Before Rolf left, Gretchen hid from her fiancé the parchment she owned: a formal Declaration against the mother country, signed this past summer, and forwarded to the king of England. She was able to obtain a copy from a printer in Trenton and couldn't help but feel pride at the words. She thought Rolf believed in the cause of Independence, until one day when she broached the subject.

"What they have done by this Declaration amounts to treason!" he scolded. "We have signed our death warrants to pompous frivolers of Philadelphia who know nothing of the cost of war. England is the most powerful nation on earth. We can never be independent of the mother country that gave us life and love, no more than one can separate from their own *mutter.*"

Gretchen wanted to discuss it more but found Rolf's staunch opposition in word and deed overpowering. Instead she silenced her tongue and bowed her head. Inwardly she gave a private voice to the words that spoke about the injustice suffered as subjects of England, the promise of a new way of life apart from tyranny, the hope of freedom. But a soon-to-be bride dared not contradict her fiancé, even if her heart felt differently. Instead it fueled her doubt over marrying the headstrong Loyalist sympathizer.

She gazed once more at the news of Rolf's death. Now there was no need for any doubt but only wonder for the future. How she wished life could be as easy to follow as the writings in a book. Even now she gazed at her mother's Bible sitting on the table beside the parchment. There were always the sacred words, giving her the answers to her questions, a peace in her heart, the joy of gladness for sorrow, and hope for a new future even if everything looked bleak. It was those words she must cling to, even if all else failed.

Gretchen sighed and moved to the table to finish rolling out the day's biscuits and then make the dough for a delicious *kuchen* dessert that Papa liked so well. Cutting out the biscuits, one by one, brought back the memory of Rolf filling his haversack with a dozen before he left to join the troops. *"These will keep me and more. There is nothing like your biscuits, Gretchen."* A smile lit his face. He turned to head out the door.

"Gott sei mit derr," she had murmured, whispering a prayer for him before the heavy wooden door closed.

Now he was gone forever. A page in her life's book had turned.

Gretchen began gathering the ingredients for the cake. Flour, brown sugar, leavening, spices, and then she noticed the empty egg basket. *I forgot to gather the eggs today!* She would need several for the kuchen, and for Papa's midday meal.

Wiping her hands on a towel, Gretchen took her heavy cloak from a hook on the wall. Hopefully the hens were still laying. It amazed her they still had chickens, what with the ongoing conflict. She had heard of people who surrendered their farms and their livelihood to soldiers from both sides. Some had their homes confiscated for use as hospitals or officers' quarters. Others had livestock taken to feed the hungry soldiers. But the battlefield was far from them, except for a small garrison of Hessian soldiers in the nearby town of Trenton. They were there to keep the peace and not cause problems, Papa had explained.

A cold wind whistled as she gingerly stepped outside, cutting through the cloak she clutched around her. A few silvery snowflakes spiraled down from the graying skies. She hurried over to the henhouse, praying there were some eggs. The henhouse was a finely crafted little building Papa had fashioned out of short plank boards. She heard the faint clucking and scratching of the hens inside. Nearby stood the barn and the horses safely sheltered within.

Out of the corner of her eye she thought she saw a dark shadow pass before the open doorway of the barn. Raw cold swept over her, and not from the December chill. She glanced again at the door but saw nothing. *It must be my mind playing games,* she reasoned, forcing herself to concentrate on her duties.

"Chick, chick, chick!" she softly called, throwing dried corn. The chickens swarmed at the seed, allowing her time to stir through the nests of straw in search of eggs. When she finished her duty, she turned and again saw a dark shadow before the barn entrance. This time the shadow did not disappear but instead came into the light of day. A man stood there, wearing a wool coat with large buttons and a tricorn hat. In one hand he held a musket.

Her knees weakened. She grabbed the doorway of the henhouse. "Oh dearest Gott, help me."

"Please! I won't hurt you."

She retreated into the henhouse, not caring that one of the hens now began pecking at her leg, tearing a hole in her woolen stocking. *Please, dear Gott, save me!*

The man now came before the entrance to the henhouse. "P–please, I only need s–some food." He was shivering so badly, the words became muddled.

Gretchen forced herself to relax, especially when she saw he had left his musket behind. Slowly she exited the henhouse yet remained a good distance from him. "I–I'm making biscuits. They will be ready soon."

"Thank you. Do you have a blanket to spare as well?"

Gretchen hesitated. She knew from his manner of speech he was not of the garrison of Hessians guarding Trenton. He had no German accent. His tricorn hat and simple coat showed him a part of this land, maybe even of the Continentals themselves. *How could that be?* she wondered. The last she'd heard, the Continental Army was somewhere in New York. She shook her head, trying again to silence the fear clawing at her. She glanced around, wondering if there were more men lurking about, men who would force themselves into their home, steal their food and the horses, and leave them destitute.

"I'm alone, I assure you," came his answer to her unspoken question. His voice trembled. "I'm so cold. P–p–please, can you help?"

"I—I will fetch some food and blankets Stay inside the barn for shelter." She hastened for the house, stopping short to look back at the barn. How could she ask him to find shelter among their prized horses? What if the man was here to steal from them? Or perhaps another of his friends lurked in the shadows, even if he said he was alone? She should alert Papa, and together they could fend off the enemy with the long rifle they had in their possession. But something in the man's trembling voice and pleading gaze told her he was only here because he could go no farther. The bitter cold had sapped his strength. He only needed warm tea, biscuits, and maybe a night's rest before he felt strong enough to travel. *It will be all right*, she reasoned, as long as she could keep the knowledge of the stranger's existence from Papa.

When she returned to the house, Papa gazed at her above his wire-rimmed spectacles and the book he had been reading. "The chores are taking you much longer to do these days."

"I. . .uh. . ." She hesitated. "Ya, gathering the eggs does take time."

He gestured to her empty hands. "And where's the basket of eggs?"

"Oh, how foolish of me. I left it inside the henhouse. I'll go back in a minute." She stole a glance out the frosted window toward the barn, thinking of the man hidden inside, shivering as he tried to stay warm. She inhaled a deep breath before casting a glance at Papa, immersed in his reading. Anxiety began to gnaw at her. She hummed a hymn from the recent church meeting, hoping to draw peace and wisdom. While the man might need bread for nourishment, she needed the one true Bread, the scripture, to calm her fear when a bedraggled soul came seeking assistance. In the least it was good Christian charity to provide for one in need. She warmed the kettle to brew tea, glancing once more at Papa to find him drifting off to sleep.

Praise be, Gretchen thought. After a few more minutes, she placed hot biscuits, ham, and a small pot of tea in a basket and then grabbed some blankets. Balancing it all, she crept toward the door and quietly opened it, praying Papa would not awaken. Carrying the items and the contents of the basket with steam swirling in her face, she wondered what she would say to the stranger. Reaching the barn door, she tried balancing the items for a free hand to open the latch, when the door creaked open to reveal the stranger brandishing his musket. She inhaled a sharp breath and nearly fled, but she followed the motion of his hand to come inside. He quickly shut the door and put the musket away. He had lit a lantern, sending a golden glow across the stalls. The four horses inside calmly gnawed at the bale of hay Papa had put out earlier in the morning.

"Thank you," he said as she served him the tea and biscuits with ham.

"I—I hope you will be strengthened soon. Papa doesn't know you are here. The sooner you leave, the better."

"Does he fear I will commit some terrible deed?" he inquired, chuckling.

"Should he have anything to fear?"

He set down his ham biscuit. She felt a chill then and began sidestepping toward the door.

He held out his hand. "Of course not," he said gently. "Please forgive my foolish words. I owe you so much for giving me food and a place to stay."

"You—you can only stay the night. With the winter weather, we rarely have need for a ride, except to town for supplies, so Papa should not enter the barn now. But he still must care for our horses in the morning."

"I can help with the horses," he offered. "I will gladly tend them tonight and in the morning."

Gretchen wondered how she would tell Papa a stranger, now occupying their barn, had offered to care for their prized herd. "How can you possibly. . ."

"Just tell him you did the chores, if you wish. I come from a large farm in Virginia. We have many horses." He reached over and stroked the muzzle of the mare they called Goldie. "They're beautiful animals. I can see you care for them well. At times I was called on to tend the general's horse. He trusted me."

"The general?"

"General Washington. He doesn't allow just anyone to tend his horse, either. He is quite particular. He said, 'Yes indeed, Jacob, you have a way with them.' After this war is over he even invited me to come to Mount Vernon and assist with his horses."

Gretchen sucked in a breath. Was the man with the Continentals? "I thought the army was far away from here. . ."

"Not that far. We escaped Long Island and. . ." He paused. "I shouldn't say anything more."

"I'm not the enemy."

"No. Far from it. Might I ask your name?"

"Gretchen Hanson."

"I'm Jake Rawlings. A pleasure to meet you. Have you lived here all your life, Miss Hanson?"

She shook her head. "No. Like many, we came here seeking a new life. But we also still cling to the old ways and the old country."

Just then Gretchen heard footsteps. Jacob hurried to hide in the rear of the barn. Papa appeared, vivid lines crisscrossing his face, his eyes wide in alarm. "What on earth ails you, liebste Tochter? I was so worried something happened to you. You have been gone a long time."

"I'm sorry, Papa. I was checking on the horses. They—they're fine."

He looked over the herd and nodded. "I fear, though, we are going to get more snow. My bones are telling me so. Maybe I should add another bale of hay."

Gretchen thought of the man Jake, hidden somewhere within, and a bale of hay tossed on him. Or worse yet, he and Papa staring face-to-face in a look of astonishment, or even anger. "Oh, I can do it, Papa. You looked so tired. And I'm already dirty."

"Very well. But come in soon. The wind is picking up, and it is turning colder."

Gretchen nodded and closed the barn door after him. She then gazed into the dim surroundings. After a bit the straw stirred and Jake stood. "Is he gone?" came his hoarse whisper. He brushed away the bits of straw from his clothing and replaced the tricorn hat on his head.

"Yes, but now you can help me with the bale, as I promised Papa."

He wasted no time assisting her with carrying over a large bale and distributing it among the individual stalls. He conversed calmly with the animals, and several nuzzled his hand when he drew close.

"You do have a way with them." Gretchen observed. "They don't even shirk."

"They're godly creatures, helpful and wise in many ways. I had a good mount named Bailey. Raised him in Virginia. Sadly, Bailey was shot in battle by a Hessian. The enemy doesn't waste any time shooting either an American or his horse."

At these comments Gretchen drew back, her hand grabbing the side of the stall to steady herself.

"Is something wrong?"

"Oh, no," she lied. But everything. The portrait of battle. Helping an enemy soldier in her father's barn. . .a soldier Rolf might have tangled with during the battle of Long Island. Maybe even the very one who had put the bullet in him, leaving him to die on the battlefield. Now she had given the enemy food and a place to stay and even allowed him to tend their horses. *Who am I? What have I become?*

An American—she knew. *Like all of us. The sooner we realize this, no matter where we all come from or the things we have been through, the quicker we can live and breathe again.*

Chapter 2

Jake thanked the Lord for this place of refuge. His hand caressed the muzzle of a horse, and he was rewarded with a nicker of appreciation. How he missed caring for the brave animals, thinking of pleasant rides through the woods of Virginia. But home in Virginia was far from here as he glanced down at his haversack containing maps and other communications. At least he was safe at a colonist's farm rather than spending a frigid night in the snow and cold. He would leave in a day or two after the weather calmed and make haste to report all he had learned of this area called New Jersey. The general and his officers would be waiting anxiously for his report.

For now Jake settled in the straw, huddled beneath the wool blankets the young woman had provided. If only he could warm the chill in his bones. His face felt hot, his limbs shaky. As he drifted off to sleep, strange dreams assaulted him. He saw armies racing toward each another, the look of fury on the men's faces, the assault serenaded by the boom of cannon. He saw men ripped apart by shot and shell, their faces white, with eyes glazed over in a picture of death. He shook with fear and awoke in a start to the heat of his body and droplets of sweat beading up on his face. This was no ordinary dream but a nightmare fashioned from some sickness suddenly gripping him.

No, this can't be happening, he pleaded. *God, help me.* Slowly he clambered to his feet, keeping the blanket wrapped tightly around him, and peered through the crack between the barn doors. Horses whinnied from their stalls as he noticed a faint golden glow from the house, like a tiny beacon of hope through the swirl of falling snow. How he wished he had a bed to rest in and the warmth of a roaring fire to ease this unending cold. He sneezed and drew the blanket closer. His body wracked with chills. He dare not be ill. What would become of the army if he failed to deliver the information they needed?

Jake paced about the barn, even as the illness rapidly turned his arms and legs into a mass of useless flesh. Many in the army were overcome with the pox or camp fever. General Washington had seen to it that as many men as possible were inoculated to keep the pox from infecting the whole army. But other illnesses still plagued the soldiers and sent many home early to heaven. He prayed the latter would not be his lot.

Soon he became hot and threw away the blankets. Again he gazed longingly at the house in the distance. If only the slight woman with the beautiful blue eyes and giving hands that presented him with tea and biscuits would come check on him. He would tell her his woes and pray she would let him seek warmth in their house.

Jake turned away and buried himself once more in the hay, wrapped up again in the blankets as chills gripped him. An uneasy sleep filled with nightmarish battles once again drifted over him. Sometime later he heard a soft voice call his name and felt gentle hands try to rouse him. "I—I can't. . ." he groaned to the faraway voice.

"But you must." A gentle hand caressed his face. "You're burning up!"

Jake tried to respond, but the illness robbed him of all strength. He heard strange words then, a foreign tongue like he had entered another world. Different hands now tried to coax him to his feet. He struggled to obey, all the while gripping the arms of a man and woman. They stepped out into the cold that sliced through him like a knife. He cried out.

"I'm sorry," crooned the woman who called herself Gretchen. "Just a few more steps to the house. You can make it." The soft voice gave him the strength to move as best he could, despite the numbing cold. Soon he stumbled into the warm surroundings and then the softness of a bed.

"Th–thank you," he managed to say before falling into the daze of sleep once more.

◆—•——•◆

When he awoke some time later, he felt like he had been thrown from a horse. Every part of him ached. He tried to sit up, but his head weighed as much as a cannon ball. He saw the young woman scurrying about, bringing a pitcher of fresh water. She wore a simple cotton dress with an apron tied over it. A mop hat hid most of her thick golden hair. When she turned to look at him, she gasped and stepped back.

"You're awake!"

He wiped his face. "My head feels awful. How long have I been asleep?"

"Nearly two days. I tried to feed you some broth, but you wouldn't take it. I feared you might die."

"Little chance of that," he said, a bit more confidently than he should considering how ill he had been. For all the ways men could die in the world, it appeared a bout of simple camp fever could rid a man of his born days quicker than anything. "Thank you for watching over me."

"Are you hungry now? I just made up some more broth. And I have fresh biscuits."

He nodded as she hurried to fetch him food. His gaze now encompassed the simple room—the bed made of feathers where he rested, the sturdy bedstead pieced together with wooden pegs, a dresser with a small mirror hanging above it, and a rocker in the corner. These were not the furnishings of an impoverished family, by any means. They did have some fine possessions. The dresser looked as if it had come from England. He wondered of their ancestry.

Gretchen hurried in, carrying a bowl of soup and a biscuit. "I'm sure you will feel even stronger after having something to eat."

"I hope you aren't spending all your time nursing me."

"Oh, no. I mean, I did what I could. But really, it is our Savior Gott who watches over us and heals our infirmities."

Jake could not argue, but he also knew disease robbed many of their lives.

"But Gott sometimes takes loved ones," she added, mirroring his thoughts. Her blue eyes took on a faraway look as if shrouded by a memory.

"You've lost someone close?"

"Yes, in the war." She again looked away, and her cheeks flushed.

"I'm sorry. War is cruel but Independence is worth the heavy price we all must pay."

She twisted her hands in what looked like a display of discomfort. Her loss must be great. How he wanted to probe her mind and find out who it was. Maybe it was her husband or beau. Or a beloved brother. He had already lost several good friends in skirmishes in the South where he came from. But the army in the North had seen the most action, from Bunker Hill to Long Island as the British slowly marched south toward the capital of Philadelphia. Yet it was the winter they dreaded most, when the cold brought about many more casualties from illness than battle wounds.

He finished the soup and biscuit. "Have you lived here long?" he asked, handing her the bowl.

"About five years. We came from. . ." She paused. "From Europe as did everyone else." Her cheeks took on a crimson color. "We have the land Papa tends, and we have our horses. Where do you come from?"

"Virginia, near Charlottesville. Home to our eloquent Thomas Jefferson who penned our famous words of freedom in the Declaration. I must say it makes me proud in many ways to be fighting for such a cause."

Gretchen hastened to the door and glanced out. "Please, not too loud!"

"Is something wrong?"

"I. . ." She hesitated. "If you must know, Papa has not sworn allegiance to Independence. He struggles like many do in making a decision." Her lower lip trembled, and she began rubbing her arms. Watching her, he wanted to soothe her fears in a gentle embrace.

"Miss Hanson, I do understand. Some think it's our duty to stand with the mother country, and if we don't, it's treason. Others hold fast to Independence. But most don't know which side to trust."

"Please don't speak of this right now. It's better for all of us."

Jake could clearly see her distress in the way she swiftly exited the room with her head down. It pained him to cause her such anguish. He assumed the people here by the river were of patriotic leanings. He knew of no Tory strongholds, but maybe he had inadvertently stumbled upon such a household. He sighed, hoping he would soon be well enough to ride out before his work was discovered.

Just then a thought occurred to him. *Oh no!* He bolted upright in bed and looked wildly around. He threw away the quilt and clambered to his feet. *Where can it be? I must have it!* The room began to spin. Pain racked his head. His legs buckled. The room's furnishings began fading from view as he slid to the cold wooden floor.

Voices erupted around him.

"*Mein* Gott!"

"Oh no!"

"*Nehmen seine arme.*"

Gretchen knelt beside Jake and tried to take his arms to help move him. Her face was so close, he could feel her breath brush his cheek. It carried a scent like cinnamon, as if she had tasted a fine gingerbread cookie. A sting of homesickness swept over him.

Tears filled his eyes with the memories: Mother baking gingerbread on the hearth, and his sister helping her make the sweets that delighted Father and him. Would he ever see them again? Or would they weep at his grave as did so many families?

The daughter and father struggled to help him to the bed where he collapsed. The bed frame swayed under his weight.

"You must stay there," the older man ordered, wagging his gnarled finger "You're too weak to get up."

"I—I was looking for something." He turned to Gretchen, searching her compassionate blue eyes. "Please. My haversack. It is very important. . . ."

"We have your musket and other belongings," she told him. "They are safe."

Jake felt little reassurance as the older man glared at him. Nothing was safe, especially if they were a Tory family, as he feared. A lump formed in his throat. "Please, I need it. I—I must make sure. . ." His voice trailed away as weakness again overcame him, making speech difficult.

"I will get it. But you can't get up again."

He shrank down beneath the blanket, under Mr. Hanson's baneful stare. The man's beard twitched as he shook his head. "Aye, *Dummkopf*," the man murmured. "Take care of him, daughter."

Jake inhaled a sharp breath when Gretchen returned with his haversack, praying they had not examined the contents. "Thank you. Did you. . .did you see. . ."

"No, I did not," Gretchen retorted stiffly, striding for the door.

Jake held out his hand. "Please, I'm sorry. It's just. . . I hold precious items inside."

"I'm sure you do. I will be back soon. Try to rest."

Jake sighed. When the door closed, he opened the haversack. Inside were maps, orders from the general, and scraps of notes. A small scope and his journal. Slowly he took out the journal and opened it to the last entry.

December 18
Without my mount, Bailey, I have no choice but to walk on foot. My shoes are barely
holding together. I must make it to the river so I can report on enemy movements
and strength to General Washington. So much depends on the information I gather.
Maybe even the future of our country.

His fingers trembled at the thought of the enemy finding these notes, which included diagrams of the garrison he had seen in Trenton, of farms and homes, road hazards and such—all the details written down by a scout working for the Continental Army. Jake licked his dry lips. He could envision the great anticipation of his arrival in the army with the notes in hand. The tall, commanding, yet gentle form of General Washington, his coat splattered with mud, would mull over the idea of a winter engagement with his officers through the information Jake provided. Could a battle plan even be feasible in the winter? It seemed unlikely with the army's badly depleted ranks. They would remain on the opposite shores of the Delaware River and wait to see what the New Year brought.

He again licked his dry lips before reaching for a tin cup of water resting on the washstand. *I need to fulfill my duties. I must leave here as soon as possible. God, make me well! I can't be the reason for our failure as an army and a nation! Please.* He tried to settle the concern but only felt the urgency rise up, draining away any remaining strength. He could no longer hold anything. His arm fell to the bedside as did the haversack, spilling its contents to the ground. Sleep quickly overcame him.

Sometime later, the sound of footsteps and a soft voice stirred him to consciousness. He opened his eyes to see a dress, covered by an apron, standing close. Again the aroma of gingerbread wafted through the air. Then he heard something else—the sound of hands putting away the contents of his haversack.

"What are you doing?" he asked, struggling to sit up.

"It had fallen. I was putting it back together." Gretchen paused. "So are you a scout?"

"I work at the pleasure of the general, yes."

"I don't understand. Why are you scouting this far west? I thought General Washington was still in New York."

Jake opened his mouth then shut it before anything vital slipped out. He considered carefully his words. "I can't say. I'm only to look over the lay of the land and report what I see." He dare not divulge any further details, not knowing their stand in this conflict. For all he knew, as a German family they could be loyal to the Hessians occupying Trenton. His work for the Continentals was far too important to risk discovering their whereabouts. Though, with Gretchen's soft blue eyes staring questioningly into his, he couldn't help but waver.

"You must have seen so much," she noted. "Surely you couldn't have traveled around on foot."

He looked away to the frosted window to see winter's fury in full force with the swirling snow. "With my horse shot from underneath me, there was no other mount available. I walked a good part of the land. As you've probably seen, my shoes have fallen apart."

"Yes. How dreadful."

"Which is why I need help. I was hoping if I could assist in tending your fine horses, I might be allowed to borrow a mount for a brief time. Just until I fulfill my duty and report back to the general. I would return it, of course."

Gretchen stared and then her hands flew to her hips. "I think you're far too ill to consider such things now, Mr. Rawlings. But when the time comes, I shall speak to Papa."

Her words were a comfort. At least she was not against his duty, as he feared she might be. "Thank you." He reached out to take her unsuspecting hand from her hip and draw it toward himself. "I don't know what I would've done without your help. You may have saved us all."

Gretchen slowly disengaged herself from his grasp. "You give me far too much credit, sir."

"If only you knew. I can't begin to say. . ."

"I—I'll bring you more soup and biscuits. Maybe tomorrow you can try getting out of bed and hopefully not fall on the floor."

Jake thanked her for everything. He knew he'd revealed far too much of his business and his position in the war to Gretchen. But somehow he felt he could trust her. The touch of her soft hand in his, her gentle eyes, the way she tended to his needs, and the questions that didn't betray an aversion to the cause but revealed understanding, all gave him confidence. But right now, he had little choice. He must entrust his life, and maybe the fate of the Continental Army, to her hands.

Chapter 3

*W*hy did I ever allow him to take my hand?

Gretchen tried to concentrate on other things as she moved about t
house, tending to the list of daily chores. Sweeping the floor. Washing t
breakfast dishes. Filling the firewood box from the woodpile. But in everything she d
she saw the dark eyes of Jacob Rawlings staring at her, and his hand folding over he
drawing her close to his heart. She shuddered at the memory. How could she have allow
such contact? What was it about him that drew her? Especially so soon after heari
Rolf's fate and trying to understand where her heart lay in the cause.

She came to the open door of Jake's room, watching him propped up on feath
pillows, reading a book. He appeared to be reading the Holy Bible. She had seen
copy of it fall out of his haversack, along with the journal and several documen.
One of the parchments on the floor revealed his work with the Continentals, a
his mission to review the land of New Jersey and all it contained. She had seen
the writings the list of farms, categorized in a way to identify which could provi
food, lodging, or assist with the wounded. Were these the documents of an enem
Or a patriot?

Staring at him recovering in bed, engaged in the Bible, he looked like no enemy s
had ever seen. Rather he appeared quite peaceful, as if the holy words imparted streng
to his weakened flesh. She thought about it and went to find her mother's Bible. S
too, needed words that gave peace in the midst of confusion, and more important
wisdom to discover what she should do with this stranger in her midst. Was she right
allowing him to take her hand like he did? Was it right to have him stay here and he
then secure a horse to do the bidding of the army he served?

She opened to Luke 6:30–31: *"Give to every man that asketh of thee; and of him th
taketh away thy goods ask them not again. And as ye would that men should do to you, do
also to them likewise."*

She glanced up to find a dark form hovering in the doorway. It was Jake, wrapped
a blanket. The heat rose in her cheeks as she hastily put down the Bible. "Are you we

"I'm better, thank you." He looked around before slowly approaching the living a
and settling into a chair close to the blazing fire. "Where's your father?"

"He's in the barn, caring for the horses." She stared at Jake sitting before her,
face enlightened by flames hungrily consuming the logs in the fireplace. He did not lo
the part of some soldier but rather one who had battled the war of disease that claim
so many. Seeing him soak up the warmth of the fire, he appeared stronger than he h

the last few days. She knew he had gained a personal victory over the enemy of sickness, and it made her glad.

"Are you hungry?" she now asked. "There are biscuits, and I will fry up some ham." She bustled about, taking out the cast-iron pan to cook the ham.

"Who are they?" Jake wondered, pointing to several paintings hanging on the wall.

"My family from the old country. Opa and Oma. My cousins, too. We gathered together and a fine artist painted them, before we left to come here to America."

"They are beautifully done. I often wondered what it would be like to sit for an artist and have a portrait painted." He paused. "And the woman? She looks like you."

Gretchen gazed at the sleek portrait of a proud woman, with golden hair and deep-set blue eyes. "My mutter. She died on the journey here to America."

Jake straightened then. "I'm sorry."

"It was ship's fever. She was never very strong. Papa thought a new place would be good for her. But the dank air of the ship proved too much." She paused. "I think of her often. We did so much together. Even to this day, I make her apple kuchen whenever I can." She paused as stray tears crept into her eyes, thinking how much she missed her.

"What is kuchen?"

" 'Kuchen' is the German word for cake."

"Hmmm, I thought you may be German."

She paused. "Does that bother you? I know there are men from the old country who fight for the British."

"You mean the Hessians? Yes." Jake stared into the fire as if the flames had ignited something within him. "They are paid by the British to wage war on us. A good friend of mine was killed by a Hessian bullet. They are all around Trenton, too, from what I've seen."

From the grating of his voice, Gretchen wished she had not brought up the subject. Not only was her life once embroiled in the Hessians, but so, too, was Jake's. The inter-section of them could prove perilous. *Why did I say anything at all?* she scolded herself. But then her gaze fell on the Bible, and she picked it up. "It is all terrible, the things we see and hear. But I know in this book there is truth and light and peace. This Bible belonged to my mutter. She left many notes in it. I feel she is near when I read what she penned on the pages."

"I'm glad you have such comfort, Gretchen," he said quietly. "It's all we can hold on to when the awfulness of war takes away loved ones. Whether by sickness or battle wounds, it's all terrible. But we have the promise of eternity if we don't lose faith." When he stood to his feet, the blanket cascaded to the floor. Gretchen came and swiftly picked it up, handing it back to him. Their hands brushed. His eyes stared intently into hers and again the color of them, dark brown and gentle, drew her in.

"Thank you." His voice softened as he took her hand. "If I had the money, I would pay you for your kindness. But there's little payment in my work and. . ."

The sputter of the frying ham sent Gretchen scurrying to turn the slices in the pan. "Nonsense. We would never accept payment."

Jake made his way to the window to see the snow-covered yard and the barn in the distance. "I must do something to help. Might I ask your father if I could help around here? I also need a mount so I can continue my duties. You mentioned asking him about this?"

Gretchen paused in turning the ham slices, wondering how she would broach the subject of Jake's need. No doubt Papa would gladly accept help with the stock. But allowing a Continental soldier to acquire one of his horses to do the enemy's bidding? How would he react to such news? Especially knowing where they hailed from and the past associations they'd kept.

"Here he comes now," Jake observed.

Gretchen held out her hand. "Please, don't mention about borrowing the horse. I'll ask him in due time. You still need to regain your strength."

Papa threw open the door then, stomping his feet to knock off the snow from his boots. "Ah, so he has arisen! You look well."

"Thank you, sir," Jake said. "And how are your horses weathering all this snow and cold?"

"Quite well, *danke*. Eating too much, as they have not been exercised. I hope I have the hay I need to stay the winter." He came over and poured out some fresh tea Gretchen had made.

She saw Jake look over at her, sensing his anxiousness to discuss his care of the animals. "Papa, did you know Mr. Rawlings is a skilled horseman?"

"Ya?"

"I am, sir," he added. "I cared for my father's horses in Virginia. We had many a fine team. I've also cared for"—Gretchen saw him fight for the words—"for special horses owned by those in authority. I've even had a job as a stableman."

"How fine, indeed." He rested in a chair and struggled to remove his boots. "Then maybe you can help us here, eh?" He chuckled.

"I would like to."

The man's salt-and-pepper eyebrows arched. "Well. . ."

"It's the least I can do, after all you've done for me."

Papa exchanged glances with Gretchen. "I'm certain we can arrange something. You may start tomorrow, if you are able."

A small smile formed on Jake's face. Gretchen breathed a sigh, thankful at least a part of Jake's request had been honored. But she knew he sought a horse to continue his work, and if Papa were to know it was for the Continental Army, she feared his angry German tongue would be heard all the way to Trenton.

Jake could hardly wait to rise early the next morning. Before the light of dawn streaked across the eastern sky, he was dressed and ready for a new day. For the first time he sensed freedom in his life, and he was uncertain why. Maybe because he felt no fear as he usually did whenever the dawn greeted him. He knew he would rise from some damp, frigid place on the battlefield or in the woods or in some abandoned barn to face another unpredictable day. He would shake off the dirt and leaves, stuff a piece of hard bread and moldy bacon in his mouth, and make tracks for whatever destination the army required. All day he would battle the fear of running into an enemy patrol, a sniper's bullet, or some other misfortune.

Before he met Gretchen, he had been scouting the New Jersey countryside. He would need to return to his work, but for now he relished in this peaceful existence. He'd enjoyed a pleasant rest in a warm bed, with a feather pillow cradling his head. He wore one of Mr. Hanson's older nightshirts instead of his own dirty clothing, and even now looked at his clean clothing scrubbed in hot water and lye soap that removed the many weeks of dirt and sweat. Gretchen had also found an old pair of her father's shoes for him to wear. Yes, life here was a fine refuge from the battle. If only it would last.

Jake ventured out to see Gretchen had risen early to make a pot of porridge for breakfast. "Good morning, Miss Hanson. May I bring in the wood?"

She turned, a ladle in her hand. "Are you certain you're strong enough?"

"Yes. I'm quite strong, thanks to such good care." He smiled, took his wool coat from off the hook on the wall, and ventured out into the frosty morning. A blanket of frozen haze lay over the fields this cold December dawn. As the sun's rays touched the farmland, wisps of clouds rose up from the brown cornstalks left as a reminder of a handsome crop earlier that year. Slowly he headed toward the woodpile and began stacking logs in his arms.

When he returned, Mr. Hanson was also awake and sitting near the fire. "*Guten Morgen,*" he said in his fine German accent. "You look stronger."

Jake carefully stacked the wood beside the fireplace. "I'm better, thank you, but I still find myself weak."

"It takes time," Gretchen said, spooning the porridge into bowls. "Come have some porridge and tea."

Jake smiled and sat down at the table, conscious of the older man quietly examining him. He wondered if the talk would turn, as it did yesterday with Gretchen, to things he'd rather keep silent about. Instead he said, "I'm most eager to help with your horses today, sir."

"I must go to town later this morning," Mr. Hanson noted. "The stalls can be cleaned when I leave, if you wish." He paused. "Surely you also had a horse at one time?"

Jake nodded. "My mount suffered a. . .that is, became injured and did not survive."

"I'm sorry to hear."

"I. . ." He hesitated. "I'm also in need, sir, of a mount to make a quick trip. Of course, when the time is right." He caught the sudden look of panic erupting in Gretchen's gaze and her head shaking no.

"I'm not sure I understand," Mr. Hanson said.

"Mr. Rawlings needs to borrow one of our horses, Papa," Gretchen explained. "I told him he might, if we are able."

He stirred in his seat. "Where will you go?"

Jake hesitated. "I—I have kin across the river. I want to inform them I'm well and in the land of the living."

To his relief the man nodded. "I think we can arrange it. Pass me the pitcher of milk, daughter."

Jake sighed, thankful the explanation satisfied the man. With all the talk of Hessians and the family's German roots, he dared not mention his allegiance to the Continental

Army. While he did not like telling a story, in a way the army had been kin to him. had many good friends serving, if they still remained in the army. Many enlistm were up in a few weeks. This magnified General Washington's fear over what m become of them in the New Year. Rumors ran rampant that the army could disinteg unless something was done.

Jake helped Gretchen clear the table then followed the elderly man to the barn assisted in helping hitch up the team for Mr. Hanson's ride to town. He wondered he had witnessed in the days leading up to his illness were true—if the Hessian tr still occupied Trenton and performed drills in the nearby meadow. Perhaps God w help him discover any new information through Mr. Hanson's visit.

Just then he felt the wisp of a breeze and found Gretchen standing beside buried in a wool cloak. "Why did you speak a falsehood?" she suddenly asked.

"A falsehood?"

"Saying you were seeing kin across the river. It's the Continentals you plan to soon, isn't it?"

"They are like kin to me, Miss Hanson. As much as can be for all we have I through these long months, while we fight to see a new country born."

"I suppose so. I do understand why you hesitate to say anything about your we She stared down the road where her father had disappeared. "Papa will no doubt into many Hessians in town today. Some are even his friends."

"I wonder how many are in the town?"

"I hear about a thousand or so. Papa says they are waiting for the British to a from New York."

"I'm sure they're also waiting for the river to freeze. Then they will hunt us d like dogs, and our country will be no more."

Gretchen turned toward him. "I see this upsets you. A part of me wishes for a become a country. But another part of me"—she hesitated—"wonders if it might be to have the mother country care for us. If we truly know what we are doing. And i can really succeed in this manner of Independence."

"Only God knows, Gretchen. It's like life. We can only walk in life's footsteps see what fate brings." He paused. "But I will say, I'm glad fate brought me here and n cold place in the woods that could have been my grave." He took her hand, which h enjoyed holding the last time, grateful she did not draw away. "Thank you."

"Always, sir." She disengaged herself, and he watched her fly into the barn li dark bird, her cloak billowing about her. His heart grew warm. Maybe as they wo he could convince her of the noble effort of the cause. Despite their heritage and affections, he hoped they would continue to draw closer. *Patience*, he told himself. *I make her fear and then take flight. Slowly, ever so slowly, with kindness and a listening show her that you respect her and honor her.*

He entered the barn to the aroma of horses and thought of Virginia. *And the God is willing, I will have her come home to Virginia, where the Blue Ridge Mountains r the sky, and all will be well in a country we will call the United States of America. Dear may it come to pass.*

Chapter 4

Gretchen wondered why the thought of Jake returning to the Continentals didn't bother her more. At times she felt guilty for not preserving the memory of Rolf. But the more she thought about it, the more she realized marriage to him would not have been right. Maybe she had only agreed to it upon Papa's desire that she be knitted to one of their countrymen. Rolf had been a fine gentleman, but his fervor for the mother county and against liberty made her uncomfortable.

She moved to her room, where she kept a copy of the Declaration and began reading.

> *We hold these truths to be self-evident, that all men are created equal, that they are endowed by their Creator with certain inalienable Rights, that among these are Life, Liberty and the pursuit of Happiness—That to secure these rights, Governments are instituted among Men, deriving their just powers from the consent of the governed—That whenever any Form of Government becomes destructive of these ends, it is the Right of the People to alter or to abolish it, and to institute new Government...*

Life. Liberty. The pursuit of happiness. The need for a new government. How the words grabbed hold of her heart. Rolf had recoiled at such things. He wanted it silenced. But there were more to these words than the print on a document. They were words that spoke of freedom and happiness and life.

She glanced out the window to see Papa and Jake busy at the barn, conversing with each other while moving around the bales of hay. She watched Jake effortlessly carry the bales, per her father's instruction, thanking God his strength had returned so quickly. What did the future hold for their country and for them? Just then Jake appeared outside the barn and turned to stare at the house. Gretchen hastily retreated from the window, feeling the heat in her cheeks. Had he seen her looking at him? She shook her head and returned to making sourdough pancakes for breakfast.

Soon the door burst open, and the men marched in with smiles lighting their faces. "We are ready for breakfast, daughter," Papa announced, thumping Jake on the back. "What an excellent worker we have. I'm sorry you cannot stay longer with us, young man."

Gretchen glanced at Jake. She knew he would eventually take his leave but didn't think it would be so soon. "We could still use help here, Papa. At least until Mr. Rawlings is strong enough to travel. And—and we can't send a soul away with Christmas so near, can we?" The stumbling words betrayed her heart. She was growing fond of him, maybe too fond. Jake looked at her, and the small smile teasing his lips revealed he knew it, too.

"Yes, that is true," Papa agreed. "Will you stay for Christmas, young man?"

"I would be honored," Jake said, flashing another grin in her direction.

Gretchen's heart sang. She made a mental note to finish knitting the new wool scarf she had begun. She'd finished Papa's long ago and was glad to have started another. It would be a warm, inviting gift for one facing the frozen elements while performing his duty. It was noble and right to love their new country and the man seeking to preserve it. The mere thought gave her peace.

After breakfast Papa went out to check on a problem with the wagon. Jake remained at the table to finish his cup of tea, all the while gazing at her in a way that made her feel excited. She tried to put aside the interest, instead gathering the dishes to wash them in the tin basin, when his voice stopped her short.

"Do you really want me to stay for Christmas?"

"Of course. I see no reason for you to go back, just to shiver out in the cold." She said it with her back to him until she felt a warm presence. When she turned, she nearly gasped at their close proximity.

Jake hastily retreated. "Thank you for having me here. I did assume you would want me to leave as soon as possible, what with your affections for the mother country, as you said."

"I was mistaken. I have been rereading the Declaration and the words of life, liberty, and freedom. I don't think we've witnessed any liberty with the terrible taxations put on us."

"No taxation without representation," he added. "This is why we fight, Gretchen. Men have already given their lives to see us set free from a tyrannical nation."

Just then she thought of Rolf and his commitment. How many on the opposite side of the battlefield gave their lives to a cause? But theirs was not for freedom. Why then did Rolf go off to war? Why did anyone, unless the cause was made clear?

"You look troubled."

"I was once engaged to a soldier with opposite views," she admitted. "He felt strongly about his duty, too. But I can truly say I have no idea why he left to fight. It was not for liberty. Or for life. Or our happiness. For what, I don't know."

Jake stood quietly, his hands in his pockets. She feared his quiet demeanor meant she had made a mistake confessing the engagement.

"It must be hard for you. Now, an enemy soldier has come into your home."

Gretchen set down the tin plate she had been washing. "Jake, you are not an enemy. You fight for what you believe. I know why you do what you do, but I never knew why Rolf did what he did. He only told me he had to, as if I should understand without explanation. Now he is gone. It is a terrible thing, and at what cost?"

"War is an awful thing," Jake said solemnly. "I have seen things no man should ever have to see. Destruction and death and the cries of suffering. But sometimes the greatest victory comes through suffering. Just like our Savior Christ, who died a terrible death only to be raised to life. If I didn't believe in the resurrection of the dead, I would never be able to do what I do. Maybe your Rolf felt the same way. Even if you don't understand why he went off to war, he was at peace with it."

His words were like strength to her soul. She felt warmth come like a flood, and a smile filled her lips. "Thank you."

Jake stepped forward. "No, I should be the one thanking you. For saving me."

"What? I—I did not!"

"You did. I've seen men die from camp fever as well as by the enemy's bullet. But we have hope in the power of God and in people's kindnesses that see us through, no matter what happens."

His tender gaze captivated her. Though his arms were not outstretched, she couldn't help but draw close. He obliged with an embrace. The kiss they shared strengthened with the feelings she nursed within—how she was quickly falling in love with Jacob Rawlings. She swiftly exited the embrace to return to her duties. The front door carefully opened and closed as Jake headed off to assist Papa once more. A part of her wanted to sing with the love bursting forth in her soul. But another part told her to remain calm and steady. *Dearest Gott, can this be Your will—to fall in love with a man who works for the Continental Army?*

◆———◆

Jake felt a certain lift to his step as he helped Mr. Hanson assess the wagon wheel damaged from an encounter with a rock. He tried to stay focused on the work at hand, but all he could envision was Gretchen's beautiful eyes staring into his, the way she had entered his arms so willingly to share in a kiss. The suddenness of their encounter did take him by surprise. Not that he hadn't dreamt of taking her beautiful form in his arms. He thought of their future after this terrible war came to a conclusion—of taking her home to the family farm in Virginia. She would look beautiful there, her blue eyes accented by the smoky-blue color of the mountains, which christened them the Blue Ridge Mountains. He would introduce her to Mother and Father, who would be glad to hear he was ready to settle down, rather than leading the life of a wanderer. She would be the answer to their prayers for them all, no doubt.

Jake used a long piece of wood to act as a lever under the axle, while Mr. Hanson surveyed the damage. Watching the older man, Jake wondered if Gretchen would ever be able to leave her father. She had not talked about other family except to say her mother passed away on the journey here and others still lived in Germany. It might be difficult asking her to leave this place, if she was the only one left to care for the man.

Soon other things crowded out his thoughts, such as the weight of his duty as scout for the Continental Army. He assumed the army would not engage in new activity with Christmas so near, but he needed to report as soon as the celebration was over. It should only take a few days at most, and then he would return.

"Ya, the wheel needs mending," Mr. Hanson proclaimed. "I need to take it to Mr. Carlson in town. He's the wheelwright."

"I'll take it to town," Jake offered. It would be a perfect excuse to have another look around and double-check his notes on the Hessian troops remaining inside of Trenton.

"Danke. That's very kind, indeed." The man stared at him for a moment. "I'm surprised a young man like yourself is not involved in this conflict. To whom do you hold your allegiance?"

Jake huffed as he continued to push down the lever, keeping the wheel raised. "My allegiance is to my Maker, sir."

"Hmmm, a wise but rather vague answer." Mr. Hanson smiled, much to Jake's relief, and began to pry the wheel off the axle. With the task accomplished, Jake used the lever to ease the wagon to the ground. He then helped roll the wheel to a small sled hitched to a horse. "I should make the journey to town, but I'm feeling rather weak today." He breathed hard while wiping his brow with a handkerchief.

Jake noticed the man's flushed face. "Rest, Mr. Hanson. I will take care of it."

"Are you certain?"

"Of course. It's the least I can do after all your kindness."

"Danke. I don't know what we would do without you."

Jake watched the man waver as he walked toward the house. Jake rushed to assist him into the home, where a wide-eyed Gretchen helped her father to his chair. Jake slipped into his room to grab his journal. He caught a glimpse of Gretchen as he headed for the door, stooping over the fireplace to heat water for tea. He prayed the man would be all right, hoping he had not given him the camp fever. He had seen such illness spread like a fire through the army and some taken away by its effects. *Please, Lord, watch over Mr. Hanson, and strengthen him. May he be well soon.*

Jake exited the house, then out of the wind he heard a voice call his name. Gretchen stood before the doorway, wrapped in a blanket to shield her from the raw wind. "You're leaving now?"

"Just to town. I'm taking the wheel from your father's wagon to have it fixed."

"Oh. I was afraid you might be going away for good. . . ." Her voice trailed off.

Jake smiled at her concern. He walked back and touched her cool cheek. Her lips responded with a smile. "I will tell you when I have a change of plans. But even when I do go, I'll return. If you want me to."

"Of course I do. I mean. . ." She blushed. "You've been helpful here and. . ." She shook her head. "You know what I'm trying to say."

"I think I do. Take care of your father. I pray I did not give him the camp fever."

"He will be all right. He's just growing slower these days. I think more and more the winters are difficult on him. We may need to seek a better place to live."

How Jake wanted to share his dream of a warm springtime in Virginia with the flowering dogwood and mountain laurel. Gretchen would look beautiful, framed by his mother's famous rose garden. He nearly mentioned the idea, but the awaiting horse whinnied, reminding him of his errand. "I'll be back soon." He took up her hand and kissed it. But as he turned for the mount and his duty, he thought of Gretchen. Hope soared that all would work out the way he'd envisioned and one day they would have a home and marriage in Virginia.

The trip to Trenton went quickly with he and the mare, Goldie, enjoying the fine day. Reaching the outskirts of town, Jake heard the sharp foreign tongue of someone in command. He looked off to his right to see several columns of Hessians drilling in the meadow. He paused to quickly count the number of soldiers and scribbled the figure in a column in his notebook. In another area he spied artillery pieces and caches of stored power and munitions. It appeared the enemy was here to stay, at least until their British counterparts arrived from New York.

After inquiring of some townsfolk, Jake found the wheelwright, Mr. Carlson, who accepted the wheel for repair. "I see there are many soldiers here in town," Jake commented.

The man shook his head. "Don't let me start babbling on about them. They come in here demanding all kinds of work on their wagons and cannons. I'm glad to work on a wheel for a farmer at last."

"Any word how long they will be here?"

The man shrugged. "I hear they are waiting for General Howe to arrive next year. Then they plan to cross the Delaware. I wish they would go back to their homeland and leave us in peace."

Jake nodded, his hand absently stroking a smooth wooden spoke to the wheel resting on the wheelwright's bench. "I also think they are waiting for the river to freeze."

"I pray it happens quickly. Then it's good riddance to them. They take up all my time with their work and don't pay in anything but worthless currency. No good at all."

Jake nodded. He wished the man good day and wandered out into the streets. He watched the villagers scurry past the soldiers walking the streets, appearing like frightened sheep amid the wolves. It angered him the way the Hessians had commandeered the town, making it their own, without any regard to those who lived here. He knew if the Continentals failed to win anything decisive in this war, they will likely see more of the British and German armies taking over towns, just as the British now occupied New York City. No doubt the nation's capital of Philadelphia was next.

Jake mounted Goldie, ready to ride out, when several Hessians walked toward him. His heart began to thump furiously. A cold sweat broke out on the back of his neck. He thought of making a dash for it but realized the horse was still hitched to the sled used to carry the wheel.

"*Was ist das?*" a soldier asked him in German. Jake feared they had seen him scribbling notes in his journal, until the man pointed to the sled hitched to Goldie.

"I used it to bring a wheel to town. It belongs to Mr. Hanson."

"Mr. Hanson?" One of the Hessians drew forward. "Josef Hanson? I know him and his daughter Gretchen."

Jake stared, unable to believe what he was hearing. He fought for the words through the plug forming in his throat. "You—you know them? How?"

"A good friend of mine, Rolf, was betrothed to Miss Hanson. He met his fate at the last battle." He turned to his comrades and translated in German, to which they all nodded. "Come have a drink with us," the man now invited.

Jake shook his head. "I—I must be getting the sled back to Mr. Hanson."

"Tell them I will come soon for a visit. We will talk more. It may bring comfort to young Miss Hanson to know about Rolf."

Jake managed to nod before quickly making his way out of town. A sick feeling of the heart swept over him. Gretchen had spoken of being engaged to a Loyalist. He had no idea her fiancé had been a Hessian soldier. . .the kind that once took the life of his friends and now stood as an invading force ready to decimate the Continental Army.

His fingers tightened around the reins. Now, more than ever, he must leave, not only to meet up with General Washington to relay what he had discovered here in Trenton but to escape the clutches of an enemy's love before he was taken over completely.

Chapter 5

Gretchen couldn't help but notice Jake's pale face and large eyes the moment he returned. Strange chills raced through her at the way he avoided speaking to her or even looking her way. The silence was dreadful. She couldn't imagine what happened in town to spawn such a reaction. She followed him to the barn where he had unhitched Goldie and was leading the mare to a stall.

"What's wrong?" she finally asked, clutching handfuls of her cloak tightly around her, trying to calm her chattering teeth and trembling limbs from anxiety rather than the December cold.

"I must leave here," he mumbled. "I can't stay any longer."

"I don't understand. I thought you would be here for Christmas."

He staggered under the weight of some unspoken knowledge. He shook his head. "I can't. They are coming."

Now her anxiety turned to fear. "Who? Who is coming?"

"They confronted me. The friends of your fiancé. The *Hessians*." He spat out the last word as if it were vile to even say.

Gretchen felt the anger and betrayal hidden within. "I—I told you I was once betrothed to another. . .," she began.

"You never said he was a Hessian. A paid enemy of our republic!"

"What does it matter? If I said he was British, would it have made any difference?" She pressed her eyes shut, trying to stem the flow of tears. "Now you think me some terrible soul? Maybe even the enemy?"

Just as quickly she felt the warmth of his arms close around her. Her eyes snapped open to see his face but inches from her own, and his dark eyes surveying her. "No, you're not the enemy. How could you be after the kindness you've shown me? But we're both caught up in this. You have friends who *are* enemies. I am with the Continentals. It's a precarious position we've placed ourselves in. I won't endanger you, and I can't be caught here with what I do for General Washington. They'll hang me."

Gretchen didn't know what to say. Of course he was right. If Rolf's friends were seeking to pay a visit, then God had warned Jake in time for him to flee before it was too late. "I don't want you to leave though," she blurted out. She thought of him day and night, the home they might have, even a child on his knee. How strange she never had such dreams about Rolf. But she found it easy to imagine a life with Jake Rawlings.

"Come with me," he suddenly said. "Several women travel with the army. Even a few families. They cook and sew and help in many other ways. They uplift the spirits of the men. And I'm sure the men would enjoy your excellent biscuits."

He winked, making her smile, until the situation drew them back to the reality of it all. "I can't, Jake. Papa has no one and. . ."

"I know." Again he held her close. "I'll miss you so much."

"At least stay tonight and take your leave on the morn. You'll be gone before they come. And we can have one last meal together."

He agreed, and her heart rested. At least they still had time before the uncertainty of this conflict forced them apart. Then a painful thought pricked her. Battles made widows, as she well knew. She had become one, although a widowed fiancée. Could she bear it if something were to happen to Jake? Maybe it was wrong to nurse love in the uncertainty of a conflict. She ought to put aside her feelings until the war ended. But seeing the smile on his face, the way he communicated to their horses and tended to their needs, the way Papa commented on his work and of course, the memory of his embrace and his kiss, all wrapped her heart in a blanket of hope. Nothing could take away hope, even with the call to battle.

They spent the rest of the day doing the usual tasks about the farm. Papa rested by the fire, reading his favorite German literature, assuring them he would be up and around soon. Jake split large amounts of firewood. His ax laying hard into the wood was a pleasant sound while Gretchen flitted about the small kitchen, preparing every dish she could think of to please him. Sausages and new potatoes and, of course, biscuits and the apple kuchen he loved so much. As she worked the dough for the kuchen, Jake came in, the cold wind blowing into the cabin, bearing an armload of wood he neatly stacked by the fireplace.

"You do excellent work," Papa observed. "I'm curious how you've managed to avoid this war when others have not."

Jake froze at the mention of the words. Gretchen felt her heart begin to pound. "Papa, you know he was ill."

"But what is it you do, sir? You said you had kin here, but. . ."

Gretchen watched Jake's eyes burrow into hers, and she sensed his concern. "Papa, he is doing what we all do, trying to live day to day with battles happening all around. And I'm glad he has been here to help us when we needed it most."

"Ya, I understand. . .," the older man began.

"I work as a messenger, sir," Jake added. "I've carried communications for those looking for news and. . ."

"Oh, how I miss hearing from my kin in the old country," the man remarked with a faraway look in his gray-blue eyes. "I wish I could send word to them. I fear, though, I'll never hear from them again." He nodded. "What a good thing, bringing news to others."

The sudden anxiety quickly faded. Gretchen breathed a sigh of relief, especially now as Papa began drifting off to sleep. She felt the brush of a hand and Jake stood just behind her. His eyes were but pinpoints.

"You know I dare not stay much longer," he said in a low voice. "Every minute that goes by, I sense danger."

"It's just for tonight. I have prepared many dishes. I'm ready to bake the kuchen you love so well. And biscuits also."

Suddenly she felt the warmth of his mouth against hers in an unexpected kiss. She tried to shrug off his embrace. "Jake, no!" she whispered furiously. "What of Papa?"

"He's fast asleep, and you know it."

"We must not—"

He pressed his finger gently against her lips. "It was merely the beginning of a long good-bye." He sighed. "I'm just grateful your father didn't ask any more questions about my work."

"He is only curious. How long will your work keep you away?" She knew the question was meant to be like a line cast into the waters to see what would come of it. She knew his deeds were noble in the pursuit of their country. But she also wanted to be a part of this, to have some important role to play. She looked over again at her mother's Bible. Mutter would have obliged her to pray. To seek the best for her fiancé, whoever he might be, and for her future and Papa's. To do what she was taught in keeping peace in the home. To be a woman of virtue, with wisdom and strength.

"I don't know," he said. "As long as it takes. But for now I only want to help you. What can I do?"

The question flustered her. She never had a man ask to help with the kitchen duties. Then she thought better. Maybe he simply wanted to spend a few precious minutes by her side while Papa napped. Their hearts could be as close as one dared in the circumstances they found themselves in. "You may cut up some apples for the kuchen, if you wish."

He obliged, taking out apples from inside a barrel and slicing them, while she patted the dough into several round tins.

"Did you ever have another love?" she suddenly asked.

The knife stopped slicing for only a minute, then continued. "A childhood friend, who lived across the valley. Her brother and I schooled together. But she married another."

"She broke your heart?"

Jake shook his head "No. Rather I think Providence wanted me to trust in another. He is the Lord of second chances. And I like what I have found here, with a caring and considerate woman."

She felt her cheeks warm. "You know so little about me. All you know is I was once engaged to your enemy." She placed the apples in a fancy ring atop the dough, then slid the pans into the small tin oven resting among the coals.

"You may have been in name only. But your heart wasn't. I think you did what you had to in honor of your father and your roots. But the Lord guided you in the end."

Gretchen agreed. The path of life did seem clearer since Jake came into their life. It made her realize she nursed other feelings. It was time to embrace new ways, much like their young country's struggle to find a new way of liberty.

"I have something for you," she announced. Jake's eyebrow raised in curiosity. She smiled and swept into the back room, bringing out a brown package. "I hope it will be useful."

"I'm honored." Slowly he undid the wrapping to find a moss-green-colored scarf she had just finished knitting. He curled it around his neck, grinning. "It is so warm. I will have no want this winter, dear Gretchen." He took her in his arms, searching again for her lips to offer his gratitude, when Papa stirred in his chair.

"I smell kuchen," he murmured.

She hurried out of his arms. "Yes, Papa. We're having a grand meal of sausages and potatoes, too." She paused. "Jake. . .I mean, Mr. Rawlings. . .must take his leave tomorrow."

Papa immediately stood to his feet, grabbing hold of the chair to steady his wobbly legs. "What? Why must you go now? Christmas is almost here."

"There are good reasons, sir," Jake began. "My kin and. . ."

"Oh yes, of course. And I remember you required a horse for a short time. You're welcome to one. You have done excellent work with them and everything else here." He pointed to the scarf still wrapped about his neck. "I see my daughter has given you a gift."

"Your daughter will not let me freeze again, sir. Which is how I came to be at your home, ill-prepared, having lost my own mount, and not ready to face the harsh weather."

"She's very thoughtful. We. . .We'll miss you. I hope you will return one day."

"I'm sure I will." His gaze met Gretchen's. Through the determination of his voice and his steady gaze, she saw his commitment. She prayed he would return to her unharmed so they might have a future together. She recalled how he spoke of his home in Virginia, nestled by the grand mountains. She envisioned them riding horses in the woods with the wind in their faces. They would pause before a stream, allowing the animals to drink their fill, then ride on through the thick woods to hidden places yet to be discovered. They would stop again at the creekside and dismount. She would splash him with water in fun, laughing all the while. He would return the favor. Then they would find themselves sharing in an embrace, and their kiss would put aside all doubt.

"I asked, daughter, when dinner will be ready?"

Gretchen whirled in a start to find a bemused expression on Jake's face as if he knew her thoughts. "Soon, Papa. I need to check on the kuchen." She bent over the small tin oven, a towel in her hands to keep them from burning as she examined each tin of fragrant cake with apple slices oozing brown juices. "They are baking nicely. They will be perfect."

"Just like you," a voice declared in her ear.

She flushed. "Mr. Rawlings, hush now."

"It will be hard to leave," he said softly. "But I must. I—I don't know when I'll return."

"I know you worry about the future. So do I."

"But you're in my heart," he whispered, "and I'll never let you go."

❖━━ · ━━❖

Jake could have stood over her all day, inhaling her fine scent, mixed with the baking kuchen. But Mr. Hanson was already gazing at them in curiosity, so he reluctantly backed away and began picking up the apple cores on the table to later throw to the pig.

He would surely miss this place. How he wished he had not run into the Hessians that reminded him of his duty. He wanted to stay until Christmas was over, enjoying the feasting and conversation and staring into Gretchen's eyes. But the encounter with the Hessians warned him not to delay, even though it pained him to leave her.

Just then a loud knock came on the door. "I'll get the door," he said to Gretchen, exchanging a pleasant smile with her.

"I wonder who could be calling?" Gretchen asked her father as Jake threw open the door. Three soldiers stood there, the snow clinging to their blue uniform coats and tall hats with stark brass plating on the front.

"*Schönen Tag!*" the men greeted.

Jake's hand froze around the wooden latch. *Hessians!* Instantly he felt weak-kneed. He fought to regain his footing and managed a soft greeting.

"*Ah, kommen und wärmt euch.*" Mr. Hanson waved the men inside and found them chairs to sit by the fire.

The soldiers thanked him in German and entered the home. Jake saw Gretchen give him a wide-eyed look until a voice interrupted them.

"How are you, Miss Hanson?" one of the Hessians inquired. "Surely you remember me. Geoff Hass, a friend of Rolf's." He removed his helmet and bowed crispy.

"Ya, I do. And I'm well, Mr. Hass, danke." She threw a glance Jake's way and slowly shook her head.

Jake could not believe the scene playing out before his eyes. *The enemy is here. . . right in our midst!* Nervously, he thought of the back room where his haversack lay on the stand, the haversack containing all his notes for General Washington. Should they find it. . .

He began sidestepping slowly toward the room.

"We met your visitor today in town," Geoff Haas said, acknowledging Jake, who paused in his tracks. "We thought of coming tomorrow evening but knew you might be busy. So we came now."

"How nice," Gretchen said pleasantly. "And we were just getting ready to enjoy our meal. I do hope you can stay and eat. Mr. Rawlings, if you don't mind helping me?"

Jake had begun inching toward the room when Gretchen called to him. He spun about and smiled slightly. Mr. Hanson engaged the men in boisterous chatter while Jake went to help Gretchen. "I have to get out of here!" he whispered fervently. "If I'm found out. . ."

"You won't be." Her gaze darted to the men who earnestly conversed with her father. "Just don't cause any undue attention. They will leave after dinner."

"I—I can't take that chance. I have to go now."

"Please, don't even consider—" She paused when the Hessian named Geoff stood to his feet and approached.

The Hessian soldier stared at the freshly baked apple kuchen, the plump sausages, the bowl of potatoes. "It all looks excellent, Miss Hanson. But the reason I came, as I told your papa, is to extend my condolences for Rolf."

Gretchen lowed her head. "Danke."

"He was a good soldier and a good friend."

Jake saw Geoff now study him. Thankfully the man said nothing to him as they all gathered around the table. During the meal, Jake thought of his plan to slip away as soon as possible. He considered making an excuse to take his leave of the situation, but decided not to tell Gretchen of his abrupt departure. He would simply disappear to avoid further suspicion. For now he tried to concentrate on the conversation shared mostly in German, with a few English phrases thrown in. Perhaps he would learn something valuable he could bring to the attention of the Continentals. But then Geoff directed a question his way.

"And how is it you, Mr. Rawlings, came to be a part of the family?"

"He was deathly sick with camp fever," Gretchen said.

"Camp fever, is it?" Geoff wiped his mouth carefully on a cloth napkin. "We suffer such illness in the military ranks."

Jake felt the sweat break out on the back of his neck, while a slow red flush filled Gretchen's face. Yet he marveled at how she maintained her composure. She piped up, "Sir, it is everywhere, and you know, even people in town have taken ill with it. Maybe because your army brought it here."

"Gretchen, what a disagreeable thing to say!" Papa admonished.

Geoff smiled. "It's all right. I meant no disrespect, Miss Hanson. But I am curious why you are not fighting in this conflict, sir," he directed to Jake.

"My home is Virginia," Jake said carefully. "It is not here."

"*Er besucht Familie,*" Mr. Hanson added.

Everyone nodded along with the exclamation, "Ah."

Jake didn't know what Mr. Hanson said, but it was enough to move the conversation to other matters. They discussed in English the weather and how the troops planned to celebrate Christmas. When Gretchen's apple kuchen was served, the men delighted in it, complimenting her on a fine meal fit for a great bishop.

At last the soldiers decided to take their leave. When the door closed and the Hessians rode out, Jake wiped the sweat from his brow and sighed. *Thank You, dear God.*

"Well, what a fine surprise, eh?" Mr. Hanson said. "Though I must say, both of you seemed very anxious."

"I—I was hardly expecting such a visit, Papa!" Gretchen was quick to say. "We…uh… the house was disgraceful, and none of us were properly dressed. It was very humiliating."

Papa stood and gave her a kiss on the forehead. "Liebste Tochter, you did well." He smiled at Jake. "And so did you, sir. It was a great celebration. Now I must rest." He nodded and moved off to his room.

Jake and Gretchen stared at each before quickly falling into a warm embrace after the sudden chill of events. They said nothing for a moment but only issued sighs mirroring what they felt in their hearts.

Finally, Jake murmured, "I can't wait any longer, Gretchen." He stood back and lifted her chin to meet his gaze. "I must leave right away."

"What will you do?" she asked nervously. "Will you send your troops to hurt Mr. Hass and his men?"

"It isn't for me to decide. I can only say I must fulfill my duty, as we all must do. In a way, I feel sorry for the Hessian soldiers. They are only hired to fight for England. They have no stake in this."

"Rolf did not believe we should be free," she said softly.

"And what do you believe?" He had to hear it once more from her lips before the call of battle drew him into the fray.

"That we are endowed by our Creator to certain rights, those being life, liberty, and the pursuit of happiness."

He kissed her before gathering his things. "I will return, Gretchen." He shrugged on the wool coat and rewrapped the new scarf around his neck.

She shook her head. "No. You won't come back."

He froze. "What? What are you saying?"

"Don't even try. We were but for a season, Mr. Rawlings."

"Gretchen, please don't. . ." He panicked. Had the Hessian visit sowed a seed of doubt?

She said nothing more but only went to the door and opened it. The blast of cold air nearly knocked him backward. He shrugged and went forward, his head bent downward to block the wind burning his face.

"Take Goldie," she called after him. "She will do well for you."

Jake whirled about. "You know I must return. I have your father's horse. Have faith."

"I know what this war does. It makes no promises in life. But I will try to have hope."

Jake returned to her side. Despite the doubts they both had, he kissed her again before heading out into the twilight. He would carry the vision of her blue eyes gazing at him, shimmering from tears. If she did not have faith, he prayed to God he would have enough for them both.

Chapter 6

Thanks to Mr. Rawlings, our plans have been confirmed." The tall form of General Washington stood to his feet, and all the officers in his company stood as well. Jake remained in the rear of the room in the house at McKonkey's Ferry, watching the proceedings under the glowing candlelight. The general pointed to the map laid out on the large table. "We will cross the river this night and attack Trenton, as outlined in the plans. Are there any questions?"

No one dared question the man responsible for keeping the army together, despite numbers barely registering four thousand. They were in desperate need of victory, not only for morale but to add legitimacy to their claim of Independence. Jake rubbed his hands together, wishing the battle lines were anywhere but Trenton and so close to Gretchen and her father. The mere thought of them in danger sent a prayer quietly rushing to his lips.

"Victory or death!" Washington pronounced.

"Victory or death!" the men replied. They saluted and hastened for their cloaks and tricorn hats.

Washington now approached Jake. He towered over him, not so much as a man of might but rather a father to a son. "I'm glad you returned when you did, young man. It served much in confirming our plans. Thank you."

All he could think of was the frightened forms of Gretchen and her father, watching the army parading by their farm. "We won't injure civilians in this. . .," Jake began, unable to bridle the concern in his voice.

"I take it you have a family in mind."

"They were good to me, sir, when I took ill. Their farm rests on the road to Trenton. They also. . . They know some of the Hessians as well. Which is how I fell into the information we needed."

"I see. Mr. Rawlings, we can only do our duty, as you have done. Ours is not to harm the population but to bring victory over our enemies. We must leave it in the hands of Providence. Now is our time to act." He nodded, placed his large tricorn hat on his head of white locks, and departed.

Jake sighed and began to pace. The general gave him no reassurance the Hanson cornfields would not be turned into a battlefield. He only prayed the Hessian friends of Gretchen's deceased fiancé remained in Trenton and away from the house. He tossed on his cloak and hurried outside to see men on flatboats preparing to ferry cannon, supply wagons, and horses, including Goldie, across the river. Upriver, Durham boats were being readied to begin the long task of carrying the soldiers across the cold waters. It was a gamble at best—to catch professional Hessian troops off guard, inside Trenton on this frigid Christmas night, and deal a blow that would turn the tide of war. Jake only wished he had not brought an innocent young woman and her father into this. If he could he would ride ahead and warn them. But he also had his duty. This engagement was to be a surprise, and he was an army scout. He had no choice but to remain with the men and see this through.

Jake hurried upriver to join the men at the second crossing point. Freezing rain began to fall, coating everything in glistening ice. The wind howled, driving the rain headlong into his face. The ground crunched beneath his feet. Men slipped and slid on the wooden dock leading to the boats. Jake waited in the rear as long as he could, stomping his feet, trying to stay warm as the storm continued to howl. Washington paced about, whispering to his officers, as time quickly slipped by. Jake inquired of a fellow soldier who had a timepiece. They were to have finished the crossing by midnight, but as the time ticked toward 1:00 a.m., with many units still to make the crossing, they knew their plans had changed. A battle at daybreak seemed likely.

"This is most unfortunate," Washington noted gravely. "We will lose the element of surprise. But there is no other way. We are committed. The outcome of this rests in the Almighty's hands."

Jake knew all too well what it meant to commit a cause into the Master's hands. Especially when doubt rose like an angry vise, ready to squeeze away hope. Watching the general observe the tedious operations at hand, Jake wished he had encouraging news to share. But he was as apprehensive as all the rest, maybe even more so when he pondered Gretchen's fate in the midst of this. If the Hessians returned to the farm—he knew the Continentals would attack, and Gretchen could be caught in the crossfire.

Suddenly Jake decided to enter the next boat set to make the crossing. No one said anything as he squeezed himself beside men while freezing rain dribbled from above. Men gripped their muskets, their large eyes reflecting an uncertainty in the lantern light. Other men lifted the heavy oars to help propel the boat across the river. Jake lent a hand with the rowing mid-river, praying forgiveness for whatever might happen this night. If only he could know the outcome of it all.

＊＊——·——＊＊

As much as Gretchen needed it, sleep refused to come this night. She should be exhausted from the whirlwind of events the past few days—the Hessians who came to visit, the emotion of Jake's abrupt departure, the Christmas festivities earlier with several neighbors who had come by to celebrate. For the last few nights she remained wide awake, and tonight was no different. Now she listened to the windowpanes rattle from the wind and rain, and a sudden prayer sprouted from her lips. For Jake's safety, for her family, for the future.

It was still dark out when she saw flickers of light play on the wooden wall. At first it was a pretty sight until she thought of fiery flames seeking to destroy them. In an instant she flew out of bed and put on a long cape, hoping not to disturb Papa, who snored in the next room. Shuffling out into the cold, dark main room, she again witnessed the play of light from outside on the road. Cracking open the door, she watched an army of men marching by in formation. No one said a word. The lights of candle lanterns reflected the frozen ground, and the gleaming ice coated everything it touched.

Just then a figure stepped out of the formation and headed toward her. She backed into the main room, the fear gripping her, and looked up at Papa's long rifle hanging above the door.

"Don't be afraid, it's me," came a voice.

She stared at the bedraggled figure coated in ice but with a familiar knitted scarf wrapped around his neck. Warm brown eyes regarded her. "Jake? Is that really you?"

"*Shhh*, not too loud. Yes. Please, are there any Hessians about?"

"Oh no. They left when you saw them go. No one has been here since."

"Hopefully they are all still in Trenton."

Gretchen looked past him to the lines of marching soldiers. "You are going to Trenton?"

He nodded. "We must act quickly while there is time." He searched her face. "Do you still agree with Independence?"

"I am not for the Hessian cause, if that's what you mean. Nor the British. I never have been. You helped open my eyes, Jake."

He smiled before his face turned serious. "I must go, Gretchen. Pray for me. For us all."

She grabbed for his coat, still covered in ice, unconcerned for the dampness or the cold cutting through her cape. She gave him a firm kiss. "You will come back to me."

His grinned. "I thank you for those words. They're much better than what you said the other night."

"I was frightened. I had no hope."

"This is a time of hope, the most I have seen in a long time. If God is with us, we will see victory this night. If not, it could be the end of our country. I will return soon."

She watched him head for the road to rejoin the troops. But soon her heart grew disquiet over the memory of another man that had bid her farewell before going off to fight for what he believed in. Would she receive the same news as she did for Rolf? Would she face once more the lonely, dark chasm of death? Prayer lit her lips until a voice startled her.

"What is this? Who are they?"

Papa had risen, holding a lit candle in his shaky hand. He stared with wide eyes at the men marching by.

"It is the Continental Army, Papa. They march on Trenton."

"But. . .the Hessians are there."

"Ya, Papa."

He stared at her. "But we must ride to Trenton and warn them!"

"No. We will not."

He backed away. The candle shook in his gnarled hand. "Gretchen! How can you say such a thing! It is our blood and. . ."

"Our blood is American now, Papa. You may have wanted to stay tied to the old country. I want to live the life God has granted me in this country. The Hessians are only paid to do the will of the British. And England has done nothing but tax us, and starve us, and hurt us, and antagonize us. Now is the time for Independence."

Papa stared, his mouth gaping in shock, before shaking his head. Gretchen didn't care. She had to say these words. For so long she had kept her feelings hidden. She never dared tell him she could not grieve Rolf's death. His was a cause she could not believe in. It always was Jake's, now and forever.

Papa shuffled off to his chair and wearily plunked into it. "The man who was here... he—he bewitched you, didn't he? He is the cause of all this. What is he?"

"He is a scout for the army. But I'd made my decision before Mr. Rawlings arrived. He only helped confirm what was in my heart." She retrieved the copy of the Declaration. "Have you read this?"

"I cannot read English, you know that."

"Then I will read it to you. Listen to what it says." For the next half hour she recited the words to a subdued father who said nothing, even when she came to the end. He sat in his chair with his eyes closed. She put aside the parchment, fearing what it may have done to him. "Papa?"

He breathed a long, slow sigh. *"Ich stimme zu."*

"What?"

"I agree with what it says."

Tears sprang into her eyes. She gave a gasp and flew to embrace him. "Papa!"

"Now stoke the fire for some tea, liebste Tochter. I am very cold."

"Yes!" Gretchen did so with joy filling her heart and a smile on her lips. *We have the warmth of freedom ringing in our hearts,* she thought in glee. *And I have the love of Jake. Oh God, help him return to me!*

Jake loaded and fired his musket as quickly as he could muster. He knew the army had surprised the exhausted Hessians, who tried to rouse from their beds after a day and night of merrymaking. Some had already been captured. Then he heard the call to gather in the meadow where the Hessians hoped to organize a last stand. They tried to ready their artillery when a blast from a Continental cannon rendered the battery useless. As Jake looked upon the defeated foe, he wondered if any of the Hessians who'd visited Gretchen's house a few evenings ago were among them or if they lay lifeless on the ground.

Just then they heard the news that the Hessian commander had suffered a mortal wound. Surrender came swiftly. The enemy troops marched in a long line to lay down their arms before General Washington, while Jake and the rest of the army looked on. They'd done it! They had secured their first major victory when all seemed lost.

Jake felt the nudge of a comrade. "We're seeing history, friend," the man said in glee. "This is better than any Christmas gift, except for the coming of our Savior Christ."

"Yes," Jake agreed with a sigh. He would feel happier, though, knowing Gretchen and her father were safe. He wanted to ride back and find out, but in the chaos of the crossing, he had lost track of the Hanson's mare, Goldie. He would need to find a replacement for Mr. Hanson before he dared return.

Suddenly he spied the proud mare being led by one of the officers. His heart leaped in relief. Immediately he hurried over. "Sir, I should like to return this mount to the colonists I borrowed it from."

The man looked at him. "This horse belongs to the Continental Army."

"I made a promise, sir."

The man shook his head. "It is no longer your concern."

"Do we now take from our people without proper compensation?" he challenged. "The horse was mine to borrow only. The victory here is hollow if we no longer practice common decency and morality."

"Return the horse to Mr. Rawlings."

Jake whirled to see General Washington, astride his mount, observing the exchange. Jake removed his hat and bowed. "Thank you, sir. May I take a temporary leave to call on the family?"

The general thought on it and shook his head. "I must deny your request, Mr. Rawlings. We are withdrawing across the river. I have need of you to ride east immediately and find out if reinforcements have been sent, as well as their position. We are relying on you, Mr. Rawlings. You could determine our next course of action."

Jake sighed, even as he gazed up the narrow road. Only a few miles away, Gretchen was staring out the window, rubbing her hands together, anxious to hear news of the battle. But he must fulfill the general's orders. There was no choice. Reluctantly, he nodded and took Goldie's reins. While he desperately wanted to ride back and look in on Gretchen, his journey lie elsewhere—to the garrison at Princeton and anything else he could uncover.

God, please keep Gretchen in Thy tender care. Help her know I am safe and that we will be reunited soon. But he knew what she would think when the army marched along the road before the house and he was not among them. She would think him lost or killed in action. The tears would come fast, and she would find herself inconsolable.

He thought then of his journal. Quickly he brushed off the crusty ice on the haversack and took out the journal, tearing out some paper and adding water droplets from his canteen to a bit of powdered ink. With a quill, he penned his thoughts to her, the way of the battle, and telling her he had survived. One of the soldiers passing by the house could deliver it. Then she would know, and her heart would be at peace.

He folded the letter, preparing to hand it off to a soldier, when an officer on Washington's staff intercepted him. "Communications, sir?"

"Yes. I was informing the lady in this area who'd nursed me through a bout of camp fever that I am well."

The man extended his hand. "Please, sir, if you don't mind. The communication."

Jake surrendered the letter, wondering if the officer himself would deliver it. Until he saw the letter torn up before his astonished eyes.

"Sir, you must realize we cannot allow such communications with nearby civilians at this time. Please take heed to your duties, sir. They are crucial to our success, as the general so stated."

Jake nearly objected before realizing the officer was right. How could he be so fool-hardy? He could not allow Gretchen's father to know the plans, especially as the man still held to the enemy's leanings and not Independence. "Of course. I apologize."

"I have loved ones, too," the officer said. "I do understand these are perilous times. But I believe Providence will reunite us with our loved ones when the time is right."

Jake sighed, praying it was so. For now he mounted Goldie, placed his tricorn hat firmly on his head, and proceeded eastward, away from Gretchen and all he knew, to regions unknown. He tucked her love deep in his heart and prayed they would soon embrace the future God had planned for them.

Chapter 7

1777

He's gone. Gott has seen fit to take him.

She could not believe it, though inside she knew it would happen. Oh, why did he ever make the promise to return when everything in her heart spoke otherwise? Why did he tell her to have faith when the only faith she could cling to was unfulfilled promises? Gretchen tried to contain the emotion until she went out to the barn to help with the horses and spied Goldie's empty stall. Only then did she let out a burst of anguish, startling the other three horses. A lump filled her throat. Goldie had died in battle with him. How she hated this terrible war. It seemed to never end but took away any semblance of future happiness.

"I'll never love anyone again," she told Crescent, the horse Papa had often paired with Goldie—named for the white crescent shape on her forehead. Gretchen lovingly stroked the horse's muzzle, allowing the tears to fall. Jake had been so certain he would survive. He wanted it to be so, and she did, too, even though she'd doubted it. Now she was proven correct. A new year began as the last one ended, without anything to celebrate. There was only the unending cold winds and winter snow, her father who nursed a cough that refused to go away, and memories of a man she had fallen in love with, and who had disappeared as quickly as he came.

She thought on the news of victory General Washington had secured over the unsuspecting Hessians in Trenton last month. The army succeeded in taking the troops completely by surprise. She had heard none of the regiments suffered casualties but prepared to head east to confront the British might. Yet, somehow, Jake's fortunes must have been different. Not long after, a description of a horse matching Goldie was found dead on the main road and the rider likewise dead of a bullet wound to the head. Gretchen wiped the tears from her eyes and tried to block the horrific image too painful to bear. Like the other losses she had endured in her life, she would give her grief to God and ask Him to take it into His everlasting arms. After all, He was much stronger to deal with such a burden. She tried to hum a hymn to give her strength until grief stifled the attempt. *Oh, Gott, help me.*

The creaking of another wagon on the road passed before their farm. Every day the wagons came, bearing families leaving Trenton to escape the growing conflict east of them. She ventured out to find the wagon had stopped and an unsteady figure had alighted. The man hobbled along on a single crutch. "Do you need some water?" she asked, ready to go to the well.

The man said nothing. He appeared disheveled, with a scraggly beard on his face, and his torn coat smeared with mud. Suddenly she recognized something—a moss-green scarf wrapped around his neck.

It can't be....

Then she heard the gravelly voice. "Gretchen."

At first she shook her head. Tentatively she stepped forward. "This must be a dream. You can't be here."

"It's not a dream. I'm here."

She began to cry softly until she saw his pant leg, smeared with deep red blood-stains. "You're hurt! Let me help you."

Jake obliged, his face tightening with every step he took. "It's not bad," he said through clenched teeth. "A bullet grazed my leg during the battle of Princeton. The general gave me leave to get help. I—I could think of only one place to go...."

She wanted to embrace him, so happy she was to have him back from the dead. But for now she helped him to the door, until suddenly he stopped short and refused to enter.

"I—I can't go in. What will your father say?"

"It's all right, Jake," she said softly. "We talked about independence. At first he didn't want to believe, but now he understands."

Jake hesitated, shifting the makeshift crutch to the other arm. "If there's any doubt..."

"There is none. Come inside. The room where you recovered once before is waiting. And so are my apple kuchen and biscuits."

He couldn't help but smile through cracked lips, parched from the harsh weather. He clung to her for balance and slowly made his way into the home, where Papa sat in his favorite chair by the fire. All at once his eyes widened.

"*Ich kann es nicht glauben*, Mr. Rawlings!" he exclaimed, unable to believe Jake had returned.

"He's hurt, Papa. He needs rest."

The elderly man stood and followed, watching from the doorway as Gretchen helped Jake into bed. "I will clean the wound and make a good tea. You will get better. I know it." Gretchen managed a smile. A part of her wanted to break out in joyous song that he was alive. But another part worried as she hurried to put on the teakettle and steep some dried herbs.

"Did he say anything?" Papa asked.

"Only that he was in the battle of Princeton."

"I heard about it. The army found the British there, and they were attempting to cut off their supplies. The Continentals had another victory." He glanced back toward Jake's room. "And what of him? Does he still spy for the army?"

"Jake is not a spy, Papa. He's a scout. And a patriot. As we all must be. This is not just Jake's fight but all our fight. And a war we can help win by caring for others." In those words she found strength and purpose. As she gathered the supplies to tend Jake's wound, she realized her purpose in this conflict. This man helped the cause, and in turn, she could help him.

Gretchen went to work immediately, taking off the old bandage dried with blood and debris and placing a poultice over the wound. She followed with a wrapping of clean linen. During the care Jake squeezed his eyes shut and grimaced. She only prayed there would not be the telltale signs of foul odor from the wound. She had seen such things in the past, when a neighbor once received a bad wound from a horse. After a week the man's leg swelled and then turned black. He lost part of his leg in the incident. Gretchen bit back any thought of such things happening to Jake. She vowed to do everything she could to make certain it healed.

"We should send for the doctor," Papa declared as she boiled another kettle to steep more herbs for a tonic.

"No, we can't. We—we don't know what allegiances they hold to in Trenton after the battle there. I can't trust a physician to care for a scout of the Continental Army."

Papa's grayish brow rose before he grunted and sat down weightily in his chair. "Are we doing what is right in this, liebste Tochter? I feel. . .I feel like I'm betraying our people. Our country. Our heritage."

Gretchen could sense his struggle. It was not unlike what she'd faced when Jake first arrived—if she had been wrong to embrace Jake after losing Rolf in the conflict. But in reading the Declaration and the Bible, she felt God leading her to seek a new way. "It is like the scripture of the old wineskins in the Bible, Papa. New wine can't be put into old skins. We are now part of this country. It is our new heritage. We can't take what's new and put it into the ways of the old country. We must embrace it all with a new heart." She glanced back to the open door of the bedroom where Jake lay recuperating. "I think God sent Mr. Rawlings to give us a new wineskin so we can embrace a new country. We would've been in a terrible conflict of the heart, torn by the old and new, if he hadn't come into our lives." She added silently, *And for that, dear Gott, I'm so grateful. I know, too, I love him for it.*

Papa said nothing, to her relief. At least he did not try to argue against what she felt in her heart. When the tea was ready, she returned to the room to see Jake dangling off the side of the bed. "What are you doing?"

"I'm not going to have you nurse me day and night. It's just a cut on my leg. I can get up and help."

"You can help much more if you rest for a few days. I don't know if the wound will get better or if we will need to find a physician."

Jake balked and swung his legs back into bed. "No physician," he mumbled.

"I understand." She gave him the tea. "But you need to be a good patient and rest. I will have biscuits ready soon."

"How I missed your biscuits." He stretched out his hand to her, and she came and took it. His large, manly hand felt warm and secure. She couldn't wait until he was back on his feet, ready to sweep her into his arms and tell her everything would be all right. But even if he did, what would become of them? He would return to the battle, and she would remain here to agonize over losing him again. She released his hand and stepped back.

"What's the matter?"

"I . . ." She paused. "I'm not certain if we should continue like this, Jake. With a courtship."

"I should ask your father properly. . .," he began.

"No, that's not what I mean." She looked out the window at the empty fields and the frost creating beautiful crystalline patterns like handblown glass. "Once you're well, you'll want to return to the battlefield."

"Gretchen, I thought I told you when I arrived. General Washington relieved me." She whirled. "What?"

"When I was wounded, he told me I had done my duty for my country. We had won great victories at Trenton and Princeton. The war's not over by any means, but he was happy with everything I'd done. We had but days to survive as a nation, and now we can continue on. It's taught me to believe in the scripture, 'If God be for us, who can be against us?'"

"Oh, Jake, I'm so happy to hear. I do pray the war will end soon, and we will be at peace."

"There is talk the French may now be persuaded to come help us. If they do, we'll have an even better opportunity of bringing this all to a quick conclusion."

Gretchen smiled. For her, she saw her dream of having a future with this man slowly becoming reality. God had graciously brought him back, and she would never let him go. "Rest for now. Everything will be all right." She slipped out of the room, her heart joyful. God was doing a great work, not only in their country but also in their hearts.

◆━━━━◆

The first warm air of the season, announcing spring's arrival, felt like a breath from heaven. Though the winter had proven harsh in many ways, not only from storms but also the effects of battle, Gretchen and Jake walked the land soon to be cultivated into vast cornfields.

"I know you don't want to stay here," Gretchen confessed as Jake walked beside her, yet with a distinct limp left from the injury. He seemed happy to be here, yet at times she caught him gazing across the way toward the river in the distance. She wondered if he missed home or his time scouting for the Continental Army or the army itself.

"I had once hoped we could make a trip to Virginia to see my family," he now said.

Gretchen continued to walk the soggy ground with him, not caring the mud had begun to coat the bottom of her skirt. It would be nice to see another area of the colonies. But Papa remained weak from the winter elements. His cough remained. She could not leave him. "You know Papa's frailty."

"Yes. Which is why I've made the decision not to return to Virginia."

Gretchen paused and turned to face him. "You won't go back?"

"I still hope to take you there for a visit one day." His head lowered as he gazed at the ground. "But there's other news I need to share."

Every hair on her head seemed to stand at attention. She grew chilled, and her teeth began to chatter. "What news?"

Jake reached into his pocket and took out a paper. "You were in the house when this note arrived by courier. It's a letter from General Washington."

The breath caught in her throat, so much that she could only whisper, "What does it say?"

"Dear Mr. Rawlings. I trust this letter finds you recuperated from your wound. We are in need of your services once more to survey the lower Pennsylvania regions. Rumors are the British might land south of there later in the year, and we look to good information of troop movements. While I do not know your present condition, I pray you will be able to again serve our country in this desperate hour.

G. Washington."

"I thought it was over," Gretchen began before quickly realizing they were but fragments of hope in her heart. Of course the conflict was not over. She could see the spark in his eyes and the look on his face as he held the letter. His heart did love her, but his sense of duty was stronger.

"Gretchen, I agonized over this when I read it. I'm not of healthy body. I have a bad leg, as you know. But I can ride. I still possess good senses and a sound mind. I know what is required. I have a gift, given to me by God. But I tell you now, if you don't want me to go, I won't."

Gretchen heard the sincerity of his words as his brown eyes drifted back and forth, searching her heart. *What is my wish? What do I say?* She then inhaled breath. *Rather, what is God's will?* "Be bold and very courageous, for the Lord Your God is with you." Tears sprang to her eyes, which she prayed he didn't see.

"I will accept, then. But there is still time. As the general says, they are not expecting troop movements until later this year. We have time to plant." His hand swept the field.

"Yes. A very good suggestion."

"And we have time to get married."

Gretchen stepped back in shock as Jake gingerly bent down on one knee. "Will you marry me, *liebe* Gretchen Hanson? Say yes, and I will be the most blessed man alive."

"Oh yes! And you are getting dirty!" She laughed as the tears now drifted down her cheeks. "Do we have time to get married?" she wondered softly.

"I will make all the time we need. If after that you still don't wish me to go, I won't."

Gretchen knew the answer. Her husband-to-be was important, not only to her but to many others. She was willing to share him with a noble cause, if only she could have him all to herself for a short time.

The kiss he gave felt like the breeze had lifted her. Only then did she realize Jake had lifted her by the waist in his strong arms and twirled her around.

"I am indeed the most blessed man."

"And our country is the most blessed country."

He set her down, and they stared into each other's eyes.

"Amen."

Lauralee Bliss is a published author of over twenty-five romance novels and novellas, both historical and contemporary. She enjoys writing books reminiscent of a roller-coaster ride for her reader. She desires readers will come away with both an entertaining story and a lesson that speaks to the heart and soul. In 2017 Lauralee celebrates twenty years of publishing.

Besides her love of writing and traveling, Lauralee's other love is the great outdoors. She is a passionate adventurer, having completed the Appalachian Trail twice, from Georgia to Maine and from Maine to Georgia, one of only twenty-five women to accomplish this feat. To this day she still avidly hikes as well as speaks about hiking.

Lauralee makes her home in Virginia, in the foothills of the Blue Ridge Mountains. Visit her website on www.lauraleebliss.com and on Facebook at https://www.facebook.com/pages/Readers-of-Author-Lauralee-Bliss.

Daughter of Orion

by Ramona K. Cecil

Dedication

Dedicated to all those who go down to the sea in ships.

Acknowledgments

Special thanks to author Louise M. Gouge, whose friendship, tutelage, and vast knowledge of New England whaling was indispensable in the writing of this story.

They that go down to the sea in ships, that do business in great waters; these see the works of the LORD, and his wonders in the deep.
PSALM 107:23–24

Chapter 1

H ow old are you?" Jacob Humphries cocked his head, his pale blue eyes narrowing at Matilda's oversized shirt and knee breeches.

"Fourteen." Matilda mumbled the lie. With her gaze fastened on the knotty-pine floor of the wharf house, she kept the ragged black slouch hat that covered her cropped hair pulled low over her face. The memory of taking the scissors to her long, dark, wavy tresses last night still hurt.

"Tall for fourteen, ain't ya?" Jacob rubbed his thumb across gray stubble that covered his ruddy, sea-weathered face. He frowned, creasing only a bit deeper the permanent crevices carved across his forehead by sun, wind, and sea.

"Yes, sir," she murmured.

Humphries' glare bored into her as he leaned back in his chair and gave a disgusted snort. "I've been outfitting the *Sea Star* with crews for more than twenty years, and you are about the sorriest applicant for cabin boy I've ever clapped eyes on. Show me your hands."

With slow, hesitant movements, Matilda stuck out her hands. Her long, delicate fingers protruded just beyond the cuffs of Mitchell's voluminous shirt.

"Palms up, you idiot!" Humphries reached across his desk and grabbed her wrist, twisting it, causing her to yelp in pain.

He examined the soft pink skin of her hand and gave a derisive snort. "Have you not done a decent day's work in all your sorry life?"

She held her breath.

Please, Lord, don't let him see through the ruse.

Jacob heaved a deep sigh laden with weary resignation. "If I had a better applicant for cabin boy I'd have already sent you packin'. Do you understand me?"

Matilda quaked, wanting to flee from his scathing appraisal. However, her legs were doing well to keep her vertical in the face of his castigation, let alone carry her from it.

His voice lowered with his grudging admission. "Truth is, there haven't been any other applicants, so I reckon you'll have to do. Maybe this trip will make a man of the pitiful likes of ya." He raked a quick, critical gaze down her form, his voice an odd mixture of contempt and sorrow. "More'n likely, it'll simply kill ya."

Matilda stood mute before his grim prediction, but her heart quickened, realizing that he'd actually accepted her for the voyage.

He turned the logbook around on the desk in front of him, shoved the inkwell forward, and flung the pen down beside it. "Go ahead, put your name or mark there."

Matilda's hand trembled as she dipped the pen into the inkwell and scribbled the unfamiliar fictitious name across the yellowed page where Humphries had jammed his grimy finger.

"At the end of the voyage, if you're still alive, you'll get a half percent worth of the whale oil take. Now, go make yourself known to Captain Dobbs."

A relieved breath forced its way through Matilda's lips as she picked up her canvas duffel with a trembling hand, slung it over her shoulder, and turned her back on Jacob Humphries and the wharf house.

Placing a shaky foot on the ship's gangplank, she feared she might collapse before ever reaching the whaling ship's deck.

What had brought her to this awful day?

One word answered.

Debt. Debt that threatened to leave her and Mother homeless.

Why, Papa, why?

The bitterness filling her chest shriveled to a lump of guilt. If Papa hadn't spent so much money on a lavish wedding for her and Mitchell, perhaps he wouldn't have leveraged their home and persuaded Mitchell to join him in gambling their fortunes on a shipload of Madagascar mahogany, which now lay on the sea floor. Perhaps he and Mitchell wouldn't have taken that last whaling voyage at the most dangerous time of year for hurricanes. And now Papa and Mitchell were gone; taken from her by the sea—the same sea to which she now trusted her own life and fortune.

The anger rolled in like the waves slapping the dock. *I never wanted an extravagant wedding. I never wanted a wedding. . . . I never wanted Mitchell.*

A new strand of guilt gnarled around her heart like the thick rope that secured the whaling ship to the dock post. She shook her head as if the motion might fling the thought from her mind. She'd wallowed enough in guilt over the past year. Guilt and regret wouldn't pay off the lien against the house. Serving as cabin boy on this whaling voyage might.

Pausing on the gangplank, she felt her stomach tighten. She hadn't set foot on a whaling ship in eight years, and then only for a short excursion to Martha's Vineyard with Papa and Mother. A day trip as a ten-year-old aboard her father's ship could in no way compare to the months-long whaling voyage ahead of her. At least Humphries had advertised this voyage as short, perhaps less than a year.

"Step lively, boy!"

Someone gave Matilda's shoulder a sturdy shove from behind.

"Either get you aboard or high-tail it back down the gangplank."

She looked over her left shoulder and into the eyes of the young man behind her. Gray eyes that, set wide in his round face framed by a mop of brown curls, held no meanness, just a lively eagerness for this impending voyage she'd begun to dread.

Matilda quickened her steps, impatient to report to the captain then slip away below deck.

"How old are you?"

She paused at the sailor's question and mumbled, "Fourteen." The lie chafed against her conscience. Jacob Humphries would likely not have hired an eighteen-year-old for the position of cabin boy, and he most certainly would not have hired a girl. But Matilda's petite stature had given her confidence that, by dressing like a male and binding her chest, she could pass for a fourteen-year-old boy.

"First voyage?" The inquisitive sailor, who looked a few years older than herself, shifted his duffel on his broad, muscular shoulder with a shrug.

Matilda squirmed beneath his discerning gaze and nodded.

"What's your name?"

"Matt Adams." Her mother's maiden name felt odd on her lips, and the lie soured in her mouth. But her married name, Daggett, or her own maiden name of Rigsby, could invite dangerous speculation.

"Tom Owens." The young man stuck out his hand.

Not in the habit of shaking hands with gentlemen, Matilda took it with a halting, tentative motion. Heat leaped to her face as she placed her palm in the calloused clasp of his large hand. His rough fingers felt strong and warm against hers.

A stiff breeze carried a whiff of Bay Rum to her nostrils while rearranging his dark curls across his tanned forehead.

"I'm the harpooner." His tone reflected his pride. "I first went to sea at fourteen myself. This is my seventh year at sea, and I've taken nearly as many whales as the years I've been alive."

Matilda doubted his boasts were empty bragging. Papa always said a man wore his honesty on his face, and she'd never seen a more honest face than the one before her.

"Well, my young friend, reckon we might as well report to old Dobbs, hey?" Grinning, he laid an arm across her shoulder. Matilda stiffened at the gesture. Not since Papa and Mitchell left on that fateful voyage over a year ago had any man touched her in such a familiar way.

She fought the urge to shrug away from his arm. Everyone on this ship, including Tom Owens, must believe she was a boy, or all was lost.

Captain Benjamin Dobbs stood expressionless on the undulating deck, his buff-clad legs planted apart, his arms clasped behind his dark wool jacket.

"Harpooner Tom Owens reporting for duty, sir."

Matilda fidgeted beside the enthusiastic sailor.

"Glad to have you aboard, Tom." Dobbs offered his hand to the young harpooner. "We should have a good take with you wielding the harpoon."

"I should hope so, sir." Tom's chest puffed out at the captain's compliment.

Dobbs's face remained a stoic mask as he turned to Matilda. "And who might you be, my good lad?"

"Matt Adams, cabin boy," Matilda mumbled. The less she talked, the less likely she'd disclose her true gender.

"Cabin boy, hey?" Tilting back his sandy head, Captain Dobbs looked down his long nose at her and snorted. "Pickin's must be gettin' mighty slim."

Holding her breath, Matilda decided not to comment.

"Well, go below and stow your gear. Stay well aft and away from the fo'c's'le." He delivered the order in a tone laced with both disappointment and pity.

"Yes, sir." Matilda exhaled a relieved breath. Holding tight to her duffel strap, she turned toward the hatch that led belowdecks with no intention of disobeying the captain's order. Papa had often described the fo'c's'le, or forecastle, of the ship as a filthy, foul place at the bow where the roughest of the crew congregated.

Stale air met her as she made her way to the stifling quarters below. The place stank of the lingering smells of unwashed bodies, rotting fish, and other aromas she'd rather leave unidentified.

Farther aft, in the galley, an old black man stood shucking oysters.

"Where should I stow my duffel?" Matilda looked around, trying to get her bearings.

"You the cabin boy?" The old man gave her a cursory glance.

"Yes."

"Old Jacob must not had no other takers." He chuckled and dropped the shucking knife into a bucket with a clatter. Turning, he scrutinized her from the top of her battered hat to her oversized shoes.

As with the harpooner earlier, Matilda squirmed beneath his stare. His bright, dark eyes appeared far too astute for her liking.

"Stow it there." A quick jerk of his gray head indicated a little cubbyhole opposite the galley. A dirty, straw tick covered the tiny space. "I'm Solomon Mays." He offered her his hand.

The name fit. She'd never seen a wiser face than the dark, wrinkled one before her.

"Matt Adams." That the lie came easier now pricked at her conscience. She accepted his hand, feeling a bit more comfortable than when she'd exchanged handshakes with the young harpooner. The firmness of the old man's grip surprised her.

"I'm cook and whatever else the cap'n decides I am." Solomon chuckled deep in his throat. "You'll be whatever I decide *you* are." He grinned, his gaze boring into her eyes. "Mostly you'll be nursemaid to the cap'n and first mate and fetch 'n' carry fer me."

Solomon Mays made Matilda nervous. Fooling the crew and even the captain would be simple compared to keeping her secret from the perceptive old cook.

"Jis' now, I want you to take that bucket o' slop up top and throw it over the side." He rammed a thumb in the direction of a foul-smelling oaken bucket on the deck floor beside him.

Holding her breath, Matilda grasped the bucket's rope handle and made for the gangway steps. A breeze blew in from the top deck, shoving the rank odor into her face, and she gagged.

"You'd best lose that sense o' smell, boy, or you'll spend the whole voyage leanin' over the side." Solomon's laughter followed her up the steps.

On deck, she gasped for breath and ran as fast as she could to dispose of the bucket's offending contents.

"Boy! Hey, boy, you'd best learn to answer when I speak!"

Realizing she was the one being addressed, Matilda snapped her head around at the harsh-sounding voice behind her.

"Climb aloft and trim that sail."

Her heart jumped, and she stifled a gasp as she looked into the green eyes of Noah Bertram.

Though they'd met but once—last year at her wedding reception—the handsome young officer had made an undeniable impression. His tanned, well-shaped features, his tall, muscular build, and his glossy black hair ensured him a constant bevy of beauties clamoring for his attention. She'd thought him somewhat of a peacock, but couldn't help feeling a bit flattered when he'd asked Mitchell's permission to dance with her.

He will know me. I'll be put off.

She could scarcely breathe for the fear tightening like an iron band around her chest. Pretending she hadn't heard him, Matilda headed for the hatch.

"Are you deaf, boy?" Noah grabbed her shoulder. "I said get you up and trim that starboard aft sail. Go on!" He gave her a hard push. "Scamper up that ratline like the little rat you are."

Amazement that he'd not recognized her eclipsed all fear of Noah's order.

"Beggin' your pardon, sir." Tom Owens's quiet voice held a tinge of controlled animosity. "I don't think the lad's ready for that yet."

Noah stiffened, his eyes flashing with anger. "He good and well better be ready for it. And I advise you to stow your impertinence, Mr. Owens. Harpooner or not, you could still be made to feel the cat-o-nine-tails."

"Bad luck to lose a man before we shove off. Just tryin' to save you some bad luck and a cabin boy." The light indifference in Tom's tone conflicted with the anger in his gray eyes, growing dark as storm clouds.

A perceptible tension between the two men suggested a less than friendly relationship. Despite his higher rank, the first mate blinked and took a half step back. Then, seeming to remember his place, he jutted out his square chin and turned to Matilda.

"I have other things to attend to, but you'd better get your scrawny hide up there and do as I say, boy!" Lifting his patrician nose, Noah swaggered away to another part of the deck.

"I'll do it." Tom started toward the ratline.

"No, the first mate ordered me to do it." Matilda set the bucket down and glanced up at the riggings. As the daughter of a sea captain, she'd learned early to never question an order or shirk a task. Jacob Humphries had hired her to work on this whaler. She might as well start now.

Tom looked down at her feet. "Then take off your shoes. The ropes are wet from sea spray. Ill-fitting shoes will cause you to lose your footing." Matilda kicked off the shoes, her innards tightening at the seaman's warning.

"Your socks will protect your feet from the rough ropes." A worried frown furrowed Tom's forehead. "Test every rope before you put your full weight on it."

She acknowledged his instructions with a nod.

"Wouldn't want to bring Jonah's luck down on us before we even weigh anchor now, would you?" His smile could not expunge the fear from his eyes.

"I can do it."

She gazed up into the rigging sketched against the blue sky like a brown spider's web. Her throat went dry. She'd climbed on the ropes of her father's ships when she was small, but never as high as Noah's order required.

Matilda dragged off her hat and handed it to Tom, then with a deep breath, she grasped the ratline. Placing a stocking-clad foot in the network of ropes, she slowly began to climb.

While the stockings did help to protect her feet from the abrasive ropes, the rough lines dug into her hands as she pulled herself up. Buffeted by the winds, she held tight to the rope ladder as she climbed, ignoring the temptation to look down.

"When you climb, you always look up toward your destination."

Papa's words, echoing in her ears, were a guiding comfort.

Willing her shaking legs to stillness, she prayed, *Dear Lord, help me do this.*

Tentatively she allowed her left foot to leave the ratline and touch the slippery rope that seemed to lead to the starboard aft sail.

"Ahh!" The strangled cry of terror sprang from her throat as the rope gave way. Matilda grasped the ratline at the last possible moment and saved herself from a deadly fall. Her quavering lungs pulled in deep, thankful breaths as her rope-burned palms clung to the life-saving ratline. For interminable moments she hung too frightened to move, her trembling body dangling far above the deck.

"Right! To the right!"

Somehow Tom's voice filtered through the din of her heart pounding in her ears. With an almost detached fascination, she watched her right foot reach out and step either toward her task or into eternity.

The rope held. She grasped the closest rope perpendicular to the one she now trusted with her full weight.

Inch by inch and hand over hand, she made her way to the starboard aft sail. Reaching out, she took hold of the rope she knew would turn the sail and bring it into the wind.

Task accomplished, she tied the sail securely with a round turn knot and two half hitches. Watching the wind fill the canvas sail, she grinned, thankful for the hours Papa had spent teaching her to tie knots as a child.

Her confidence buoyed by her success, she scampered with ease down the ratline. Back on the solid deck she met Tom Owens's ashen face with a broad smile then snatched her hat from his hands and plopped it back on her head. "See, I told you I could do it."

"For a minute there, you almost caused me to get religion," he said, his voice a bit unsteady.

"Then I'm glad, if by 'religion' you mean trust in the Lord. I would say that is exactly what you need, Mr. Owens."

His lips slipped into a crooked grin. "What I need Master Adams, is a green willow switch to apply to your legs, you cocky scalawag! You just took five years off my life with that stunt."

" 'I can do all things through Christ which strengthens me.'" Quoting her favorite verse from Philippians, Matilda pushed her stocking feet into the scuffed pair of her late husband's shoes.

Tom's grin stretched across his handsome face, and Matilda's heart quickened. "I'd say you'll bear some watchin', my little man-of-the-cloth, if you are to return to New Bedford after this voyage."

Matilda picked up the bucket, turned, and made her way toward the main hatch, feeling the harpooner's gaze on her back. She attributed her pounding heart to the fright she'd experienced in the rigging and the exhilaration of conquering her fear. With God's help, she *could* do anything. With God's help, she could endure whatever this voyage demanded.

Down below, Solomon's dark gaze followed her every move. "Could'a dumped a dozen buckets of slop an' got back sooner."

Matilda's voice swelled with pride. "First Mate Bertram ordered me to trim a sail."

"Is that right. . .*boy*?" The old man's eyes narrowed as they bored into her.

Matilda felt the blood drain to her toes. He knew.

Chapter 2

"Y ou got nothin' to fear from me." Kindness softened Solomon's quiet voice as he took the bucket from her fingers, frozen with fear.

"Reckon you got your reasons." He set the bucket down in the galley.

Rising stiffly, he turned a stern face to hers. "Try to walk more like a boy, keep away from the crew, 'specially at night, and pray to the Good Lord that none of 'em finds out you're a girl."

Matilda nodded.

"Here!" He thrust another bucket into her hand. "Dump these shells over the side and don't 'spect no slack from me." Despite his stern voice, she caught the kind twinkle in his dark eyes.

When she remembered to breathe again, Matilda exhaled a painful breath.

She climbed to the top deck, her heart lightened. Knowing she wouldn't need to maintain her deception around the cook relieved her burden. Perhaps God had given her an ally in Solomon.

Matilda lifted her face to the azure sky.

Dear Lord, please help me do this.

◆— —◆

A strong, gentle hand on Matilda's shoulder stirred her awake.

"Matt, watch. Up with ya now."

At Tom's voice, Matilda's heart quickened as she sat up and squinted against the light of the lantern in his hand. "Already?" She blinked and yawned into his smiling face. A month into the voyage the interrupted sleep of the four-hour-on and four-hour-off schedule still felt jarring.

"Already, my little mate." Since her harrowing climb that first day on the ship, Tom Owens had made good on his comment that she'd "bear watching," tending to hover near her when on deck and even requesting the same watch. While his insistent watchfulness often grated against Matilda's independent nature, she couldn't deny that she enjoyed the handsome harpooner's company. His perpetual good humor, ready smile, and sweet nature drew her to him while his patience in teaching her tasks had proved a godsend.

"What time is it?" She sat up on the straw tick and ran her hands through her short-cropped hair, chasing out the cockroaches that scurried from the light in all directions.

"Does it matter?" His teeth flashed like pearls and his gray eyes danced with fun in the soft light.

Matilda's heart quickened, a now familiar response to his nearness, which always precipitated a flash of guilt. Over their short engagement and scant month of marriage, Mitchell had never evoked such feelings in her. She shrank back into the shadows to hide the blush warming her cheeks.

"It's midnight." Grasping her arm, he hauled her to her feet.

"I'm coming." Matilda twisted from his grasp, irritated at her own flustered reaction to his touch.

"You sure are a grouch when you wake." His soft chuckle sent her heart hammering again.

He thinks I'm a boy. I must never forget that he thinks I'm a boy. The reminder blared through her head as she followed Tom up the gangway to the main deck.

Above deck Matilda inhaled a lung full of fresh sea breeze—a delicious relief from the stifling dead air below deck.

"Good to breathe again, ain't it?" Tom grasped the rail, gazing out into the vast darkness.

Joining him, Matilda lifted her face to the canopy of stars above them. The bright, winking heavenly bodies looked like diamonds strewn across black velvet.

"Look." Encouraging Tom's gaze to follow her fingertip, she pointed toward the night sky. "It's Cetus, the whale."

"You know the stars?"

She almost giggled at his surprise. "Of course. My father was a seafaring man. He taught me all the constellations. It will be December, though, before we can see my favorite, Orion."

"And why is that one your favorite?"

The compassion in his quiet question made her heart thump, and laced her tone with sadness. "When my father was alive, we'd always look for it together at Christmastime."

"Your father was lost at sea?" The kindness in his voice made her want to cry.

"Yes, he was a whaleman." At the last moment, Matilda stopped herself from adding that her husband had also been a whaleman. She looked up into the starry sky through the mist of tears stinging her eyes as memories of studying the constellations with Papa flashed through her mind. "The Christmas Eve when I was six, he showed me how to find Orion, 'The Hunter.' He told me that like Orion he, too, was a hunter. A hunter of whales." She swallowed hard. "We vowed to always look together for Orion on Christmas Eve, even when we were apart."

"Well, with the son of Orion aboard, we should have a good take." Tom laid a warm, comforting arm around her shoulder, and the temptation to rest her head against his chest became so strong she had to pull away.

Daughter of Orion. The urge to correct his description of her tugged hard, but such a careless slip could jeopardize her voyage. Instead, she focused on the more troubling part of his comment. While she appreciated Tom's attempt to comfort her, it bothered her that he would attribute a successful voyage to anything other than God's grace.

She looked up at him, and her voice strengthened with her conviction. "If the *Sea Star* has a good voyage, we will have God alone to thank."

A good-natured chuckle bubbled from his well-shaped lips. "Perhaps you're right, my little man-of-the-cloth. And perhaps you are better suited for the pulpit than a whale ship."

Matilda's heart raced like a wounded whale as she gazed at his lips drawn up into a lazy grin. *I wonder what they would feel like against. . .* She shook her head as if to toss the troublesome thought from her mind.

"No?" He misinterpreted her gesture. "You do not think a pulpit is in your future?"

"No."

"Then you plan to become a whaleman like your father?"

"No." Matilda gazed out at the dark ocean. She must stop looking at him.

"Well, if you don't plan to be a whaleman or a preacher, then what sort of man *do* you see Matt Adams growing into?"

No man. No man at all! The words clawed at her lips, aching for their freedom. She swallowed them down hard. "I don't know."

"Don't you think your father would want you to follow in his footsteps?" Tom's soft voice nudged.

Matilda gazed into the black infinity while the deck rolled gently beneath her feet on the calm sea. Memories of Papa came washing over her like the ocean waves. The creaking of the ship's timbers, the occasional slapping of the billowing sails, and the soft *lap, lap, lap* of the sea against the side of the ship filled the silence. When she finally spoke, her whispered reply felt more to the September night than to the man beside her. "I think my father was more concerned that I develop a strong character and love for Christ than how I chose to make my living."

"Sounds like you were right fond of your father." His soft words wrapped like a warm blanket around her heart.

"Yes."

"You say he was a whaleman, yet the name Adams is not familiar to me, and I know every whaleman in New Bedford."

Matilda didn't want to lie. There'd been too many lies already. "He sailed out of Nantucket." It was the truth. Her father's last voyage *had* sailed from that harbor.

"I have sailed several times from there, myself." An odd somberness weighted his words. Then, with a grin and a shrug, his voice lightened. "But then, I don't know *all* the Nantucket whalers."

"I don't care to speak of it further." Matilda cleared her throat a little too delicately, so added as deep and masculine a sounding cough as she could muster.

"Best ask Solomon to give you something for that cough." He brushed past her and picked up a harpoon lying near a bucket of coiled rope. "Old Solomon's got a concoction for most every ill—that is, if you can keep 'em down." Tom chuckled as he seated himself on an upturned barrel and began restringing the rope along the harpoon's shaft.

Watching his handsome profile silhouetted in the pale moonlight, Matilda's heart quickened, and immediately a gust of guilt smote it. While Mitchell had never made her heart dance, he *had* been her husband. She'd embarked on this voyage barely out of widow's weeds. Surely she could control her emotions enough not to dishonor her dead husband by allowing a handsome face to set her heart aflutter.

She turned her face from Tom and lifted it again to the glittering heavens. She must school her heart and mind to think of Tom as a friend, and nothing more. Besides, hadn't she vowed to never again give her heart to a seaman? Years of watching Mother endure loneliness during Papa's absences had soured her on the notion of marrying a seafaring man. So when Papa had encouraged her to accept his first mate, Mitchell Daggett's, offer to court her, she'd balked. But, in the end, as always, she'd given in to Papa. Courting turned to engagement, and engagement to marriage.

Marriage to a man I didn't love.

A new wave of guilt rolled over her, drenching her heart. Sweet, boring Mitchell. She'd scarcely known him. Perhaps, as Mother had counseled on Matilda's wedding day, love was a journey and Matilda would have reached the destination over time. But a scant month past her wedding, Mitchell and Papa had left on the voyage that took their lives. Papa had chosen her first husband, but if Matilda ever wed again it would be to someone of her own choosing, and he wouldn't be a seaman.

She glanced back at Tom working with the harpoon a few feet away, and her rebellious heart did that odd little twirl again. Grasping the ship's railing hard, she blinked back tears and stared toward the horizon. Ruling her heart might prove as difficult as ruling the sea, because while the night sea remained calm as glass, her heart felt caught up in a tempest and headed toward dangerous waters.

◆──────◆◆

"You sho' do put a powerful lot o' store in your Bible readin'."

Sitting cross-legged on her mat, Matilda looked up from the Bible in her hands to Solomon, who stood across the galley. Reading the scriptures and faithfully keeping an account of their voyage in her journal had helped Matilda fill the monotonous hours.

"Yes, I find the scriptures a great comfort." She caressed the soft gray fur of the ship's cat curled in her lap. "You like it, too, don't you, Ambergris?" Smiling, she petted the affectionate animal then glanced at the cook. "Did you name him for his color, Solomon?" The hue of the cat's coat did resemble the highly prized gray substance found on rare occasions in the intestines of whales.

"No." Solomon looked up from cleaning a fresh catch of cod. "It's 'cause he's worth his weight in gold. If it wasn't for him, you'd be chasin' rats off your face each mornin' 'stid of roaches."

"Then I like him even better." Laughing, Matilda stroked the cat's back until he arched and purred, gently kneading her knee with the soft pads of his front paws.

Her thoughts returned to the cook's comment about her Bible reading. "Don't you find the scriptures a comfort, Solomon?"

"Can't read, but me and my mammy, we worked for Quakers when I was young. They was always readin' to us from the Bible. Bein' young, I soaked it up like a sponge. Reckon I carry my Bible here." He thumped a gnarled finger against his chest before dropping a handful of small fish heads to the galley floor. "Here, puss!"

Ambergris abandoned Matilda's lap to pounce on Solomon's offering.

"Are you a Christian, then?" Matilda's heart filled with joy to learn that the old cook, who'd become her confidant and friend, shared her love of the scriptures.

"Yes, young'un. Don't you worry none 'bout this old man's soul. Sorry as it is, it belongs to the Savior."

They shared a glad smile.

Solomon had never asked about her true identity, or why she'd chosen to masquerade as a boy aboard a whaling ship. It also heartened her to notice how he took care to never address her in the feminine gender. Without question, he'd offered her his help and friendship, so it didn't surprise her to learn of Solomon's strong faith. The old cook embodied the teachings of Christ.

"Read some to me." He cocked a grin in her direction.

Matilda turned her attention back to her Bible. "I was just reading from Psalm 107."

"Ah, one of my favorites." Solomon's wrinkled face relaxed into a tranquil smile in anticipation of the passage.

Matilda's fingertip slipped down the page until she came to verse twenty-three.

" 'They that go down to the sea in ships, that do business in great waters; these see the works of the Lord, and his wonders in the deep. For he commandeth, and raiseth the stormy wind, which lifteth up the waves thereof. They mount up to the heaven, they go down again to the depths: their soul is melted because of trouble. They reel to and fro, and stagger like a drunken man, and are at their wit's end. Then they cry unto the Lord in their trouble, and he bringeth them out of their distresses.' "

Her voice faded. Although she'd always loved this passage, it now reminded her of the storm that took Papa's and Mitchell's lives. "Do you think we are apt to run into a gale on this trip?"

"Young Mister Owens done told me 'bout your pappy." Solomon's dark eyes softened with sympathy. "Don't you worry none, young-un. Don't 'spect we'll see any real bad storms as far north as the cap'n plans to keep us. But as long as you belong to the Savior, He'll keep you safe in this life and in the next."

Lifting his face and closing his eyes, Solomon recited the twenty-ninth and thirtieth verses of the Psalm. " 'He maketh the storm a calm, so that the waves thereof are still. Then are they glad because they be quiet; so he bringeth them unto their desired haven.' "

"Do you think Tom is a Christian?" The question had troubled her since that first day when Tom helped her with the sails, but she hadn't found the courage to ask him.

A slow grin crawled across Solomon's lips, and his eyes twinkled. "Mister Owens is a right fine young man. Would make a good catch for the right woman."

"That's not what I asked." Feeling a warm flush suffuse her face, Matilda turned from his astute gaze.

"Reckon you'd have to ask Mister Owens that." Solomon turned his head but not quick enough to hide a knowing grin.

"Ask Mister Owens what?"

Matilda jerked her head up at Tom's voice, her heart beating like the wings of a captured bird. "I—I was just wondering if you are a Christian."

"This boy's meant for the pulpit for sure!" Tom's laughter boomed in the little galley.

"Well, are you?" Matilda looked him in the eyes.

Fidgeting, Tom cleared his voice. "Well, I believe in God. I'm not a heathen, if that's what you mean."

"No, that's not what I mean." Determined to not allow him to evade the question, Matilda pressed him for an answer. "Have you given your heart and soul to Jesus?"

His gaze bounced around the galley, avoiding hers. "When you put it that way, I reckon not. Never been much on religion," he mumbled, frowning.

A desperation she'd never known seized Matilda's heart.

"But what if you were lost? We will reach the whaling grounds soon. What if one came up under your boat? What if. . ." She found herself unable to finish the thought, let alone the words.

Tom's mouth slipped into the half-grin that always turned her insides to jelly. "I'll think on it, Matt, I promise." He reached down and tousled her hair.

At the touch of his fingers on her head, Matilda's heart ran a gamut of emotions. Shock, anger, and frustration melted into a sweet caring she wasn't prepared to attach a name to.

She clutched her Bible to her chest as she watched him walk toward his berth with the hint of a limp she'd noticed in his gait.

Even his distinctive walk had become dear to her.

Rogue tears filled her eyes. She turned her head from Solomon's perceptive gaze as an errant tear dropped onto the black grainy cover of her Bible.

Dear Lord, please keep him safe until I can persuade him to accept Your salvation.

Resting for a moment against the handle of the deck swab, Matilda lifted her face to the salty breeze. Her heart ached with a quiet desperation.

In the two days since she'd talked to Tom about becoming a Christian, neither of them had mentioned it again.

Winning him to Christ was her mission. She could see it as clearly as she saw the dolphins jumping out of the waters just off the port side of the *Sea Star*, glistening like arcs of silver in the sunlight. Somehow she must make this good man, this sweet man, understand the importance of giving his heart and soul to Jesus.

She closed her eyes, feeling the Lord's presence in the warm sun on her face and the gentle fingers of soft breezes gliding through her hair.

Lord, give me the right words to make him see.

"Master Adams!"

Matilda's eyes flew open and her heart jumped to her throat at Noah Bertram's voice.

"See that rope bucket?" A quick jerk of his dark head indicated a bucket lying on its side, a few feet away.

"Yes, sir." Matilda's voice sank at the sight of the bucket, its rope spilling out onto the deck.

"Is that your doing?" His ominous quiet tone reminded her of distant thunder before a storm.

She didn't remember having bumped the bucket, but she might have. Her hand trembled on the swab handle as she turned back to Noah's angry face.

"We're nearing whaling grounds, Master Adams." He made the clipped words sting like the end of a lash. "That rope needs to be ready for the whale boats. Is it, Master Adams?"

Paralyzed with fear, Matilda stood mute, her bare feet awash in the seawater she'd been using to swab the port-side deck.

It came like a blur before she could answer. With a backward swipe of his hand, Noah landed a solid blow against her left ear that would have sent her sprawling across the wet deck if she hadn't grabbed the railing, keeping her on her feet.

"You clumsy little brat!" Noah towered over her with clenched fists. "I want that rope picked up and wound properly in its bucket, do you hear?"

Shaken, Matilda could hear little but the ringing in her left ear. Clinging to the rail, she touched her hand to her throbbing face and raised her tear-filled eyes to his.

The hard line of his mouth twisted into a vicious sneer. He enjoyed inflicting pain. Matilda could scarcely believe that these cruel green slits were the same eyes that had gazed admiringly into hers a year ago at her wedding. The same hand that smote her face had once lifted her hand to his lips for a tender kiss. The angry man before her held no resemblance to the dashing seaman with whom she'd shared a dance at her wedding party. Noah Bertram was a monster.

"Are you all right, Matt?" Matilda felt Tom's strong, reassuring hands grasp her shoulders from behind.

"Y–yes," she managed, her voice shaky through the ringing in her ear.

His hands left her shoulders, and he walked around her to face Noah.

"Matt didn't knock that bucket over. It was already on its side when he came up on deck." Anger quivered through Tom's voice and his fists clenched, making his tanned biceps ripple. "You strike that boy again for no reason, Bertram, and I promise you a taste of your own medicine!"

Noah blanched in the face of Tom's steely glare. Then he stiffened and lifted his chin in an arrogant tilt. "Your impertinence has just bought you a taste of the lash, Mister Owens!" His gaze darted about the deck. "Mister Prescott! Mister Davitts!" He screamed at the two burly seamen who'd just descended to the deck from furling the mizzenmast sail. "Strip Mister Owens to the waist, and lash him to the mizzenmast. He wants to be reminded of his place on this ship."

Chapter 3

No!" The word tore from Matilda's throat in an anguished croak.

Captain Dobbs strode toward them, his face a thundercloud. "What is the meaning of this? Let this man be!"

He glared at the two seamen who chorused "Aye, aye, sir," as they released their grips on Tom and scurried away.

Matilda's quaking knees threatened to buckle as a wave of relief washed over her.

"Mister Bertram!" His countenance a study in controlled fury, Captain Dobbs confronted the first mate. "We are all but upon the whaling grounds, and I need my harpooner in good shape."

Noah lifted his square chin, his voice steeped in righteous indignation. "Mister Owens threatened me with bodily harm when I attempted to discipline Master Adams."

The captain turned to Tom. "Is that right, Mister Owens?"

"Yes." Tom's unflinching gaze met his captain's. "He hit Matt for no good reason."

"The clumsy brat knocked over the rope bucket, yonder." The ugly scowl on Noah's face deepened.

"Did you?" His voice toneless, Captain Dobbs turned an unreadable face to Matilda.

"I don't know." She pushed the honest answer past her constricting throat. "I don't think so. Tom said I didn't."

"And you believe him?"

Matilda swallowed down her heart that had jumped to her mouth. "Yes, I do."

Would Tom be beaten? Would she? Would her masquerade be discovered?

"Then so do I." The barest hint of a smile lifted the corner of the captain's mouth, sending a flood of relief through Matilda.

His features hardening again, the captain turned to the two men. "Mister Bertram, Mister Owens. I'll have no more of this, or the pair of you will be put ashore and replaced when we reach the Western Islands. Is that understood?"

"Yes, sir," Tom and Noah said in near unison.

"Now, be about your chores, the both of you." The captain's stern look bounced between them.

Matilda watched the two young men's glares cross rapiers one last time before they turned and strode away in opposite directions.

"Master Adams."

Standing alone before the captain, Matilda swallowed hard.

When he spoke, the gentleness in his voice surprised her. "Go below. Solomon should be able to find something for you to do. And from now on, try to give First Mate Bertram a wide berth."

"Yes, sir," she mumbled before sprinting to the main hatch.

Below deck, Solomon looked up from his perch on a barrelhead where he sat shining the first mate's spare pair of boots. "What happened to you?"

Matilda touched her left ear that felt swollen and hot. "First Mate Bertram hit me because he thought I knocked over a rope bucket." Sniffling, she smeared a tear from her cheek with trembling fingertips.

"He's a bad'un, that one." Solomon's wrinkled brow furrowed even deeper and his hand stilled the buffing cloth as he watched her pull on her socks and shoes with shaky hands. "Not worth cryin' over, though. He ain't worth. . ." He finished the thought by spitting on the toe of the boot then rubbing the spittle hard into the leather.

"I'm not crying because Noah hit me." Matilda sat cross-legged on her straw tick and picked up Ambergris, who'd jumped into her lap. She rubbed her injured face against the cat's soft, gray fur. "Tom nearly got a beating for coming to my rescue. I was hoping to teach him the scriptures. Now he will probably stay as far away from me as possible."

"Oh, I don't 'magine that'll happen." The old cook grinned at the tears slipping down her face. "That boy's right fond of you." His dark eyes twinkled. " 'Cept, I reckon, he don't rightly know why."

With her heart feeling like someone had lashed it to an anchor, Matilda wished she could believe Solomon as she watched his hunched figure carrying the shined boots shuffle off toward Noah Bertram's cabin.

Her hopes of talking to Tom about Christ's salvation withered. Despite Solomon's opinion to the contrary, Tom would likely spend the rest of the voyage avoiding her.

Opening her Bible, she retreated into the sweet comfort of the Savior's words.

"Are you all right?"

At Tom's soft voice, Matilda's head snapped up. Her racing heart snatched away her breath. "I'm sorry I caused you trouble. You shouldn't have challenged Mister Bertram. If not for Captain Dobbs, Solomon would be treating your back with one of his smelly concoctions."

Tom's easy chuckle dismissed her concern. "Guess I'm not much of one for turnin' the other cheek." He nodded toward the Bible in her lap. "Reckon, too, it would've been worth a beatin' to mop the deck with that horse's behind."

"You *do* know the Bible!"

"A little."

"Would you like to know more?" Her enthusiasm to minister to Tom revived, Matilda seized with gusto the opportunity God had presented to her.

"Sure." Tom gave her a good-natured grin and dropped to the floor beside her. "Preach to me, my little man-of-the-cloth." He settled with his back to the cubbyhole wall, his arms crossed over his chest.

Thank You, Jesus!

The prayer fluttered from Matilda's happy heart. She began reading the account of Christ's Sermon on the Mount from the book of Matthew, hope blooming in her voice.

At length, Tom heaved a deep sigh. The grin had left his face, and his brow furrowed in thought. "Lot of things to remember. Lot of things I don't think I can do, like turnin' the other cheek and lovin' my enemy. Don't think it's in me. I'm a seafarin' man."

Undaunted, Matilda hastened to dismiss his illogical conclusion. "Peter, James, and John all followed and loved Jesus. They were all seafaring men, too. Would you like for me to read you the account of when Jesus called them to be fishers of men?" The pages of the Bible whispered as she searched for the familiar scripture.

"Tomorrow." Laughing, Tom stood and gave her hair a playful muss. "Right now I have work to do." His gray eyes turned serious and his voice softened. "You'll make a preacher yet, Master Adams, and who knows, you just might save my sin-blackened soul after all."

Watching his back disappear through the main hatch, she whispered, "I hope so."

◆━━◆━━━━◆━━◆

Turning from the rail, Tom glanced down the main deck and smiled to see his young friend walking toward him, Bible in hand. He couldn't help admiring the lad's persistence.

While he generally preferred to keep to himself during a voyage, something about this cabin boy had drawn him—something he couldn't quite get his mind around. He'd found the boy's interest in religion at once irritating and amusing. At first he'd agreed to listen to Matt's Bible reading and preaching simply to humor the lad. However, as the days passed, he realized he'd begun to look forward to their sessions, though he'd sooner be keelhauled than admit it.

He'd found the passages about forgiveness especially interesting, and his heart had reached out for them as if they were life buoys. Was it possible for Jesus to wipe away what Tom had done? Could He restore Tom's sense of peace that the sea swallowed up a year ago?

Tom's heart softened at the sight of Matt's young face. Pink cheeks and large blue-green eyes, shining with childlike enthusiasm.

Matt believed it. But Matt didn't know what Tom had done. And Matt had never felt responsible for the deaths of a ship full of whalers. How could Tom expect God to forgive what he couldn't forgive himself?

"Tom, I found another scripture about forgiveness." Matt plopped down on the deck beside him. "Yesterday you seemed interested in that subject, so I've been searching for more verses concerning it."

Tom fished the pumice stone from his pocket and began applying it to the blade of his harpoon. "Preach to me." He angled a grin at Matt.

"It's from the book of Colossians." Matt's delicate brow wrinkled with determination as he leafed through the pages. At last, he began to read, tracing the words with his finger. " 'Giving thanks unto the Father, which hath made us meet to be partakers of the inheritance of the saints in light: Who hath delivered us from the power of darkness, and hath translated us into the kingdom of his dear Son: In whom we have redemption through his blood, even the forgiveness of sins.' "

Forgiveness of sins. If only such a thing could be true. Tom stopped his work with the pumice stone and looked at Matt. "All sins? Aren't some sins worse than others? Wouldn't you reckon—"

"Thar she blows!"

The familiar cry Tom had waited for sailed down from the crosstrees, interrupting his thought.

Both Tom and Matt swung their faces up toward the top of the mizzenmast.

"Where away?" Captain Dobbs cupped his hands around his mouth, directing his shout to the rigging above.

"Four points off the lee bow, sir!" The answer floated down to the deck.

"Sing out! Sing out every time!" Through his cupped hands, Benjamin Dobbs transmitted his orders amid a thunderous rush of human feet, scurrying about the deck like so many roaches caught in the sudden light of a lantern.

Matt grasped Tom's arm. "I want to go, too."

Tom met his young friend's pleading eyes with a full understanding of the boy's feelings.

"She breeches!" wafted down from the crosstrees. "She white-waters! Thar she blooows!"

Tom felt a tug-of-war within him. He'd experienced the excitement of the hunt and the lure of the sea at Matt's same age. Yet, whaling was dangerous work. Could he put this boy at risk? Could he bear the burden of another death?

"Please." Matt's voice turned urgent.

Conflicted, Tom glanced about at the whalers dashing to their posts, then turned back to Matt. His resistance crumbled in the face of the cabin boy's huge, hopeful eyes.

God, if You can hear me, please don't let me regret this.

"I reckon, if it's all right with the captain. I went out first at fourteen."

"I'll put my Bible away, then I'll be right there!" Matt shouted over his shoulder as he ran toward the main hatch.

"Better hurry," Tom hollered back. "Whale boat waits for nobody!"

Consternation balled in Tom's gut, followed by a flash of irritation. He needed to stop feeling responsible for Matt Adams. He'd signed on to this voyage as a harpooner, not as nursemaid to some kid. He raked his thumb across two days of chin stubble. So why did he feel so protective toward him?

Something...

He didn't have time to worry about it. Grasping his harpoon, he hurried toward the port side. Somewhere out there a whale waited for him.

◆—————◆

Matilda stuffed her Bible in her duffel and flew back up the ladder, the companionway gang passing in a blur.

While she had no desire to watch the killing of a whale, the thought of waiting and worrying about Tom's safety felt unbearable.

"Lower away!" Captain Dobbs's shouted order spurred her on and she sprinted to the port side where most of the crew had gathered.

She ran up to the captain, the words of her breathless request tumbling over one another. "I want to go, too, sir."

"Maybe next time, son." Smiling, he placed a hand on her shoulder.

Her hope ebbed then rose again on a wave of determination. She wouldn't allow him to dismiss her out of hand. "Please, sir. I need to go. I *have* to go."

His soft sigh and half smile told her she'd won. "All right. Watch your seat, and mind Mister Bertram."

"Thank you, sir!" Matilda didn't wait for him to change his mind, but hurried to follow Tom down the rope ladder draped over the side of the ship.

Dropping the last four feet from the end of the ladder into the whale boat, she struggled to get her balance in the little rocking vessel.

"Keep your hands and arms away from the rope once I've stuck him," Tom said. "Once it starts payin' out around the loggerhead, I've seen it take off an arm just like that." He snapped his fingers in her face.

She gave him a solemn nod then took the seat in front of him.

The boat quickly filled, with Noah Bertram the last person to come aboard. As first mate, he would act as boat header. Standing at the bow, he'd handle the rudder and sing out orders.

Matilda's heart raced with anxious anticipation, but Tom's nearness offered a measure of calm.

Dear heavenly Father, please protect us.

As the prayer formed in her mind, Noah gave the order to lower the sail.

The crew took up their oars. Though at first Matilda strained with the exertion, her muscles soon remembered the rowing lessons Papa had taught her as a girl. Except for strength, she felt confident that her rowing skills matched that of any man in the boat.

"Put your backs into it, you maggots! Row! Row!" Noah's hateful, raspy whisper urged the crew to a faster pace.

Struggling to keep up with the rhythm of the crew, Matilda strained harder, pushing then pulling the smooth, round oar chaffing against her palms.

"Hold back, hold back!" Noah's frantic whisper told her they must be nearing the beast. "Take up the paddles. Be quiet with those oars."

Matilda's hand shook as she let go of the oars, allowing one to bump against the side of the boat.

Noah shot her a lethal glare. "You make one more sound, Master Adams, and I'll wring your scrawny neck!"

Quaking at his rasped threat, Matilda found comfort in the reassuring pressure of Tom's knee against her back.

The boat began to rock as the sea started to undulate in a way that felt nothing like the regular rhythm of the tides.

"Hold, hold. . ." Noah's voice tightened.

At last he looked at Tom. "Mister Owens, stand and give it to him."

The boat rocked as Tom took his place at the stern.

Matilda turned and watched him place his thigh against the clumsy cleat—the sturdy board with a concave cutout that allowed the harpooner to steady himself. The muscles of Tom's right arm flexed as he grasped the harpoon.

A large gray hill like a small island rose from the waters a few feet away, and Matilda stifled a gasp. Tom's arm flew forward like an iron spring. With a *zip*, the harpoon left his hand.

Nothing happened.

Had he missed?

The boat jerked and began to move across the water at an ever-increasing speed. In terror, Matilda grasped the side of the boat as they skimmed across the waves from crest to crest. Remembering Tom's warning, she kept her hands away from the rope that emitted a shrill whistle as it paid out at a deadly rate from the two tubs. All her life she'd heard Papa and other whalers speak of the "Nantucket sleigh-ride." Now she prayed to survive it.

Sea spray drenched Matilda's back as she held tight and prayed for the whale to tire. She lowered her head away from the whipping wind and water, her heart racing as much from excitement as from fear.

For almost a full hour, she guessed, they sped across the water. When she thought she could bear it no longer, the boat began to slow.

How far the whale had pulled them from the ship, she couldn't guess. The thought of towing a forty-plus-ton whale back to the *Sea Star* felt daunting.

"Pull, you lazy slugs, pull!" Noah stood. Matilda, along with the other members of the crew, pulled hard on the rope that was attached to a dying whale somewhere out in the ocean.

At last they drew up alongside the mortally wounded behemoth. Their boat came so close Matilda could have reached out and touched the whale's side.

An unexpected sadness gripped her. There would be time enough to touch the hide of this poor giant creature.

"Move away! Move away, I say!" Noah pushed his way toward the stern where he would administer the lethal lance.

Passing Matilda, he gave her shoulder a rough shove. Punishment, she suspected, for her earlier offense with the oar.

Tom stiffened and glared at Noah, but he said nothing. As the two men passed in front of her in the cramped quarters, Matilda could almost hear the air sizzle with their mutual loathing. For a moment, she feared they might actually go after each other right there in the whale boat.

"To the bow, Mister Owens." Noah ground the words between clenched teeth before taking his turn at the clumsy cleat.

Hefting the lance, Noah pressed his leg against the board's concave cutout and rammed the lance into the wounded, exhausted animal.

In agony, the beast reared its great tail and, in its death throes, what the whalers called its "flurry," brought it down hard next to the whale boat.

Matilda grabbed the side of the bobbing boat, fearing it would either be capsized or smashed to splinters. While the colossal tail missed a direct hit on the boat, it managed to graze it, drenching the crew with a shower of seawater and sending a mighty shudder through the small vessel.

To Matilda's horror, the blow catapulted Tom into the air. He landed in the ocean with a splash then disappeared beneath the crimson waves, stained with the whale's blood.

"Tom!" She screamed his name, her heart contracting as if squeezed by an iron fist. "Man overboard! Man overboard!"

In desperation, she turned to Noah, still goring the dying whale.

"Please, Mister Bertram. Mister Owens has been thrown out!"

Noah met her frantic pleas with an annoyed scowl. "Then someone fish him out! I have work to do."

With tears coursing down her face, Matilda raced around the edges of the whale boat, scanning the bloody ocean for any sign of Tom. Not since she'd learned of Papa's and Mitchell's deaths had she felt such utter despair.

The other three seamen in the boat joined in the search, poking their oars into the water.

"Tom! Tom!" Her lungs and throat burning, Matilda continued to scream his name as she peered into the murky depths.

Dear Lord, please don't let him be lost. He's not yet accepted Your Son. Please don't take him yet.

Chapter 4

A violent rocking of the boat brought Matilda scrambling over all obstacles to the starboard side.

"Tom!"

Relief surged through her at the sight of his brown curly head poking up through the water. His gray eyes sparkled with fun as the two Portuguese seamen hauled him into the boat like a landed carp.

"Worried?" Standing now and drenched with sanguine-stained seawater, he grinned down at her.

Spent, Matilda slumped to the closest rowing seat. Looking up at Tom's grinning face dripping with seawater, she wanted to scream. She wanted to beat her fists against his chest for frightening her so. But what she most wanted to do, she couldn't. She couldn't throw her arms around him and weep and kiss his neck. Instead, she hugged her arms around her shaking body and said the obvious, hoping the sea spray obliterated her tears.

"I thought you were gone."

Tom chuckled between sucking in deep breaths. "Not me. I'm not ready for Davey Jones's locker yet. Not by a long shot!"

The trip back to the *Sea Star* with the dead whale in tow proved as long and arduous as Matilda had feared. Her arms, shoulders, and back ached beyond anything she'd ever experienced, but her joy swamped all discomfort. Hymns of praise and thanksgiving winged their way to heaven from her grateful heart.

Tom was alive.

She could no longer deny the feeling surging through her, nor did she desire for God to take it away. With all her heart, as much as God allowed her to love another human being, she loved the man who sat rowing behind her.

Matilda set her mouth in a determined line. A renewed urgency to win Tom to Christ gripped her. While the news of Papa's and Mitchell's deaths had cleaved her heart, she at least had the comfort of knowing they belonged to Christ and were safely in the bosom of the Lord. She had no such reassurances concerning Tom. And for all his casual bravado, he'd come very close to losing his life today.

Dear Lord, make him see. Please, make him see.

At last, they pulled near the *Sea Star*.

Through pure will, Matilda pulled her spent arms and legs up the rope ladder dangling from the side of the ship.

"Step lively, Master Adams. Old Solomon could mount it quicker," Noah growled behind her. "Move those feet or I'll grab one and throw you back to the sea!"

From the *Sea Star's* deck, Tom shot a glare over Matilda's shoulder at Noah. "Do, and you'll follow directly behind him." He grabbed her hand and hauled her to the deck of the whale ship.

"Well done, Mister Bertram, Mister Owens," Captain Dobbs said as he strode to the starboard-side deck to congratulate the whaling party. "A nice-sized right whale! A fine start, I'd say."

He turned a rare, unrestrained smile to Matilda. "Survived your first hunt, I see, Master Adams."

"Yes, sir. Thank you, sir." The long punishing journey back to the ship and the climb up the side had drained the last ounce of Matilda's energy. Digging deep, she found strength she never knew she had and somehow stayed on her feet.

"You've all earned a good couple hours' rest before the cutting-in."

Acknowledging the captain's offer with a mute nod, Matilda headed for the main hatch hoping she could remain vertical until she reached her little straw tick.

At the bottom of the companionway, she turned to Tom who had followed her down. Looking into his tired gray eyes, she fought the urge to throw herself into his arms and hold him against her. Instead, she managed a weak smile. "I'm glad you made it."

The corner of his mouth quirked up in that lopsided grin that always melted her heart like butter on a hot griddle. "You didn't think I would miss the cuttin'-in and tryin'-out, did you?"

"It makes what we've been talking about even more urgent, don't you think?" Today he had faced death. Hopefully, the scare would prove the catalyst to bring him to a decision about Christ.

Tom sighed. "That again."

Gazing into his eyes, she prayed for divine guidance. "Any of us could have our lives taken without warning. We need to be ready." It took every bit of willpower she had to not take his hand into hers. "*You* need to be ready. Just like that first day on the ship when I nearly fell from the rigging."

Her words erased the grin from his face.

"I wanted to live, Tom, but I might have died. I know I'm ready to meet my Savior. I want you to be ready, too."

His sweet smile broke her heart. "Get some rest, my little man-of-the-cloth. As soon as the cuttin'-in and tryin'-out starts, rest will be scarce."

She watched him walk toward his bunk behind the galley. The weary slump of his broad shoulders blurred with her gathering tears. Falling to her mat, she surrendered to quiet sobs of exhaustion, frustration, relief, and sadness that she couldn't reveal her true feelings for Tom.

◆•———•◆

For the next three days, Matilda experienced what she would later describe in her journal as "a glimpse of hell."

While the crew cut the blubber from the dead whale lashed to the starboard side of the ship, she carried countless armloads of wood to feed the try-works. There, in the large brick oven near the bow, pieces of blubber rendered in huge, bubbling try-pots.

Bible reading, journal entries, and even general conversation gave way to the work at hand, which demanded all her time and energy.

The six-hours-on and six-hours-off shifts operated twenty-four hours a day.

And then there was the smell. The inescapable, all-enveloping, indescribably horrible stench of the rotting and rendering whale flesh. It permeated everything.

As a child, Matilda had first gotten her sea legs on her father's ship during short excursions. She'd taken pride in having not become seasick on this voyage. But now the sickness came with a vengeance. She spent her waking hours either hanging over the side or gagging on her knees down in the blubber room.

There, she learned to cut blanket pieces—huge slabs of blubber—into more manageable hunks called horse pieces. These were scored into "bible" leaves, ready for rendering.

"It's not a shame to be sick." Tom's soft voice and gentle hand on her shoulder offered blessed comfort during her latest bout of sickness at the rail.

Trembling, Matilda wiped a shaky hand across her mouth and turned to face him.

Covered in black, greasy soot, Tom looked almost indistinguishable from the Verde Islanders, except for his soft, gray eyes.

"Can't keep your biscuits down, Master Adams?" Noah's mean laugh cut through her as he passed them.

"Noah Bertram needs a beating," Tom said in a low growl.

"Leave it be, Tom." She laid a restraining hand on his arm. "I don't want you to get in trouble because of me."

Drawing a deep, quivering breath, she hitched up her courage. "I need to get back below." However distasteful the work, she'd hired onto this ship to do a job, and with God's help she would do it.

"Maybe there will be some days between this tryin'-out and another catch when you can preach some more to me." The encouraging tone in his voice made her ache to hug him.

Though no moon shined in the inky-black sky above them, the burning try-works washed the deck in an eerie orange glow. Tom's teeth flashed a white gleam in the midst of his blackened face. "I think maybe I need to hear about that 'turnin' the other cheek' thing again."

Wanting to reward his efforts to make her feel better, Matilda managed a weak smile. "Maybe," she whispered, before turning toward the main hatch with a sore stomach and an aching heart.

━━━◆━━━━◆━━━

Matilda looked at her reddened hands that stung with the lye she'd used to scrub the portion of the deck between the windlass and the try-works. The three days of processing the whale had proved the most horrible of her life. Somehow with God's help and the blessing of Tom's presence, she'd borne the agonizing drudgery.

Despite her need to earn a tidy wage on this voyage, Matilda couldn't help dreading the next whale sighting.

Her lips slipped into a wry grin as she dunked the scrub brush into the bucket of soapy water. At least for the moment, the secret of her identity seemed safe. Surely no one would suspect that the filthy, scrawny figure on its knees scrubbing the greasy, sooty scum from the deck, the rails, the yardarms—everything—was anything other than a scroungy cabin boy.

"Matt."

At the sound of Tom's voice, she jerked around.

"Most of the crew is taking a swim in the drink to wash off the whale." He wrinkled his nose as he grabbed at his grimy shirtfront. "Wanna come?"

"I—I don't think so." Matilda's mind raced to think of an excuse. "I can't swim," she blurted, silently begging forgiveness for the lie.

As tantalizing as a swim in the ocean sounded, she couldn't risk exposing her ruse and rendering all her labors for naught. Solomon had promised her a bath in the galley this evening. He'd even saved rainwater for her to wash her hair.

"That's all right." Tom gave a dismissive shrug. "I'll watch out for you. I'd say it's high time you learned to swim."

"But—but. . ." Matilda's heart pounded as he took hold of her arm and towed her toward the cutting stage where several of the crew had gathered and were already diving into the blue-green water.

"Look, it'll be fun." Tom tugged harder on her arm, cocking his head toward the men laughing and frolicking in the calm sea.

Matilda's heart filled with terror at the mischievous glint sparkling in his eyes. Whatever happened, she couldn't allow him to dump her into the ocean.

"No, Tom, please no!" She wrenched her arm from his grasp and backed away, her breath coming in short, painful puffs.

His grin melted into a kind smile. "All right, my little man-of-the-cloth, but one day I will teach you to swim." Laughing, he dove into the ocean.

Matilda watched him for a while. His strong, lithe body skimmed through the waves with power and grace, not so unlike the whales he hunted and just as beautiful.

He belongs to the sea. The thought brought a stab of sadness.

◆━━━━◆

"You jis' take your time, missy," Solomon whispered, pouring another bucket of hot water into the large wooden tub he'd positioned in the middle of the galley floor.

Blinking back tears at his kindness, Matilda nodded and thanked God for His servant, Solomon Mays.

"Old Solomon'll jis' stand down by the gangway ladder. Nobody's gonna get past me, I promise."

A few minutes later, Matilda luxuriated in the warm rainwater, soaking the weariness from her muscles as she soaked the grime from her skin and hair. Solomon had even found her some lye soap he'd scented with ambergris.

"One of my concoctions," he'd said.

Settling against the end of the tub, Matilda laid her head back and breathed a contented sigh. Soon, they'd put into port at the Western Islands to take on fresh water, fruit, and vegetables. Her heart leaped with the anticipation of walking on solid ground again and finally getting to post the half-dozen letters she'd written to Mother.

Thoughts of home and Mother washed over her like the warm bathwater, bringing with them pangs of homesickness. How had Mother fared alone in the two months since Matilda went to sea? Visions of Mother struggling to bring in enough sewing and laundry work to pay the monthly mortgage assailed Matilda's heart.

Shaking off the troubling thoughts, she dried her hair with the large cotton towel Solomon had provided. She shook her head, allowing her damp locks to hang in dark waves. Her hair had grown. Unwilling to cut it again, she had chosen to simply pull it back in a queue.

"Where's Matt?"

At Tom's bright voice, Matilda's fingers stilled in her damp hair.

"He's takin' a bath," Solomon said in a firm tone.

"So?" Tom's unconcerned voice sounded closer.

Her heart pounding, Matilda wrapped herself in the towel and held her breath.

Chapter 5

He don't want nobody to bother him." Solomon's voice broached no resistance.

Tom chuckled. "He's a good, hardworking lad, but he sure is an odd one."

After a long moment, the sound of Tom's steps continued alongside the galley, diminishing in the direction of his berth, allowing Matilda to exhale a shaky breath.

◆———◆

Three days later, Matilda walked along the sun-washed deck with her Bible in hand. Her frights at the close calls with Tom and the horrors of processing the whale seemed to float away on the sweet ocean breezes wafting across the calm blue seas. Since the ship's cleaning—not to mention her own—both her mood and her health had improved.

With a spring in her step, she approached Tom who sat cross-legged on the port-side deck, his back against the afterhouse wall. At the sight of him, her heart leaped like a happy dolphin.

"What are you doing?" Smiling, she glanced down at his hands holding a small knife, with which he scraped something that looked like a bone.

"Scrimshaw." He made another gouge in the ivory-colored material.

"May I see?" Curious, Matilda leaned in closer. She'd seen some of the beautiful carvings sailors had rendered on whale bone and teeth, but had no idea that Tom did such work.

He scooted farther away and covered the work with his hand. Whether attempting to hide the scrimshaw or simply to make room for her to join him, she couldn't tell.

"In a bit." He angled a grin at her.

Intrigued, but wanting to respect his privacy, Matilda sank to the deck and sat cross-legged beside him.

"Can't wait to put in at Fayal." He cast a crooked grin in her direction. "First thing I'm goin' to do is get myself the biggest, juiciest orange I can find. How 'bout you?"

"An orange sounds wonderful, but I'm most eager to mail my bundle of letters to my mother."

"Reckon you miss home a lot, huh?"

"Yes, I'm all my mother has now. Don't you miss your home?" Matilda realized how little she knew of Tom's past, or of his life ashore.

"Reckon the sea is my home."

"Why? Don't you have a home somewhere onshore?"

Tom fixed his gaze on his hands, busy with the carving knife. "I was orphaned at the age of ten. My grandmother took me in for the next four years. When she died, I went to sea. That's where I've spent most of my time since." He gave her that little smile she loved. "Reckon the captain and crew of whatever ship I'm on is my family now."

"Then you plan to stay at sea?"

"Only for as long as it takes."

"As long as it takes for what?" Intrigued, Matilda watched his eyes grow distant.

"As long as it takes for me to earn enough money to buy my own ship, or at least, buy into one."

That Tom had ambitions to captain a ship didn't surprise Matilda. With his good sense, kind heart, and even temper, he'd make a fine captain.

The memory of her father's absences flooded back, and Matilda voiced her thoughts. "Captains are at sea, too."

"Oh, I may captain for a voyage or two, but what I really want is to own a fishing fleet. Galveston Bay, down on the Gulf of Mexico, that's where I'm headed. I believe whalin's seen its best days—no future in it." His face clouded for a moment then brightened again. "Yes, siree, I've had enough of New England winters. Gonna live out the rest of my life in a warm clime."

Matilda felt her jaw go slack. She would never have imagined that Tom harbored such lofty goals.

His gaze turned pensive. "One day I'm goin' to own a whole fishing fleet and build a fine home on Galveston Bay." He reached out his hand holding the carving knife and gestured toward a vision that only he could see. "I can see m'self sittin' on a fine veranda, warm breezes off the Gulf of Mexico blowin' in my face. I'll watch my fleet o' ships sail out o' Galveston Bay then back again with my fortune, all from the front porch o' my home. My own home. . ." His voice turned quiet.

"And would you live in that home alone?" Her throat tightened. Perhaps he had a sweetheart back in New England. She'd never even asked. She'd never considered the possibility. The thought gouged at her heart.

"Not if I can find a good wife to share it with me." He grinned. "But you're a bit young for this conversation."

When Matilda's heart began to beat again, it raced.

Me. Tom, I want it to be me!

It didn't matter that she knew nothing of Galveston, Texas. She would follow Tom anywhere. Galveston, the moon, it didn't matter.

"Ain't ya gonna read more o' that to me?" He jammed his thumb toward the open Bible on her lap. "Reckoned since you ain't saved my soul yet, and the next whale just might swallow me right down like old Jonah, maybe you'd better." He shot her a teasing grin then puffed out a breath to blow dust from the carving.

"If you'd like." Bristling, she couldn't keep the chilly tone from her voice. How could he act so unconcerned about something so serious? The urge to get up and stomp away pulled at her. But she couldn't. Like it or not, God had laid this mission on her heart. Whether or not she'd ever see Tom Owens again after this voyage, it didn't change the fact that she loved him. She would always love him. She couldn't bear the thought of worrying for the rest of her life that he wasn't safely in the arms of Jesus. She had to try her hardest.

"I'm sorry," Tom said, seeming to sense her irritation in the ensuing silence. His lips slipped into that familiar lopsided grin. "Preach to me, my little man-of-the-cloth." Tiny lines crinkled at the edges of his gray eyes, glinting with fun.

The gentle ocean breeze continually rearranged the soft brown curls framing his tanned face.

Matilda felt her heart do a somersault at the handsome vision of the man beside her. With difficulty, she dragged her attention down to focus on the scriptures and began reading from the eighth chapter of the gospel of Matthew, the account of Jesus stilling the tempest.

"It'd be right helpful if He could do that nowadays." Never looking up from his work, Tom draped the comment in an uncharacteristic somber tone.

"But He can!" Matilda's voice leaped with her heart. This was the opportunity she'd been hoping for—a chance to show Tom that Jesus was just as alive today as in Bible times.

Her fingers fanned the pages until she came to the thirteenth chapter of the book of Hebrews. " 'Jesus Christ the same yesterday, and to day, and for ever.'"

"Alive or not, I wouldn't reckon Jesus'd want to have much truck with me." Tom's gaze narrowed and his voice turned cynical. "Don't reckon churchgoin' people would, either. Good people, who don't lie or cheat and ain't done nobody harm. No." He shook his head. "They wouldn't want no truck with the likes of me."

While the defeated tone in Tom's voice troubled Matilda, at least he seemed serious. And wasn't that what she'd wanted, for him to become serious about Christ's message of salvation?

Yet her heart throbbed with compassion at the despondency in his voice. She longed to smooth away the furrows etched across his forehead by an unspoken pain.

"No, Tom. You're exactly who Jesus wants!" She recounted with enthusiasm the passage of Jesus rebuking those who criticized him for eating with publicans and sinners. "He told them that the sick need a doctor, not those who are well. Jesus wants to forgive all your sins. All you have to do is ask Him."

She ached at the sadness in Tom's sardonic chuckle.

He snapped a quick nod in the direction of her Bible. "Maybe that book's got all the answers, and maybe it don't. All I know is, there are things a body does in this life they can't ever take back. Things that leave marks that won't wash away."

She rose from the deck, her limbs feeling as leaden as her heart. She hadn't gotten through to him. She'd failed.

Perhaps Tom's heart was the rocky soil that Jesus had spoken of in the parable—a place where the Word wouldn't grow. No, she simply wouldn't accept that. She'd seen the sweet softness of his heart.

Why couldn't he accept God's love? What awful specters from the past tormented his soul? She couldn't begin to guess.

"You're wrong, Tom. No one who goes to church is perfect, and many are not even good."

Her shoulders sagging, she turned to leave. "Solomon will be looking for me."

"Don't you want to see?" Tom held his carving out toward her.

Matilda reached down and wrapped her fingers around the small, smooth object. Her incredulous gaze shifted from the carving on the whale tooth in her hand to Tom's smile. "It's me."

"Thought you might like to have a souvenir of your first whaling voyage."

Tears welled in Matilda's eyes. The gesture was so sweet, the gift so personal.

She wanted to hug his neck and kiss him. Instead, she cleared her throat. "Thank you."

There was nothing else to say, nothing else she could do. In truth, she would rather have had his likeness on the memento instead of her own. But that would have been unnecessary. Tom had already carved his likeness into her heart as indelibly as if he'd done it with a scrimshaw knife. It would be there forever.

Later, Matilda lay wide awake on her mat, unmindful of the cockroaches crawling over her unmolested. Ambergris slept against her side, his furry stomach rising and falling to the rhythm of his soft purring.

Clutching the whale tooth in her hand, she ran her thumb lovingly over the rough ridges Tom had carved there.

Guilt gnawed at her heart. What would Tom think of her if he knew she was living a lie? She, who presumed to teach him the scriptures.

When she left New Bedford, she'd felt sure this voyage was God's will. She'd heard so clearly the divine whisper, sanctioning her decision. Now, that surety had dimmed in a fog of guilt and uncertainty.

Perhaps when they reached the Western Islands she should go to the captain and tell him the truth.

But what of her mother and their debt? Mother, too, depended upon this voyage. And what would Tom think if he learned the truth?

Matilda's heart sank at the vision of his dear face twisted in disgust at the unveiling of her deception. All her efforts to convince him to become a Christian would surely be lost if he viewed her as a hypocrite.

She rubbed the whale tooth against her wet cheek as her heart crawled in pain and confusion to the mercy seat of her Lord.

Lord, tell me what to do. Please, just show me what You want me to do.

Chapter 6

Tom grasped the port-side rail and watched the diminishing harbor of Fayal as the *Sea Star* weighed anchor and headed out to sea. Above him, black-headed gulls glided in lazy circles against the cloudless blue sky.

Despite the warm sun on his face, an inexplicable unease wrapped around him, permeating his being like a chill fog. He couldn't quite put his finger on the cause of his discontent—a vague ache he couldn't identify. But his instincts told him that the vexing feelings were in some way linked to Matt Adams.

"It's all his pesky Bible readin', that's what it is."

He shook his head as if the motion might throw off the elusive torment. Yet his own words rang false in his ears. Indeed, he'd come to so enjoy the scriptures Matt shared with him, he'd even bought a Bible of his own at a Fayal mercantile.

He blew out his frustration in a long sigh. No, it was something else. Why had he felt an intrinsic responsibility to protect the boy? By carving Matt's features into the whale tooth, he'd hoped to rid himself of the disconcerting feelings of attachment.

During his years at sea, a half-dozen cabin boys had crossed Tom's path. All others had evoked nothing more from him than a passing acknowledgment of their existence. So why was this boy different?

Why?

Bewildered, Tom mumbled his regret. "Should'a kept to myself like I usually do on a voyage. Should'a—"

"Tom, I thought maybe we could study the scriptures together, now that you have your own Bible."

Startled from his reverie, Tom whirled to face the cause of his unease. His brow slipped into a scowl as he met his young friend's hopeful eyes.

The troubling questions boiling inside him suddenly exploded like water from a whale's blowhole. "Why don't you just leave me be, you aggravatin', Bible-thumpin' little whelp? Go bedevil somebody else for a change, why don't you?"

Matt's eyes filled with tears, and Tom's insides twisted with regret.

"Tom, what have I done to make you angry?" The lad's delicate chin quivered beneath features crumpled by shock and hurt. "Whatever it was, I'm sorry. I never meant to. . ."

Tom winced as his heart rent, then steeled his resolve. He had to rid himself of this feeling. He had to.

When Matt stepped closer, Tom threw out his hand to push him back. "I said, get away!"

When his hand touched Matt's chest, an unmistakable, soft roundness met his fingertips. Recoiling in shock, he yanked his hand back as if he'd touched the blazing side of a try-works.

"Don't tell. Oh, Tom, please don't tell." Horror widened his friend's eyes.

His—*her* trembling plea filtered through the cacophony of stunned confusion screaming through Tom's brain.

"No, I won't—of course I won't." The words stumbled from his lips as he reeled from the discovery.

In a frantic attempt to assimilate what he'd just learned, Tom rubbed his fingers across his forehead as if to gather his jumbled thoughts.

This person he thought he knew was being transfigured before his astonished gaze.

How had he missed it? The feminine features of her large blue-green eyes fringed by thick, dusky lashes. The delicate line of her jaw and the soft pink fullness of her rose-petal lips made her gender suddenly obvious.

Tom's heart soared with the seagulls. He wanted to laugh and shout. He wanted to dance a hornpipe. His heart had recognized what his mind had not comprehended. All the feelings swirling inside him made perfect sense now.

Then the enormity of the task this mysterious girl had undertaken hit him like a ballast. What awful desperation had brought her to this whaling ship? What absolute courage had kept her here? The profound respect he felt for this amazing girl began to deepen into something far sweeter.

Grasping her hand, he drew her between the mizzenmast and afterhouse then shot quick glances about to ensure himself that they were indeed alone. "Why? How. . .?" There were too many questions. He had no idea where to start.

"I'm not a fourteen-year-old boy, and my name is not Matt Adams. I'm Matilda Daggett, the eighteen-year-old widow of Mitchell Daggett and the daughter of Captain Barnabas Rigsby."

She lowered her gaze with the remorseful confession. A large teardrop clung for a moment to her long lashes then fell, to slip slowly down her soft pink cheek.

Her voice unsteady, she continued her astounding admission. "My father was a whaling captain and my husband his first mate. Just before their last voyage, my husband and father incurred a large amount of debt. To satisfy the debt, my father took out a lien against our home. When their ship went down in a hurricane, my mother and I struggled to pay the mortgage." Her fingertips trembled across her tear-streaked face. "The only way I could see to pay off the mortgage and keep a roof over our heads was to go to sea."

Tom's heart seized as joy collided with terror. *This is Captain Rigsby's daughter?* How excruciating to have the budding hope of building a new, and far different, friendship with this girl cut down before it ever had a chance to blossom.

"Solomon knows. He knew almost from the beginning." A sad smile trembled on her lovely lips above her quivering chin.

His heart writhing, Tom watched in helpless agony as she turned and walked away.

A growing fear soured the sweet ache burrowing deep inside him.

This brave, beautiful, wonderful girl must never learn that he had caused her husband's and father's deaths. His actions had forced her to endure the horrors of this whaling ship.

Chapter 7

In the days following Tom's discovery of her true identity, Matilda wallowed in regret and despair. If only she'd bound her chest that day as she usually did despite how dirty and smelly the bindings had become. Her worst fears came to fruition. Tom seemed to take pains to avoid her, and with each passing day, he became more distant.

She missed their Bible study sessions until she ached, but had scant hope that he'd care to resume them.

"You done planted the seed, missy. Pray God will allow it to grow and the harvest will come." While kind, Solomon's encouraging words offered scant comfort. Matilda did pray. In obedience to the admonition of the apostle Paul in his letter to the Thessalonians, she prayed without ceasing.

Ironically, the awful work had become a blessing, she realized on her knees in the blubber room.

Two days out of the Western Islands they'd caught and butchered three whales in quick succession.

The reeking whale ship once again robbed Matilda of her appetite. Today, she'd managed to eat only a couple of hardtack biscuits and drink a little tea at Solomon's insistence. She'd lost that, half an hour ago.

Laden with a basketful of horse pieces, she ascended the ladder to the top deck. Her heart quickened, knowing Tom would be manning the midnight shift at the try-works.

It had been days since they'd spoken. Pain stabbed at her heart. Their friendship, once close, warm, and easy, had disintegrated into the cool, formal posture of strangers.

The blazing try-works bathed the midnight deck in an unearthly orange glow. Tom's unmistakable silhouette turned at the soft pat of her bare feet on the wet planks.

"Have you had anything to eat today, Matilda?"

"A little." She handed him the hideous basket of whale flesh, surprised to hear him use her real name. The sound of it caressed her ears. In his soft, caring tone, she heard again the friendship they'd shared for nearly four months.

"You must rest when you can and try to eat something." His soot-blackened face looked drawn and weary in the light of the try-work's flames. "There are still some oranges that are good yet."

"I know." She forced a weak smile.

"That hymn you and Solomon were singing earlier this evening is one my grandmother used to sing."

"If it bothers you, we won't—"

"No, I like it. It's been a long time since I was sung to sleep."

"My mother and I used to sing hymns every evening while I played the piano— until we had to sell it to help pay the mortgage." Swallowing hard, she blinked back tears at the memory.

"You have the fingers for it." He lifted her hand in his, caressing the backs of her fingers with his thumb.

Her heart jolted at his touch then beat like a metronome gone mad. Did he have any idea what his touch did to her? How could he?

Perhaps he didn't hate her. But did he still possess the Bible they'd chosen together for him in the Fayal mercantile? She didn't dare ask for fear of the answer.

Turning to hide the tears streaming down her face, Matilda retreated to the main hatch and the dark, stench-filled purgatory of the blubber room.

Tom's heart wrung as he lowered a forkful of whale blubber into the bubbling try-pot.

Matilda seemed to weaken with each passing day. According to Solomon she hardly ate, and what she did eat, she couldn't keep down. Tom was tempted to miss the next whale just to allow her a few extra days to recover before another round of cutting-in and trying-out.

She was stubborn. He couldn't help smiling. So like her father. Tom's stomach churned as guilt twisted through him.

Gazing out over the placid, dark ocean, he no longer saw the gentle waves rocking the *Sea Star*. Instead, he saw a mountain of angry waves crashing against a helpless whale ship. As the sea opened its greedy mouth and swallowed the little ship down its dark gullet, Tom winced. Grasping his head in his hands, he tried to expel the scene from his mind.

Why? Why had he taken such a foolish chance? He could see himself as in a dream, stepping up on the clumsy cleat of the whale boat instead of leaning against it as he should have. He wanted to scream at the vision. *No! Get down! Get down!*

The first mate, Mitchell, had screamed those words too late.

Once again, Tom saw the great gray tail looming above him as if suspended in motion. Droplets of seawater glistened on the murderous fluke, falling like rain on everyone in the whale boat.

Pain. Tom reached down to rub his right leg just below the knee. The massive tail had crashed down, throwing him from his precarious perch, snapping his leg like kindling against a rope bucket.

"If only. . ." He whispered the useless words of regret to the dark ocean.

If only he'd stood against the cleat as he should have. Maybe he wouldn't have broken his leg. Captain Rigsby wouldn't have had to drop him off at the Western Islands and pick up another harpooner. The *Voyager* wouldn't have taken an alternate route, sailing directly into the hurricane's path.

Tom released a ragged breath. Each time the scene played out in his mind, he came to the same conclusion. His stupid, cavalier stunt had cost the lives of everyone on that whale ship, including Matilda's husband, Mitchell Daggett, and her father, Barnabas Rigsby.

"Matilda." *Sweet, beautiful, wonderful Matilda.* Her name tasted sweet in his mouth.

Fear shuddered through his heart as his trembling hand slipped across his greasy, soot-covered forehead.

Please, Lord, if You can hear me, please keep her safe. Don't let her sicken. And please, please, just don't let her find out.

Chapter 8

Matilda stopped swabbing the deck to watch Captain Dobbs squint at the horizon's green hue. His brows furrowed, he clasped his hands behind his back, fingers twitching.

The captain's features held the same intense look she'd seen on Papa's face when he'd gazed at thunderclouds building on the horizon. To her, it meant one thing: hurricane.

The waves had become choppy, bouncing the whale ship like a bobber on a pond. The *Sea Star* groaned as it strained against its anchor. A gale was coming. How soon? How bad would it be? The captain's job required him to determine those answers.

Captain Dobbs lifted his face, studying the rigging. The ropes whistled as they whipped in the intensifying breeze. His gaze swung down to the deck, surveying the many barrels of whale oil cooling there.

"Mister Bertram." A deep furrow cleft between the captain's eyes as he turned to Noah. "How much longer do you think is necessary for the oil to cool?"

"Just a few more hours, sir. I think the barrels could safely be stored away by sundown." A hesitancy in Noah's voice lacked conviction.

Pushing the mop, Matilda worked her way to the corner of the afterhouse, concealing herself from their view. Her tightening chest constricted her breath as she waited for the captain's decision. The entire whale oil take as well as all their lives were at stake. If the barrels of oil were put in the hold while too warm they'd contract, causing them to leak. Only on deck was there room enough for the ship's cooper to adjust the bands on the barrels until they'd sufficiently cooled.

"Sundown it is, then, Mister Bertram," Captain Dobbs said. "I do not believe the gale will reach us before then. Perhaps not before midday tomorrow."

That afternoon, Matilda lay on her straw tick, unable to sleep. A little earlier, she'd enjoyed her first bath in a month. The interminable cutting-in and trying-out had, again, come to a halt.

Remembering the look on the captain's face, she fought back the fear threatening to overwhelm her. They'd come too far. They'd worked too hard. Surely God would not allow them to lose it all now.

She hugged her arms tightly around her emaciated form as cold chills rippled through her. Her fingers pressed against her protruding ribs. She doubted even her own mother would recognize her now.

The stench of the rotting whales still hung heavily in the stale air belowdecks. But now that she no longer handled the whale flesh hour after awful hour, her appetite had returned to a small degree, and with it, some strength.

She winced, remembering Tom's gentle voice the other night urging her to eat something.

She breathed his name in the darkness and shifted on the straw tick, comfort eluding her. Tears slipped unbidden down her face. His changed attitude left no doubt about his altered feelings toward her. He seemed to avoid her at all costs.

She reached out and grasped her little, worn Bible beside her mat and clutched it close to her chest. She still prayed daily for Tom to accept Christ, and daily read her Bible alone.

With the advent of December, a fresh bout of homesickness had gripped her. Thoughts of Mother and their home in New England inflicted an ache only prayer and the precious scriptures could ease.

Next week would be Christmas. The thought of New Bedford blanketed in snow and their front door and parlor decorated with festive greenery and fruit filled her with longing. Other memories assailed, bringing tears to her eyes—those of climbing with Papa to their home's widow's walk to search for Orion on Christmas Eve then exchanging homemade gifts with her parents.

Regret that she had no gift to send Mother this Christmas pricked her heart. But she did have a gift: this voyage that could save their home. This voyage that pushed her to her physical limits and dealt as brutally with her heart and spirit as it had with her body.

Again, her mind drifted to Tom—always to Tom. Try as she might, she could not tear away from the grasp he held on her heart.

Even if he hadn't found her hypocrisy disgusting, how could he ever see the scrawny bag of bones she'd become as the "good woman" he dreamed of one day sharing his life with? The thought ripped a new tear in her tattered heart.

Pressing her wet face in the crook of her arm, she drifted off to sleep whispering his name in the sanctuary of her cubbyhole.

"All hands on deck!"

Noah Bertram's frantic cries jolted Matilda awake as he ran past the galley.

Sitting up blinking, she glimpsed the flash of his black boots before they disappeared up the companionway steps.

Outside the ship, the wind screamed like an angry beast.

Matilda tried to stand, but the violent pitching of the ship threw her back to her mat. Struggling again to her feet, she stumbled toward the companionway steps.

A hand on her shoulder stopped her, and she turned to face Solomon's disapproving frown.

"You got no business up there wrestlin' them there oil barrels. That's man's work."

"First mate said 'all hands,' and I have two perfectly good ones." Shrugging off his restraining grip, Matilda climbed to the deck.

The instant she stuck her head through the hatch the sea spray stung her face like a million needles. It took all her strength to climb onto the deck against the force of the wind. Once there, the ferocious gusts made it almost impossible to stand upright.

Her courage flagged as she squinted against the wind and water smacking her in the face.

Loose ropes from the rigging whipped about like lethal lashes. The barrels of oil rolled helter-skelter while the frantic crew stumbled about attempting to corral them and store them below. Some of the barrels had smashed, spreading their slick contents across the rolling, pitching deck, making moving about or even standing treacherous.

"Get below!"

Matilda turned to see who'd hollered into her ear over the howling winds. "I want to help, Tom!"

"It's too dangerous! Get below, now!" He took hold of her shoulders and turned her back toward the hatch.

"We need every pair of hands up here. He can work!" Noah yelled into Tom's face.

Tom gave his head a violent shake. "He's not strong enough!" he screamed over the tempest.

Veins popped out on Noah's wet neck. "I don't have time to argue, Owens. Obey me now or face the consequences later!"

"Mr. Bertram's right, Tom. I can help." Ignoring Tom's pleas, Matilda reached for the closest barrel and began rolling it toward the forehatch. There, waiting hands pulled it down below deck.

Tom's angry glare from farther aft where he struggled with two barrels didn't dissuade her. Determined to be of use, Matilda grabbed at another rolling barrel. If he couldn't respect her integrity, he'd at least have to respect her sense of duty.

Clinging to the barrel, she didn't have time to react as a great wave broke over the deck. With bone-jarring force it smashed her and the barrel against the ship's rail, splintering the barrel and sending her sliding across the deck on its oily contents.

Flat on her back, Matilda looked up toward the sound of a loud crack. In paralyzing terror, she watched the mizzenmast snap near its top. In another moment it would come crashing down upon her.

Lord, help me, she prayed, wondering if Mitchell and Papa would meet her at the gates of heaven.

Strong arms grasped her waist, pulling her clear an instant before the mast crashed to the deck. She and her rescuer rolled over and over until they came to rest against the midship shelter.

Trembling in Tom's arms, Matilda pressed her face hard against his chest, feeling the rapid thumping of his heart beneath his sodden shirt.

Small mountains of cold black sea washed over them in an icy deluge, mixing with a rush of horizontal rain.

When the wall of water retreated, Matilda gasped, desperate to suck fresh oxygen into her lungs before the onslaught of another wave.

Planks from the midship shelter above their heads flew into the air as if ripped off by the hand of a raging giant.

The roar of the wind and the pounding of the sea swallowed the sound of Matilda's screams.

With what had to be Herculean effort, Tom moved them closer against the outside wall of his cabin. "Hold on to me. Don't let go!"

Matilda clung to him with all her strength, knowing her life depended upon it.

Though his arms held her in an iron-tight grasp, even Tom's strength couldn't match that of the hurricane. The storm's relentless clutches continued to pull them asunder as it sucked them toward the hungry sea.

Chapter 9

As Matilda's heart cried out in silence to the Lord for help, she heard Tom put voice to her pleas.

"Sweet Jesus," he hollered above the din, his chin pressed hard against Matilda's head. "Please save us and still the tempest as you did in the Bible. But if you see fit to take us, then take us together. Matilda belongs to you, and I ask that you count me as one of yours, too. Please, Lord Jesus, don't let us be separated—not in this life or the next."

Matilda clung to the man she loved, her sobs lost in the hurricane's wail, her tears mingling with the sea and the rain. *Thank You, Jesus! He's come to you at last.*

As if in answer to Tom's prayer, the winds subsided. The waves, though still reaching foamy tentacles across the debris-strewn deck, lost much of their potency.

Matilda sat up, blinking at the miracle. Before her terror-frozen mind could make sense of the situation, Tom leaped to his feet, pulling her after him.

"The eye. We're in the eye." His arm around her waist, he guided her toward the main hatch. "We must get below before it starts again."

Matilda hurried down the companionway steps as fast as her shaky legs would carry her, with Tom following close behind.

Her heart soared, drenched with happiness at the words of Tom's prayer.

Her next thought quelled her silent jubilation. Did he really mean what he'd said? *Lord, please let him mean it.*

A sudden jolt snapped her prayer short as the hurricane's winds resumed.

Unprepared, Matilda pitched forward, but Tom caught her securely in his arms. For one sweet, brief moment, their eyes locked, and mutual understanding swept away all uncertainty. Her heart stood still as she watched his eyes close and his head lower.

His tender kiss grew softer as it deepened, and Matilda felt as if she were sinking into folds of velvet.

At length, she emerged from a fog of bliss and pushed away from his embrace.

The question screaming through her mind would not be still as she searched his eyes' gray depths. "Tom, I have to know. Did you mean the prayer you prayed up on deck?"

"Every word, my sweet girl." His gaze, as soft as his whispered words, caressed her face. "I've been reading my Bible—the one you chose for me in Fayal. I believe it, my darling. I believe Jesus can forgive my sins, and I believe He has."

His fingertips gently brushed a strand of wet hair from her eyes. "My heart's been telling me something more. It tells me that I love you—that I love you beyond anything or anyone else on the face of this earth."

Happy tears rolled down Matilda's cheeks. The storm continued to buffet the ship, but a deluge of joy extinguished her fear.

Frowning, he let her go and turned away. "It's you, my darling Matilda, who I fear will never be able to forgive me." His eyes refused to meet hers.

Confused at his words and the dejection on his face, Matilda's heart and hand reached out to him, and she touched his arm. "Tom, I love you. There is nothing you might have done in your past that I couldn't forgive. You must believe that."

He whirled toward her with a look so fierce it sent her heart leaping to her throat.

"I killed your husband and your father, Matilda," he blurted. "I'm the reason you're on this ship!"

The blood drained to Matilda's toes and she felt as if she were drowning. She couldn't breathe, she couldn't move, she couldn't think. A loud roaring filled her ears. Perhaps the hurricane had intensified. What could Tom mean?

"Well, well. What have we here?"

A harsh voice intruded on her pained confusion and she turned to face Noah Bertram.

"Mister Owens." Noah's glare bounced from Tom to Matilda. "And *Mistress* Adams, or whatever your true name might be, the captain will see you in his quarters." His mouth twisted in a gleeful smirk.

Still dazed by Tom's startling words, Matilda walked half the length of the ship as if in a dream—a horrible nightmare from which she couldn't awaken. Noah must have witnessed her and Tom's conversation and overheard him call her Matilda. The moment she'd feared since embarking on this voyage had come. She allowed Noah's hand on her shoulder to propel her toward the captain's cabin. Tom, however, shrugged off the first mate's grasp with an angry growl.

Inside the captain's quarters, Captain Dobbs regarded Matilda and Tom with a stern look down the length of his aquiline nose. "It would appear that the two of you have perpetrated a deception on me and this ship."

Matilda's heart hammered in her chest. With her ruse discovered, she would surely be put off the ship. Worse, she'd doubtless forfeit her earnings that could save her and Mother's home.

Noah's mouth lifted in a smug grin. "I found them in a passionate embrace. It appears that Mr. Owens, wanting some female company on this voyage, brought his paramour aboard in the guise of a boy."

Tom swung toward Noah, his face twisted in fury. "Watch your mouth, Bertram. You dare malign Matilda and I'll—"

"It's not that way at all!" Matilda blurted as anger at Noah and fear for Tom swelled in her chest. She deserved whatever punishment the captain chose to mete out, but he needed to know that Tom wasn't involved in the deception.

Captain Dobbs ignored Matilda and looked at Tom. "Is this young woman your sweetheart, Mr. Owens?"

Noah's face screwed up in an indignant scowl. "Of course she's his sweetheart! I caught them kissing." He crossed his arms over his chest and glared at Tom. "I heard Owens call her his sweet girl. His darling Matilda."

Captain Dobbs kept his focus on Tom. "Well, Mister Owens, how say you? Is this woman your sweetheart?"

The smile Tom gave Matilda brought tears to her eyes. "Yes, she is."

Matilda stepped forward, her words tumbling over one another in a rush. "I am to blame in this, not Tom!" She had to make the captain understand. "Tom didn't bring me aboard. Until after we caught that first whale, he knew no more of my true identity than you did."

Captain Dobbs's attention swung from Tom to Matilda. Though still stern, his voice and demeanor softened. "Then, young woman, I'd say it's high time you gave a full accounting of yourself. Who are you, and why have you perpetrated this fraud?"

Matilda swallowed the knot in her throat but lifted her chin and met the captain's gaze. "My name is Matilda Daggett, widow of the late Mitchell Daggett and daughter of the late Captain Barnabas Rigsby." Tears sprang to her eyes and she looked down. "My father took a lien against our home and died before he had the chance to repay it." She looked back up at Dobbs. "I signed on to this voyage to earn enough money to save my mother's home from foreclosure."

"I suspected as much." A slow grin, one of the few Matilda had ever witnessed on Benjamin Dobbs's features, spread across his face.

She gasped. "How long have you known?" Her words came out in an incredulous whisper.

"I was just a twenty-year-old harpooner when I first sailed with your father, but I never forgot his lovely little dark-haired daughter with eyes the color of the sea." His rare grin stretched wider. "I realized at our first meeting there was something familiar about you. The first twenty-four hours of this voyage confirmed my suspicions."

"Solomon told you?" The thought of her friend's betrayal felt like a stab in the heart.

"No, Solomon didn't tell me." Captain Dobbs shook his head with a soft chuckle. "But I'm not surprised he knew. Nearly impossible to conceal anything from Solomon. No, Mistress Daggett, it was your mannerisms, courage...and the way you tie knots," he added with a grin. "You reminded me very much of my old friend Barnabas."

His pale blue eyes clouded. "I had no idea you'd married. Mitchell Daggett was a good man. Sailed with him once on the *Venture*." He gave his head a sad shake. "May I offer my condolences at your loss, my dear girl, late though they be?"

"Ma—Matilda Rigsby?" Noah's jaw hung slack and his eyes had grown to the size of half-dollar pieces.

The captain glanced at Noah. "Mr. Bertram, you are dismissed to further assess the extent of our damages."

Noah still stared at Matilda as if frozen, requiring the captain to repeat his order.

When Noah finally blinked and staggered from the room, Captain Dobbs looked at Tom, and the hint of a grin touched his lips. "Since there's no crime in a young man kissing a lovely young lady, you are dismissed as well, Mr. Owens." His expression turning somber, he looked at Matilda. "As for you, Mistress Daggett, you must know that however sympathetic I might be to your financial plight, deceiving both a ship's owner and captain carries serious consequences."

Tom, who despite his dismissal still lingered, piped up. "Forgive me for sounding impertinent, Captain, but Matilda has worked as hard as any of the crew. She's earned her share."

Captain Dobbs sent Tom a steely look. "Thank you, Mr. Owens, I'll take that into consideration. I believe you've been dismissed."

With a concerned glance at Matilda and a nod to Captain Dobbs, Tom left the room.

Benjamin Dobbs gazed for a long moment at the empty doorway. Turning back to Matilda, he regarded her with a weary sigh. "Mistress Daggett, Mr. Bertram is doubtless sharing the news of your revelation with the crew as we speak, rendering your further presence on this ship impossible. By midday today, we will put into the Jamaican Islands for repairs. So now we must discuss what is to be done about you."

The gray clouds on the horizon blushed with the soft pink of early dawn when Matilda stepped onto the top deck, her heart feeling as battered as the ship around her.

She walked toward Tom who stood at the rail, his back to her. The words he'd uttered before Noah hauled them to Captain Dobbs's quarters echoed through her tortured mind. Though dread knotted her stomach, she needed to know what he'd meant about having killed Papa and Mitchell.

"Tom."

His back stiffened, but he kept his gaze on the horizon. "I was the harpooner on your father's last voyage." He turned to her now. The anguish in his eyes ripped at Matilda's heart. "It was the first whale of the voyage." His gaze shifted back to the open sea. "We'd gone farther than we'd expected for the first sighting. Reckon I was overanxious."

"Tom, you mustn't—"

"Yes, Matilda, I must." His jaw set, Tom's eyes locked on hers. "We won't ever get past this unless you know."

His head sagged and his shoulders slumped. "God knows, I prayed that you'd never find out. But His Word kept reminding me that I needed to tell you. I took a stupid chance to get that first whale. I climbed up on the clumsy cleat to get a better shot at it. When the tail came down there was nothing to save me and I fell against a rope bucket. Broke my leg." He reached down and rubbed his right leg. "You've wondered about my limp."

Matilda didn't dispute his statement.

"Without a harpooner..."Tom raised his hands in a helpless gesture. "We were near the Western Islands, so your father sailed there. I was put ashore and another harpooner hired on for the rest of the voyage." He winced at the memory. "I learned later that your father took a more dangerous, alternate route for the hunt. A route that promised lots of whales, but notorious for hurricanes." A palpable agony rippled through his voice. "They sailed right into the path of one. I wouldn't blame you if you couldn't forgive me."

Myriad emotions tangled inside Matilda. Could she separate the man she loved from the man whose actions had precipitated Papa's and Mitchell's deaths?

Through a mist of tears she watched despair dull Tom's eyes. Now she understood his interest in scriptures that spoke to the subject of forgiveness—the same scriptures that now challenged her own faith. She either accepted Christ's command to forgive or she didn't.

At the agony etched on Tom's dear face her heart rent and the sunshine of God's love flooded in, drenching it with peace. "Our Lord commands us to forgive as He forgives us. God forgives us because He loves us. I love you, Tom Owens. How could I profess to follow Christ and not forgive you?" Sobbing, she fell into his arms.

Matilda felt his tears mingle with hers as their lips met. Tom's arms tightened around her, holding her as if he'd never let her go. His kiss lingered, deepening with a sweet urgency.

When at last he released her mouth, he murmured against her ear, "I love you, Matilda. I'll love you every day for as long as God gives me breath." Taking her face in his hands, he brushed away her tears with his thumbs, his gaze melting into hers. "Will you marry me and share my life and the home I promised you I'd build one day?" He swallowed hard, his voice saddening. "I only wish I could ask your father for your hand."

"Of course I will marry you," she said through her tears.

His voice tensed. "But what did the captain say? Are you to be put off the ship?"

"Captain Dobbs said that it would be impossible for him to allow a single woman to remain on the ship." She grinned. "But he said that a married lady with her husband aboard could remain on the ship."

The muscles in Tom's face relaxed as he drew her into his embrace and nuzzled his face against her hair. "Then I'd say we make you a married lady as soon as possible."

Snuggling in her beloved's arms, Matilda marveled at the amazing journey on which God had taken her. When she learned of Mitchell's death she'd vowed to never again marry a seafaring man, but God knew better. He had other plans for her—far better plans. The words of Proverbs 16:9 flashed into her mind: "*A man's heart deviseth his way: but the LORD directeth his steps.*" Another scripture followed it—God's promise from Jeremiah 29:11: "*For I know the thoughts that I think toward you, saith the LORD, thoughts of peace, and not of evil, to give you an expected end.*"

Feeling blessed beyond all expectations, Matilda thanked God for a second chance at love as she whispered against Tom's heart, "And I have no doubt that Barnabas Rigsby would approve."

Epilogue

Matilda's heart raced as she stepped from the carriage onto County Street. The two-story brick facade of her mother's home—a sight she hadn't seen for almost two years—dimmed through her tears. To know that Mother now owned it free and clear thanks to Matilda's earnings made the sight even sweeter.

Tom's arm around her waist, secure and comforting, calmed her as they climbed the steps to the front door. Next week, Christmas Day, would be their first wedding anniversary.

Gazing at the fruited wreath on the dark walnut door, Matilda's mind flew back to that wonderful day on the Jamaican beach.

Again, she pictured the azure sea heaving and sighing softly behind them, its foamy fingers caressing the sparkling white sands. There, she and Tom had pledged their love and lives to each other before God and their shipmates.

Despite the buffeting of the New England winter winds and her sturdy shoes that encased her feet, she felt again the soft, warm sand between her toes. Wearing a white lace dress borrowed from a Christian missionary's wife, and a fragrant pink hibiscus blossom in her hair, she'd wed the man who owned her heart.

To her astonishment and delight, Tom's heart had become a raging fire for the Lord. Even when the work aboard ship left him so tired he could hardly hold his eyes open, he'd insisted they continue their evening scripture reading.

The sound of Tom rapping on the door mimicked Matilda's pounding heart.

The door swung open to reveal Mother, who stood gaping with wide eyes. "Matilda!" With tears streaming down her face, she pulled Matilda into her arms.

After tearful hugs and introductions, Tom looked at Mother.

"Did it come?"

"Yes." Mother led them to the parlor.

Matilda gasped and her heart seemed to stop for a long moment. The most beautiful piano she'd ever seen stood in the corner. Her eyes brimming, she looked first at Mother then at Tom.

"A late wedding present, my love." Standing behind her, Tom wrapped his arms around her and bent to press his cheek against hers.

"Oh, Tom, I do love you so much!" Twisting in his arms, Matilda smiled at her husband through happy tears that he kissed away.

Still clinging to Tom, she turned to her mother. "You were right, Mother. God did take care of us. And I know He will continue to take care of us. All four of us."

Mother gasped. "Matilda, do you mean. . ."

At Matilda's nod, Mother's face bloomed with excitement. "You certainly are your father's daughter—a surprise a minute."

"Yes, she is." Tom's gaze melted into Matilda's. "Daughter of Orion."

Ramona K. Cecil is a wife, mother, grandmother, freelance poet, and award-winning inspirational romance writer. Now empty nesters, she and her husband make their home in Indiana. A member of American Christian Fiction Writers and American Christian Fiction Writers Indiana Chapter, her work has won awards in a number of inspirational writing contests. Over eighty of her inspirational verses have been published on a wide array of items for the Christian gift market. She enjoys a speaking ministry, sharing her journey to publication while encouraging aspiring writers. When not writing, her hobbies include reading, gardening, and visiting places of historical interest.

The Substitute Husband and the Unexpected Bride

by Pamela Griffin

Dedication

A heartfelt thank-you to my critique partners—Theo and Mom. Also, thank you to Dad, who's been such a huge financial support to me and mine through the years, and to my son Joshua for his input on guns, and my son Brandon for his help in other areas. . . . As always, dedicated to my Lord and Savior, Jesus Christ, who's so patient with me when the storms of life come and I struggle to keep the faith, and without whose guidance I would be lost.

Chapter 1

1864, Seattle

Cecily McGiver stood near the prow of the *Kidder* and stared anxiously out over the dark water at the long stretch of wilderness that would become her home.

Over a week's delay in Panama City, due to the leaky boiler of a ship they had planned to take, forced them to miss the monthly steamer. Rather than wait for the next, Asa Mercer found passage for his small expedition on a lumber bark bound for Puget Sound. From there, they boarded this sloop and now arrived, in the dead of night, on the final leg of their two-month journey.

How could relief be found coiled up in the bindings of such fear?

"Nothing like our reception in Teekalet, is it?" Sarah, one of her traveling companions mused. "Those loggers were so happy to see us, all that hootin' and hollerin' and carryin' on—and here, it looks as if barely a soul came to greet us."

Sarah voiced Cecily's thoughts, though only one man's presence mattered.

It had been a full decade since she'd last seen Zeke. Was his one of the ghostly, dark shapes standing on the wharf? She doubted she would recognize him. Even back then she'd barely known him.

"Say, she doesn't look so good."

Sarah's worried tone snapped Cecily from the past, to her ten-year-old sister who fiercely clutched her hand.

"Gwennie?" Cecily crouched down to see her face. Pale and drawn, it bore dark circles that had ringed her eyes since midjourney and were apparent in the lamplight. "Are you not feeling well?"

"I'm fine." Her voice came as fragile as a will-o'-the-wisp, barely heard over the constant slosh of water.

Cecily squeezed her hand. "Only a little longer and we'll see you tucked snug in bed with a warming pan at your feet. I promise."

The sloop soon docked, but Cecily felt no better for their arrival. Her legs wobbled, her balance precarious. Gwen clutching so tightly to her hand did not help, and she feared she might fall into the water and take her sister with her.

Cecily listened with half an ear as a stout man holding a lantern greeted them, detaching himself from the small welcoming committee that had assembled—several men and women, one of whom eyed Gwen with suspicion. A protective instinct led Cecily to edge with Gwen to the back of the group. Her mind no longer felt connected to her body, which perched on the brink of mutiny to her ebbing will. If she didn't find somewhere to sit down soon...

She turned to scan the area.

A distant shape bearing a lantern broke from the darkness of clustered trees. Her shipmates had their backs to Cecily, too absorbed in the spokesman's effusive salutation to notice the stranger. Cecily watched the shape take the form of a man. He approached, his face indistinct in the flickering lantern light, the hat he wore concealing his features. His spry step and lean build suggested him to be younger than their greeters.

Cecily took a hesitant half step when the newcomer came close.

"Zeke?"

He eased his hurried advance into slow, determined steps.

"You must be Cecily."

His voice came rich, warm, and deep, and she looked up in confusion. What she could see of his hair hanging below his ears was dark, not fair, and he was much taller than she remembered. Of course, he would be. They had been children when he saved her from the bully who pulled her braids, and the passage of time would account for such changes.

"Yes, I'm Cecily. And you must be Zeke?" she inquired a second time, still uncertain.

He looked over her head to the group behind.

"May we go somewhere and talk?" he asked in the cautious, quiet tone reserved for breaking bad news. She had heard just such a tone a little over two months ago and eyed him warily.

"I prefer to remain here. Why will you not answer? Are you Zeke?"

"No, miss. Please, if you'll just step with me there, over by those crates, I'll explain."

Suspicion weighed her down, and her legs felt ready to bow beneath their load. "No, I don't think so. Where's Zeke?"

He hesitated. "I'm sorry, Zeke is dead."

He got no further. The boards on which Cecily stood seemed to cave beneath her feet, carrying her into a fog of dark oblivion.

◆ ● ———— ● ◆

Garrett barely saved the woman before she hit the ground or toppled into the black water. The rapid flutter of her lashes had warned him, and he stepped forward and caught her with one arm in the nick of time. Holding her against him to gain better balance, he set down his lantern then shifted her slight weight to lift her fully into his arms.

A tug at his coat made him look down. Wide green eyes in a wan face regarded him solemnly.

"Please, mister, is Cecily going to die?"

The wobble of fear in the woebegone voice touched his heart, and he gave the girl a reassuring smile.

"She's just a mite weary, I reckon. Hasn't got her land legs yet. Let's take a seat on one of those crates. Grab the lantern and come along."

At least he hoped Cecily McGiver would be well, not having foreseen her reaction and not sure whether weariness or shock was its cause. Like the child, the young woman also looked and felt like a bundle of skin and bones. Did they not feed them on this excursion?

No one had noticed her quiet swoon, and Garrett carried his precious cargo, leading the little girl to a short stack of crates. He set the woman on one, using the side of another to prop her back, then took the lantern from the child. Kneeling before the woman, he took gentle hold of her face, noting her fine features in the lamp's golden glow. Hair that blazed like flame and skin as flawless as cream. Like the child, dark circles shadowed the skin beneath her eyes he recalled being a deep green.

"Miss. . ." He slapped her cheeks lightly to rouse her.

She groaned and struggled to open her eyes.

As green as the sea in the shallows on a summer day. . .

Seeing him loom close, with his hand on her jaw, she jerked back in shocked alarm.

"It's all right," he soothed, releasing her. "Are *you* all right?"

She pushed herself up to sit taller. "I. . .just dizzy." Memory made her frown. "What you said—about Zeke?"

"I'm sorry to be the bearer of bad news. I was on my way to my cabin when I saw the boat docked. I wanted to be the one to tell you. Zeke was a friend. He spoke of your arrival."

"Oh." She stared ahead at nothing, shaking her head as if in a daze. "I hardly knew him, really. We were from the same town of Lowell, in Massachusetts. I saw his ad, and. . . Oh, sweet mercy, what have I done?" she whispered. "I should never have come here. What shall I do?"

The question seemed more self-directed than a plea for advice, but he answered, hoping to reassure her. "I understand teaching positions are reserved for all the women."

"But I'm not one of them, not really. I traveled with them, yes, but I can't teach, I have no certificate and. . ." Her eyes widened. "Where's Gwen? Where's my sister?"

"I'm here," a small voice piped up behind Garrett. The girl stepped into the pale circle of light.

Cecily reached for her, drawing her close. "Are you okay, sweetheart?"

The child nodded, wrapping both arms around her sister. "You won't die, too, will you?" she asked plaintively.

"Now, what kind of talk is that?" Cecily retorted lightly, though Garrett heard the tremor in her words. "I'm of strong stock, at least that's what Auntie always said. And so are you. We're McGivers, you and I. We made it across an ocean. We'll do just fine."

A ghost of a smile lifted the child's pale lips.

Garrett watched the emotional interaction between sisters, not unmoved. "Is the girl ill?" he asked Cecily.

"No more than a wretched case of seasickness."

He nodded in sympathy. He'd seen grown men three times the girl's size succumb to the devilish waves.

"What will you do now?" He asked the question she earlier posed.

"The hotel will put us up for tonight, according to our welcoming committee. Tomorrow I'll find other arrangements."

Garrett knew that several families offered to take in Mercer's girls upon their arrival but had a bad feeling, call it a hunch, about the plight of these two waifs. He'd been taught never to bypass a soul in need and wasn't about to start now. Yet the idea that sprang to mind rendered him speechless, and he wondered if long hours poring over books had addled clear thought. One somber look into two pairs of anxious eyes set his mind on a trek that would surely knock his world flat and send the whole of it catawampus.

"If I might make a suggestion. . ." he said when he gathered the nerve to speak.

Cecily nodded for him to go on.

One part concern, one part need, and more than his fair share of guilt bolstered him to say the rest.

"Marry me."

Chapter 2

Cecily shrank back from the stranger as if he were a wild native wielding a hatchet, though he made no move to touch her.

"You cannot be serious," she whispered. "I can't marry you!"

His earnest expression showed him to be quite sincere.

"I make a decent enough living as an accountant at the lumber mill; I have a cabin nearby and can provide for both you and your sister." He calmly rattled off his assets as she continued to stare in shock. "My offer isn't made without a mutual need, Miss McGiver. I have a small son who requires a mother. My wife died two years ago, and Zeke was a good friend. I feel beholden to give aid to the woman he was set to marry. Given your situation, I believe the plan ideal."

Aid was one thing—but *marriage*?

She gathered her wits and struggled to stand as quickly as she was able, ignoring the hand he held out to assist. "Thank you for your offer, Mr. . . ." A little hysterically she realized this man offered a lifetime commitment, and she didn't even know his name! Though clearly he knew hers.

"Forgive me for the oversight. Hunter. Garrett Hunter."

He tipped his hat. The alarming thought swept through her mind that he might be aptly named. A hunter, indeed. And she felt cornered.

"Yes, well, thank you, Mr. Hunter—"

"Garrett, please—"

"But I see that my group is leaving, and we must join them." She held out her hand for Gwen to take. "Thank you for telling me about Zeke." She realized that she'd not even inquired how he died, but she refused to linger. She would ask around later. "Good-bye."

With a flustered parting nod, she hurried away, toting her sister along, relieved when they caught up to the others. As they took the path to the hotel, she couldn't resist a peek over her shoulder. As suspected, as she'd *felt*, Garrett Hunter stood where she'd left him—looking in her direction.

Cecily hastened her steps.

A quarter-hour later, once they were settled in a room at DeLin's Hotel and Gwen slept in her first real bed in months, Cecily paced the cold floorboards and brooded over her conversation with Zeke's friend. The man had been considerate, certainly no threat. Nor had he behaved the least bit indecently. Yet she had treated him like a wolf stalking sheep that had strayed too far from the pen.

She sighed and rubbed her forehead and the ache that settled there. It had been a difficult year. Her plan to sail alone changed when Aunt Jocasta died unexpectedly a week before Cecily was due to depart. A wealth of determination with no meager amount of pleading persuaded the captain to take Gwen at a lower fare, all that Cecily could afford after booking her own steep passage, the bulk of it paid by Zeke. The promise to share meals with her sister prodded the captain's eventual agreement, though what little food Gwen ate at sea often failed to stay down.

With concern, Cecily eyed her frail sister lying fast asleep and clutching her rag doll, all she'd been allowed to bring—save for one carpetbag packed with as much as Cecily could stuff into it. Gwen hardly resembled the active, rosy-cheeked child of three months ago, and Cecily grimly resolved to do all she must to bring that little girl back to life.

◆—————◆

With less than two dollars in her reticule, Cecily set out the next morning to procure permanent living arrangements. She soon learned that polite determination along with a promise to help in any capacity needful offered poor enticement where fear and superstition ran amok. Though she'd left Gwen behind to rest, assuring a swift return, word had spread about her sister's illness—*false* word to be sure. Cecily no more than mentioned Gwen, and all of a sudden potential boarders were without a spare bed. In some cases, it was likely true. At a few homes she'd been advised to try, she noticed fellow shipmates had found shelter. But Cecily was always turned away, albeit politely.

She couldn't afford a second night's stay at the hotel. Finding a place to lodge in this unknown township was paramount, as was the need to secure work. She had hoped to obtain both by the afternoon. If only she had applied herself better to her schooling and acquired a certificate to teach! She was reasonably intelligent, knew the fundamentals of reading and writing but very little arithmetic, the bane of her existence. Her attempts at sewing bordered on pathetic, certainly not worthy of securing employment as a seamstress's assistant.

Like most women, she yearned for a husband and children. Lowell had been scarce of men since the War Between the States took so many away to fight and die. Reading a friend's circular with adverts from a handful of men looking to find a wife willing to live in the Pacific Northwest, then spotting Zeke's name, had seemed like a godsend. Though at times, like now, Cecily questioned if God was truly listening.

The evening sun hung low in the sky when Cecily approached the mercantile. The township wasn't as populated as Lowell but, after hours of traversing muddy roads and skirting scattered stumps to arrive at suggested locales only to receive nothing but bitter disappointment, it felt gargantuan in size. Men clearly outnumbered women in this part of the world, and most of the former appeared rowdy and wild. Once, she even needed to scurry across the street when a fistfight broke out ahead of her. Throughout the day, she received numerous looks, some curious, some lewd, but thankfully no one approached. Her stomach churned with hunger and nerves. She'd had no more than an apple a kind woman offered—eating half, saving the remainder for Gwen—but despaired returning to the hotel until she met with success.

The matronly storekeeper was kind but apologetic, explaining that she and her husband barely had space for themselves in their home above the shop. Nor did they need help, and dejected, Cecily exited the mercantile. She eyed her surroundings, wondering where on earth to go next. The endless blue ocean sparkled between buildings across the street, the vast wilderness of towering deciduous and evergreen forest flanking the rest of the settlement. One snow-flecked mountain stood prominent across the water, beautiful—but the entire vista felt like yet another obstacle, making her feel trapped.

She had exhausted all suggestions given and strongly considered knocking on each and every door she saw. Zeke had been a lumberman. He wrote in one of the two letters she received of his plan to build them a cabin near the logging camp. In desperation, she wondered where the cabin was located, and if she and her sister might find shelter there.

The agitated whinny of a horse brought her attention to the street. A young woman had just escaped being run over by a wagon, darting in front of it to cross the road, judging by the irate driver's harsh expletives. He shook his fist at her and drove away. Another man bent to help her collect belongings that had fallen from her basket then tipped his hat in farewell and continued in Cecily's direction. The girl turned to watch him.

Cecily inhaled a soft breath when he noticed her in front of the mercantile and crossed the street to where she stood.

"Good evening, Miss McGiver." Garrett Hunter tugged at his hat brim. "I hope your day has met with success."

Feeling foolish for her panicked behavior the night before, she politely smiled, in need of a confidante. "Actually, no, I cannot find lodgings. I nearly met with success a few times, and then I mentioned my sister. The gossips have been busy. Everyone here seems to think Gwen has the plague!"

"She didn't look all that well."

"Only from being seasick and half starved," Cecily said wearily, having used the explanation all day. "Added to that, we recently lost our aunt who took us in when Gwen was a babe. She took her death very hard."

"I'm sorry, but don't take any bad reactions to heart. There recently was something of an epidemic, nothing fatal, but it was nasty. People are afraid to take the risk."

Cecily sighed, fully understanding such logic, but it didn't help her predicament. "I should have asked last night, but how did Zeke die?"

Garrett studied the activity across the street. "An accident while logging."

"Oh." She thought about that. "What kind of accident?"

He grew silent a moment then looked at her. "Ever hear of a widowmaker?" She shook her head and he went on. "A thick branch fell from a tree and hit him in the head."

Cecily winced. "How long ago?"

"About a month now."

"I see." She felt sorry to hear it and not only because it left her with no place to go. "Zeke mentioned a cabin he was building for us. Any idea where it is?"

Garrett squinted at her in alarm. "You can't live there, if that's what you're thinking. Not only is it unfinished—no roof—you wouldn't last a week."

She drew herself up in offense. "I'm a lot tougher than I look, Mr. Hunter. Last night's swoon was simply a fluke."

"This is a different land than what you're accustomed to, Miss McGiver, with predators native to this forest, wild animals you've never encountered, and you without a weapon to fight them off. Such a choice would be doubly harsh on your sister."

He was right, not that she would admit it.

"I'm only trying to find a solution."

He pursed his lips, nodded once, and looked her straight in the eye. "Have you considered my proposal?"

She stared at him in disbelief. "You mean—to marry? *You were serious?*"

"As the sun is to rise at dawn and the moon to light a path by night."

Taken aback by his lyrical reply, she shook her head. "I don't even know you!"

"You said you didn't know Zeke that well, and it's what you came here to do. Marry."

"Yes, but at least I knew *about* him, since we grew up in the same town. I heard things. I knew of his disposition. I know absolutely *nothing* about you."

"Oh, well if that's what it takes to set your mind at ease, come with me." He motioned to the door she'd just exited. Wary but curious what he was up to, Cecily retraced her steps inside.

"Garrett!" The woman behind the counter greeted him with a wide, nearly toothless smile. "Haven't seen much of you lately. Been burning the midnight oil over them books?" She glanced at Cecily, a curious light in her eyes to see her again so soon, but included her in her smile. Her husband, stick-thin where she was plump, stood beside her, arranging a box of shaving brushes on the counter. He nodded to Garrett in greeting.

"You know me too well, Mrs. Crabb. I was hoping you could inform Miss McGiver here, well. . ." He paused, suddenly uncertain. "If you could tell her a little about me?"

Mrs. Crabb looked back and forth between them, a dozen questions popping up in her eyes, but nodded briskly. "I'd be happy to oblige." She focused her attention on Cecily. "Garrett, here, is one of the kindest souls you'll meet. A gentleman if ever I knew one, and a God-fearing man besides. Goes to church meetings as often as they hold them. And if there's a body in need, Garrett's one of the first to meet the call. Why, when old Mr. Flaherty's home burned to ash, Garrett here was the man in charge of rounding up volunteers to build him a new one. I *know* he was responsible for footing the bill for the lumber, though he never admitted to it," she said in an aside to Cecily, *sotto voce*, as if revealing a confidence. "When Mrs. Jenkins lost her husband to consumption, Garrett here helped with repairs to her home, even finding a milk cow for the young'uns. . . ."

Garrett fidgeted, clearly uneasy. "Thank you, Mrs. Crabb—"

"He's honest, hardworking, and a more devoted father you'll not find," the storekeeper continued. "He dotes on that adorable tyke of his. It's a right shame he hasn't found a wife, though the handful of unmarried ladies in these parts tried to turn his head more than once, I daresay."

Garrett's face, by this time, had turned berry red. "Yes, well, I think that's enough—"

Mr. Crabb chuckled, and Cecily struggled not to grin, enjoying this impromptu testimonial to his character.

"Did I mention he's a good listener? Always has time to pass with us old folks, plays checkers now and then with my man Frederick here. And you'd have to be blind not to see what a handsome fellow he is—strong, too. Why, I've seen him lift a full barrel of molasses as if it was eiderdown."

"I think Miss McGiver has the general idea," Garrett said hastily. "Thanks for your time. We must be going."

Cecily made no objection as he took her arm and hurried her out of the mercantile.

Outside, she could no longer withhold the light laughter that bubbled so near the surface.

Garrett looked at her awkwardly. "Yes, well. . ." He cleared his throat and matched her smile. "She's prone to exaggeration, but I hope you feel more at ease about the prospect."

Given what she already knew about Garrett Hunter, Cecily didn't think the woman exaggerated in the slightest. "I do," she admitted.

His eyes flared a little wider, and Cecily took note of them for the first time. Gray-green, with a dark rim framed by darker lashes. Heavy, neat brows the shade of his hair, what she could see of it beneath the hat. Dark brown with a curl at the ends. He stood a half head taller than her, lean of build, his shoulders broad, clearly strong, but with gentleness in his demeanor.

"Does that mean you accept?"

She studied him, surprised to consider it. "If I agree, what would you expect of me? As a wife?"

The nervous tone of her words made clear what she was asking.

"In all honesty?"

She nodded.

"I won't ask for more than you're willing to give. I won't demand that you share my bed, leastways not yet. That is, I won't pressure you, not until you're ready."

She was sure her face achieved the cherry color his had in the mercantile. Oddly, he showed more ease than minutes ago—still nervous but appearing calmer as he clarified his expectations. But then, he had been married before.

"I'm not going about this very well, am I?" He chuckled ruefully. "Let me try again. You're a lovely woman, Cecily, and you possess a pure soul. You're determined and fiercely loyal. I like that. The bond of marriage is everlasting as I see it, and one day I would want you as my true wife."

Hearing her name so softly leave his lips and the earnest candor of his chosen words sent prickles of warmth shivering up her spine and tingling to her toes. How could he know those things about her on such short acquaintance, barely a day? Attraction clearly wasn't an issue for either of them, but Cecily needed more. "I—I couldn't possibly consider consummating—not *now*."

"I don't expect so. But I would hope, maybe one day. . ."

Her face grew more heated with her choice of words, and she felt a little breathless as she looked up into his eyes full of question.

"Yes. . . I—I mean. . .one day. Maybe."

She felt as if she floated in a dream—good or bad she had yet to decide. Were they truly having this conversation? Had she just agreed to become this man's wife?

Garrett smiled. A slightly crooked tooth did nothing to diminish his pleasant appearance. "Then I shall be content with that. Let us embark on this venture in friendship. I vow you'll always have a home and your needs met, you and your sister."

She tilted her head in puzzlement. "Why are you not concerned like everyone else that what Gwen has might be catching?"

"Call it a hunch, but I believe you're right and she's just bone weary. I would like Doc Maynard to look her over, regardless."

Cecily nodded in relief to hear the town had a physician.

"Well, then?"

The glowing pink ball of the sun had nearly met the horizon. She was out of funds to stay at the hotel and out of time to search for other prospects.

Garrett's offer was, quite literally, all she had left.

Taking a deep, nervous breath, Cecily once more took a step into unfamiliar territory, hoping it wouldn't send her plummeting into an abyss of regret.

"Very well, Mr. Hunter, I accept your proposal."

Chapter 3

G arrett stood motionless, not sure he'd heard correctly. Had she finally agreed? For an instant he struggled with misgiving and wondered again if the late hours he kept at the mill office had made him a little loco.

Perhaps he shouldn't have offered marriage. Perhaps he was being too hasty.

True, he *did* know more about Cecily than she knew about him. Zeke had been most forthcoming with her letter—the sole correspondence received, that one letter. It had been a many-paged missive sharing a goodly portion of her character. Garrett knew from those lines that she was loyal, hardworking, God-fearing. Resilient. Determined. That she was a pleasure to the eyes was a bonus. Still, she was a slip of a girl, much too thin, and he wondered if she possessed the stamina to take care of a lively two-year-old. But she had spirit, and deep in his being, he sensed this was the right choice.

He owed it to Zeke.

"Well, then." Garrett cleared the hoarseness from his throat. "We might as well do this. It'll be dark before you know it." He had no wish to sully her reputation by giving her shelter without first having a ceremony.

Cecily's eyes went huge with apprehension, but she nodded her agreement.

"I must return to the hotel for Gwen and—and to pack our things."

"I'll accompany you then make the necessary arrangements."

"Yes, all right."

She kept quiet during the walk and barely acknowledged him when he left her outside the hotel door with a parting remark that he'd return within the hour.

Preacher Dawson and his wife both questioned him, sure they'd heard wrong. Despite that he had interrupted their supper, they were both beside themselves with what amounted to stunned glee.

"You're sure, Garrett, *you* want to get *married*? Tonight?"

"Yes, ma'am."

"And it's one of Asa Mercer's girls, from the boat?"

"It is."

"Oh, my." The preacher's wife patted her ample bosom as if she'd become short of breath. "But you hardly know her."

"I know enough," he said decisively.

The preacher chuckled. "When you get it in your head to do something, you don't waste time."

"No, sir." Garrett smiled, aware his request was a lot to absorb. The well-meaning matrons had tried to interest him in taking a wife for over a year. Those suggested were the Widow Abercrombie, ten years his senior, and Chelsea Ritter, barely a woman, just turned sixteen.

"Will you do it?" Garrett asked, not having received a solid answer.

Preacher Dawson considered. "We can waive the preliminaries. You'll still need to see the registrar, but yes, we can manage a wedding."

"If you hurry," Mrs. Dawson added, "you and your bride can share a nice slice of buttermilk pie with us after the ceremony."

"Thank you kindly, ma'am."

He replaced his hat and exited their tiny parlor.

Generous souls that they were, they likely wouldn't have balked to take in Cecily and her sister, ignoring rumors, unfounded or not, of the child being ill. Yet the Dawsons had no true room to spare, and what food they received was often given in charity. Garrett owned a cozy cabin and provisions, certainly enough to share with two waifs in need of both.

He looked up the road toward the hotel, lowering the brim of his hat against the setting sun. In less than an hour, he would again be a married man, this time to a woman he barely knew.

God help them both.

◆—————◆

The next hour passed like a dream most bizarre.

Cecily at least felt reassured that Garrett was a good Christian man, from what little she'd seen and heard. Gwen showed no surprise or reservations at the new arrangement. One near stranger for her sister's husband was quite equal to another, Cecily supposed.

Preacher Dawson and his wife were a congenial pair, and Mrs. Dawson surprised Cecily when she slipped a posy of bright blue wildflowers into Cecily's damp hand.

Vows were exchanged—if not from hearts of love, at least with earnest giving—and before Cecily knew it she was Mrs. Garrett Hunter. In the two weddings she'd attended in her nineteen years, the groom kissed his bride at the conclusion of the ceremony. She felt relieved when Garrett made no move in that direction, only giving her a slight nod and smile. The nervousness in his eyes oddly calmed her fears somewhat, to know he was just as apprehensive of their future together. No longer a farfetched notion, but now ordained by God and carved in stone.

At the invitation to dessert, Cecily declined, certain her churning stomach wouldn't hold a bite, but at the hopeful glint in her sister's eye, she nodded for Gwen to go ahead. Garrett also declined pie but waited patiently while Gwen shoveled forkfuls of the pastry into her mouth, barely swallowing before taking another bite. Now that they were on dry land, her appetite had thankfully returned.

Garrett made small talk with the preacher while waiting for Gwen to finish. Once she did, Mrs. Dawson rushed to intercept them before they could make their farewells and exit through the door.

"You can't leave without a lantern to light the way." She thrust one toward Garrett. "It's as dark as a bat's wing out there. You may know the way with your eyes closed, but you wouldn't want your new wife stumbling about, since she can't say the same."

He reddened slightly but took the lantern. "I'll return it tomorrow."

"Will we see you at Sunday meeting?" Mrs. Dawson looked at Cecily. "We gather in a nearby clearing on sunny days and inhabit the schoolhouse on rainy ones." Without missing a beat, she brought her attention back to Garrett. "I should be most pleased to introduce your lovely new wife and sister-in-law to the other ladies."

"Della, my dear. . ." Preacher Dawson's amused words came from behind. "Perhaps we should let the newlyweds hasten on home? The little one looks tuckered out."

In concern, Cecily glanced at Gwen, thankful she didn't appear ill, only tired.

With the lantern that Mrs. Dawson had given them, along with her well wishes and offer of help should Cecily ever need anything, the new family made its way along the path to Garrett's cabin.

Cecily felt grateful for Gwen's hand in hers as they walked behind Garrett, her qualms getting thicker the farther they traveled into the dense wood. The moon barely made a dent through the branches, and she was thankful for the lantern's light. It put her in mind of a favorite psalm of Aunt Jocasta's: "Thy word is a lamp unto my feet, and a light unto my path."

God's light certainly would be useful to cut through the encroaching darkness of confusion that seemed intent on spreading through her mind. Not for the first time Cecily wished for the strong faith her dear aunt possessed. Her imagination took wild tangents impossible to curb. Had she been too hasty? She had heard of incidents where strangers turned out to be murderers, and here she walked, following a man she barely knew deeper into the dark wood.

Garrett turned suddenly, the lamplight going full in her face, and she jumped back, keeping a tight hold on Gwen's hand.

He remained silent. Cecily, blinded by flame, couldn't make out his expression in the shadows.

"The cabin is just beyond that rise," he said. "Not much farther."

Cecily managed a nod, and Garrett resumed leading them.

Telling herself she was being foolish, she managed to calm down. The storekeeper had nothing but good things to say about Garrett, and the preacher and his wife treated him as a favored son. Again, she was letting her fears get the better of her, and she stiffened her shoulders in resolve to show some common sense.

Couples often wed, sight unseen, through arranged marriages, and from what she knew, they turned out all right.

Her heart pounded like a trip-hammer once his cabin came into view.

Built of logs, it looked small, and once he led them inside, her assessment did not waver. One room. A stone hearth. Shelves with staples and dishes. The furnishings consisted of a table with benches, a woodstove, and a rocker. Behind that, a wool blanket acted as a curtain that hung from ceiling to floor and must hide the sleeping area.

Seeing no bed, she could not wrench her focus from that blanket, with the sure knowledge of what lay beyond. Gwen suddenly yanked her hand from Cecily's, wiping it on her dress. Cecily's palms had gone from damp to drenched, and surreptitiously she wiped them on her own skirts.

"You mentioned you had a son?" Cecily worked to keep the tremor from her voice.

"Paul, yes. The Widow Brown is looking after him for the night. She does that when I work late. I'll leave word in the morning for her to bring him home."

"And when you're not working late?"

"When Paul was an infant, I took him with me. I laid him in a bin at the mill office, but he's at an age where he gets into everything, and that's no longer possible. He stays at the Widow Brown's during the day. If I'm not working late at the books, I bring him home. I expect that will change now, the need to leave him there."

He studied Cecily as if uncertain she could manage. Small wonder, since his first impression had been for her to swoon from exhaustion and have him need to catch her.

"Would you like anything to eat before retiring? There's not much in the larder. We'll need to replenish supplies, but there's bread and a slab of butter, along with some dried pork."

"Thank you, no." Cecily had barely eaten all day but dared not make the attempt now. "Gwen, are you hungry?"

Her sister shook her head. "I'm sleepy."

"The bed is back there." Garrett motioned to the blanket.

Gwen did not wait to be told twice. Cecily watched her pull back the drape and crawl onto the mattress.

"I should see to her." Cecily excused herself.

"Go on to bed as well. You've had a long day."

"Oh, but—" She brought her words to an awkward halt, suddenly uncertain of what she intended to say.

"You needn't keep me company," he reassured her, saving her from the need to speak. "I could use an early night. I'll sleep in the rocker until I can rustle up something better."

"All right, then. Good night."

Cecily followed her sister into a cubbyhole, barely large enough for the bed. The mattress was lumpy but soft, and big enough to fit two comfortably. A long cradle sat at the foot. She kissed Gwen's forehead and covered her with a blanket, noticing a second one. Thinking a moment, she grabbed the spare and pulled back the curtain.

Now hatless and coatless, Garrett stood with his back to her and stared into the fire. The flames brought out golden and bronze highlights in his hair, a softer brown than she'd first thought, and the damp air caused it to curl more tightly at the ends.

At her step, he turned. She held out the blanket.

"So you don't get cold," she whispered.

A half smile twisted his lips. "The fire will warm me. You don't have that advantage. Keep it."

"No, please, I insist."

It was bad enough she was kicking him from his bed, when the law—both God's and man's—decreed that she should be reposing on that soft, lumpy mattress with him.

Flustered by the thought, she thrust the blanket at his chest.

He grabbed it, to keep the coverlet from falling to the floor when she abruptly let go. His eyes, luminous in the lamplight, caught and held hers a breathless moment before she wrenched her focus away.

"Well, then, good night."

Cecily took hasty refuge behind the blanket before Garrett could echo the sentiment.

Chapter 4

The incessant knock on the door entered Cecily's dreams, jarring her awake. She sat bolt upright, uncertain where she was and how she got there. Gwen stirred beside her, and memory returned with the second set of loud knocks. Realizing Garrett must not be available to answer, Cecily vacated her warm haven and hurried in stocking feet to open the door.

A woman stood on the other side, smartly dressed, young and pretty, with dark upswept hair and big eyes of remarkable violet, a shade lighter than her day gown. Clinging to her neck, a small tot with fair hair, almost white, regarded Cecily with a solemn blue stare.

With her own hair a mass of tangled curls and dress rumpled from being slept in, not to mention lack of footwear, Cecily felt and looked like a misplaced ragamuffin.

One finely arched brow lifted high as the violet eyes took surprised inventory.

"I was left word to bring Paul home," the woman said, her voice soft and well modulated with a Southern twang. "I'm Alice Brown, a friend of Garrett's. Is he here?"

So, this was the Widow Brown. Definitely not the elderly granny with gray hair that she had expected. "No, I don't think so."

"You don't *think* so?"

"I only just woke."

"I see...."

From the sun's placement through the trees, Cecily could tell few hours remained of the morning. She hadn't intended to sleep so long and rarely did.

"And you are?"

"Cecily."

"Garrett didn't tell me he had family visiting."

"Oh, I'm not. I mean... Well, I suppose I am," Cecily blundered, recalling the evening ceremony. "I'm his wife."

The words came whisper-soft, still hard to believe, much less say—but well heard by the Widow Brown. Her impossibly huge eyes grew wider. "His *wife?* Garrett is *married?*"

For the briefest moment, Cecily thought she saw a glimmer of hurt there.

"Well, what do you know about that," the woman mused with a sunny smile, making Cecily wonder if she had imagined any dismay. "I assume you're one of those girls newly arrived? I didn't see you at the celebration at University Hall yesterday."

"Cecily?"

At Gwen's anxious cry, Cecily half turned to look then again regarded her visitor.

"I'm sorry, I must go. Thank you for bringing Paul."

She held out her hands for the boy. He turned his face away, burying his cheek in the Widow Brown's shoulder.

"He doesn't cotton well to strangers," Alice said, her tone bordering on supercilious.

"We'll manage." *Somehow*, Cecily added silently, and took the child, pulling him forcefully away while being as gentle as she could. He whimpered and wriggled to get down, but Cecily held him fast to her side. "It was nice meeting you."

False words but polite, as Garrett would expect. He had given her his name and a place to live. She wouldn't embarrass him with bad behavior by slamming the door of his cabin in this snooty woman's face.

Closing the door softly, she took the blubbering child back to the bed. Gwen sat up, her eyes wide as saucers.

"Is everything all right?" Cecily asked her sister.

"Who's that?"

"This is your nephew, Paul." Cecily plunked the tot in the middle of the patchwork quilt. He looked at his familiar surroundings and the unfamiliar little girl who sat in his papa's bed.

"Doh 'way!" he commanded, the word coming out garbled with tears. "Doh 'way!"

"What's he saying?" Gwen bent toward him and poked his belly with her finger. Startled, he stopped crying and looked down at Gwen's hand then giggled when she smiled and did it again, wriggling all her fingers.

Cecily chose not to respond that she thought the boy might be telling them to go away. She hoped the day would progress better than it began.

◆━━━━◆

After a tiresome afternoon of transcribing page after endless page of worn ledger, Garrett arrived home near sunset.

Opening the door, he spotted his new bride on a bench before the low fire, her arms crossed on the table and used as a pillow for her head.

He closed the door softly. Regardless, it woke her.

She lifted her head and blinked. "Oh. . ." Hastily, she straightened. "Oh!"

"I didn't mean to startle you."

"I must have dozed off, Mr. Hunter. I'm terribly sorry. You must be hungry. What would you like to eat?" She scrambled off the bench, smoothing her skirts.

"Garrett. And please, sit. I know there's not much—we'll remedy that once I get my wagon back. For tonight, I brought meat pies from the bakery."

He set a canvas sack on the table and withdrew two huge pastries.

"There's *a bakery* here?"

Garrett grinned at her astonishment.

"Opened just this year by Charles Terry and his wife. They own much of the business district. You'll find this part of the Northwest Territory isn't the uncivilized jungle it was purported to be in the flyers back home. Oh, at first it was nothing but wilderness. I'm sure the stumps scattered about town tell their own story, but we've made progress."

She nodded. "And your wagon? I didn't know you owned one."

"A cracked axle. A friend is seeing to it. I also loaned him my horse. That's why I was on foot the night we met. Truth is, I only recently acquired both wagon and horse and need to see about building a shelter to house them soon."

She took two plates, two forks, two knives, and two checkered napkins from the shelf and set them on the table. He raised his brow at the amount.

"The children ate earlier and are sleeping. I haven't the heart to wake them. Paul's been rather fussy."

Hearing the tension in her voice, he eyed her closely. "Bad day?"

She shrugged, attempting a smile. "Your son doesn't like me much."

"He doesn't know you. Give it time."

"Time, yes. . ." Her gaze settled on the curtain that hid the slumbering children, and he sensed Paul's rejection wasn't all that troubled her mind. Her next words confirmed it.

"I should put him in his cradle, I suppose. I'm sorry to keep you from your bed." She blushed. "It doesn't seem right."

Garrett sat down across from her. Solely to comfort, he laid his hand over hers that rested on the table, surprised by the little shock of warmth the contact generated. She must have felt it, too, with the manner in which her eyes jumped to his and widened.

He said grace over their meal but didn't move his hand, instead giving hers a slight squeeze. "Cecily, I meant what I said. We'll take this slow. There's no need to vex yourself with worries. I suggest we spend these evening hours conversing and getting to know each other."

A smile lifted her lips, putting a glow to her face and a shine to her eyes, and once more he was struck by her beauty.

"Well, then, Mr. Hunt—er, um, *Garrett*, I should like to know more about you."

"What would you like to know?"

"Everything."

He grinned. "Fair enough." He cut a slab of his beef and potato pie, grateful that steam rose from the broken crust and it hadn't cooled much. "I was born in Chicago on April 5th of 1841 to Myra and Grant Hunter. My father worked at a factory."

"Really?"

Noting her sparked interest, he hazarded a guess. "Your father was a factory worker also?"

A wistful expression crossed her features. "No, a schoolteacher. I lost my parents when I was young. In a fire. Gwen was just a baby, and we were staying with Aunt Jocasta. We never left her home after that day, not until she suddenly passed on the week before our journey here. Her heart."

"I'm sorry for your loss."

She nodded, brushing away a tear. "It's why I brought Gwen with me, though that was never the plan. But I couldn't very well leave her behind."

"Of course not."

"I showed interest in the factory because I worked in one, too. As a mill girl at a textile factory. I worked there until it closed. They could no longer get the cotton needed from the South due to the War Between the States." She tilted her head curiously. "You do know there's a war going on?"

A smile teased his lips that she would think them so cut off from civilization not to be aware of something so pertinent. He somberly nodded. "The war erupted shortly after our arrival. We get news from back home weeks, even months after the fact, but we're not completely cut off. And soon, from what I read in the *Seattle Gazette*, we hope to have a telegraph line."

"You have a newspaper here?"

"We do." He grinned at her shock. "As a matter of fact, there was a short column about your arrival."

Her eyes widened in alarm. "Please say they didn't mention me or Gwen by name. I specifically asked them not to."

He drew his brows together. "Why ever not?"

"I don't want attention drawn to us, especially now, not after what Gwen's been through." She wrinkled her nose and picked at her crust with her fork. "It may seem foolish, but I don't really feel like one of them—what they call us. Mercer's girls. I bought my ticket with a plan in mind and a bridegroom waiting, while the other women were more daring, coming here with their futures virtually unknown."

He sat back and regarded her. "It seems to me you sell yourself short. To travel across the country alone, by train and by ship, to take a man you barely recall as a husband—all of that conveys its own brand of courage."

She flushed prettily. "I just don't like all the fuss."

"You needn't worry. They didn't mention names."

She smiled in relief, and they ate a moment in silence before she again spoke.

"Why here? Seattle. What brought you to these parts?"

Garrett thought about that, opting to give her a heartfelt answer rather than his usual vague one. "I didn't want to be a factory worker like my father. I saw what it did to his health. The lure of a new land still in its birth pangs and owning a small parcel of it was too tempting to refuse while living in the filth of a city that had become over-crowded. I tried to convince my parents to come, but they said they were too old, and Mother had no desire to move away from my two sisters. Both are married and living in Chicago."

"Were you married long? To your first wife." Her skin went a shade rosier, and flustered, she tried to retract her words. "I'm sorry. It's none of my business."

"We were wed the day before we left for Missouri and the Trail. She discovered she was with child a month after we arrived. The journey was difficult, and she was. . . delicate. Paul's birth depleted her health. That winter she took on a fever and died. We were married little over a year."

"I'm sorry."

He nodded but said nothing a moment, staring into the fire. "I won't pretend it wasn't difficult, that I didn't grieve her loss, but I've come to accept what cannot be changed." He looked up. "Don't feel you can't ask questions, Cecily. It *is* your business. You're my wife and should know who you married."

She looked at him with curiosity. "You're very forthright. I don't think I've ever met a man quite like you."

He grinned. "I'm not, actually. But it's important we get to know each other, so I'll make the exception."

They talked well into the evening until Cecily yawned and offered an embarrassed apology. Somewhat surprised by just how much he enjoyed their conversation, a glance at his pocket watch showing him it was later than expected, Garrett suggested they retire. While Cecily cleared away dishes, Garrett fashioned his makeshift bed. Cecily solemnly watched him at his task, and he considered it progress that her smile seemed genuine enough as they exchanged the pleasantries of good nights.

Chapter 5

Two weeks passed, and married life with Garrett grew more manageable if not altogether comfortable. Once he left for work each day, Cecily struggled to learn the basics for their home to run smoothly, having no one to instruct her. She'd done chores for Aunt Jocasta, but running a household, even a small one, and in these wilds, was far different. Garrett did whatever she quietly asked of him, Cecily still not feeling she had the right. She might be a wife, but hardly felt like one. He took her to the mercantile and waited patiently while she made selections, then stowed the items in the back of his wagon.

On days absent of rain, few and far between, buckets of water needed to be hauled from the stream that trickled a short distance behind their cabin, not pumped as she'd done in Lowell. Thanks to a healing tonic prescribed by the doctor—more than a week's rest, and good food, pink again tinged Gwen's cheeks. Cecily delegated the task of fetching water to her sister, sure the daily walk would aid in getting her back to full health. Cecily used copper and silver coins to purify the water she boiled, as Aunt Jocasta had done, and used this for personal cleaning and household washing, first separating a pitcher for drinking and the coffee Garrett required on his arrival home.

She had just ground beans for that stout brew and dumped them in the coffeepot to heat when she heard a horse whinny. Knowing it was too early for Garrett's return, Cecily stepped to the sole window, its boards open wide to let in the light, and peeked through the calico curtain.

She groaned to see her visitor and pushed a damp strand of hair into place, swiftly repositioning a pin. Casting a derisive eye over the topsy-turvy state of the room and her dirty apron, she whipped the latter off and hung it on its peg.

Taking a calming breath, she waited for the inevitable knock then opened the door.

"Good afternoon." The Widow Brown smiled, once again the picture of fashion with every hair held in place beneath a matching blue hat. In one gloved hand she held something covered with a cloth napkin. The other was gripped by a dark-haired boy, perhaps two years older than Paul. "I brought a pie. I hope this isn't a bad time."

Cecily managed a smile. "Come in. Please excuse the mess. I've been baking bread."

"So I see." The woman's sharp gaze took in the flour-spattered table and floorboards, landing on Cecily's sleeve. Cecily looked down to see flour streaked there and brushed at it, feeling she had been judged and found wanting.

"We've missed you at Sunday meetings." The widow came straight to the point. "I do hope you plan on attending soon. People talk, and well, you wouldn't want anyone getting the wrong idea that you're a heathen, you being so new here and all."

The words were delivered sweet as syrup, laced with bitter venom in their ring of false concern. Gwen's ill health had kept Cecily away the first week, a bad headache the second. Justifiable excuses both, but not at the heart of her avoidance. Anxious of what others must think of her, marrying Garrett as swiftly as she did, she knew she was at the hub of the current chin-wagging. The curious and suspicious stares she received when they went to town were proof, and she was willing to bet this woman started that chain of gossip.

A harsh notion, and Cecily felt instant remorse for her unkind thought. She smiled. "Please, take a seat, Mrs. Brown. I'd offer you coffee, but I just put it on."

"Oh, do call me Alice." The woman perched carefully on a clean part of the bench then looked around the room. "Where's Paul? Surely you haven't lost him already."

Cecily kept her smile plastered in place. "The children are outside playing."

"Children?" One arched brow lifted.

"My sister is with Paul. I'm surprised you didn't see them."

"Oh, dear. I do hope they haven't gone far into the woods."

"I told Gwen not to stray. They're probably behind the cabin."

"Not near the stream, I hope?" Alice tsked. "I never understood why Garrett chose to remain here when he could have made a lovely home in town. There's always the danger of bears, you know."

No, she didn't know, and when the door flew open, admitting the two missing children, Cecily felt relief—a relief immediately squashed when Paul's eyes lit up and he ran straight for Alice Brown.

"Mama!"

Cecily tried to ignore the fleeting look of triumph in the widow's eyes as she hugged the child to her bosom. Of course Paul felt close to this woman, having spent days and nights in her home. Hearing her offspring address her with the title, it stood to reason Paul would do the same. But that logic did not dispel the painful stab in Cecily's chest. And her own small victory to reach a point where the boy no longer cried or fidgeted to get down when she held him dissolved to dust.

The older boy pulled at his mother's arm. "I wanna play."

"Well, I suppose," Alice agreed. "Stay in front of the cabin. Don't go past our wagon."

All three children scrambled for the door.

"Keep an eye on them," Cecily called.

"She's awfully young," Alice pondered once they were again alone.

"Gwen is older than she looks."

"I heard something about her being ill."

"She's better," Cecily staunchly said. "More so every day."

"That's nice, dear. It's quite distressing to be encumbered with a sick child." The

Widow Brown looked up at a crudely framed sampler hanging on the wall, catty-corner to Garrett's mounted shotgun. "I'm pleased to see you kept Linda's things about. Mrs. Pettigrew was sure you'd dispose of them, but I hoped you wouldn't. Linda was a dear friend, such a sweet soul. A true angel. It would be a shame to lose any part of her left."

Cecily sank to the opposite bench, her legs suddenly weak.

"She had such skill with a needle, spent most of her time in the months before Paul's birth sewing and knitting. She made those curtains—they certainly cheer up the place, don't you agree?"

Cecily looked at the yellow calico wafting in the breeze. She had worked in a factory that made the cloth to craft such curtains, but her own prowess with a needle was nil.

"Linda was the picture of sunshine, with her bright, golden hair. And flowers—why Linda used to fill the place with wildflowers. On the table, on the mantel, fresh flowers every day. She even put them in her hair." Alice fondly chuckled then sighed. "Such a tragedy, her taken from us so unexpected-like. Garrett was heartbroken. I didn't think he would ever marry again. It was quite the shock that he did."

Alice pinned Cecily with a narrow-eyed look. "You really are quite brave to take all this on."

"Brave?"

"To have her things about, knowing how Garrett adored her. It can't be easy for you, knowing you'll never measure up." Alice raised her fingers to her lips in remorse, though Cecily doubted the woman's sincerity. "Oh, dear! I shouldn't have said that. Do forgive me. It might take a while, but I'm sure, in time, things will work out for you."

Cecily stood on the verge of asking why she should suspect problems when the door swung open to a squalling Paul. At a glance she could see his skinned knee. Not to her surprise, he ran straight to Alice for comfort, and the invisible knife in her heart twisted a little deeper.

"Jeremy pushed me," the boy cried.

"Now, Jeremy, that wasn't nice," Alice reprimanded in a silken tone.

Jeremy scowled, tugging on Paul's arm to try to pull the boy from his mother's embrace.

"I wanna go home," he whined.

Alice sighed. "I suppose we should. Your sister will be home from school soon."

The Browns left, amid Paul's miserable entreaties of "Don' go!"

Cecily struggled to pull her battered emotions together and dabbed at his scraped skin with a damp cloth that he repeatedly pushed away.

◆•——•◆

The sun had not yet set when Garrett strode into the cabin. He sent an uncertain glance to his son, sitting on the floor near the door and pitifully sobbing, then noticed the flour-strewn table and floor, his wife's face, bodice, and sleeves streaked with the same.

Paul jumped up and practically leaped into his arms, clutching his neck. "Papa!"

Testing the waters, noting Cecily's taut features, he made a stab at a greeting. "Bad day?"

She grimaced as she set a dish down with a clunk. "About as well as can be expected."

Hoping to cheer her, he inhaled appreciatively a whiff of the pastry on the table. "Mmm—rhubarb pie. My favorite."

To his shock, her eyes grew wet with tears.

"Of course it is!" she exclaimed between clenched teeth, her eyes shooting daggers at him as she stormed from the cabin.

At a complete loss, he looked after her then at Gwen who sat on the far side of the room with her rag doll.

"Mrs. Brown came by earlier," the girl said quietly. "She brought the pie."

Garrett winced at his blunder, now noticing the napkin beneath the pastry—white with embroidery and not checkered. He scooped the filling that oozed from the baked crust with a fingertip and offered it to Paul. Instantly the boy's whimpers ceased as he eagerly latched on to the offered treat and smiled.

With his son pacified for the moment, Garrett set the boy down and went in search of his slighted wife.

Garrett found her just outside, staring at the trees that blocked the view into town.

"Why didn't you tell me that rhubarb pie was your favorite?" she asked without turning.

"Preference of food isn't a subject that's come up in our fireside chats. We can remedy that tonight if you wish."

"Did you even like the custard one I made last week?"

"I did."

He stood behind her, debated the idea, then took her gently by the shoulders and turned her to face him. She didn't pull away and, liking the soft feel of her, he kept his hands where they were.

"What's this really about, Cecily?"

Her face went a charming shade of rose. "Too foolish to mention. I'm embarrassed by my behavior in there, Garrett. Please just forget it."

"You're my wife, and I'd like to know when something vexes you. Marriage is about sharing."

"I'll try and remember that."

She smiled, the green of her eyes lit up from within. He noted just how lovely she was when she did that, flour-spotted, tousled hair, and all. His thumbs drew gentle circles against her sleeves, and her expression softened.

A loud clatter and delighted squeal from the cabin broke them apart.

"Paul! What have you done?" Gwen shrieked as Cecily hurried inside, Garrett right behind her.

His imp of a son sat on the floor covered in globs of gooey pie from the dish he'd pulled off the table. A huge smile spread across his red-streaked face as he ate the filling off his fingers then stuck his hand out in invitation to the adults gaping at the door.

"Yum!"

"Oh, mercy. . ." Cecily clapped her hands to her cheeks.

Garrett couldn't help himself. Throwing back his head, he roared with laughter, the little ladies joining in until the cabin rollicked with the sound.

Chapter 6

I like him," Gwen said decidedly. "He's nice."

Cecily nodded, her focus across the clearing shaded by sweeping boughs of evergreens, oaks, and maples, where her husband spoke with a Mr. Sanderson. Her sister's approval of Garrett came as no surprise. The man had been nothing but patient and kind. What astonished her was how quickly Gwen had discarded her shyness in his presence. And Paul had become her baby doll, the boy pleased as punch to nestle at his aunt's side or hold her hand, as he now did.

"It's a pleasure to finally meet you," a voice said near Cecily's elbow, and she turned to greet the wife of one of the lumbermen. "I'm Lorraine Truett, my husband is Samuel. We were so sorry about Zeke, but I'm happy that Garrett took a wife, as unexpected as it was."

Her words were kind, and Cecily smiled, the icicles of fear that had pierced her in approaching this day having melted with the late morning sun.

A fourth week passed before she gathered the courage, but her decision proved worthwhile to witness Garrett's pleased approval when she announced over breakfast that she would like to attend today's meeting with him.

Preacher Dawson's message of endurance through faith under fire, inspired by the distant war going on between the North and the South, provided food for thought, and along with the congregation, she sympathized with one woman who received recent word that she'd lost two brothers in battle months ago. Cecily found herself saying a silent prayer for those men she'd known from Lowell who'd also gone off to fight.

The minister's wife approached, her enthusiastic welcome making Cecily regret she'd given in to foolish qualms and waited this long to join them. The women talked about town matters, Cecily listening with interest, though she still did not feel comfortable enough to join in. Mrs. Dawson excused herself to speak with another parishioner, and Lorraine drew close to Cecily.

"I'd watch that one if I were you. That bit of poetry that Lizzie Doter wrote in the *Gazette* a month back—'Mistress Glenare'—could have been written about the likes of her. 'Three parts serpent, and one of the dove. . .'"

At first Cecily failed to understand the low warning until she looked to where she'd last seen Garrett. The Widow Brown stood close to him, the two alone, and Garrett inclined his head toward Alice as if to hear her better. Cecily clenched her free hand into a fist in her skirts, certain the woman spoke in dulcet tones so he would do just that. A possessive feeling came over her, and she struggled not to march over there and snatch her husband's arm from the woman's fingertips, perhaps even take his hand in her own.

Lorraine's warning was hardly necessary.

Faith under fire.

However, sometime in the last year Cecily misplaced her faith that God actually cared about the little details of her life, though Alice Brown could hardly be called a little detail. A big glaring stain was more apt, and she wasn't entirely sure God cared about those, either.

The ride back to the cabin proved awkward, and from the corner of her eye Cecily noticed Garrett glance over at her in curiosity more than once. She was afraid to speak, to air something better left unsaid, and kept her silence.

<hr>

Not until the children were put to bed did Garrett act. With a hasty good night, Cecily brushed by where he sat on the bench, startled when he grabbed her wrist to prevent her escape.

He rarely touched her, and she stared at him in curious shock. His eyes were grave.

"What have I done, Cecily, to cause you to go quiet on me?"

"I'm not sure what you mean." She barely got the words out, his hand burning her skin and causing warmth to spread through her body.

"You don't want to have our talk?"

Their evening chats had become the part of the day Cecily most looked forward to, but she shook her head. "Not tonight. It's been an exhausting day, and I wish only to go to bed."

She averted her eyes, feeling horrible for causing the hurt she glimpsed in his, and wished they had the kind of close relationship where she felt comfortable asking him uncomfortable questions. Namely, of his involvement with a certain beautiful young widow.

"Then I won't keep you."

His reply came distant, almost cold, and he released her hand.

She found she missed its warmth.

A long time later, Cecily stared wide awake at the opaque curtain, the red glow from the dying firelight illuminating the cloth. Garrett's grim words and the reason for them weren't all that kept her awake. She rued drinking a glass of water shortly before retiring and didn't think she could wait until dawn's gray light to tend to nature's persistent call.

She considered taking a candle, but that would be difficult if not impossible to manage, and she certainly had no wish to set the surrounding forest ablaze. The lantern sat on the mantel, but to reach it she would literally have to step over Garrett. She would simply make do and trust her eyesight not to fail her in the dark.

Cecily approached the door with stealth, glancing only once toward the fire's embers and the dark bulk that lay stretched out on the floor, to reassure herself that he slept. Quietly she opened the door, wincing at the creak of wooden hinges, and slipped outside. She was immensely grateful that the moon shone bright enough, positioned above the trees, so that her surroundings could be seen.

To her consternation, on her return from the outhouse the fickle moon hid behind a long, thick cloud, forcing her to pick her way along, and she chided herself for not putting on her shoes, the ground prickly beneath her bare feet. She was halfway to the door when she heard a loud, long rustle behind. Stifling a small yelp, she spun around, not wishing to present her back to the claws of whatever creature stood beyond sight. Slowly she backed up toward the cabin, her eyes frantically scanning from left to right for any moving mass of shadow poised to attack.

She ran into something hard and unyielding and let out a startled scream.

"Cecily!" Garrett muttered, quiet so as not to rouse the hearing of any living being but harsh enough to command silence. "It's me."

At the knowledge he stood there, she melted against him. Still trembling, she turned and clutched folds of his nightshirt, pressing her cheek against his chest. His heart pounded rapid but reassuring. Her mouth went dry at the feel of his hand pressed against her lower back. He was warm and solid, and amid the myriad feelings that fluttered inside, she felt safe in his arms.

"Is it a bear?" she whispered.

"I don't know, but we should get inside."

His arm tightened briefly before releasing her, and they entered the cabin. She noticed then that he carried a shotgun in one hand.

"I tried not to wake you."

She watched him replace the weapon atop its pegs in the log wall. His nightshirt hung almost to his knees, and she glanced at his pale calves. From the experience of being held in his arms, she knew the rest of him must be as well sculpted.

"I wouldn't have minded if you did."

Flames heated her face and neck at the direction of her thoughts. She also stood clothed for slumber, her nightdress voluminous and opaque from throat to ankles, but felt grateful the room lay in semidarkness lit red only by the last glowing embers of the hearth.

Before she could offer a hasty good night, he turned and slowly covered the short distance between them. She shivered as he cradled one hand against her jaw.

"At least you should have taken the shotgun. These woods can be dangerous at night."

"It wouldn't have done me much good. I don't know how to shoot."

"No?" he asked quietly.

"There isn't much cause for it in Lowell."

Tingles of warmth prickled along her skin as his thumb made a slow caress against her cheek, running faintly over her lower lip. The air felt suddenly charged, her senses heightened and sharp, like the fine hairs that stood on end seconds before a lightning strike.

"Well, then, we'll have to remedy that."

"Yes," she whispered, barely aware she spoke or that her chin had tilted up to him, both from the faint lift of his fingers and her own volition. Her eyes flickered to his mouth.

In the next instant, his lips were on hers, soft and cool as the brush of silk then firm in gentle demand, growing warmer and parting her lips. Again she clung to his shirt.

Eventually he broke away, but she kept her eyes tightly shut, anxious to open them and look into his. Nervous of what she might find there. But most of all, troubled by this strange tumult of sensation that made the room feel suddenly too hot. She did not feel ready to share his bed, but was it right to deny him a wife?

"Good night, Cecily."

His words came strained, and when she opened her eyes, she found him in profile, bent to the fire and stirring it with a poker.

Feeling relieved by his unexpected dismissal yet oddly disappointed by his abrupt distance, she wasted no time in escaping to the borrowed bed.

Chapter 7

He had promised her.

Garrett recited the reminder in his head at least a dozen times a day.

He had promised Cecily he would make no demands, would not woo or persuade her until she was ready, and it became a constant struggle to keep his word. Three nights ago he failed, the kiss a result of relief at finding her in one piece after her late-night scare. Their close embrace had sharpened the desire to take his wife in his arms and teach her all the ways a man could love a woman. He might have, too, had he felt her kiss in return, but upon pulling back he'd noticed her eyes tightly shut with nervous dread. Reminded of his vow to her, he gave her what she wanted. Distance. But Garrett wasn't sure how much longer he could live with her in a cabin that had gone past being cozy to cramped and confined. He was a man, and she was a woman, his woman. His *wife*. How long was he supposed to ignore that?

And when had he fallen so hopelessly in love with her?

He feared she might never feel the same about him, no matter how patient and understanding he tried to be, no matter how much time and distance he gave. He had only touched her with intimacy twice since they met—the night her ship brought her to him, when he carried her close, and three nights ago, when he held her in his arms and kissed her soft lips, wishing to partake in all the things a man did with his wife.

"How am I to manage this?" He rolled his eyes up to the space of blue sky seen amid the top boughs of towering trees. "I fear I will fail and kiss her again, I want to so badly, every time I see those big green eyes smile back at me, but I don't want to scare her away. Is this how life will always be with us? Am I being *too* patient? Or am I required to learn to live in a loveless marriage? Well, not loveless," he muttered. "More like a love unrequited."

He had cherished his first wife with an affection deeply returned, had cruelly lost her, and never thought to love again, surprised that he could and did. Was it so much to ask that after two years of avoiding all possible and impossible matches the well-meaning matrons tried to arrange, that the one woman he'd chosen to share his life with would return his feelings? He ached to tell her how he felt but feared doing so would scare her away.

Collecting the boards brought from the mill, he piled them near the table he had dragged outside and reached for his saw.

Maybe his concern had no basis. It had been little over a month since they married, and their fireside chats, though coming less frequently with the need to finish tasks before winter, had been beneficial in getting to know each other. He still wasn't the best conversationalist in town, but he had enjoyed every moment of learning more about the woman who was his wife.

Garrett continued with his task, a bed for a child, and hoped the reason for it would be understood. His thoughts wandered as he worked, and then fire suddenly shot through his thumb as his hammer missed the nail.

"Confound it!" A short stream of more colorful words left his lips. He shook his hand, instantly contrite, and looked up to the skies again. "Sorry about that."

His eyes lowered, caught and held to the slight figure who'd just come around the side of the cabin where he'd strung a rope between trees on a sunny patch of ground for a clothesline. In her arms Cecily carried a basket of linens. They stared at each other a moment before she moved to go inside.

With a weary breath, Garrett tackled his work with a vengeance, striving not to let his mind wander.

"Garrett?"

Startled by her voice so near, he narrowly missed pounding the hammer into his thumb a second time. He turned swiftly, his expression fierce, and she backed up a quick step.

"I'm sorry," she apologized. "I thought you heard me coming."

He worked to calm his features, remorseful for frightening her, and wiped the sweat from his brow with his forearm. "No, it's all right. Was there something you needed?"

"I brought you some water. You've been working out here awhile."

Taking the cup, he faintly smiled in acknowledgement and drank a few long gulps. "Much appreciated." He handed her back the cup, but she made no move to go.

"I was wondering. . ." She looked at the boards he had nailed together on the table. ". . .where we're to have our supper?"

He thought a moment. "I'll need the table for the next couple of days to saw lumber. I want to get as much work done as I can during these few months of frequent sunshine. The cabin's a mite crowded, and I want to build on before winter comes."

"Oh."

He wished he knew what put that pensive look in her eyes.

"How about a picnic inside?" he suggested. The ground was still muddy and messy from rain two days before.

"That sounds delightful." She looked back to his project on the table. Her brow furrowed momentarily, but her eyes sparkled when she again looked up. "I'll lay a blanket on the floor to make it more picniclike. Gwen and Paul will love it."

"I'll bring a jar of ants."

"What?" She blinked in confusion.

He winked. "Can't have a picnic without them."

She giggled, and his heart lifted at the sound. He realized then how rarely she laughed, and decided to do what he could to change that.

❦————❦

Cecily reclined on her side on the blanket, her hand supporting her cheek with her arm braced to the ground. Her husband rested across from her, one long leg stretched out, the other bent at the knee, while he casually leaned back against both arms. Between them lay the remains of supper. He stared into the fire while she stared at him.

She had been doing quite a lot of that lately.

With the children tucked into bed, Cecily posed a question that piqued her curiosity. "You said once that you were a lumberman turned bookkeeper. How did that come about?"

He let out a soft, amused snort. "One of the boys told the boss about my gift for numbers. When he fired the previous accountant, he came to me."

"Your gift?"

His skin turned a shade darker. "I sum them up in my head."

Her brows puzzled into a frown. "Can't everyone?"

"Not long ones." At her intrigued glance, he nodded. "Go ahead."

She rattled off two numbers, each containing five digits.

He thought a moment. "Ninety-five thousand, five hundred and seventy-eight."

She stared at him. "You do realize I have no way of figuring if that's correct."

He chuckled. "There's a pencil and paper in the box on the shelf."

"No, that's all right. I'm terrible at math," she confessed. "I see more than two numbers to add and I break out in hives."

He laughed at her little joke, and she smiled to hear it.

"So, I married a mathematical genius. And with your commitment, the long hours you've spent at the mill, they're twice as lucky to have you."

He fidgeted, uncomfortable with her praise. "I had no choice. The ledger was left unprotected—it's to be wrapped in oilcloth when not in use. The rains came, the ceiling sprang a leak, and the ledger got wet."

She lifted her brows. "You work for a lumber company, and they didn't fix a leak in their own building?"

"They have since. It's not much. A shack really, smaller than this cabin and hastily built. I had just taken on my new role, and my first chief task was to transfer what could be deciphered of the blurred entries into a new ledger. I finished with that a few weeks ago—that's why you don't see me spending any more nights there."

Cecily remembered. In the first week they were married, Garrett returned home late every evening. She remembered, because she had lain in bed next to Gwen, unable to sleep, until she heard him come home. Not out of fear for herself but concern for him, which was rather odd. At the time, he'd still been so much a stranger, and she felt she had no right to ask how he kept himself occupied. His current explanation eased a burden in her soul. She didn't really suspect him of drinking, gambling, or seeking out loose women, not after the storekeeper's accolades of praise. But she had wondered if the Widow Brown might have been a recipient of his visits.

As if he, too, suddenly thought of those long nights he'd been away, leaving her alone with the children, he spoke: "I'm teaching you to shoot tomorrow."

Startled, she looked at him. "If you think it necessary."

"I do."

Cecily recalled the night that prompted his decision and the breathtaking kiss that followed. Her face warmed, not from the flames.

"Garrett, why did you marry me?"

He stared at her, clearly thrown by her change of topic.

"I told you why."

"Yes, that you needed a mother for Paul and I needed a home." She hesitated, uneasy, but having talked herself into this corner, she resolved to say what had been on her mind for more than a week. "While there is a shortage of marriageable women here, and the men do far outnumber them, and I understand why Mr. Mercer felt the need to, er, fulfill such a mission. . . ." She sought for clarification, realizing she was going about this badly. "The town isn't exactly absent of women suitable for marriage." She bit her cheek not to say the Widow Brown's name. "And, well, we were nothing more than strangers when we met. I learned quickly you're the gallant type, but marriage is a lot to offer, a lifetime commitment, and I just don't understand why you would do such a thing when you could have had your pick of anyone out there."

She hoped she hadn't mangled the expression of her thoughts and also wished she could read his mind as well as the look in his eyes, which during her discourse had gone from curious to pensive to somber, staring at her intently.

"Do you have regrets, Cecily?"

"Goodness, no! That's not what I meant at all. I mean, well, of course when we first met then married, I was—I wouldn't say frightened exactly, more apprehensive and unsure." She still felt uncertain. "I knew you to be kind from my own experience and what others said. But, Garrett—why *me*?"

He went quiet a long moment, too long.

"Never mind. You don't have to—" Cecily began, sitting up to smooth her skirt.

"I did it out of guilt," he said at the same time.

"Guilt?"

She stared at him in curious shock. He smiled sadly.

"Those needs you mentioned, they factored in, of course, but the underlying reason for all of it. . ." He looked away and inhaled deeply. His troubled eyes went to the fire. "I felt responsible for Zeke's death."

"Responsible?" She winced, realizing she was beginning to sound like a mindless echo. "Why would you feel—"

"I pushed him too hard," he replied so fiercely that Cecily jumped a little, taken aback. He looked at her and unclenched his jaw. "Forgive me. I didn't mean to scare you. I seem to do that a lot."

"You didn't. . .don't."

Nothing about Garrett truly frightened her, now that he was no longer a stranger and had become a friend. But she'd never seen him this upset.

"I shouldn't have asked."

Briefly he closed his eyes, letting out a hoarse laugh that sounded more woeful than happy. "You've every right to hear the truth, Cecily. I should have told you that first day. Zeke was a good man, a friend, but he lacked motivation. When the time drew near for your arrival and he had barely laid the foundation for the cabin, also developing a pattern of showing up late to work, I sat him down and gave him an ear-scalding lecture. Told him he must work harder and play less at cards. Must stop getting into brawls and frittering away the empty hours. I told him if he didn't shape up, he would lose it all. He took me at my word—I had recently taken on the bookkeeping and had the boss's listening ear. I think he presumed I would speak against him. I never would have, unless his actions endangered a life, but I let him go on thinking that, satisfied to see a change. He worked to the point of exhaustion. He wasn't careful. I should have spoken. I didn't see the danger until it was too late, or maybe I just closed my eyes to it."

Cecily wanted nothing more than to reach across the wide gap and lay a reassuring hand on his arm.

Abruptly, he straightened. "It's late, and I have a full day's work ahead," he said gruffly, pushing himself up to stand.

He hesitated then walked toward her and stretched out his hand. Butterflies madly fluttered in her midsection as she accepted his help, his palm warm in hers. Once she was on her feet, before he could release her, she brought her other hand to cup his.

"It wasn't your fault, Garrett. You did nothing wrong. You only wanted the best for Zeke. I'm sure he wouldn't want you to blame yourself for what amounted to a bizarre accident."

Something flickered in his eyes that she couldn't define. His smile came faint as he brought his free hand to cover hers.

"Thank you, Cecily. It means the world to me, to have your forgiveness."

"There's nothing to forgive."

They stood like that for a time, hands clasped in silence, a silence not intrusive but tender, before she withdrew and they said their good nights, each settling into their own bed.

Cecily stared long into the darkness, sleep refusing to come. She heard a scuff against the floorboards and peeked through the curtain. Garrett half-reclined before the low fire, clearly burdened with the same problem.

The affinity that was getting stronger the more she grew to know her husband urged her to go to him. . . .

But a whisper of doubt held her back.

Chapter 8

An unexpected cloudburst delayed the shooting lesson, and in the days that followed, a host of minor problems requiring attention interfered. More than a week passed before Garrett gave Cecily her first lesson.

At first, she handled the shotgun as if it were a snake ready to sink its fangs into her hand. He patiently described each part to her and how it worked, also explaining the dangers and how to prevent them, and she soon eased enough to hold the weapon without looking as if she might drop it at the slightest provocation.

Two weeks later she hit the tin can dead-on, knocking it from a distant pile of rocks where he'd set it. Garrett was proud of her accomplishment, surprised that she learned so quickly what at first had seemed would take months to perfect.

"I did it," she exclaimed in quiet shock then turned with a squeal where he stood close behind. "Garrett—I did it!"

"You did," he agreed, taking careful hold of the shotgun she wildly swung, and tossing the weapon to the ground. "I'll make a sharpshooter of you yet."

Her smile rivaled the sun that peeked from the treetops, her eyes bright green and shining with the delight of her triumph. Before Garrett could think, he acted, cradling her head and pressing his lips passionately to hers. She gasped, the warmth of her breath soft against his skin and playing havoc with his senses. He deepened the intimacy, feeling her melt against him, her hands clutching fistfuls of his shirt. Slowly, shyly, she returned his kiss.

With his heart pounding against his ribs, he pulled back to look into her eyes. They remained closed, like last time, not squeezed tightly with nervous dread, but her reaction served as a reminder that he'd made a vow to wait and that perhaps she wasn't ready. All the same, should he apologize for kissing his wife? For *wanting* to kiss her?

After a moment she opened her eyes, and he saw the uncertainty there.

"I should go," he found himself saying and could have kicked himself when she flinched as if he'd shouted the words. He collected his shotgun from the ground. "I'll be back by suppertime."

"Are you going into town?"

"Did you need me to get something?"

"No, I just wondered."

"I'm going to deliver Alice the new bed I crafted for Jeremy. He has outgrown sleeping with his sister, and as the little man of the family, he should have a bed to call his own."

"You made Alice Brown's son a bed?"

At her startled question he glanced her way.

"Yes, in appreciation for all her help with Paul these two years, since Linda passed."

Garrett moved to hitch the wagon, deciding not to tarry until tomorrow, as had been the plan—to deliver the bed on his way to the mill.

He left Cecily where she now stood in the doorway and felt her gaze until the wagon disappeared from sight. Distance might be hard to manage, but he thought it best to give them both some peace of mind.

Cecily tried not to let his gift of gratitude toward the widow affect what existed of her expectant mood at learning of his plans to enlarge the cabin.

She tried to behave like it didn't matter when Garrett returned that night, and with palms sweating, she made an awkward attempt to discuss what happened between them.

"About earlier, when you, um, kissed me—"

"I shouldn't have done it," he said before she could say more. "I apologize."

His reply surprised her and she spoke without thinking. "A man shouldn't have to apologize for kissing his wife."

Her face warmed with her words, and he looked away from the fire and in her direction. "No, but with us it's not quite the same, is it?"

His response came pensive, sounding somewhat miserable and making her wonder. When she could think of no adequate reply, he stood and gathered his blanket for a bed.

"I have to get an early start tomorrow," he said. "Good night."

And that had been the sum of their fireside chat.

Over the next few weeks, Cecily tried not to let it matter when he barely spoke to her and spent his time involved in other things. *Important* things, she reassured herself, the process of his latest project fascinated her.

He felled a tree a short distance from the cabin, chopping into logs the trunk he'd hewn, and notching the ends. Then, with the aid of two men who joined him from the mill, he erected a room entered from the wall with the hearth. A bedroom that Garrett stated he would inhabit. Once all gaps were filled with a mixture of moss and mud, making the walls weather-tight, he built a bedstead, much larger than the first one he crafted—the child's bed she mistakenly thought was for Paul.

Garrett did not ask her to join him in taking ownership of the new room, did not even ask if she wanted to, and that only increased her guilt at not being a proper wife and stirred her doubts that he still wanted her as one.

Nor did she try to let it matter each time she ran across the path of the stylish Widow Brown, whose dulcet comments with their double-edged sting served to make Cecily feel even more of a failure as a wife and stepmother. Mistress Glenare, indeed. . . She, too, had read the poem on the front page of the paper about the self-righteous, fault-finding woman, even discussing it with Garrett her first week with him, a love of poetry something both she and her husband shared.

After one harsh encounter with the widow at the mercantile that left Cecily's nerves frayed, she abruptly rounded on Garrett where he sat eating his meal.

"Those curtains—I don't like them. May I arrange for new?"

He held his bread in midair, stilled from taking a bite, and looked at her with confusion in his beautiful smoky-green eyes. "This is your home, Cecily. You may do whatever you like with it."

Tears formed at his benevolence in response to her foolishness. Always, he was so kind and patient, making her feel horrid for her petty words.

"Never mind, the curtains are fine. I don't know why I said that," she managed before she stepped outside, to pull herself together.

She had never begrudged Garrett keeping Linda's things. Never felt envy, having understood his first wife would always hold a tender place in his heart. The Widow Brown stirred the pot of these foreign jealousies and uncertainties, and for more reasons than innuendo of Cecily's failures as a wife and stepmother.

Alice Brown was all that stood between Cecily's complete surrender to Garrett. For as summer abruptly changed into autumn one morning, so Cecily came to understand her heart.

She loved Garrett and wished to be his wife in every sense of the word. Wished to bear his children and be a true family. She no longer wanted to be the permanent fixture of a guest in his cabin.

This awful new distance he had forged, since the day he delivered the bed, made Cecily question if he was unhappy with his choice of a bride. She did not think him unfaithful. He simply wasn't the type. There didn't appear to be an ignoble bone in his trim, muscled body. But in his thoughts did he wish Alice Brown occupied the space at the table where Cecily sat night after night? Did he wish that the widow sat beside him in the wagon when they drove into town and that Alice shared his new room and new bed?

"I struggle to keep my faith in this," she confided to the pastor's wife one afternoon after a short trip to the market. Garrett had taught her to drive the wagon, and she felt the need for advice from someone trustworthy to give it.

"It has always been difficult for me," she added.

"My dear. . ." Mrs. Dawson patted her hand. "Give it time. The two of you met and married in the most unusual of circumstances, but these things have a habit of working themselves out. I've seen the way he looks at you, and I do believe you have nothing to fear. Alice Brown. . ." She sighed. "Well, that woman could stand a mighty heap of prayer. It's true she and Linda were friends—they met in the wagon train that brought them. But I highly doubt Garrett wishes she was in your place. If Pastor Dawson were here. . ." She directed a concerned glance toward the door. "He would tell you that faith rarely comes easy but is precious to God and attainable by hearing His Word. Keep attending church meetings. I guarantee it will help."

Pastor Dawson soon entered, and his wife rushed to embrace him, taking his coat and hat and stating she'd been worried when he didn't come home from his nightly vigil. He affectionately patted her shoulder, saying she had no reason to fear, that he was needed at the bedside of a dying man and would always come home to her.

Cecily furtively watched them, wishing in her heart of hearts that could be her and

Garrett someday. How many times had he been absent from the cabin, long hours into the night, and she'd been filled with worry that he'd been hurt, robbed, or eaten by a bear?

That night after supper, Garrett excused himself and headed to bed.

"You're retiring so soon?" Cecily blurted, setting down the dirty plates she had gathered.

He looked at her in question.

"We haven't talked for some time. . . ." She sought for something to keep him there. "It's Paul. He's outgrown his cradle. When he lies on his back, his head and feet are almost flush against the wood." The boy was small, the cradle built generous in length, but the time had come to put it aside.

She felt her face warm with the hope that someday it would again be put to good use.

He sighed, and she heard his exhaustion. "We'll talk another time. I have to get an early start. I used all the lumber but will look into it soon. Good night, Cecily."

Once he left the room, she sank to the bench, wondering how many "early starts" she must contend with. Early starts never posed a problem before, during the many lovely nights they had engaged in their fireside chats, long weeks ago that seemed ages. Clearly, these early starts must be a devised excuse to quit her presence.

She missed his company, missed his entertaining anecdotes and sudden laughter. She missed him.

"Faith," she whispered pensively and looked up at the ceiling. "Father, I have so little, but what I have I commend to Thee."

Garrett perched on the edge of his new mattress of his new bed of his new room that he wished his wife would acknowledge as theirs and stared up at the ceiling.

"I don't know how much more patience I can extend, Lord. I love her. I want to hold her in my arms and show her how much I love her, but I made that blasted vow. . . . Forgive me." He cleared his throat and brought his gaze to the closed door where he heard Cecily move about, clearing their supper dishes.

He had not fibbed to her about his need of an early start each time he'd said it. These last weeks he had formed the habit of leaving for the mill office before Cecily awakened, when it was still dark, to get a jump on work there, so he could leave early and tend to matters at home. Namely, the building of this room and a small stable to house his horse and wagon, all necessary before winter barreled through with its dark, gloomy days and icy drizzle. There were other odd and sundry tasks still awaiting attention, but his "early start" had become the handiest excuse. If she had shown any sign of needing him. . .of *wanting* him, he would have stayed. Yet after that last kiss, he didn't trust himself in her sole company and definitely not when they sat together before a cozy fire.

He was no fool. He knew this couldn't continue. Should a fierce winter storm hit, they would be trapped inside the cabin. He couldn't very well hole himself up in this room—well, he could, but that seemed a tad asinine. Or perhaps he was the bigger dim-wit not to just flat-out tell her he loved her.

How would she react? Would she pale and stare in awkward horror? Flush and shut her eyes in nervous dread? Stutter an apology that she didn't feel the same?

With a weary sigh, Garrett reclined on his back, crossing his arms behind his head, and stared at the ceiling.

He dared not take the risk. They had come too far, despite the distance he recently forged. She now treated him as a dear friend, no longer a casual stranger. Somehow, that would have to be enough, for as long as it took, though hopefully not forever.

"I don't have the patience of Job, Lord," he muttered, "but I'm surely trying."

Chapter 9

Autumn waltzed in with a blaze of glory, the trees dressed with leaves of bronze and russet fire that danced in the wind amid the tall evergreens of pines. Cecily had seen more magnificent displays of foliage back East, it was true, but she loved their little cabin surrounded by these woods.

With the passage of weeks, her miserable outlook eased and she began to hope, though the days themselves grew gloomy. Garrett had conversed with her after supper the last few nights, his manner congenial and easygoing, and she cherished every minute of time shared. His eyes often remained on the fire, which he zealously tended as they spoke of many things—life, poetry, the children, the town, the people in it, but never about themselves. Every so often she would catch him staring, her heart giving a jolt to see on occasion what looked like longing in his gray-green eyes. But then he would look away, his behavior as relaxed as before. She never questioned, but it did make her wonder if she imagined his deeper interest.

Her interest had become almost tangible. She found that her gaze often strayed to and lingered on various aspects of his person, when he remained unaware of her fascinated attentiveness. His hands were lean, his arms toned, his fingers long and often stained with the ink from his trade, and she wished to feel their brush against her cheek and along her neck as he had so seldom done before. His build was trim and nicely muscled, fit, and upon looking at the strong line of his shoulders, she recalled the safety in his embrace, and the warmth of new feelings stirred. The recollection of his mouth against hers kept her awake many nights, and for a long time now, whenever he entered the room, her stomach would flutter, her heart quickening at his nearness.

Paul had slowly warmed to Cecily, no longer fussing to be held, though his preference for Gwen remained intact. It no longer bothered Cecily much, her chief emotion relief that the children got along well. The women she spoke with after Sunday meetings were kind, opening their circle wider to receive her, and Cecily almost felt like one of them now. The sole thorn in her side continued to be the Widow Brown, and this afternoon, the thorn burrowed deep. Her syrup-filled words had flowed like poison, spreading into areas highly vulnerable, all of them having to do with Garrett and the woman's conjectured notions that not all was right within their marriage.

"How could she have possibly known?" Cecily muttered to herself as she whisked the broom along the planks in a stir of dust, dispelling tracks of mud, long dried.

"Surely Garrett wouldn't have told her?" she fretted as she immersed the plates and swiped them one by one in a pan of dishwater.

"Am I so transparent that the vindictive woman can see through me like window glass?" she asked the ham hock she cleaved, the choice meat part of her reason for making the trip into town in the first place.

Behind her she heard the sound of someone choking and spun around in curious alarm.

"Paul?"

The boy sat on the floor near Garrett's room, gasping for air, his chubby hand at his throat.

"Paul!"

She threw the cleaver to the table and raced toward him. Dropping to her knees, she reached for the boy's shoulders and shook him. Paul's face went darker. Horrified with shock, she quickly pulled him up to stand as she also stood. She struck his back, a little harder than if she were burping a babe. The boy continued gasping for breath.

"What do I do?" she whispered in panic. "Dear God, what do I do!"

Gwen walked into the cabin. "What's wrong with Paul?"

"He can't breathe!"

"Hang him upside down."

"What?" Cecily snapped in confusion.

"Like the midwife did when Mattie's baby sister couldn't breathe! Hold him by the legs upside down."

The idea sounded ludicrous, but Cecily was in no position to argue.

She grabbed the boy beneath the arms and laid him on his stomach, picking him up by the ankles. Paul wriggled frantically, still gasping, heavier than before, and Cecily struggled with all her might to raise him from the ground and keep a good hold on him.

Sweet Lord Jesus—help us; it's not working!

Gwen suddenly struck the boy on the back, harder than Cecily had done, not once but repeatedly. Suddenly Paul coughed and Cecily felt something hit her skirts.

The boy's strident wails were music to her ears, proof of his clear breathing.

"Oh, sweetie," she cooed as Gwen helped her set the boy upright on his feet. "I'm so sorry."

Still crying, Paul allowed her to pet him and kiss his brow but turned into Gwen's arms for comfort.

"How did you know to do that?" Cecily asked her sister.

Gwen smiled a bit sheepishly. "Last year, Mattie and I peeked through the door and watched when Mrs. Mathison stopped screaming and it got quiet. That's what the midwife did, and the baby started squalling."

Shaken that they could have lost Paul, *that Garrett could have lost his son*, Cecily sank to the bench, her entire body trembling. Her attention dropped to the floor and the small round object Paul had coughed out. Bending over, she plucked it up. A button from Garrett's shirt. The same one she'd sewn on last week—she could tell by the slight chip at the edge.

In her earlier agitation, she had done a shoddy job of sweeping away debris, an even shoddier job of mending the shirt.

Paul had almost died because of her carelessness.

◆━━━━━◆

Garrett arrived home weary. It had been a miserable day, tempers on edge, and he just wanted a nice supper and a moment of quiet. It really wasn't much to ask.

Opening the door, he saw Gwen and Paul on the floor, playing with the blocks he had carved last Christmas. Paul smiled up at Garrett, holding out a block. Tracks of dried tears were apparent on the boy's face, his nose pink and runny.

"Where's your sister?" he asked Gwen.

The girl looked up, her eyes solemn. "She was upset and went for a walk. Paul choked on a button."

Garrett took in the information, concern for his son secondary when he could see the boy recovered and calm, while his wife remained missing in the darkening twilight.

He reached down to ruffle the boy's fair curls then retraced his steps to the door. "I'll find her. You stay here with Paul."

There weren't many places Cecily would wander. Not finding her at the outhouse, Garrett felt relief to spot her at the stream. Hearing the crunch of his footsteps, she turned. He could see that she'd been crying.

"Why did you marry me?"

Not the first time he'd heard the question, but this time he sensed more lay beneath her words than simple curiosity.

"You needed a home. I needed a mother for Paul."

"Ha! Some mother I turned out to be. I almost killed your son!"

Garrett covered the rest of the distance between them. "It was an accident, Cecily. Gwen told me what happened."

"I should have paid better attention," she insisted. In the remaining twilight the tears on her cheeks faintly glistened.

He took firm hold of her arms above the elbows, gently forcing her to look at him. "The boy is always getting into things, you know that. He's fine—"

"And you should have married the Widow Brown!"

Stunned that she would even think such a preposterous thing, let alone speak it, he could only stare. "Why on God's green earth would you say that?" he asked at last.

"She's perfect." Her eyes avoided his, looking to the stream. "She's a good mother, always smartly dressed, clearly she dotes on you and Paul, and I'll wager she can sew buttons that stay on clothes!"

Perfection wasn't a word he would associate with Alice Brown.

"If I had wanted the Widow Brown, I would have proposed long ago. Women like that don't interest me. She's too polished and difficult to please and rarely satisfied with what the Good Lord's given her."

Her eyes flitted back to his. "But I've failed at so much since coming here!"

"I don't see it like that. You're learning a new way of life. Things like that take time."

"I can never be like Linda."

Her words came small, a whisper he almost didn't hear, and they tugged at his heart.

Lifting one hand to her chin, he gently tipped her face upward to meet his eyes.

"I don't want you to be." Her eyes flared a little with shock, and he went on. "I loved Linda, but she's my past. You're my wife now, and you have many worthy qualities. You're kind and loyal and considerate—do you recall the first night I brought you here when you were frightened to death of me but drew near to insist I take the blanket? And how many more times have you put others before yourself? With Paul? With your sister, always taking such good care of her? She told me of the arrangement made with the captain to bring her along and how you shared your meals. That sweet, selfless generosity, that family loyalty I see in you every day, is part of what drew me to you from the start."

Her face had achieved a rosy hue of embarrassment, much like his must have looked that evening in the mercantile to hear his traits glorified. But he meant every word, and suddenly he knew she needed to hear him say it, needed his affirmation. He only wished he had spoken sooner.

"I can still be quite the hoyden," she argued softly. "That's what my aunt called me when I was Gwen's age."

He chuckled. "I like your fire and spirit. It keeps things interesting."

"Really?" She looked at him with suspicion.

"A perfect match to all that fire-red golden hair."

She quirked her lips, more a smile than a pout.

"You're beautiful, Cecily. Your eyes alone could stir a man to forget his name and sink forever into their depths."

At his solemn words, those lovely sea-green eyes grew wider.

He ached to kiss her, to feel her mouth, soft and warm, beneath his, to learn every enticing bit of her mystery—ached also to tell her that he loved her. But he'd made a promise—to her, to himself, to God—and he had no wish to upset her again, now that she had calmed. He had no desire to see her eyes flinch or fall shut with dread and uncertainty.

He never wanted to see that look again.

Instead, he cradled her face between his hands and pressed his lips to her brow, keeping them there a moment and settling for a weaker expression of his feelings.

"All of that is the crux of why I married you. The truth is I've come to care for you a great deal."

◆━━━━━◆

As Cecily cleared away the supper dishes, she watched Garrett, who sat with his back to the table. Paul sat on his lap as Garrett told both children a story of his own hair-raising adventures when he'd been new to the Pacific Northwest. Gwen sat at his feet, adoration for her new big brother apparent in her eyes. Ever since the night Garrett swept into their lives, Gwen had not shown one ounce of fear to be near him, accepting him more readily than Cecily ever did.

He thought her beautiful. He told her he cared for her. . . .

And he had no leaning toward Alice Brown, responding with something akin to horror that she would suggest it, proving the idea never even crossed his mind.

"You really saw a bear up that close?" Gwen's eyes were wide.

"Sure did. Carlson swatted it on the nose with a branch, and it took off running."

"Do you think I'll see one someday?"

At her excited tone, Garrett grew serious. "It's likely, but you don't want to try, Gwennie. If ever you should run across one's path, never approach it."

"Will it eat me?"

Garrett smiled. "We trust God that it won't, and your sister and I both know how to use a shotgun, but it's wise to be cautious."

"Can I learn to use a shotgun, too?"

"Maybe someday."

Once Garrett's story drew to a close, Cecily made her decision. "Time for bed, children. Another day will be here before you know it."

With only a mild murmur of complaint, Gwen scrambled up from the floor and gave Garrett a hug and kiss on the cheek. Paul did likewise. Gwen took the boy's hand and approached Cecily. She crouched down to hug both children then looked at Gwen.

"Let Paul sleep in the bed," she said for her sister's ears alone. "The cradle's gotten much too small for him. And don't forget your prayers."

Gwen nodded, and both children slipped behind the curtain.

Cecily resumed putting everything away and watched Garrett finish his mug of cider.

"Would you like to talk tonight?" he asked.

Her heart pounded so loud she could hear it. "No, not tonight."

She sensed his disappointment, but he smiled. "All right, then. I'm off to bed. Like you said, a new day will be here before you know it."

Not too soon, she hoped.

"Garrett?" she quietly called to him once he opened the door of his bedroom.

He turned to look at her, a question in his eyes.

Her palms had gone damp and she found it a struggle to breathe. She moistened her lips and slowly approached. There was much she wished to say, but more than anything, there was something she wanted—*needed* to do.

Coming to stand before him, she lifted herself on her toes and pressed her hands to his face and her lips to his.

He remained as still as a post, but she felt his shock in the jump of muscles in his chest. At her shy attempt to part his lips and deepen the kiss, he softly groaned. His strong arms came swiftly around her, his mouth teaching her what she was so eager to learn. He tasted of cider and warmth and home, and she kept her eyes closed to savor the moment.

"I love you," she whispered once he pulled away so they could again breathe. "I do."

Her mind whirled with the passion of their kiss, her body warm against the heat of his, and she was thankful for his arms to support her, for surely she would have melted to the ground without them.

"My sweet Cecily. . ." His voice came low, a slight waver to the words, and she felt the tender touch of his lips against each closed eyelid. "I have loved you almost since the moment I met you, maybe even then."

She opened her eyes. "Truly?"

"As God is my witness. Another reason I wanted you for my wife."

She returned his smile, pressing her mouth again to his, finding it impossible to curtail the need now that she'd surrendered, a need that only seemed to grow.

"I want to be your wife, Garrett," she whispered nervously. "Your *true* wife."

His hands slipped around her back and legs, and he swept her up into his arms. She rested her palm against the warm column of his neck.

"You always have been, Cecily. You just needed to come to that understanding."

"That you love me?"

"Always and forever. I thought of you as precious cargo when I held you in my arms that first night the boat brought you here. My opinion hasn't wavered, only that you are now *mine*."

"Take me to bed, husband."

Sweet words melted into more heart-stirring kisses as he carried her into their bedroom and shut the door.

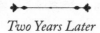

Two Years Later

"I see it!" Gwen cried with excitement.

"Where? *Where?*" Four-year-old Paul craned his neck to look out over the expanse of silver water.

Gwen picked the skinny boy up, her arms crossed against his middle with his back to her chest. "See that dark shadow in the distance?"

The boy squealed. "I do! I do!"

Garrett chuckled at the children's exuberance, and Cecily turned her head toward him with a shared smile.

Holding Baby Annette, her adorable daughter of ten months named after her mother, Cecily stood with her family near the dock, Garrett's arm protectively around her. Hordes of people had gathered on this fine, clear day, and the air felt alive with celebration. Quite the opposite of Cecily's nocturnal entrance into town, but even if such things were possible, she wouldn't go back and change her circumstances for the world.

Had matters gone differently she might never have found Garrett, and that would have been to suffer a most miserable fate indeed.

Paul still preferred his aunt Gwen, but he'd grown to accept Cecily, and her heart turned over with thankfulness the day he called her Mama. No longer the baby of the family, it took him awhile to accept his little sister, but each night he bent over the cradle to give her a good-night kiss atop the wisps of red curls on her head.

Gwen had yet to see her bear, but Cecily felt secure in the knowledge that if ever the day should arrive, and in these rugged wild hills they well might, both she and Garrett could protect their family—which would be growing by one come winter. Something she had yet to tell her husband, and she smiled with her secret.

Life in their small neck of the woods had been rich with harmony and abundant with blessing that made even the worst of storms that blew their way bearable. The Widow Brown still singled her out to find fault and offer suspect advice, but her jibes no longer troubled Cecily, because she'd found security in her husband's love. She truly wished the "Mistress Glenare" well and that she might find her own happiness someday.

The SS *Continental* drew closer. The moment had arrived.

Cecily handed Annette to her husband, who regarded his wife with an approving eye.

"You are still the most beautiful of all the belles," he whispered.

They shared a brief kiss before Cecily moved to join the others of the welcoming committee. Mrs. Dewhurst smiled at her, and they exchanged pleasantries. Having taken a more active role in the community, Cecily had been voted by the women of her church to partake in the honors, herself having been in just such a position once, what felt like another lifetime ago.

She brushed her hands against the skirt of her best dress, smoothing wrinkles from where she earlier bounced Annette on her knee, then stepped toward the cluster of travel-weary women who'd just stepped off the ship of Asa Mercer's second expedition. Each of Mercer's Belles, the moniker they'd been given, regarded the rugged territory with mixed looks of anticipation and fear. Cecily chose the most nervous looking of ladies to greet first.

"Welcome to Seattle," she said brightly with a reassuring smile, extending her hand to clasp the newcomer's. "We are so pleased to have you join us and make this your new home. . . ."

Pamela Griffin lives in Texas with her family. Her main goal in writing is to help and encourage those who know the Lord, and plant a seed of hope in those who don't, through entertaining stories. She has over fifty titles published to date, in both novels and novellas, and loves to hear from her readers. You can contact her at words_of_honey@juno.com.

The Prickly Pear Bride

by Pam Hillman

Chapter 1

C ole Rawlins rode alongside Prickly Pear Creek, his sheepskin coat tied to the back of his saddle.

The late spring runoff had the creek escaping its banks. The sun was shining, pink and purple flowers were starting to bloom, and the entire mountain range was dotted with lush green meadows.

Grinning, he took a deep breath of the fresh mountain air. Prickly Pear Creek was everything his uncle had described in his letters. A cowman's paradise. His cattle would grow fat and lazy in these mountains.

A splash followed by a yell pierced the air, and Cole jerked back on the reins. Another splash and a round of barking had Cole spurring his mount forward. He broke through the sparse trees to see a man in baggy breeches and a slouch hat struggling to wrestle a sheep across the rising stream. A small black-and-white collie nipped at the sheep's hooves.

Cole shook out his lariat and tossed it to the hapless sheepherder. "Grab hold."

Instead of saving himself, the man tied the rope around the sheep's neck. "Pull."

Shaking his head, Cole did as he was told, hauling the sheep out of the water, the shepherd pushing. The shaggy animal came unwillingly, much like an ornery calf, but it did come. The sheep stood on the bank and Cole shook his lariat loose, but before he could toss it to the shepherd, the man turned back, crossing back to the other side of the stream.

Cole coiled his rope, frowning. What now? He looked beyond the man and spotted half a dozen sheep stranded on a tiny outcropping lush with grass. Steep banks rose behind the sheep. Another collie crouched in front of them, keeping them from climbing the banks.

Cole's gaze swept the quickly moving current. If the water kept rising, the sheep would be cut off from safety, and the shepherd and his dogs with them. And if there was a flash flood—

The shepherd grabbed another sheep and wrestled it to the edge of the rushing stream. Cole swung his rope, tossed it over the stream, and the shepherd tied it to the sheep. Fighting them every step of the way, it took awhile to get the ornery critter into the water, but once there, Cole pulled her right on across. Working together, the shepherd and his dogs rounded up the remaining sheep, and they repeated the process.

Finally, only one was left, a big ram that had evaded their efforts. Cole coiled his rope, ready to toss it over, but the ram was having none of it. Even in the few minutes that they'd been there, the dry land on the opposite bank had shrunk to half the size.

Cole frowned. It was time to get that shepherd and his ornery critter back across to safety before a flash flood swept both of them away. He spurred his horse across, the water sweeping inches below her belly.

His mare clambered up the opposite bank, and Cole swung a wide loop, the rope settling over the ram's head. He rode his horse close to the shepherd and held out a hand. "Let's go. The water's rising."

"Go on." Head down, the shepherd waved him away then headed toward the stream, splashing into the fast-moving current. The dogs followed, swimming quickly across.

Cole shook his head. The old coot was a prickly sort.

But he was likely to get them all killed.

Cole urged his mare into the water, dragging the ram along behind his horse, the mare fighting her way across the fast-rushing stream, the shepherd stumbling along beside them.

But his cow pony had the stamina of a mountain goat and didn't give up easily. Neither did Cole. He gritted his teeth and spurred his horse, determined to see the stubborn shepherd and his sheep to safety and be on his way.

As they reached the middle of the stream, the current grabbed the shepherd, and he lost his footing. Cole grabbed the man by the collar and pulled him up.

He flailed against Cole's hold, clawing at the saddle. His slouch hat sailed off his head, landed with a splash and whirled away downstream. Cole pulled the gasping man up and out of the water, marveling at the slight form.

Wide green eyes stared up at him out of a heart-shaped face with a smattering of freckles across a pert little nose, and a long braid of honey-blond hair trailed into the rushing stream.

Cole almost lost his grip on the shepherd's collar.

Wasn't a man under that getup.

No way. No how.

"You're a woman."

+•————•+

"Yep."

Safe on land, but freezing from being dunked in the ice-cold runoff from the mountains, Evelyn Arnold nodded at the cowboy. Then she whistled for Skittles and Blue Boy.

Dark brows dipped over brilliant blue eyes. "Why didn't you say something?"

"Look, mister, I appreciate your help and all, but right now I need to get these sheep back to the others then get out of these wet clothes."

"Yes, ma'am." With jerky movements, he coiled his rope and reined away. "Let's get at it."

Thankful for the help, Evelyn herded the sheep away from the creek. Teeth chattering, she called out commands to her dogs. Out of the corner of her eye, she watched the cowboy and his well-trained horse herd the sheep forward.

Even she could see the benefit of knowing how to use a lariat and having a horse to cover some ground. One glance back at the creek, and she shivered, partly from the cold seeping through her clothes down to her bones, and partly from the realization of how close she'd been to meeting her Maker.

The creek bed had been dry as a bone this morning, and the sheep had wandered across looking for the fresh, tender grass growing in the rich, fertile soil. But the runoff from the mountains had filled the stream quickly. If it hadn't been for the stranger riding through, she and her grandfather's sheep might well have perished on that exposed patch of green.

By the time they reached the line shack, Evelyn's teeth were chattering, and she couldn't control the shivers. She cast a longing glance at the small tendril of smoke curling out of the pipe from the stove but then steeled her resolve. The sheep needed to be safely returned to the others before she could get out of these wet things.

Skittles, Blue Boy, and the cowboy herded the strays back to the flock, and they went along peacefully enough. Relieved, Evelyn turned to her rescuer, feeling like a drowned rat in her grandfather's overalls and sheepskin coat. Teeth chattering, she muttered, "Thank you. Much obliged."

He eyed her, frown still firmly in place. His gaze cut toward the cabin. "You'd best be getting inside before you catch your death from a chill."

Evelyn nodded then moved that way, barely able to put one foot in front of the other. Now that the sheep were safe, she knew she had to get. . .to get warm. She had to. . .

The porch seemed so far away. She barely registered when the cowboy reached out an arm and circled her waist, half carrying her the rest of the way to the porch. She swatted at his arm. "No. You can't—"

He held her upright, his blue eyes glittering. "Ma'am, I mean you no harm. Just let me see you inside. Then I'll build up the fire and leave you be."

Embarrassed at her weakness, but knowing she needed the help, she searched his gaze then nodded. "Skittles, Blue Boy, come."

Evelyn allowed the cowboy to lead her into the cabin, then moved toward the stove, hovering close to its warmth. The dogs plopped down close by, watching her every move. "I didn't catch your name."

"Cole Rawlins." He strode to the stove, opened it, stirred up the embers and tossed two more pieces of wood inside. "And yours?"

"Evelyn Arnold." She took off the heavy sheepskin coat and grabbed one of her grandmother's quilts off one of the cots. Wrapping it around her shoulders, she moved toward the stove, hovering close to its warmth.

"Pleasure to meet you, Mrs. Arnold."

"Miss." Evelyn winced. There'd been no need to tell the man that she wasn't married. No need at all.

"Sorry, ma'am." He glanced around the one-room shack, the evidence of Grandpa's shaving supplies on the shelf, his trousers hung on a peg, and an old pair of boots next to the door. "I just assumed that your husband would be back soon."

"Grandpa—" Evelyn hesitated. No need to tell him that Grandpa wouldn't be coming back to the line shack, at least not until his broken leg healed. "I live with my grandparents."

"I see." He stood, his frame dwarfing hers in the small space. "Will you be all right until he returns?"

Evelyn looked away. "I'll be fine."

"All right. I'll be getting on, then." He rubbed a hand along his neck then placed his hat on his head. "Good evening, Miss Arnold."

Chapter 2

When Sunday morning services dismissed, Evelyn stood rooted to the spot, not moving, not twitching, not even breathing as everyone crowded around Ollie Rodgers, his wife Angie, and their baby.

Out of the corner of her eye, she saw Mrs. Michum exchange a sly smile with Mrs. Vincent. Mrs. Michum moved to Evelyn's side before she could slip away. "Evelyn, dear, come see the baby."

"Yes, ma'am." Evelyn forced her legs to move, to join the crowd, to smile, to act like she was happy for Ollie and Angie.

And she was. Happy for them, that is.

But it was the look in Mrs. Michum's eyes that made her want to run and hide. Mrs. Michum patted Evelyn's arm as if she needed reassurance. And she guessed she did.

It wasn't often that a jilted groom got to show off his new baby to his former sweetheart.

Ollie wouldn't look at her, but his sweet little wife smiled shyly at Evelyn and held the baby out for Evelyn to see. Evelyn kept the smile on her face, hoping it didn't look as rigid as it felt. "She's beautiful."

Angie beamed. "Thank you."

"You're welcome." Duty done, Evelyn dipped her head, smile still firmly in place, and turned blindly toward the open door of the church.

If she could just escape. Escape the stares, the whispers, the looks of pity from her neighbors. But there was no escape. Not unless she left Burnt Sage, Montana, for good. She stifled a hysterical laugh as she stepped outside. While the higher elevations along Little Prickly Pear Creek afforded a nice cool breeze, the heat was already being felt in Burnt Sage. By late summer, the sun would wither everything in sight, just like the name of the town implied.

Burnt sage, burnt crops, burnt dreams.

And burnt reputations.

Burnt the day she'd walked out of this very church, leaving Ollie Rodgers at the altar.

She searched the crowd for her grandmother, spotted her talking to Mrs. Vincent, and groaned. Mrs. Vincent wasn't quite as catty as Mrs. Michum, but she ran a close second. "Granny, it's time to go. I need to get back to the line shack before dark."

"Line shack?" Mrs. Vincent's eyebrows lifted. "The sheepherder's cabin up on Beaver Ridge. Dear girl, what on earth are you doing up there?"

"I'm taking care of the sheep. There's no one else, ma'am. Not with my grandfather laid up."

"What about the sheepherders? Surely one of them can help until he's well."

"Yes, ma'am. Someone should be arriving any day to take over. As it is, Billy Wilson, the tender, is with them today. But I need to get back so he can deliver the rest of the supplies to the other sheepherders in the mountains."

"Well, I never. A girl has no business tending sheep all alone up in those mountains."

"She's safer with those sheep and her dogs than she is in most places around here. I've tended sheep many a day."

"Minnie, it was different back in our day." Mrs. Vincent shook her head, her gaze landing on Ollie and Angie as they exited the church. "A pretty young girl like Evelyn needs to be courting, getting ready to have a family, not holed up in some sheep camp all year."

"Clara, she's not going to be there all year. Just for a few days until another sheep-herder arrives."

"Well, I hope you're right." Mrs. Vincent patted Evelyn on the shoulder. "Evelyn is the only single girl in these parts other than Rosemarie Nelson—and as much as she'd like to think differently, that girl is much too young to think about courting. Surely there'll be some eligible young men at the Fourth of July picnic. Why, I heard that Hiram Danvers is looking for a wife."

"Good day, Clara."

Evelyn's grandmother sailed across the churchyard toward their wagon, Evelyn trailing behind, trying not to laugh. As her grandmother picked up the reins, she muttered, "Hiram Danvers has never hit a lick at anything in his life. Poor Susette—God rest her soul—worked herself to the bone to keep them in house and home and birthed all those children at the same time. Eligible? Ha! I don't know what Clara thinks is eligible, but I wouldn't put Hiram Danvers in that category, not in a million years."

As they left the churchyard, Evelyn spotted Cole Rawlins standing next to his horse. Their eyes met, and a slight smile tipped up one side of his mouth. He touched the tips of his fingers to his hat as they passed and Evelyn gave a short nod of greeting in return.

Face flaming, she sat on the hard bench seat, waiting for her grandmother to grill her on the newcomer. But thankfully, her grandmother was so wrapped up in what Mrs. Vincent had said that she hadn't even noticed the handsome cowboy.

◆━━━━◆

Cole stood off to the side under a canopy of trees, watching as Miss Arnold left the church with an elderly woman. It was her all right, down to the last freckle across her cute little nose.

But the ragtag shepherdess had been transformed. Instead of baggy britches and an oversized sheepskin coat, she wore a pink, flower-sprigged dress that hugged her waist and swished about her ankles as she helped the older woman into a wagon at the edge of the churchyard.

As they drove off, two matronly women strolled past, barely acknowledging him before continuing their conversation.

"Did you see the look on her face?"

"Yes. Can you believe she still carries a torch for Ollie, after what she did?"

"Oh, she's much too prickly for dear, sweet Ollie."

"She hasn't always been that way. It was only after—" The woman saw him watching, clammed up right quick, then dipped her head in greeting.

"Ladies." Cole tipped his hat then stood aside, letting them pass.

Turning back toward the church, he spotted Uncle David and Aunt Lily on the porch steps, bidding the last of their flock good-bye. Beside them was his cousin Angie with—with a *baby* in her arms?

Uncle David spotted him just as Aunt Lily reached for the child, cooing. His uncle bounded down the steps, hand outstretched. "Cole? My dear boy, is that you?"

Cole strode forward, letting his uncle grab his hand then pull him into a tight hug. "It's me, Uncle David. Good sermon this morning."

"You were there?" His uncle's brow furrowed. "I didn't see you."

"I slipped in the back after church started."

Intentionally. Uncle David would have called him up to the front of the church, introduced him to the entire assembly, and insisted he sit with Aunt Lily and the rest of the family.

Cole preferred to meet the residents of Burnt Sage on his own terms, not as a specimen on display. He didn't relish the thought of being on exhibit before the entire town.

The rest of the family gathered around, and he gestured at the bright eyes staring at him from Aunt Lily's arms.

"Who's this?"

"That's Rebecca." Angie hugged him then turned to the tall, slender man standing next to her. "And this is my husband, Ollie Rodgers. Ollie, this is my cousin Cole."

"Pleased to meet you." Cole shook hands with Angie's husband, assessing the softness of his hands, his pale complexion.

Angie smiled up at her husband. "Ollie and his mother own the mercantile down the street."

"If you need anything, Mr. Weaver, just stop by the store."

The Weaver family burst out laughing, and Cole grinned. Angie's husband flushed, his gaze bouncing from one to the other. "What? What did I say?"

Aunt Lily placed a hand on Cole's arm. "Cole is a Rawlins. He's my sister's son."

Ollie twisted his hat in his hands, a flush splotching his face. "Pardon me, Mr. Rawlins. I just assumed—"

"No harm done. And call me Cole." He nodded and winked at Angie. "Since you're married to my cousin, I reckon we're practically kin."

Uncle David clapped his hands together. "Well, we could stand here jabbering all day, but I think I smelled fried chicken this morning, and the boys are already gone. We'd better get on over to the house before that chicken grows legs and walks off. Please join us, Cole."

"I don't want to impose—"

"I won't take no for an answer." Aunt Lily gave him a look that reminded him of his mother.

"Yes, ma'am."

"Come on, Angie, you can help me get the food on the table. Here, David, hold your granddaughter." Aunt Lily handed the baby to Uncle David and headed down the street toward a small, whitewashed house.

Uncle David wrapped the blanket around the baby and tucked her under his arm, following his wife down the street. "What brings you to Burnt Sage, Cole?"

Cole walked along beside him. "Land. I'm going to start a ranch, Uncle David."

"A ranch?"

"Yes, Ma shared your letters about the grazing land along Prickly Pear Creek, and I wanted to see for myself."

His uncle's eyebrows drew down into a frown. "Where are you going to get that kind of money?"

"My employer, Malcolm Mangrum, is going to partner with me. But in a few years, I hope to buy him out completely."

"I've heard of Mangrum. He owns the Double M, doesn't he?"

"Yes, sir. He's one of the biggest ranchers in these parts."

"Do you trust him to do right by you when the time comes?"

"I think so. He's a good man, and he's helped others get started."

Uncle David clapped him on the back. "Sounds like a good plan. It'll be good to have you here."

◆━━━━◆

Granny clucked to the mules, urging them to go faster. They increased their pace for the space of a heartbeat then settled right back to the same slow plod as before. "I don't know why Clara and Dottie can't leave well enough alone. That business with Ollie was two years ago. It's over and done with. But you don't help matters any."

Evelyn jerked her gaze toward her grandmother. "Me? What have I done?"

"Every time you see Ollie and his wife, you go rigid as a poker." Granny gave an unladylike snort. "If you wanted Ollie, why didn't you marry him when you had the chance?"

"I don't want Ollie, Granny. I'm the one who called off our wedding, remember."

"Without so much as a by-your-leave to anybody." Her grandmother eyed her askance as if she couldn't believe even Evelyn had that much gall. "I'll never understand you, Evelyn Arnold. Why did you agree to marry him in the first place?"

Evelyn shrugged and sighed. She couldn't tell Granny the truth. It was better that everyone thought badly of her than of Ollie and Angie. But from the moment Angie had come to town with her sweet, gentle ways, Evelyn had known Ollie was smitten.

"I realized that just because we'd known each other all our lives, it was no reason to get married."

"Well, you could've realized that a lot sooner than on your wedding day, if you ask me."

Evelyn had realized it a lot sooner. She'd begged Ollie to call off their wedding, but he wouldn't. He'd said it wouldn't be honorable. But when she'd walked down that aisle and seen the tired look in her childhood friend's eyes and the barely contained misery on Angie's face as she played the organ, she'd known she couldn't go through with it. Ollie and Angie were meant for each other, and she wouldn't keep them apart in spite of Ollie's determination to honor his commitment to her. Why couldn't Mrs. Michum and her grandmother just let the past be buried? Ollie and Angie were happy, and that's all that mattered.

Evelyn watched the creek roll by. The road curved along the creek bed, the grass shades of pale and bright green. Everything was fresh and new and springlike. But she felt old and withered and prickly, just like the prickly pear that grew in patches alongside the roadbed. She shrugged. "It just wasn't meant to be. I don't begrudge Ollie and Angie their happiness."

"Well, it don't matter none that ya don't, child. The fact that everyone else thinks you do is what matters. Ollie's moved on, got him a wife and a cute little young'un, and you're still moping around like a cat with a sawed-off tail."

"I am not moping around."

"You could've fooled me."

"It's just that Mrs. Michum delights in poking barbs at me."

"She's always been like that. Always will be." Granny flicked the reins. "We're going to have to do something about it, that's for sure."

"Like what? Leave Burnt Sage?"

"Of course not." Her grandmother glared at her as if she'd lost her mind. "We'll just have to get you married off, that's all."

Evelyn jostled her grandmother's shoulder. "There's always Hiram Danvers."

"Over my dead body." Granny scowled. "Nope. We'll find somebody else."

Evelyn choked back a laugh. "Granny, really, you do get the strangest notions. It takes two to marry, and I haven't seen any single men around lately."

Which wasn't entirely true. Cole Rawlins was probably single. But he was a cowboy, and cowboys and sheepherders didn't mix.

Chapter 3

The bell over the door of the mercantile jingled when Cole pulled the door open and stepped over the threshold Tuesday morning.

Angie greeted him with a smile. "Cole, how are you?"

"I'm fine." He handed her a list. "Could you fill this for me?"

"Of course." Angie glanced over the scrap of paper and then started gathering the items. "Are you going into the mountains?"

"Yes. I wanted to scout out the grazing land on the other side of Antelope Pass."

"Oh, would you mind dropping off a package for a friend of mine?" Angie measured out a pound of coffee.

"Sure."

"Wonderful." She hand him a small parcel wrapped in plain brown wrapping paper and tied neatly with twine. "Evelyn's been waiting for this to come in."

"Evelyn? Evelyn Arnold?"

"Yes, have you met?"

"Yes, we've met."

Angie smiled. "That's good. Ollie can tell you how to get to the line shack. He's much better at giving directions than I am, and besides, he's lived here all his life. I'm not sure I could find Mr. Arnold's line shack if I had to."

Ollie stepped inside, carrying a crate. "Why do you need to find the line shack?"

"Cole's going to drop off some supplies for Evelyn. Isn't that nice?"

"Very nice."

"Tell him how to get to the cabin."

"I know where it is."

Ollie and Angie both stared at him. "You do?"

Cole laughed. "I fished her and her grandfather's sheep out of Prickly Pear Creek the other day."

"My goodness." Angie looked surprised. "I wonder why she didn't mention it to anyone?"

Ollie slid two cans of beans across the counter. "If she had, it would have been all over town by now."

Angie nodded. "That's true enough. You know how Mrs. Michum and Mrs. Vincent like to talk."

Ollie's gaze cut to Cole then back at his wife. "They mean well."

"Humph." Angie reached for the beans and tucked them into a tote sack. "Maybe they do, but I worry about Evelyn up there at that line shack all alone."

Cole's head snapped up. "Alone? I thought she lived with her grandfather."

"She does. And with her grandmother. But not at the line shack. They live in a little frame house a couple miles out of town."

"I don't understand." Cole frowned at them. "Then why is she up there all alone?"

"Her grandfather broke his leg, and somebody has to mind the sheep until the sheepherder he sent for gets here." Angie pulled the strings tight on the tote, patting the bulging pack. "Here you go. All packed up and ready to go."

Frowning, Cole hefted the pack and headed toward the door. Miss Arnold had said she lived with her grandfather. But she hadn't said at the cabin. At least someone was on the way to take over the job so Evelyn could return home.

He didn't like the thought of her staying up on that ridge all alone.

Evelyn whistled, and the sheepdogs herded the sheep away from the streambed. They wouldn't step into the fast-moving current, but after getting stranded the other day, she wasn't taking any chances.

With the sheep grazing contentedly, she plopped down on a rocky outcropping and pulled out an egg sandwich on thick slices of her grandmother's homemade bread. As she ate, she eyed the sparse grass in the meadow.

If the shepherd Grandpa had hired didn't come soon, she'd have to take the sheep to higher pastures. Grandpa had made her promise not to leave the cabin, but it looked like she might not have a choice in the matter.

Skittles stood, gave a short bark, and faced the path that led down the mountain. Evelyn reached for the rifle she kept nearby, but relaxed when Skittles's tail began to wag. Whoever or whatever it was, the dog was happy to see them, so there was nothing to be afraid of. Maybe the sheepherder had arrived after all. She shaded her eyes against the afternoon glare.

Her heart gave a happy little skip when Cole Rawlins rode free from the tree line, his horse picking her way along the rocky edge of the stream.

Nervously, she tucked her flyaway hair up under her hat, trying to remember if she'd brushed it this morning. She didn't think much about trying to look presentable here in the mountains, as the only living things that saw her most days were the sheep and her dogs, and the occasional mountain lion or coyote.

And the camp tender who came around on Saturdays. But old Billy had known her since she was knee-high to a gnat and didn't care much what she looked like.

She jerked her hand away from her hair. She shouldn't be so happy to see Cole. Cowboys and sheepherders didn't mix. She'd heard the tales of violence between the two, of cattlemen running sheepherders out of the country, of border wars and bloodshed. But surely no one would be interested in her grandfather's flock, small in comparison to the big outfits that ran thousands upon thousands of sheep.

Her gaze narrowed and she cradled the gun. It wouldn't hurt to be on her guard all the same.

Cole rode up to her, tipped his hat, and rested his forearms on his saddle. "Afternoon, ma'am."

"Mr. Rawlins." She fidgeted. "What are you doing up this way again?"

He shifted in his saddle. "I'm looking for Antelope Pass. Do you know where it is?"

"Antelope Pass? Why are you looking for that?" Evelyn blushed. "I'm sorry. That's none of my business."

"Mr. Pinson, the assayer in Helena, says there's a wide-open tract of land on the other side." He shifted in the saddle, his gaze taking in the scruffy tufts of grass left in the wake of the sheep's heavy grazing. "I hope there's more grass on that side of the pass than here. This doesn't look like much."

"That's just because the sheep have grazed it down. It's time to move them."

"I'd say it's past time." He cocked a brow at her.

She tugged her hat low, hoping to hide the blush that stole over her cheeks. "I'll be moving them soon."

"I see. Will you need help?" His intense blue gaze bored into hers, a hint of accusation in the look. "Angie said you were up here all alone. Your grandpa is down with a broken leg."

Evelyn lifted her chin. "I never said Grandpa lived here."

"But you didn't say he didn't."

Evelyn cradled the gun. She wasn't afraid of Cole Rawlins. He meant her no harm, but still, she didn't really know him. She licked her lips. "Mr. Rawlins—"

"No need to apologize, ma'am. I was a stranger, and you were right to be wary." He pushed his hat back. "Well, I reckon I'd better be on my way."

Apologize? That was the last thing on her mind. "You thinking of running cattle on the other side of the pass?"

"Maybe. Have you been through the pass? Seen the land on the other side?"

"A few times."

"What did you think? About the land? Is it good for grazing?"

"It's fine land." Evelyn stepped back. "Don't let me keep you."

"You don't seem to like me, Miss Arnold." He eyed her. "I guess it's my turn to apologize. If I've offended you in some way, I'm sorry."

"It's not that." Evelyn shook her head. "It's just that sheep and cattle don't seem to mix."

"I don't see any reason why they can't. And besides, there's not much likelihood of them mixing if the cattle are on the other side of Antelope Pass, now is there?"

"I suppose not." She shrugged. "We'll likely not even see each other again."

A tiny smile kicked up one corner of his mouth. "I suppose not."

"Good day, Mr. Rawlins."

"Oh, I almost forgot." He reached for a bundle tied on his saddle horn. "Angie asked me to give you this."

He held out the package, and Evelyn stepped closer, her fingers brushing against the warmth of his in the transfer. "Angie? You've gotten mighty familiar with Mrs. Rodgers to have known her for such a short time."

He chuckled. "Oh, Angie and I go way back."

"You do?"

"Yes, ma'am. She's my cousin." He grinned, his blue eyes twinkling. "You have nothing to fear from this saddle tramp, ma'am."

"I'm glad to hear it." She lifted her chin and gave him a tight smile. "Good day, Mr. Rawlins. You'll have a lot of riding to do if you make it through the pass before nightfall."

He tipped his hat. "Good day, Miss Arnold."

Evelyn clutched the package to her, watching Cole Rawlins ride off, leaving her alone with her dogs, her sheep, and a coveted copy of *Little Women*.

Chapter 4

The grass was gone, and the sheep bleated, walking around in a bit of a daze looking for grass where there was none.

Cole Rawlins had been gone four days and the sheepherder hadn't shown up, either. Evelyn couldn't leave the sheep to go get help, and she couldn't wait for someone to come.

Before dawn on the fifth day, she'd finished packing the sheepherder's wagon. Small by most standards, it was big enough for her and the dogs. The going would be slow as she'd have to drive the wagon and herd the sheep at the same time, but she'd do the best she could.

Her grandfather would not be happy, but what else could she do?

The sun was barely peeking over the horizon when she closed the cabin, making sure it was locked up tight against any varmints snooping around.

She whistled for Blue Boy and Skittles and jerked her chin toward the sheep. "Walk on."

The dogs didn't need any other urging. Clicking to the mules, she followed along behind as the dogs herded the sheep away from the cabin into the mountains. It didn't take long to realize the error of trying to handle the mules, call commands to the dogs, and keep the sheep in a tight-knit group. Neither the dogs nor the sheep were used to taking commands from someone on the seat of the wagon. In fits and starts, they made their way along the trail.

The going was slow as the sheep nibbled grass along the way, and Evelyn let them. They might as well get their fill as they meandered along. When the sun was directly overhead, she ate from the wagon seat, keeping her eye out for stragglers, but as the day wore on, she began to worry. She needed to find a safe place to bed the sheep down for the night.

As she followed along behind the meandering flock, the lead ram with his bell tinkling, she realized the sheep weren't just randomly going along. They seemed to be heading for a particular place, with Skittles and Blue Boy bringing up the rear, nipping stragglers along and corralling strays. By midafternoon, the sheep rounded an outcropping of rock and spilled into a grass-filled meadow, scattering to continue feeding.

The dogs sat back on their haunches, looking pleased with themselves, and she pulled the mules to a stop near the stream under a grove of aspens. She chuckled when she spotted a ring of rocks and the remains of an old fire. The dogs and the sheep had led her straight to a common way station on the trail to summer pastures high in the mountains.

She jumped down from the wagon and scratched Skittles behind the ear. "Good girl."

Blue Boy sat on his hunches, tongue lolling, a satisfied grin on his face. She patted him then gave him a good scratch when he tilted his head, exposing his left ear. "You, too, Blue Boy."

Evelyn made camp then skirted the perimeter of the meadow, familiarizing herself with every nook and cranny. The dogs trotted along behind her as if it was their duty to show her around.

As she circled back toward the wagon, Evelyn's worry clung to her. There was enough grass here for two, maybe three days, and then they'd have to move again. She had no idea where the next meadow was or how long it would take to get there.

And she couldn't leave the sheep to scout ahead.

Later, after the sheep had bedded down all around the wagon, she bowed her head over an unappetizing bowl of lukewarm beans and hard biscuits and prayed for help to come.

❧———•———❧

Perplexed, Cole shifted his weight in the saddle.

Evelyn was gone, and so were the sheep, the cabin locked up tight as a drum.

Had the sheepherder come to relieve her, moved the sheep to new grazing, and she'd gone back to her grandparents' home? He sure hoped so. He turned away from the empty cabin and headed down the mountain.

He'd be in Burnt Sage before nightfall, and he couldn't wait to tell Uncle David of his findings. There was plenty of grazing on the other side of the pass, as far as the eye could see. And he'd located an abandoned cabin with a sturdy barn that wouldn't require much work to be habitable. He'd send a letter to Mr. Mangrum first thing tomorrow. The sooner they got a herd in here and started grazing, the better off they'd be.

He was barely out of sight of the cabin when he heard the singing. If you could call it that. Caterwauling was more like it. And it was headed straight toward him.

The sight that greeted him around the next bend brought him up short. A grizzled old mountain man rode toward him, a string of heavily loaded pack mules trailing behind him.

The off-key singing broke off as the man spotted Cole. "Howdy, stranger."

"Howdy."

The old man cradled a scattergun that looked like it would blow a hole clean through the middle of the mountain at Cole's back. "Name's Billy Wilson. I'm camp tender for these here sheepherders out here."

"Mr. Wilson."

"Just Billy." The muzzle of the gun shifted just a bit toward Cole, making him uneasy. He rested both hands on the pommel of his saddle, easy-like and nonthreatening. "Don't reckon I caught yore name, sonny."

"Cole Rawlins."

"What'cha here for?"

It wasn't any of the old coot's business, but the scattergun made Cole a bit more inclined to be neighborly. "Cattle. I'm planning to run cattle on the other side of Antelope Pass."

"Hmpf, wonder what the sheepherders will think of that?"

Cole shrugged. "It shouldn't matter what they think. Miss Arnold seemed to think—"

"What you know about Miss Evelyn?" The edge in the old man's voice grew more menacing, and his eyes darted up the trail toward the cabin. "If you hurt a hair on that gal's head—"

"Look, mister, I haven't touched her. But she's not there, anyway. I reckon that sheepherder came by and she headed on down the mountain to her grandparents."

"She ain't done no such thing. I jist came from the Arnolds', and she ain't there." He motioned with his scattergun. "Now you jist turn right around and mosey on back to the cabin so I can have a look-see."

Cole did as he was asked, and not just because of the gun. Had Evelyn herded the sheep farther into the mountains? If the old man was right, she must have. But they weren't going to get far until the man trusted him.

"Do you know Reverend Weaver?"

"Met him."

"He's my uncle."

Silence met Cole's pronouncement, and he risked a look over his shoulder. The gun hadn't wavered.

Billy squinted at him. "And jist because you say the preacher is your uncle means I kin trust you?"

"I'd hoped you might." Cole turned around and kept riding.

They stopped in the empty yard outside the cabin. Billy edged around to the side of the barn. "Wagon's gone."

"That means she's gone farther into the mountains with the sheep, doesn't it?"

"Yep." Billy scowled, his gaze following the path that led higher. His gaze shifted, came to rest on Cole. "You kin to the preacher, you say?"

"Yes, sir."

The scattergun lifted. "I reckon you can head on down the trail, then. Unless—"

"Unless what?"

"Unless you want to ride along with me until we catch up with Miss Evelyn. Then you can ride back to town with her in the morning—provided she's agreeable. It's bad enough that she's been up here at the cabin these last few weeks, but out in the sheep wagon, that's a different story altogether."

At least he and the old man agreed on something.

"Lead the way."

◆— • —◆

With the sheep bedded down for the night, Evelyn got out her book and read a few pages, but it wasn't long before the shadows made reading impossible. So she put her book away and contemplated heading into the wagon to sleep. Nervously, she poked at the fire as the darkness closed in around her and a coyote howled in the distance.

She'd never spent the night out in the sheepherder's wagon alone. With her grandfather, yes, but she'd never had to take the wagon out by herself.

It was all a bit unnerving.

She patted Blue Boy on the head. At least she had the dogs to keep her company. Skittles and Blue Boy would take care of her and of the sheep.

Blue Boy's ear's perked forward, and he growled low in his throat. Evelyn's hand stilled. "What is it, boy?"

She reached for the rifle kept close by for wolves and coyotes when she heard the strike of hooves against rock. Relief filled her as a string of pack animals materialized out of the darkness. She put the rifle down and ran toward Billy. "Billy, am I glad to see you!"

But it wasn't just Billy riding up to her camp. She stopped when she realized that someone else rode alongside the tender. The light from her fire spilled on Cole Rawlins. "Mr. Rawlins."

He pulled to a stop, resting his forearms on the pommel of his saddle. "Miss Arnold."

Billy rode the rest of the way to the wagon then dismounted. "Where's the sheepherder?"

"He never showed."

"So you just took it upon yourself to move the sheep on your own?"

"I had no choice. They needed grass."

"It's Saturday. You knew I'd be at the cabin today, and you could have waited a few more hours."

"And risk not getting them to pasture before nightfall?"

Billy grunted then turned toward one of the pack animals. "Got any coffee?"

"I'll brew up a fresh pot. And I've got some leftover beans if you're hungry."

"I could eat. Rawlins, help me with these pack mules."

"Yes, sir."

While they unpacked the mules and hobbled them, Evelyn stirred up the fire and had a fresh pot of coffee boiling by the time they returned. She'd opened another can of beans and stirred up a pone of corn bread as well.

As she dished up the simple fare, she wondered why Cole Rawlins was traveling with Billy.

Billy ate with gusto. "So, you're gonna run cattle on Antelope Pass."

"Yes, that's the plan."

Billy grunted.

"Do you know something I don't?" Cole asked.

"Not really. Just that good grazing land in June might not be so good in August. And might be near impassable in December."

"Because of snow."

Billy nodded.

Cole scooped up another dipper of beans and sank to the ground in front of his

THE Second Chance BRIDES COLLECTION

saddle. "Is there a better place to winter cattle on the other side of Antelope Pass?"

"Maybe."

Evelyn sipped her coffee, hiding a grin. Billy wouldn't give up his secrets easily.

Cole sighed. "Do you think you could show me?"

"Maybe." Billy scraped his tin plate clean then rinsed it in the bucket of water hanging on the side of the wagon.

"Billy, I don't think I'll go down the mountain tomorrow. It's a much longer trip now that I'm not at the cabin."

Billy skewered her with a look. "Your granny's expecting you, gal. If you don't show up, she'll worry."

"I suppose you're right."

"And besides, Cole here said he'd ride along with you. He's new to these parts, and might need somebody to show him the way."

As she topped off Billy's coffee cup, the coyotes yipped again, then an entire chorus of calls sounded. Blue Boy's ears perked up.

Billy squinted at her over the rim of his cup. "Evelyn, girl, now that you've had to move the sheep, you've got to tell your grandpa that sheepherder ain't showed up yet."

"Do we have to tell him, Billy? He'll head up here himself, and he's in no condition to be traipsing all over these mountains."

"It was one thing when you were at the line shack and another to be out here in the open like this. It ain't proper."

Chapter 5

Early the next morning, Cole had his horse and one of the mules saddled and was waiting on Evelyn when Billy approached him. Billy grabbed his arm and pulled him away from the wagon.

"Sonny, you tell that girl's grandpa that he needs to find someone to herd these sheep. You heard them coyotes last night. Most of the lambs have been born, but there are always a few ewes that are late to give birth. Them coyotes know they'll be easy pickings."

Cole scowled. Just like newborn baby calves, but a sight easier. "I reckon so."

Evelyn exited the wagon, a tote in one hand. "Billy, are you sure you don't mind watching the flock until tomorrow night?"

"I'm sure, missy. My bones are aching from traipsing all over these mountains, delivering supplies to the camps. Them sheepherders don't know how good they've got it. Just sitting there night and day, resting their bones next to a good fire. All the hot coffee they can drink. Beans, beans, and more beans."

Evelyn grinned, eyes twinkling. "Then maybe you should give up tendering and start herding."

"I just might do that, missy." Billy scratched his beard, his gaze on Cole. "If your grandpa and the others can find some young whippersnapper to take over my job."

Cole held up his hands and backed away. "Don't look at me. I'm here to run cattle, not deliver supplies."

"How long's it going to be before you get cattle up in that valley, sonny?"

"I don't know, but there's a lot to do before the cattle get here."

"Like what?"

"Like—" Cole glared at the old man, unable to think of a single thing he needed to do.

"Like I figured, there's not a lot to do until the cattle get here. There's grass and there's water. Not much else you need to know about Antelope Pass." He chuckled and turned to Evelyn. "You'd better get on. Your granny's probably worried sick by now. But you tell 'em what I said."

"Let me get my hat." Within minutes, she was back. Cole stepped forward to help her mount, but she swung up on the back of the horse before he could offer assistance. "I'll be back in the morning."

"Don't rush on my account. Them other herders can wait a few hours."

Cole and Evelyn headed down the mountain, following the trail alongside Prickly

171

Pear Creek toward town. The going was easy since the sheep had marked the trail the day before.

They rode into a farmyard, and the same elderly woman Cole had seen with Evelyn at church came rushing out, drying her hands on her apron. Her questioning gaze landed on Cole but skittered straight back to Evelyn.

"Where have you been? Billy left in plenty of time to get to the cabin before dark."

"Well, he had to go farther than the cabin. I had to move the sheep."

The old woman pressed her lips together. "The sheepherder didn't show, then?"

"Not yet."

"I knew that man couldn't be trusted. He kept asking for half a month's wages up front, and when Delbert wouldn't give it to him, he asked for a week's worth." She shook her head. "Now tell me what a sheepherder needs money for up in them mountains? He's probably down in Helena now having himself a good ol' time."

"He'll show up, Granny. This week. I'm sure of it." Evelyn glanced at Cole then placed a hand on her grandmother's arm. "Don't tell Grandpa that I had to move the sheep. I don't want him to worry."

Her grandmother's mouth flattened into a thin line. "Evelyn, I won't lie—"

"Of course not. But if he doesn't ask, what will one more week hurt?"

Granny speared Cole with a look. "And who might you be?"

Cole whipped off his hat. "Cole Rawlins, ma'am."

She squinted at him. "Reverend Weaver's nephew?"

"Yes, ma'am."

Her gaze flitted from Cole to Evelyn and back again. "Hmpf. Don't reckon there's any need to ask why you're riding with my granddaughter."

"Granny, Cole's thinking about running cattle up on Antelope Pass. Billy asked him to ride back with me."

Evelyn's grandmother plopped her hands on her hips. "You might as well get down and set a spell. Delbert will want to meet you, ask about the grass in the high meadows."

"Yes, ma'am." Cole dismounted.

Evelyn's grandmother pointed to a rocker. "Wait here."

Cole glanced at Evelyn, but she ducked her head and hurried inside.

Hat in hand, he waited. Not long after, he heard a thumping sound heading toward the door.

"Now, Minnie, quit your hovering. I can manage on my own."

"You don't want to fall and break your other leg, old man."

"I'm not going to fall."

The door opened, and Evelyn backed through. Mr. Arnold came right behind, on crutches, but looking like he had little control over the contraptions. His wife brought up the rear, a plush cushion clutched in one hand, the other holding tight to the back of her husband's work shirt.

Cole held his breath until the women had the elderly man safely seated in one of the straight-back chairs. Mr. Arnold stretched out his injured leg, and his wife rushed toward a low stool.

"Here, ma'am, let me get that." Cole grabbed the stool. "Where do you want it?"

"There." She pointed toward Mr. Arnold's foot.

Once they had Mr. Arnold's foot propped up, Mrs. Arnold shooed Evelyn toward the door. "Come on, granddaughter, time for your bath. I've been keeping water hot all morning."

Cole waited until the women left then sat back down in one of the rockers.

"Minnie tells me you're planning to run cattle on the other side of Antelope Pass."

"Yes, sir."

"What's the grass look like?"

"Lush and green." Cole spread his hands. "Two feet tall in some places."

"It'll all be dead by midsummer. Your cows will have a hard time finding much to eat on the Antelope then."

Same thing Billy had said, in so many words. Cole placed his forearms on his knees and eyed Mr. Arnold. He didn't get the impression that either Billy or Evelyn's grandfather was trying to convince him not to bring cattle into the area. They seemed to know what they were talking about. "You've been here a long time, Mr. Arnold. Do you think I can successfully run cattle in these parts?"

"It can be done, sure. You'll just need to keep rotating your cattle to the best grazing spots year-round. And since there aren't any sheepherders on that side of the pass, you shouldn't be competing for the grass there. But I still think you should wait until spring to bring in cattle."

Cole clasped his hands, disappointed. When he'd seen that grass, tall enough to scrape the belly of his horse, he could just see the high mountain valley dotted with cattle. Cattle that would someday be his. He nodded. "My partner is coming to look over the setup, and I'll see what he thinks. He's run cattle in and around Helena, and I trust his judgment."

"The moneyman, huh?"

Cole chuckled. "Yes, sir."

The muffled sound of women's voices reached them from inside the home, and Mr. Arnold shifted his leg on the pillow. "So that sheepherder didn't show, then?"

"No, sir." Cole resisted the urge to tell Mr. Arnold that Evelyn had to move the sheep. It wasn't his place to meddle. He cleared his throat. "The tender was adamant that you find someone to take over the sheep for Evelyn. He's not happy with her being up in the mountains alone."

"He's right. But until I can locate another sheepherder, there's not much I can do other than go up there myself."

"He also said he'd be willing to stay with the sheep if you could find someone willing to deliver supplies."

"You volunteering?"

"No, sir. I'll be herding cattle."

"Fair enough."

173

Chapter 6

A prickly pear can't hold a candle to that girl."

Evelyn's face heated, and she inched to the left so that a stack of dry goods hid her from view. She tried to keep her attention on the red calico her grandmother held out for her inspection.

"I should have known she'd have an excuse not to help plan the Fourth of July picnic."

"Just like she didn't attend the last quilting bee and bowed out of the latest round of canning. I don't see how Minnie puts up with her shirking her duty like that."

"Mrs. Michum, can I help you?" Even from her hiding place behind the dry goods, Evelyn heard the disapproval in Angie's tone.

"Evelyn, are you listening?" Her grandmother's pinched mouth showed she'd also heard the catty remarks.

"Yes, ma'am."

"With some white ribbon, or maybe blue, this would be perfect for the Fourth of July picnic." Her granny held a swatch of blue ribbon against the red cloth. "Oh, and I could add some matching ribbons to your straw hat. Wouldn't that be festive?"

Evelyn eyed the red material with tiny white flowers. "It's very pretty, but a bit too bright and bold, don't you think? I'd feel uncomfortable wearing it to church later."

"Nonsense. You'll look lovely, and no one would bat an eye at red calico in church."

Sighing, Evelyn reached for a length of blue. Granny was determined to make her a new dress, and the blue was decidedly less flashy. "What about this instead?"

Mrs. Michum and Mrs. Vincent finished their shopping and sailed out of the mercantile. Angie closed the register and hurried toward Evelyn and her grandmother. "I'm sorry, Mrs. Arnold. Evelyn. What can I do for you today?"

Granny draped the red calico over Evelyn's shoulder. "Don't you think this would be perfect for the Fourth of July picnic?"

"Or this one?" Evelyn pleaded with Angie to choose the blue.

"The red is very festive," Angie conceded, "but the blue is cheaper."

"How much?" Granny fingered both pieces of cloth, her eyes widening when Angie named the prices.

"Granny, I don't need a new dress."

"Of course you do, child. You have one good dress—"

"That's all I need."

"And you wear it every Sunday." Her grandmother picked up the blue. "Very well.

174

I'll take the blue. You're going to have this dress, and you're going to wear it to the picnic."

"I'm not going to the picnic. I'll be taking care of the sheep."

"Hogwash. Delbert will have found another herder by then. Mark my words."

Evelyn squirmed. "Granny, that seems unlikely at this late date."

Her grandmother clucked her tongue against the roof of her mouth. "I declare, Evelyn, if I didn't know any better, I'd think you'd rather stay up there with those sheep than attend the picnic on some handsome man's arm."

"Granny, there won't be any handsome men at the picnic."

"Well, you never know. Some of the sheepherders might be there."

Evelyn cringed. Most of the sheepherders were old and grizzled, and she couldn't imagine attending with any of them. "They have to stay with the sheep, too."

"Angie, maybe you can convince your cousin—what's his name?—to attend the picnic. Even though I'm not sure anything could ever come of it, him being a cowboy and all."

Angie covered her mouth, stifling a giggle.

Evelyn shook her head. "Granny."

"Well, it's true. A sheepherder's granddaughter and a cowboy? Hardly a match made in heaven. Angie, I'll take enough of this blue to make Evelyn a dress for the picnic."

"Yes, ma'am."

The back door opened, and Ollie's mother walked in, carrying the baby. Mrs. Rodgers smiled. "Minnie. Evelyn. What a pleasant surprise."

"Katherine." Granny moved across the room and smiled at the baby. "Hello there, sweetie."

The baby gave her a toothless smile, cooing, leaving them all smiling. Ollie's mother lifted the baby to her shoulder and patted her on the back. "Oh, Minnie, I wanted to show you the pattern we've chosen for our next quilting bee. Do you have a moment?"

"Of course."

Evelyn reached for the baby. "Here, let me hold her."

"We'll be right back."

Her grandmother and Mrs. Rodgers slipped out to the small clapboard house that she shared with Ollie and Angie next door, and Evelyn cradled little Rebecca against her. Angie measured out yard after yard of the blue calico, smiling at the two of them.

"She's right, you know."

"Who?" Evelyn lifted her gaze to Angie. "About what?"

"Your grandmother." Angie cut the cloth, a smile playing on her lips. "Cole is quite handsome."

◆—•————•—◆

Cole tossed his reins over the hitching post and stepped onto the porch of the mercantile. A calico cat dozed in a patch of sunlight, eyes at half-mast.

The bell over the door to the mercantile jingled as he stepped inside. His gaze landed on Angie and Evelyn, both staring at him from the back of the store.

Eyes wide, Angie glanced from him to Evelyn. She lowered her gaze, a smile playing across her face before she started folding a length of blue calico. "Afternoon, cousin."

Cole nodded. "Angie. Evelyn."

"Cole." Even in the dim interior of the store, Cole could see the bright red flush that heated Evelyn's cheeks. She nodded a greeting but then quickly turned her attention back to the baby.

Cole looked at a display of pocket watches while Angie finished folding the cloth and wrapped it in a piece of butcher paper. "What can I get for you?"

"Do I have any mail?"

Angie stepped behind the counter, reached for the mail in a cubbyhole behind the counter and started thumbing through it. The baby let out a cry and Evelyn threw Angie a panicked glance, jiggling the baby in her arms. Angie grabbed a knotted piece of cheesecloth and handed it to Cole. "Here. Let her chew on this. There's a bit of sugar soaked in it."

Cole crossed the store to where Evelyn tried to comfort the baby. The moment she latched her mouth on to the sugar-soaked dummy, she stopped crying, and her big blue eyes locked on to Evelyn's face.

Evelyn's gaze met his, a wide smile on her face. "She likes it."

"Yep. Looks like she's happy now." Cole took one of the baby's hands in his and her chubby fingers curled around his finger.

For a long moment, they stared at each other, the baby between them. Then Evelyn looked away, her attention falling to the baby in her arms. Cole let his gaze wander over the smattering of freckles on her lightly tanned skin, her strawberry-blond hair that she'd pulled into a severe bun but that had somehow slid down to the nape of her neck leaving loose strands framing her face.

A woman with silver-streaked hair entered the store, followed by a younger girl who could only be her daughter. Her gaze landed on Cole, Evelyn, and the baby, one eyebrow raised. Suddenly Cole realized how intimate a picture the three of them presented. Clearing his throat, he eased his finger out from the baby's grasp and moved away.

The woman turned her attention to Angie. "Ah, Mrs. Rodgers, could I have a moment of your time? I'm in a hurry and need some cloth."

"Yes, Mrs. Nelson." Angie thumbed through the mail. "I'll only be a moment."

"I'm sorry that I've just now made it to town. We've been so busy out at the farm and just couldn't make it back before now." The older woman kept talking as if she hadn't heard and headed toward the dry goods, the girl trailing behind her.

"Excuse me, ma'am." Cole stood aside, letting the ladies pass.

"Now, Rosemarie, which cloth did you want for your dress?"

"The blue calico." The girl huffed as if her mother knew perfectly well which cloth she wanted.

She gave her daughter a fond smile before addressing Evelyn, who still stood beside the table gently rocking the baby back and forth as she sucked contentedly on the sugar dummy. "Well, Evelyn, you look like a natural holding that baby."

"Thank you, Mrs. Nelson." Pink tinged Evelyn's cheeks, but if anything, the heightened color on her cheeks made her even prettier.

Cole turned away, placed both hands on the counter and focused on Angie. "Found anything?"

"Ah, here it is."

"Thanks, Angie."

He leaned on the counter and ripped open the missive. Disappointment filled him when he read that it would be another couple of weeks before Mr. Mangrum could get up to Burnt Sage.

"Oh, no." Cole let the letter dangle in his hands at the panic in Mrs. Nelson's voice. She tossed bolts of cloth aside, searching through the modest selection. Finally, she unfolded a small swath of blue calico Angie had folded and set to the side.

"Is there a problem, Mrs. Nelson?" Angie asked, looking concerned.

"It's gone." She waved the small square of material. "There's hardly enough here to make a doll blanket, let alone a dress."

"Mama, I told you I wanted the blue calico." The girl folded her arms and pressed her lips together in an angry pout, glaring at Angie. "And they sold it to someone else."

"Now, Rosemarie—"

"I never get anything I want." Hiking her skirts, the girl rushed toward the door and Cole moved to the side to let her pass.

"Mrs. Nelson, I'm sorry, but Evelyn—"

"Not to worry." Evelyn picked up the brown paper–wrapped package that Angie had been wrapping when Cole had entered the store earlier. "Angie had just wrapped up the cloth before you came in the store. Perfect timing, wouldn't you say?"

"Well, this is a pleasant surprise." A smile bloomed on the woman's face as she clutched the package to her. "Mrs. Rodgers, you saved it for us just like Rosemarie asked. Would you put it on our tab?"

Angie glanced toward Evelyn then nodded, looking none too pleased with the turn of events. "Yes, ma'am."

Mrs. Nelson headed toward the door, giving Cole a quick nod. "Good day, sir."

As soon as the door shut behind her, Angie turned to Evelyn, crossed her arms, and gave her a steely-eyed look. "Now why did you go and do that? Rosemarie never told anybody that they'd be back for that cloth, and besides, I can't hold dry goods on the whim of a thirteen-year-old."

Evelyn shrugged, gently rocking Rebecca back and forth. The baby had miraculously gone to sleep during the exchange. "What else could I do? Rosemarie had her heart set on the blue calico. If I'd shown up at the picnic—or anywhere else, for that matter—wearing it, she wouldn't have been happy. I wouldn't upset the poor girl that way."

Angie jerked up a length of red cloth sprinkled with white flowers and smoothed it out, straightening the disarray caused by Mrs. Nelson's frantic search for the blue calico. "Well, you'll just have to pick out something else, then."

"Oh, Angie, there's no need. I'm not going to the picnic."

"Your grandmother will not be happy."

"I won't be happy about what?"

Cole straightened as Evelyn's grandmother entered from the back.

"Evelyn let Rosemarie have the blue calico."

"She did, did she?" Mrs. Arnold's brows lowered. "Well, young lady, you won't get off that easy."

Snatching up the red material, she turned, her attention landing square on Cole. She unrolled a couple of swaths and held the cloth up in front of Evelyn, whose face rivaled the color of the material. "Mr. Rawlins, would you say that this color looks fetching on my granddaughter?"

"Yes. . .uh. . .yes, ma'am." Cole swallowed the lump in his throat. "Mighty fetching."

"Then it's settled. The red it is." Mrs. Arnold handed the cloth to Angie and marched toward the exit. Almost there, she stopped, pivoted, and pinned Cole with a steely-eyed look. "We'll see you at the picnic, won't we, Mr. Rawlins?"

"Yes, ma'am." He whipped off his hat. "And it's just Cole, ma'am."

Chapter 7

Cole plucked his hat off a peg at the back of the church and followed the rest of the crowd out into the bright spring sunshine. Settling the hat on his head, he joined Angie and Ollie next to their buggy. The baby gave him a toothless grin and lunged toward him.

Angie held her out. "Do you want to hold her?"

"Looks like I don't have any choice." Cole laughed as the baby leaned toward him, her grin growing even wider. As soon as he had her in his arms, she zeroed in on his string necktie, her chubby hands reaching for the black ribbon. She missed the tie and grabbed a handful of his shirt, immediately stuffing it in her mouth.

Angie laughed then reached to untangle her daughter's hands from Cole's shirt. "She's going to get your shirt all wet."

Cole smiled at the baby as she batted him with both hands, fighting her mother's efforts. "I don't mind."

"Miss Arnold?"

Cole lifted his gaze in time to see a man approaching Evelyn, a trail of youngsters in his wake. The man whipped off his hat as Evelyn turned, the same faded pink dress she'd had on last week swishing around her ankles.

Angie huffed, whispered so low that Cole barely heard her. "Hiram Danvers, don't you dare."

Mr. Danvers mangled his hat between meaty paws. "Miss Arnold, would you—would you let me escort you to the Fourth of July picnic?"

Was it his imagination or did the entire churchyard grow silent?

"I—" Evelyn's gaze swept across the crowd, looking for all the world like a trapped rabbit.

"Cole, do something." Angie hissed.

Cole did the only thing he could. He handed the baby to Ollie and headed toward Evelyn.

◆—•———•◆

"I—" Evelyn snapped her mouth shut when a male hand attached to a blue-striped sleeve jutted out toward Hiram Danvers.

"Danvers, isn't it?"

Cole's voice. Cole's arm. She wanted to sink into the hard-packed churchyard, knowing the entire community stood around ogling the three of them. Hiram's gaze ricocheted from hers to Cole.

Once. Twice. A third time.

Finally, he reached out and took Cole's hand, nodding. Cole gave him a hearty shake then clapped him on the shoulder. "Sorry to beat you to the punch, Mr. Danvers, but, well, Evelyn's grandmother asked if I'd be at the picnic. You understand, don't you?"

"Of course. My apologies." Hiram backed away, his face red. "Good day, Miss Arnold."

He turned and fled, leaving Evelyn and Cole standing in the middle of the church-yard surrounded by—well, by *everyone*.

And nobody was talking.

Cole gazed down at her, a slight smile on his face, but his gaze was dead serious. Evelyn's gaze was drawn toward the dimple in his cheek. He held out his arm, one eyebrow lifted. "Ready?"

With nothing else to do other than cause a scene, Evelyn placed her hand in the crook of his arm and let him lead her to the wagon.

Quiet pockets of conversation started again as if the congregation hated to talk too loudly in case they missed something else. Her grandmother joined them, walking a few steps behind.

"Cole—"

"We'll talk about it later."

His voice was low, intimate, and meant for her only. He handed her up into the wagon then helped her grandmother up.

Doffing his hat, he nodded. "Ladies."

Evelyn had never been so humiliated in her life. Well, maybe once. When she'd left Ollie at the altar in that same church in front of those same people.

But she'd known what she was doing and was willing to live with the censure and the talk in order to give Ollie and Angie a chance at happiness.

Granny clicked at the mules to pick up the pace. "Well, I reckon it's a good thing I bought that red calico."

Evelyn didn't answer, and her grandmother lapsed into silence. The closer they got to home, the more determined Evelyn was to get back to the mountains.

As long as she stayed with the sheep, the townspeople had no reason to mock her. Hiram Danvers couldn't ask her to the picnic with the intention of courting her to be a mother to his children.

And Cole Rawlins couldn't embarrass her making promises he didn't intend to keep.

◆—————◆

To her credit, Granny didn't mention the incident at church again. The two of them rode home in complete silence, each lost in her own thoughts.

After dinner, Granny pulled out her measuring tape. "Here, girl, let me get your measurements. You've lost a bit of weight traipsing all over those mountains following those sheep."

"Not that she had any to lose, that's for sure." Her grandpa patted his own bulging stomach. "Unlike her old grandpa."

Evelyn held up her arms, submitting to her grandmother's will. Finally, the measurements were done, and Granny cleared the table and laid out the red material. Evelyn pulled out her pack and started preparing for the return trip to the mountains.

Granny eyed her as she laid out her paper pattern she'd used to cut Evelyn's last dress. "You're packing mighty early."

Evelyn shrugged. "I thought I'd get an early start. No need to wait until morning."

Grandpa sat with his foot propped up on a chair, his pipe in his hand.

Granny snipped at the cloth. "Delbert, have you heard anything from that no-account herder?"

"Not a word."

"Well, I don't like it."

Evelyn ignored them and kept packing.

"I've wracked my brain trying to find someone to watch the sheep, but it's not easy. Not just anybody can do it."

"Blue Boy and Skittles know what to do."

Evelyn closed the pack and opened a second one. "Sure they do. You trained them well. But it wouldn't take long for some yahoo who doesn't know a thing about dogs or sheep to undo everything we've done."

Her grandpa sucked on his pipe then waved it in the air. "That young feller who brought you home the other day said Billy wouldn't mind watching the sheep for a few months if I could locate another tender. What do you think of that?"

"Billy Wilson give up his job as tender?" Her grandmother laughed. "That'll be the day."

"Well, he's getting on up there in years, Minnie. Just like you and me."

Her grandmother harrumphed.

"Well, none of that matters much right now." Evelyn stood, hefted the pack and dropped it near the door next to the first one. Then she turned to face her grandparents. "It's up to Billy and me. One of us has to stay with the sheep and the other one has to deliver supplies to the other herders. That's all there is to it."

An hour later, she waved good-bye and headed into the mountains, breathing easier with each passing mile.

Chapter 8

Evelyn's grandmother stood on the porch eyeing Cole.

He'd just missed Evelyn. She jerked her chin toward the trail that meandered along Prickly Pear Creek. "You can catch up with her easily if you're of a mind to. I'd be obliged if you ride along and make sure she makes it back safely."

"Yes, ma'am." He doffed his hat and headed into the mountains. He caught up with her a mile from the line shack.

She turned in the saddle, gave him a nod. "Cole."

"Evelyn."

They rode for a few minutes, and he let his gaze wander over the creek to his right, the mountains in the distance. But eventually his gaze landed on the woman at his side. She'd abandoned her dress in favor of the baggy pants and oversized shirt more suitable for herding sheep. A floppy, sweat-stained slouch hat hid her face from his view.

He cleared his throat. "Evelyn, don't you think we need to talk?"

Finally, she glanced at him, her green eyes wary. "About what?"

"About this morning. About the picnic."

"Why did you do it?"

"Angie—" Cole clamped his mouth shut. Somehow telling Evelyn that Angie had insisted he do something about Danvers didn't seem like a good idea. "You—"

"I what?"

"You looked like you needed help."

"I can take care of myself."

The cabin came into view and Evelyn urged her mule faster. Cole followed, dismounting when she did. "Why are you stopping here?"

"I need to get some things." She stepped up onto the porch then turned to him. "Look, Cole, I appreciate what you did with Hiram, but you don't have to go to the picnic with me."

He gaped at her. "Why not? I said I would. Did you want to go with him?"

"No."

"So, let me get this straight. You don't want to go to the picnic with Danvers, and you don't want to go with me. Seems to me like I stuck my foot in my mouth when Angie—"

"When Angie what?"

Cole felt his face redden. He ducked his head and ran one hand around his neck.

"Well, Angie was determined that you not go to the picnic with him, so I stepped in. I thought you'd be happy about it."

Evelyn sighed. Then she stepped down off the porch and met his gaze head-on. "Thank you, but you've just made things worse."

"How so? I don't understand what's going on with you and Angie and Ollie and all those busybodies in town. Why are they all so determined to make you look bad?"

"Angie doesn't want me to look bad. She's trying to help."

"Well, she has a funny way of showing it." Cole shook his head. "So, you're determined not to attend the picnic? You're going to stand me up."

"I think it's for the best. You just asked because Angie pushed you into it." She shrugged. "And I have a good excuse not to go."

"The sheep?"

"Yes."

Cole eyed her then motioned toward the cabin. "Get whatever you need, so we can get to the camp before nightfall."

"You don't have to ride along."

"I promised your grandmother that I would."

Soon they were on their way again, and Cole pondered Evelyn's determination not to attend the picnic and her equally stubborn determination not to tell him why.

Billy was willing to look after the sheep for her to make a weekly trek home to see her grandparents and attend church, so he'd be willing to watch the sheep for her to go to the celebration.

No, there was some other reason that she didn't want to attend. She just wasn't willing to tell him what it was.

◆•——•◆

Evelyn peeked at Cole from under the brim of her hat. She could tell from the scowl on his face that he was unhappy with her answer.

But she couldn't tell him the truth.

She couldn't tell him that every time she set foot in church or in town for that matter, she could feel everyone's eyes on her. It was bad enough to face the stares and the whispers once a week when she attended church with her grandmother, but Granny didn't give her a choice. Her grandmother had agreed to let her take over care of the sheep when her grandfather had broken his leg with the condition that she promise to come home and attend services every Sunday.

She didn't mind church—she loved being there to worship—she just minded the busybodies who liked to take jabs at her for letting Ollie Rodgers slip through her fingers.

They rounded the bend and came on the open valley where they'd left Billy. As she expected, the grass was almost gone. Billy waved at them, and Skittles and Blue Boy trotted toward her, tails wagging.

"How's it been?" she asked.

"Fair to middlin'. The grass is getting sparse, though, so the sheep are starting to wander off." Billy eyed Cole. "Glad to see you came back, young feller. We need to move these sheep to a bigger pasture, somewhere they can stay for the rest of the summer. An extra pair of hands to drive the wagon and herd sheep is mighty welcome. It's a far piece, but if we push 'em we can make it in one day."

"I'll do what I can."

"All right. First thing in the morning, then."

Billy had them on the move come daylight. Cole led the pack mules, while Evelyn drove the wagon and Billy herded sheep. Midafternoon, Evelyn convinced Billy to switch places with her, and she walked the rest of the way. The sheep were weary by the time they descended into a large valley filled with plenty of shrubs and grass.

As darkness fell, Billy and Cole bedded down outside, and Evelyn took her place inside the wagon. She stretched out, and within minutes was sound asleep. She woke to a start, the panicked bleating of sheep mingled with the yelping of coyotes galvanizing her into action.

She jerked on her boots and stumbled out of the wagon, gun in hand. Cole and Billy were already on their feet as well. Sounded like the coyotes were attacking both flanks of the sheep.

Billy took charge. He pointed to the left. "Evelyn, you and Cole go that way. Take Skittles with you. I'll take Blue Boy and check this side."

"Skittles. Come!" Evelyn ran, following the sound of bleating, Cole and the dog right on her heels.

The darkness closed in around her, and she slowed, listening to the sheep, letting them guide her way. Suddenly, the coyotes stopped howling, but the sheep milled nervously, eyes wide as they stared into the darkness.

"They're out there," Cole muttered.

"Yes."

The sheep remained unsettled, and Cole and Evelyn continued to walk the perimeter of the flock. On the far side, they met Billy coming from the other direction, a scattergun cradled in his arms.

"See anything?" he growled.

"Nothing."

"Why don't you two go on and get some sleep and the dogs and I will keep watch."

"Billy, it's my responsibility. I should do it."

"Oh, don't you worry none, Miss Evelyn. You'll get your turn to keep watch before daybreak."

She eyed the old man, barely able to see his features in the dark. "If you're sure."

"Sure as rain. Now be off with you."

Evelyn and Cole headed back to the campsite. "Maybe we all should stand watch."

"Billy's right. If something happens, he'll alert us. It'll do no good for us all to stay up."

"I suppose."

They were halfway back to the wagon when an explosion of bleating and panic erupted up ahead. Cole whipped out his pistol and put a hand on Evelyn's arm. "Stay here."

Before she could protest, he was gone. Skittles whined at her side. Panicked over the thought of her dog getting shot in the dark, she called out, "Skittles. Down."

Skittles immediately crouched full-belly on the ground at her feet. As they waited, the sheep milled about, bleating. Skittles growled, her attention focused toward the brush to Evelyn's left.

"Come away." Evelyn backed away, trying to see into the darkness. But it was no use. Skittles stood, moved in front of her, and gave a short bark of alarm, backing with her but staying between her and the threat in the bushes.

Evelyn held the rifle at the ready, but she'd never been a very good shot. If the coyote charged—

She screamed as a blur of gray shot out from the shadows, but instead of charging toward her, the coyote headed straight for Skittles. Evelyn jerked the rifle to her shoulder and fired off a shot. Missed. The next thing she knew, the coyote and Skittles were at each other's throats. Evelyn gritted her teeth and tried to draw another bead on the coyote, but it was useless. She couldn't risk hitting Skittles.

Dog and coyote parted, and a shot rang out and the coyote fell dead. Skittles rolled away then stood. "Skittles. Come."

The dog limped to her side and Evelyn ran her hands over her coat, searching for injuries. She encountered a sticky wetness next to her throat.

"Is she all right?" Cole knelt by her side.

Evelyn shook her head then whispered, "I don't know."

He scooped up the dog. "Let's get her back to the wagon."

As soon as they reached the camp, Cole laid the dog down.

Billy and Blue Boy came charging in from the other direction. "What happened?"

"A coyote jumped Skittles, but Cole shot it."

Cole grabbed his saddle.

"What are you doing?"

"I'm going to ride herd on these sheep just like we do on cattle. The coyotes are skittish of horses and aren't as likely to attack."

Before Evelyn could say more, he'd saddled his horse and mounted. Blue Boy stood, looking like he might follow. Cole whistled, and to Evelyn's surprise, the dog trotted after the man and horse.

"Well, I'll be." Billy shook his head. "I wouldn't have believed it if I hadn't seen it."

Evelyn watched until the night swallowed up Cole and her dog. "I hope he doesn't confuse Blue Boy with the wrong commands."

Billy laughed. "I don't think Blue Boy's gonna get confused. He probably went along to make sure the cowboy didn't harm his sheep."

Evelyn laughed. "You're probably right."

Billy turned to Skittles. "Evelyn, let's see how bad Skittles is. Bring me the lantern."

After they'd cleaned Skittles' wounds, all minor, Billy sat back. "She's gonna be sore for a few days, but she's gonna be fine."

Evelyn ran a hand down the dog's back. "She saved my life."

"Along with that cowboy out there riding herd on your sheep."

"Yes."

"He's a good man, that Cole."

Chapter 9

The sun was just rising over the horizon when Cole rode up to the campsite where Billy had the fire going. The sheep were all bedded down, calm and quiet. The dog lay down, ears perked forward, staring at him.

"Light a spell." Billy reached for a coffeepot and poured Cole a cup of coffee.

Cole dismounted. "Don't mind if I do. How's the dog?"

"She's gonna be all right. Just a few scratches."

"Did you get some sleep?"

"I dozed."

"Evelyn?"

"She's sleeping. I finally convinced her to turn in."

Cole squatted next to the fire, and eyed the old man, who looked tired but would never admit it. "I've been thinking. . . ."

"I figured you might."

"After last night's encounter with the coyote, I don't think we should leave Evelyn alone, and I'm not sure that she'd welcome me staying here overnight."

"Delbert Arnold wouldn't, either. You can head out first light." Billy scrabbled around and unearthed a piece of brown wrapping paper. "I'll draw you a map where all the other herders are."

"It shouldn't be that hard. There are trails all up in here."

Billy scratched out a rough map, showing the easiest path to each camp. When he finished, he handed the map off to Cole, a satisfied gleam in his eyes. "And when you come back on Friday, you can escort Evelyn down the mountain."

Cole tucked the map into his shirt pocket and chuckled. "I thought you might say that."

◆•——·——•◆

Soaked to the skin and covered with mud, Evelyn struggled to extricate a lamb from the muddy mess down a steep incline. The lamb's dam stood on the bank bleating for her baby.

It had been raining for three days straight, and Evelyn was sick and tired of fighting with the mud, rescuing lambs, and fighting off coyotes. But for the moment, the rain had stopped, and she hoped they were in for clear weather for a change. Blue Boy padded back and forth behind her, whining.

As she pulled and prodded the lamb up the bank, she prayed that they wouldn't lose any more lambs, that the rain would stop, and that her grandfather would find another herder to help.

If he didn't, she didn't see how he could manage another growing season, and the sheep were their livelihood. She'd been so foolish to think that her grandfather could keep herding sheep forever at his age. His broken leg had just brought his advancing age to the forefront of her thoughts.

Bleating, the lamb stood on wobbly legs and tried to wriggle out of her grasp. "No you don't."

She gritted her teeth and held on, even as the moisture-laden clouds opened and dumped more rain down on her. Just fine and dandy. She'd left her slicker back at the wagon. Slipping and sliding, she crawled up the muddy embankment, holding the kicking, squirming lamb to her.

By the time she reached the top, she was exhausted, covered in mud, and feeling like a drowned rat.

"Here. Let me have it."

Cole. He'd come back. With a sigh of relief, she shoved the struggling bundle of muddy fleece the last few feet toward him. He got a firm hold then pushed the lamb away from the bank toward its mother. Blue Boy didn't waste any time herding the two back to the flock. The muddy lamb huddled close and started nursing right away.

Cole reached down, grasped her by the collar, and pulled her the rest of the way up. Rain sluiced off his hat and ran in rivulets down his slicker, but otherwise, he looked none the worse for wear.

He started unbuttoning his slicker. "Here. You're getting all wet."

"No. No need to get your slicker all muddy, too. I'll just change into dry clothes." Evelyn backed away, hands held out.

She felt her feet slipping as she teetered on the uneven ground, saw Cole's eyes widen as he grabbed for her outstretched hands. The next thing she knew, they were both tumbling down the embankment.

They landed in a heap. Evelyn lay on her back, the rain bathing her face and washing away the mud. She glanced at Cole, only to find his nice clean slicker covered in mud and his head bare. He'd lost his hat.

She snickered. "I guess I'll take your slicker now."

Cole loomed over her, leaning on one elbow. Rain peppered his hair, the moisture running in rivulets down his face. He blinked, swiped at the rain on his face, and ended up smearing more mud on his face. A crooked grin kicked up one side of his mouth. She sucked in a breath when a dimple appeared in his mud-spattered cheek. "Nope. Too late now."

She felt an answering smile spread across her face.

Slowly, his grin faded, and his gaze roamed over her face, stopping at her mouth. Evelyn stopped breathing as it hit her that he might kiss her. No, he couldn't. He—they shouldn't. She blinked, looked away from his mesmerizing gaze.

For a moment, time stood still, the only sounds the splat of rain against Cole's oilskin slicker and Blue Boy's whining as he looked down on them.

In one fluid movement, Cole rolled away and stood, reaching out a hand to help her up. Hesitantly, she took his hand, risking a glance at him. Her stomach roiled at the scowl on his face.

"You need to get in some dry clothes."

◆——————◆

"She's not coming to the picnic?"

Cole eyed Angie over the counter. "That's what I said."

"But—but she's got to." Angie threw a panicked look at Ollie, who was busily wielding a crowbar against the lid of a crate. "Did she say why?"

Cole felt his face heat up. It might have had something to do with the fact that he'd almost kissed her. He shrugged. "She said that with the rain and the coyotes after the sheep she didn't want to leave Billy alone. That's why I agreed to come after the supplies for Billy. I don't have anything else to do until I hear from Mr. Mangrum."

"Ollie, we've got to do something." Angie whirled toward Ollie.

"Now, Angie, if Evelyn's made up her mind not to come, then there's nothing you can do about it." Ollie gave his wife a tender smile. "Maybe it's best to leave well enough alone."

"But it's not well enough. Nothing's good about the way Mrs. Michum and Mrs. Vincent treat her." Angie's eyes filled with tears. "And after this, they'll be even worse, saying she ran out on Cole, too. Evelyn deserves better."

Cole placed both hands on the counter, his gaze shifting from one to the other. "Don't you think it's time somebody told me what's going on?"

Angie glanced at Ollie, and he looked at the crate as if getting to the contents inside was the most important job in the world.

"Well?" Cole persisted.

"We've got to tell him. Please, Ollie."

"We promised Evelyn we wouldn't."

"That was before. This is now."

Ollie sighed, dropped the crowbar on top of the crate, and walked over to the counter. "Evelyn and I were engaged to be married. We grew up together, and it seemed like a good idea at the time. So many of our friends had married, and that just left the two of us. Neither of us knew what love was. We were friends, and that seemed like enough."

"Then Angie's pa came to be the new preacher, bringing his family." Ollie's mouth softened as his gaze landed on his wife. "It didn't take long for me to realize that I was falling in love with Angie."

Cole's gaze went from one to the other. "So you called off the wedding?"

"No." Ollie's mouth tightened into a thin line, and he shook his head. "But there are days that I wish I had."

Cole frowned and shook his head. "I'm confused."

Angie placed her arm around Ollie then patted his chest. "Ollie wouldn't call off the wedding because he didn't want to hurt Evelyn. He was determined to do the right thing and honor his commitment to her."

"Then—"

"Evelyn called it off. I tried to hide the way I felt about Angie. I wouldn't even talk to her and certainly didn't attempt to see her. But Evelyn sensed that something was wrong. A few days before the wedding, she asked if I was sure about getting married, and I assured her I was." Ollie cleared his throat and stared out the large picture window at the front of the mercantile. "On the day of our wedding, when Evelyn entered the back of the church and started down the aisle, she paused. It was as if time stood still. She looked directly at me, then she looked at Angie seated at the piano playing the wedding march, then back at me waiting at the front with Reverend Weaver, and it was as if she knew. She just smiled, turned around, and walked out."

"Did she ever tell you why she did it, or did you just know?"

Ollie chuckled. "Oh, she told us all right. A few days later, she asked me to meet her at the old swimming hole. I went, thinking I'd get some answers. When I got there, she had Angie with her. She put my hand in Angie's and said that she could tell we were meant to be together, and that's why she'd done it. She looked me in the eye with that prickly look of hers and said that she'd called off our wedding because she realized she didn't love me. That if anybody asked, that was reason enough. They didn't need to know anything else. Then she hugged Angie and walked off.

"She was braver than I was. I thought I was doing the right thing by going ahead with the marriage, but I was the coward. If I'd called off the wedding, the busybodies would have left her alone." Ollie looked disgusted with himself. "As it is, they talk about me as if I'm some kind of saint. Poor Ollie this, and poor Ollie that. Sometimes I just want to—"

"Now, Ollie, kicking up a fuss now would just give them something more to talk about." Angie patted his arm, and then she shifted her attention to Cole. "But now we have a new problem. If she doesn't show up at that picnic on your arm, then tongues are going to wag more than they ever have before. She'll be a laughingstock all over again."

Cole glared at his cousin. "Angie, you sure do have a lot of faith in my powers of persuasion. Just how do you think I'm going to convince Evelyn to come to the picnic when she's already said she wasn't coming? And with good reason, I might add."

"Well, the reason she said she wasn't coming was because she didn't want to leave Billy alone, right?" Angie smiled. "I've got a remedy for that. The weather's cleared and the sun's shining, and I've got two little brothers who'd jump at the chance to spend a couple of days with Billy out in that wagon."

"Will Uncle David let them go?"

"Of course. It was his idea. I've been trying to come up with a solution to Evelyn's problem of herding sheep. He went out to talk to Mr. Arnold yesterday, and Evelyn's grandfather agreed. Even Mama came around to the idea when she realized it would keep those two out of trouble for the rest of the summer."

"And who's going to be the tender if Billy and the boys are sheepherders?"

"You, of course."

Cole lifted an eyebrow. "So you've got it all figured out?"

"I do." Angie gave him an angelic smile. "All you have to do is convince Evelyn she's no longer needed to herd sheep, and she won't have an excuse to stay up in the mountains."

Chapter 10

Evelyn knew the minute that Cole rounded the bend because Blue Boy gave a short yelp in greeting and started wagging his tail. The sheep dog had never taken to anybody as quickly as he had to Cole.

Heart beating out a happy dance, she kept stirring the pot of stew over the open fire. Why was she so happy to see him? She needed to get her emotions under control. As soon as the cattle showed up, he'd herd them through the pass and would forget all about her. She'd likely never see him again unless he just decided to drop in at church on Sundays, about the only day she was in town herself.

Blue Boy's tail wagged faster and faster as Cole and the pack train drew closer. Unable to help herself, Evelyn glanced up. As expected, Cole rode into view, leading Billy's pack animals loaded down with the weekly supplies needed for the herders scattered throughout the mountain meadows.

But she didn't expect the jolt that seeing him gave her stomach.

And she didn't expect to see the two boys riding alongside him, grinning from ear to ear.

"James? John?" Evelyn straightened, shading her eyes against the sunlight. "What are you boys doing here?"

The boys slid off their mounts and ran toward her. John, the spokesman of the two, blurted out, "We're here to learn how to herd sheep."

Evelyn glanced at Cole. "Herd sheep?"

He shrugged then dismounted. "Your grandfather and Reverend Weaver thought they'd enjoy it." Cole dismounted. "Billy could use the help, and these two might stay out of trouble for the summer."

"I see."

"Sheepherders, huh?" Billy joined them, a stout walking stick in his hand, Skittles close to his side. He leaned down and scowled at the boys. "What do you know about sheep?"

James and John faced Billy, mute.

"I see." Billy slapped his hands on his knees. "Well, nothing like the present to find out. Come on."

At Cole's nod of encouragement, the boys followed Billy as he walked toward the flock of sheep. "You boys mind Mr. Billy, now, you hear?"

"Did you see my grandparents?"

"Yes. We stopped by on our way out of town. Your grandmother was disappointed that you didn't make it home but said she understood."

"And Grandpa?"

"He's getting around much better. I think he would have headed this way himself, but when he saw the boys with me, he simmered down. Said they'd be a big help, much like you used to be in the summers."

"I used to love to spend the summers with Grandpa up here. Not that I got to spend the entire summer with him, but I'd beg and beg, and finally Granny would relent." She smiled, stirring the stew. "I looked on it as a big adventure, but looking back, I remember Grandpa napping under the wagon in the afternoons. He'd tell me that I was on guard, and that if anything happened, I was to wake him immediately. I felt so important. I'd take the dogs, walk among the sheep, making sure none wandered off. Rarely did anything happen. It was years before I realized that Grandpa was up and about all during the night while I slept."

"Was it the sheep, your grandfather, or the mountains you loved being around?"

Evelyn looked around at the wide-open valley stretched before her. She smiled. "All of it. I just love being up here away from people. And I love the sheep."

Cole grabbed one of the packs and brought it over to the fire. "I have to say the constant bleating of the sheep would drive me crazy."

"Don't cows bellow a lot?"

He glanced at her, a funny look on his face. "I can't say I've ever noticed it, but yeah, I guess they do when they're hungry or thirsty or when we're on a cattle drive. But other than that, they're pretty quiet."

"It's the same with the sheep. Like now. They're quiet because they're napping. Just like Grandpa used to do."

"I reckon you get used to their routine just like you do with cattle." Cole cleared his throat and moved to her side. "Evelyn, I know you said you didn't want to go to the picnic, but will you reconsider now that the boys are here to help Billy? Everybody's expecting you to be there."

"Everybody? Or just Mrs. Michum and Mrs. Vincent?"

His blue eyes searched hers. "Why can't you just go to the picnic and enjoy it without worrying what they might think?"

She shrugged, unable to tell him the truth.

He reached for her and turned her to face him, a deep V pulling his brows down in a frown. "Evelyn, it occurs to me that I might have overstepped in assuming you didn't want to go to the picnic with Hiram Danvers."

She shook her head. "No, you didn't overstep."

"Then, I'm asking you again." His gaze searched hers, and she couldn't look away. "Will you go to the picnic with me?"

"Why?" Her breath caught in her throat.

"Because I want to see you in that pretty red dress your grandmother is making."

"You do?"

"I do." He tipped her chin up then lowered his mouth to hers. Evelyn sighed as his lips closed over hers in a kiss as sweet as the clear mountain air surrounding them.

◆—•——•◆

Cole couldn't wait to get back to Evelyn's camp. He tried to convince himself that he needed to see how the boys had gotten along, but the truth was that he wanted to see Evelyn. He'd thought of little else in the five days he'd been gone.

When he rode in, the camp was neat and tidy. The rain had moved out, and the mountainside had bloomed with flowers and fresh green grass. The boys regaled him with tales of what all they'd learned since he'd been gone, and Evelyn smiled shyly at him when she served up beans and corn bread.

The next morning, Cole and Evelyn rode down the mountain, and he left her at her grandparents with a promise to see her the next day at the picnic.

After dropping off Billy's pack mules at the livery stable, he headed to his Aunt Lily's. He rapped on the door, and she let him in.

"Cole, so good to have you back. How are the boys?"

"They seemed to be enjoying themselves. I imagine they'll be tired of sheepherding in another week, though."

She eyed him up and down, wrinkling her nose. "You could use a shave and haircut as well as a shower if you're going to attend the picnic tomorrow."

"I was thinking the same thing."

"Well, come on in to the kitchen, and I'll heat some water."

The aroma of cinnamon, sugar, and butter made his mouth water. He reached for the door on the pie safe. "It smells good in here. Is that apple pie?"

"Don't you touch it. That pie is for the picnic tomorrow. I've got some leftover ham and biscuits in the pantry. But"—she pointed to the enclosed back porch, one eyebrow raised—"get cleaned up first."

"Yes, ma'am."

Two hours later, he was clean and shaved, and his aunt had plopped him in a chair in the backyard right off the kitchen, snipping at his hair. He closed his eyes and let her do her magic, glad not to have to pay a barber for the service.

"There you go. All done." Aunt Lily whipped the bedsheet off him. "You're all ready for your big day tomorrow."

"My big day?" Cole stood, lifted a hand to his neck, his fingers touching the bristly strands in the back.

"Well, of course." She flapped the sheet and tufts of his hair fell to the ground. "You'll have the prettiest girl in Burnt Sage, Wyoming, on your arm, and, well—"

"And well, what?"

"Nothing." His aunt shrugged. "I was just woolgathering. It's nothing. Really."

"Aunt Lily. . ."

"Oh, all right." His aunt folded the sheet, looking uncomfortable with the conversation. "Did you know Ollie was engaged to Evelyn when we moved here?"

"I heard about it." Cole wasn't sure how much his aunt knew about what had transpired, and he didn't feel at liberty to share what Ollie and Angie had told him, so he didn't add more.

"Well, there's something strange about Evelyn calling off the wedding like she did.

Just up and left Ollie standing at the altar and all. I've always wondered. . . ." Aunt Lily pursed her lips. "Well, that's neither here nor there. What's done is done, and it worked out for the best, I suppose. But Evelyn is a sweet girl, and I'm so happy that you see what I see in her. She deserves a special day and a day to show those—"

"Cole!" Ollie rode into the yard. "I'm glad to see you here. Mr. Mangrum arrived in town earlier today. He wants to see you first thing in the morning."

"This is wonderful. Where's he staying?"

"At Mrs. Michum's boardinghouse."

Bright and early the next morning, Cole knocked on Mrs. Michum's front door.

"Mr. Rawlins."

"Ma'am." Cole whipped off his hat. "May I come in?"

"Of course." She swung the door wide. "You're here to see Mr. Mangrum?"

"Yes, ma'am."

She led the way into the parlor. "I'm afraid he isn't feeling well, but—"

"Cole?"

Cole turned at the familiar voice. "Helen! I didn't know you were coming with your father." Quickly, he crossed the room, and Helen lifted her cheek for a kiss. Cole obliged. "How is he? Mrs. Michum said he's not feeling well."

Helen patted his arm. "Oh, he'll be fine. Just too much of Mrs. Michum's fine cooking last night, if I don't miss my guess."

Mrs. Michum preened at the compliment. "Speaking of cooking, I'd better get back to the kitchen. I've got a cobbler in the oven."

Cole turned back to Helen. "Maybe I should come back later after Mr. Mangrum is feeling better."

"That might be best." Helen arched a delicate brow. "But in the meantime, Mrs. Michum tells me that Burnt Sage is having a delightful picnic today to celebrate Independence Day."

"Would you like to attend? I'm heading that way soon myself."

Helen beamed. "Oh, Cole, I'd love to. Will you wait while I get ready?"

"Of course. Take your time."

Chapter 11

Evelyn made five trips from the wagon to the picnic tables with food that she and her grandmother had spent the entire morning preparing. She tried not to be too obvious as she searched the scattered groups of men for Cole.

"Evelyn!"

She turned to see Angie hurrying toward her. Angie hugged her then held her at arm's length. "You look stunning! Red is definitely your color. Wait until Cole sees you in that dress."

Evelyn blushed at the compliment and looked down at her new dress, the first she'd had in ages. Her grandmother had taken pains to add little touches of ribbon and lace, giving it an extra special flair. She'd even sewn white eyelet around the neckline and threaded thin blue ribbon through it, tying a bow front and center. She felt feminine and very patriotic. "Do you think he'll like it?"

"Of course he will." Angie grinned. "He won't be able to keep his eyes off you."

Evelyn blushed, remembering the way Cole's eyes *had* lingered on her, the touch of his lips on hers. Her gaze swept over the tables set up between the church and the creek. People were arriving from all around Burnt Sage, families in farm wagons, buggies, horseback, and on foot. But Cole was nowhere to be seen. The butterflies in Evelyn's stomach took a nosedive. "Maybe he decided not to come—"

"No, it's nothing like that. Remember Mr. Mangrum, the man who's going to help Cole get started in the cattle business? Well, he arrived yesterday and is staying at Mrs. Michum's. He wanted to see Cole this morning. Cole will be along shortly."

"Oh." Evelyn didn't take time to examine her relief.

Angie gave her a teasing smile. "Were you afraid he might not come?"

"It did occur to me."

"Cole wouldn't do that. He likes you. And. . ." Angie searched her gaze. "You like him, too, don't you?"

"Of course I like him."

"Enough to marry him if he asked?"

Evelyn's mouth fell open. "I don't think we know each other well enough for that."

"Sometimes it doesn't take long to know you're meant for each other."

"And sometimes it takes longer than you'd think. I don't want to make the same mistake I made—" She bit her lip, face heating up. "Before."

"You mean with Ollie? Ollie wasn't a mistake. I have no doubt the two of you would have been very happy had I not come along when I did. But I'm glad things turned out like they did." Angie hugged her.

"Me, too."

Two years had shown her a lot. Enough to know that she cared for Ollie as a friend but not as a husband.

"I just wish you wouldn't take all the responsibility for what happened on your own shoulders."

"It's better this way. You know how Mrs. Michum is. She would have crucified Ollie if he'd been the one to call off the wedding." Evelyn couldn't help but smile. "But I'm like the prickly pear. I can take her needling."

"Evelyn, you shouldn't say such things." Angie swatted Evelyn on the arm as the two of them shared a laugh. A faint cry drew their attention, and Evelyn looked up to see Ollie threading his way through the crowd, a red-faced and very unhappy baby clutched against his side. He juggled the baby, his frantic gaze searching for Angie. Spotting her, he headed their way, Rebecca's cries growing louder with every step. "I've got to go. Looks like Rebecca wants her mama."

"Go, take care of that sweet baby. I need to help Granny put out the rest of the food."

Evelyn spent the next half hour draping tables with sheets, arranging pots of dump-lings, fried chicken, pork chops, corn bread, and an endless array of vegetables. Her mouth watered when she placed her grandmother's burnt-sugar cake on the dessert table.

"Oh, my, look at all these many desserts." Angie's mother plopped an apple pie on the table with a flourish. "Honestly, I'm tempted to just skip the main meal and go straight for the desserts."

Several ladies laughed as she reached for Granny's cake. "I'll just take this and go hide under a wagon."

Angie sidled up to her mother, the now-content baby sleeping in her arms. "Let me get a fork, Mama, and I'll go with you."

"Make that two," someone chimed in.

Evelyn smiled at the good-natured ribbing as the women cut the cakes and pies and finished getting the meal ready for the picnic.

Finally, Mrs. Weaver stepped back and placed her hands on her hips. "Well, ladies, I think we have everything ready. I'll find that preacher husband of mine and ask him to bless the food so we can eat. I've worked up quite an appetite this morning."

Angie pulled Evelyn to the side. "Did you bring a quilt?"

"A quilt?" Evelyn frowned. "What for?"

"For your picnic with Cole." Angie all but rolled her eyes. "Oh, never mind. I brought an extra just in case. I'll give it to Cole and tell him to find a quiet spot for you two."

"Angie!" Evelyn hissed, feeling a blush swoosh across her cheeks.

"Shh! Father's saying the blessing."

Evelyn clamped her mouth shut and closed her eyes as Reverend Weaver blessed the food. But she couldn't close her mind or corral the butterflies that had taken flight in her stomach at Angie's teasing.

Would Cole find a secluded spot for them away from the others? Or would he put the quilt down next to her grandparents, or even close to his uncle and aunt? Would his actions determine how he felt about her?

By the time Reverend Weaver finished the blessing, Evelyn's stomach was tied up in knots. She didn't even know if she'd be able to eat anything at all, and she still hadn't seen Cole. Maybe he'd gotten tied up with Mr. Mangrum and wouldn't be able to make it after all.

Her stomach roiled. No, she wouldn't borrow trouble. He'd be here. He'd promised. She stood back out of the way as the crowd jostled for position along the tables, filling their plates. And that's when she saw him. He alighted from a well-appointed buggy then reached up to help someone down.

A woman. A stranger. A beautiful woman with hair as smooth- and silky-looking as the top of her grandmother's burnt-sugar cake, her tiny waist accentuated by the elegant cut of her dark blue dress. She paused on the steps of the buggy, her gaze taking in the festivities. Her dress looked like silk, or taffeta, or something that Evelyn's rough fingers would rip to shreds.

The woman smiled and said something to Cole. Then he lifted her down as if she weighed nothing and tucked her hand into the crook of his arm.

As he turned, the crooked smile on his face that Evelyn had learned to adore, she faded back behind the crowd, heart pounding.

Chapter 12

Cole escorted Helen toward the crowd. "Come on, there's someone I'd like you to meet."

"A girl?" Helen teased.

"As a matter of fact, yes."

"It's about time you settled down." Helen patted his arm, smiling.

Cole searched the crowd for Evelyn but didn't see her. He made the rounds, introducing Helen to his aunt and uncle, to Evelyn's grandparents, to others he'd met in the few short weeks he'd been here.

She'd already met Mrs. Michum, but as he wove through the crowd, there were others who wanted to welcome her to town. They all expressed concern over Mr. Mangrum's health and hoped he'd be well enough to attend church on Sunday.

But Evelyn was nowhere to be found.

He spotted Angie holding Rebecca as Ollie spread a quilt in the shade of a large oak. He led Helen over to them.

"Helen, this is my cousin Angie Rodgers and her husband, Ollie." Cole tickled the baby under her chin. "And this little cutie is their daughter, Rebecca. Angie, this is Mr. Mangrum's daughter, Helen."

"Delighted to meet you, Angie." Helen nodded at Angie and the baby. Rebecca squealed and reached for her. Laughing, Helen held out her arms. "Oh, she's adorable. May I?"

Angie smiled. "Of course, Miss Mangrum."

"It's Mrs. Secrest. But, please, call me Helen."

"Angie, have you seen Evelyn? I've looked all over for her."

"The last time I saw her, she was over by the tables helping her grandmother get the food on the table for the picnic. And before I forget," Angie reached for a quilt and shoved it at him. "Why don't you find a nice quiet spot for yours and Evelyn's picnic. Somewhere down there, perhaps." Eyes twinkling, she pointed at a grove of trees down by the creek. "Mrs. Secrest, you're welcome to share our quilt."

Helen hugged the baby to her. "I'd be delighted to spend more time with this little darling. Now, Cole, run along and find this mystery woman of yours. I can't wait to meet her."

Cole made the rounds, not finding Evelyn anywhere. He spotted Mrs. Arnold and Mrs. Michum in line. He headed toward them. Maybe Evelyn's grandmother knew where Evelyn had gotten off to. "Mrs. Arnold, ladies."

"Oh, Cole, we thought everyone had gone through the line already." Mrs. Arnold handed him a plate and reached for another one. "Where's Evelyn? I thought—"

"That's what I came over here for. Have you seen her?"

"She was here just a moment ago."

Mrs. Michum's gaze swept the sea of faces, then widened. "Minnie, where is that granddaughter of yours?" Her eyes widened even more. "Surely she hasn't—"

"Hasn't what, Dottie?" Evelyn's grandmother glared at Mrs. Michum.

Mrs. Michum huffed. "Well, Minnie, she does have a tendency to run off, doesn't she? She ran out on Ollie on their wedding day, and now she's done the same thing to this nice young man."

"Begging your pardon, ma'am, but this isn't our wedding day," Cole interjected, hoping to head off the woman's barbed comments.

"That might be true, but maybe it's for the best." Mrs. Michum tilted her chin up as those around them stopped filling their plates and listened. "Leaving one man at the altar is enough, don't you think? Better this happened now rather than later. Embarrassing poor Ollie like that in front of the whole town—"

"That's enough." Ollie stood there, Angie at his side. He looked around then at Angie. She nodded. Taking a deep breath, Ollie turned back to Mrs. Michum. "Mrs. Michum, Evelyn called off our wedding because she realized that I was falling in love with Angie, and she didn't want to stand in the way of my happiness."

"And she made us promise not to tell anyone why she'd done it." Angie stepped forward, her gaze firmly planted on Mrs. Michum. "She didn't want blame to be cast on Ollie. So if you want to talk about anybody, talk about me."

"Or me. Not Evelyn." Ollie moved to Angie's side and wrapped an arm around her waist.

Mrs. Michum's mouth opened and closed like a fish left on the bank, gasping for breath. Finally, she huffed and stalked off in a fit of embarrassment. "Well, I never."

Angie's mother glared at her daughter and son-in-law. "Well, it took you two long enough to break your silence."

Ollie's mouth flattened into a thin line, his gaze on Mrs. Michum's retreating back. "I should have done it from the get-go."

Angie pulled Cole to the side. "I think I know why Evelyn left so quickly."

Evelyn rode along the trail toward the line shack, fighting the tears that threatened to blind her to the rough path.

She was right back where she'd been two years ago, but this time her heart was involved. She'd told Angie that she liked Cole, but that wasn't exactly true. She more than liked him. She was falling in love with him.

She choked back a sob. Wouldn't Mrs. Michum have something to talk about now? Evelyn had thrown Ollie over and then spurned Hiram Danvers in favor of a handsome newcomer. It didn't matter that Cole had only asked her to the picnic at Angie's urging and to keep Hiram Danvers out of the picture. Mrs. Michum would spin the tale in whatever way would get the most mileage as far as gossip was concerned.

It wasn't that Mrs. Michum hated her. Evelyn knew that. The woman just thrived on gossip, and Evelyn had been her target since the wedding fiasco.

Evelyn could hear it now.

How she'd got her comeuppance.

What goes around, comes around.

Yep, that's exactly what Mrs. Michum would say.

And she'd be right.

Evelyn had let herself dream of a future with Cole. But it had been a foolish dream. It was better to surround her heart with the thorns of a prickly pear than to fall in love with Cole, only to have him throw her over for someone else.

The line shack came into view, and she slowed her mount, swiped at her tears, and took a deep breath. She dismounted, but instead of heading inside, she walked down the grassy knoll toward the bend in the creek where she'd first met Cole.

She wrapped her arms around her waist, the tips of her fingers pressing against the crisp feel of her new dress, and let the tears flow.

"Evelyn?"

Her heart stuttered at Cole's voice. Swiping at her face, she tried to erase the evidence of her tears. She didn't turn around. "You shouldn't have come."

"I thought you might need rescuing." His voice was closer, and he sounded amused.

Evelyn shook her head. "Not this time."

"I disagree."

His voice sounded so close that she was certain if she turned, she could reach out and touch him. But she didn't turn. He put his hands on her shoulders, and fresh tears sprang to her eyes. Why had he come? Why hadn't he stayed at the picnic with the beautiful woman on his arm instead of coming up the mountain to find a poor sheep-herder who spent her days wearing her grandfather's worn-out britches and patched and tattered shirts?

Gently turning her to face him, he tipped her chin up with his thumb and forefinger, forcing her to look at him. His blue eyes, as bright as the sky overhead, searched hers. "Why'd you run away?"

She shrugged then whispered, "Who is she?"

A chuckle rumbled up through his chest. A spark of indignation flared in her chest, and she glared at him. "It's not funny."

He schooled his features, but a hint of amusement still lingered about his lips. "She's my boss's daughter. And she's married. Very, very happily married."

A ray of hope pierced the gloom lodged in Evelyn's chest. "She is?"

His gaze swept over her face, and he reached up to smooth back a strand of her hair. Evelyn shivered at his touch. "Yes. Mr. Mangrum wasn't feeling well, and I offered to escort Helen to the picnic. I've known her and her husband since we were kids—a lot like you and Ollie—and she's dying to meet you."

"She is?"

"Is that all you can say?" He arched a brow.

Evelyn laughed then winced. "I'm sorry I took off, and now Mrs. Michum has something else to talk about."

"Actually, Ollie is now the object of Mrs. Michum's gossip. He told everyone why you called off the wedding."

"He did?" Evelyn frowned. "He promised—"

"Ollie Rodgers can take care of himself." Cole snaked an arm around her waist and pulled her closer. All thoughts of Ollie, Mrs. Michum, Angie, or anyone else, fled. "Right now I want to talk about us."

"Us?"

"Yes, us." He grinned, the dimple she loved popping out on his cheek. "Actually, we can talk later."

And then he kissed her, right there on the banks of Prickly Pear Creek.

CBA bestselling author **Pam Hillman** was born and raised on a dairy farm in Mississippi and spent her teenage years perched on the seat of a tractor raking hay. In those days, her daddy couldn't afford two cab tractors with air conditioning and a radio, so Pam drove an Allis Chalmers 110. Even when her daddy asked her if she wanted to bale hay, she told him she didn't mind raking. Raking hay doesn't take much thought so Pam spent her time working on her tan and making up stories in her head. Now, that's the kind of life every girl should dream of. Visit www.pamhillman.com.

The Widow of St. Charles Avenue

by Grace Hitchcock

Dedication

For Dakota, my inspiration for all heroes.

Acknowledgments

To my agent, Tamela Hancock Murray, for her encouragement and dedication; to Becky for believing in this debut author; to my faithful betas, Theresa and McKenna, and my critique partner, Ramona, for their sincere feedback; to my husband and family for always supporting my writing; and to the Lord for His steadfastness.

"I am the bread of life. Whoever comes to me will never go hungry, and whoever believes in me will never be thirsty."
JOHN 6:35 NIV

Chapter 1

May 1895
New Orleans, Louisiana

F or goodness' sake, smile a little. You'll insult our hostess," her sister whispered,
giving her a poke with her silk fan.

Colette Olivier pasted on a smile, hoping she appeared to be enjoying mingling with the other dinner guests.

Julia rolled her eyes. "Have you completely forgotten how to act? As the wife of Robert Olivier, you were one of the most influential socialites. What happened to your confidence and blasé demeanor?"

"It's been over a year and a half since I've truly been out in society," Colette returned, smoothing the front of her blush frock, "so I'm a little out of practice." *And I was only a glowing socialite because Robert wanted me to be. If it were up to me, I would have stayed at home half the time with a good book and a cup of white tea,* she thought. "I wish I hadn't let you dress me in such a vibrant color. Did you see the looks I received at dinner? Honestly, I feel as if every lady in the room is judging me," Colette whispered, her pale cheeks turning warm. She tucked back a golden strand that had managed to escape her austere, high coiffure, which she was certain Julia would've altered as well if they hadn't run out of time. *At least the ladies might've thought my hairstyle befitting a widow, if only it didn't refuse to stay in place.*

"I know. I'm sorry I cajoled you out of your plum gown and into one of my own." She sighed. "Everyone knows that such a young widow isn't expected to complete the *full* two years in mourning. It's not as if you are shaming your husband's memory by accepting an invitation for a dinner party. The socialites are only upset because their daughters will have to compete with a rich widow for a husband sooner than anticipated."

Colette glanced up and saw yet another gentleman advancing to greet her now that her gown announced her return to society and the market.

"I'm beginning to understand some of the benefits of mourning colors. Do you want me to divert him?" Julia flicked open her fan.

"Please, divert away!"

"Mr. Carlson," her sister drawled as she grasped his arm and steered him in the opposite direction. "Have you tasted the pastries? Mrs. Lemoine's Italian chef makes a positively delectable cannoli."

Wishing with all her heart to blend into the room as she usually did, Colette poured herself a cup of coffee and, smiling to the hostess, sank into an armless chair in the farthest corner of the parlor. Closing her eyes to the fearsome glares of the older socialites, she inhaled the deep scent of chicory, praying for strength to make it through the rest of the evening.

"Why, Miss Fontaine! It's still Miss Fontaine, isn't it?" A deep voice broke her reverie.

Startled, she met the hazel eyes of her childhood friend Norman. "Mr. Hartley! What a pleasure." She stood and gave him a curtsy, careful not to spill her coffee. "But, I'm called Mrs. Robert Olivier now."

"*Mrs. Olivier?* Ah. Well, I can't say I'm surprised you were snatched up." He smiled, disappointment edging his words. "I haven't seen Robert in years. He and my father were friends back in their days at the university, so I know Father would be glad to hear of our meeting again. Where is old Robert anyway? Still stuck at the office?"

I knew I shouldn't have let Julia talk me into this dress. Anyone who saw me yesterday would've known not to ask. Longing for the comfort of her dark gown, she took a deep breath. "My husband passed almost two years ago. He was involved in a boating accident." At Norman's look of abject shock, she lifted her hand to halt his oncoming apology. "Please, don't be distressed in your inquiry. You happened to find me on my first attempt at attending a dinner party out of mourning colors." She laughed softly as she regarded the room. "But, I'm afraid, I may have startled some of the other ladies with my choice."

"I'm sorry if I caused you pain," he sighed as he raked his hands through his blond hair, "but I think it would've been a pity to deprive society of seeing you in such a sweet color that sets off those crystal-blue eyes I remember so well."

She felt her neck grow warm. It had been so many years since he'd left for New York that she'd forgotten how his flattery affected her. "You haven't changed a bit. You always were ready with a compliment. So, tell me, what brings you to New Orleans?"

"That would take a bit to explain. May I call on you? It's been far too long since we've last visited."

She glanced across the room at Julia, who gave her a small nod of encouragement as if she were reading Norman's lips. "I think it would be splendid." Colette smiled up at him, thinking how the past six years made him even more handsome as he had matured into a man. "How does afternoon tea next Saturday sound? Your aunt has my address."

"I'd be honored." Norman gave a little bow. "It'll be like old times."

A touch of mischief played at the corner of her lips. "In which case, I'll have the cook retrieve the pecans out of the storage pantry and make you some of those praline confections you loved so much as a boy." She caught sight of the whisking fans of the ladies in the corner with their heads together, chatting as they gawked in her direction.

Colette's stomach turned. *What am I thinking? I can't have a caller so soon.* She snapped open her fan to hide from the scrutiny of the other women. "I'm afraid I'm feeling a little tired and must fetch my sister home, but I look forward to continuing our conversation and hearing all of your news."

"And I yours. My mouth is already watering for those pralines." Norman reached for her gloved hand, pressing a kiss atop before she slipped away.

Wrapped in her cloak, Colette exhaled as she and Julia leaned against the tufted leather seats of her carriage. "Thank goodness that's over."

"You were splendid," Julia gushed, giving a little clap. "Not that I'm a bit surprised. But *Norman Hartley* returns for not even a day and he already asks to call? To have that kind of talent to call upon. . ." She looked heavenward and inhaled. "I would be jealous if not for your history."

"Julia. . . ," she cautioned.

"What?" Julia raised her brows. "Norman was only twenty when he left for New York, and I distinctly remember him tearing up at our gate when he came to say good-bye. I was surprised he didn't marry you then and there and take you with him."

"While he did shed a tear, it was because we had been best friends since childhood." Colette smiled at the sweet memory as she stared out of the carriage window at the mansions on St. Charles Avenue, gaslights streaming through the windows.

Norman, her boy next door, had been the most eligible bachelor in New Orleans when she had first come out into society, but when he had moved to New York for business without asking for her hand in marriage, her parents gave up trying to match them. She had known long before her parents that while Norman may have liked her and maybe even loved her for a brief moment, he couldn't afford to marry a highborn girl who wouldn't raise his wealth with a significant inheritance. She'd understood then, and she wasn't about to become a romantic like Julia and envision a life with Norman now that their paths had crossed once again.

"He simply wishes to chat, so I won't have you getting your hopes up for anything more," she admonished Julia's enthusiasm. "I'm not that girl anymore who gets sweaty palms and a racing heart at the mere thought of Norman Hartley coming to call. I don't expect anything to come from it, and besides, he's probably seeing someone."

"I checked with his sister for you and he *isn't*. I'm so happy you're getting on with your life and receiving a caller. You are far too beautiful to let yourself wilt away in your widow's weeds." Julia grasped Colette's hands, squeezing them. "Now that you've captured the attention of the dazzling, wealthy Mr. Hartley at long last, you can help your baby sister find her own beau."

"Well, since I have my husband's fortune, I don't necessarily *need* to marry," Colette reminded her as the carriage rolled to a stop in front of the impressive Olivier estate.

"Why wouldn't you wish to remarry?" Julia twirled through the door with her hands clasped above her heart. "To love and be loved is all I could ever want in life."

"Just take care to fall in love with a man who can always keep you dressed in the latest of fashions," Colette teased as she pulled the tie from her cloak, glancing down at her borrowed gown. "Speaking of fashion, I'll need to make an appointment with the dressmaker for a new wardrobe." She handed her cloak to the maid, murmuring, "Thank you, Belinda."

Julia smirked at Colette's concession. "I knew you were ready to come back to society. All it took was a little bit of color to bring you to life and a beau to your parlor."

"I feel so strange attending social events three months early. I fear what people will say." She rubbed her forehead. "Maybe I should wait on ordering those gowns."

Julia gave an unladylike growl of frustration as she kicked off her blue silk evening slippers. She carried them into the parlor, where she sank onto the red-and-gold settee as Colette chose Robert's old, oversize leather wingback chair. "People shouldn't judge you." Julia scowled. "You're too young to be so secluded from society."

"People will always judge a widow returning to society no matter her age, but I suppose you're right about getting out more. However, I don't want to be besieged with desperate bachelors who are fortune hunting. I'm not ready." She groaned as she, too, slipped off her shoes. Tucking her legs beneath her, she gazed into the glowing fireplace, which was lit more for ambiance than practicality in the warm New Orleans' night air. "I'm just thankful I can attend church without scorn. Those first few months after Robert's death were wretched, forced to being isolated and discouraged from even attending service."

"Hmm." Julia tapped her chin. "Well, what if you get involved in church as a means to ease into society again? You could volunteer as a Sunday school teacher or something of the sort. If I recall, you used to love working for charity and—" She left off her sentence as the maid rolled in the tea service. "Ah, lovely." Julia reached for the pot without waiting for Colette to formally do the honors and poured herself a cup, plunking four lumps of sugar into her tea. When the maid closed the door, she continued, "Why did you stop volunteering in the first place?"

Colette watched the steam curl as she slowly poured and considered revealing her secret. Leaning back, she took a long sip. "When Father presented me with Robert, I didn't allow myself to question if marrying an unbeliever was best because Father said it didn't matter. . .but it did. I should've prayed for guidance before I married Robert, but instead, I followed Father's advice without question." She looked down at her tea and swirled the dregs around in the cup. "My whole life I was told that as merely a woman, I wouldn't know what was best for my future and that I must listen, but I should've listened to the Lord."

"But, Robert wasn't harsh, was he?" Julia pressed her hand to her heart at the news of her sister's less-than-happy marriage.

"Robert was kind when we were courting, and because he thought me pretty, he didn't mind my small inheritance," she answered, stroking the handle of her teacup with her thumb, "but after we married, he became very strict. Things grew difficult when Robert stopped attending service. It created a barrier in our relationship, but I had hope that he'd eventually come with me again until one evening when I came home late from volunteering. Robert had made spontaneous plans for us to dine with a potential investor and his wife, which I ruined by not being home and not leaving a note letting him know where I was working that day. He was so angry that he forbade me from ever serving again."

Julia dropped her teacup in the saucer, sloshing its contents. "I didn't know. I thought you gave it up because you were too busy being a wife to Robert, and now to hear. . . No wonder you don't wish to marry again. Why did you wait so long to tell me?"

"Because I was ashamed," Colette admitted. "And I didn't return to my charity work after his death out of respect to his memory. I long to go back, but I still feel so trapped by his and society's disapproval. I never was good enough in their eyes for Robert and his fortune, and tonight probably solidified their opinion of me by my attempting to come out of mourning three months early." She took a sip of tea to steady her nerves. "But, maybe it's time I go against his wishes and volunteer again."

Julia reached out and gently squeezed her arm. "You should. Write to the pastor tonight and see what happens. If Norman doesn't cause your heart to pitter-patter anymore, which I doubt because the man is almost prettier than you, maybe you'll meet someone through the church who will steal your heart right out of your chest before you even know it's in danger."

✦━━━●━━✦

The doorbell rang again. "Belinda?" Colette called up the stairs as loudly as she dared for fear of being overheard by the guest at the door. *Where is everyone? I need to dress for dinner.* After waiting another minute for the maid or butler to appear, she smoothed down any strands of escaped hair and opened the door herself.

A tall, ruggedly handsome man stood on the porch, and upon seeing Colette, he swiped off his hat, revealing his unruly auburn curls as he gave a small bow. "Good morning, ma'am. I'm Malcolm Reilly. Pastor Wilson mentioned you were keen on teaching Sunday school?"

"Uh, yes," she started, unsure of why he was asking.

He brandished a letter from his coat pocket. "This is from Mrs. Wilson, explaining why I am at your door."

Goodness, already? It's only been three days. "Yes, thank you." She accepted the letter. "I'm sorry. Where are my manners? Won't you come inside?" Colette asked, holding the door open.

He gestured to the clear blue sky. "It's a beautiful day. Why don't we sit on the porch? I'd hate to trudge any dirt into your parlor. I came from the warehouse district, as I was out of the office today observing the workers and am not parlor friendly at the moment."

Colette's gaze fell on his filthy work boots. "Oh, yes. Please, do sit down." She stepped out onto the veranda and sank onto a wicker chair as she broke the sealed letter and scanned it. "You're the pastor's son?"

"Yes, ma'am," he replied as he rubbed the brim of his hat.

I wonder why he doesn't go by the same surname. Memories of the wild pastor's son dipping her curls in ink flooded her memory. Smiling at the recollection, she wondered if he knew that she was the victim of half a dozen of his antics as she motioned for him to continue. "Please, tell me about your Sunday school class."

"Well," he chuckled, "it's more of a Bible class since we meet on Friday afternoon because the children attend their own service on Sunday. I was hoping to find another teacher to help me restore order. The boys can get quite rowdy."

"Boys?" Her voice squeaked.

He grinned at her surprise, causing her heart to jump unexpectedly at the sight of his dimpled cheeks. "Yes, I teach the ten- to fourteen-year-old boys over at St. Mary's Orphanage. Mother left that out of the letter?"

"Ah." She inhaled through her teeth. "I had thought I'd be teaching the young ladies of the church as I'd have more to offer with my finishing school experience." She cleared her throat as she folded up the letter, disappointed that she wouldn't begin serving so soon after all.

He leaned forward in his chair. "You see, that's where I think you aren't giving yourself enough credit. Most of these boys only have the influence of their male teachers and a handful of nuns who work so hard that they don't have as much time as they'd like to nurture the boys. I believe you'll provide a calming presence and teach them how to behave in front of a lady, which"—he smiled—"the nuns will appreciate."

She gave a short, disbelieving laugh. *Either he has vastly overestimated my skills, or he is desperate, but I can't possibly work with a man. Mother would have an attack.* "Be that as it may—"

He held up a large, rough hand. "At least come with me one time on Friday before you turn it down altogether. I promise that when you meet these boys, you won't ever want to leave them."

She felt her resolution waver at his confidence. *Well, maybe just this once, and with the nuns present, I'm sure it'll be more than proper.* "What time shall I meet you?"

Chapter 2

W here are you going, Mr. Reilly?" Colette called to him as he passed the waiting carriage in front of her mansion.

"I thought we'd take the streetcar to the orphanage," Malcolm replied, shifting her heavy-laden basket of baked goods in his grip. "No sense in having your driver wait for over two hours while we give our first lesson together."

Colette swallowed at the thought of taking public transportation. Even though the St. Charles Avenue line had a stop steps from her drive, she had never needed to use it, and Robert would've never approved even if she had. "Is it, uh, quite safe?" she questioned, as she hadn't been on the newfangled electric line yet since it was installed right before Robert's accident.

Malcolm laughed and offered her his elbow to cross the street. "It's much faster than the old bobtail line and safer, as we don't have to rely on the whims of the mules, but we can take a hired carriage back if you discover it is too much."

Waiting on the neutral ground, Colette judged the safety of the red streetcar as it screeched to a halt. Malcolm handed her the basket, stepped up to pay for their passage, and then extended his hand down to her. Stepping inside, she eyed the wooden seats, searching for a spot with the least amount of grime.

Malcolm's eyes laughed at her as he waited for her to choose a row and set her basket of baked goods beside her before he took the seat opposite. The streetcar jerked as it began rolling down the line, swaying with each turn of the wheel. She gripped the windowsill, grateful that all the windows seemed permanently lowered to allow the fresh, humid air, and not the scent of the passengers, to fill her lungs.

To distract herself from becoming sick from the motion, she attempted to break the awkward silence of being alone in public with a man she hadn't spoken to since she was a girl. "So, what caused you to become interested in teaching Sunday school to orphans, Mr. Reilly? Even if you are the son of a pastor, most young men I know are more interested in their horses, stocks, and planning their next hunting trips on their time off." *Besides, you were hardly pastoral when you were busy tying Theresa Ann's and my braids together in Sunday school class.*

Malcolm grinned, his dimples causing her heart to dip. "Well, it may help explain things in that I don't live on St. Charles Avenue or Royal Street as your acquaintances do. I was raised at St. Mary's Orphanage until I was ten, when Mr. and Mrs. Wilson adopted me."

Attempting to conceal her shock in not recalling that rather sizable detail, she dropped her gaze and smoothed her dove-gray skirt, unsure of what to say next. "So that's why you serve at an orphanage?"

He nodded. "After I was adopted, we continued to serve at the orphanages weekly, and through my time under the Wilsons' wing, I realized education would be the only way of giving myself a fighting chance to make something of myself. Even though I'm now the son of a pastor, people still see me as the orphan waif of very low birth."

Colette wished she could negate his statement, but she knew society was ruthless in whom they accepted as worthy in their circles.

"Because of the many charities my parents supported, money was always tight, so when Miss Sophie Wright opened her free night school for young men, I was one of the first in attendance. In her classes, I began to dream of becoming a teacher to the lower classes, but as that required more training than I was receiving, I settled for working as one of the clerks in the shipping office until I can save enough money to attend college classes and earn my teacher's certificate."

Respect for this ambitious, generous man filled her. She knew socialites who wouldn't hesitate in dropping charity work if they had a spontaneous teatime to attend. Her cheeks warmed, knowing she had done the same more than once. The streetcar halted, jostling her chapeau, and she was grateful for the excuse to fidget as she repositioned her hat and gained control of her coloring, hoping he wouldn't notice her shame.

"We have to change lines here," Malcolm stated, extending his arm to her. "It's just a short walk."

When they had settled into their new streetcar, Colette pressed her handkerchief to her neck, patting away the perspiration from the "short" walk, before prompting him to continue his story. "So even with your working and saving for classes, you still find time for the orphans every Friday?"

He smiled, nodding. "About thirteen years ago, Margaret Gaffney Haughery, one of the only adults who cared about me before the Wilsons, passed away. Her husband and only child died in the yellow fever epidemic that left so many orphans. As a childless widow, she dedicated her fortune and life to taking care of the motherless children."

Her brows rose at the thought, and she couldn't help but ask, "And her remaining family supported her endeavor?"

He shrugged. "Probably not, but the children of New Orleans became her family. I like to carry on the tradition in honor of 'the bread lady,' as she fondly became known as to us orphans. She left her estate in the stewardship of the Daughters of Charity for the orphans of New Orleans, so her legacy lives on to this day."

Her heart clinched as envy filled her. *To be allowed to spend one's fortune without expectation.* "She sounds like quite the woman. Not many would spend their life much less their money on such an endeavor."

"Mrs. Haughery was my guardian angel. I try to do as much as I can, but it's hard to make a difference when the people seem to have forgotten the plight of the orphans," Malcolm replied, rising as they had reached the end of the Dauphine Street line. "St. Mary's is two blocks south."

"But aren't there quite a few orphanages and homes in New Orleans with benefactors to provide for them?" Colette asked, knowing she attended at least one charity event a year devoted to benefiting the orphans. Feeling a slight breeze, Colette found herself across the street from the Mississippi River as they halted at the corner of Chartres and Mazant Streets in front of a large gray building.

Malcolm shrugged as he rang the bell. "There's always a need. No matter how many children are sheltered here, there are always more on the street."

The door creaked as it was wrenched open an inch by a pair of withered, spotted hands. "Yes?"

"Sister Joan?" He tucked his cap under his arm.

"My dear Malcolm! I couldn't remember if you were coming by today." She smiled, her forehead wrinkling beneath her wimple as she beckoned them into the hallway. She threaded her hands around Malcolm's muscular arm. "The children will be happy to see you as always." Her gaze fell on Colette's mauve chapeau and gray dress with its heavy lace, and understanding lit her features. "And who is your friend?"

"Sister Joan, may I present Mrs. Olivier? She's here to help me with the boys."

"Wonderful!" She patted Colette on the arm. "We can always use another pair of willing hands. If you'll follow us this way, Mrs. Olivier, we'll introduce you to the children."

Colette's heels clicked on the hardwood floors as she caught sight of the once glorious crown molding bowing away from the ceiling with small patches of mildew and watermarks trailing down from its cracks onto the wall. While the floors were spotless and the rooms kept tidy, the estate was in desperate need of funds.

Passing by an open door, she spotted a small boy standing on an overturned crate, peering through the windowpanes onto the street below with such a forlorn look on his little face that she had to pause. Lightly tugging on Malcolm's sleeve, she pointed to the dark-haired child. "Do you know him?"

Sister Joan leaned through the door to see what had caught Colette's interest. "Oh, that's Darvy. He turned seven last month and was transferred from one of the city's infant asylums."

"Transferred?"

"The infant asylum only keeps the children until they are seven. The girls have a specific orphanage they are released to, but the boys go to wherever there is an opening, regardless if they know anyone or not. There are always more orphans than space," Malcolm expounded before he crossed the room and crouched down by the lad.

Colette stiffened in the doorframe, hesitant of what to do, for she had no experience with crying children.

"Hello there." Malcolm extended his hand as if greeting a man. "It's Darvy, isn't it? What's wrong?"

The child turned his attention to Malcolm and gave a hesitant nod as he sniffed back a tear and accepted Malcolm's handshake. "I miss Mary. They said she couldn't come here."

Malcolm wiped away a rolling tear and placed a hand on Darvy's thin coat. "I'm sorry, laddie, but that's because you're growing up to be quite a man now. In fact, I think you are so old now that you should join the older boys today in our Bible class. Mrs. Olivier here"—he nodded toward her, and the boy's soulful gaze flitted over to her—"is going to tell you a story about another brave lad from the Bible who was also on the small side but became a king. Would you like to hear the story?"

Nodding, Darvy followed them from the room, and sensing him draw near, Colette looked down as he slipped his tiny hand into hers. Something inside cracked at his touch. *He needs me*, her heart whispered, and at the thought, her breath caught. *No one has ever needed me before.* While she longed to wrap her arms around the little fellow and kiss away his tears, all she could do was reach into her basket and pull out a cinnamon roll. "Hello there, would you like a baked goody?" she asked, bending down to his level.

For an answer, he hungrily snatched the roll from her fingers and stuffed it into his mouth, the icing smudging his pale cheeks as they entered the designated classroom.

Colette barely kept herself from gasping as she beheld the hunger in the children's faces when they locked on her basket of iced cinnamon buns. As Malcolm introduced her to each child, she handed out a roll, chastising herself for not contributing sooner as the boys crowded over, awaiting their portion. *If only I could do something more than just fill their bellies for a day.*

◆━━━•━━◆

The sunset's glow through giant oak trees called to her, and feeling rather restless, Colette had the hired carriage drop them off five blocks from her house.

"So what did you think?" Malcolm asked, walking with her down the avenue with the Spanish moss gently waving in the branches above.

Colette ran her gloved fingertips across the black cast-iron fences with their ornate fleur-de-lis topping each rail. "You were right. They've completely stolen my heart."

Malcolm grinned. "So you'll accept the position and teach alongside me?"

"As long as you promise not to dip my curls in ink," she teased as she nodded to a lady passerby.

He stopped short, his jaw dropping.

She turned to him, a girlish laugh escaping her lips. "You honestly don't remember? You terrorized me and my poor hair ribbons in Sunday school class before they split us into a girl class and boy class."

"I could never forget," he admitted, sheepishly raking his hand through his curls as he paused by her gate. "I'm just surprised you remembered."

"I don't know how I ever forgot," she replied before dipping into a small curtsy. "I'll begin preparing the lesson plans, but I'll see you on Wednesday evening to go over Friday's class?"

He returned a bow. "I'll be here at six o'clock sharp, and I promise not to ruin another set of your hair ribbons."

Closing the gate behind her, she knew her heart was already counting the days until she would see him again.

Chapter 3

N orman Hartley is getting out of a carriage in front of your house!" Julia giggled as she poked her head through the parlor door. "You didn't tell me he was coming today, or I never would've stopped by unannounced."

Colette's head snapped up from her lesson plans to the grandfather clock. Grimacing at the time, she hurried from her writing desk to the looking glass above the mantel, smoothing her hair and pinching her cheeks.

"You should've changed out of that hideous frock," Julia lamented, stepping into the room.

"I lost track of time, and besides, the only gowns I have are in widow's colors until the seamstress can come," Colette replied as she noticed an ink stain in between her writing fingers. *Blast.* "The color isn't that repulsive, is it?"

Julia pinched the bridge of her nose and inhaled. "You would've never asked yourself this question when you were eighteen. It's not the color. It's the heavy black lace and that dowdy high collar. I wish you wouldn't wear Grandmother's old shell cameo. It's positively common. Why don't you get a carved gem cameo, one that befits your status?"

"Well, I'm not eighteen anymore. I'm a five-and-twenty-year-old widow who has forgotten how to be courted. Besides, I happen to love this piece. It reminds me of *Grandmère.*" She plucked a yellow flower from the vase on her desk and tucked it into her bun. "Better?"

Julia pulled a blond curl loose from Colette's low coiffure and drew it over her shoulder. "It's the best we can manage for now, but I'm going to check with the seamstress to ensure her promptness in attending to your sad wardrobe."

"Mr. Norman Hartley to see Mrs. Olivier," the maid announced with a curtsy as Norman's confident stride sounded in the hall.

"Mrs. Olivier, you're looking quite fetching today"—he gave Colette a smile and a deep bow before turning to her sister—"and you are as pretty as ever, Miss Julia."

"Thank you, sir, and as much as I'd love to stay and visit with you, I must be on my way." She twirled out of the room before he could respond, but not before she gave her sister a conspiratorial wink.

Colette motioned for him to take a seat and signaled to the maid that she was ready for tea. "I trust your Sunday was relaxing?"

"Quite," he replied as Belinda rolled the tea cart to her mistress's side.

Colette filled his cup, worrying that they had forgotten the ease of old as the silence enveloped them. After a few minutes of stilted *tête-à-tête*, Colette noticed his cup sat in its saucer untouched. "Is something wrong with your tea, Mr. Hartley? Would you like me to send for another flavor? Perhaps a rooibos?"

"You found me out." He chuckled and set the cup aside. "I don't even drink tea anymore, but I didn't want to miss the chance of seeing you."

"Oh." She set her cup on the tea cart and rose. "Well, how about a turn in the garden instead? I usually go for a stroll at this time with Beignet."

"Beignet?" he asked, his brows wrinkling.

"My little dog," she explained and took his offered arm. "He's probably playing in the garden."

At the sight of the little golden dog with white markings on his face dashing about the garden in a whirlwind, Norman grinned. Beignet's antics broke the strangeness between them and they began chatting away as old friends, dropping the stiff formality of surnames as he reminisced on their mischievous childhood.

"It's nice to see you again, Colette." He tucked a loose strand behind her ear. "And now that the shipping business is growing, I'll hopefully be seeing more of you, as I've hired a manager for my New York office. I can finally move back and set up an office here in the warehouse district."

She halted, turning to face him. "Really? How wonderful for your mother and sisters to have you home again."

"And for me to have you almost next door again."

She blushed, recollecting when Norman was the sole thought of her girlhood musings of love.

"You are different than you used to be," he murmured as they sank onto the bench under the giant magnolia tree, the gentle fragrance of its large ivory blossoms wafting down to them.

"Oh?" Her hand fluttered to the tiny crease in the corner of her eye that had come from Robert's incessant displeasure over something she had or had not done.

"You were always so carefree as a girl. What happened to that spirit of adventure that had you longing for more?"

Colette toyed with her cameo, staring past Beignet. "I was married and was widowed. Bereavement takes a toll on one's spirit."

His hand rested on her forearm. "I wouldn't have mentioned it, but Julia hinted that your marriage to Robert was not a happy one."

She pulled away and stood, wishing she could throttle Julia for divulging something she had shared in confidence. "Then why did you ask about my spirit? Did you wish to cause me pain by having me admit it?"

"I'm sorry." His face fell as he rose with his hand at her elbow. "I rather bungled what I was going to say."

Colette shied away from his touch and resumed walking.

"Please forgive me. I merely wanted to know if you still harbored dreams of adventure after your marriage with Robert or if you were content to spend the rest of your days here...single."

She exhaled, forcing herself to release her anger. "You're forgiven. If you must ask, now that I am nearing the end of my mourning period, I've been beginning to feel as if something is about to change." She contemplated mentioning her time with the orphans, but as it was still so new, something held her back from confiding in her old friend. She didn't want to tell him about Malcolm or her precious Bible class for fear he or society would dissuade her again.

"I've been feeling the same." At her tilted head, he raked his hands through his locks and continued, "If I wasn't such a fool as a lad, I would've realized what I was missing."

"You did what you thought best at the time, as did I."

"It has been my constant regret that I did not pursue you, Colette, and that I stood by and let you marry that man." His fists clenched. "After what Julia told me, I could've flogged myself for what my cowardice caused you to endure with a man twenty-odd years your senior."

Her heart caught in her throat. *Is he confessing that he actually loved me when we were younger? That he cared for me as much as I cared for him?*

"He should've treated you like a queen," he growled. "I know I would have."

"Robert was as kind as he could be, but I couldn't give him what he really wanted, and I think that's why he was so verbally. . ." She cleared her throat and picked up her pace a bit. *We can't do this. It was too long ago. Besides—*

He turned to her and grasped her hand in his, the warmth of his touch shooting up her arm. "All I ask for is a chance to prove to you that I don't care about your change in fortune. Give me the opportunity to woo you as I should have seven years ago. I never should've listened to my father. He wanted me to marry for wealth and so I tried to find a bride who met his expectations and my hopes for love. Yet, I never loved anyone as I knew I could've loved you if given the chance." He held her hand to his chest.

"Norman," she cautioned, her guard mounting as he stepped closer. "I'm not the same girl I once was. I've changed."

"Please," he begged, the swift beating of his heart under her hand distracting her. "I know my timing couldn't be worse, but I will make it my crusade to prove to you that money doesn't mean anything to me."

As if against her will, she found her old hopes and dreams rising to the surface. *Is this my chance to finally be loved. . .to be wanted by a man?* Malcolm's winsome grin came to mind, and with a shake of her head, she tried to dismiss his dancing Irish eyes to focus on a man who she should actually consider, who would be accepted by her family. "I warn you it will be difficult."

"And I warn you that I never give up." He bowed and tenderly kissed her fingertips.

Chapter 4

M rs. Olivier!" Sister Joan greeted her, surprise in her voice. "I'm not expecting you, am I?" She rubbed her hands together. "Goodness, the sisters were right. I'm getting quite forgetful in my old age."

"Oh, no! I'm sorry to come by unannounced, but"—Colette cleared her throat at her own impropriety as she clutched her storybook in one arm and her basket in the other—"I couldn't wait until Friday to see the children, so I thought I'd use a basket of fruit as an excuse to come visit." She raised her peace offering for her lack of manners. "I hope their classes are over for the day. I wasn't sure what time they concluded, so I guessed."

The elderly woman smiled, opening the door wide for her to enter. "My dear, you never need an excuse to visit the children. I'll tell your class to meet on Darvy's floor." She winked at her. "I know he's already captured your heart as he has mine. He reminds me of Malcolm with his sweet eyes."

Malcolm certainly does have sweet ey— Colette felt her face color, but thankfully, Sister Joan had already turned toward the stairs, and within minutes, Colette was surrounded by her boys. She playfully tossed oranges to the group, happy that she'd brought more than enough for her Bible class so she could share with the younger children on Darvy's floor.

Darvy's amusement at her liveliness lit his face, but he didn't smile. He took his orange and sat in the corner, studied Colette's instruction on how to properly peel an orange, and slowly consumed his fruit as Colette opened her storybook.

Experiencing the joy of the children over an afternoon with a simple treat and a story, Colette pulled Sister Joan aside afterward and asked for her assistance in putting a smile on Darvy's face.

On Friday, Colette met Malcolm on her way out the door with a giant basket of food on each arm and Belinda trailing behind with two more, grunting under the weight.

"What's all this?" Malcolm chuckled.

"Well, I noticed some of the boys seeming a bit glum," she panted, smiling all the while, "so I spoke with Sister Joan, and we thought it might be fun if I arranged to have the Bible lesson outside in Jackson Square today with a picnic lunch for the class."

"Sister Joan agreed to it?" Malcolm took the baskets from her. "Good heavens, did you bring the entire storehouse with you?"

Colette shrugged. "I wanted to be sure they'd have enough. And of course she did, as we planned it together. Do you think the boys will be surprised?"

"I think they'll be thrilled, but with fourteen boys, it'll take three carriages to carry us all to the square, as I don't trust them to take the streetcar and not get lost."

"Then it's a good thing I've arranged for my drivers to take care of that." She gestured to the row of carriages at the side of the house ready to depart.

"And then there is Mother Superior to ask," he added.

"Sister Joan has already spoken with her, and she's given us her permission and seemed quite excited for the boys' outing." She gave him a victorious smile.

"Well, then." His bright eyes met hers as excitement lit his face. "What are we waiting for?"

Her list of things to do muddled in his gaze. Shaking her head to break through the clouds, she motioned for the drivers to store Malcolm's and Belinda's loads as the butler appeared with two more baskets of dishes and blankets.

Within the hour, the rowdy group of boys poured out of the carriages onto Jackson Square. Belinda and the butler set up the white picnic blankets and spread out the food, and Colette laid down a blanket for her and Sister Joan to sit on and keep an eye on the boys while Malcolm readied the materials for the Bible lesson.

Watching the boys play tag on the lawn, Colette smiled. "They are so content with small pleasures."

"This is likely the most fun they've had since arriving at the orphanage," Sister Joan replied. "We work hard at St. Mary's to keep the boys happy, but this is a luxury for them."

Colette chewed the inside of her cheek, thinking as the boys tumbled on the grass. "I wish they could be this happy every day."

"You can't take them on picnics all of the time," Sister Joan said, laughing, "but I know that they will cherish this day until you are as a fairy godmother in their retellings."

Heat crept up her neck. "I'm so nervous about my little part of the lesson today that I'm afraid their retellings will have more to do with how my voice shook the whole time or my dreadful execution."

Sister Joan smiled, patting her on the arm. "I'm sure you'll do fine, my dear. And if you get nervous, look to me or"—she winked—"to Malcolm."

Colette blushed in earnest as she plucked a blade of grass and proceeded to rip it into tiny pieces.

"They're too quiet by that tree," Sister Joan groaned as she stood. "I best go find out what mischief they've already managed to find."

Spotting Sister Joan, the boys waved their arms as they piped their findings of a strange insect.

Laughing at their antics, Colette leaned back on her hand, but feeling a sting, she drew it back sharply, gritting her teeth against the biting pain as she flipped over her hand to inspect it.

Malcolm's gaze flashed over and caught her pinching her palm together. "What happened?"

"It's nothing." She dismissed his concern and attempted to pull out the splinter herself, grunting as it burrowed itself deeper.

221

He knelt by her side, tenderly took her hand in his rough one, and, with the greatest care, removed the splinter. Instead of releasing her, Malcolm brought her palm up to ensure he had removed all of it.

Colette felt herself drawn to him, and with him bent over her hand, she took the opportunity to study his strong jawline, which had a hint of strawberry-blond stubble. With his broad shoulders so near, she couldn't help but think of what it would be like to have such a man to cherish her as his own.

He glanced up, their faces merely inches apart. "I think you'll survive," he murmured, a grin spreading over his face at catching her examining him.

"Is everything okay over here?" Sister Joan called as she crossed the green toward them.

"Thank you," she murmured and slipped her hand from his, glancing over to Belinda. "I think lunch is ready. Will you call the boys, Sister Joan?"

Helping her to her feet, Malcolm directed the charging boys over to the large blankets. The older fellows, eager for first pickings, beat out the little ones to the blankets, and after every lad was filled, Belinda presented each boy with a miniature chocolate pie with a whipped topping.

When almost every face bore evidence of the chocolate treat, Malcolm glanced up at the clock at the top of the St. Louis Cathedral. "We best begin our lesson because it's almost time to head back. Mrs. Olivier?"

Nervous to take the lead, she pasted on a smile. "Today's lesson will be short, but it's very important, so please scoot close." Colette patted the blanket beside her and motioned for the boys to crowd together. Darvy snuggled up next to her, and she couldn't help but look to Malcolm and smile.

"We're going to talk about John 6:35 where our Lord Jesus Christ tells us, 'I am the bread of life: he that cometh to me shall never hunger; and he that believeth on me shall never thirst.' Today, we gave you cake and milk and filled your bellies, but as you know, boys will get very hungry again by nightfall. Jesus is talking about food for your soul"— she tapped Darvy's chest near his heart. "For a long time, I felt alone, and I searched for a way to fill the hole in my heart because I was hungry for something more. I tried to fill the void being the very best girl I could manage, which as you know can be difficult when others tempt you to retaliate when teased."

At this the boys poked each other, and Malcolm had to intervene to turn the attention back to Colette.

Clearing her throat, Colette continued, "But being good wasn't enough to make the hole go away. I needed something more, *Someone* more." She glanced at Malcolm, who gave her an encouraging nod. "Do you want to know how I stopped feeling hungry and alone and how you can, too?"

Some of the boys seemed a little restless, but her gaze locked on the young Italian boy, Luca, whose eyes were bright with thirst. *Please, Lord, let me get through to them.* "If you believe in Jesus as your Savior and pray for Him to enter your heart, you will never again feel hunger in your soul, for He will fill that void inside." She pressed her hand to her chest as her voice wavered.

Malcolm reached over and gently squeezed her hand. "Thank you, Mrs. Olivier. Let's bow our heads." With a brief prayer, Malcolm dismissed the boys, and as they dashed away for one last romp, she overheard Luca asking Malcolm for a moment alone later.

"See? It wasn't so bad," the old nun whispered with a smile, her wrinkles creating a halo over her brow. She clapped her hands and herded the boys back into the carriages.

As Colette bid each boy farewell at the orphanage, her heart filled at their overwhelming gratitude. Ruffling Darvy's hair, she thought, *If only I could bring all these boys home with me.* She turned in the doorway, relishing Darvy's laughter as Malcolm gave his animated interpretation of the day's events to Mother Superior. *It's not as if I don't have the space, time, or funds.* She chewed the inside of her lip and turned away.

It was almost dinnertime when Colette arrived home, and stripping off her gloves, she sighed with exhaustion as she spied a gentleman's small calling card on the silver tray in the hallway with its top left corner folded. Flipping it over, she found Norman's name with a request for dinner in his fancy script and felt a twinge of guilt that she hadn't even thought of him all day.

Chapter 5

Norman held the gilded back of her chair as she slipped into her seat in the lavish hunter-green room with gold trim. *Antoine's* ornate golden chandelier lent a delicate glow that caught the crystal glasses on the tables, making the walls sparkle.

Taking his place across from her, Norman lifted his glass and ceremoniously clinked it against hers. "I believe this is the first time we've ever dined together in public without a family member or your old nurse as a chaperone."

"I think I can take care of myself." Colette winked at him, lifted her menu, and located her favorite creole appetizer, *chair de crabes au gratin*.

"You most certainly can." He reached across the table and clasped her hand. "You look breathtaking."

Her mouth watered a bit at the thought of the breaded crab dish. "I'm sorry, did you say something?"

He chuckled and released her hand. "Well, that hasn't changed." At her raised brow, he expounded, "Until you get food, you can't carry on much of a conversation."

She grimaced and set aside the menu. "I'm sorry. It's been far too long since I last came here with Robert."

"Ah, yes." He shifted in his seat, uncomfortable with any mention of Robert.

"I do have a bit of news that I'd like to share with you." She smoothed her amethyst silk skirt before draping the fine linen napkin over her lap. "I'm helping with the Bible class at the boys' orphanage, St. Mary's, and—"

"Really?" His glass chinked rather loudly as he hit the rim of his plate in setting it down.

"Well, yes," she stumbled in her haste to explain, "I wanted to volunteer at the church, as I used to do it all the time, but shamefully, I haven't for years because, um—" She paused, not knowing how to politely phrase, *Since I was married and Robert forbade me from it.* "Well, let's just say that things didn't work out. After visiting the orphanage, I found myself wishing there was more that I could do as the orphanage is so crowded and the children almost never get a chance to play off grounds, so I brought the lads on a picnic yesterday."

"How kind of you." Norman gave her an almost patronizing grin.

"Thank you," she pressed onward, ignoring her agitation, "but I wanted to discuss something with you. After the picnic, I began thinking—"

"Sorry I'm late," Julia panted as she joined them. "I couldn't decide on which dress to wear as a chaperone. I figured my emerald-green dress was as austere as I could manage."

"Miss Julia!" Norman dropped his napkin from his lap in his haste to rise and bow, but as she was already seated, he managed a half bow.

"I may be a widow who can take care of herself, but I haven't forgotten the proper etiquette for dining with a gentleman." Colette leaned toward him and whispered dramatically, "You don't think I want the socialites to catch wind of secret rendezvous with a mysterious suitor, do you?"

"Funny." Norman smirked.

"Have you ordered yet?" Julia motioned for the waiter to fill her glass.

"I was waiting for you." Colette handed her menu to Julia as her stomach growled. "Please tell me that you already know what you want." She pressed her hand to her corset, praying her stomach would mind its manners.

"Of course. Now, you two pretend that I'm not here." Julia rattled off her order to the waiter before he turned to take Norman's and Colette's.

Taking Julia at her word, Norman returned to the topic at hand. "So, you brought these boys out to Jackson Square on your own?"

"Oh, no." She inwardly cringed at the thought of wrangling all the boys by herself. "I teach with a gentleman named Malcolm Reilly. He makes certain the boys stay in line."

"Reilly? Never heard of an Irish *gentleman* by that name. Is it proper to teach alongside him?" He motioned at Julia, his nose pinching. "I mean, you've known me your whole life, yet you teach with this man alone."

"Sister Joan is usually present for their lessons." *But not all the time.* She thought of Malcolm's hand caressing her palm and realized Norman might be right to question her. "It's not as if he were taking me to dinner," she reassured him as much as herself. "Besides, it was the pastor's wife, his mother, who enlisted my help, and as the nuns adore him, I feel that is as good a character recommendation as one could get."

"Oh, the nuns approve of him? Sounds like quite the catch," he mumbled sarcastically as he buttered his sweet potato roll.

"Anyway, to continue my story, when I saw how happy the children were outside of the orphanage, I began thinking that I have so much room in my mansion, it's really a shame to keep it all to myself."

Norman choked on his drink and Julia pressed her napkin to her mouth, a snort escaping. She waved them onward. "Sorry, sorry! I'm not here. Keep talking."

"You can hardly have them in your home," Norman replied with a slow smile.

"And why not?" she retorted, disappointed at the mockery her dreams were receiving.

"Really, Colette. Mr. Hartley will begin to think you're serious," Julia interrupted, forgetting her silent role as she dabbed away her tears of amusement.

"But I am serious. I have more than enough room, while they barely have a place to lay their heads or enough food to go around. The caretaker said that they scarcely have less than four hundred children at a time."

"It's not as if you can fit that many in your home, either," Norman muttered.

"No, but I can fit at least twenty boys, and if I finish out the half story, I can fit another six boys," she continued, her heart pounding as she confided her dream of a school for the first time.

"Twenty-six? Why would you want so many to fill your mansion when an orphanage could get the job done more efficiently if you *donated* your funds? I know a few of the men on the board at St. Mary's, and I'm sure they'd appreciate your sizable donation."

"Sister Joan sparked an idea that has been brewing in my head for the last twenty-four hours. I could transform my mansion into a legitimate school and teach the boys a trade, provide cotillion classes, and raise their stations in life through education." Her eyes glistened with excitement. "While I may not be able to help *all* the boys at once, I can change the lives of dozens and then, over time, hundreds."

"That's my sister. Always so generous at heart that she fails to see the logic in the moment." Julia patted her on the arm. "You've never been a mother, and heaven knows, with only a sister, you've never experienced rearing boys. It was a very sweet thought, my sister, but surely you can understand why we can't take you seriously?"

Colette opened her mouth to protest, but Julia gave her a little kick under the table, pursed her lips, and sent her a pointed stare as the waiter set their plates before them. Colette clenched her jaw and stared at her appetizer. Since Robert's death, she hadn't thought anyone would try to control her desire to serve again. . .much less her sister or Norman Hartley.

◆—————◆

Over the next few weeks, Colette did not bring up the school to Norman again. Instead, she prayed and planned over her school in the quiet of her home until she was certain it was not in fact, as Norman suggested, a passing fancy. When she was certain of the Lord's hand, she hired an architect to draw up the plans to convert her home, and upon delivery of his work, she tucked the plans into a portfolio and left for Malcolm's office.

"Mrs. Olivier"—concern lit the green flecks in Malcolm's eyes as he rose from his desk—"is everything okay? I thought we weren't meeting until tomorrow afternoon."

"Oh, yes, but I had something that couldn't wait." The high collar of her dress stuck to her throat from the heavy morning humidity. "I know I've only been helping you for a short time, but I'd like to ask you something."

He motioned for her to have a seat, giving his full attention.

"I was praying about what else I could do for the boys at the orphanage, more than teaching classes and the occasional picnic."

His brows shot up. "Oh?"

She laid her portfolio on his desk. "I've been thinking that I'd like to turn my home into a school for boys where they can learn a trade and have a foster mother along with a houseful of brothers."

He blew out his cheeks. "Colette, er, Mrs. Olivier," he corrected his slip, "I don't know what to say."

"I know you studied at Miss Wright's night school, so I'd like to offer you a job as one of the teachers and my counterpart." She cleared her throat. "I know, it's a strange position I'm proposing, but I could think of no one I'd rather have as my partner in the day-to-day operations of the school."

His jaw slacked as he crossed his arms and leaned against his cane-back chair, exhaling.

"I hope I haven't offended you." She dipped her head. "I—I know you work hard at your office here, but I remembered how you said you wished to teach, and I was hoping you could put to use what Miss Wright taught you and guide me in operating a school for boys."

"I'm not offended at all." Malcolm laughed, running his hand through his hair. "I'm simply speechless."

Colette let out her pent-up breath. *Thank goodness.*

He rested his hand on her arm before thinking better of it and pulled away. "You're sure about this? Because once the school is open, it'll be hard to turn back without upsetting the lives of a lot of boys."

"I've prayed extensively about this, and I believe that it's what I'm to do for the rest of my days. I had been wondering how I could use Robert's fortune, and this is the obvious route."

"You know that no one in your family will approve"—he drummed his fingers on the desk—"and I'm sure your friends won't look kindly on your decision, either."

Friends, meaning Norman? "No, but I'm done bending to their opinions. I must listen to the Lord. I've ignored Him in the past, but I won't again."

He took her hand in his; the roughness of his skin seemed to peel away the layers of protection she had spent years forming. "Then, Mrs. Olivier, you mustn't let anything stand in your way."

"Would you like to see what I have in mind?" She grinned, happy to share her news, as she rose and opened her portfolio.

"Absolutely." He stood and leaned on the desk to peer over her prints.

Taking him through the plans, floor by floor, Colette explained how the first floor would be for classrooms, the second floor's west wing for the youngest children and the teacher, the third floor for the middle grades, and the half story for the oldest boys.

"So what do you think?" she finished breathlessly.

"Quite the undertaking for just the two of us." He rubbed the base of his neck.

"Yes, but with your help and with another teacher, we can manage." She slowly turned to the sketch of the garden house, her heart racing. "I thought that for propriety's sake, it would be best to have the old gardener's house turned into a comfortable home for you, offering you privacy, but, uh...that is"—she paused, biting her lip in the fashion Robert had hated—"if you even *want* the job." She turned to him, the seriousness of her question weighing her shoulders: "Will you be my partner in raising these boys?"

He stuck out his hand. "I'm your man."

At those words, she slipped her hand into his, and her heart stirred as it hadn't in years. *Yes, you just might be my man.* She took a deep breath, reminded herself of Norman, and banished the thought. "Wonderful. The interviews for the teaching position begin tomorrow morning at nine o'clock sharp."

Chapter 6

Colette groaned into her hands. "How is everyone we've interviewed so far so ill suited for teaching boys?"

"Let's hope this next person will be conducive, because she's the last candidate." Malcolm leaned back on the two legs of his chair.

A pretty girl with dark locks poked her head into the doorway. "Good morning, I'm—"

Malcolm's chair legs slammed onto the hardwood. "Katie?"

"Malcolm Reilly?" She gasped as he stood and extended his hand.

"I thought your name sounded familiar. Patrick's little sister all grown up. So good to see you! The last time I saw you was when you were in pigtails."

She laughed. "It's been quite a long time, and as you can see from my references, I go by Katherine now." She turned her attention to Colette and curtsied. "Mrs. Olivier, thank you so much for agreeing to see me."

Colette nodded and gestured for her to have a seat. "We were eager to meet you, Miss O'Dell, but as you and Mr. Reilly have already met, why don't you tell me a little bit about yourself?"

Miss O'Dell bubbled with enthusiasm, describing her studies and how even though she lacked experience in the classroom, she was more than ready to take on the challenge of teaching a class of rowdy boys from her experience of growing up in a houseful of brothers.

At the end of the interview, Colette knew Miss O'Dell was the one for the job even though she was slightly annoyed by how much Malcolm seemed to enjoy the young lady's giddiness.

When Malcolm returned from taking rather a long time to show Katherine to the door, he reclaimed his seat, swiveling to face Colette. "Well, that was a pleasant surprise. She's studied at a fine school, and while this will be her first teaching position, I think she'll be a great fit." He brushed off his hands as if his job were done.

"You're certain the boys would respond well to someone so. . .young?" she ventured, testing to see if he thought she was indeed as pretty as her imagination led her to believe.

He grinned. "It may actually work in her favor, as they are more likely to behave for such a bonny face."

Bonny face? She fought back a grimace, trying not to dislike the girl before she even started working. Colette stretched her back. "Well, we know for sure that the first five candidates will not be a suitable match for our school."

"And your thoughts on Miss O'Dell? Is there anything holding you back from hiring her?" Malcolm's brow creased.

Besides the fact that she's gorgeous? "Her age," she settled, leaving out her youthful glow and bright blue eyes devoid of crow's feet.

"The boys will be respectful. I'll see to it," he assured her in a shielding tone, causing her heart to twitch.

Upset by her own jealousy of Malcolm's protectiveness toward the pretty teacher, she examined her hesitation. "Well, in that case, let's hire Miss O'Dell."

He grinned, scraping back his chair as he stood. "I'll go to her house at once and tell her the good news myself, and we can get started on ordering some supplies tomorrow morning."

"Marvelous." Colette returned his smile, praying her heart would catch up with her head.

◆——————◆

As they walked about the parlor, Colette jotted down instructions on her notepad for the removal of the Persian rug and the antiquities, how many desks they needed, and the possible placement of the teacher's desk.

"And speaking of the teacher's desk," Malcolm interjected, "have you given mind where the new schoolmarm will stay?"

"I was planning on giving her the largest west-wing room and having a sort of sitting area set up in the corner of her room. Do you think that will be to her liking? Or will she expect two rooms?"

"Miss O'Dell isn't picky." He pointed at a spot between the front windows. "I think she'd like to have the morning light on her papers, so let's place the desk there."

"You know her well enough to know that?" She bit back a snort and again questioned her animosity toward Miss O'Dell. *She's been nothing but sweet to you, so behave.*

"When I stopped by her parents' house last night, they invited me to stay for dinner and I learned a little bit more about her," he replied, seeming not to suspect her reaction.

"That's nice," she murmured, thinking that it was quite the opposite of nice, and turned her attention back to the schoolroom and away from this troubling turn of events. "So, what do you think about adding bookshelv—"

"So it's true. You really are turning your home into a school," Norman stated from the doorway, gripping the brim of his hat. "I didn't think I'd be hearing such life-altering news from Julia."

Colette crossed the room, rested her hand on his arm, and lowered her voice to keep Malcolm from overhearing. "I hadn't planned on announcing it yet. The school won't be ready until mid-August."

"Then don't. It's absurd to devote the best years of your life to a houseful of children," he growled, his brows knitting together.

"You forget that you were the one who encouraged me." Colette gave him a wink to smooth his temper as she threaded her arm through his and led him out to the garden, hoping the fresh air would cool his temper.

He frowned as he flung open the garden gate, stepping onto the public sidewalk.

"You're angry with me, aren't you?"

He looked down at her, the darkness in his features fading as he cupped her cheek. "I'm merely concerned and a bit hurt you didn't feel the need to confide in me of your plans and that I had to find out about this from your sister."

She inclined her head, understanding his point of view. "I'm sorry. I should've told you in person, but when I tried to tell you at the dinner, you dismissed it."

"I didn't know you were so serious about it." His voice strained, and clearing his throat, he tugged on his hat. "I suppose you still need an hour before the dinner party to dress, so I'll take a walk."

"Won't you wait for me in the parlor? I lost track of time, but I can be ready in a half hour." She attempted to stay him.

"I could use the walk to calm down. I won't be much of a dinner partner if I'm sullen." He dug his fists into his pockets and trudged down St. Charles Avenue. "I'll see you in a bit, Colette."

❖——·——❖

Her family did not take the news well. After an awkward dinner of her parents trying to convince her to fulfill her calling in a less expensive way, she flung her skirts behind her as she stepped down from the carriage onto her drive, ignoring Norman's offered hand.

"Colette." He grasped her by the elbow, stopping her. "Please don't be angry with me. I was taken aback by your determination to open this school. I had thought that you were taking time to recover after your mourning period, but now that you're spending most of your fortune on this place, I think it's time I step in with some advice."

"You already tried that at dinner and it didn't quite work out for you." *So you best bide your tongue*, she finished in her head.

"Yes, and I wish to apologize for my overbearing tone earlier," he replied, drawing her hand in his.

"Oh?" The tension in her shoulders lessened a fraction.

"However, I do believe in the message I was attempting to convey," he finished.

Unbelievable. She dropped her hand from his grasp and marched toward the garden, fearing what she might say in her anger. "I don't need your approval." She shoved open the iron garden gate. "Honestly, Norman, I thought you would be more supportive, especially after you defended me at dinner tonight."

"Your father's friends had no business offering their opinion, but as we are courting, I believe I can be concerned!"

She clenched her jaw, swallowed back her retort, and barely resisted slamming the gate between them. "You are crossing the line."

"Crossing a line? I thought we were more than casual acquaintances. Doesn't that give me a right to an opinion?"

Her cheeks flushed. "An opinion, yes, but authority, no. Until all of this settles down, I think we need to take some time to reevaluate our relationship."

He inhaled deeply as he halted her promenade, grabbing her hand and gently pulling her toward him. "Colette."

Norman gave her the smile that she knew melted girls' hearts everywhere, except tonight. It wouldn't work. She looked down to avoid his hypnotic stare and keep her thoughts clear. "No. I won't discuss this with you any further tonight."

"I think, my dear Colette, that we are just too different."

Her startled gaze met his. "What?"

"We want different things. Even though it's your spirit that has always drawn me to you, I'm too traditional for you, my dear girl." Norman stroked her cheek with his thumb. "I want to be with you, but not enough to share you with a houseful of boys that are not ours."

Colette's shoulders caved as the wind left her lungs. *Surely he isn't leaving me a second time?* "Are you certain?"

He lifted her chin and tenderly kissed her cheek. "I'm sorry, but I think we are better off as friends, and if you really think about it, you know I'm right."

The doubts she had not wanted to admit having rose, and instead of being crushed once more, she knew he was right. "I'm sorry." She reached up to brush a curl from his forehead. "I'm sorry I could not be the girl you left behind."

With a tender smile, she slipped inside to find Malcolm packing away the last of the parlor's antiques in an open crate. "Oh, you didn't have to do this. I was going to finish up tonight," she said, setting down her reticule on the settee and stiffly peeling off her gloves, still in shock over Norman.

"I don't mind," he replied, tucking a figurine in the straw. "How was dinner?"

She laughed without mirth. "Well, between Norman and Julia, the news was released prematurely. One would have thought that I was committing a felony with the way everyone responded." She removed the last vase from the fireplace mantel and handed it to Malcolm.

"Well, I'm sure they did think of it as a crime," Malcolm replied as he hefted the crate into his arms.

"What on earth do you mean?" she asked, following him up the stairs to the east wing.

"They raised you to marry into a fortune, and now that you have access to do what you will with it, you are doing the very opposite of what they intended," he surmised, setting down the crate outside her door.

"The opposite being?"

"Spending it on the family or using it to raise your station in a way that would still support them. You have to be strong in your decision. The school opens in two weeks, so now is the time to back out if you need to."

"No, absolutely not. I've tried their way before and I was miserable." She leaned against her door and looked up to him. "Do you think I've taken leave of my senses? That I'm letting my feelings carry me away?"

He took her hands in his, and with kindness in his voice, he whispered, "I think what you are doing is a mighty fine thing. You're going to change the lives of hundreds."

At his words, she found herself flooded with strength. She thought of Norman's aversion to her calling and of Malcolm's opposite reaction. *Is this what love is meant to be like? If only I'd had Robert's support, how different my life would've been.*

Chapter 7

With the rooms complete and the last chalk tablet set on the school desk, Colette was eager to open the school and welcome her boys.

At the sound of carriage wheels crunching the gravel drive, Malcolm peeked behind the schoolroom's lace curtain. "Katie, I mean, Miss O'Dell is here!"

Colette checked her watch pin. "We have just under an hour until the boys arrive, so would you mind walking about to ensure all is prepared while I get her settled into her bedroom?" She smoothed the front of her new navy gown and straightened her cameo, which was fastened to a ruffled lace jabot.

"Certainly." The front door opened, and Colette watched his face grow bright at Katherine's presence. "Miss O'Dell, welcome home."

The pretty teacher untied her cloak and dropped into a small curtsy. "Mr. Reilly and Mrs. Olivier, I must tell you it's *such* an honor to be working as one of your first teachers," she babbled, her hands fluttering in the air. "Who would've thought that *I* would be appointed as head schoolmarm on my first job?"

Colette smiled at the girl's enthusiasm. "We're honored to have you, and while the duties of the head teacher shall rest mainly with you, Mr. Reilly and I will be here to help ease your burden with his classes and mine."

"It's wonderfully clever to teach such a useful class as Mr. Reilly's trade workshop," Katherine replied as the underbutlers appeared with her rather worn trunk between them.

"I hope the boys will only ever learn things here that are useful," Colette replied quietly. "As a debutante, I was taught all manner of impractical things."

The young girl blushed, abruptly aware of her faux pas.

"If you'll follow me, I'll show you to your room." Colette smiled to put her at ease, gesturing her toward the stairs.

In the hall, Katherine complimented the ornate wallpaper, and when Colette swung open the west-wing bedroom door, the new teacher gasped.

Colette paused, trying to read her expression. "Is it not to your liking? I wish I could've given you two rooms for a bedroom and parlor set, but I needed the other room for the boys, and I thought a breakfast nook in the corner would suffice—"

Katherine pressed a hand to her mouth. "It's beautiful. I've never had a bedroom to myself before, and I never imagined living in one half as grand."

Colette cleared her throat. "Well, um, I'm very glad it pleases you. Shall I send one of the maids to help you unpack?"

"Maids?" She giggled, stroking the heavy curtains as she passed. "It wouldn't be worth the time for them to climb the stairs for I only have a trunk of dresses, as the other trunk is full of books and school things that I thought might prove helpful." She knelt down and pried open the lid with a grunt. "It gets a little stuck sometimes." She gave a nervous giggle and shook out a serviceable gown of navy and spread it out on the bed, followed by a brown frock and a gray.

Pleased that Katherine had such sensible gowns to keep the distractions at a minimum, she nodded with approval. "Well, I'll leave you to get settled, and then I'll give you the tour with the boys? They should be arriving soon."

"Oh? I'll come with you, then," she said, tossing a stocking back into the trunk. "I don't want to miss the grand opening of Mrs. Olivier's School for Boys."

Colette warmed to her enthusiasm and knew they could become friends if only. . . She paused with her hand on the mahogany stair rail. *Am I jealous?* She attempted to dismiss the ridiculous notion. *I've nothing to be jealous of. Malcolm has no commitment to me other than being my employee and is free to see whomever he likes.* To her chagrin, her rebellious heart clenched at the thought of Malcolm and Katherine together, and she wished that society's rules weren't quite so limiting. She bit her lip. Thinking how her parents had reacted to the news of the school, she could just imagine how they would respond if she acted on her growing feelings for Malcolm.

"They're on St. Charles Avenue, Mrs. Olivier," one of the maids called up to her, breaking her reverie. "The underbutler was on the lookout for them."

Hastening down the stairs and out the front door, she found Malcolm already on the bottom step. "I can't believe our first set of boys are here." Colette clasped her hands in front of her satin skirt as she waited for the two carriages to pull into the driveway with two boys from each grade from first to sixth.

"There's no turning back now." Malcolm smiled down at her.

"I would never want to," she returned. *Give it a week and I'm sure you will think differently,* she could almost hear her mother say if she were present.

"When will the rest be arriving?" Katherine asked.

"I checked with St. Mary's, and they said they'll be sending the additional fourteen boys from the seventh to twelfth grades this afternoon. We wanted to have time to settle the younger group," Malcolm explained to her.

Spotting the carriage, Colette barely contained a squeal as she grasped Malcolm's rough hand. He looked down at her, surprise lighting his eyes. Colette dropped his hand, her face flushing, and turned her attention to the halted carriage.

Darvy leaned out of the window and yelled and waved both his arms in the air. "Mrs. Olivier! Mrs. Olivier!" The small dark-haired boy hopped down from the carriage, skipping a step, and ran straight into her arms as they both giggled and began chattering away.

Kissing his cheek before releasing him, Colette focused on the other eleven lads and Sister Joan, who had agreed to chaperone the boys until they reached her care. "Hello, I'm Mrs. Olivier, and I want to welcome you to Mrs. Olivier's School for Boys, your new home and your new family. Let's get you established in your rooms, and when you hear the gong, meet us at the foot of the stairs for the tour of the grounds."

The boys cautiously climbed the stairs to the second and third floors, some with distrust in their expressions and others with fear as Colette showed the boys to their assigned rooms. Keeping the six youngest boys on the second floor in case they grew afraid at night, she directed the rest of the boys to the third floor, saving the large half story for the eldest lads.

After fifteen minutes of orderly chaos as each boy settled into his bed, Colette had Belinda sound the gong, bringing the boys tumbling down the stairs and sending Beignet into a bouncing barking fit at the invaders of his house. The boys snickered at the little dog's hysterics with Darvy imitating the sound, much to the maids' annoyance as they pressed their hands to their ears.

Colette overheard Katherine giggle from behind and whisper to Malcolm, "They're going to have to get used to the noise, or I'm afraid Mrs. Olivier might find herself in need of replacements within the week."

"Let's pray that isn't the case, else you and I will have our hands full," Malcolm returned, teasing in his voice.

Raising her hands, she called for the boys' attention, and as they already knew Malcolm, she introduced them to Katherine, who gave them a brilliant smile and curtsy. Colette thanked her with a small nod. "Now, I know that some of you"—she looked to the twin third-graders who had lost their final parent to illness—"have suffered a great loss recently and others, in the distant past. I may understand a little of what you're going through as my own husband died two years ago, leaving me quite alone in this house. It was my greatest wish to have a child, but as you see"—she gestured to her empty arms with a little laugh—"I didn't until this day. I want you all to think of me as your mother, or if you can't, maybe at least your favorite auntie who loves you all more than she can express. My door is always open to you."

As if shy by her warmth, the boys shuffled their feet at the end of her speech, but Darvy sidled up next to her, slipping his hand in hers.

"Well, enough of that. Let's explore, shall we?" She released Darvy's hand with a gentle squeeze and brought the group of twelve boys through to the classrooms, tailed by Malcolm and Katherine, who she noticed kept their heads inclined toward one another, whispering to each other.

Sister Joan came up to her elbow, shaking her head as she chuckled. "With all that sweet talk, these boys are going to attempt to run right over you"—she nodded to Darvy—"especially that one. He's already got you wrapped around his finger."

Colette's face warmed as she scooped up the still yapping dog in an attempt to quiet him. "Did I sound foolish?"

Sister Joan rubbed the top of Beignet's head, her gold wedding band catching in the light. "You sounded genuine, my dear. However, be prepared to love them with not only gentleness but firmness." She laughed at Colette's tilted head. "In other words, don't let them get away with murder. You won't be doing them any favors when they leave here." She nodded toward the group. "You better give the tour. I fear they're getting restless."

Colette clapped her hands and led the group through the classrooms, listing off which classes would be taught by which teacher. Seeing the boys' noses wrinkle at the mention of her cotillion classes and hearing disgruntled mumbles about frilly lessons, she bit back a snicker as Beignet wriggled in her arms. "And beyond the dining room, the doors lead out into the gardens," Colette called, setting down the dog and swinging open the french doors.

The boys hooted as they flooded outside behind the dog and ran over the manicured lawn, rolling in the grass and climbing the large oak and magnolia trees. One of the boys picked up a fallen bunch of Spanish moss and draped the gray filth over his head to form a beard.

"Tommy! You want to give the school lice on the first day?" Malcolm shouted and scrambled over to him, swiping it off his head.

Colette cringed, remembering Mother's prediction that the boys would cause the place to swarm with insects, ruining her costly Parisian furniture.

"Mrs. Olivier?" Belinda called from the veranda, panting from her haste. "The last of the carriages are pulling into the drive with the older boys! They're two hours early! What are we going to do?"

Letting Malcolm and Katherine deal with the lice-infested moss for the moment, Colette gathered her skirts and hurried toward the front of the house with Sister Joan and the maid following closely behind. "We're going to take it one day at a time."

◆•————•◆

Colette tossed and turned until she knew slumber was not going to visit her unless she had some chamomile. Pushing aside the mosquito netting, Colette slipped on a loose ivory blouse and stepped into her pink skirt but left her hair spilling down over her shoulders. Grabbing her blue silk shawl embroidered with bright flowers, she tiptoed down to the kitchen in her bare feet to brew some tea.

With the kettle on to boil, she rested her head in her hands on the rustic kitchen table and began to pray for each and every boy, beginning with the youngest. She paused in her petitions when she came to the names of the seventh-graders. *Good heavens. What are their names?* Feeling like quite the terrible mother for forgetting their names, she jumped up to fetch her ledger, when she heard a scratching at the side door of the kitchen.

Knowing all the children were in bed, she gripped her teacup, ready to fight should a robber endanger her children. The lock popped and the door clicked open. With a frightful yell, she hurled her tea and the hot contents into the face of the intruder. The robber ducked, avoiding the cup as it shattered into the wall, steeping him.

"What on earth?" Malcolm wiped off his shirtsleeves.

Her shoulders caved as she pressed a hand to her pounding heart and leaned on the table. "I thought you were a burglar!"

"And you were going to fight him off with a cup of hot tea?" He chuckled, swiping a rag from the counter. "Good thing you have me to watch out for you."

"What are you doing prowling about at this time of night?" She crossed her arms over her chest, aware of her hair flowing down to her waist.

He paused before answering, his gaze lingering on her golden curls before he looked down, rubbing his hands on the rag. "I was hungry and I left my key inside, so I used my lock kit." He lifted a small, rolled-up leather pouch.

"Why do you have a loc—"

"My grandfather was a locksmith. I don't remember him too well, but it was the only thing I had when I was brought to the orphanage, so I learned how to use it."

"I bet you gave the nuns a frightful time with that little toy." She giggled. A sudden weakness from the fright of Malcolm's unexpected appearance gripped her and she sank down onto the kitchen chair, clutching her silk shawl to her neck.

"I had it taken away more than once." He grinned. "Well, I'll leave you to your tea and come back later."

"Would you like some chamomile tea? I made a fresh pot, and it would be a shame to only share it with the wall when you could use some to help you sleep." Warning bells sounded, but she ignored them. "And I spied some leftover cinnamon rolls under the glass dome, over there." She pointed to the corner of the kitchen.

"Chamomile would be nice," he admitted as he retrieved the sweet roll and two teacups, taking a seat as Colette poured him a cup. "Don't know why I'm so awake. Must've been all the excitement of the day."

"Me, too," she agreed, lifting her cup in a salute. "Day one is over, but our journey is just beginning."

"Here, here." He clinked his cup against hers. His gaze caught Colette's, and it seemed as if he was trying to find the right words when one of the maids appeared in the threshold.

"Oh! Excuse me, Mrs. Olivier," she gasped, clutching her robe, no doubt shocked at seeing her mistress with her hair down and alone with Malcolm.

With flaming cheeks, Colette grabbed her teacup and saucer, made her excuses to them both, and vanished upstairs, reminding herself that she had done nothing wrong.

Chapter 8

A nd, one-two-three-four and one-two-three-fou—" She gritted her teeth as Tommy's foot slammed onto her toes.

"Sorry, Mrs. Olivier," he mumbled, stepping away to let her catch her breath as she limped it off to keep from crying out.

Six weeks of dance lessons and he still can't manage the simple step. She smoothed the front of her canary-yellow dress to compose herself. With its lace cuffs and ruffles, she knew her dress was a bit ostentatious for a dance lesson, but she tried to convince herself the color was for her own sake and not because Malcolm was about the house and she wanted to look her best. "It's quite all right, Tommy. You need to practice, though, to be ready for the cotillion dance in three weeks if you want to impress the girls' Sunday school class."

A chuckle came from the parlor's doorway, and she spied Malcolm attempting to wipe the grin from his face. "Mr. Reilly," she almost sighed with relief, "I think it might help the class"—she gestured to the older students that she was endeavoring to prepare for being released into society—"if you demonstrated." She lifted her hands into position, waiting for him to step into her arms.

Malcolm shrugged. "Tommy seems to be doing well enough."

"Yes, but"—she waved him over, with her right hand still in position—"it will help them to see it executed without flaws."

He averted his gaze. "I'm sorry. I can't."

She dropped her hands and turned back to Tommy, her pride smarting. "Well, then. Since Mr. Reilly isn't available, let's try this again, shall we?" She instructed Luca to play the pianoforte, starting the piece from the middle.

"Mind if I cut in?" Norman asked, stepping over the rolled-up carpet to claim her.

"Mr. Hartley!" She gasped as his arm wrapped around her waist and he whirled her around in the waltz, saving her poor feet from further injury. "You know just when to rescue a girl, don't you?"

"Your poor, dainty toes." He looked down at her feet, spotting the black boot marks on the tips of her dancing slippers. He captured her eyes with his somber ones. "Can you ever forgive me? I'm a wretched oaf. I was so focused on my bullheaded, so-called logic that I didn't even consider your calling to raise these boys," Norman whispered into her ear. "Give me another chance, my darling. Say yes, and I'll never give you cause to doubt me again. To begin, allow me to take you to dinner tonight?"

Seeing now that Malcolm had no interest in her, she intended not to make a further fool of herself. *Why should I pass my chance of love in the hopes Malcolm will eventually want me?* "You know I never could stay angry with you for very long." She lifted her voice and her smile to the class, "See, lads, how Mr. Hartley guides me about the room? His grip is confident, yet gentle."

"Dancing is all about making the lady shine," Norman added, mischief tainting his voice. "You're merely an instrument to display her beauty, making you the object of envy of every man in the room."

Colette rolled her eyes as the boys cackled at his instruction. "Really, Norman," she whispered. "Such ideas you will give them."

"It's true, though. With you in my arms, I am the envy of every man."

Blushing, she turned her focus back to the boys, catching Malcolm sauntering off behind them with his hands shoved in his pockets.

◆—————◆

Standing in front of the class, Colette rubbed her sweaty palms discreetly on her yellow skirt. "I suppose you are all wondering why I am here. Miss O'Dell just received word that her father has taken ill, so I gave her the next few days off. Mr. Reilly is currently working on unclogging the plumbing"—the boys chortled and pointed to Tommy, but she ignored them, continuing—"so I'm taking over her class."

She directed everyone to take out their arithmetic books. *Lord, help me. I haven't looked at a mathematics problem since I was a girl.* The rain plinked against the wavy glass panes as she cracked open Katie's teacher's guide and cringed. As a socialite out for a rich husband, arithmetic had been grossly neglected at her finishing school. The only math she had needed to know was how to count how many girls she was competing against for which eligible bachelors.

After an hour of trying to teach twelve grades of arithmetic to a class of fidgeting boys, she felt as if her head might explode. A golden ray fell onto her page, and glancing up, she realized it had stopped raining. *Thank God.* "Let's take a quick recess while there's a break in the rain." The classroom erupted, and sinking back into her chair, she rubbed her temples. *How does Katie do this? It's excruciating.*

Pulling the bell cord for some much-deserved tea, she heard footsteps on the stairs. She pinched her cheeks and drew her curl over her shoulder before she reached for the nearest book, wishing to appear as collected as Miss O'Dell. Feeling slightly silly but not enough to drop her carefree charade, she turned the page without reading it.

Hearing shouts from outside, she rustled to the french doors and peeked through the lace curtains to see the twins in an all-out brawl. "Joshua and Jordan! Stop that at once!" she cried as she dropped her book and dashed down the veranda steps. The boys ignored her and fell to the ground, grappling in the soggy grass, turning it into a mud pit.

Gritting her teeth against the mess, she attempted to wrench the two apart, but a misplaced punch knocked her off her feet and face-first into the mud. Colette gasped as she raised herself onto her elbows, feeling the cold mud seep through to her skin.

The horrified twins halted their fight as a pair of strong hands assisted her to her feet. "We're so sorry, Mrs. Olivier," they cried, attempting to wipe off her gown while she scraped the mud from her face, groaning as her cheek was already growing tender.

Malcolm gripped her shoulders, and turning her to inspect her face, he grimaced. "You're going to have quite the shiner."

Colette tried to tip her chin out of his hand. *At least the mud hides my flaming face.*

"What on earth is going on?"

Colette froze at the shrill voice.

"I asked, what is going on? Will someone be kind enough to explain why my daughter is covered in mud?"

Colette turned, smiling through the mud to her mother. "Mother, how kind of you to stop by unannounced. I was just explaining the minerals of mud to the class, of course."

The boys snickered at Mrs. Fontaine's revolted expression.

Colette shot them a scowl, quieting them at once. "There was a small scuffle, but it's all sorted. Allow me to send for some refreshments for you while I clean up a bit."

Mother followed her up the stairs, stating her disapproval in no uncertain terms as Colette had the maid prepare a bath.

"Mother, I'll be at least a half hour. Can't we visit another time?" she called through the crack in the bathroom door as Belinda peeled off her ruined clothing.

"I'm concerned about your reputation. People are beginning to talk," her mother replied.

Clutching her robe to her neck, she poked her head through the door. "What are they saying?"

"Apparently, your own staff has been making comments that you're far too friendly with Mr. Reilly and"—she pursed her lips—"that he's an opportunist."

Colette turned to Belinda, who shrugged and mouthed it wasn't her. Sighing, she lowered herself into the rosewater as her mother listed her iniquities from the other room. After a hasty bath, Colette made herself decent while her mother continued, informing her how stories of Malcolm's low birth were circulating and that he only educated himself enough to snatch up a rich, vulnerable widow of St. Charles Avenue.

"Mr. Reilly has been nothing but a gentleman to me," she gasped, holding her wet braid out of the way as Belinda fastened the last button of her gown.

"Be that as it may, you need to preserve your reputation at any cost for the sake of the school if you want to see it succeed." Glancing at her gold watch pin, Mother rose. "Escort me to the door, dear. I'm afraid I haven't any more time to spare. I'm supposed to meet the seamstress in a quarter of an hour for a fitting for your little cotillion next month."

Leaning against the door, she groaned, relieved at her mother's departure but her head spinning at the news that could ruin everything. *Why, Lord? Why does society have to keep poking their nose in my business and forcing me to do things that aren't needed?*

"We need to get some steak on that eye," Malcolm called from the classroom, mistaking her groan for pain and not dread.

Her hand fluttered to her cheek, and she flinched upon contact. "I'm sure it's not that bad."

His brows rose, silently affirming that it was much, much worse. "I sent the twins to the kitchen with a month's worth of extra chores. And as for you, I was thinking that after a day like you've had, you and I could take a drive to the French Quarter to *Café du Monde* for some coffee and beignets to discuss how we want to handle Katie's classes for the rest of the week. We might want to inquire if Sister Joan can come and help us in Katie's absence," Malcolm suggested, following her into the next room.

She fidgeted with the papers on her desk in their shared office space as the comments made about her relationship with "the help" flew to her mind, along with her mother's parting warning. "Thank you, but I can't as Norman will be calling tonight. However, go ahead and ask Sister Joan if she is able to come."

"That's still going on?"

Startled, she dropped an invoice. "Excuse me?"

"Sorry, I thought that since he was so, um, against the idea of your school that you would've sent him packing by now." He retrieved the bill from the floor, handing it to her.

"We've reached an understanding. Norman simply needed time to get used to the idea. He is quite supportive now." Lifting her paper, she cleared her throat. "Now, if you'll excuse me, I need to see to this bill right away." Ignoring his baffled look, she brushed past him. *I can't let any man hinder me in my work. Be it on purpose or by accident, no one shall stand in the way of my calling again.*

◆— • —◆

Thankful for the children's early bedtimes, Colette ducked into the schoolroom to fetch her Bible for some much-needed quiet time before her late dinner engagement with Norman, but seeing a flicker through the french doors, she stepped out onto the veranda. The delicate perfume of her favorite flower embraced her as scattered gardenia blossoms filled every surface from the door to a candlelit table where Norman stood, a bouquet of gardenias in hand.

"I remember the first time I saw you. Your hair was a bit wilder then, but your free spirit will never change." He reached out and lightly brushed her bruised cheek with his hand.

Her heart fluttered at his compliments, but she wasn't sure if it was love or if it was the scent of gardenias that clouded her mind.

"I wish I could say I've loved you from that moment, but it wasn't until I had to leave you that I knew I had lost something precious." Norman took her hand in his as he guided her to the table. "I cannot express how much I respect your work, drive, and sweet nature. My darling Colette, I think you know what I'm about to ask."

Her hands trembled as she became a girl again, crying over Norman's departure and her cold marriage that never brought her the warmth she had hoped it would.

"When I was away all of those years, I compared every woman I ever called upon to you. The way they made me laugh, or didn't. The way they looked, walked, acted. . .they all made me think of you, and I don't think I could ever be happy with anyone else."

To her surprise, the words she had longed to hear didn't cause her heart to race the way she'd imagined they would. "Norman—"

"Please, let me finish. I was a coward, afraid of marrying without money."

She sobered at the mention of money. "But, you do realize I'm dedicating my fortune to this school, to these boys, don't you?"

"Of course. I love your drive to follow the Lord's calling, but why do it alone when you can have someone by your side?" His hand wrapped about her waist. "To comfort you at night after a long day. To kiss you because you are too pretty not to be kissed." He leaned toward her, his warm breath on her lips. "Marry me."

She hadn't been kissed since she had married Robert, but she hadn't *really* been kissed since that one evening so long ago before Norman left. His lips pressed into hers and she waited for the electricity of old to shoot through her spine, but it felt different from before. It felt forced. She pressed her hands against his chest and gently broke their kiss as the crickets sang about them. At the sound of a window shutting, she twisted about, hoping that Malcolm had not witnessed their kiss.

Norman cupped her chin, returning her focus to him. "You don't have to answer now, but I wanted you to know that, should you choose to become my wife, I would always have your best interest at heart, no matter what."

She started to reply, but Norman rested a finger on her lips. "Sleep on it, my darling, and let me know your answer in three weeks when I return from Charleston."

Chapter 9

S he gazed over the classroom of boys bent over their etiquette test. Norman's question seemed to never leave her as she weighed her options, but she knew she had to decide soon, as he expected her answer at the cotillion ball tomorrow night.

She glanced down at her sketch, which was supposed to be of Norman but had taken a very Malcolm-like turn. She added a fallen curl to the forehead, hoping it would begin to resemble Norman again. *All those years, I dreamt of Norman asking for my hand. Even when I was engaged to Robert, some part of me still hoped Norman would ride up and declare his love for me as an impediment at my wedding ceremony, saving me from a marriage of convenience. Yet even now, Norman didn't mention loving me.* She twisted her pen between her thumb and forefinger. *But, he did say that he'd support my dreams. What other motive but love would cause him to propose since he knows my fortune is going to the school? Lord, please give me some direction.*

"Mrs. Olivier?" One of the seventh-grade boys called to her with his hand raised.

She snapped her sketchbook shut. "You have a question, Jeff?"

He pointed to Julia in the door.

Giving him a nod of thanks, she scooted her chair back and crossed the room. "What's wrong?" she asked in a low voice.

"I need to talk with you"—she gave Colette a pointed stare—"about you know what. It's urgent."

Seeing as the boys had lost all concentration, she rubbed her forehead and announced, "Let's call this test a practice round and have an early recess, shall we?"

The boys hooted as they charged past Julia, heading for the backyard and freedom.

Julia pressed her hands over her ears. "How do you bear such violent din? Is it possible to find a quiet spot?"

"This way." Colette led her sister up into her private parlor where they could not be overheard by little ears. "After a while, you don't notice the noise so much and it becomes more of a hum." She chuckled at Julia's horror. "If it ever *is* quiet, *then* you have a problem." She pulled the bell cord and motioned for Julia to have a seat. "So what was so urgent that you had to interrupt my class?"

Julia sank onto the settee. "You can't trust Norman."

Confused, Colette clicked the door shut. "Why would you say that when you are the one pushing me to accept his hand?"

"Yes, but I overheard him talking with Father in the study last night, and"—Julia dipped her chin—"Father requested that, once the marriage certificate is signed, Norman seize your assets."

"What?" Feeling the room spin, she sank next to Julia. "But he promised I could keep the school."

"Which Father hopes will close in six months' time without the proper funds."

"And Norman?" She pressed her fingers to her lace jabot as Julia gave her a pained stare.

"While he didn't agree to Father's plan, he feels you will choose to close the school on your own volition when you tire of the novelty."

The breath left her lungs and she was left with one thought. "Are you sure?"

"Positive," Julia whispered, drawing her handkerchief from her sleeve. "I wish I wasn't, but it's all true."

She rose and went to the window, letting her forehead rest against the warm pane. *Well, that was quick.*

Her sister came and wrapped her arm around Colette's shoulders. "Were you so very in love with him?"

Colette gave a shaky laugh. "I'm more relieved than anything."

"What?" Julia drew back.

"Norman promised me everything I wanted, but something was holding me back, and now I know why." Her gaze found Malcolm in the side garden, creating a raised bed for part of the agriculture class.

"Oh." Julia tucked her unused handkerchief into her reticule. "Well, I'm glad you took it so well. And it's not as if he were the only eligible bachelor who is interested in you. They've merely taken a step back out of respect for Norman." She gave Colette a peck on the cheek. "We will find you a new suitor who respects your school, never fear."

"Is it so bad that I only wish to marry again if I absolutely adore the man I am to wed? Marriage to Robert was so hard, but I know it can be wonderful." She watched as Malcolm stooped to help Darvy plant his vegetable seeds. "I know it can be sweet. I want that." She turned to Julia. "Is it too much to hope that a widow like me could have a second chance at love?"

Julia clasped her hands around Colette's. "If anyone deserves to be cherished, it's you."

"For all his faults, Norman would've tried to cherish me, but I know now that we could never make each other happy. I'm too independent for him, and he is too set in his ways for me. If I am ever to marry again, I'm going to wait for the Lord to bring me my husband. I've tried society's ways and they failed me. It's time to trust in Him with *every* aspect of my life."

At Julia's departure, Colette opened her inkwell to pen Norman a letter, thanking him for his offer but firmly refusing. Feeling no need to accuse him of scheming with her father, she signed her name with a flourish and descended the stairs to set it on the mail tray.

Hearing Luca practicing on the piano, she paused in the doorway to find that he wasn't alone. There, with the afternoon light spilling onto her beautiful, dark locks,

Malcolm held Katie in his arms as they waltzed about the music room. Colette stiffened, feeling her heart drop into her stomach. She had a hard time swallowing back the lump in her throat as Malcolm stepped on Katie's hem and, giggling, she fell against his chest to avoid having her skirts ripped.

"Really, Malcolm, we've been dancing for weeks. If I didn't know any better, I would think you were *trying* to tear my skirt." Katie winked boldly at Malcolm as he righted her.

Before she could be spotted, Colette slipped into the shadows of the hallway and deposited her letter, feeling cold. *If I'm to be alone, so be it. Lord, help me bear it.*

With tears stinging and her lungs burning, she turned away. Then she heard something shatter in the direction of the kitchen. Exhaling, she swiped at her cheeks and changed course to find Tommy and the twins covered in flour and Davey and Darvy fighting over the bowl of batter. "Boys! What on earth?"

Darvy silently pulled his finger from the batter, and the boys shuffled in the flour for an explanation.

"Why didn't you ask the cook for a snack if you were hungry?" She lifted her skirts to avoid the flour on the floor and reached for a clean rag to wipe off their faces.

"We wanted to surprise you—" Davey began but stopped as Darvy elbowed him in the ribs.

"Surprise me? Well, indeed you have, but for what occasion did you want to surprise me?" She bit the inside of her mouth as she ran the rag over Darvy's face.

Relieved that she wasn't angry, Tommy shrugged. "The cotillion ball is tomorrow, so we wanted to make a chocolate cake to say sorry for almost breaking your toe five times."

The door swung open, and Ralph, the eldest boy, halted in his tracks at the sight of Colette standing in the middle of the mess. "I said to wait for me, fellows. I'm sorry, Mrs. Olivier. I guess they"—he glared at the others—"got too excited to wait while I dug up my ma's old recipe."

Her heart warmed at the boys rallying together for her. Grinning, she grabbed an apron. "Ralph, you're the teacher tonight, because my mama never let me near the stove. Let's get baking!" The Lord had seen to it that she would never be alone on this earth again.

+•————•+

Dressed in a new satin cerulean gown with a low, square neck, pointed waist, and short puffed sleeves, Colette felt rather exposed after wearing such dowdy clothes in public for years, but as it was for the cotillion ball, she hoped her guests would deem it appropriate. Giving one last twirl in the ballroom looking glass, she surveyed the room, checking that everyone and everything was in its place.

Not a minute too soon, Katie brought in the boys and instructed them to stand tall in their formal wear as Mrs. Wilson heralded in the girls from her Sunday school class along with their chaperones. Colette laughed behind her fan as she watched the boys halt their fidgeting and become uncharacteristically quiet while the girls gathered on the other side of the room and the musicians began to play.

To get the dancing started, Colette and Ralph began the first waltz. The young man led her about the room with confidence, and Colette was filled with pride that he had made it through the dance without a single mishap. With a curtsy, she whispered her congratulations and pointed him in the direction of a pretty raven-haired girl.

Jumping at the touch on the small of her back, Colette turned to find Norman. "Mr. Hartley!"

"So formal." He grinned. "May I have the honor of this dance, *Mrs. Olivier?*"

She felt the blood drain from her face and glanced around for Julia, hoping her sister could save her. *Why is that girl always late?* "You wish to dance with me?"

"Please." He gave her a bow. "I've dreamed of little else during my business trip."

He didn't get the letter, she thought with horror. "Wait!"

Norman pulled her onto the dance floor. "I had thought I'd get a better welcoming than this," he teased, "all things considered."

"Norman, can we go outside and talk?" she whispered, feeling frantic as he whirled her about in the candlelight.

"Eager to kiss me again, are you?" He winked at her. "Well, you'll have to wait, little lady. I have been dying to hold you close, and as dancing is the only means of doing that until we are wed, I plan to keep you on the dance floor all evening."

The heat rushed to her cheeks as she attempted to put a little distance between them as they waltzed. "Norman. . .I know what Father asked you to do."

He missed a step and his grip tightened. "Regarding?"

"The school," her voice strained. "He asked you to consider seizing my assets."

"But I didn't agree to it," he replied, eyes wide as if he was more taken aback over being caught than ashamed of the conversation that transpired.

"But you didn't say you wouldn't," she whispered, almost apologetically. "And how can I trust a man who won't even stand up to the bullying of my own father? I sent you a note explaining everything. Didn't you get it?"

"No. I came straight from the station so as to not miss your school's debut dance." He pressed his lips into a thin line.

"May I cut in?" Malcolm tapped him on the shoulder.

At the sight of the Irishman, Norman looked as if he might begin throwing punches, but he clenched his jaw and gave her a slight bow. "Let's talk more later."

"I'm sorry," she replied, truly meaning it, "but there's nothing to discuss."

Malcolm placed a hand on her waist and waltzed her a little stiffly about the room with the rest of the class, sending the chaperones twittering behind their fluttering fans.

"I thought you said you didn't dance." Although relieved at his timing, she couldn't help but jab, still stinging from his rejection.

"I didn't, but I've been practicing in the hope that one day, I could do this"—he twirled her out onto the veranda.

"What on earth do you think you are doing?" she whispered. "We need to get back inside at once before people begin to talk."

"I heard about Norman's proposal. You can't marry him."

"That, sir, is *none* of your business." She moved to head back inside.

He took her by the elbows, turning her to him. "You can't marry him because he doesn't love you."

Is it that obvious? Hurt filled her features as she tried to pull away.

"I do," he whispered and reached out, stroking her cheek.

"What?" Her voice caught in her throat.

"I love you, Colette Olivier. Am I foolish to think you feel the same? We are from two completely different worlds, but I can't help thinking that we belong together. . . even though everyone is pushing you toward someone more suited to you." He took her hand in his. "But no one can force you to marry this time."

"What about Miss O'Dell?" she fumbled.

"Katie?"

"I saw you two dancing with only Luca as a chaperone. You didn't seem to have any trouble asking her to dance for the last few weeks." She lifted her chin.

Malcolm inhaled sharply through his teeth. "You saw that, did you?"

She gave a curt nod, disappointed he apparently had attempted to hide it from her.

"Nothing happened between us. She is seeing a close friend of mine."

"Then why—?"

"We were dancing because I felt bad that I couldn't help you in your cotillion class. I know the dances of the middle class, but your upper classes have a different way of doing things, so I asked Katie to teach me how to dance like a proper gentleman."

"Oh." She blushed, dazed by how far he went out of his way to please her.

"I love you, Colette, and I believe in our calling to raise these boys, but I don't see why we can't do it together as husband and wife. People may say I'm an opportunist, but I don't care one whit about your money. I want you to spend it all on our legacy, our boys and our school. And if you ever had doubts of me. . ." He pulled a single pink ribbon, stained on the ends with faded ink, and draped it in her palm.

She traced the ribbon. "Is this. . . ?"

"Aye. It's only ever been you in my heart, Colette," he whispered, his hands at her waist, drawing her near as the violinists began to play "Love's Old Sweet Song," its enchanting lilt floating out and enveloping them. "Say you'll be mine and let me cherish you forever."

She couldn't breathe. All she could think of was kissing this man who loved her.

"If you need to think about it, I understand." Malcolm misinterpreted her silence.

"I don't."

"Oh." His expression fell as he stepped back. "I see."

"Because I want everything you want." She closed the distance between them. "I want to love and be loved. I want someone who will treasure my boys, teach them to be men, and do anything to protect them and me. You have my hand and my heart, Malcolm Reilly." Wrapping her arms around his neck, she lifted her lips to his and lost herself in his kiss only to find the warmth and tenderness she had been dreaming of for years.

Epilogue

Feeling like a bride for the first time, Colette took a deep breath as she lowered her veil and accepted her wedding bouquet from Julia. Smiling so much her cheeks hurt, she descended the stairs and followed the path of rose petals out into the garden, where Malcolm waited under the giant moss-trimmed oaks.

The boys filled the chairs, and as Luca began playing the violin, they rose, their eager faces finding hers as a few hoots and hollers passed their lips. Katie shushed them, and Colette couldn't help but laugh, as she wished to shout herself. In the front row, she found her mother's supportive smile and felt the lack of her father's presence, but with time, she prayed he would come around to accepting Malcolm into the family.

Leaving all thoughts but Malcolm behind, Colette placed her hand in his and promised to be his forever.

Grace Hitchcock is a Louisiana Southerner living in Colorado with her husband, Dakota. She is a member of ACFW and has a master's in creative writing. *The Widow of St. Charles Avenue* is her first Barbour novella. Visit Grace on her website at GraceHitchcockBooks.com.

Married by Mistake

by Laura V. Hilton

Acknowledgments

I'd like to offer my heartfelt thanks to the following:

To my critique group—you know who you are. You are amazing and knew how to ask the right questions when more detail was needed. Also thanks for the encouragement. Candee, thanks for reading large amounts in a short time and offering wise suggestions.

And to my husband, Steve, for being a tireless proof-reader and cheering section. To Jenna for reading over my shoulder and editing as I wrote— also for naming the horses.

To Loundy: my favorite song.
To Michael: my adventurous one.
To Kristin: my darling daughter.
To Jenna: my sunshine.
To Kaeli: my showers of blessing.

To God be the glory.

Chapter 1

Mackinac Island, 1902

A kiss.

The sea spray touched Bessie O'Hara's face as gently as she imagined he—whoever he might be—would someday brush his lips across her cheeks.

She couldn't wait.

If only she could skip all the tiresome courtship rituals like monotonous parlor visits and chaperoned strolls. She'd also eliminate the formal calling cards and fluttering fans society demanded and go straight to the happily-ever-after.

It wasn't that easy. She glanced at her two cousins, giggling behind their fans, as they stepped off the ferry onto the dock leading to the island. They looked toward some gentlemen who'd come to meet the boat. Judging by the men's clothing, they were there for the summer season as well. They certainly weren't employees hired to drive the buggies and wagons.

Bessie smoothed her dress. Splotches of water dampened the material under her touch. With a sigh, she looked around for her family's carriage. Papa had wired ahead and told the driver when to meet the ferry. She didn't see the carriage, but a large crowd blocked her view.

She didn't want to do this. Not that she minded visiting her family's vacation home on the island, or escaping the stifling August heat of Grand Rapids, or even spending time with her cousins. But this was so much more than a summer reprieve. Henrietta and Rosella were husband-hunting and dragging her along, completely against her will.

And worse? Her parents completely agreed with her cousins. It was time she got married. That was a woman's highest calling—to manage a husband and a household.

Or so she'd been told.

She'd been looked over so many times before, she was afraid of facing another rejection. Was she somehow defective because her hair wasn't pale blond like Rosella's or a deep, dark red like Henrietta's? She dreaded being put on endless display in the "meat market" and found lacking over and over during the tiresome rituals.

If only she could have said husband handed to her, dropped in her lap, maybe even delivered, gift-wrapped with a ribbon and a card reading, "Here he is. Treat him well." Instead she'd been forced to endure countless teas in stifling parlors from her usual place on the fringes.

Bessie hurried to catch up with her cousins who already neared the end of the dock. She didn't want to be left behind. A gentleman wearing a plaid cap stood in her way, talking to someone. She stepped to the side to keep from hitting him, but he turned sharply and bumped her in the side with his elbow. Her foot landed on the edge of the dock. She groped for something to grab on to but came up with nothing but air. She gulped a breath that emerged as a high-pitched squeal, and tumbled toward the water.

A strong hand grabbed her by the back of her dress, jerking the fabric up tight, and she flailed. Was this how a fish on a hook felt? She eyed the cold, fishy water she'd almost fallen into. Seconds later, another hand closed around her elbow, the grip tightening as the hand on her dress released the material, grabbed her around her waist, and hauled her back against a firm chest.

Shock raced through her body like the rise and fall of waves crashing against the shore during a storm. His arm firm against her, the man loosened his grip on her elbow. Then the arm wrapped around her waist slid away.

Slid—the fingers took a leisurely tour of the silky fabric covering her abdomen. There had to be something improper about this, but the touch set her senses on fire, charring her thoughts almost before they formed. She tried to take a deep breath and light-headedness made her dizzy, overwhelmed with how quickly her situation had changed from impending bath to rescue.

"Watch where you're going." The voice was brusque, hardly matching the rest of the sensations. And with those harsh words, he released her. Her feet were set firmly on the wood planks, and she was set free from his disturbing touch.

Bessie jerked her shoulders in an angry twitch as she turned carefully around and moved away from the edge of the dock. She didn't want a repeat performance. "Watch where I'm going? Let's try being more careful, Mr. . . ."

Her voice trailed off as she stared into grayish-blue eyes, the color of the water on a winter day. Stubble shadowed the man's chin, and his equally dark hair, a bit on the long side, peeked out from under his plaid cap.

He adjusted the brim as a muscle jerked in his jaw.

Wait. He was the man who'd stood on the opposite side of the ferry and stared at her during their ride over to the island, his gaze boring into her until she turned to fully face him.

He'd quickly looked away.

Her fingers had itched to sketch his portrait. Strong. Dark. Handsome. And dangerous. She tried to memorize his features, but he'd glanced back at her and caught her staring.

Then it had been her turn to look away and try to distract herself by listening to another half hour of her cousins giggling about potential prospects.

"You." The single word sputtered out without warning. She resisted the urge to clamp her hand over her mouth. Maybe she should apologize for being so rude. But then she'd need an explanation for why she'd said it, and she had none. Other than. . . well, he drew her and made her long to get to know him. Not that she'd ever admit it to anyone.

He bowed, his lips twisting into something resembling a grimace, and he waved his hand. "Ladies first."

Thomas Hale averted his gaze from the swish of aqua skirts, fighting the urge to rush after her and explain his rude behavior. It had been aimed at himself, not her. He had no right to notice a woman. No right to look. Not after. . .

Well, his chances were over, that's all. And nothing would change it. He was ruined. And any woman—well, at least one like her—would run in the opposite direction rather than have her name associated with his.

As soon as his groceries were unloaded from the ferry, he'd stow them in his buggy and go to the one place he was safe.

He blew out a frustrated breath, wishing for the umpteenth time he'd sent his housekeeper to do the shopping for him so that he wouldn't have to cast a shadow on the socialites descending on the island in droves. A cooler place to spend the summer. The place to be seen.

A place to hide.

"Tommy." A hand closed on his shoulder, drawing him to a stop.

Swallowing his annoyance, Thomas turned—and met the concerned eyes of his best friend, Archie. He'd met Thomas at the ferry a few moments earlier to see if he might be interested in any of the debutantes.

They had been standing on the dock, talking, Archie studying the beauties in colorful dresses, Thomas ignoring them. Until he'd gotten sidetracked by the beauty in aqua. He'd noticed her on the boat, but prior to that, at the dock on the mainland, bending down to pet a stray dog and feeding it bites of her sandwich after another passenger kicked at it. And after a porter was screamed at by the same passenger for being so inept, she'd been quick to thank him for handling her luggage so efficiently and had even gone to speak to the porter's boss about his excellent service. That said much about her character.

The fact that she wasn't giggling behind her fan and making eyes at eligible bachelors said even more.

She was someone he wanted to know.

"You could meet her if you would go to the social events in town." Archie tilted his head in her direction. "I know you've received invitations."

There was a very good reason he'd not responded to the many invitations he'd received. If Pauline came to the island and spread her ridiculous stories about his being a spy as well as her lies about him accosting her lady's maid, it would be her word they'd believe. Not his. Especially if any of them had witnessed the loud, angry, hateful words she'd spewed at him. And the equally unkind words he'd shouted in reply. And it would define him. Better to let the silence define him instead.

Besides, the wounds were still too fresh. Or maybe he'd simply allowed them to fester. It had been a year.

"I need to go. Must. . ." His breath came in gasps as if he'd been running. No! He wouldn't allow himself to fall apart in public. He'd be the talk of the town for the rest of the season—and beyond.

Breathe.

"I still need to talk to you." Archie squeezed his shoulder. "Can we meet sometime? Come to my house. Soon."

Thomas nodded, his gaze drifting again to the girl with honey-colored hair.

He had received an invitation to some event to take place that very night. What was it? He'd probably thrown the thick, embossed card away.

But maybe she'd be there.

And while he shouldn't—wouldn't—approach her, there was no harm in looking.

Bessie settled her skirts around herself as she sat down on the piano stool. She let her fingers trickle over the keys while the servants unloaded their luggage.

Henrietta stood at the door and barked orders. Rosella had gone upstairs, after the servant carried her trunk up, yelling for her maid so she could start getting ready for the masquerade ball tonight at the Grand Hotel.

It promised to be a lot of fun. If one liked that sort of thing.

Fun.

Ha! It was a meaningless game, guaranteed to hurt someone. Why should she flirt with members of the opposite sex when she hadn't any idea if she'd like them or not in real life? The one suitor who'd been gentlemanly and attentive to her in the parlor turned into something else when she saw him on the street a few days later berating a delivery boy.

How could one even imagine falling in love when meeting like this, with everyone on their best behavior, dressed up and acting? She was sick of pretending, and faking her smile. It was getting harder and harder to feign interest when yet another young man rambled on about his family's vacation home in the Adirondacks, when what she really wanted to know was if he noticed the colors in the sunset or found joy in a gentle breeze on his face.

Bessie shifted on the seat and let her fingers crash onto the keys.

Henrietta winced as she glanced at her.

"The piano needs tuning." Bessie stood.

"You don't need to screw up your face so. Or break the keys in the process."

Bessie rolled her eyes. "When Jackson comes by, ask him to please find a piano tuner. I'm going to take a bath and prepare for tonight."

"You? Prepare before us?" Henrietta fanned herself then laughed. "Did you see someone at the dock who interested you? Do tell."

"No." But the image of the man who'd stared at her, the one who'd saved her from drowning—though it was his fault she almost did—flashed through her mind. "Besides, even if I did, how would I recognize him? We'll be disguised." Except she might recognize his dark hair. And those stormy blue-gray eyes would still be visible through a mask.

"If you did? *If* you did? Oooh, sounds like it's pretty definite, then. Who is he? Were you formally introduced? Why weren't we introduced? Oh, and where were we? Seems we would've noticed this man, too. What's his name?"

Bessie waved off her cousin's questions as she went past.

"Rosella and I will be watching you tonight," Henrietta warned.

"You'll be too busy flirting with your own potential beaux to pay any attention to me and mine." Hopefully.

Because she definitely would be looking for someone.

Chapter 2

The crush of people in the Grand Hotel ballroom overwhelmed Thomas to the point he wanted to turn around and have his driver take him home. Immediately. If not sooner. Even if it meant giving up or missing out on meeting *her*.

But he'd already shown his invitation and been admitted. And after he'd hunted everywhere for the invitation, finally finding it tossed carelessly on the piano keyboard in his music room, he didn't want to waste his time.

Of course, if *she* wasn't there, it would be a waste of time anyway.

He hadn't attended a masquerade ball in over a year, but he still remembered how it worked. They'd keep up their disguises until midnight, when all would be revealed. He simply needed to find *her*, flirt a bit, maybe share a dance, and disappear before midnight. Remaining anonymous suited his purposes. Especially since this flirtation would—could—go nowhere.

But even though he kept telling himself it was wrong, he felt a need to feed this attraction to the first woman who'd captured his eye in the past year.

"Do you see her?" Archie stood beside him. They'd arrived, not exactly together, but at the same time.

Thomas scanned the crowd, hoping she wasn't one of the women in the concealing masks and overwhelming hats covering the hair with ostrich feathers soaring to impossible heights. If she was, then he'd never be able to find her.

And. . . There. His gaze grabbed hold of a woman wearing a sparkly, cream-colored dress, her mask held by a stick in one hand, her honey-colored hair loose around her shoulders.

His heart thudded, racing faster than a deer trying to escape a pack of hungry wolves. His breath came in spurts. Women didn't have this effect on him. Not even Pauline, and he'd courted her with an eye toward marriage. Thank God he hadn't proposed. But he'd been planning to.

And then it all went bad. Worse than bad.

He shook his head. Maybe he should look for Pauline before he approached another woman. She would jettison his future before it could even set sail. She hadn't been on the ferry late that morning, but that didn't mean she hadn't arrived earlier in the week. After all, she normally came once or twice in a season for a brief appearance. She hated being on the island and having no escape except by boat but seemed to feel obligated to be seen.

If she was at the ball, she'd effectively disguised herself beyond recognition. Which, of course, was the point.

He looked back at *her*. Was she meeting someone there? Was that why she wore a simplistic disguise? So she would be recognized—as Pauline had done at their last masquerade ball together? "You'll know me by the single blue feather in my hat," she'd said with a wink. And he had.

"I have the most brilliant of ideas," Archie said, interrupting Thomas's thoughts. "When you come over tomorrow, I'll discuss it with you. Maybe the beauty in white would be willing to help."

"Help with what?" Thomas asked. He hadn't meant to reveal the woman he had an interest in. But given the way he'd been staring at her, it would be amazing if everyone didn't realize who it was. At least she hadn't had a male chaperone approach and demand to know his intentions.

"All in good time, my friend. All in good time. Why don't you ask her for a dance? I'll catch up with her later." Archie walked two steps away, stopped, then turned back. "On second thought, I'll ask her now. It'll take you some time to work up your courage. *You* can catch up with her later." He winked and headed the opposite direction.

Toward *her*.

Thomas let him go. But the thought of holding her in his arms for a waltz. . . He could be persuaded.

On the other hand, there was no way they could be anything more than acquaintances, so why torture himself?

Because it would give him pleasant memories, that was why. Something to remember during the long, cold, lonely nights that ruled his future.

He hunted deep inside for an ember of courage, fanned the flame to life, then followed Archie, or at least attempted to. A hand to his upper arm stopped him. The woman wore a reddish-black dress that emphasized her considerable charms. Was this Pauline? His heart stuttered, and he studied her closer. The mask disguising her face and the huge feather-adorned hat covering her hair rendered her unidentifiable.

"May I have this dance?" Her voice, a grating falsetto, had been altered somehow, either by the mask or by her own efforts.

He nodded and led her onto the dance floor, positioning himself as near to Archie and his partner as possible.

And maybe, if God smiled on him, they could switch partners.

◆—•——•—◆

Bessie twirled around the room on the arm of yet another man. Her toes were sore from being stepped on a few too many times, but that was probably her own fault for stepping forward instead of back at the appropriate times. She'd been too busy watching the other dancers instead of paying attention to the leading of her partner.

She'd looked for the man with the mesmerizing eyes she'd seen at the wharf, but none she gazed into were familiar. And none of the arms that held her sent tingles up her spine.

Maybe she was wrong to want to become acquainted with a man solely because of his physical appearance and aura, but warm thrills were preferable to repulsion. And she'd experienced that enough times. She excused herself to the next man who asked for a dance, accepted a glass of lemonade as she passed the concession table, and made her way to the doors leading to the hotel gardens.

She stepped outside and descended the stairs leading to the gardens and the lake, letting the mask fall to her side.

"Dangerous for a woman to be outside unchaperoned, don't you think?" The familiar voice whispered out of the darkness.

It's him! Bessie stumbled and then righted herself just before she fell. Her lemonade sloshed and she set the cup down on a bench. She glanced around then belatedly jerked the mask into place. No one appeared for a long, endless, heart-pounding moment. And then—a dark shadow emerged from the night farther down the path.

"Plenty of chaperones around, sir." She made a point at glancing back toward the hotel. She saw nothing but dark forms moving past the windows on the outside and the brightly lit people inside.

"I guess you're right." He moved closer. "I've been watching you."

She raised her eyebrows but said nothing. Really, she couldn't think of anything to say. Except for maybe expressing her joy that he'd looked for her. Located her. And made a point to approach her.

"I wanted to ask you to dance. But you've suffered from no lack of partners."

Or sore toes. At least she hadn't danced holes into her slippers. She winced and subtly shifted.

"I needed fresh air." Her voice finally emerged. She didn't mean to sound breathless. But he'd *found* her and asked her to dance.

"It's stifling in there," he agreed. Strains of music from a new song, "The Woodland Waltz," filled the air, mixing with the gentle sounds of the waves on the lake. He held out his arms. "May I have this dance?"

She smiled. And stepped into his arms.

◆•———•◆

Ah. Heaven. Thomas drew her nearer, his pulse pounding harder with every breath. "Couple dances are nicer than group dances." Thomas kept his tone casual, but his racing heart didn't need convincing. He encircled her waist with his right arm and held her right hand in his left. A shiver coursed through his body at the closeness of her. How many times had he dreamed of this moment—dancing in the moonlight with *her*—without even knowing whom he dreamed of? Just some cloudy vision of a woman—the one who made him spring to life in every way possible.

He could barely believe he held her—even if it was at arm's length and not in an embrace. And he didn't even know who she was. Not her name—nothing. Just that she was *the one*.

The music played, and their feet moved together in rhythm. *One-two-three and one-two-three and one-two-three.* She attempted to keep her face covered with the stick-held mask but gave up, maybe believing the darkness hid her. And it would have, except for the moon. His gaze never left her face. She nearly took his breath away. Those hazel eyes, her skin glowing in the moonlight. The not-too-full, not-too-thin lips. How was she not yet some lucky man's wife?

"Am I making anyone jealous?" The question escaped before he could bite back his curiosity.

She peered up at him from under long, dark lashes. "I doubt it."

"Don't be so sure. You don't know the effect you have on a man's heart." His voice turned husky without his permission. He jerked his gaze away and struggled to hide the emotion that probably was written all over his face—thank goodness most of it was hidden behind his mask. But he couldn't escape the scent of her. The faint fragrance of lilacs washed over him, and he drank it in.

She seemed oblivious to the spell she'd cast on him, but temptation was driving him mad. As highly improper as it was, he wanted to kiss her. But he knew that once he did, he'd never again be able to think with his head and not his heart.

It wouldn't be right.

Once Thomas had trusted that God had a perfect plan for his life. He'd assumed a year ago that Pauline would be part of it. Now he wasn't at all sure.

" 'Pride goeth before destruction, and a haughty spirit before a fall,' " he muttered as the dance ended.

"Excuse me?" Her eyes widened.

He shook his head. "Talking to myself."

He bowed as he released her and stepped out of the moonlight, choosing the darkest path that could take him away from her.

Chapter 3

Bessie stood on her tiptoes, her muscles straining, and searched for the man who'd danced with her in the moonlight. It was after midnight and the revealing had occurred. And while people had begun to depart, they were leaving so slowly it was like a herd of turtles moving through peanut butter.

Nowhere did she see someone who might be *him*.

It had been the man from the ferry and the dock who danced with her in the moonlight. Though she couldn't see his uncommonly intense eyes, she'd recognized his voice. The feel of his hand.

She hadn't seen him at all after their dance. Not even when she strolled through the crowd, looking, searching. Hoping for a sign that even if she didn't recognize him, he'd recognize her. Maybe give her a wink or a special look. Something to indicate he might feel the same interest in her as she did in him.

No one. Nothing.

Had he left? Or maybe she'd imagined the romantic dance in the moonlight, a couple gazing into each other's eyes?

The warmth where he'd touched her lingered, suggesting otherwise.

Henrietta leaned close. "We should be inundated with invitations tomorrow. This is going to be so much fun." Her voice ended in a tiny squeal that she quickly smothered with her hand.

An answering wave of excitement washed through Bessie. Tomorrow, while they were at home, maybe she'd while away the quiet time by sketching a couple dancing in the moonlight, with the lake sparkling behind them. But she'd have to be very careful not to reveal herself as the female in the picture, or her cousins would tease her mercilessly. Thank God they'd been inside and hadn't seen her dancing with the stranger.

But *him*. . . Yes. He would be there. And her. She'd paint herself from behind. Or the side, maybe.

"Did you meet someone?" Rosella asked as she joined them. She glanced from Henrietta to Bessie. Her cheeks were bright, her eyes twinkled, and a slight smile curved her lips.

Henrietta gave Rosella an answering grin. But Bessie looked away from her cousins and scanned the crowd one more time.

The mysterious stranger must have been her imagination.

She looked up at the stars in the night sky and pinpointed one that shone bigger and brighter than the others. It reminded her of a new nursery rhyme she'd read to her niece before she left for the island. *Star light, star bright, first star I see tonight. . .* She might get better results if she were to pray. *Dear God, someday I'd like to dance in the moonlight with my future husband. Someday. . .*

And with that prayer on her lips and in her heart, she followed her cousins to the buggy.

◆━━━◆

As Henrietta predicted, they woke the next morning to a stack of invitations. The last one they opened was to tea and croquet that afternoon hosted by Mr. Archibald Asparagus.

"What do you think?" Rosella waved the invitation. "This afternoon. We don't have anything else going on then, and croquet sounds fun. But I don't remember meeting a Mr. Asparagus last night, do you?"

Bessie shook her head. She certainly didn't remember meeting a man named after a green vegetable. But what if it was *him*? Though with such an unfortunate name. . .

Bessie Asparagus?

But still. What if it was *him*?

Bessie Asparagus? Ugh.

"I think we should go." Henrietta snatched the invitation from Rosella.

Rosella shrugged. "He might be new money. I agree. We should go. What can it hurt? And it might be fun. Bessie?"

Bessie nodded. At the very least, it would settle the question of whether or not her mystery dance partner was named after a vegetable.

◆━━━◆

Soft voices wafted in from the parlor as Thomas approached.

"Thomas Hale," the butler announced.

Archie stood from the edge of the chair where he had perched. "Tommy, my man. So glad you could join us. You know my brother, Junior. And these lovely ladies are Miss Henrietta Johnson, Miss Rosella Everson, and Miss Bessie O'Hara of Grand Rapids."

"Nice to meet you, Mr. Hale," one of the women said.

Thomas nodded, his gaze skimming over the ladies. He hesitated, backtracking, as Archie gave a low chuckle. The lady in the pale green afternoon dress—Miss Bessie O'Hara—was the woman who'd haunted his dreams last night. The misty lady on the ferry. His moonlight dance partner.

The owner of his heart.

Well, a bit presumptive on his part, considering they didn't know each other. But as unbelievable as it seemed, his heart recognized her.

It was crazy, but. . . He smiled and extended his hand. "Miss O'Hara."

"Thomas is of the Hale Mining Company, operating out of Marquette," Archie explained.

Thomas held her hand a second too long as he bowed over it.

"Mr. Hale." Her voice sounded breathless. His probably did, too. *Bessie.* Was that a diminutive for Elizabeth, Beatrice, or Bessandra?

He released her hand as he remembered the other two twittering, fidgeting ladies waiting. He struggled to remember their names, but years of society mingling kicked in.

"Miss Everson. Miss Johnson." He bowed over each hand as he said their names.

"Mr. Hale," they repeated in unison, still giggling.

He took his seat and the ladies resumed chattering. Except Bessie. She sat quietly, her face flushed. But everything about her screamed his interest was reciprocated.

"Ah, our tea is here," Archie murmured.

"Would you care for some refreshment, Mr. Hale?" A maid appeared at Thomas's side, a silver tea tray in her hands. She set the tray on a small round serving table and reached for an upside-down teacup, one with gold trim and gold- and silver-colored flowers delicately painted on the fine china. Thomas eyed the mismatched cups and saucers, but Archie made no apologies. Thomas supposed the eclectic character of the pieces added to the charm of the tea setting. His mother had the same type of collection in their family home in Marquette. The Upper Peninsula city was near the mines and the shipping company, and within view of Lake Superior from where they shipped the iron ore.

The iron ore that was the cause of his life falling apart.

Even Father didn't completely understand Thomas taking a sabbatical to "hide" for a year on Mackinac Island instead of staying home and helping run the family business as he should.

Now that the newest flock of debutantes was flooding his island sanctuary in waves, Thomas's determination to hide here to lick his wounds no longer made sense. He had first come in the winter, when the only inhabitants were the year-round residents.

He shook himself out of his memories and glanced at Archie in time to see his cousin's head tilt, a sure sign he'd asked a question. "Beg your pardon?"

"I asked if you wanted to play in two teams of three, or individually?" Archie set his teacup on the tray.

Thomas opened his mouth then shut it. The ladies should choose.

But Junior grinned. "I think two teams. Men against women. Either that, or I'll take the lovely Miss"—he scratched his chin—"Everest as my partner."

The two girls giggled behind their hands again. "Everson," one of them corrected.

Archie shrugged. "Men against women might be best. But that's kind of an unfair advantage against us men." He winked, but Thomas didn't know at whom.

"I think individually would be fine. I'm not very athletic and would hate to hurt anyone else's score," Bessie said.

"I'll be glad to help you, Miss O'Hara." Thomas set his half-full cup down on the tray. He wasn't a big fan of tea and preferred the bitter sludge of coffee. He reached for the last remaining scone. He sliced it open and spread butter and an odd-colored jam across both sides. "What kind of jam is this?"

"I think Cook said blood orange. It's quite good." Junior frowned at it then pulled his watch from his pocket and frowned again as he headed to the door. "I hate leaving you in the lurch, but I just remembered something I was supposed to do yesterday and shan't be able to do tomorrow."

"Nice seeing you, Junior. Anyone want the other half of this scone?" Thomas asked.

Archie waved it off as Junior left, and the giggling duo shook their heads.

"No, thank you," Bessie said. "Besides, you haven't had any yet, and the rest of us have."

What she'd said. . . Thomas glanced at the tray again. The empty teacups, the scones, gone, except for what he'd just taken. How much had he missed? He grimaced. "I didn't mean to be rude." But he couldn't think of any way to explain his sudden lapse of attention.

◆━━━━◆

Bessie studied the handsome man across from her. The one who'd stared at her on the ferry. The one who'd come across her in the darkness and danced with her beside the moonlit waters. So romantic.

Mr. Asparagus summoned his maid to have the remnants of tea removed, then stood. "Shall we adjourn to the backyard for croquet?"

"We must excuse ourselves for a moment first." Henrietta rose and grabbed Rosella's hand. They scurried from the room, following the directions of the maid.

Mr. Asparagus smiled. "Perfect. I needed to talk to you both. As Tommy knows, I'm thinking of opening my family home as a resort."

Bessie glanced around. "That would be lovely."

"I want to retain a photographer to snap a wedding on the premises, with flowers in bloom, the lake in the background, a beautiful reception. If we post photos in the newspapers of larger cities across the nation, it would help my dreams materialize. I was thinking of the two of you posing as the happy bride and groom. That white sparkly dress you wore to the masquerade ball last night, Miss O'Hara, would be perfect. That is what made me think of it. Would you be agreeable? I'd see that you are rewarded handsomely."

Mr. Hale coughed. "You want us to pose as a bride and groom? Miss O'Hara and me?"

"Yes, of course. It is perfect. I'll invite everyone summering on the island to be our guests for a. . .a. . .a reenactment."

"Exactly what would we reenact?" Mr. Hale's voice hardened.

Did he object to posing with her specifically, or to the idea in general? His voice reminded her of when he'd quoted scripture about pride before disappearing into the darkness.

"My grandparents' wedding at this very place, many years ago." Mr. Asparagus grinned. "It'd be loads of fun, and completely innocent. I'll design the invitations myself tonight. Arrange for someone to stand in for a preacher. Chairs. Flowers."

Bessie blinked. "It's just pretend, right? You want to go to all that trouble for just a few pictures?"

"Absolutely. We'll invite people to a party with a surprise reenactment as part of the program. It's all in fun and a good business plan, I think. What could possibly go wrong?"

Chapter 4

The temperature outside was pert near perfect. Thomas stood back and watched as the other four players chose their matching mallets and balls. Miss Everson scooted ahead of everyone, picking a bright green set. Archie waved Miss Johnson forward. She chose orange, which made Thomas think of his childhood Christmases and the lone orange with a handful of nuts and either a shiny red apple or a grapefruit tucked into his stocking. The only time of the year they had oranges when he was growing up. His mouth watered.

Miss O'Hara chose a sunny yellow, and Archie reached for the black. "At least I'm not going to get the color matching my name this time."

A few nervous—or maybe embarrassed—titters from the ladies followed his comment.

"In a book I read a few summers ago," Bessie said, "the heroine in the story played croquet with the queen. But instead of using balls, they used hedgehogs, and instead of mallets, they used flamingoes. They didn't follow any set rules, either. Everyone just played when they wanted. In fact, if I remember right, the hoops were all soldiers bending over backward."

Archie blinked at her. "We have no hedgehogs, flamingoes, or soldiers here. The fort was abandoned seven years ago."

"So you like to read, Bes. . .uh, Miss O'Hara?" Thomas asked. That would be a plus on the long, dark, frigid Upper Peninsula nights.

"She's a regular bookworm," one of her cousins said dryly. Thomas didn't catch which one.

The tiny tip of Miss O'Hara's tongue caught his attention as she ran it over her lips. She dipped her head, her face flushed.

What? It wasn't anything to be embarrassed about. "I like Mark Twain's writings. And Charles Dickens."

She glanced up, a tiny smile flickered then grew. "I love to read."

Obviously, since she'd been described as a bookworm, but that was a start at having a conversation. He grinned back at her. "What else do you enjoy, Miss O'Hara?"

She looked away.

"She's quite an accomplished pianist." Miss Everson lined her ball up in front of the first set of double hoops and took aim. But it wasn't a very good shot, and the green ball stopped halfway through the first hoop. But since it was halfway, it counted as going through, so she got another shot.

"I can't wait to hear you play sometime. Maybe I could come calling." What was he thinking? He'd been much too bold, and his face heated. He should deflect some of his attention toward the others, as if he meant the trio, not her personally. "Are you ladies taking callers?"

"That would be lovely." Miss Everson straightened after tapping her ball. "We arrived ahead of our families. They're assuming all the events we attend will be well chaperoned." She shrugged. "But our mothers will arrive within a few days, and our fathers at the end of the month. Perhaps then we could send you and Mr. Asparagus an invitation to dinner."

"Perfect." With a smirk, Archie lined up his black ball and hit it through both hoops, knocking the green ball so that it rolled several feet away from the hoops. Two free shots for going through the hoops, and those shots put him through the next hoop.

He moved quickly through the course, hitting the ball through the double hoops at the end, hitting the stake, then moving the ball enough to knock it back through the hoops.

Thomas swallowed the urge to tease Archie in order to throw his game off. Maybe he could complain that he went out of bounds. But since they hadn't established boundaries at the beginning, he didn't want to offend the ladies and make them think he was grumbling. Especially not Bessie—Miss O'Hara.

Bessie took aim with her mallet, sending the yellow ball through both hoops.

Archie stopped in the middle of the playing field and put his hands on his hips. "My turn wasn't done. I still have two free shots for knocking the ball through the wickets."

"Perhaps I want to play with no rules, like in the story I told you about." Bessie flashed a cheeky grin toward Archie.

Thomas took his chances, defending Bessie. "You went out of bounds anyway." He pointed to where Archie's black ball rested at the base of a tree. "You can move it into the playing area, but you forfeit your move."

Archie smirked. "Of course, you'd take the side of the ladies, Tommy. No rules it is, then, Miss O'Hara. And may I suggest changing it to a game of Poison? If I hit your ball, you're out of the game."

Bessie's chin rose. "You're on."

"That's not exactly fair." Miss Johnson clutched her mallet close to her chest.

"Perhaps we could postpone the game of Poison until after the current game," Thomas suggested. "And we could play by the rules this round."

"And I suppose you'll be the judge and jury about whether we do or not." Archie tilted his head, the smirk still in place. "Want to establish the boundaries, too? Goes along with being a bigshot businessman, does it not?"

Thomas glowered at Archie. He didn't want to talk about this. Wasn't it the business that had caused the embarrassing public breakup with Pauline and his self-induced exile to Mackinac Island?

━◆━━━◆━

Bessie had never enjoyed a game of croquet more. Of course, flamingo mallets and hedgehog balls might have made it more interesting, with the hedgehogs unrolling themselves and wandering off and the flamingoes trying to bite or peck, or whatever that type of bird did. The birds probably wouldn't have appreciated being held upside down and used to whack hedgehogs.

But between Mr. Asparagus and Mr. Hale playfully arguing over whether a ball was out or not and trying to keep track of who got a ball through the hoops and how many extra turns they got, the game was interesting enough. Mr. Asparagus had even tried to teach Henrietta how to aim the mallet, since her ball usually only rolled an inch or two before it abruptly stopped. She claimed the ball had it in for her.

"Sorry, Miss O'Hara." Mr. Hale put his mallet behind the matching ball—which was behind hers—and with one solid thump sent her ball flying off into the bushes.

"Of all the…" She scampered off, fighting her way through skinny twiglike branches loaded with leaves and tiny red berries. The bush honeysuckle plants were every bit as tall as she was. It seemed as if a bright yellow ball would be easy to find, like sunshine in the shadows, but she appeared to be wrong. She couldn't see it anywhere. Not even a hint of yellow.

It might have rolled down the incline and into the water. A terrible thing. Unlikely though, since it would have to go through the bushes, followed by a field of weeds, then a rocky beach before it reached the lake.

She didn't want to be responsible for ruining Mr. Asparagus's set.

Bessie looked down at her dress. Would she get stains on it if she dropped down to crawl around under the bushes? She'd have to take her chances. Maybe if she didn't sit all the way down, but kind of crouched…

She hiked up her skirt and squatted, bending over to peer under the other nearby bushes. Nothing.

Branches moved, stabbing at her.

"Sorry." Mr. Hale joined her in the bushes and sat beside her. "I didn't mean to hit it so hard. I certainly didn't mean for it to go flying off into this impenetrable abyss. Things roll under here and are never seen again."

A shiver worked through Bessie that had nothing to do with fear. "Really?"

"Oh, yes. Super dangerous. Especially for innocent young ladies. And croquet balls, of course. Badminton birdies, too. Not sure how many of them have flown in here. Never found a one of them." He shook his head, frowning. But his lips twitched.

Her eyes narrowed as he focused on glancing around again. His presence beside her made her thoughts hazy. All she could think of was him, and the warmth that worked through her. Not to mention the minty scent of him, as if he'd chewed some peppermint leaves before joining her.

Something caught her attention and she looked closer. Was that… Maybe…

"I think I see it." She pointed. "There's something yellow, about five feet ahead. Of course, it might be a dandelion. There are a bunch of them."

"Where?" He brushed some branches out of the way and narrowed his eyes. "Ah, a field of dandelions. Don't tell Archie. He thinks they're weeds. Personally, I like dandelion salad. Do you?"

"I don't know." She started to rise, but Mr. Hale touched her hand, sending sparks all the way up to the elbow.

"I'll go see. We certainly don't want you falling into the abyss."

Bessie wasn't sure if the fluttering movement of his lashes was caused by a wink or if a leaf-laden branch had caught a breeze and moved.

But his lips quirked and he squat-walked through the bushes toward the field of yellow and carefully unearthed the ball from among the dandelions. The ball gripped in one hand, he held up a birdie in the other.

"Badminton. Maybe we should go crawling around back here another day. No telling what we'd find." This time, a wink did accompany the words.

There wasn't any reason for the shivers to work through her again, but they did.

❖•———•❖

Thomas followed Miss O'Hara around the croquet game like a besotted pup the entire afternoon. Rescuing her runaway ball when it went out of bounds again. Suggesting ways to position herself for the best possible shot. He couldn't resist, even though she didn't need much help. She was a much better croquet player than she gave herself credit for. Better than her cousins.

Archie won, of course. Nobody ever beat Archie at croquet. Except Thomas. Once. But that was only because he'd hit Archie's ball out of bounds during a game of Poison—his, and everyone else's balls, making Thomas the automatic winner.

Miss O'Hara had a great sense of humor, teasing when appropriate then discussing books and music and the masquerade ball last night—though she didn't mention their moonlight dance beside the softly lapping lake water. Maybe she didn't realize it had been him. Probably just as well.

Plus, she knew when to be quiet—at least compared to her giggling, twittering cousins. She certainly didn't talk as much as Pauline had. The more Thomas witnessed, the more he liked. Whatever had attracted him to Pauline? It must have been the way she latched on to his arm, his life, and didn't let go until he failed to meet her expectations. But what had she intended him to do? Father had sent him to Europe for business. He'd done as his father requested—even though Pauline's father advised against it. Thomas had made the arrangements and signed the contract. Mission accomplished.

At least until. . .

Thomas sighed, assailed by memories of Pauline's shrieks of rage and horror followed by all sorts of false accusations. He'd almost expected police sirens to wail. Escorts to prison. . . He shook his head, forcing the thoughts away. He'd never marry, thanks to Pauline. His reputation was ruined. Ruined!

Maybe Archie's idea of a wedding reenactment wasn't such a bad idea. Thomas would stand next to her—the woman of his dreams—in the field of dandelions—well, maybe not there—and pretend Bessie really was his bride. And he'd have the picture to prove it. Or maybe not prove it, but to continue fooling himself into believing such a fairy tale could possibly come true, if only in his dreams.

But wishing wouldn't get her into his arms.

Nothing but a miracle of God would accomplish it.

And God had abandoned him on a busy street in downtown Berlin, Germany.

God and the rest of polite society.

Only Archie hadn't abandoned him. Archie, and these lovely ladies who apparently didn't know about his ruined reputation. The lies and distrust surrounding his name. And when they did. . .

If God heard him, and if He listened, then he'd pray, and say something like, *Lord, please let the wedding go off without a hitch.*

But it wasn't a prayer. God didn't listen or hear him.

And the marriage would be as real as the polite smiles and kind words murmured in public. As the lies discussed in private.

He shoved his hand into his pocket. It closed around the badminton birdie he'd stuffed in there and forgotten to give to Archie. He crushed it in his grip then eased it out of his pocket and handed it to his best friend.

His only friend these days.

Archie tilted his head. "Where did you find this?"

"In the dandelion field." Thomas nodded toward the bush honeysuckle plants. "Before the slope down to the water. And if you don't have another place for the wedding reenactment in mind, I would love for it to be among the dandelions."

Archie's lips quirked. "You'd be off to a weedy start."

Thomas expected nothing more.

Chapter 5

It amazed Bessie how quickly Mr. Asparagus put together the wedding reenactment. And he did it in style. Now, two days later, she looked around at the chairs set up among the dandelions, along with a wigwam skeleton made of pristine white pine and decorated with a strand of roses artfully wrapped around two of the front poles. Rose petals lay scattered on the ground underneath. A minister waited for her inside the teepee. Archie had even gone to the trouble of securing a piano and moving it to the hillside above the lake. A photographer stood off to one side. Every seat was filled. Though she saw several familiar faces, there were also many she didn't recognize.

It was a beautiful setting, one she'd love to re-create for her real wedding someday if she were allowed to have what she wanted.

Delicious aromas came from the big house, too. Mr. Asparagus's staff must have worked all night, cooking and baking for this resort-opening party.

She smoothed her hands over the sequins stitched to her white dress as she tried to wipe the moisture away. It wasn't a real wedding, but with Mr. Hale's gaze fixed on her so intently, a half smile on his face, and the crowd of "well-wishers" rising with the beginning of the wedding march, it seemed as if it might be. Butterflies and bees swarmed in her stomach. Her knees wobbled.

She didn't dare look for her cousins. They were somewhere in the front, giggling as they had been all morning. Their comments ran through her thoughts in refrain. "Not every girl gets to playact the entire wedding ceremony. What great practice for the real thing when it's time."

But her real wedding wouldn't be beside Lake Huron, with Round Island Lighthouse in the distance. No. It'd be in a dark cathedral in Grand Rapids, music from the pipe organ filling the room.

Yet this lakeside ceremony was much more romantic.

Her heart pounded as she began the slow, hesitant wedding march toward the fake preacher and her make-believe groom. His gaze held hers the entire time, a strange light in his eyes that made her wish things were different. Maybe even real and not pretend.

His smile grew as he held his hand out to her. After a moment's hesitation she took it. Warmth spread up to her shoulder and beyond.

The preacher cleared his throat. "We are gathered here today in the sight of God and angels, and the presence of friends and loved ones, to celebrate one of life's greatest moments, to give recognition to the worth and beauty of love, and to add our best wishes and blessings to the words which shall unite Thomas Hale and Elizabeth O'Hara in holy matrimony."

Her heart skipped a beat then raced. The preacher used their real names. Not the ones of the people they were representing. But maybe Mr. Asparagus had forgotten to mention it to the pastor, or maybe since they were just posing for pictures of a fake ceremony it didn't really matter. At any rate, it would be rude to interrupt and tell the preacher he had the names wrong.

She glanced at Thomas as his hand tightened around hers. He still smiled, his gaze on her, as if he was trying to soak up every moment of this day.

She moistened her lips and his gaze dropped to them, his smile faltering.

No. Surely they wouldn't include the lines about kissing your bride. . . . Her heart stumbled then revved like one of those newfangled motorcars. Mr. Asparagus couldn't be so crass as to want a picture of them kissing.

The photographer shifted the camera a little and a puff of smoke or something rose from it. The preacher droned on, talking about verses in Ephesians and comparing marriage between husband and wife to Christ and the church. Did she need to listen closely since this was a trial run for her future wedding, somewhere down the road?

"Repeat after me. I, Thomas take thee, Elizabeth, to be my wife. To have and to hold, in sickness and in health, for richer or for poorer, and I promise my love to you forevermore."

Mr. Hale, Thomas, repeated the words with reverence.

Bessie's breath lodged in her throat.

If only he meant them.

The preacher turned toward her.

"I, Elizabeth, take thee, Thomas, to be my husband. To have and to hold, in sickness and in health, for richer or for poorer, and I promise my love to you forevermore."

His hand tightened, his thumb sliding across the back of her hand. Tingles raced up her arm. She repeated the preacher's words, hating that she couldn't control the huskiness in her voice. Her cousins would tease her about it mercilessly.

"Thomas and Elizabeth, as you this day affirm your faith and love for one another, I would ask that you always remember to cherish each other as special and unique individuals, that you respect the thoughts, ideas, and suggestions of one another. Be able to forgive, do not hold grudges, and live each day that you may share it together—as from this day forward you shall be each other's home, comfort, and refuge, your marriage strengthened by your love and respect."

A pause. Somebody coughed.

"With the power vested in me, I now pronounce you man and wife." Then, "You may kiss your bride."

◆━━━━◆

Thomas stared down at Bessie's—Elizabeth's—upturned face. The correct thing to do would be to thank her for a realistic display, and end this charade. But. . .he wanted to kiss her. Wanted to eke every bit of enjoyment out of this as he possibly could. A kiss would be one more thing to remember her by.

But then again, it might ruin her, being kissed in a pretend marriage ceremony. Why hadn't Archie warned him about this?

Someone in the crowd giggled, and Reverend Stout cleared his throat. "Go ahead now. Don't be shy."

A chuckle came from somewhere on Thomas's side of the seated guests.

A pretend kiss. On the cheek would be enough.

Thomas dipped his head, catching the scent of lavender. Brushed his lips across her oh-so-soft cheek, achingly close to her lips. Then pulled away.

"I now present Mr. and Mrs. Thomas Hale."

"Step over here." Mrs. Stout—who matched her name and her husband in appearance—waved at them from the piano bench as she rose to her feet. "We need your signatures." She shoved a piece of paper and an ink pen across the top of the piano. She kept her hand covering the top of the page.

Thomas—his hand still wrapped around Bessie's—headed over to her. "What's this?"

"Just so we get your names right for the paper." A man Thomas recognized from the newspaper pushed his way forward.

The camera was shuffled again for another shot as they signed. Thomas rolled his eyes. If Archie paid this much attention to detail, his resort was sure to be a success.

Thomas nodded, took the pen—it scratched—and scrawled out *Thomas Edward Hale* then handed the pen to Bessie.

Her hand shook as she took the pen, and she hesitated. "Should I sign my real name or what everyone calls me?"

"Your real name, dear," Mrs. Stout said.

She glanced shyly at Thomas then leaned closer and wrote *Elizabeth Cordelia O'Hara*. He caught the scent of lavender and roses. Breathed it in so he could recall it during the long, lonely nights ahead of him.

Mrs. Stout's hand shifted, revealing the calligraphy at the top of the page. It read "Marriage Certificate."

Thomas reached for the paper, but Mrs. Stout jerked it back and put it in her songbook. "Thank you, dear. It's all taken care of."

Yes, but. . . Internal alarms rang. A contract was legal and binding. . . .

"Refreshments are in the house, I understand." The preacher's wife gathered up the songbook, clutched it tightly to her side, and headed in that direction at a fast clip.

Thomas extended his elbow to Bessie. He'd visit the preacher and sort out the wording of the paper later. Because surely. . .there wasn't any way. . .

No. He was mistaken. Had to be.

◆—————◆

After a moment's hesitation, Bessie tucked her hand in the crook of Mr. Hale's arm and allowed him to escort her to the house. Really, though, it seemed as if they'd gone beyond the formalities, and into a closer relationship. Probably all due to the structure and order of the wedding ceremony, even though it was fake. And all for the sake of getting pictures so Mr. Asparagus could advertise his resort.

She looked around for the cameraman, but he'd vanished, along with his camera.

Seemed they could have taken the pictures without actually performing the ceremony. Preaching the sermon. Playing the wedding march. Not to mention the kiss, which had been as sweet and gentle as she'd imagined on the ferry. Yet lacking, because he'd missed her lips.

How many photos did they need for one brochure or newspaper article? And of so many different events? Though it was conceivable that Mr. Asparagus would want several different shots so he could choose which he liked the best.

Mr. Hale escorted her into a lavishly decorated dining room. White tablecloths, napkins folded in the shape of swans, vases filled with white roses and lilacs on the table. He seated her where the butler indicated then sat beside her.

Much too close.

Their elbows would become intimately acquainted during this meal. The reenactment would give her the chance to get to know him better without her cousins criticizing her behavior. The giddiness she felt reminded her of the moonlight dance, and of getting lost in his eyes and his wink behind the honeysuckle bushes near the dandelion field.

After a prayer offered by the preacher, the maids served the first course of smoked salmon with horseradish and caviar along with a small garden salad.

The main course was pork tenderloin with roasted rhubarb, wild rice with mushrooms, and garden-fresh steamed green beans with pearl onions and bacon bits.

Slices of a white wedding cake decorated with cherries rounded out the meal.

Mr. Hale leaned close, his breath warm against her ear. "The whole meal and the wedding cake seem overdone. Are they even taking pictures of the food? If they are, it must be in the kitchen."

Bessie barely controlled a shiver caused by his warm breath and the intimacy of the moment. She didn't know anything about how or why Mr. Asparagus planned things. She hoped it helped his resort, though. The house and grounds were nice, and people likely would love staying here.

As the evening drew to a close, the preacher's wife came up and wrapped Bessie in her arms. Bessie stiffened, pulling back a little, but the woman leaned close.

"I hope you and Tommy will be very happy together. He deserves some goodness in his life. And you seem like a very sweet young lady."

What? Did she believe they were really married?

Chapter 6

Sunday morning, Thomas woke up in the predawn gloom. Three days after the wedding, he still woke from dreamland reaching for the other side of the bed and finding nothing but cold, empty sheets. He ached with the loss of a pleasant dream, as if somehow part of him was missing. Odd, since he'd known the wedding on Thursday afternoon was pretend. But even though he tried to convince himself it had only been fake and not reality, it wasn't easy.

Especially since he didn't want to wake up alone.

He stumbled out of bed, flung open the shades. The day stretched drearily, with no wife to walk along the beach with. . . . No one to share his life with.

He dressed, and went downstairs to the dining room.

"Good morning, sir." The maid placed his breakfast in front of him and left. He stared at the empty chairs around him and imagined Bessie sitting next to him. He could imagine her smile brightening the room as they shared the meal. But he blinked and she was gone. He groaned and put his fork down. He didn't want to eat alone. Not with the memories of Bessie beside him, sharing the wedding meal and conversation.

He stood and walked over to the window and stared out at Lake Huron. At least some things weren't pretend. He could recall every detail of that beautiful day. Bessie's hesitant walk. Her lovely hazel eyes locked on his as if drawing from his strength.

She'd been so beautiful. Like a royal princess as she glided down the rose-petal-strewn makeshift aisle toward him, her glittery white dress sparkling in the sunshine. Her hair had been up in a loose bun, curling lazily around her ears, a flowery tiara in the honey-colored locks.

Pure beauty.

He never should have agreed to Archie's harebrained scheme. The harsh contrast of the dream with his lonely reality was enough to make him want to go home to Marquette to "heal" from this misadventure. But maybe. . . If he could just see her one more time. She probably wasn't as sweet and wonderful as she had appeared when he spent all afternoon with her two days before the ceremony, and then a good portion of the day together on their wedding day. Pretend wedding day.

Today was Sunday. She'd likely be in attendance for the service. He hadn't darkened a doorway of a church in over a year, but maybe today should be the exception. Even if he could only catch a glimpse of her, even if he couldn't get near enough to speak. He'd sneak in the back. Hopefully, Reverend Stout wouldn't faint at the sight of him inside the building. After all, the preacher visited him every Wednesday without fail, inviting him to services, urging him to attend, warning him of the dire consequences of staying away. He always arrived promptly at teatime, and, of course, stayed long enough for a cup of coffee and cookies. The preacher always cleared the platter, single-handedly, as if his wife kept him half starved at home.

Thomas checked the time. Yes, church today would be good. Reverend Stout would believe Thomas's presence was the result of his faithful weekly visits to empty the cookie jar, even though the truth was that Thomas wanted only to see the woman he longed for.

After he prepared, he climbed into the buggy and had his man, Jonas, drive him to town. The church doors stood wide open, letting the cool lake air into the building.

"Amazing Grace" played quietly from inside the church. A few other late arrivals climbed the steps ahead of him. Thomas slipped inside behind a fashionable lady with a big hat and found a seat on a hard pew at the back. Maybe he'd escape notice.

Except he wasn't as late as he'd planned. He arrived in time for the before-church fellowship. Conversation stopped as people turned to stare at him.

He didn't think he'd been considered that much of a backslider. Unless this proved Pauline's attack on his character had far-reaching effects.

Then again, of course it did. He'd known he was ruined. And had hidden for a year as a result.

Reverend Stout paused in the midst of his visit with someone several rows up, excused himself, and came back to greet Thomas, hand extended. "Good to see you, Mr. Hale."

Thomas rose and shook the preacher's hand. Maybe this would eliminate the need for a weekly tea party. Or another well-meaning lecture about the "dire consequences" of not attending services. "Lovely day, Reverend Stout."

"I saw your beautiful bride walk in earlier with her cousins." The preacher looked around. "There she is, on the other side of the church. You should be able to slip in next to her." He leaned close. "People will think you've had a honeymoon tiff if you don't. Excuse me a moment. I must speak to someone else." He moved away.

A honeymoon tiff?

That would involve having had an actual wedding night. . . .

Thomas's whole body heated. He was sure he was almost as red as the Harvard beets Mrs. Stout served at every church potluck Thomas had ever attended. He shuddered. Vile things. But maybe they were indications of how well Mrs. Stout cooked and why her husband always emptied Thomas's cookie jar.

Thomas couldn't keep from glancing in the direction the preacher indicated. An older woman with a rapidly fluttering fan stood beside Bessie. Her mother? Bessie wore a light green dress today and a matching hat. It must do wonders for her beautiful eyes. She didn't look his direction, and he sat back down, alone, as the organist hit a loud chord of a different song indicating visitation time was over. At once, the people in the church found their places.

His neighbors from two houses down the road sat in the pew in front of him. The wife turned to him with a bright smile. "Good to see you here, Mr. Hale. Congratulations on your marriage. Is Mrs. Hale not here today?"

They'd been at the ceremony. Had the invitations not said that it was only for publicity at the resort?

Or. . .

It *had* appeared to be an authentic marriage certificate. They'd signed their real names. What if. . .

Yes. It was what he wanted. Hoped for. Desired.

Her reaction? He swallowed. That he feared.

A hard knot formed in his stomach.

But he was equally fearful that it wouldn't be true and he'd truly be alone for the rest of his life.

How many people had stopped to congratulate her on her marriage? It seemed everyone in the church had wandered by Bessie's pew to welcome the bride and inquire about her husband.

Mother, who'd arrived late yesterday afternoon, now fanned herself as if she was near to suffering heatstroke. It might be July, but it wasn't terribly hot on Mackinac Island. Much cooler than the city, at any rate. All the color had washed out of Mother's face as she politely informed the first well-wishers that they were mistaken and Elizabeth wasn't yet married. She'd gotten a pitying look in return. Bessie wished she'd taken the time to tell her mother about her role in the advertising scheme, but it hadn't seemed important. It was playacting. Not reality.

The other lady had gone off and whispered something to her friend, and Mother had refrained from comment afterward. But as the number of well-wishers surpassed the fingers on both hands, Mother's narrow-eyed glare and rapidly waving fan told Bessie she'd hear plenty when they got home.

Yes, she'd have a lot of explaining to do. And yet there was nothing she could say. Bessie smoothed her skirts as she squirmed into a more comfortable position next to Mother in the pew. Would her mother accept "all in fun" as a good enough excuse, or "helping out a new friend"? Or maybe Bessie should say she was encouraging economic growth, so the escapade could be considered her civic duty?

Her cousins were enjoying her discomfort too much to be of any help.

Mr. Asparagus had said she'd be handsomely rewarded, but he hadn't specified how. And she hadn't asked. Besides, it had been rather fun. . .though confusing. Why all the pomp and circumstance for a make-believe wedding? Maybe he would let her and Mr. Hale see some of the photographs they took when they were deciding which ones to use for the brochure or newspaper ads.

Rosella leaned near her, knocking Bessie's hat askew. "Don't look now, but Mr. Hale is staring at you."

Heat burned Bessie's cheeks as she pondered his response if even half the people who'd come by to congratulate her had stopped to offer the same to him. And did they wonder why they weren't sitting together as Mrs. Stout had warned?

When Mrs. Stout began pounding out the first stanza of "A Mighty Fortress," Bessie glanced over her shoulder to see if Thomas was indeed staring at her.

She couldn't see him. Too many people and big hats were in her way.

Mother poked her in the ribs. "Stop squirming. You should know better."

Yes. She did. And now she knew that with so many big hats between them, there wasn't any way Thomas could stare at her. Rosella was just trying to get a rise out of her.

But maybe they'd see each other after the service. Spend a stolen moment greeting each other—as polite society dictated—then go their separate ways.

It wouldn't be enough.

It had to be enough.

She twisted around further to peer at the foyer. Her eyes met the stormy bluish-gray stare from the back pew.

Thomas winked. Ever so bold.

Her pulse jumped in response.

◆——•——◆

It was Tuesday before Thomas had an opportunity to go downtown and discover if he was *really* married.

The sun was high and bright, and society was out in full force, wandering down the main street, browsing shops, and enjoying the island fudge. Mainly, they just wanted to see and be seen.

Would Bessie be out in the crowd today? Or were they receiving callers this morning?

Would he be a welcome visitor?

Likely not, if he got the news he feared.

His stomach clenched.

To say he longed for it would be more accurate.

Though that news would certainly send Bessie, all her family, friends, and even acquaintances into a tizzy.

His, too, if he was honest. Mother and Father would be hurt he hadn't invited them. His sister would probably cry for weeks. Perhaps it was selfish of him to hope it was real, all things considered. But if it wasn't, his dreams would be shattered.

He grimaced at his own exaggeration and parked his buggy in front of the courthouse, tied the horse to the post, then went inside. Something needed to be done.

Attempted, at least.

A heaviness of heart made him stop at the doorway to the clerk's office. He didn't want to do this. He'd rather live in blissful unawareness.

His heart folded in on him. He fought for air, turned the knob, and walked in.

"Mr. Hale, what are you doing out and about this fine day? Seems as if you and your bride should still be on the honeymoon." The clerk's eyebrows waggled.

Still be on. . .? They hadn't even left. Because. . .

Thomas heaved a great sigh. "Then, it's true. The marriage is real?"

"Well, of course it is. Silly of you to think otherwise, wouldn't you say? The good preacher and his wife delivered the marriage certificate bright and early Friday morning. Mrs. Stout told me to be sure to get it legalized right away. Legalized." He laughed. "As if it wasn't legal enough when you signed it. But I'm sure she meant filed."

"I suppose it's too late to tell you it was supposed to be a reenactment of Mr.

Archibald Asparagus's grandparents' wedding, to advertise the resort?"

The clerk pursed his lips. "Is that what they told you? You were rather gullible to fall for it, don't you think? You know Mrs. Stout has been trying to marry you off for the past year. Ever since you came skulking onto the island."

Skulking? And here he had imagined he'd stridden in with his head held high.

The clerk shook his head. "I don't know what happened back then. All I know is when you arrived on the island, the good preacher said, 'Thomas Hale needs lots of prayer. We need to do what we can to reach out to him and help him through this valley.' What valley did you go through?"

Thomas shook his head. He hadn't even shared his problems with Archie. By no means would he divulge such information to a man he didn't know. What was his name anyway? Thomas glanced around for a nameplate. Nothing. "Can we get it annulled?"

The clerk's mouth dropped open. "Why would you want to do that? Maybe you ought to check with the wife first. She'd want some say in it."

He was quite positive she'd insist on an annulment as soon as she found out.

"Besides, Mrs. Stout told me not to let you cut off your nose to spite your face."

He sighed. "I'll check with Miss O'Hara—"

"You mean Mrs. Hale."

Frustrated, Thomas shook his head. "And I shall return." After he delivered the good—make that, bad—news to Miss O'Hara.

Hopefully, she wouldn't swoon when she found out they were *married*.

Chapter 7

Bessie paced to the piano, wishing she could play something calming instead of listening to Mother complain to Aunt Samantha that everyone at church believed Bessie was married. Aunt Samantha had been there, too, and had been just as shocked. Horrified, even. And they all were at a loss. How could they ever stop the rumors?

But the pretend ceremony had been five days ago. Five. With the way people gossiped, it seemed someone would have discovered the truth and broadcasted it. But the lie, that Elizabeth O'Hara had married Thomas Hale, was juicier than ever.

"Mr. Thomas Hale." The butler appeared in the doorway with a calling card.

"Show him in and ask Sally to bring tea." Mother sighed, stabbing her needle into her embroidery. "I can't concentrate anyway. I do hope Mr. Hale is here to explain this so we can discuss how best to put the rumors to rest."

Aunt Samantha laid aside her own needlework. Beside her, Rosella grinned and placed hers on her lap. Unlike Bessie, Rosella hated creating works of art in any form. She'd rather dance the night away.

Bessie would rather not. Unless it was in the moonlight alone with her pretend husband.

Henrietta and her mother had gone shopping this morning instead of receiving. Henrietta wanted a new hat, and probably a new dress and shoes to go with it.

Mr. Hale strode into the room, his hat clutched in front of him with both hands. Bessie couldn't read his expression. His eyes were dark, worried, sad. But a dimple lurked on the right side of his mouth. A half grin was in place. Conflicting signals, for sure.

"Have a seat, please." Mother waved toward a wing chair—Father's favorite when he was on the island. "I've called for refreshments."

Mr. Hale sat then his gaze drifted to Bessie, skimmed over the piano, then came back and rested on her. A light appeared in his eyes for a moment then died.

Sally bustled into the room with tea and still-warm shortbread cookies. "Fresh from the oven," she said before she left the room.

The cookies explained the buttery-caramel scent filling the house that morning. Bessie's stomach rumbled. She rested her hand against it in a feeble attempt to muffle the embarrassing noise. Her face heated.

Thomas's eyes remained locked on Bessie, his lips pressed together as if he wanted to say something but kept the words inside.

"How do you take your tea, Mr. Hale?"

He didn't look away from Bessie. "One sugar cube and a spot of cream, please."

Mother sighed again as she passed him a cup of tea. "I do hope you are here to discuss how to settle this issue of whether you and Elizabeth. . ." She covered her mouth with a handkerchief.

"Quite right." Mr. Hale's hand wobbled, and he set the teacup down with a clatter. "It turns out the rumor is true. We are wed."

❦━━━━━❦

Thomas leaned forward and clasped his hands together between his knees as Bessie gasped, her hand clamped over her mouth.

"How can that be?" Her mother fluttered her handkerchief as if it were the fan she waved so quickly at church. The color drained from her face. "How could you possibly allow yourself and Elizabeth to be put in this position?"

Bessie's other hand moved to rest on the piano, and she leaned on it, as if that were all that kept her upright.

Of course, he'd known she'd be shocked. He wouldn't be surprised if she swooned. He glanced around for smelling salts but didn't see any.

His gaze returned to Bessie. Being her husband wasn't a hardship for him. She was definitely easy on the eyes. A lovely girl—woman. Her color had faded, as if she might be dangerously close to fainting. She'd be even more overwhelmed if she'd been privy to the conversations he'd had with Mrs. Stout and Archie after he left City Hall. They'd admitted they planned the whole escapade, believing it was past time for him to move on from his self-imposed solitude. It hadn't been a reenactment at all, but a real wedding. He deserved some happiness, they'd said, and even if they had to take matters into their own hands, they'd see him settled.

Settled!

Unbelievable. And Miss O'Hara had been an unsuspecting pawn in their carefully laid schemes for him to have a second chance at love.

Of course, so had he.

He never would have guessed his best friend and the pastor's wife would be accomplices in crime. Had Reverend Stout known it was real all along, too?

"*So* romantic." Miss Everson sighed.

Bessie's head began a slow shake as words, objections, or something formed. Probably the word he dreaded. . .*annulment*. He imagined the word running through her mind.

A lump rose in Thomas's throat. Words wanted to come out, but shouldn't. He had no say in this, of course. They wouldn't want Bessie married to him, if they knew how Pauline had. . .

No! He clenched his fist. He wouldn't think of it—just as he wouldn't think of annulment. Still it became a roar in his head, repeating over and over. *Annulment. Annulment. Annulment.*

His unspoken argument grew, pressing against his throat until he couldn't breathe. Until he had to say what he thought or die from strangulation. Until. . .

"No. Absolutely not. We said 'I do' before God, for better for worse. We signed a legal, binding contract. And I'm. . .I'm not—I'm not going to let—let you go." He burst to his feet with the force and intensity of the words.

Okay, maybe he hadn't meant to be so harsh, determined, or demanding. It was still her choice. But he'd. . . Well, marriage *was* before God. And if He'd been looking down on them, and witnessing the ceremony, He'd expect them to honor the vows.

Or maybe God recognized it as the deceit it was, chuckled a little at the joke, and then would look the other way when it was quietly annulled.

"I–I–I think I lo—"

Bessie's eyes widened, her knuckles whitening on the side of the piano.

He swallowed the rest of the endearment. It would be inappropriate to speak of his feelings, and well, he *thought* he loved her. He *determined* to love her. He *would* love her. But Bessie still hadn't said a word. Maybe he should find out what she thought first.

"I'm confused. 'No, absolutely not' what? Divorce?" Miss Everson said weakly, fluttering her sewing in front of her face. "Annulment?"

"Never. I'll not have the shame of a divorce. Though annulment is a possibility under the circumstances." Mrs. O'Hara frowned at Thomas as if this predicament were entirely his fault. And maybe it was. After all, he hadn't heeded the warning alarms when they blared, complete with emergency flares. "I have no idea what your father will say about this." She snapped her handkerchief in Bessie's direction.

Thomas could imagine. The same thing his father likely would say. *You did what? With whom? How could you. . .?* At least none of the women here were prone to the vapors.

"Then. . ." Bessie drew in a breath, straightened, and removed her hand from the piano. "May I speak to my. . .husband alone? Maybe in the garden?"

Her mother waved her away as Thomas moved closer to Bessie and extended his arm.

After a slight hesitation, she tucked her hand into the crook of his elbow.

◆━━━━◆

Bessie opened the doors to the back patio then led the way down the steps. This house, like Mr. Asparagus's, sat on the lake, with a dock for her father's boat. Not that he used the dock for anything except fishing. And maybe quiet evening walks by her side when they discussed beaus.

Father would be coming soon—and what would he say to her now? His desire for her to be married hadn't turned out as anyone had expected.

But God did have a sense of humor. The day she'd arrived on the ferry she'd wished she could skip the courting and have a husband handed to her with the instructions to treat him well. Now her husband stood beside her, and she had no idea how to start.

What did he expect? A real marriage with all that involved? Or did he want a marriage in name only since they didn't love each other and didn't know each other and. . .

Or did he want an annulment?

Mother was right. She couldn't take the shame of a divorce. She'd be ruined. But she didn't exactly feel comfortable being married to a virtual stranger unless it was a marriage in name only, even if he was extremely attractive. And even if he appealed to her in every way. Even then, how did women handle marrying complete strangers—if anyone actually answered those newspaper advertisements? *Handsome, twentysomething, dark-haired, blue-eyed man, heir to—whatever he was heir to—looking for wife willing to vacation on Mackinac Island. Must know how to play croquet and waltz by moonlight.*

She smiled at the silliness of her thoughts.

"I suppose it will be a marriage in name only, then?" The words hurt her throat. "Although, if we're to be married, even temporarily, shouldn't we know something about each other?" She peered up at him. "Other than the fact that you're good at croquet and waltzing under the stars?"

He smiled, a slow, gentle curving of his well-shaped lips. The same lips that had brushed oh-so-gently against her cheek at their turned-out-to-be-real wedding. The kiss she'd wished had been more. . .ardent. Maybe now that they were married, he would kiss her properly. . . .

"Reverend Stout has said often enough that love is a decision. Based on that, I have decided that since we're married"—he caught his breath—"and we can do nothing about it for now, I am determined to love you as Christ loved the church."

For now. Bessie frowned. Father would definitely insist on an annulment under the circumstances.

Thomas rubbed his jaw. "Though, to be perfectly candid, I'm not quite sure how I can love you only temporarily, because the Bible says that Christ loved us enough to say, 'I will never leave thee, nor forsake thee.' It's very hard for me to believe in a love like that, because I could echo the cry of Jesus, 'My God, my God, why hast thou forsaken me?' I have often felt that God has forsaken me." He sighed. "That is probably too brutally honest. I apologize. Sunday was the first time I've been in church for a year. A year, Bessie. And the only reason I went was to see you."

Bessie's mouth dropped open and she stared at him, unsure what to say about him going to church to see her when he was so blatantly heathen. God had a good reason for turning His back on His Son. He couldn't look on sin. And if He'd turned His back on Thomas, then. . .

Were his sins that wicked?

That was a frightening thought. Very frightening.

Who was this man?

"I'll send my man around to collect you and your belongings this evening," Thomas said, before turning and striding around the house. He didn't pause and didn't look back. Just left.

This evening? Did he even have a piano?

Of course, a musical instrument should be the least of her concerns.

Because if he did send his man, an annulment would be impossible.

Bessie expelled a heavy breath and turned for the house.

She was halfway inside before she realized he hadn't agreed—or disagreed—about a marriage in name only.

Marriage to Thomas Hale excited her much more than it should.

Chapter 8

Thomas sat in his buggy, parked outside Bessie's family's vacation home. He hadn't signaled for his driver to leave but instead told him to wait. For what, he didn't know. He couldn't quite decide the next step. Home, to make the house ready for his beautiful, blushing bride—or to Reverend Stout's house to demand to know if he was aware of what he'd done.

He hated having spilled so much of his spiritual condition to Bessie. He had no right to, and, considering they were strangers—even if they were married—he'd undoubtedly horrified her. Wouldn't he be shocked if he were a good Christian man and she had confessed to being forsaken by God? He could only imagine what had gone through her mind.

And then he'd terrified her by insisting she come home with him tonight, as his bride. But if they were to be married, she wanted it in name only, and that hurt. Really hurt.

But she would likely be ruined, her reputation in tatters, even if it was annulled. People would always imagine they'd spent time alone together. They believed what they wanted, as if the truth didn't matter in the least. He knew it well enough. He needed to be man enough to take her in and shelter her. Protect her.

Love, honor, and cherish. And get to know her and maybe convince her to be his real wife. . . .

Oh, yes. He was willing.

If he were still a praying man, he'd. . . What? Pray? He almost snorted. God had proved multiple times that He didn't hear Thomas. After all, He'd allowed Pauline to rip Thomas's reputation to shreds with both the European and American elite. And all because he obeyed his father's directives. Honored the contract. A legally binding contract. One Thomas had no problems with, other than the fallout. And the lies.

And hadn't Thomas prayed—begged God to return Pauline to him so they could marry, as he'd planned? Well, that prayer had been answered with a resounding "no."

Thomas sighed. In hindsight, that was a blessing. He wouldn't want her now. Not after meeting the woman he'd been dreaming of for as long as he could remember.

Jonas shifted on his seat. He probably was getting restless. And undoubtedly wondering if Thomas were in his right mind.

Yes, he needed to talk with the preacher, for more than one reason. And he would, too, if the man's involvement in this scheme hadn't effectively obliterated any trust Thomas had in him. He ejected another heavy sigh.

"Something wrong, sir?" his driver said cautiously, turning around and peering at him.

"Quite so. Everything is. Or maybe nothing at all. I don't know."

And that cleared it up nicely. Thomas could have laughed at the confusion on Jonas's face, except it wasn't funny. Not a bit.

"God sees you. Hears you," Jonas said quietly.

If only it was true. "Take me by Reverend Stout's place."

Because he needed to give him a piece of his mind.

❖—————❖

Bessie's stomach fluttered, dipped, and dived like a fish discovering its fins for the first time. Despite the worry and fear, excitement swirled. Married to Thomas—the man who still noticed her after meeting her much more vibrant, beautiful cousins.

But she would have a lot of explaining to do when Father arrived on the island. He would be livid. Upset she'd somehow gotten married—by mistake.

How was it even possible?

But that aside, she'd gotten married without his approval. Without him walking her down the aisle.

And how would Thomas's family react? Would they even like her? Or would they find her lacking? Light brown hair instead of delicate blond or fiery red. Hazel eyes instead of blue or brown. Average height and curvy instead of tall and willowy like Henrietta, or petite and delicate like Rosella. Boring instead of beautiful.

Inside the house, she drew a deep breath and went to direct the help to find her trunk and repack it. They wouldn't need to know why. But then again, with the gossip mill the way it was, maybe she should explain it to them so they'd know the truth—that she had been duped into marrying a complete stranger, attractive and appealing as he was, when she thought she was only helping with the grand opening of a resort.

Keeping quiet was probably the best plan.

Jackson sat at the kitchen table, a steaming drink in front of him and what looked like a hot fruit turnover on his plate. He stood as she hesitated in the doorway. "Yes, miss?"

"When you finish, would you please put my trunk in my room and ask my maid to repack it? I'm leaving tonight."

Curiosity lit his eyes, but he didn't comment, other than another, "Yes, miss."

Bessie returned to the parlor where Mother, Aunt, and Rosella pretended to focus on embroidery. She sat on the settee next to Rosella and picked up her own piece of sewing.

The door burst open and Henrietta blew in, ripping off her gloves. "I saw Miss Pauline Chapman downtown."

Pauline—another beautiful debutante Bessie couldn't compare with. All the men would notice her. Probably Mr. Hale, as well.

"Guess what? She told us all kinds of juicy tales about Mr. Hale. Turns out, he's a spy!"

It didn't surprise Thomas to find Archie already at the preacher's house when he arrived. He probably planned to warn Mrs. Stout about Thomas being onto them and their wicked plans. But Mrs. Stout already knew. Thomas was sure of that since, when he'd seen her in town, she'd darted into a nearby gift shop in her feeble, obvious attempt to hide from him.

Silly, considering he was a man on a mission. He'd caught up with her anyway.

Archie hadn't attempted to hide, but probably only because Thomas had approached him in the middle of the street. Well, that, and because Archie was a man. Men didn't go running into gift shops to get away from their best friends.

And now Thomas needed to talk to the preacher about more than one thing. His agenda included both the marriage mistake and his own personal relationship with the Lord. Though with the preacher's integrity in question. . .

Thomas rubbed his jaw.

Maybe the "relationship with the Lord" problem could wait until Thomas found a preacher he could trust. God would understand, right? Because Thomas needed answers to spiritual questions that would remove all doubt.

Reverend Stout answered the door. A big smile lit his face and his hand rested on Thomas's shoulder. "Good to see you, Thomas. Where's the lovely bride?"

Behind him, in the manse, Mrs. Stout gave a startled glance at Thomas, jumped to her feet, said something to Archie, and with a furtive look behind her, darted into the kitchen. He heard the back door slam shut.

Archie stood. "Nice to see you again, Tommy. I need to help Mrs. Stout with something in the garden. I shall return, I'm sure." He followed the direction Mrs. Stout had taken.

"What can I help you with?" Reverend Stout took a step back to allow Thomas entry then peered into the road where the buggy waited. "Where is your lovely wife?"

Thomas sighed. "My lovely wife is at home with her family, probably still wrestling with the fact that she somehow managed to get married against her will."

Reverend Stout blinked at him. "What's that you say?" He scratched his head. "Against her will? I'm quite sure I didn't see any shotguns there."

So, the preacher truly didn't know? Thomas approached the settee where Archie had been seated, and sat without an invitation. "What exactly were you told about this wedding?"

Reverend Stout shrugged. "Mrs. Stout told me that you'd come by to ask me to officiate your wedding. Of course, I was more than pleased to do so. She also said you wanted the ceremony at Archie's house, though I questioned that. You have a lovely home of your own, you know. I was also rather surprised at the suddenness of the marriage, especially since you weren't waiting for your families to arrive, but my dear wife told me time was of the essence." His face colored.

Thomas gaped, his own face heating.

"Needless to say, I agreed. We didn't want that bit of scandal getting out. But you're saying she didn't want to marry? She'd rather be ruined?"

Thomas's mouth worked as he tried to find his tongue. "Um. . . . She's not. . . We didn't. . ." Jolly bad spot they'd been put into. "She's not. . . I barely know her. We haven't even been alone together." Not quite true. They *had* danced, alone, in the moonlight. Thomas sighed and scrubbed his hand over his face. What had he gotten into? More important, how was he going to get out of it?

Not that he wanted to.

"Are you saying Mrs. Stout lied?" Reverend Stout's voice hardened and his eyes narrowed.

Was he? Thomas looked down, trying to remember the preacher's exact words. *Time was of the essence.* Mrs. Stout could argue that what her husband assumed wasn't what she meant and claim misunderstanding. . .but the intent to mislead and manipulate was undeniably there.

Or was it? That could be argued, too. How could he know or guess her thoughts?

Thomas raked his fingers through his hair. "No, I'm not saying she lied. I'm saying she misrepresented the facts and landed us in a fine mess. And I'm not entirely sure how to proceed."

Or maybe he did know.

"You see, Archie asked Bessie and me to reenact his grandparents' wedding as a publicity stunt to advertise the opening of his resort."

"Then why the marriage certificate? Why was time of the essence? I need to call my wife in. We need to see if we can undo this." Reverend Stout stood.

"We're willing to stay married to avoid further scandal." Thomas grimaced. Maybe he shouldn't have said that. But *he* was willing at least.

He had no reason to believe that Miss Bessie O'Hara—Mrs. Thomas Hale—would be going home with him that night.

Maybe not any night.

"Speaking of further scandal. . ." Reverend Stout reclaimed his seat. "With all the rumors whispered about you being some sort of a spy, not to mention dishonoring Miss Chapman in some manner—well, perhaps you could offer a bit of explanation so I could try to understand?"

Thomas sighed. "There's a very large German munitions company in Europe owned by a family named Krupps. Among their many holdings is a factory in Berlin that supplied arms to the Boers in the war in South Africa. Miss Chapman's father somehow had vested interest in this war, on Great Britain's side, and he warned me not to sell iron ore to the Boers, who had earlier negotiated a contract with my father. I had no interest in the war and didn't particularly care about whether Mr. Chapman did or not. I traveled to Germany, per my father's wishes, and completed the sale." He frowned, and clasped his hands on his knees. "As a result, I was wrongfully accused of being a spy for Germany. Miss Chapman publicly accused me of such, in addition to accusing me of having improper relations with her lady's maid. She trampled my name in such mud that I fear it'll never wash off."

"Improper relations with her maid, you say?" The preacher's eyebrows rose.

"Lies. I don't even know who her maid is, and I have never had relations—proper

285

or otherwise—with anyone."

"To get this straight, you're saying that because you supplied the Krupps with iron ore, which they in turn sold to the Boers for their war against England. . ." Reverend Stout rehashed the story. It sounded just as ridiculous when he told it.

Chapter 9

Bessie forced herself to recline against the back of the chair, even though everything inside of her longed to lean forward as Rosella had.

"A spy? How exciting. Do tell." Rosella fanned herself then apparently caught her mother's frown. "This changes everything, of course. You can't be married to a spy."

What Bessie knew of Mr. Hale didn't remotely match her mental image of a spy. Though what, truly, did she know?

"Pauline used to be engaged to him, you know. They were going to marry last June," she said. "A big, lavish wedding in Grand Rapids followed by a yearlong honeymoon in Europe." Henrietta tossed her gloves carelessly on the piano keyboard and lowered herself into a chair across from Bessie.

"Engaged...to Pauline..." Rosella breathed.

Somehow, the information stabbed Bessie's heart. Sharp pain filled her. She'd never compare favorably to Pauline. Neither physically nor financially. Her dowry would be far smaller.

"What happened?" Rosella scooted closer to the edge of her seat.

Bessie's aunts and mother sat quietly, not even attempting to feign disinterest. This would be the biggest scandal since—well, since five days ago. Her marriage currently held that distinction.

Henrietta hesitated, accepting the tea the maid poured for her and taking several small sips until Sally left the room. "Pauline says he was spying for either the Krupps or the Boers. Probably the Krupps, because she knows he delivered information to them in Germany. It's a miracle he wasn't arrested and thrown into the deepest, darkest dungeon in the emperor's castle."

"What? What emperor? Emperor Wilhelm's castle?" Bessie probably shouldn't have asked. "Surely you mean King Edward's castle. If he was spying against the British." If Henrietta was wrong about a basic fact, she could be wrong about other things, too.

"King, emperor, same thing." Henrietta waved her hand in dismissal. "Pauline says her father warned him to not meet with the Krupps, but Mr. Hale insisted." She shook her head sadly. "Probably King Edward will come here to arrest him after President Roosevelt finds him. Do you imagine the president would attend a ball in his honor if he's here arresting Mr. Hale? We need to start planning. Issue an invitation to the royal family and Mr. Roosevelt. We'll be the talk of the town. Oh, maybe we should disclose Mr. Hale's location. We might be invited to the White House for a party in our honor."

This volume of confusing information was quite dizzying. The royal family? Bessie wasn't quite sure what or who the Boers were. She vaguely remembered hearing Father's conversations with his fellow businessmen of a war in South Africa where the British were fighting some farmers over something. Of course, she might be wrong, but she didn't think Henrietta was any nearer to correct. Still, if Mr. Hale were truly a spy, he would have been arrested in Europe. Not a year later on Mackinac Island. Bessie shook her head. "I don't think Mr. Hale is in any danger of—"

"Fiddlesticks! We shall be the belles of Washington. Everyone will ask for our hands in marriage, because we single-handedly apprehended a dangerous criminal." Henrietta's eyes widened. "Do you think he carries weapons?"

"Oooh, and he was in this house," Rosella wailed, her fan flapping.

All three mothers stared with wide, horrified eyes at Bessie.

"We need to warn Jackson not to admit him, ever again. Oh, Bessie, you married a criminal!" Rosella stood. "Jackson!" Then she crumpled to the floor in a heap.

"And that is my side of what happened," Thomas said.

Reverend Stout frowned while Mrs. Stout twisted her hands in her lap next to him. Archie twirled his hat on his finger, as if whatever happened here was none of his concern.

"And what is your side, my dear?" The preacher looked at his wife.

"Just a simple misunderstanding, of course. Mr. Asparagus approached me about Mr. Hale and Miss O'Hara marrying at the grand opening of his new resort. He already had the photographer lined up for a certain date, and so time *was* of the essence. I didn't mean anything improper by it. And I helped by picking up the marriage certificate for him and asking if you'd officiate the wedding. It's not my fault things went wrong." Mrs. Stout's eyes were wide.

"But you're the one who filed the marriage certificate at the courthouse, and you're the one who told them not to let me 'cut off my nose to spite my face,'" Thomas said.

Mrs. Stout jerked her shoulders, as if taking offense. "But of course, Mr. Hale. It is high time you got over your hermit ways. Mr. Asparagus told me you seemed quite enthralled with Miss O'Hara, and it was the first time he's ever seen you so taken by a woman."

Thomas didn't bother denying it. All he knew was that if he took Bessie home with him tonight, he'd have to acknowledge the warmth he'd felt in her arms. Something he'd gotten along without all these many years.

"And that dreadful Miss Chapman you were engaged to—"

"Not engaged. I never asked her to marry me," Thomas corrected her.

Mrs. Stout rolled her eyes. "Well, to hear her tell it, you were engaged and ready to marry last June and were going on a yearlong honeymoon to Europe. She was proclaiming it to everyone downtown today, the hussy, along with the deliciously scary information about you being a spy and how someone needed to warn that poor naive girl you took up with at the masquerade ball."

Ah, as he'd thought. The woman he'd danced with initially had been Pauline. "She told everyone I'm a spy?"

"Oh my, yes, and Miss O'Hara's cousin, Miss Johnson, was there. I'm sure Miss O'Hara knows by now."

"Did Miss Chapman mention a scandal with her maid?" It hurt to ask.

Mrs. Stout gave him a puzzled look. "Men will be men. Being a spy is quite enough. You'll have to undo some damage, but she's worth working for. Besides, you can't never always sometimes tell. The marriage is legal and binding, after all. Maybe she feels for you what you feel for her."

"You can't never always sometimes tell," Thomas repeated slowly as he shook his head. He resisted the urge to scratch his head. He'd puzzle over that comment later. "Quite right. Thanks for that. And now I think I'll take myself off to give an explanation to Miss O'Hara. I only hope the cannons at the fort aren't loaded and aimed to shoot me when I get to her residence."

Archie chuckled. "Haven't been soldiers here for seven years, remember? The only danger you're in is the Queen of Hearts screaming 'Off with his head!' I'll go with you, if it'll bolster your confidence."

"Much obliged. Of course, then she might scream 'Off with *his* head, too!'"

Archie laughed. "I'm much too lovable."

Thomas raised his eyebrows, which only made Archie laugh louder. But despite the teasing, the "Off with his head!" comment worried Thomas.

If Pauline had already gotten to Bessie, what would he walk into?

A nest of vipers might be less dangerous. And considerably more welcome.

◆━━━━◆

Bessie rose from where she'd knelt beside Rosella, having waved smelling salts under the woozy girl's nose. Jackson helped Rosella, still pale but conscious, into a chair as Sally brought in a glass of water. The drama over—for now, all three mothers sat side by side, heads together as they discussed this newest issue. And how the marriage simply *must* be annulled.

Bessie wasn't quite sure what to think. Mr. Hale intrigued her. He *noticed* her. And he was willing to honor his marriage vows. He'd said he was determined to love her. . . .

Not quite as romantic as she'd dreamed when Mr. Right proposed, but then this wasn't exactly a proposal. It was an after-the-fact declaration.

And the way he'd looked at her when she walked toward him on the rose-and-dandelion-strewn path at the pretend-but-real wedding still made her heart race.

He just couldn't be a spy. Could he? Maybe she ought to look into this further. Miss Chapman was just as prone to exaggeration as her cousins—and probably herself, too, if she was honest. Mr. Hale most likely had a legitimate reason for being in Germany—not that he needed one. After all, everyone traveled abroad. And surely he could explain what happened to earn both the reputation of being a spy and Miss Chapman's disdain.

When he came back for her tonight, Bessie would go, whether he'd honor the marriage-in-name-only request or not. He likely needed an heir. And honestly, the thought of him sweeping her into his arms and kissing her—really kissing her—

Oh, my. Her face heated, and she fanned herself.

Jackson appeared in the doorway with two calling cards. "Mr. Hale and—"

Already! He must be anxious to start their life together.

Chapter 10

Thomas handed the butler their cards. The butler took them then invited them to wait while he went to announce them.

Would Miss O'Hara even admit them?

Thomas's stomach churned and he pressed a hand against it while waiting for the butler to return. It seemed to be taking a while. Was he about to be turned away from this home, having left it only an hour before?

He needed to undo the damage Pauline had intentionally done, and then tell Bessie she wouldn't be going home with him after all. At least not now, and likely not ever. On the way over, he'd stopped to send a telegram to her father. He had to believe that the man would find some way out of this fiasco without ruining her reputation. Thomas's reputation, on the other hand, was of no account. Pauline had already destroyed it, first by publicly humiliating him in Europe, then by flaunting his perceived sins around their peers. His wants and desires didn't factor into this decision, although yes, he did want a second chance at love—with Bessie. He sighed heavily.

"Don't worry so much. With God, all things are possible," Archie said quietly.

With God, all things are possible. If only Thomas could believe it. But then, who was Archie to talk about trusting God when he and Mrs. Stout had taken it upon themselves to make sure Thomas married instead of waiting for God to move when He was ready? If Archie and Mrs. Stout had left him alone, Thomas wouldn't be trying to make amends now. He was not grateful for their interference. Not in the least.

Unless, of course, Miss O'Hara decided to honor their marriage contract.

And then—then he might be tempted to throw a party in their honor.

Archie bowed his head. Could he be praying?

If God was listening, it'd be wise for Thomas to pray, too. He bowed his head. *Oh, Lord, my Lord. . .* Did those words assume an intimacy that wasn't there? Nausea built. *If You hear me, please—*

"Follow me, please," the butler said, likely not realizing why the two men were bowing their heads before him. If he had, he surely wouldn't interrupt a long-overdue conversation with God.

Fine, talking with God would come later. At some point, He and Thomas somehow had to get over their impasse.

Thomas swept off his hat and bowed slightly as he entered the room where the ladies still sat. His eyes sought Bessie, but a loud gasp interrupted him.

He jerked his gaze toward Miss Everson, who paled. A glass toppled to the floor, splattering water all over the oak boards.

"We're all going to die!" She slumped against the seat, her fan flapping only a little slower than a hummingbird's wings.

Thomas blinked. "I see my greatly exaggerated reputation has preceded me."

Bessie giggled.

Maybe she didn't believe the worst of him. Maybe there was a spark of hope that she'd want to make the marriage work.

She approached them, a smile lighting her eyes. "I'm glad you came. Would you like some tea?"

Not especially. What was it with this infernal offering of tea when he called? He may be half Brit, but he didn't inherit the necessary genes that would make him a die-hard tea drinker. "Thank you, no. I just had some at the manse." And if he drank any more in the next twenty-four hours, the Boston Tea Party would be reenacted on Mackinac Island.

"I do hope you've come with some sort of explanation." Mrs. O'Hara speared him with a glare. "But do sit down."

Archie dropped into a wingback chair.

Thomas sat in the chair closest to the piano. "Yes, ma'am. First of all, I took it upon myself to send a telegram to Mr. O'Hara, informing him of this emergency situation. Secondly, it seems you've been served a heaping helping of lies. Miss Chapman and I have never been and will never be engaged."

Miss Johnson gasped. Or was it Miss Everson? He wasn't sure.

"We did cohort with the same group of peers, and I did briefly court her, but a year ago we had a very public breakup over my refusal to follow her father's demands."

Despite the fact that she'd not been summoned, the maid bustled in with tea.

Thomas pressed his lips together, accepted the cup and saucer as gracefully as he could, and set it down beside him on the bench. Then he looked at Bessie. "I won't ask you to come home with me tonight."

She withdrew, her expression shuttering.

"I need to speak to your father first."

She nodded, her smile returning.

"Her father will agree with me. The marriage will be annulled," Mrs. O'Hara said.

Thomas nodded and looked back at Bessie. "If he doesn't, or if it can't be done, I want his blessing. He needs to know who I am and decide for himself if I am worthy of his daughter."

Bessie's gaze softened.

"What about the spy accusations? I'm tempted to tell President Roosevelt where he can find you so he can take you off to prison." Miss Johnson firmed her shoulders, her voice hard.

Archie chuckled. Bessie leaned forward—as if this point concerned her somewhat. Maybe she had considerable worries after all.

Thomas was tempted to roll his eyes. "Yes, Miss Johnson, but those are unfounded lies. I am not now nor have I ever been a spy. The truth is my father owns Hale Mining

Company of Marquette. One of the metals we mine is iron ore. Because I sold iron ore to a German company who then sold it to the South Africans fighting the British, Miss Chapman somehow made the incorrect assumption that I'm a spy. Or perhaps she purposely devised the story. But despite the scandalous rumors she started, the reality is not quite so exciting, I'm afraid."

Thomas glanced at Archie and saw the staunch support there, and then he looked at Bessie and found boldness and freedom in telling the truth.

"We're not going to die?" Miss Everson's fan slowed.

Miss Johnson slumped. "You're not a spy? We're not going to be applauded in Washington at a big gala? We won't be the belles of the country?"

◆━━━━━◆

Bessie could barely contain another giggle at those absurd questions from Henrietta and Rosella and the confused expressions passing over both men's faces.

They exchanged glances, and then Mr. Hale stood. The cup rattled in the saucer on the bench, but he didn't look at it. "You aren't going to die at our hands, Miss Everson. And Miss Johnson, all three of you lovely ladies are undoubtedly the belles of the nation. But if you'll excuse us, we'll take our leave. I just wanted to make sure you knew the truth, so you wouldn't be tempted to believe the rumors longer than you already have."

"Thomas is an upstanding man and my best friend." Mr. Asparagus stood also. "I came along with him to tell you, Miss O'Hara, that I'm sorry for my part in this whole fiasco. I did want Thomas to stop hiding from society and to marry. When I saw his immediate and unprecedented reaction to you, I did a quick appraisal of your character. I discovered only good things about you. You are the woman God intended for him. I have no doubt of it. However, I should have let God handle it rather than forcing His hand. But I am going to use some of the photos to advertise my resort, with your permission. The rest will go into an album as my wedding gift to you both."

Bessie stood and extended her hand to Mr. Asparagus. "Thank you for your kind words." She released him and turned to Thomas, taking one of his hands in both of hers. "And thank you for coming by and putting the rumors to rest."

For an insane second she wanted to offer to go with him after all, but Father needed to know and to bless their union first. If he would.

Thomas folded his other hand over hers. "I should have addressed the issue when I first came to Mackinac Island a year ago instead of becoming a hermit. But I was convinced God didn't hear me, and the breakup with Miss Chapman was ugly, humiliating, and devastating. I needed time to heal. I hadn't even told Archie. But honestly, I'd like the rumors and lies to die. It seems a bit belated to handle them at this stage."

"I admire your courage in talking about it now." Truly, she did. The way he'd handled the situation spoke volumes about him. Thomas was shaping up to be a man she'd be proud to call her husband.

Unless, of course, he publicly lost his temper and berated delivery boys on the street.

But he hadn't even gotten angry over the wedding fiasco. He contacted her father, wanting his advice and approval. He treated her with kindness, respect, and, oh, the way he looked at her made her long to be his wife.

Thomas bent over her hand, brushed his lips over her knuckles, then straightened and left the room, taking her heart with him.

◆•———•◆

Thomas glanced at his best friend as they rode away from the O'Hara house, toward the side of the island where Archie lived. Archie had sent his own driver home when he decided to ride with Thomas on his errands. It made sense, since Thomas's home lay beyond Archie's.

"I am sorry for interfering." Archie apologized again as he had at the Stouts' manse. "I shouldn't have. And I surely didn't mean to cause this big mess—not for Miss O'Hara, and certainly never for you. I don't know what I was thinking. Maybe I just let Mrs. Stout sweep me in when I mentioned your attraction to Miss O'Hara and my plans for a reenactment. We spoke of how wonderful it would be if it were real and things just went from there. But with the silly Pauline saying you're a spy and that you might kill people, the rumors just snowballed."

Thomas nodded. Despite how crazy and out of control the rumors were after Pauline spread her story, they had easily folded under the truth. His ego and infatuation had truly been out of control as well. But God had saved him from Pauline, using a vision of a dream girl he couldn't help but compare to the poison of a society viper.

"Out of control. Quite so." He looked out the window, catching glimpses of Lake Huron as they passed by beautiful cottages and homes. He didn't want Bessie to be forced into this marriage, with the idea that she had to or be ruined. But, oh, he wanted her with every fiber of his being. Ever since he first laid eyes on her at the ferry, something about her made him take notice. And he knew she was the one, the fuzzy vision he'd dreamed of since he was old enough to notice women, to think about marriage, to dream of a future with a woman.

And with that in mind, why, why, why had he allowed Pauline to draw him into her web? She really had been like a poison, a substance he couldn't get enough of, but that in the end had almost destroyed him. She had caused him to believe himself abandoned by the one who had made him.

Why couldn't he admit this to his best friend sitting beside him?

He didn't know how to bring it up.

Maybe if he just blurted it out. He closed his eyes so he couldn't see the censure. The judgment. "I've felt abandoned by God. I believed He couldn't hear me, couldn't see me, and didn't care what happened to me so long as I stayed out of His way. I asked God to help me get Pauline to see the truth or to make her lies disappear. But they only got worse, and so I thought if God didn't care enough to answer my prayers, then I wouldn't care about Him. That if He wouldn't help me, I'd save Him time and stop asking for help."

Archie turned to look at him.

Jonas slowed the horse to a walk as they turned into the driveway in front of Archie's house.

"Jonas told me that God is the God who sees me. He's the God who hears me. That means He knew and cared what was best for me, even when I ignored Him. And it hit me that He's the kind of God I want, the kind I need. A God who cares about the littlest thing that happens to me. And the one who gives me the woman of my dreams, even when I've turned my back on Him."

From the driver's seat Jonas nodded. "God loves you more than anything."

His mother's words when he left home replayed in his thoughts. *"He more than cares, Tommy. He loves you. He loves you so much, you were the one He saw when He sent Jesus to earth as a little baby. You were the reason Jesus suffered and died. You were the one on His mind when He was resurrected from the dead, and He's watching you from the right hand of God even as we speak. He's given His angels special charge over you. He loves you beyond anything you could ever know."*

Thomas swallowed the lump in his throat. "I need to pray."

The buggy came to a stop in front of Archie's house as Thomas got onto his knees in front of his seat.

Chapter 11

Today's the day. Bessie straightened as Jackson announced Thomas and the elder Hales's arrival. And while she wished she were alone with Thomas, this meeting would be the means to the end. If both sets of parents agreed.

Thomas had come by every day, courting, wooing, and causing her to fall deeper in love with him. But today he came for a different reason. She glanced at her father, smoothed her skirt, and then welcomed Thomas in with a smile. If only she could rush over and throw her arms around him the same way her two-year-old niece greeted her. Overly excited, but acceptable in one so young.

He had his hands behind his back, and as she stood, he presented her with a bouquet of red roses.

A man, an older version of Thomas, entered behind him, closely followed by a woman. His father—and mother. Bessie swallowed. *Lord, let them like me.*

They introduced themselves, and then Thomas's mother wrapped her arms around Bessie and gave her a hug. "You are the woman who won my son's heart."

Bessie hugged her back, a smile building and growing. "And he won mine."

"Let's talk. Please, take a seat." Her father extended his arm and motioned toward the chairs.

Polite. Overly polite. Bessie cringed. She thought Father understood how much she wanted to be with Thomas. But he didn't seem to be making this easy.

Thomas's eyes darkened with undefined emotion. A muscle worked in his jaw.

Father turned to Thomas. "I received your telegram."

Thomas nodded and leaned forward, clasping his hands between his knees. "I don't know what Bessie has told you, but she and I were duped into getting married under the guise of doing a favor for a friend." He hesitated, his eyes softening as he glanced at Bessie. "But Bessie is the woman I've always dreamed of. Since we married, I've been courting her, and I've fallen deeply in love with her. I'm asking your permission to marry her. Properly this time."

"Bessie has told me about it. Rather presumptuous of your friend. But I appreciate your decision to court my daughter, to take the marriage vows seriously, and to ask my blessing." Her father glanced at her and smiled.

Bessie's heart pounded. Hopefully, the smile meant a blessing sooner rather than later. And not an annulment. If only she could hold Thomas's hand as they awaited the verdict.

"Most couples don't know each other as well as they think they do when they marry.

They learn everything after the vows are taken." Father took a breath, frowned.

Oh, no. Would Father refuse them now? She wiped her trembling hands against her skirt.

"Bessie tells me she loves you, too. And so I give my permission for you two to marry. . . ." The frown faded and he chuckled. "Or rather, to renew your wedding vows, this time in front of family."

Thomas grinned. "Thank you, sir." He stood and took a few short steps forward then dropped to one knee in front of Bessie. "Elizabeth Cordelia O'Hara, I love you incredibly much. Will you give me the honor of becoming my wife?"

Bessie's breath caught. She leaned forward, wrapping her arms around Thomas's neck as he straightened and pulled her up. "Yes, yes, a thousand times, yes."

Thomas glanced at their parents, sitting around the room. "Will you excuse us while I take my wife for a walk to discuss the future?"

The older folks chuckled and started chatting about arrangements while the happy couple slipped out the side door.

Hand in hand they strolled toward the lake. "How soon do you think we can renew our vows?" She glanced up at him.

"As soon as possible. We'll spend a few days here then leave for our honeymoon before we move to Marquette to help run my family business."

Bessie breathed in the scent of the water as she had the day they met. On the day she hoped someone would deliver her a husband wrapped up with a bow and tell her to take care of him.

When they were well away from the house, Thomas stopped in the shade of a tree and caught her close in his arms. He lifted her up and swung her around. "Dreams do come true." His lips brushed hers then came back to claim them more fully. "I love you, I love you, I love you."

Each "I love you" was punctuated by a kiss.

"And I love you, Thomas Hale."

She'd made no mistake in marrying this man. God had it in His plans all along.

Laura V. Hilton is an award-winning, sought-after author with almost twenty Amish, contemporary, and historical romances. When she's not writing, she reviews books for her blogs, and writes devotionals for blog posts for *Seriously Write* and *Putting on the New*. Laura and her husband Steve have five children and a hyper dog named Skye. They currently live in Arkansas. One son is in the U.S. Coast Guard. She is a pastor's wife, and home-schools her two youngest children. When she's not writing, Laura enjoys reading, and visiting lighthouses and waterfalls.

Fanned Embers

by Angela Breidenbach

Dedication

To all our heroes unknown, unsung
All the statues as yet undone
The Lord sees all and will not forget
Earthly sacrifice and commitment.

Acknowledgments

I'm grateful to my family for riding the Hiawatha
three times with me for research and fun!

Thank you, Tamela Hancock Murray and the hardworking people
of Barbour Publishing, for helping bring this story to readers.

Thank you to those who have gone before, battled deprivation,
tamed the wild, that we may enjoy our lives today!

Chapter 1

July 4, 1910
Adair, Idaho—Deep in the Bitterroot Mountains
Milwaukee Railroad Western Extension, Montana-Idaho Border

Juliana Hayes squinted against the sun breaking over the sharp rock outline of the Bitterroot Mountains. Each escaping ray ratcheted up the thermometer in the early Pacific Northwest morning. Giant cedars looming above eighty-foot white pine should offer refuge and shade. Instead they represented the immobile bars of her prison. In the distance, the forest closed so tightly it looked like rolls of dark green velvet. Such beauty hiding the malevolent nature of the area's extreme dangers. As dangerous as some of the men Juliana cautiously avoided since being stranded.

How much longer until she could break out of the harsh existence that had held her captive for over two years? The deep snows in winter and the fires in summer, extremes she could do without. The oncoming train puffed out clouds of smoke against the sky so blue and clear it resembled a lake more than the heavens. But she'd also ridden that train many times praying they'd make it to the next mining camp through heavy snow and bitter cold. Did there exist another place so wildly inhospitable?

"Anot'er hot day, Mrs. Hayes." The baggage handler lifted his flat cloth cap and rubbed a gray cotton sleeve across his forehead. "Who knew America would be such a hot place?" He flopped the cap back on his head as he waited with her on Adair's plat-form for the train to sidle up.

She'd join the morning shift change on the train headed for the mines dotted through the wilderness settlements and narrow, serpentine valley to deliver her quota of baked goods. "We've never had a summer as hot before, not that I can remember." Was he Austrian, Belgian, Croatian? She didn't ask. He obviously wasn't Chinese or Japanese with his blond hair. She tried not to wrinkle her nose. It was blond, wasn't it? Hard to tell when these men likely bathed only on their day off. He stood tall enough to stick out among the Japanese who mostly inhabited the tent city of Adair nowadays. "After the avalanches in the spring, I don't think anyone expected this drought."

"I heard da winters here are hard. You do good wi' dem?"

She nodded, avoiding too much conversation. There must be more than seventy dif-ferent nationalities working on the rails and the mines here on the border of Montana and Idaho. Some nationalities were so close they spoke similar languages; only the col-ors or sometimes a piece of native clothing distinguished them one from another. This mishmash of humanity from every known continent all with the same hope—to make their fortunes, whether to bring over more family or get rich quick or hide from the law. Money drove these desperate men.

His clothing suggested another Austrian. They tended to band together, each of these different nationalities. It helped with communication overall as the foremen spoke English and the native language of their crews; sometimes a few others did as well. The mixed-pigeon varieties were endless, and sometimes humorous, but the pigeon languages helped bridge one group to another unless they clashed. They often clashed. Tempers were as hot as the rail spikes in the sun, after a day of working in the excruciating cold, wet work deep in the rocky mountainsides. As important the sense of togetherness inside a group was, it was ironic how that togetherness habitually incited aggression and animosity toward outsiders. Why couldn't they all just get along?

Juliana did her best to be as neutral and invisible as possible, down to wearing dull clothing and keeping her long hair tied up under her baker's scarf. But as a young woman, that worked as well as a queen bee in a hive. She hated developing the stinger that went along with the unwanted attention buzzing around her like soldier bees. But she'd been left with little other protection when her husband died.

Not long now. She calculated her time left based on her weekly pay envelope. She could shed the protective veneer in nine weeks, six days, and twelve hours—give or take the time it took to leave the mountains behind. She'd have her trunk on the very next train to Helena without a second glance. There'd be no salt pillar of Juliana Hayes in Adair, Idaho, or any other debauched mining town in this forsaken place.

This Austrian, or whatever, was new on the job in a constantly changing mass of men. He'd met her at the brick dome ovens in Adair the last few days to help load a converted mining cart with the staples she baked for the workers up and down the line. At least she could understand his English—and he didn't seem to be a Montenegrin by the look of him. Those vicious men tended to work in Rowland and Taft, on her Tuesday and least favorite route. Why did she have to feed the very men who murdered her husband? A shiver ran down her spine. She'd have to deliver the bread order to them tomorrow. Each week she considered adding sawdust, or worse, to the dough—and each week she mashed the desire down deep as she punched the bread into submission. Twenty loaves, untainted by her dark desire for vengeance. *"Vengeance is mine. . .saith the Lord."* She repeated that verse each time the snake's temptation squeezed its coils around her heart.

"I hear said da snow gets deep as the depot roof."

Juliana nodded again and graced the man with a quick, courteous smile, careful not to encourage anything. Too nice a response would garner yet another proposal or a lewd proposition. No response and she'd have to lug all four heavy freight baskets onto the train herself to the next stop on her daily deliveries. Her pay packet from the railroad would be reduced if she cost precious production minutes, she knew from experience when she first started for the Milwaukee Railroad. The company didn't care that she was a new widow. They cared she kept up with her quotas.

"Too bad we don't have a little snow left over," she mumbled as pleasantly as possible, under the circumstances. "I hope we don't see a fire season so dangerous again as that one two years ago." She didn't want to relive a summer like that for more reasons than the spot wildfires. Her grief had been as thick as the smoke trapped by the jagged peaks.

"Was bad, *ja?*"

"Yes."

The engine whistle blew three long shrieks as metal on metal squealed a high-pitched complaint, braking the train to a stop. The nearness of the rocky mountain slopes amplified the sounds. The conductor, in overalls and brimmed summer hat, leaned out the caboose porch. He leaped onto the wooden platform and ran nimbly along the train before it had a chance to stop, bellowing, "All 'board! Let's be movin', folks." He inspected the waiting cargo, including the amount Juliana brought aboard. "Mornin', Widow Hayes."

"Good morning, Mr. Kelly." She handed him a couple of buttermilk biscuits filled with apple butter, wrapped in cheesecloth. The conductor often missed meals for train delays. "There's one for the engineer also."

"Yer a good woman, ya are." He tipped his hat and strode at a fast pace toward the front. "Johnnie, we been visited by the Angel of Adair! Looky the size of them biscuits!" Only he called her that, and only he was allowed. The older man, stronger than his wrinkles led one to believe, had shoved more than his share of miscreants off the train for interfering in her duties.

Johnnie Mackedon tooted out his thanks on the whistle. One of his signatures. Stay long enough and each engineer could be recognized by the way he pulled the train whistle.

She laughed and gave him a quick wave as she called out, "You're welcome, Johnnie."

The burly handler lifted the heavier basket laden with oversized loaves and walked with Juliana toward the steps leading into the first passenger car.

As he shifted to pass another up to the top step, he said, "Mizz Hayes, I been meanin'—"

Juliana made a show of focusing on raising her skirt to climb the steps. Three days it took him. Must be a record. "Oh look, the front seats are open. Mr. Kelly keeps them clear for me, you know." Prime space to settle in with her tasty cargo that still wafted the fresh-baked aroma of oat bran, whole wheat, and honey all around her. The rich scent of baked goods helped to mask the constant smell of the muck of the mines. She always rode in front. First on and first off to keep deliveries moving and the unwanted scent of unwashed bodies blown behind her by the open windows. In the front, she avoided eye contact. They might approach her with odious offers, but none would dare take a Milwaukee Railroad baker's chosen space. The company provided the best grub in the country for their workforce, supplementing the regular camp cooks. Bellies held priority until full. Then it switched to other appetites. Appetites she refused to fill.

All eyes devoured her as if she were a Sunday cinnamon raisin bun. How unfriendly did she have to be to protect herself? It seemed the colder she behaved the harder some men tried. She'd heard the dares and the bets and chose to ignore them. One at a time, she could rebuff the advances.

"Mizz—"

"I don't want to keep you from your other freight or we'll both get docked for delaying the shift change." Not today. She didn't want to be targeted by teeming crews snatching up the handful of women as wives or worse. No, she couldn't stomach it, today of all days. She lifted the nearest bread crate and stowed it.

"Ma'am, the party tonight, if you're of the mind—" His voice soft, pleading.

He might even be a nice man. But Juliana didn't want a man here, nice or otherwise. She took the last crate from him and backed away, setting the bread on the front seat beside her. The length hung well beyond the edge. With those stacked on the floor near her feet, another across the aisle, they formed a sort of protective fencing. A small fortress protecting her personal space.

The whistle blew, sounding departure. She couldn't give him a hair of a chance to spit the rest of the words out. "I'll bring a few loaves of hearty dark rye in the morning. I know that's a favorite with the wild onion and venison sandwiches. I heard your bunkhouse got a big buck the other day. Maybe a trade for some meat?" The extra work would be worth it if she could supplement her pantry and not spend out of her savings. And steer the conversation away from what she knew came next.

"Good, ja, to be sure. Would you—"

The conductor pushed through the entry. "Get on back to loading, Jack." He jabbed an elbow into the baggage man's ribs, whose name was something more like Jacques, if one could get the accent right. "The Widow Hayes got 'er job and yous got yers. Move it, man, get those supplies loaded and leave room for them pack horses!"

A moment later, Juliana escaped the first proposal of the day by luck and by golly. At least he'd tried to be nice. Three stops to dispatch last night's labor, and a basket of buttermilk biscuits for the highest weekly production, then the ride back to Adair. Tomorrow she'd deliver to Rowland, and the cycle would continue six days out of seven. The Rowland baker from down the line would overlap schedules for her one day off on Sunday, as the others did for all the mining camps stretched through the long valley along the tracks. Juliana rarely saw the other women, as they worked one another's days off. Most had marital and family duties to catch up on. Each baked for her camp and three to four more that either didn't have an oven and baker, or only worked part-time due to other responsibilities.

Juliana slid against the seat back, savoring the air flowing in from the window. So many days lately the air stood still as a deer at the crack of a twig. Her only relief came from the train window. Juliana split her schedule and baked half her quota well before dawn during the summer to avoid the intense heat of the huge brick ovens in the late afternoon, the hottest part of the day in the Idaho panhandle.

She had little chance of avoiding several more marriage—or unmentionable—invitations with the significance of the holiday for citizens and immigrants alike. She smoothed the worn white apron over her tan cotton work skirt. She'd have on black still, but that brought the men out of the tunnels and mines as much as the whiskey called them to the saloons. A black dress meant a woman had no man, fair game in this most beautiful of desolate places. Mary, a new baker, had been carried to the preacher within days of arriving last summer. Carried. That miner wasn't taking a chance of cold feet or bridal theft. Bridal theft could get a man killed in these parts as much as having the precious commodity of a bride, if she were particularly desirable. Most respected marriage, though they'd line up to pay respects at any married man's funeral in hopes of walking the new widow right past her home and into theirs. Women like her friend Astrid picked a new husband quickly, especially if she had children to support. These mountains could be ruthless in weather and with wild animals.

This summer poor Mary nursed a newborn and baked. She managed to give away one of her days to another miner's wife, a previous canary, that wanted honest work rather than the bawdy house her husband had found her in. *Not me, Lord. Be it Your will, I'm getting out of here come the end of September! I am not raising a family here. If You ever grace me with a good man again, let it be in a city! Strike that. I'd rather just have a city life.*

Some days Juliana felt more like a lone stalk of grain in a herd of buffalo bulls all snorting and ramming one another. After this summer ended, she'd have enough to move on before the harsh winter hit again. She'd take this very train into Helena, Montana, the Queen City of the Rockies, and never look back. Maybe she'd continue to Minneapolis or keep going as far east as Chicago. With the mastery of mass baking she'd gained, her own pastry shop would serve cookies, cakes, and anything to break the monotony of wheat bread and sourdough, four days a week, cinnamon raisin or another sweet bread on Saturdays for their Sunday meals, and the dark rye to the weekly winners of extra rations.

Only a short ride between towns, the train wove beside the St. Joe River that flowed low from the heat and lack of rain, and around the wide bend before pulling into Kyle. Deliver into the depot, climb on the next train to Stetson. Deliver, climb on the next train to Avery. Then home to Adair to start the dough for tomorrow. The cycle didn't slow. Mix dough, bake bread, deliver bread to miners and railroaders. Keep them working. Juliana stared out the window at the white pine, cedar, and river flashing past as they rode deeper into the rugged realm. Why couldn't she have fallen in love with a man who would stay in the city the first time? She could have avoided this day. While everyone else would celebrate the country's independence, Juliana marked the second anniversary of her husband's death.

"Get outta my way!" The shouts erupted several rows from the front.

"I got dibs!"

Juliana rolled her eyes heavenward but didn't bother to look at the skirmish. She already knew what caused the fight. She plunked her elbow on the window ledge and dropped her chin into it, staring at the passing landscape. Nine weeks and six days. . .

Chapter 2

L ukas took a headcount of his newly hired crew as they boarded the back of the railcar from the Kyle platform. He breathed in relief as he followed them inside. He'd pick up a few extras from the other foreman, if he had them, and head back to Rowland. Better to be prepared for attrition. Any given day a man walked off the job without a word.

A whiff of fresh bread floated from the front of the car, wafting in the air between bodies pushing for seating. He closed his eyes and inhaled deeply. He'd like one good day this month. Just one. It'd be topped off with a hunk of that bread and the ability to concentrate on the actual job rather than refilling empty positions for the company. His stomach rumbled. Bad coffee reheated from last night didn't make the best breakfast. Perhaps the baker would have a bite to spare in her bundles?

As the crowd in the aisle diminished, one lummox shoved another backward. "I ain't givin' way! She ain't got a man an' I ain't got a woman. I'm tired o' spendin' money on canaries."

"An' you ain't gettin' betwixt she an' me!" The targeted victim, righted by his buddy behind him, used the upward momentum and shoved back, sending his opponent flying across two other men.

Shouts and curses turned to bets on the winner as the crew tossed the rivals into the middle.

"That don't make you the one she wants!"

In less time than the breadth of a horse hair, the first man fisted and decked the second guy.

Not ducking out, the punched man recovered, again with the assistance of a buddy, and flew into battle. The rest of the crew leaned over seats, egging the two on, cheering for their favorite, and passing money to the man nearest the fight, who acted as the bank.

By the time Lukas made it through the tangle of bodies blocking his progress, the culprits were on the floor trying to strangle one another over a woman. Not the first fight he'd seen, since females were as rare in this rugged country as trout in the low river. The job challenged the strongest men physically, mentally, and spiritually. After a month as the hiring foreman, he'd discovered the most grueling job, his, was keeping the mines running against the constant loss of manpower from giving up or getting beat or moving on. Men could take the hard work. They could handle the extremes in temperature. But the lack of womankind wreaked havoc in a way he couldn't have fathomed when he agreed to the contract. Men forged the roads, built the towns, answered the call of adventure. But women—they tamed hearts, settled men, and created civilization.

The production reports took a backseat to order, discipline, and the act of production. Two months of reports from the last foreman never happened. Now he knew why. His first had yet to be finished for the company. But if he lost any more men, he'd be down in the mines working an empty shift again. Though he'd earned respect by doing it before. Now this mess—before the day even started. He pushed the gawkers in the inner circle back into their seats, a firm hand on a shoulder if one protested. They took one look at who dared and backed down. Many here stood taller than average and sported physiques built out of years on farms, railroads, mines, or prison. All came for the opportunity, but few boasted the equivalent of Lukas's height and frame—the epitome of a European man who'd worked hard through his boyhood. That fact alone stopped many problems. He had the additional benefit of an excellent education and leadership skills. His deep voice cinched it for the rest.

Lukas grabbed a handful of shirt collar and hauled the bigger brute up in one yank. The man landed on his feet, staring up into his foreman's darkened glare. "You will stop." The other contender leaped to his feet and launched forward, fists primed. Lukas extended a flat palm with such force toward the oncoming attacker, he knocked the wind out of him. "You will also stop."

Never once did he raise his voice above a low growl as he spoke in his native language. His height alone commanded attention. Add the muscular body of heavy labor since childhood, and most would-be challengers remained just that. He had a resonant baritone that, when raised in worship, filled a church with beauty, but directed in discipline, shook the recipient to the core. As head foreman in charge of men pushed past human endurance, when decency in the ranks didn't last long, Lukas had no choice but to be half father and half bouncer. What he couldn't afford to be was too close of a friend, not given these intense conditions. Enough familiarity to build connection and enough command to build respect. Something his father had taught him about managing their holdings while tutoring Lukas to take over.

"What was this about?" He asked the man whose scruff he still held.

"Her." He pointed at the baker in the front row, wooden bins of bread all around her making a kind of blockade. She faced forward with a stiffened spine, pointedly ignoring the scene not far behind her, arms wrapped tightly around her torso. Did she know the fight was over her, or couldn't she understand the language?

One of the miners nearby laughed, and explained, "Ain't no big deal. Someone's always makin' a play for her. She ain't givin' the likes o' those two no never mind. Gotta be a rich man to catch a gal like that one. I'll get me rich and then get that gal for my personal canary." The fellows around him slapped him on the back. "You'll all be jealous, then."

The bakers, hired directly by the Milwaukee Railroad, were hard to find and hard to replace. If Lukas wanted bread for his crews, that lady needed protection from the men she had to feed.

He switched to English, hoping the woman would understand he had everything under control. "You will all leave the baker alone. If not, you will answer to me." He narrowed his eyes, looked at each man, and asked, "Do we understand each other?"

Lukas caught a flicker of movement in the front row. Had she glanced over her shoulder?

"Ja," the one who could speak said as he nodded.

Letting the man go, Lukas pointed at the bench several rows back. Then he turned to the smaller culprit. *"Und?"*

He nodded.

Lukas released him.

The fellow sputtered, wheezed, and worked his way down the aisle doubled over, to sit as far away from Lukas as he could get.

Lukas stared down the entire compartment. Then he shook his head. One perfect day. This wouldn't be it. He searched for a seat, catching hold of one he passed to balance as the train swayed around a bend. All full until he reached the front.

"May I?" he asked the pretty bread baker. The company of a sweet soul with kind words would do a lot to ease the stress today.

She turned from the window, sized him up with caramel-brown eyes in a flash that rocked him as hard as dynamite blasting a mining shaft. "No."

He'd caught a glimpse of freckles across glowing cheeks and honey-colored hair under her baker's scarf. Eyes he hadn't seen in the month he'd ridden behind the baker or in a different car dealing with new men, paperwork, and supplies. He'd seen her from a distance. He knew of her. Until now, he'd no idea what she looked like. Only the rumor that she was a looker. Sometimes Lukas missed the train altogether when he had to roust employees out of a bordello, likely still drunk. But those eyes needed studying. He understood now what the men fought over. A chance to capture the light in those eyes—or to be the man that put it there.

The train ratcheted around another curve, jostling Lukas into a giant basket, almost spilling its contents. He righted it without losing a loaf or the perfect packing order, and then held out a hand. "Terribly sorry, Miss—"

"It's Mrs." The woman held up her hand, displaying a plain gold band on her fourth finger. She reached across the basket and pulled it back from Lukas. Then she turned away to the window without another word.

A choked snicker transformed into a cough when Lukas turned to look. The miner fixed his eyes on the floor, suddenly fascinated by his boots. More now than any time, Lukas had to establish authority with the replacements or risk costly disrespect. That could mean lives. He lengthened his scrutiny with disapproval until the man inched toward the window like a naughty puppy. Expanding to include the others in the vicinity, he quelled any further laughter intended to minimize his leadership. Sometimes he felt sorry for his past teachers. This must be similar to how they felt with a bunch of unruly adolescents.

"My apologies, ma'am." He lifted the basket off the bench across the aisle. "Would you mind if I held this for you while I sit here?"

She glanced over her shoulder, took in the packed passenger car, and then at him. "That would be fine, as I see no other option."

"I'm Lukas Filips." He thumbed toward the other passengers, half already snoring. "They shouldn't bother you again."

"Yous got that right," the conductor said as he arrived, coming up through the train. "I ain't got the time to be runnin' through my train to keep the peace." He shook his head. "From now on, any o' your lot rides an' yous gonna be ridin' or y'all be walkin'!"

Lukas furrowed his brow. "I can't—"

The conductor shrugged. "Suit yerself." He leaned down toward the woman and peered out the window at the thick brush along the river. "Guess them boys want to work up a good appetite fer yer baked goods since they'll be addin' a couple miles' walk through the brambles." He chuckled as he straightened, but that low laugh held a tone of finality.

She rewarded him with a raised eyebrow. "Could make for an uncommonly pleasant ride, Mr. Kelly."

"You know I have to keep my men working. I can't—"

"No siree, ain't gonna tell yous yer business. Jes tryin' to help as best I can in the circumstance." He held his palms up. "You 'n' me, we got our jobs. Mine is to get my passengers, cargo, and the baker ladies to their destinations. When yer fellas make my job harder, ain't much of a leap fer me. I like her cookin' more than I like bustin' up a boxin' match ever' mornin' and noon. Get me?"

One more log to roll out of the way in the jam piling up. He'd have to ride from Rowland and make the loop every day to ensure the early crew arrived until their bunkhouse, closer to the mine, was completed. "What if we strike a deal? I ride for a short time. If there's no problem, we call it solved." The hour, plus travel time, would cost him in yet later reports. But if helping this one very pretty woman helped him manage his crew better, then so be it.

"Knew he'd see reason, Widow Hayes. Yous let me know if you got any problem." The conductor pulled out his pocket watch. "Back to it, then." He flipped it closed as he left Lukas and the caramel-eyed widow staring at each other.

Lukas curbed the desire to shout, and spoke low enough for the two of them. "How am I supposed to get any work done or manage my crews?"

Her eyes widened like an oasis emerging from the sands, and just as surprising, "You think I've no work to do? It's your men that often delay me." She rose with hands on hips. The train jockeyed for its position, snaking round another bend. "I have bread to get to—" Another quick jolt to the left and the beauty flopped down on her bench as if the hand of God brushed against her, plopping her in a most unladylike fashion to finish the conversation. "Never mind." She turned away. "I don't want to talk about it."

"Wait, Widow Hayes." He slid a basket off the seat and sat beside her. "How do my men make you late?"

She stared at him. "How would you manage in this female-starved environment if you were me?"

She expected him to answer that other than he'd advise her to get married? "I don't understand." Maybe it was a nuance in the English language he had yet to learn, though his education had been thorough in English, Russian, French, Croatian, Italian, and his own mother tongue. "What do you mean?"

"Was that not you breaking up the fight?" She tilted her head. "That's only one example. When that kind of thing happens, I'm often blocked from getting deliveries through the crowd and miss a train. Or, heaven help me, I get stopped just for a chat." Her voice mimicked the gruffness in many of the men. "As if I don't know what that means. What do I have to do to avoid all the manhandling?"

"I—"

"If I wanted to work in a bawdy house, that's where I'd be. I've chosen to bake." She folded her arms. "That's all."

"I—"

"Of course, the drunks on the train each day that make it harder to get on and off or try to follow me home have to be the worst. Then again, you did say you would personally stop the poor behavior. Why don't you tell me how you'll do that if you aren't on board?"

Would she breathe and let him speak? For a woman who didn't want to talk about it, she said a lot.

"Well?"

Oh, his turn. "I'll be on board. My men will not bother you."

"Fine." She arched a brow that proved she didn't believe in the possibility. The train pulled into the makeshift station at Stetson. "If you'll hand the basket down, please, I'll be right back. Unless you'd extend your protection into the depot?"

He assessed the silent car. Not one man dared break a grin. But all eyes were on him. If he wanted to show these men how to behave, now he had the chance.

"Ma'am." Lukas stood with her, stepped aside to allow her to pass, and followed her off the train, carrying the massive basket. He heard a low whistle and then, "Look at that, will ya? I ain't sure if'n the Widow Hayes tamed the foreman or the foreman is tamin' the Widow Hayes."

"I'll take that bet." And the ruckus started, money passing back and forth, plainly visible through the windows to anyone on the depot platform.

Lukas closed his eyes for a brief moment and breathed deeply. He could and would be a gentleman. He could and would be the example the men needed. Hopefully, she hadn't heard that last bit in English.

She turned back toward the noise, studied the apparent nonsense, and said, "I'm not sure you'll be able to manage that lot. Perhaps you won't want to get back on the train, either, Mr. Filips."

His hackles rose at her challenge, and he drew his brows together. First the conductor and now a woman he'd never met before. "You'll leave that to me." With this many men vying for her hand, surely she could simply solve the problem before he'd have to do much more. Especially since she no longer wore widow's weeds. "However, it seems you should simply choose a husband. Plenty will be at the celebrations tonight. You can take your pick."

The widow spun on her heel before she crossed the depot threshold. One hand on her hip and one pointing right into his chest. "You hear me good. I will never, not ever, will not even consider a ruffian the likes of these!" She flicked her hand outward toward the audience. Her eyes narrowed, "No trainman or miner or any man. . .no, no, no! Why can't you all leave me alone?"

He'd hold his hands out to show he'd meant no offense, but they were full of her bread. Then he realized the entire train could see him getting an earful. Could she make his job any harder today?

"And you! You're just like all of them, aren't you?"

"My bet is on the widow, Foreman Filips!" At least that jest was in his mother tongue. Laughter roared out of the open windows behind him.

But from the irritated expression on her face, she likely caught the gist anyway. Did she speak more than English?

She tightened her lips and went inside.

Yes. She could make it harder. Lukas growled under his breath as he went inside the cooler log building, dropped the load where she directed, and walked her back to the train in silence.

Chapter 3

The train chugged down the track to the next stop. They repeated the delivery in near silence, only speaking for directions or to acknowledge the other out of courtesy. His men watched every detail.

Juliana settled into her seat. He'd helped her finish the delivery even though she'd yelled at him in front of all those men. Embarrassed him, after he'd already broken up a fistfight. After he'd agreed to keep her safe, on a daily basis. The guilt poured over her heart and festered like yeast in sugar water.

"I'm sorry." The words squeaked out. She cleared her throat. "I'm sorry I snapped at you." She snuck a sideways, upward glance across the aisle at his surprisingly clean russet hair and stoic profile. A fine-looking face, for a miner, she allowed with a tad bit of realism. She liked his clean-shaven chin with the small cleft.

He inclined his head without turning to look at her. "Accepted."

He still clenched his jaw, a small muscle popping in and out. "You've accepted my apology, but have you forgiven me?"

No response.

"Mr. Filips?"

He searched her face. "You have made my job more difficult." He gestured back toward his crew. "But, yes, I choose to forgive you."

She smiled, and when he smiled back, Juliana's heart warmed. Of course, the sunshine streaming in through the window had everything to do with feeling overheated. It certainly wasn't the handsome mining foreman whose gray-blue eyes twinkled at her like sunlight winking on a lake. Juliana slid a finger around the high collar of her shirt blouse. She needed a cold drink of water.

Their mutual smiles brought attention. One of the men who'd been fighting yelled toward the front, "You oughta get in line, Foreman. Ain't no cause for you to swoop in and steal the girl from them what's been tryin' all summer."

Mr. Filips turned, his arm across the back of his bench. "The man drew the short straw on smarts," he said quietly to Juliana, causing a giggle to burst from her. He gave her the most intense momentary stare as if the sound of her laugh entranced him. Then he raised his baritone. "Rowdy, I know you need this job, since you've been let go from two other foreman. You want a third boot?"

That sent a guffaw around the men who'd boarded at the new stops along the ride.

The depth of that look, penetrating behind her wall, sent Juliana scurrying to reinforce the safety zone. She mentally built a heavier barrier to his masculinity.

"I'm grateful for your help today and your willingness to help in the future." She gathered the baskets and stacked them on the bench to keep distance between them. He'd done nothing untoward, but the way he looked at her sent sparklers to her stomach. Since she had no plans of attending the holiday celebration this evening, she didn't want to see fireworks in a new relationship, either. She needed to get home and not dream of a tall handsome man when she slept away the afternoon heat. She needed to finish the first rising and then bake tonight. All the railroaders and miners would be busy celebrating. She wouldn't have to fend off anyone between the oven and her quarters while they were at the saloons. Enough celebration for her. Then she'd prep the next batches for the ovens after the stragglers wandered through to the bunkhouses. She'd be done in time for the baggage man to tote it all to the platform, ready for the train.

"Mrs. Hayes, we're going to be riding for at least an hour every morning, maybe more. Would it be a better idea to become friends?"

Juliana wished she could say yes to this intriguing man. But the risk outweighed the momentary relief. *Good things come to those who wait*, she told herself. She was waiting for a life outside the camps. "It's not better for me." She swallowed at his disappointed expression. Not wanting to be friends would hurt anyone. With as much courtesy as she dared, Juliana apologized. "I'm sorry. But you don't know what I've been through."

"I don't. But friends can listen and ease the burden."

He had a genuine manner and a handsome face. . .and manners. His offer tempted Juliana beyond her expectations. At the roar of laughter over a ribald comment, she retreated from the offer. These men were transients. Her lonely life would be done, gone by September. Nine weeks and six days left till freedom from camp life, by her calculations. She'd have been here just over three years then. The one year James had promised and then the two on her own. Long enough to have earned a better life, albeit without the husband and children she'd imagined. But she'd be established. Then building a new life would come naturally.

"I'm not in need of a listening ear."

"Ah, you already have someone to share your thoughts."

His words drilled a little light through her wall. To have normal conversation about the day? About her dreams? She tightened her heart. Not now. Not so close to her escape.

"Surely you can see how it doesn't work, with the transient nature of your business." Other men had paid her kindnesses, and she'd responded at first. All it did was encourage them to try and win a wife or a wanton. They all had ulterior motives. Men wanted their houses cleaned, their bread baked, and their—needs met. All expectations without the pay or the freedom she wanted. Even her sweet husband had changed once he'd brought her to this dismal camp life. He'd planned to make enough money to build her a house in Spokane so she could be close to her family.

"How can that be true?"

"It is true, for me." She lifted her chin at his scowl of disbelief. "Mr. Filips, it is true for me."

"Will you at least tell me why? I only mean to—"

She had to tell him or make it the business of everyone. Juliana lowered her voice. "Because I am not staying. I want no strings to this place. When I leave, I am not coming back. Though it's not likely, I do not want to miss anyone here."

"Many people move on. But friendships...we need others." He reached out to touch her hand to console or convince.

Juliana pulled her hand back as if a bear tried to maul her. "I do not need anyone else in my life."

"Then you don't need me to help you each morning?" He sat back and crossed his feet. "That will make my life so much easier."

Her eyes flared wide, and despite the suffocating heat, she blanched. "You promised."

"Ah, but only as long as I was needed." He gave her a polite smile. "You have said I am not. I'll let Conductor Kelly know when we reach the next stop."

"No, I didn't mean it that way." She glanced over her shoulder and saw that half the men snored from working all night, and the day crew seemed suddenly fascinated by the conversation from the front of the car. Panic swirled in her throat. Left to her own devices, she'd be fighting off continual problems again each time she boarded the train.

"I'm sure you'll be fine. After all, you said you'd been doing this a long time."

Yes, she had, and it grew harder by the day. The transitory nature of the Bitterroot mining camps brought out the roughest in the male species. Most lacked the common civility of citified folk. The kind of people she'd chosen to leave behind when... It didn't matter. *What's done is done.* She dropped her gaze into her lap and twisted the gold wedding band. This entire time since she'd been widowed, she hadn't had as peaceful a delivery route. Pursing her lips, Juliana braced to admit it.

"Hey, widder woman, you gonna be at the party tonight?" The voice called from the very back, over the noise of the train. "I got a spot on yer dance card, ya hear?"

"I got her dance card right here!" another yelled in response.

"Oh yeah, Jonesy?" One more joined in the taunting. "Who needs a dance card? I got these here two arms to sweep her off her feet and right to the preacher. She'll fit right nice in 'em, and we'll see if anybody else can take her out once I got her." He struck a pose, showing his biceps.

Gritting her teeth, Juliana closed her eyes and then heaved out the frustration in a weighted sigh. Maybe it wasn't just the men from Rowland she wanted to feed sawdust.

The foreman, in a lithe move, stood and faced the men. "There will be no sweeping Mrs. Hayes off her feet!" He thundered out the words.

Juliana couldn't help herself. She stared in astonishment at her protector. Any other time, that phrase would have sounded comical. Somehow Foreman Filips made it sound downright heroic.

"If there is a dance card, it belongs to me and me only."

"You stakin' a claim on that gal, Foreman?"

He looked at her then at Jonesy. *"Ona je moja žena."*

Except for the part where he claimed her all of a sudden. Now what?

The car went silent a moment. Then Jonesy said, "I gots ya. She's already goin' wit' choo. You been up there sweet-talkin' her all the while, h'ain't ya?"

"What d'ya gotta do round these parts ta get a break?" another groused.

"Figures. Gotta be management fer a woman likes o' her to go sparkin'."

Juliana tried to take it as a compliment. But words like that weren't meant to compliment. These men acted like wolves over an elk calf. She chose to keep her dignity and sat up straighter while snapping face forward. How did she end up with the pack leader?

"Fine, then." Jonesy gave way. "If she goes with you tonight, I'll find me another. But I'll be watchin' fer my chance, ya hear?"

"She's going with me tonight. Or shall we have a private discussion when the train stops?"

"When ya put it like that. . ."

"Wouldn't wanna cause no trouble."

"I got my eye on another missy."

The whistle blew and the train pulled into the Adair platform, letting the men off to their intended destination of either mines or temporary barracks. Foreman Filips had not sat back down. He'd folded his arms, planted his feet, and blocked the way to the front exit going by Juliana. The car emptied fast. No one seemed to dawdle.

She waited for all the men to clear the platform. "I can't, you know." She looked up from the seat. "I have to work." Tonight she did not want to celebrate.

"Well, Mrs. Hayes, it's like this. I can't do my first hour of work each day until I ride you around this track. So it seems fair that to make my job easier, you'll show up for an hour tonight with me to keep all those hounds off the scent of an unattached female and their minds on the job so I might finally finish overdue reports."

"What did you say to them? The part I couldn't understand."

He looked a bit sheepish. "I said you were my girl."

"You—but I'm not anyone's girl."

The whistle blew for departure.

"What's it to be? We help each other so we both can do our jobs, or are we done here and now?"

She opened her mouth but closed it at his serious expression. "I'll see you tonight, Mr. Filips."

"It's Lukas." He hunkered down near her while taking the stack of bread bins.

His hands rested for a moment on the top of the baskets, near her knees, while those blue-gray eyes watched and waited.

His nearness was the closest she'd allowed a man in two years. Her mouth went dry. "Mr. Filips, I—"

"Lukas, or no one will believe you."

She nodded. Then with a light tap to her collar, she said, "Juliana."

He broke into one of those heart-flipping grins. "Juliana. I'll pick you up about seven, as long as the train is on time." He carried the empty baskets to the platform, placing them into her waiting handcart that now sat in the shade of the depot. "Maybe then you'll at least allow me to become a friend. I could use one outside of the crews, you know."

She watched him run, swing up onto the train as it chugged away toward Grand

Forks, Rowland, and Taft. "No, you of all men cannot be my friend. And not on this day." She had to find a way to keep him at a distance. He was different, almost cultured, though he spoke English with quite a romantic accent. Not one she recognized. Lukas Filips behaved like a gentleman, a rare breed in these mountain mining operations. She pushed her oversized handcart toward the path. What was he doing here?

Chapter 4

Juliana punched down the dough. "A dance. Like I have anything to wear to a dance." With her wrist she pushed back dangling hair that escaped its updo. Folding, kneading, and then shaping the mound of honey wheat bread helped her work out the worry. She squeezed off a handful, rolled it into a ball, and smashed it flat. Then she set it aside for a few moments to finish dividing the rest into greased bowls for rising. Each huge bowl had its own damp cheesecloth laid over the top to keep out the bugs and keep the dough from drying out as it rose. Picking up her small piece, she fried it in butter in a cast-iron skillet. A simple dinner of fry bread, honey, and a few garden vegetables would suffice until Jacques traded venison for the extra loaves tomorrow.

Juliana had sold her pretty dresses long since to build up savings for her escape. It'd take more than her trousseau to open a pastry shop. She owned four dresses, not including her wedding suit. Two skirts for work, one for Sunday best, and her widow's weeds that cost her too much and proved to be wasted. The black skirt and blouse hung on pegs acting as the wardrobe on the back wall of her cabin. Could she dress up the skirt if she wore a white blouse with it? The sun wouldn't set till past ten, though the shadows would be long thanks to the ragged mountaintops and tall trees. That skirt was the only clean one. Laundry day wasn't until tomorrow when she could get to the river because she didn't have extra loaves to bake on Wednesdays. Then she assessed the blouse she wore. She couldn't wear it, either. It would never dry fast enough with the time she had left. There was one other option. The ruffled shirtwaist from the walking suit she left home in when she married.

Walking slowly to the small bedroom space behind the blanket, Juliana opened the cedar trunk at the foot of the wrought-iron bed. She moved aside the winter down quilt and lifted out the pink velvet jacket trimmed in crimson cording. She ran her hand over the softness that rivaled finely milled cake flour. She draped it over the edge of the trunk. Though white as the others, the shirtwaist's tiny pleats layered one another with delicate lace around the waist and bodice. The memories flooded back of trembling in anticipation while she fought the small seed pearl buttons for that lovely afternoon party. The day of her first kiss. Would wearing the delicately made blouse for tonight's sham spoil the memories? She looked at the soiled clothing in the basket. Like her choice to marry, some decisions brought value beyond the cost. One year with James had been worth it. One night wearing this outfit could likely ease the next nine weeks. Wearing her memories could bring her solace and peace, too.

Decision made, Juliana rinsed away the day and washed her hair in cool rosewater.

She left her thick hair down, pulled into a pink ribbon, to finish drying or she'd be chilled in the middle of the night when the mountain air turned colder for a few hours. Black skirt pressed, white ruffled top, and polished black kid-leather walking boots. She smoothed her long skirt, longer than the ankle-length work wardrobe, a little self-conscious of the difference that almost two years passing made. But no one would notice it was a few years out of style here.

At his knock, she startled. Did she have to continue this farce for the entire time, or could they relax once they'd given the impression of being sweet on each other at this event? Rather than invite him into her private space, Juliana went outside. She raised her eyes as she crossed the threshold and stopped mid-step. Lukas's clean blue shirt, denims, and freshly brushed-back dark hair smelled of soap and fresh mountain air. She didn't want to like both, but did. Heaven help her, she definitely did.

"Goodness, you certainly wash up well. Not to say you needed a bath. . . ." She didn't know how to do this. "I'm sorry. I'm embarrassed."

Amusement danced around his lips. "Good evening, Juliana." His voice was as luscious and smooth as whipped honey butter on hot bread.

Her breath caught. Lonely. She'd been very lonely. That's all these awkward feelings were. She cleared her throat. "Good evening, Lukas." Why did her voice sound more like a croaking frog?

"You look. . ." He paused and blinked. "Quite beautiful."

He made it easy for her to smile. "Thank you."

"Aside from our plan, I'm proud to escort you to the Independence Day dance."

Proud, goodness. Something was very different about Lukas Filips besides the fact he bathed more than once a week. Juliana took his proffered elbow and walked through the makeshift wood and canvas town that once held more than four hundred men. Over half of the people had moved to other mines for the competitive pay. Adair had a few logging crews, but the mine didn't need the same roll call.

"This camp never built up with decent buildings, except one or two. I find it ironic your cabin and the Loop Saloon seem to be the best built. There are other possible living arrangements. What keeps you here rather than one of the better built towns?"

She saw what he saw. Broken-down two-by-fours with canvas torn and not repaired on many empty sites. But she saw what he didn't—fewer men to fend off. Less worry over whether she'd be grabbed unawares while baking to fill those bellies. And then she saw the sadness of it all. The death of a town when the work or mine came to an end. If this one closed, she'd move to the next—as long as it wasn't Rowland or Taft.

"The logging helps some stay. Enough I don't fear a bear or wolves. Few enough I fear the men less here when they congregate in droves needing to prove themselves."

"What do you do for amusement when you're not baking?"

"I attend chapel, read, and plan my future." Juliana reminded him, "I haven't needed to build a big life here, because I'm not staying." A short break from the drudgery would give her the ability to finish this trial well. Tonight, the curtain opened on the final act in the tragedy. But what had been would not be her future. She trusted the Lord would use what she'd been through for her good. Hope sang in her heart as they waited the few minutes for the train heading to the East Portal YMCA, a few miles up the track. She would have her happy ending, just not the true love in all the fairy tales of childhood.

◆•——•—••◆

The piano jangled another upbeat tune along with East Portal's best fiddler, joined by other musicians from up and down the valley. Lukas held out his hand. "Would you care to dance another jig?"

"Could we sit this one out? I feel like I've had enough in this heat."

He noticed the fatigue around her eyes. "How about a little punch and then I get you home. I think we've made our point."

She gave him a grateful nod. "That would be perfect."

As he returned from the punch table carrying much-needed drinks, she reached out for the cup, thanking him. "I have enjoyed myself. It's just been a long day with a long week ahead."

He covered her fingers with his palm. "It's been an honor to spend a little time with you." He held her eyes with his. "Maybe we can get together more before you go."

"Maybe," she whispered as she took a sip of the red punch. Her lashes fluttered, shading those pretty eyes. "But I think—"

"Hey, buddy, you gonna share that canary?" A new fellow, with a friendly, overly loud Scottish accent, clapped his hand on Lukas's shoulder.

Lukas brushed off his hand. "Mrs. Hayes is not a woman for hire."

The man's words slurred together from both alcohol and heavy brogue. "Sure, she is. That bunch over there told me so." He thumbed over at the corner where several men who'd ridden the train earlier in the day enjoyed the joke on the unsuspecting logger. "Said I needed to get on her dance card." He stumbled against Lukas, sending the full glass of punch flying out of his hand. The cup spun at their feet as if whirling to its own tune.

Lukas shook his head, keeping his eyes fixed on the intruder, not daring to back down, but held his temper. The Scot may be heading toward a headache in the morning, but it was an obvious accident. "I'm telling you they're pulling your leg. Get on your way now."

"I wan' on her dance card." The man's slurring deepened, as did his tone of belligerence.

Lukas went nose-to-nose with him. "Listen, there is no dance card. The lady is with me."

"I'll hear it from the canary first. She can speak for herself."

"I've said it nicely. The lady is not a—"

Juliana put a hand on his bicep and tugged, not budging him a bit. "Lukas, let's leave."

In that moment, the drunk grabbed at Juliana's waist, getting a fistful of lace that lined the tiny pleating design. "Gimme a li'l smooch."

Before the drunk could plaster a wet kiss on her, Lukas gripped the man's wrist and twisted him away. But in the process, Juliana's ruffles ripped off, ruining her blouse. The drunk swung wide, shredded ruffles between his knuckles, and punched at Lukas.

Face darkening, his eyes narrowed, Lukas closed his fist. He clocked the man,

319

sending him straight to the floor. Putting his boot on the man's chest, he said, "I wouldn't get up if I were you."

The Scot scrambled backward like a mouse who'd discovered the trap when Lukas removed his foot. "She's all yours."

Lukas stared down the opposite side of the room and took a stride forward. "Who else needs a reminder?"

Heads shook or men stared at the ceiling, avoiding eye contact as soon as he looked at them. The instigators hid grins behind their drinks.

"Kindly take me home, Lukas." Juliana's soft voice came from very close behind him.

He turned around and took in the shambled remains of lace hanging off her torn blouse like rivulets of a weak, end-of-the-summer waterfall, stained with his sticky red punch. Still modestly covered, but her outfit was as wholly ruined as her dripping hair. But it was the sad resignation in her expression that sucked the air out of his lungs.

No tears on her pale, punch-covered cheeks. She simply raised her chin and said in a resigned manner, "I think the point has been exceedingly well made."

He stepped back and allowed her to leave ahead of him, which she did with the dignity of a queen in the silence after the skirmish.

Lukas pulled a red kerchief out of his back pocket and handed it to her. "I'm very sorry."

She closed her eyes and made the smallest shake of her head. "I knew better than to come." Then she opened her eyes and dabbed at the already drying mess on her face and neck.

"Juliana—"

"Please. Let's just catch the next train."

"Yes." Trains ran often to keep crews working, freight and supplies moving, twenty-four hours a day. At the least, they could find a spot on a platform out of the wind if there wasn't a passenger car. Her position afforded privileges with the Milwaukee Railroad. Under the circumstances, any one of the conductors would help her home the few miles between camps. But Lukas felt both the responsibility and the desire to see her all the way home.

"I suppose there's no saving this." She fluttered her hands in front of her body and then handed him back the soiled kerchief.

"No, I wouldn't think so. But I'll replace it. You shouldn't spend the money you've worked so hard to save." He stuck his hands in his pockets.

"I can't replace what it meant to me, but thank you for the offer."

"Isn't it just a blouse? Surely—"

The lack of emotion in her face belied the intensity of her words. "This, Mr. Filips, is not just a blouse. I had my first kiss and married my husband wearing it." Pink crept into her cheeks, barely perceptible in the fast-coming dark. Mountain shadows had long since blocked the setting sun, though the sky still held a glow, turning high, thin clouds peach and gold.

"I'm truly sorry for my part in destroying your outfit." He hung his head. "My intention was to defend your honor, not hurt and humiliate you."

"I know." She gave him her full attention, caramel-brown eyes sticking to his soul. "This was all my fault. I knew better. But now you know why I keep to myself." She touched the missing lace and loosely hanging bodice. "Also, now you know why I'm grateful you travel with me." She shivered. "What if that man had caught me alone? What if he'd been a merciless Montenegrin?"

"A what?" What did she have against Montenegrins?

"Never mind. I shouldn't have said that." She turned away and watched the track for the train as if she could will it there faster.

"Please share why you feel Montenegrins are merciless."

She remained quiet, only shaking her head, refusing to speak further.

Someone had hurt her terribly. "There are good and bad people everywhere, Juliana."

"And there are some I choose to avoid." She folded her arms. "Press me further and you'll be one of them."

"Could you consider forgiving whatever happened?"

She gave him a glacial glare. "I'll see myself home."

He lifted his hands in surrender. "No. I'll not press."

She nodded as the train came through the tunnel. "Thank you. Some things should be left alone and in the past."

How could he find out more if she wouldn't talk about it? Once they sidetracked and turned the train, Adair, on Loop Creek, would be two stops and a few minutes. He had a very short time to smooth over the strain between them.

"Will you bake tonight?"

"Once I clean up."

"Is there some way I can help ease the burden?"

"You want to help me bake? You know your way around a kitchen?" She arched a brow. "You really don't strike me as kitchen help."

"Well, I'm not such good help in the kitchen, but I will do anything to make this day end better for you."

The stress on her face relaxed into bemusement. "In all this time, not one man has offered to help me other than get me to the train. And that has been because the station master requires it of the freightman in order to deliver the bread on time. The other bakers have husbands or, well, they have someone." She tipped her head as she thought about his offer. "Would you consider moving bags of flour for me while I clean up?"

"Juliana, I will do whatever you need."

"Thank you, I accept your offer." The train slid into the East Portal stop. Juliana took a second glance at Lukas. "You know they weigh up to fifty pounds each, right?"

"Not as much as your handcart when it's full, yes?" He smiled. "I think I can manage."

She boarded the train and sat in the front row, pulling her skirt aside so Lukas could join her on the bench of the very nearly empty passenger car.

Ah, progress. Without words, she'd invited him to take the place beside her that he'd wanted from the moment he'd caught sight of Juliana Hayes. But if she found out he was Montenegrin, would she really disassociate? Surely she'd know him well enough to overlook such a blanket prejudice. He sat, mulling over options.

By the time they'd reached Adair, she'd rewashed her sticky hair and changed, and he had moved three large bags of flour from the storage shed to her work space, Lukas had decided not to reveal his origins. At least not until Juliana and he grew closer. For the rest of the time God graced him with the responsibility to protect her, Lukas would find a way to build her trust through acts of kindness. Then he would tell her and overcome her bias because she would have his constant examples of goodwill. He would win her heart as well. But first he needed to find out why she distrusted his people.

Chapter 5

Early August

"What do you know about the Widow Hayes?" Lukas asked Conductor Kelly while he waited for her to arrive at the platform. He'd asked around where he dared the last few weeks, but no one seemed to know much about her. She kept to herself except to deliver the required bread rations and the disastrous dance. But the rides with her had been pleasant, the conversation kept to general topics. Lukas wanted to know her, truly know this woman. "How long has she been alone?"

"I ain't know'd her that long, sorry." He shrugged. "I been here 'bout a year. You could count it like dog years compared to most in this here valley." He laughed at his own joke. "She been widowed all that time, I figure. Weren't wearin' widow's weeds when I came." He looked at his watch, then in the direction of Juliana's cabin and brick ovens, and shook his head. "If'n she don't show up right quick, we gonna have to leave her to the next train." He shook his head again. "Hate to do it to a good woman. But I can't risk a pay cut. That ain't gonna bode well with the company when she misses the shift change."

"I'll see what's keeping her."

"Three minutes and I blow the whistle." He went to close a freight car door on his way to inspect for departure.

Lukas jumped off the train, jogged to the dirt path leading away from the platform to see down the direction she should be coming from.

She struggled with a handcart to push her load up the last small incline, brown skirt hem dragging in the rocks as she leaned hard into the steel handle.

Why wasn't anyone helping her? He ran the hundred yards to help. "Here, let me."

"The path is just rough here." But she sidestepped out of the way and used the apron corner to wipe her brow. The sun rose early and hot, getting hotter and the air drier by the hour.

"We have about two minutes to get you and your cargo aboard." He took off at a clip with her right behind. "Karl, Simon, lend a hand!" he called out as he reached the front of the train. The two gave him less guff than the others as a general rule. He assumed it might have something to do with having wives. A woman settled a man. He glanced at Juliana. He wanted to be settled by her. Jonesy was right. He could get in line behind a couple hundred others vying for her attention. But none of them had daily access to build a relationship like he did.

The men jumped to the stairs at their foreman's command, Karl on the bottom step and Simon at the doorway, grabbing the first basket of ten fat, nourishing loaves and passing it back to another as the whistle blew for departure. The men moved the other baskets on board as the widow shoved her cart out of the way. Then the train's wheels budged and rolled forward until they had to run alongside.

Lukas seized the handle, swept an arm out, and swung the surprised widow, skirt billowing like a sail, onto the step with him, pulling her in close to his body.

The train bumped heavily on the track heading into a turn. He instinctively pulled her tighter against his chest—purely to protect her from the jostling train—but he had to fight the desire to lower his head and taste her lips. The little rusty flame sparking in her heated eyes tempted him so much he had to look away or he'd blow the plan he'd painstakingly thought through. She hadn't given him the chance to look that deeply into her eyes, not even when she'd begrudged him a dance just for show. He more than liked this perspective. With patience, his plan would open her heart. Act rashly, and he'd have as much chance as the hundreds she'd already rebuffed.

"You could have dropped me." Juliana's gaze slid past his shoulder and watched the track behind them fall away faster as she clutched his shirt.

"Never." He inhaled the scent of rosewater, honey, and fresh bread that emanated from Juliana. The scent that clung so satisfying and welcoming to a man. The scent of home. "You will always be safe with me."

She pushed back with shaky hands when the train moved off the curve and onto a straightaway, but stopped at his words and whispered, "Until you aren't here just like—" She frowned, dousing the fire in her eyes. "Never mind."

"I will be here for you." Lukas moved his arm away before she could push again, settling his hand in the small of her back to protect her from losing her balance as she climbed the last two steps. She looked a bit rattled the way she stood instead of sitting. He didn't know whether from their acrobatics or that the baskets all ended up on the left bench so only one space for the two of them remained. Or could she be feeling a little like him, shaken from their closeness a moment ago?

"Way to go, Foreman! The next camp won't miss their grub."

"Shoulda been a trapeze artist," Rowdy joked, instigating laughter around him as he had instigated the Scot at the party.

"Already feels like a three-ring circus here to me with you clowns," Lukas shot back, raising the level of laughter all the more, but this time directed at Rowdy.

Karl clapped him on the shoulder. "Where's Harry English and his camera? That'd a made the front page as downright heroic."

"Wouldn't have had a picture without you boys." He thanked Karl and Simon. "It's all in the teamwork." Then Lukas sat beside Juliana.

He watched as she scooted away as far as possible on the short bench without making it noticeable to those behind them and clasped her hands in her lap. With his size, she didn't have much room to move. But his closeness must have done something to her.

"That's good," she said, not looking him straight in the eyes. "The way you build up your men."

"Always give credit where credit is due. My father taught me that. A man will give his best when it's appreciated." As he brushed the dirt from the cart and the train off his hands, he said, "Now tell me, please, why you had no help today."

Her chin turned slowly, until their eyes met. "You don't know?"

"I should know?"

Juliana looked confused. "You really don't?"

"I don't."

"Oh." She glanced away and then back at him. As if not wanting the rest to hear, she leaned in toward his ear. "You remember Jacques? The baggage man working the Adair depot?"

"Yes?"

"He decided to take another job down the line as a firefighter. The pay is pretty good, I hear."

"Well that's not uncommon. The men move around as needed."

"I know, but now they can't fill this one at Adair."

"Really?" He raised his brows. "Why?"

"The men are all afraid of you after, well, after the way you knocked down the brute at the dance. Jacques was there, and after he'd pestered me for a date, he figured you'd come for him next. When the new jobs posted. . ." She shrugged, the rest understood.

"Ah, I see." He grinned. "So they don't want to be seen bothering you in order to avoid tangling with me."

She swallowed and looked away. "You're the problem. No one wants to come near me now."

"I'm the problem? Seems I'm the solution. Unless you can make it to the departure on time, in addition to making sure you are safe on the train, I need to get you to the train."

She tucked a few strands of loose hair up into her scarf. "I don't know how you want to handle it. But I can't bake any faster than I already do. My workload is growing with the firefighters coming in for the spot fires."

He thought for a few minutes. "If you can be ready, the train is here long enough for me to get you and the cart up the path."

"I can be ready." She slumped against the seat, seeming defeated. The largest publicly visible movement she'd made since they'd met. "I hate asking for help, but with so many loaves to deliver each day, I can't do it myself."

She wasn't a small woman, reed thin with a waist as tiny as a wasp like the corseted socialites he'd met. Healthy and shapely from the physical demands of baking and living in these harsh mountains, but small, relative to his size. She had strong arms and shoulders, even for a woman of average height. Lukas admired Juliana's tenacity and strength—and the beauty of how that looked all put together along the length of her bare arms, thanks to the summer heat and her baking position. She wore short sleeves and calf-length skirts, making it hard for him to look away. But a wooden handcart lined with steel meant for lighter trips in the mines, plus the load that overflowed the cart's bucket with each loaf weighing two pounds, landed a tad above the top of her abilities. Grown men felt the weight of that equipment.

"I'll come, before the start of my shift each day, for as long as you need me."

She looked up. "The company added Sundays to help with the fire crews. I'm to provide extra loaves each day of the week and a full order on Sunday as well. You realize that may be the rest of the summer."

His lips turned up slowly. "I hope so, Juliana. I told you I will be here for you."

She searched his face. "I believe you." She blushed. Then she added, "With the extra work, I might be able to leave sooner than I'd planned."

"Sooner?" His stomach coiled.

"Yes." She glowed with anticipation. "Maybe as much as a few weeks."

He needed more time. As much time as possible before she left him to a cruel winter without her. Time to win her promise to wait for him.

"If this keeps up, and the fires stay way down the line, I'm thinking the first of September." Her eyes lit up with joy. "Won't that be wonderful? And you won't have to ride with me anymore."

How should he answer that? She didn't know the conductor told him he could ease up—a conversation Lukas requested be kept between them, earning him an elbow in the ribs from the older man. He'd said, "I'd keep that gal lassoed myself, if I was yous."

"Juliana, I like our rides." He couldn't quite meet her eyes or she'd see the deep emotions stirring. "I hope you'll change your mind and stay. I'll miss you when you go."

Chapter 6

Lukas took the worn envelope from his box at the Rowland Depot. For a moment, he couldn't do more than stare at the handwriting. It felt like ages since he'd stood on home soil. A year working as a translator at Ellis Island, then he'd worked his way west, always sending funds home to help support the estate.

He jumped on board, greeting the conductor. "It's going to be a good day, Kelly."

"Did ya see all those boys headin' home all week? They're lettin' a few thousand off fire duty. Yep, gonna be a good day."

Lukas closed his eyes and leaned his head against the seat back for a moment and thought of Montenegro. He remembered what the manor looked like, the massive stone fireplace, and the velvet trappings around the windows pulled back to allow guests to walk in the gardens during parties. The way it looked when he was a child, full of people and the wonders of the world waiting for him. Though he'd held off as much loss as he could, working the remains of the estate after his father's death, they needed to sell it before the economy crashed altogether. His sister would never get the promised dowry from the government. That infusion of Russian money, along with the rest, had long since disappeared, never making it past the prince's coffer to the people the donor had meant to support. Prince Nikola continued taunting Russia with a teasing dalliance with Austria as a display of independence. The fine steps of his dance had eroded the fortunes of the Filips family and many others over the years until many Montenegrins, like him, struck out to find alternate means to support their families. If the prince wanted real independence, he'd learn how to manage the economy rather than living off other countries. He'd give teeth to the 1905 constitution so his people could prosper.

But now, with the blessings God poured out on him, Lukas's family could focus on building a life in America—without the land, deteriorating manor, and title. A new life full of opportunity. He'd proven that as he took higher paying positions with each move. In Montenegro, his title held him back in spite of the higher education he'd been given. Here, all he had to do was survive the coming cold, snowy winter and he'd have enough to set up a home and soon a school for Montenegrin immigrants. So many here needed a good international education. He could at least plan on tutoring in the six languages he spoke. His mother and sister could emigrate as soon as the estate sold. He broke into a smile at the thought of young men learning etiquette from the stern duchess who'd often visited at court with her senate husband. If he only had his mother to instruct his crews. The vivid image brought a snicker. He sobered. What would his family think of Idaho and Montana—and of the woman he loved?

Lukas sat up as the train pulled into Adair. Juliana had her own plans. Would she consider altering them to include him? Or would she be shamed by an abdicating duke? Touching the letter in his breast pocket, he could think of nothing better than to surround himself with the love of family—and Juliana. With the fires dying down, perhaps she wouldn't have to work Sundays any longer. He'd ask her to spend her first Sunday off with him, picnicking by a tributary, away from prying eyes. They could talk freely and plan the future together.

Lukas greeted Juliana for their morning delivery ride despite the growing summer storm. "Good morning." Clouds overhead grew in thick, heavy formations, trapping in the remaining smoke from the dregs of distant fires. The winds picked up, but no rain yet in the early morning. "Looks like we're getting a break from the heat. Let's hope the rain comes with it."

Growing gusts buffeted dingy canvas shelters, snapping the tent flaps in the makeshift town and creating a scene of rolling waves like whitecaps on the sea. He normally carried his coat and gear in a pack for deep mine supervision or pulling his weight on an undermanned shift, but today he might have to wear it.

"Morning," she said with happiness lighting her face. "I love the breeze. Last night when it started, I savored the cooler air. It pushed out all that stale smoke left over from those spot fires." She leaned in to tell her secret, smelling of rosewater and the cinnamon she'd baked into the Sunday rolls. "I let my hair down and let it blow wild. It took me half an hour to comb it out."

How he wished he'd been there last night to see her hair stream out behind her, to run his hands through it. He'd been stuck indoors finishing his second round of monthly reports.

She laughed as she wrapped a thick brown shawl around herself, overlapping it to tuck into her waistband. "It was worth it. We seem to be getting a little relief from the smoke." She glanced at the darkening clouds. "And some moisture to break the drought, by the looks of those."

"That would be blessing indeed with how dry it's gotten around here. I know we've needed them, but it's been hard to find enough seats for my crews since they've been sending so many firefighters up and down the line. And the pack horses take up space in the freight cars. I heard on the train this morning that they let quite a number of firefighters go home now." He shared her elation. "Looks like the scare is over and the fires are mostly out."

"Couldn't be better news." She lifted a large picnic basket, hanging it over her elbow and balancing it on one hip. "All those extra batches have added to my savings, though I'm worn out. I haven't had a Sunday off the last three. The fire camps have needed five hundred loaves a day!"

"I hope there's a raisin cinnamon roll in there for me," he teased while pushing the load onto the path. The aroma of sweet fruit and spice curled into his nostrils. "Otherwise my weakened muscles may give way under this load and the wind will blow me away."

She assessed his arms and shoulders as if at a military inspection, with a light of admiration in her eyes. "Tsk, tsk. We can't have you waste away, now can we?" She brought a large cinnamon bun out from under a tea towel. "Will this do?" She pursed her lips to keep from breaking her straight face.

"Most definitely." He stopped and held out his hand to accept the edible gift. The cart had a mind of its own, rolling backward into his shin. "Ow, ow, ow. . ." He hopped backward as he grabbed at the handle to halt building momentum. His pride felt the smash more deeply than his leg.

She pressed one hand against her mouth, holding back the mirth. "I'm sorry, really." But as she spoke, a giggle burst out. "I hope that won't spoil your day." A gust blew her skirts against her legs, outlining her slender, athletic form. "I'll just carry this to the train for you."

Drawn to the sparkle in her eyes, Lukas spat out the first thing he could think of before snatching her up and kissing her. "I have a letter from home."

"How wonderful!" She beamed joy through his soul with her beautiful smile, as if the common eagles overhead lifted him up on the drafts where they hung, suspended. "Did you get good news?"

"I haven't read it yet."

"How could you not?"

"I'd have been late getting to you."

Her cheeks blossomed rosy red. Would she consider a real relationship with him in the future if she knew not only his origins but his family obligation? Surely every woman wanted to marry well. In America, titles didn't seem to matter. Only the ability to provide a future held importance. Her dream of a bakery could blend perfectly with his dream of a school. She might want to take students to learn the trade as assistants.

Once on board and all her wares stowed, Lukas, and most of the other passengers, closed their windows against the strengthening wind. "It's really picking up out there." He sat down and accepted the roll made just for him.

Juliana patted his arm. "Go ahead now. If I had a letter from home, I couldn't wait to open it."

After he finished eating, he pulled out the letter and read in silence, savoring the news. He shared a surprise tidbit. "My mother and sister will come soon." His smile grew with each line. The estate had a potential buyer, an Italian.

She turned from watching out the window. "They will? That's wonderful!" She looked at the letter and envelope in his hands.

"There are rumors the prince will proclaim himself king."

"A king. They're overseas, then?" She pointed at the postmark. "I haven't seen one like that."

He realized too late his folly of sharing the letter. America didn't have a prince, and he was from the one place Juliana couldn't tolerate. "I've been sending money to help with expenses."

"Lukas, where is home?"

Had the time spent together built enough trust for what she asked now? He steeled himself. "Juliana, do you trust me?"

"Why would you ask that?"

"Because my homeland is Montenegro."

Her eyes opened wide as she pushed her back against the corner of the seat, near the window. "Montenegro." She looked away, as if the regular movement onto the side track making room for the eastbound held a special fascination. "You tell me this now, and you ask me for trust?"

"I hoped you'd see that where I'm from doesn't determine our friendship."

He saw the wall rebuilt between them in the space of seconds as she retreated behind it. "Where you're from. . ." she said in her quiet, too calm way. "Yes, it matters very much where you're from to me."

He kept his voice down as well. He'd prefer this conversation in private, but a niggling doubt warned him it wouldn't happen. Best not to let it fester. "At least tell me why you feel so strongly. I feel I've earned that much. Do we not share a mutual respect?"

She sized him up much like she did when they'd first met. Her eyes held pain though, not aloof anger. This time, those eyes planted grief in his heart. Grief, because he saw her pull away. Grief at the loss he felt coming. The grief might prove dangerous to his heart. He could not allow it to take root. "My husband died because he broke up a fight between Montenegrins. It was a horrible accident, but not his fault. He didn't start it. His job was to keep men working, keep them alive, not get murdered because Montenegrins can't behave like civilized people. They fight with Italians. They fight with Serbians. They fight with one another. Is there anyone a Montenegrin won't fight with?" She paused, scalding him with judgement. Without waiting for his response, she added, "I think not."

"How many were in that fight, Juliana? The entire country? How is it you don't feel that way about the Scotch? Remember, it was a Scot that assaulted you at the dance and a Montenegrin, me, that stopped it."

"You've conveniently forgotten it was Rowdy and his Montenegrin gang that set the Scot up. Who was really responsible?"

"I've been here all summer working with men from all around the world. Of the seventy-plus different nationalities, I have at least six under my command, including Montenegrins, Italians, Croatians—sometimes more. I haven't had nearly the trouble foremen in the past have had, even with the constant rotation. Is it possible leadership is the issue and not one group of people?"

"Now you're casting aspersion on my husband's character?"

"That's not my intention. What if you could determine there were ten good Montenegrins like those who have helped you on and off the train? Or those who are grateful for the food you provide?" Lukas caught her stormy gaze. "What if there was one? Me." He caught her hand. "That's why I didn't tell you. I wanted a chance to prove to you through serving. Serving your needs has been an honor. You've met my men. Simon and Karl have helped you before."

Confusion lightened her features from the betrayal. "I'd say you were trying to get around what I know. You ordered them to help."

"But they did help. Would you condemn them all for a few?"

"Reality is reality. I condemn no one."

"Don't you? Don't you condemn me now?" He lifted her hand to his heart. "See me. I'm more than where I was born. I'm the man who—"

Juliana tugged her hand away. "I would have, but then you intentionally deceived me for weeks." She stood as the train came to a stop.

How could he get through to her? "I will do this as I have, without fail." Lukas took hold of the bread bin handles. "I have not changed, Juliana, simply because you know where I was born."

Her eyes clouded, but she turned without a word. Then she stopped at the top stair and looked back. "You have helped me beyond what should have been expected." She cleared her throat. "I know that."

Thank You, Lord! She was softening, beginning to come around.

Conductor Kelly met them on the Falcon platform, yelling over the howling wind. "Just got given a telegraph fer ya, Foreman. Sounds like ya got a situation back there in Rowland." A streak of lightning cracked across the sky followed by an intense boom echoing through the valley. The wind kicked up as if it'd absorbed the energy between Lukas and Juliana.

With the delivery basket in his arms, Lukas raised his voice above the wind, "What's it say?" He tipped his head in the direction of the depot to get them all out of the storm. "Tell me inside."

Lukas set the crate near the area where Juliana unloaded each morning, filling several bunkhouse baskets. They'd be picked up by the various cooks in Falcon at the end of each shift to round out the crew meals.

The conductor continued, "You're down two men on the morning shift up at Rowland. Been a scrape 'tween yer night and day crews."

Juliana stood and turned around, her face bland as she said, "So there's been another fight."

"Yep, a big one sounds like."

Lukas could hear the death knoll on their future. He tried to end the conversation. "I'll get on it. Thank you."

Picking up a freight list from the communication board, the conductor added, "Gotta give it to 'em, they're a tough bunch. You been keepin' it better controlled than we seen in the last three, four years." A sprinkle, more like a spit or two, darkened the wood outside the door as he opened it to head back to the train. "Maybe the rain will help. This heat's been makin' things worse. Only so much a man can take."

Lukas nodded, acknowledging the praise while his hope deflated. The squeeze in his chest built at the look in Juliana's eyes. He ran a hand across the back of his neck. Sure, he'd had a few skirmishes over the summer. The job, conditions, and temperaments that came with this kind of back-breaking monotony had occasional pressure releases. But that didn't speak for his people, only the situation. She had to see the unforgiveness she held on to was unreasonable. But this situation with his men had to be handled or it would escalate. "I'm sorry, Juliana, I have to go back and take care of this. But we'll finish our talk when I get back."

"No, I think we're done."

"Juliana—"

"You need to go." She picked up her empty basket and walked past him. The wind whipped at her shawl and skirt as she boarded the train on the side track headed to Kyle and Stetson.

The lightning and thunder picked up their efforts, creating a massive show in the heavens. He blew out a heavy sigh. At least God knew how he felt. Lukas climbed the stairs on the eastbound. *Lord, please grant me the chance to make this right.*

Chapter 7

Juliana startled at the double crack of thunder as lightning flashed close enough to reverberate through the tracks. She pressed her cheek against the window to see if the strike left. Lightning mixed with the high winds was not a good combination. They needed a deluge to get the forest good and soaked.

The conductor came on board. "Sorry, folks, schedule change means everybody off." A groan ran through the car. "We gotta head down the valley and pick up folks at Avery. They got a wildfire startin'. Everybody off."

Grouchy and grumbling workers, who'd been breathing smoke from surrounding fires for weeks except when underground in cold, damp conditions, stumbled and shuffled off the train, their fatigue evident. This night crew wouldn't get back to their bunks for a while.

Juliana caught the conductor's attention. "Mr. Kelly, I have to make the deliveries to the camps." She pointed to the hundred loaves, more than double her normal quota since they'd added the fire camps. She'd been contemplating hiring a boy to deliver if this volume kept up. "Can't I stay?"

"Sorry, Mrs. Hayes, we don't got the time for the extra stops. See the smoke comin' up down yonder?" He pointed at a distant dark plume that thickened as they spoke. "They got a bunch o' lightnin' strikes south of Avery today. We got a telegraph sayin' they're closin' the tracks except fer firefighters after this here train. The wind is winnin' down at St. Joe City, and the fire looks to be headin' this way into the valley."

"I understand." Juliana shivered, whether at the unexpected chill from the overcast skies, or fear, she couldn't tell. "What about all that bread?"

"Since we ain't stoppin', just leave the bread. If the fire stays back, I'll get the baggage men at Stetson and Kyle depots to help unload on the way back. We'll pick you up once we got the folks at Avery out of danger. But we ain't takin' anybody closer to it." He leaned out the door, keeping an eye on his work. "Best bet's gonna be an hour or two. We'll lay her out and make it a quick trip. Might as well get a good meal down ya. I think they're gonna work ya to the bone after this."

Juliana smiled at him as she took the steps down toward the platform. She turned back. "Just come back safe, Mr. Kelly. What you're doing is heroic. I'll keep you all in my prayers." She waved at his salute as the train pulled out. Hot food hadn't held any interest most of the summer. She ate to keep up her strength. But with the cooler day, she took the conductor's advice and headed over to the Falcon dining room while lightning and thunder flashed and boomed down the valley. She ate to keep her mind off the howling winds, increasing lightning strikes, and the threat.

Strong gusts weren't unusual through the winding valley. This, though, was somehow a different kind of blast, carrying heat from miles away, ending the mild cooling with a suffocating pall.

❖——•——•❖

Lukas arrived at Rowland, three long whistles alerting the town and depot workers. The telegraph operator ran to the engine, waving a sheet of paper the wind tried to yank away. "Johnnie, you gotta go back now!"

The engineer, Johnnie Mackedon, shouted out his window, "What's wrong?"

"They're shutting down all the mines and log camps. The fire converged and blew up at Avery." The operator climbed up far enough to hand off the full message.

Lukas jumped off the steps and ran toward the railroaders to better hear the emergency. He had men in camps all along the line—and Juliana, where was she? Had she gone down past Stetson to Avery, or did she get warned in time and stay in Falcon?

"We got word that the wind has fanned embers into a massive fire back southwest of Avery. Hurricane-force winds blasted through St. Joe City into the backcountry. A wall of fire is headed this way."

"Get the passengers off and unhitch those full freight cars. Let's turn her around and get as many out of there as possible!"

"There should be a slew of people heading up toward Falcon. The tracks closed about thirty minutes ago downline from there."

Lukas grabbed the telegraph operator's arm as the man jumped down. "Send a message. Tell everyone to get to the depot platform. We'll get them from there."

Panic bit his belly, spreading the poison of terror.

"Johnnie, I'm with you! The Angel of Adair is down there."

The engineer agreed by pointing Lukas to the coupling.

He signaled back he understood. Adrenaline poured into his bloodstream as he raced to assist. He bounded on the first car as they put all the full freight cars in the hole on the side track. With the forest service out of the threatened area this last week, Juliana's regular delivery, from Adair to the small camp town of Falcon, took a deadly turn. Could he find her and get his men out before the wall of fire did?

Johnnie leaned out the window and yelled, "Aboard or not, we're pulling out!" He pulled several short whistles—signaling emergency—and set the train on its rescue mission, Lukas hanging on the side. He slipped behind the fuel load as the smoke darkened, getting heavier as they rode down the track. Coughing, Lukas tied his kerchief over his face. The winds built, slamming into them, slowing the progress of the powerful engine. *Lord be with us; we're riding into the beast.*

They passed Adair in record time, Johnnie laying on the whistle sounding the emergency.

❖——•——•❖

An hour in, full tables waited for the train with nowhere to go when the hurricane winds hit Falcon. The wooden dining hall creaked under the onslaught. Noise, so loud people covered their ears, seemed as palpable as the trees bending.

"Fire!"

She had no idea who yelled out the warning, but Juliana rose in the ensuing panic and fought to get to the door. As soon as the first person swung it wide, the door was ripped off its hinges and flung into the storm. Sparks and ash fell like a fine mist.

A cook ran in from the stoves. "Help! My babies are in the school. My babies!"

An off-duty mine foreman took charge. "Crew Three, get the kids out of the school! Crew Four, go through the town. Tell 'em all to get to the depot."

"They're so little the wind will blow them away!"

"Tie 'em to you, then. Whatever you have to do, but get the kids to the depot. Their folks can meet them there." He bellowed out, "Move!"

The crews that had been groggy, waiting to get to their bunks, shot into action. In less than fifteen minutes the entire town and unexpected guests, over a hundred men, women, and children, banded together on the Falcon platform, straining to hear a train whistle over the roaring winds. Trees exploded, sending fireballs into the sky like Roman rockets as the fire raced up the canyon. Then a tornado of fire and wind whipped up, heading right for Falcon.

Juliana's scream ripped out of her throat, stolen, as the spinning monster took out a line of trees at the edge of town. The dining hall went up in flames along with the school and several bunkhouses. The smoke thickened until everyone coughed, eyes watered, and rivulets of ash mixed with tears trickled down cheeks. Massive chunks of burning wood landed all around them. Juliana kicked at them to send them into the dirt like she saw the others doing. The roof on the depot caught and flamed one log after another, like a candelabra. The smoke and ash forced her to cover her mouth and nose, breathing through her shawl.

The train was nearly on top of them before anyone at Falcon could hear or see it through the smoke. Flames licked at the dry wood platform as the engine backed onto the side track. The crowd ran for it only to discover no cars.

Engineer Johnnie Mackedon leaped from the front, shouting to someone to help hook up the empty logging flatbed.

A shadow moved through the smoke, assisting, then disappeared to appear again on the platform. "Let's go! Get on and get down!" he yelled through a wet red kerchief tied to cover his nose and mouth. "Juliana! Juliana, are you here? Ju-li-an-a!"

She vaguely heard her name over the gale. Lukas? She ran to him. "Lukas!"

He threw his arms around her, shouting over the din. "I'm here. Let's go!"

The entire crowd clambered off the burning railway platform onto the flatcar.

Juliana helped him hand children up to outstretched arms. When all were aboard, Lukas lifted Juliana and then jumped up after her.

"Down! Everyone lie down!" He pushed as many on their bellies as he could reach, motioning for them to do the same all the way up the flatbed as Johnnie rolled the train out of the station, heading for safety.

Juliana lay on the very edge, inches to spare. Lukas covered her body with his, holding tight to the side as the car swayed back and forth, buffeting in the sixty-plus-mile-an-hour winds. As far as she could tell, they'd saved everyone from Falcon. But the wall of flames licked up the mountainsides like a hungry wolf coming after them, with a ferocity through thick undergrowth and trees so dry from the drought that the furnace could rival Hades.

Johnnie seemed to be gaining ground as they approached Tunnel 28. The hurricane winds battered the passengers with debris. Tree branches, falling trunks, pieces of tent material flew into the crowd. As fast as they could, burning their hands, they threw pieces off the train and off one another.

A chunk of burning wood landed on Juliana's skirt. Lukas lifted up on his elbow and kicked it off her, keeping it from burning through as the engine chugged into the tunnel. Water dripping from the tunnel ceiling wet the clothing of all exposed. The tunnel hadn't yet lost its cold, fresh air to the vortex sucking the life out of everything in its path. For a few moments, Juliana and Lukas gulped in oxygen.

The hot mega gust hit them coming out the other side as the train raced uphill to the trestle ahead that crossed a tributary into Loop Creek. Lukas lost his grip. In a tangle of skirts, he and Juliana flew off the end of the flatcar into the underbrush. Her scream echoed back from the tunnel.

Chapter 8

Though the unburned branches protected them from broken bones, Juliana's face and neck felt scraped and bloodied from the dry, sharp pine needles. Her scarf had blown off somewhere in the fall. She had nothing to keep the smoke from her lungs or her hair out of her face.

"Can you run?"

She saw the smoke puffing through the tunnel. The fire would be on them in no time. "Yes."

"We have to go down." He pointed to the water below. "Tie up your skirt, run to the trestle, and start climbing."

Her eyes went wide as she traced the trestle's beams and bars. "That's more than a hundred feet. I don't think I can."

"Either you do or you don't trust me." He took her face between his hands and made her focus on him. "I'll go first. I'll be with you the whole way. Just slide down each one and I'll catch you before we go to the next."

She nodded, tears pouring down her cheeks and her hair whipping all around them.

"We go to there." He pointed over the edge to the earthen bank. "Not so far, right?"

She nodded she understood.

"Once over the edge, move in the direction of the bank. We can work our way down to the water hanging onto the bushes and trees."

The roar of the fire grew closer, drowning out his last words. Fireballs sailed overhead like comets as the train shrank into the distance.

"What?"

"Now!"

Juliana grabbed his outstretched hand and ran to the edge of the trestle. She yanked the bottom of her skirt through her legs and jammed it into her waistband, creating wide trousers. Then after tying the shawl around her waist, she followed Lukas onto the first rung. She slid her foot until she felt his hand on her ankle, and he steadied her descent. Her low-heeled boots helped by acting as a hook to find the next foothold. Her hands were strong from two years of kneading dough. But that didn't help the fact that she hung far above the river rocks, shaking in terror. Her waist-length hair blocked her view of Lukas. She froze in place.

"Faster, Juliana! We have to get in the water!"

The air sucked up, up into the demon above, pulling all her hair upward, twisting toward the sky.

Lukas motioned to her to start moving toward the side where the trestle met the built-up earthen foundation.

Her arms felt the strain and the insteps of her feet would bear the bruises for days, if they survived.

The fire laced fingers across the top of the tunnel, cresting the mountain as they neared the valley bottom. Juliana's foot missed a rail and her arms gave out. She slid, smacking her chin on the next bar, until she landed in the circle of Lukas's arms where he clung to the trestle a yard below.

"I've got you," he soothed her as she pushed the hair out of her face. The fire leaped onto the trestle above. "Let's go, three more rails." They crawled down together to see flames curling down the hillside in front of Tunnel 28, as if blown by a dragon.

Lukas picked Juliana up and ran for the water. He jumped in feetfirst, splashing Juliana into the shallow stream onto her side. Then he rolled her to completely soak her clothing and hair. She came up sputtering as he dove down, doing the same to himself.

He was up in a split second, hauling her up with him. "Now we run! Stay in the water. We can keep dunking ourselves until we find safety."

"How? How do we get to safety?" she yelled over the cacophony.

"We'll follow the creek north to the next train station we can find. If we hurry, we might catch them at Moss Creek. They still have to pull uphill through Adair. That switchback takes long enough, we can get to them using the logging road, as long as it's clear."

They fought through the rocky stream, stumbling and coughing, with the fire chasing their heels like a hound scented on a fox. The animals, though, had already run for higher ground.

Juliana fell for what must be the umpteenth time. Lukas wouldn't let her stay down except to soak her clothing again and again, the heat drying them too quickly. "My shawl is wool, Lukas. I can't keep going with the weight of it if you keep getting it wet, too."

"You have to keep it. That may mean life or death if the smoke gets so thick again." He dipped it into the stream, wiped her face to clear the smoke and ash from her eyes, then tied it around his own waist. "I'll carry it for you."

She nodded and took his hand.

Three hundred yards more and they crossed onto the logging road. They ran as hard as they could into the clearing leading to Moss Creek. They didn't have to go all the way to know they were too late. Everyone was long gone—or dead. The fire sizzled away the canvas, structure beams collapsed, burning like stacked campfires. No more trains were coming up the track through the wall of fire that chased them, consuming every ounce of life in its way.

"We cannot stop." He grabbed her elbow and turned them due north, away from the fire rushing in from the south and toward the mountains ahead still unmarred by the dragon's breath behind them.

The smoke, thick as heavy fog, burned Juliana's throat as she tried to keep pace with Lukas's long legs.

He looked behind them and scooped his arm around her, propelling her forward. "Keep moving."

"If the fire doesn't get us, I think my heart will give out." She doubled over, hacking and wheezing as ash snowed all around, cinders setting off dry brush wherever it landed.

"Juliana." Lukas stooped down and pulled the red kerchief off his face, close enough to shout over the storm and see her eyes. "You are my heart. If yours stops, then mine does, and I will not let that happen." He brought her knuckles to his lips.

"I can't keep going."

"I'm not moving without you. So if we stay, it's your choice. This is your chance to get retribution on a Montenegrin." He took his hands away. "I surrender. Is that what you want?"

Flaming projectiles soared overhead. She screamed, "No! I want you to live!"

"Good!" He grinned, infusing her with his optimism. "I have plans for our future, and I think God gave them to me. Do you at least believe in God?"

She doubled over again, hands on her knees and nodded, her chest heaving.

Lukas ripped off an already torn sleeve, pressed it against the damp shawl at his waist, and then tied it around Juliana's nose and mouth. "Look up there."

She searched the area, following where he pointed to the swell of rocks of the mountain. A tunnel! Cool, fresh air!

"Let's go."

She straightened her shoulders. God had sent this man into her life to give her courage for this trial. She would trust God and trust the gift of a heroic man. If she should perish, at least she gave her all as he did for her. Juliana held out her hand. "Lead on."

◆— · —— · ◆

Halfway up the mountain, Lukas guided Juliana into the mouth of the tunnel. The beams held up boulders above the entrance. The tunnel had been blasted out of sheer rock. But the outside light reached a back wall. The air was already warming, though still fresh. For how long?

"Take a short rest, Juliana." He removed their kerchiefs. "Then we have to head out."

"What?" She leaned over the pack mule path they'd just clambered up. The fire below wouldn't have fuel up close to the boulders around the abandoned tunnel. "We should be safe here, shouldn't we?" She stumbled toward the inner sanctum, leaning heavily on the wall. The sweet air relieved the burning pressure in her chest.

Lukas bent over, both hands on his knees, and sucked in oxygen. He shook his head. "Not enough room in here to shelter us."

As she recovered a bit from the run, Juliana knew he could make it out if it weren't for her slowing him down. "Why did you come?"

"What do you mean?"

"You're educated, have manners, and can do just about anything. Why here?"

"Because I have responsibilities that require funding."

"So this isn't about getting rich quick for you?"

"No. It's about helping my people." He cocked his head, listening. "Do you hear that? There's water in here." He lifted a hand, feeling along the rock walls for weeping, moving deeper into the tunnel. "Why didn't you go back to your family after your husband died?"

She pressed her hands to the rock on the other side of the narrow shaft. "My father told me that if I married James, I should not come back."

"That's harsh."

"When I wrote home to tell them I was widowed because he was murdered by a Montenegrin, my mother wrote back that my father had died of a heart ailment."

"So those men deprived you of your husband and then you were dealt a further cruelty of finding out your father died."

Her voice cracked. "I'd broken his heart with my decision, and it's too late to reconcile. I'll never see him again." She took another breath of air, though it seemed not as cool as before. "Then my mother said she was going home to Helena, Montana, and I should follow her there."

"So you are going home." He moved his hand back to squeeze her fingers. "That's a good choice."

"I was. We sent letters back and forth, communicating again. I was so happy." She turned her hand palm up and held his, needing human contact. "My mother died last summer of the flu. I couldn't get to her in time."

"You're an orphan and a widow. You've been doing this all alone." He took two strides, pulling her to him and holding her tight. "I'm so sorry."

Her cheek pressed to his chest, she nodded. "I still have an aunt and uncle there. But they can't support me."

In the hazy light, Lukas tipped her head back, searching her eyes.

"You know none of those men were on my crews, don't you?"

She nodded. "The sheriff arrested the man who did it almost immediately." Her lungs ached, but the anger and unforgiveness pressed harder on her soul. "I don't want to hate anyone anymore."

His palm caressed her soot-covered cheek as his lips touched hers, stinging and chapped, and yet electricity sang through her veins. She found herself as thirsty for his love as for water, and that shot panic through her body. She stepped back, feeling for the chiseled rock. Her fingers slid into a crevice, and water trickled over them. "I found it!"

Spinning around, Juliana cupped her hands, pointing the tips of her fingers into the fissure, funneling the cold water to her mouth. It ran pure, almost freezing her throat as it spilled down her bodice. Pulling away, she invited Lukas to share. "It's sweet and so good."

He did the same, taking turns with her until they had enough.

"Juliana, we have to go. The smoke is getting heavier outside the tunnel." He pointed toward the front. "And the air inside is getting hotter. Soon it's not going to be safe. The fire is going to feed on the air from this shaft and suffocate us. Get as wet as you can." He knelt and splashed at the mud puddle on the ground while she pressed her body into the running rivulets. Then he took his kerchief, the makeshift kerchief from his sleeve, and her shawl, wetting them as best he could.

"When we get out of this, you're marrying me."

"No." She shook her head. "I've saved for two years. I'm opening my pastry shop in Helena."

He folded her back into his arms. "It's all gone by now, Juliana, all gone."

Everything destroyed. Her dream up in flames. "I'm lost, then. I have no future."

"You have me, and you are my heart. We can rebuild our lives together." He leaned down and kissed her. "Say you'll marry me. Give me the hope to get us out of here alive."

They'd never make it. Smoke already billowed into the cave. "I'll marry you, if we get out of here alive."

"A Montenegrin?"

"You have proven to me that a good man is a good man." Hope sprang up in her at the joy in his face. She'd make good on that promise—if they survived.

He grinned, white teeth almost glowing against his dirty, soot-covered face. "God is not finished with us. If you will not trust me to save your life, then trust God. He put us on this journey toward each other. He's not going to let it end like this. Yes?"

"Yes."

Lukas tied their kerchiefs on. Then he put his arm around her again and let her lean into him as they moved into the path of the fire.

They saw smoking mountains, blackened forests, and a rolling cloud of smoke encroaching as the blaze flattened and scorched all creation. For a moment, neither could move at the sight of hell on earth coming to swallow them up. For Juliana, hope exploded like the massive cedars sending shreds of bark sparking high into the sky. Then she felt Lukas yank her from the ridge.

They slid and rolled down to a creek, smaller than the last, that flowed toward them. "We're heading toward Wallace, Idaho." As the haze shifted, Lukas and Juliana dunked as best they could.

"Don't drink that." Lukas blocked her as she cupped her hands. "It's full of the fall-out and getting too warm." His eyes grew enormous. "We've got to move." He pointed at the fire spreading into the trees about to circle their location. "There, head up again!"

Juliana's thigh muscles burned and her calves felt like hot pulled taffy, but she kept moving. Lukas stayed behind her and splayed his hands around her hips, giving her momentum until the hill flattened out into a mule trail. Then her legs gave out. She hit the ground, rocks biting into her skin.

Lukas slipped his arms around her and lifted. "Arms around my neck. Press in as close as possible. I need your weight as close to center to help me."

She squeezed tightly to his shoulders and whispered, "I'm so sorry. I have nothing left."

"We're going to make it." He took off, following the trail. "There has to be a longer mine around here. You say the prayers. That's going to keep us going."

She obeyed, closed her eyes, and prayed with her head tucked into his neck, her mouth just below his ear. "Lord, see us. Help us. Strengthen Lukas, and guide us to safety." She repeated the same words over and over as he stumbled through the rough terrain. She tried not to cry out when he tripped.

Visibility dropped to a few yards. If Lukas couldn't see, they'd likely run off a cliff.

"A horse! I see a horse, and someone is on it!"

She turned her face forward. A long line of men with picks and shovels shuffled ahead on the mountain trail. Firefighters! By the time Lukas caught up to where they'd been, they'd disappeared.

"In here!" a voice called.

Lukas spun in the direction of the thin sound, finally finding a man looking down from the mouth of a dark tunnel. "Juliana, look! If I put you down, can you climb that outcrop?"

He'd been carrying her. She could crawl up a bunch of rocks. "Yes."

The voice called again, "Go back ten feet and come up there."

A steep, overgrown trail tramped down by men and horses led right to the mine shaft. Lukas set Juliana ahead of him. They half crawled, half climbed the couple of yards to the six-by-ten opening surrounded by overgrown shrubs. Both collapsed from exhaustion.

A man an inch or so taller than Lukas leaned down and picked up Juliana from her knees. "Glad to see more alive. Let's see if we can keep it that way."

Lukas nodded but couldn't stop coughing.

"Ed Pulaski. This here's my fire crew." Ed motioned him farther back. "Catch your breath and get your woman to the back where she'll be safest."

The tunnel ended in another dead end, but it'd been dug at least a hundred yards deep before abandoned. Heavy beams reinforced the ceiling. A few lanterns illuminated two horses and men strewn all over the floor. There was a small puddle here and there, but not much weeping water as in the last mine.

"Will we have enough air?" Juliana asked as tendrils of smoke snaked into view. Soon the black smog would follow.

"I don't know. But it's the best chance we have. The fire's coming on too fast."

At the entrance, Ed Pulaski formed a sort of bucket brigade. "Get any blankets you have out of your packs. Find the puddles and soak them. We gotta cover these posts and this exit."

Men scrambled into action. While they worked, Juliana searched the saddlebags for canteens. Finding one, she found a slow drip high on the wall and held the canteen under it.

"Who has any tent pegs or horseshoe nails?"

Men produced anything they could find. Lukas grabbed an ax and helped pound tent spikes to anchor the makeshift door into the walls at Ed Pulaski's instructions. "If that wood burns, we're in trouble." He turned to everyone. "Fill your hats with as much water as you can get and keep these things wet."

With no hat or helmet, Lukas and Juliana turned to the injured men leaning against the tunnel walls. He found another canteen, dry as a bone, and started filling it as she helped a downed man sip out of hers. Then they switched.

The fire raged, sucking under the blankets at the clean oxygen and singeing them. Steam floated off the wool leaving dry patches. "No!" Ed yelled. He called for more water as he held the edges tight. "Get down low and stay down. The lower you are, the more likely you'll survive!"

One of his men panicked and ran like he'd tear his way out. Juliana screamed. The horses tried to rear and break for the entrance, but Lukas grabbed one and a firefighter snagged another.

Ed had his revolver pointed at the terrified man. "You try it and I'll shoot you down."

The terrified man backed away. "We're gonna die in here."

"We're going to live." Ed kept his gun up, slowly aiming around the cavern. "I'm getting home to my family, and so are you."

Juliana could plainly see the blisters and burn marks on his hands. His sleeves were blackened to his shoulders, moustache and eyebrows nearly gone.

"The next man who tries to leave the tunnel, I'll shoot." He stared them all down the way Lukas did his miners on the train. "The only job you have is to get water up here to keep this all wet."

He stood there, guarding the door the rest of the night as the mountains roared like a thousand freight trains behind him, as far as Juliana could tell—until she passed out. . . .

Chapter 9

Juliana's throat felt like glass shattered inside it. Her head ached as she tried to sit up, but she couldn't move. Heavy, dry wool smothered her face. She fought to get away from it, and rolled on the rocky ground into a body.

Lukas threw the hot, dry shawl off them and turned his head toward her. "See? It worked." Sometime after she'd passed out, he must have soaked her shawl and covered them.

He looked past her at the entrance, spilling in sunshine, without raising his head off the ground. He croaked through parched lips, "We lived."

She turned to follow his gaze. The blankets had burned off the posts, charred remains hung in tatters. Ed Pulaski lay nearest the exit. No sounds. Not even the heavy breathing of the horses. Was anyone alive besides them?

She sat up slowly, unable to hold back hacking coughs.

Lukas did also and, though coughing hard, moved to block her view of the horses. "Don't look." He put his hand up and curved his palm around her cheek. "Let's see if there's anyone we can help."

Juliana's lips trembled, but she nodded.

A few others stirred until most were making their way to the front.

Groggy, sick from the smoke inhalation, Lukas and Juliana joined the others who could move under their own power.

Lukas counted those that would never rise again. "Five men down, and the two horses."

"Looks like Big Ed didn't make it, either," one of the firemen called back as he hunkered over Pulaski's still body. "The boss is dead."

"No, he's not." Ed Pulaski groaned and lifted onto his elbows. Most of his hair had been burned off and blisters covered his eyes. But he lifted his chin to savor the fresh air circulating through. "Might need some help getting home."

A collective sigh sufficed as a cheer.

Lukas wrapped his arms around Juliana. "Let's get going. We have a wedding to get to. You do plan to keep your promise?"

Juliana raised on tiptoe, touched his sooty cheek, and in a scratchy voice said, "I do."

◆•————◆◆

"I now pronounce you man and wife. You may kiss your bride." The preacher laughed with them over their torn, scraggly clothing. "Though I've never seen a couple in such condition. I'll be glad to look back on this day that something good came out of that big blowup."

Lukas gently rubbed his thumbs across his wife's scratched knuckles and then leaned in and touched his lips to hers. As he pulled back, he said, "Sooty and scratched, you are the most beautiful bride in the world." He smoothed her tangled hair away from her cheek.

She smiled into his eyes. "You got us safely out. I will follow you anywhere." Then she took a long look around what remained of Wallace, Idaho. "But where do we go from here?"

The preacher pointed to the coming train. "I hear folks in Montana are welcoming survivors in Missoula and Helena. There's a lot going on over there for an industrious couple such as yourselves."

Juliana searched Lukas's face. "Do you suppose they'd like a baker and a teacher there? Or do you have to go back and rebuild?"

"That's up to you," Lukas answered.

The preacher took a step down from the altar. "I hear they're growing so fast they need all sorts. Most folks need to make their own opportunities. You could make as much there as working for the mines, if you do it right. Sounds like you both have the skills."

"Opportunity, yes. This is why I came to America." Lukas put an arm around Juliana. "This is what we'll do. Yes?"

"Yes," she whispered, rapture and relief washing over her adorably dirty face.

The preacher stretched out a hand. Lukas took it and they shook. "Might not be the best wedding supper, but the ladies of our church have good food ready. They've been feeding all the firefighters and survivors since yesterday. You'll be a bright spot if you'll let them feed you before catching the train."

They followed the minister out of the redbrick chapel and around the side toward the back.

Juliana's eyes misted. "What about your mother and sister? Everything is gone. How will you bring them now?"

Lukas stopped and hugged her. "They're already on the way."

"They are? How?"

"I sent tickets earlier in the week. I've always kept my funds away from the camps. Too much desperation and too much risk. The company agent deposits my pay in the bank and has set aside funds for my family all summer."

"I did, too—deposit with the agent, I mean."

"You did?" Lukas shook his head. "I thought you said you'd lost all your money in the fire."

"No. I lost all my kitchen tools." Her voice dropped into a husky tone. "And my memories." She lifted a hand to his scruffy chin. "But I didn't lose you or our future."

"I'm sorry you lost all those things, though."

"Me, too." She touched her fingers to her temple and then her heart. "Those memories are here and here forever. But I suppose the pastry shop will start out a little smaller than it would have. Maybe I'll be able to buy some used items."

Lukas kissed her. "Oh, my lovely wife. . . You haven't met my mother yet. She may very well have everything you need."

"She would bring kitchen utensils all the way from Montenegro?"

He shrugged. "She may have already heard about your dream. I wrote to her, after I first looked into your eyes. I kept writing. She wrote back that she would sell all but her best utensils and bring them for you as a wedding gift. We may have lost our land, but the manor had an extensive kitchen."

"That was mighty bold of you." She plopped her hands on her waist. "What if I'd never agreed to marry you? You'd have had a trunk full of useless pots and pans."

"No. I would have done this—" He scooped her up to a flurry of giggles. He held her close as her arms tightened around his neck, and strode toward their waiting meal, carrying her over the threshold of the fellowship hall.

"I see, Mr. Filips, you would abscond with my heart?"

"Mrs. Filips, I already have." He kissed her before setting her on her feet to receive the good wishes of a room full of strangers. Strangers that shared the joy of a future and a hope amid the smoking mountains.

Angela Breidenbach is a bestselling author, host of *Lit up!* and *Grace Under Pressure Radio*, and the Christian Author Network's president. And yes, she's half of the fun fe-lion comedy duo, Muse and Writer, on social media.

Note from Angela: "I love hearing from readers and enjoy book club chats. To drop me a note or set up a book club chat, contact me at angie.breidenbach@gmail.com. Let me know if you'd like me to post a quote from your review of this story. If you send me the link and your social media handle, I'll post it to my social media with a word of gratitude including your name and/or social media handle, too!"

For more about Angela's books (especially more Montana-inspired romances) and podcast, or to set up a book club chat, please visit her website: http://www.Angela-Breidenbach.com, Facebook/Instagram/Pinterest/Twitter: @AngBreidenbach

From a Distance

by Amber Stockton

Dedication

To all of you who have experienced love from a distance and ever wondered
if you'd get a second chance. Love can come in the
most unexpected times and places.

Acknowledgments

To Grace Hitchcock for allowing me to be in this fantastic collection, and to my
agent Tamela Murray for suggesting that I get involved. Thank you, ladies, to you both!
A special thank you also to Jeanne Leach who helped me with facts and details about
Breckenridge. And of course, I could not continue to do what I do without the support
of my husband, who wrangles the kids while I'm on a deadline. Thank you, honey!

*"But this I call to mind, and therefore I have hope: The steadfast love
of the Lord never ceases; His mercies never come to an end;
they are new every morning; great is Your faithfulness."*
LAMENTATIONS 3:21-23

Chapter 1

Breckenridge, Colorado, 1925

Trevor Fox rammed the shovel into yet another pile of soiled hay. Mucking out horse stalls certainly didn't rank high on his list of desirable work. A soft whinny sounded from the Pied Piper where he stood behind the crossties in the space next to the stalls.

"Yes, boy, I'm getting your home all freshened up." Trevor gave the former wild herd leader a sideways glance. "Of course, if you would learn to take your business outside, it sure would make keeping this barn clean a lot easier." He dumped the mound of hay into the wheelbarrow and twisted around to fill the shovel yet again.

The mighty Appaloosa raised his head and stuck his muzzle into the air, shaking his flowing mane as if Trevor's suggestion was ludicrous. The Piper served this ranch well, and everyone who worked here treated him like a king. Taking care of his needs was a task bestowed on only a trusted few. Trouble is, the horse knew it. And Trevor could think of at least a dozen things or more he'd rather be doing. How in the world had he gone from servants waiting on him hand and foot to *being* the servant to a ranch full of animals and livestock?

Oh, right. Charles Logan. Trevor jammed the shovel into the hay again and transferred it to the wheelbarrow. He could blame it all on Charlie.

"*Come out to Colorado,*" his longtime friend had said. "*It will give you room to breathe, fresh air.*" And a chance to clear his head as he freed himself from the endless line of eligible young ladies being paraded in front of him, all hoping to secure themselves a piece of the Fox empire. He had room to breathe, all right. Plenty of it out here in Breckenridge. The country had fought in and won the Great War just seven years ago, but it seemed as if the residents of this town couldn't be bothered with things like that.

Trevor turned to look out the barn doors toward the towering range of mountains rising above the ranch, like guards keeping watch night and day. And all the fresh air he could ever want. Thinner here than back home but definitely cleaner. The mountains and the ranch lands went on for miles in almost every direction. A far cry from the crowded streets and avenues of New York City and the mass of buildings several stories high, crammed into every available space. The slower pace took a bit to get used to, but it sure beat the pressures of racing to win all the time.

After sticking the shovel into the mound of hay piled in the wheelbarrow, Trevor grabbed his pocketknife to snip the bindings on the fresh bale outside the stall and threw a few armfuls into the enclosed space. He spread it out all across the dirt floor and stepped back.

"Okay, Piper, old boy," he said as he unhooked the crossties and reached for the horse's lead rope. "Let's go." He gave two clucks of his tongue and Piper immediately walked forward, turning without hesitation to enter his stall.

The "royal highness" looked to the left and right before nodding several times and stamping his hoof twice.

Trevor chuckled. "Well, I'm glad you approve, fine sir," he said with an exaggerated bow before the equine.

A moment later, he slid the stall door closed and locked it. Pied Piper stepped forward and extended his head through the opening. Trevor reached out and scratched the horse's forelock.

"Well, Charlie was right about one thing," he said as he cupped Piper's cheek and stroked from crest to muzzle.

"Are you talking to yourself again, Fox?" Charlie asked from the doorway. "People might start to question your sanity if you aren't careful."

Trevor turned to see his childhood friend saunter into the barn like he owned the place. Not much different from the well-respected leader of every class in school they ever took together. Charlie knew how to command an audience, and his strong work ethic had earned him every bit of the respect others paid him.

"Just talking to Pied Piper here," Trevor replied.

Charlie propped one booted foot on a bale of hay and rested his forearm on his thigh. "So, what was I right about?"

"Huh?"

Charlie jerked his thumb over his shoulder toward the main doors. "What you were saying a moment ago just before I showed up." He jutted his chin toward Piper. "You know, when you were talking to the horse."

"Oh, right," Trevor said with a nod. "I was ruminating about the difference between working here and working in my office at my father's company in New York. Quite a change."

"But a good one, right?" Charlie widened his eyes, waiting for an answer he likely already knew Trevor would give.

"Without a doubt," Trevor said. "I never knew how much I needed the change until I let you convince me to pack it all up and move here."

Charlie curled his fingers as if to inspect his nails then blew on them and brushed them against the shoulder of his chambray shirt. "That means I've still got it."

Trevor gave his friend a wry grin. "And what is it you think you have?"

"That *je ne sais quoi* that makes people follow me, no matter what I say or do."

"You've got something all right," Trevor answered. He gave his friend a mock punch to the shoulder, almost causing him to lose his balance. "You and the Pied Piper here are like a matched set." He nodded toward the horse. "Both good leaders and both of you convinced you're the best thing that's happened to everyone around you."

Charlie grinned and winked. "It's a gift." He paused for a second. "But, hey!" He whacked Trevor lightly with the back of his hand. "Don't sell *your*self short. Not every-one can turn his father's company into a financial triumph by doubling profits in just two years, then shed the business suit for a pair of jeans and boots and within a couple of months make some excellent suggestions to streamline the management of a ranch."

Trevor shrugged. "I just pointed out a few areas where I saw the need for improvement. Cutting costs, increasing percentages per acre, and improving the reproduction quotients."

His friend pointed at him. "That's exactly what I mean, Trev," he replied. "I came out here to help my uncle with an extra pair of hands. You arrive and you've got this ranch prioritized for profit in less than two months."

"It's a gift," Trevor said with a grin, throwing his friend's words back at him.

Charlie guffawed and slapped Trevor on the back. "Well, speaking of that gift, you realize we got paid today. Some of the guys and I are headed into town to see what kind of trouble we can find. Wanna join us?"

"Just try and keep me away!" Trevor pulled off his work gloves and tossed them in the bin, and then he reached for the cowboy hat he'd hung on a hook. A hat that at one point had felt so foreign on his head and now seemed more like a second skin. He smoothed his thick sandy-brown hair before setting the hat on his head. "Ready when you are," he announced.

"Great," Charlie replied. "We're taking the Woodie so we can all fit. Let's go!"

About thirty minutes later, Charlie parked the truck near the Fireman's Hall bell tower, and everyone hopped out of the back. Four of the hands took off with barely a wave, but Charlie's cousin Jesse waited on the wooden sidewalk for Charlie and Trevor.

"So, where to first?" Jesse asked.

"Well, I have to go to Sumner's for a couple things," Charlie answered, "but then I thought we could go next door to the Denver Hotel and see if we can join one of the Faro tables on the main floor."

"I like that idea." Jesse grinned.

"You would," Trevor countered, reaching out and tousling the younger lad's shaggy blond hair. "More than just a luck of the draw for you, for sure." He pointed toward the red-and-white-striped pole a few buildings down from where they stood. "But I think you should head in to see Frank first and get yourself a trim."

"Yeah," Charlie chimed in. "Getting a little shaggy there, cousin."

Jesse ducked his head and gave them both a sheepish grin as he reached up and touched the hair in question. "I guess it couldn't hurt to tidy it up a bit." He started to head for the barbershop then paused. "Meet you at the hotel?"

"You bet," Charlie replied.

Once Jesse left, Charlie and Trevor crossed the street and walked in the direction of the grocery supply store. Trevor nodded at several folks who passed by. More than once, he thought he caught some whispering as they watched him. Two young ladies held a newspaper in their hands and smiled big when he acknowledged them. Another young lady clutched her mother's arm and boldly pointed right at him, exclaiming something Trevor couldn't hear. Just before he and Charlie stepped inside, he stopped Charlie with a hand on his arm.

"All right. At first I thought it was just me, but there is clearly something going on here in town, and it appears I'm the subject of conversation." He narrowed his eyes at Charlie. "You have any idea what it might be?"

Charlie shrugged. "No. Are you sure you aren't just imagining things?"

Trevor looked around, only to find several people watching him, some of whom averted their gaze when he glanced their way. Others nodded, and at least a half-dozen young ladies smiled in a shy but flirtatious manner.

"No, I'm not imagining it."

His chest tightened. Word of who he was hadn't traveled this far west, had it? He had been extremely careful to not say anything about his past to anyone. People didn't read the *Post* or the *Wall Street Journal* this far out, so there wouldn't be any articles about his family's business or financial holdings. He'd pretty much kept to himself at the ranch, and he hadn't done anything to draw attention to himself. So why all the stares and hushed conversations?

"Uh, Trev?"

Charlie's cautious tone drew Trevor's attention back to his friend, who stood in front of a wooden box outside Sumner's, looking down at whatever was inside.

"What is it?"

"I think I figured it out."

Trevor stepped up next to Charlie and also looked down. Darkness crowded around his peripheral vision and the *clip clop* of horses' hooves mixed with the rumble of automobile engines faded as his heartbeat pounded in his ears.

"What on earth?" he exclaimed.

There, in black and white, on the front page of the *Breckenridge Bulletin*, was a rough sketch of his face just below a headline that read, "BRECKENRIDGE'S MOST ELIGIBLE BACHELOR."

Charlie picked up a copy and chuckled. "I can't believe he actually did it."

"Who did what?" Trevor asked.

"George Mitchell." Charlie tapped the paper. "The one who wrote this article."

So Charlie was on a first-name basis with a reporter? When had that happened? And what did it have to do with him? Trevor wrapped his fingers around Charlie's upper arm and squeezed.

"So, you *do* know what's going on, then. The looks, the whispers, the smiles, the pointing." Trevor jabbed his index finger into the paper. "What is the meaning of this?"

Charlie pried Trevor's fingers loose from his arm and took a step back. "Relax, Trev. It was all in good fun. I didn't think George would actually run the article."

Trevor's blood heated. "You mean you gave him the idea?"

"Well, not exactly," Charlie hedged. "A couple of the guys and I wanted to get something about our ranch in the *Bulletin*. With your great ideas about increasing production and decreasing costs, I figured it was the perfect angle. Something like a special interest piece, touting your skills and insight and highlighting the improved productivity at the ranch." He gestured toward the paper. "Never thought he'd put this kind of spin on things."

Trevor peered at the paper and skimmed the article. His heart pounded faster and louder with each sentence he read. "This thing's got me sounding like the manager of the ranch, poised to take over ownership any day now! No wonder all these ladies are eyeing me like a prize to be won."

Trevor took off his hat and slapped it against his thigh then raked his free hand through his hair. He didn't even want to think about the many strands likely now standing on end. Another young lady passed them and offered Trevor a demure, yet hopeful smile. He dipped his head, forcing a polite smile even though the last thing he wanted to do right now was be polite. He didn't need this kind of attention or notoriety. Next thing he knew, his real identity would be revealed, too.

"It's like being back in New York all over again," he grumbled.

"Hey, Trev, I'm real sorry." Charlie tossed the paper back into the box then removed his own hat and ran his hands around the brim. "If I had known George was going to do this, I never would've agreed to the interview in the first place."

"Don't worry about it." Trevor waved off his friend's apology. "I know you didn't mean for things to get out of hand."

But Charlie sure could've checked with him first before giving personal information to a reporter. Those guys were always looking for an angle, a way to sensationalize their articles to attract more readers. He'd been down this road way too many times.

"You still joining us at the hotel?" Charlie asked.

"Nah, I think I'm going to take a walk and clear my head." Trevor gestured toward Sumner's. "You go on and do what you need to do. I'll meet you back at the truck in a bit."

"Okay." Charlie disappeared inside the pharmacy.

Trevor stood on the sidewalk and stared up and down Main Street. Clear his head. Sure. And where, exactly, would he do that? If he stayed outside, he'd no doubt encounter any number of attempts to attract his attention, or perhaps thinly veiled introductions covering up their real intentions. No, he didn't want any part of that. He had to find a place to disappear, so he reviewed the storefronts again.

The post office; Kistler's; Theobold's; George C. Smith, Jeweler. None of those held any appeal. Wait a moment. What was that one? He narrowed his eyes and focused on the letters painted on the glass. Jooge's? Jacque's? Jacquie's? Yes. It said Jacquie's. Trevor looked up and down the street then crossed to the other side. As soon as he stepped up onto the sidewalk, two women—a mother and daughter, he presumed—exited the grocery to his right. It took the mother only a moment to recognize him, and then she flashed him a cordial yet sly grin as she nudged her daughter. In a low tone, she admonished the young woman to stand up straight. He gave both women a cursory glance. The younger was definitely attractive. Were circumstances different, he might be inclined to make her acquaintance. Not with the way things were now, though. Not today.

He had to find a way out of this mess. And he had to get away from the optimistic expressions of nearly every young woman who crossed his path. He stopped in front of Jacquie's. An assortment of handcrafted jewelry, fine art, woven baskets, various carvings, and unique clothing adorned each window. Peaceful and calm. This looked like the perfect place to gather his thoughts and devise a plan.

Chapter 2

Anna St. Claire stared at the rough sketch in the *Bulletin*. It had to be him. The likeness was too strong to be anyone else. The bell above the door jingled as someone entered her shop, and she looked up. Her breath caught in her throat. Trevor!

The man who had been sketched for the paper now stood less than twenty feet away from her. Still as breath-catchingly handsome as the last day she'd seen him, perhaps more so in blue jeans and boots instead of a suit jacket and tie.

"Morning, miss." He gave her a polite nod.

And still completely unaware of who she was or that they shared a past. . .even if most of it was in her imagination.

"Good morning!" She forced a welcoming smile. Best to not appear startled by his appearance and presence. He might start asking questions, and she wasn't ready to answer anything right now. "Welcome to Jacquie's," she said instead. "Authentic jewelry, art, crafts, and quilts made by the local Ute Indians. Is there something I can help you find?"

Trevor clasped his hat in his hands and gave her a sheepish grin. "Please forgive me, but I honestly came inside to avoid an uncomfortable situation out there." He nodded toward the door. "This was the first place that caught my eye."

Divine guidance? Maybe. At least on her behalf. Certainly not for a seasoned Casanova like him. But wait. He'd said something about a bad situation.

"Oh." Anna furrowed her brow. Someone wasn't threatening him, were they? "Is everything all right?"

"Yeah." He turned and glanced out the storefront windows as he rubbed the back of his neck. His hair was a bit longer than she remembered. "Just some friends who meant well and their plans went slightly awry." He faced her once more and flashed his familiar, confident, take-charge smile. "It's nothing I can't handle."

Ahh, that smile. The one that no doubt charmed investors and employees alike at his father's company. Like clay in a potter's hands, people were swayed by his opinions and enticed to do his bidding with ease.

"I'm glad to hear that," she replied. "Please feel free to stay as long as you wish." *The longer the better*, she thought to herself. "And if I can be of any service, please do not hesitate to ask."

"Actually, since I'm here, I might as well take a look around." He gave the little shop a decisive perusal, as if sizing up the merchandise in one quick sweep of his eyes. "You have some unique items here, and they appear to be superior in craft and style."

Anna couldn't determine if he was surprised at the quality or making the remark because he was impressed. She imitated his visual inspection from one side of the shop to the other. She could identify each and every item on display and knew the story behind each one.

"Yes. Everything we have here is handcrafted and consigned to me for sale in this shop." She moved her arm in a sweeping motion across the store as she spoke. "From the woven baskets, to the jewelry, to the pottery, there are no two pieces alike."

"That's amazing." Trevor hooked his hat on a mannequin then reached out and picked up one of the woven baskets.

Anna moved from behind the counter and took cautious steps toward where he stood at one of the side tables. Could she bear to be so close to him again without giving herself away? She could if she focused on her work and not on him.

"That one was made by twining the peachleaf willow branches," she offered, touching the colored pattern threaded throughout. "It's done by threading the vertical and horizontal strands for a tighter and stronger weave. They dye the branches with pastes made from various plants or vegetables to create their designs."

"I've never seen anything like it." He tilted the basket to the left and right, inspecting every facet. "The craftsmanship is spectacular." He turned his head to look at her. "And you say each one is unique? These aren't mass-produced in any way or manufactured?"

"No. Awendela brings me new items each week, and I either provide her with food to take back to her camp, or she uses her portion of the money earned to purchase items for bartering and trading."

The idea of goods made without the benefit of machines was likely a foreign concept to him. It was for her, too, before she moved here. Now, more than a year later, she had grown accustomed to this new way of life.

"Who is Awendela?" Trevor asked.

"She's a member of one of the local Ute Indian tribes in the area."

His eyes widened. "You've had interactions with the Indians here?"

Anna covered her mouth as a giggle escaped. "Yes. There's no reason to be alarmed. They are quite friendly, and we haven't had—"

Trevor raised a hand. "No, no. That's not what I meant. I'm actually fascinated by them, not concerned in any way."

Heat climbed up her neck and warmed her cheeks. "Oh. I'm sorry."

"It's all right." He touched her arm. "You've never met me before, so you would have no way of ascertaining my level of interest or worry."

Oh, but she *had* met him before, more than once. He just didn't remember because he'd been too smitten with her older and far more beautiful sister, Maggie.

"I actually work on one of the biggest ranches outside of town," he offered. "So I'm aware of the local tribes. But I've only been here a couple months, so I haven't yet had the fortune of meeting any of them."

Anna glanced down at where his fingers lightly grazed her sleeve. Trevor followed her gaze and immediately withdrew his hand, though she wished he hadn't.

"My apologies," he mumbled.

If only she could tell him she didn't mind, that she actually enjoyed being this close to him and talking with him. She had tried more than once when they both lived in New York, but her attempts had all been for naught. She might as well have been a speck of dirt on men's clothing for as easily as they all dismissed her when her sister was present. And she hadn't minded. . .until she'd seen Trevor.

"Awendela is an unusual name." Trevor spoke, drawing her out of her brief reverie. "What does it mean?"

Anna blinked a few times and took a deep breath to clear her head. "It means 'morning mist or dew' and is another name for Morning Fawn, but she says her people have also called her Awandela Alameda, to honor when and where she was born. Alameda means 'grove of cottonwood,' something we have in abundance in this area."

He chuckled. "Ah, yes. I've witnessed it firsthand on rather windy days." He plucked an imaginary speck from his chambray shirt, as if a piece of cottonwood fluff had somehow been stuck to the material. "Those cotton seeds get everywhere."

"Once or twice I've had to rid the shop of them when I've had a fair number of customers on those windy days."

Trevor glanced back at the door. "I can imagine," he said, as he stared out into the street.

Was he still concerned about that situation or issue he hadn't yet explained? How long would he be in her shop? She didn't mind, of course, but with each passing moment, she continued to worry that he might somehow recognize her and remember who she was. She had been present at every social event where he and other gentlemen had been holding court with Maggie. None of them had paid much attention to her, though. So, why would Trevor somehow remember her now?

"So, tell me about the jewelry you have here." He stepped past her to the glass case on the front counter where she'd been when he entered. "I gather it's quite valuable if you feel the need to keep it in a locked case."

If he was still concerned about what brought him into her shop, he did a good job of hiding it. Anna pivoted so she could resume her place and stand opposite him once more.

"I never would have thought items such as these would sell so quickly, but being a mining town, we attract a unique set of people here." Anna pointed to the collection on the top shelf. "Tourists from all over come to visit this shop, whether they are staying for a few days or just passing through. These items are among the most popular."

Trevor bent over and hunched his shoulders as he peered into the case. "The colors are excellent, and the designs are fascinating."

"I agree. In this area, we have a lot of silver from the mines that has found its way into the streams and rivers. The Indians take the silver and other minerals and hammer them into shapes. They can depict animals, geological elements, revered spiritual figures, and other important symbols."

"And what about these?" Trevor pointed at the collection to his left.

"Those are quite a bit more valuable. They come from experienced and skilled craftsmen within the tribe." Anna stepped back and unlocked the door to retrieve one of the pieces. She held it out to him in her open palm and pointed out specific features. "It isn't easy to fashion beads, animal bone, turquoise, pieces of pottery, hair and fur, and a variety of other elements into brilliant pieces like this."

"I believe my mother and sister would love something like this." Trevor fingered the hand-painted bone and feather earrings she held. "Or perhaps one of those pendants with the feathers." He pointed to the lower shelf. "I've been meaning to look for something to send back to them ever since I arrived here." With a wink and a grin, he continued. "Now, thanks to you, I believe I have found the very thing."

If a sudden snowstorm delivered two feet of snow outside her door, Anna would still be happy. Trevor was grateful for something she had done, and he was actually seeing *her* for the first time in her life, not her sister.

"Would you like me to package your purchases and mail them for you?"

He frowned. "How did you know I needed to send them through the mail?"

"You mentioned sending them back and talked about arriving here," she replied. "So, I gathered you haven't been here very long."

Trevor nodded, admiration shining in his warm, chocolate eyes. "I did say that, didn't I? You are quite observant, Miss. . . Oh. I'm afraid I never introduced myself or asked for your name. Please forgive my horrible manners."

Anna touched her fingers to her lips. "Oh, my! You're right. I apologize as well."

"Let's remedy that, shall we?" Trevor extended his hand. "Trevor Fox," he said. "And who might you be?"

Anna placed her hand in his. "Anna S. . . Clairmont," she replied, hastily covering up almost slipping and giving him the St. Claire name. That would have ruined everything for sure.

"Well, Miss Clairmont," he stated as he raised her hand to brush her knuckles with his lips, "it is a true pleasure to meet you and make your acquaintance." He lowered her hand then released it. "And, yes, I would greatly appreciate your boxing up those two items and preparing them to be sent out."

She could still feel the warmth of his fingers and the touch of his lips on her hand as she reached under the counter for a suitable box and paper to wrap up his purchases. "Trevor Fox," she began. "That doesn't sound like a name I've heard around here, and it certainly doesn't sound like any cowboy I've met so far."

Once again, Trevor rubbed the back of his neck. He grinned. "No, and that's because as you noticed, I'm not from around here. I've only been here for two months."

"Which pendant did you want?"

"That one." He pointed. "With the turquoise stones in the center and the blue and brown feathers."

Anna carefully wrapped the pendant and placed it in the box, nestled in more paper to cushion and protect it. Next she reached for the bone and feather earrings. "Where were you before you came here?"

Maybe if she pretended to not know anything about him, it would increase her chances of remaining unknown to him. She wrapped the earrings and packaged them with the pendant as she waited for his response.

"Believe it or not, I've spent all of my life in New York City."

"New York? Really?" She tried hard to sound impressed. "That's quite a long journey from here."

"Yeah," he replied.

"What brought you to Colorado?"

"Charlie Logan." Trevor pressed his lips into a thin line. "We've been friends since we were boys, and when I spoke to him about needing some space, he suggested I come out here for a bit. Change of pace and scenery. His uncle owns a ranch near here, so he invited me to join him."

Logan. Now, why did that name sound familiar. Oh, right! "The Logans. That's Red Hawk Ranch, isn't it?"

"Yes." His face brightened. "You've heard of it?"

"It's the largest spread between here and Frisco." Anna smiled. "I'm fairly certain everyone in the area has heard of that ranch."

Trevor puffed out his chest and stood tall. "Well, we do provide beef to all the mining camps, and our ranch hands come into town on payday."

Anna nodded. "Just like the miners." She grimaced at the thought of the obnoxious ruckus all those men made each week. "It's those nights and early mornings when I don't get much sleep, as my home is above this shop."

His shoulders drooped a bit. "Oh, Miss Clairmont, I'm sorry about that. Guess I hadn't thought about merchants such as yourself living right here in the center of town." He reached for her hand again and enclosed it in both of his. "Now that I've met you, though, and am aware you're here, I'll be sure we limit our shenanigans to down by the hotel."

Anna smiled. Charming and appeasing as always, complementing the Casanova behavior he employed with the young ladies he frequently courted back in New York. Movement outside the store caught her eye, and Anna looked over Trevor's shoulder to see two young ladies pointing through the window at the two of them, small pouts on their lips. She slowly withdrew her hand from his and drew her eyebrows together. Why would those ladies be upset with the two of them talking?

Trevor noticed her expression, and he turned around. An immediate groan mixed with a sigh sounded from him. "I'm never going to get away from them now," he spoke low.

"Get away from whom?" Anna asked. "Do you know those ladies?"

He faced her once more, his jaw clenched. "No, I don't. And that's the reason I entered your shop in the first place."

"I don't understand."

"I'm not sure I fully understand it, either," he replied. "But, remember that friend, Charlie, I mentioned a few minutes ago?"

"Yes."

"He and some of the other hands at the ranch wanted some publicity, so they spoke with a reporter for the *Bulletin* and told them about some suggestions I had to improve profits at the Red Hawk. The reporter twisted the story a bit, and somehow, I ended up being named the most eligible bachelor in Breckenridge." He ran his hand across his face then raised both hands to his temples and started rubbing, as if his head ached. "Now, thanks to that article, I am beginning to see young ladies show a great deal of interest in me, everywhere I turn."

"Oh." Back in New York, he didn't seem to mind being the center of attention and courting more than one lady at a time. Now he wanted to avoid that? "Can't you simply tell them you're not interested?"

"The only way that would work is if. . ." He stopped. Then his entire countenance changed. Light entered his eyes, and a smile formed on his lips as his chest filled with the large intake of air he breathed. "Miss Clairmont, please forgive me if this is being too forward, but might I have your permission to court you?"

Court her? Had she just heard him correctly? She'd dreamed of this very moment for years, and it had finally happened. But it wasn't real. He only needed her to make the other ladies believe he wasn't available. Then what? Could she bear to have her heart broken again once the reason for his request no longer existed?

"I realize my asking you comes as a surprise," he said, interrupting her musings. "And under normal circumstances, I wouldn't be so bold with someone I just met. But it would only be for a short while, until the gossip dies down and they find something else to hold their attention."

Anna didn't believe in happenstance. She'd put more than two thousand miles between them, yet somehow he'd not only ended up in the same state to where she'd fled, but the same town, too. There had to be a reason for it. If she could in some way help him, she would. Of course, being courted by him held its own level of appeal. In her mind, it was a benefit to them both.

"Yes," she finally said. "If you need my help for a short while, I'm happy to give it."

Trevor beamed a wide smile at her then leaned across the counter and planted a quick kiss on her cheek. "Thank you!" She must have looked surprised, because he immediately backed away and instead reached for her hand. "That was too bold, wasn't it? Forgive me." He raised her hand to his lips once more and touched a soft kiss again to her knuckles. "I will return soon." He released her hand and took two steps backward. "We can begin by taking a walk together, get to know each other better." He almost tripped over the baskets on the floor and ran into the glass door as he rushed to leave. "This is going to be perfect. You'll see."

Anna watched him stumble again on the sidewalk, but he righted himself and looked through her window as he waved at her before disappearing from view. In the silence that followed his departure, she tried to make sense of all that had just happened. First, Trevor Fox surprised her by showing up in Breckenridge and coming into her shop. Next, she agreed to let him court her so he could avoid unwanted attention and she could fulfill a long-held dream. But had she truly thought through the ramifications of her acquiescence?

What had she done?

Chapter 3

So, did I hear right?" Charlie led one of their horses out of the barn and over to the forge where Trevor grabbed a new shoe. "You've gone and found yourself a girl already and have started courting her?"

"Yes," Trevor replied. "But it's not what you think." At least, that's what he kept telling himself.

Charlie grinned big. "You don't waste any time, do you?" He clapped Trevor on the back. "Just like back in New York."

"Thanks to you, I didn't have much of a choice, did I?" Trevor parried.

"Yeah, good point." Charlie looked at him across the back of the horse, speaking low and settling the mare to prepare for shoeing. "But, hey, I did apologize, and from the sound of things, it hasn't turned out to be all that bad."

Trevor moved the stool and positioned himself to the side of the mare before reaching for her rear leg. He'd learned the hard way right after arriving on the ranch why it wasn't wise to stand behind a horse. Wouldn't be making that mistake again. . .ever.

"So, what exactly did you hear?"

Charlie moved to stand at the mare's head, holding tight to the lead rope to keep her still. "Not much, to be honest. Just that you were seen keeping company with the proprietress of the Ute Indian goods and jewelry shop." He handed Trevor a farrier's knife. "My aunt is friends with the owners of the tailor shop two doors down. She said the Bernats' daughter saw you talking with the young woman, and there were indications it was more than mere pleasantries being exchanged."

Trevor jerked his head and stared at Charlie, who stood there with a knowing grin on his face. He held up his hands in mock surrender when Trevor narrowed his eyes.

"Hey! I'm just reporting what I heard," Charlie protested. "Don't look at me like I had anything else to do with this."

Great. So not only had he become the talk of the town because of the article, but the quick choice he'd made trying to deter all those young ladies had only stirred up more gossip. At least it was somewhat accurate, though.

"I know." Trevor sighed as he changed tools and grabbed the horseshoe pullers. "I only wish I hadn't been forced to make such a rash decision." He placed the pullers under the shoe and rocked the tool back and forth to loosen it. "Miss Clairmont was merely a convenience," he said, grunting a bit with the exertion. "And she happened to be in the right place. . ." He took a breath and worked the tool. ". . .at the right time," he finished, popping off the shoe.

"Well, maybe this won't be such a bad thing," Charlie stated. "You having a young lady to hold your attention for a bit."

Trevor glanced at his friend and grinned. "Are you saying the work on this ranch isn't enough for me?"

"Come on, Trev. You know as well as I do that ranching isn't your thing." Charlie handed Trevor a brand-new horseshoe. "I mean, you've picked up on things faster than I thought you would, but you're far more at home in a suit and tie, negotiating deals and brokering financial affairs, than you are interacting with a bunch of horses and cattle and cleaning up their messes."

Trevor set the shoe on the mare's hoof and grabbed the nailing hammer. "You're right about that." Working on a ranch had taken him far out of his element and challenged him in a way nothing else had. The physical labor alone had nearly done him in those first couple of weeks.

"Not that I and my aunt and uncle don't appreciate how you've jumped right in without complaint and done any task we asked of you." Charlie passed over a box of nails. "Better than some of the other cowhands we have around here."

"You know I hate being idle," Trevor said as he began hammering the nails to secure the shoe to the hoof.

"Exactly," Charlie agreed. "Which is why I said this courting thing with. . .Miss Clairmont, was it?" At Trevor's nod, he continued. "It's why I said this might not be a bad thing after all."

"I'll be meeting her again on Saturday, so we'll see if it'll work out like I hope."

"Saturday, huh?" Charlie grinned. "So, tell me a little more about this young lady. Did you choose her because she was the first one you saw, or was there something about her that caught your eye?"

Trevor grabbed the clincher and folded over the nails like Charlie's uncle had shown him. Then he reached for the rasp to trim up the hoof and round the edges for a smooth fit.

"Miss Clairmont isn't like any of the ladies back in New York. There's something about her that's refreshing and pure." He worked his way around the hoof, testing each side. "She put me instantly at ease, and we settled into a comfortable rapport I don't ever remember having with anyone else in the circles we used to travel."

"What does she look like?"

Trevor grinned. He wondered when Charlie would get around to asking that. With all the ladies they met and invited on outings, Charlie always pointed out their looks first. Trevor noticed appearances, too, but he also looked for someone who could carry on a conversation with him and who asked intelligent questions. He didn't merely want someone to hang on his arm and look pretty. Unfortunately, far too many of the ladies he'd met in the past had been just that. They only expressed interest in him for the status he could offer through his position in the Fox company.

"Well?" Charlie interrupted his musings. "Are you gonna tell me or not?"

Trevor moved the stool around the mare to the other side and prepared to repeat the shoeing process. "I will tell you she would stand out a great deal back in New York. And not just because of her clothing." He didn't have to try hard to conjure up an image of Anna in his mind's eye. "She has this long braid of brown hair that hangs down her back or falls over her shoulder."

"So she hasn't given in and gotten one of those short bobs we've seen almost everywhere."

"No," Trevor replied. "And I kind of like it."

"Ah, more traditional, then," Charlie quipped.

"Yes, and not only that, but there's intelligence in her eyes. She knows a lot about the area and can initiate a conversation without being prompted."

"Color?"

"What?"

"The color of her eyes," Charlie amended.

"Oh." Trevor looked upward. "As blue as the Colorado sky."

A low whistle sounded from the other side of the mare. Trevor leaned over and peered around the horse's chest at his friend. His gaze met a bemused expression on Charlie's face.

"What?"

"She's definitely caught your eye." He snorted. "And maybe more, too!"

"But I know hardly anything about her." Even his own protest sounded weak to his ears. "We just met."

"That's why they call it attraction, my friend." Charlie waggled his eyebrows. "You don't need to know anything about her. You only need to *want* to."

Well, he certainly had that. In abundance, in fact. He couldn't put his finger on it, but something about her made him want to find out more about her. What a change from how he usually regarded the ladies who spent time by his side. There wasn't much difference between them. He might be considered a Don Juan or a Romeo to some, but they didn't understand his situation or his circumstances. They didn't know he paraded through all those ladies because he searched for a relationship with meaning, one that inspired and excited him. So far, he had yet to find that.

Trevor checked the other two hooves. They didn't need any repair or cleaning. He stood and nodded at Charlie. "Go ahead and take this girl back inside."

Charlie gave the lead rope a tug, and Dusty Sunrise swung around to walk toward the barn. Just as they reached the edge of the shoeing area, Charlie paused.

"The real question is our little unassuming shop owner." He looped the rope around his wrist. "I wonder what she's thinking about you right now."

"*If* she's thinking about me," Trevor corrected. "I don't know that she's even giving me a second thought right now."

"Aw, come on. Handsome and charming guy like you? Most eligible bachelor in Breckenridge," he added with a wink. "Asking to court whom I can only guess from your description is an attractive young lady?" Charlie nodded. "She's most definitely thinking about you."

Trevor grinned. He could certainly hope.

◆•————•◆

"Miss Anna? Did you hear my question?"

A tap on her arm startled Anna from her thoughts and she looked up to see Morning

Fawn staring at her, a concerned expression on her light brown face.

"I'm sorry, Morning Fawn. I must have been daydreaming." She offered a soft smile. "Please forgive me. What question did you ask?"

"I wish to know if you will put the new jewelry in the case with the others, or if you want me to put it with the clips and ties for the hair on the table over there."

Anna looked at the items her friend held. They might fit well with the hair clips and ribbons, but with the embellishments and added mineral elements, they needed to be kept close at hand. She reached for the tray. "I believe these are far too delicate and beautiful to simply sit on a side table. They deserve to be featured and allowed to shine."

"You are too kind, Miss Anna," Morning Fawn said with a smile. "I am happy it is you who I met on the road one year ago. What my people make is being seen and bought by so many different people, and we have a new purpose in what we create. We owe you a great deal of thanks."

Who would have thought she could make such a difference in the lives of so many simply by suggesting an idea that popped into her mind? Anna couldn't have been more surprised herself by the turn of events that brought her to Breckenridge and led her to not only being on her own at twenty-four but being the owner of a shop unlike any other in the vicinity.

"I, too, am glad we met," Anna replied. "You saved my life in more ways than one that day."

Morning Fawn gave her a puzzled look. "I do not understand. You were in no danger."

Anna chuckled as she set some of the newest items inside the glass case and arranged them in an eye-catching array. "No, that's not what I meant. Saving my life can also be a way of saying you helped me figure out a solution for a problem I was having."

"Oh, yes." Morning Fawn nodded. "You speak of the life you ran away from and the new life you have found here."

"Yes, exactly."

"But your old life is still very much alive, and you will have to find a way to make peace with it before you will ever be able to move forward with your new life."

During conversations like this, the wisdom of Morning Fawn's years spoke out loud and clear. At other times, Anna forgot Morning Fawn was old enough to be her mother. The wise woman did have a daughter around Anna's age, about to be joined that summer to a noted brave from her tribe. He had already presented his horses and other bartered treasures to Morning Fawn's husband in what Anna's circle of friends would call a dowry. . .even if it was being given instead of received by the soon-to-be husband. Why couldn't things be that simple for her and her friends? Why did they have to endure all the emotional upheaval and the Ferris wheel of interest from gentlemen in their lives? Around and around they went sometimes, neither one saying what they were feeling.

"Miss Anna? You are doing it again," came Morning Fawn's gentle chiding.

Anna blinked several times and shook her head. "I do apologize. I don't know where my head is today."

Morning Fawn extended her hand and reached for Anna's, leading her over to a velvet-cushioned settee by the front window. They both sat, and Morning Fawn turned toward her.

"I have seen that look on the face of my daughter many times. She lived many moons with her head in the clouds after Avanaco—Lean Bear—asked to marry her." The older woman touched Anna's cheek. "Now, tell me about the young man who has put the stars in *your* eyes."

Anna hesitated. How much should she share with her friend? It wasn't as if Trevor would have cause to meet any of the tribal members or speak to Morning Fawn. So, whatever she said she was certain would be held in the strictest of confidence.

"I didn't expect to ever see him again," Anna began. "All of a sudden, he is here, and he is asking if he can court me so he can avoid the attentions of the other young ladies in town."

Before she could stop it, the entire story poured out. Everything from when she first met Trevor back in New York all the way to the moment she'd agreed to let him call on her. Morning Fawn listened, never interrupting, and never making any sounds at all. She only nodded and allowed Anna to let it all out.

When she was done, Anna took a deep breath. She hadn't shared that much with anyone since before she left New York. Morning Fawn touched a finger to Anna's cheek and caught a tear about to fall. "Your heart and your mind are very tormented, little one."

Anna scrubbed at her eyes. She hadn't even felt the tears form as she poured out her story, but her friend had seen them.

"This Trevor Fox, he is a part of your past life?" Morning Fawn asked.

"Yes." Anna sniffed and reached into her pocket for a lace handkerchief. "We knew each other when we both lived in New York."

"And now he has come to be part of your new life, too?"

Well, Anna didn't know if she'd put it that way, but he had definitely walked into the life she had begun to lead separate from the one she'd led in New York. Whether he would remain a part of it remained to be seen.

"He is here now, yes," Anna replied. "And it appears we will be spending some time together in the coming weeks."

Morning Fawn clasped Anna's hands in her own. "Does this make your heart happy?"

"I don't know for sure," Anna said. She took a deep breath and released it. "A part of me is excited at the possibilities now that we are both away from the life that kept us apart, but another part of me wonders if I should risk my heart getting broken again by believing Trevor might choose me."

Morning Fawn placed her hand on Anna's chest. "It is only a heart open to love that can truly blossom. You cannot allow fear to be your guide." She smiled. "I know you talk to the Great Spirit. Be still and listen for the direction He will give you."

"But how can I be sure?"

"Trust your heart, little one," Morning Fawn replied. "When the time is right, you will know. But you will still need to make peace with the worries of your old life. If you do not, the new life you try to live will forever have a dark cloud following it." She patted

Anna's hands. "Awendela wants sunshine and healing rain for Miss Anna, not storms."

Anna clasped her friend's hands and gave them a squeeze. "Thank you." She leaned forward and placed a soft kiss on the woman's weathered cheek. "I don't know what I would do without you."

"You would find a dog or a cat or a horse or maybe a cow." The older woman laughed. "You would tell all your secrets to it and wait forever for a reply."

Anna laughed, too, and stood. She couldn't keep Morning Fawn away from her people and her responsibilities any longer. And they still had a bit of work to do. The wisdom she'd received today, though, would last long after her friend left. Anna only hoped she'd know when the time was right to put it to use.

Chapter 4

The rumble of mining trucks sounded along Main Street as the workers headed to the mines on Saturday morning. Anna stood outside her shop, watching them pass. Business had been rather slow that week, so she didn't have any problems closing the shop for the morning. She'd contemplated hiring an assistant, but would there be enough reason for her to be away from the shop to warrant having someone take over for her? Anna raised her hand to shield her eyes as she peered down the street in search of Trevor. He'd left her a note three days ago asking to meet that morning, and she had sent her reply that she would be there.

Had he forgotten?

Had something happened to prevent him from coming?

She covered her mouth as a yawn escaped, and blinked several times, scrunching her eyes tight to clear the sleep from them. Another Friday night, and more revelry beneath her window into the wee hours of the morning. Despite Trevor's promise to keep the cowboys away from her shop, he had no control over the miners and other riffraff who came into town. Thank goodness for the strong tea she'd bought from Evans Pharmacy. Otherwise, she might still be sleeping and miss out on meeting Trevor.

It had been less than a week since she had reunited with him and agreed to this ruse, yet she had thought of nothing else since. On Wednesday, after she'd received his note, the anticipation of this morning had been hard to tame. Now Saturday morning had arrived, and she stood waiting for Trevor. She glanced down at her simple skirt and blouse. Should she go back upstairs and change into something a bit nicer?

And what about her hair? She reached to touch the brown braid that hung down her back. Should she pin it up like she had so many times back in New York? Or maybe it was time to follow the fashions and styles she'd seen so many other ladies imitate. She pulled her braid over her shoulder. But that would mean a rather drastic cut of her hair to the shorter, cropped styles that had been slowly traveling west from the bigger cities to the east. No, for now, she'd leave things as they were. Besides, a shorter hairstyle might make her look too much like Maggie.

Anna glanced down the street to the north again, looking in the direction where she knew the ranch was located. She stretched up on her tiptoes hoping to see farther. She lowered her heels and pivoted sharply, only to come to an abrupt halt when she ran into someone who had been standing right behind her. Two strong hands held her elbows until she regained her balance.

"Were you by chance looking for me?" a familiar voice asked.

Anna smoothed the front of her skirt and looked up to see Trevor standing there with a cowboy hat on his head, his hands in his pockets, and wearing a rather mischievous look on his face. "Yes. I thought you would be coming from the other direction."

"I took a shortcut."

"Do you always sneak up on unassuming young ladies?"

He winked and sent a devilish grin her way. "You've discovered my favorite pastime. Now we don't have a choice. We must go for our walk and begin our courting lest you change your mind and leave me to fend for myself with all of those matchmaking matrons walking about town, looking for suitable matches for their daughters."

Anna grinned. He sounded so much like the Trevor she knew from New York, with his quick wit and easygoing charm. But the image of that man wasn't the same as the one that stood before her now.

Scuffed and worn boots peeked out from the legs of his blue jeans, which were fastened with a wide belt and hugged his long legs better than the pants of any suit ever had. He wore a light green chambray shirt today, which stretched across his broad shoulders and tapered down to a narrower waist. Top that off with his hat sitting atop his sandy-colored hair at a crooked angle, and he looked every bit the picture of trouble.

In fact, he reminded her of a grown-up version of little Dominick, the scrappy street urchin who spent most of his time hanging out by the Denver Hotel looking for dropped coins and other treasures misplaced by hotel guests. Every time she'd seen him get caught, he managed to talk his way out of any consequences and convince the would-be punishment enforcer to forgive him and continue on their way.

"Is this a good time for you?" Trevor asked, breaking her from her silent observation. "You look lovely this morning, by the way."

"Thank you," she replied, feeling a hint of warmth steal into her cheeks. "The time is perfect."

"Who is watching your shop?"

"I decided to close it this morning. Business has been a bit slow this week."

"More time for our walk, then," he said with a grin. "You won't be needing to rush back at any specific time."

She couldn't argue with him on that. She had taken the freedom of a more leisurely pace into consideration when she'd made her decision to close the shop. This way, she could follow whatever lead Trevor decided to take.

"Shall we?" He extended his arm, and she placed her hand in the crook of his elbow.

"We shall," she replied with a smile.

Anna fell in step with him. She looked at the cloudless blue sky and reveled in the warmth from the sun above. There were far more clear days like this than what they had back in New York. When storm clouds filled the skies above her there, she'd felt trapped with nowhere to go. Here, even when storms came, they passed quickly, and there would be blue skies yet again. The only unfortunate part was the mud in the streets and sometimes the threat of mudslides from the mountains surrounding them, but so far, there had been no disasters.

"So, tell me more about your shop and how you came to own it," Trevor said. "How long has it been open, and how did you meet. . .Awendela, was it?"

"Yes. Her name is Awendela," she replied, waving and smiling at Mr. Evans as they passed the pharmacy. "I met her the first day I came to Breckenridge."

Trevor looked down at her.

"Like you, I'm not from here," she continued. "Several friends of my family who had traveled to Colorado returned, highly recommending a visit. They made it sound so amazing and so beautiful, I had to see it for myself."

"And how did you end up in Breckenridge?"

Anna giggled. "That part is a bit funny."

Trevor placed his hand on hers. "Please tell." He paused and held her back as a rather boisterous person shoved through the main doors of the Denver Hotel and stomped out onto the sidewalk.

Anna watched, wide-eyed. The man didn't even excuse himself for walking in front of them. She doubted he saw them at all. As Trevor started them walking again, she brought her attention back to her story.

"I arrived by train in Denver planning to travel south to Colorado Springs to visit the Antlers Hotel or perhaps see the Broadmoor. Word of those impressive hotels had reached all the way to the depot stop in Kansas City, and it made me want to see them."

"What did you think of them?" Trevor asked.

"I never saw them. When I arrived in Denver, I happened to overhear another passenger talking about a beautiful road through a valley to the west, full of stunning views and the chance to see a good sampling of Colorado wildlife." She shrugged. "I didn't exactly have a time line for anything, and I was here, so I thought it would be a good idea to travel this road. Turned out, it wasn't such a good idea, as the wagon ended up getting stuck around the reservoir and prevented further travel."

"And when was this?"

"A little over a year ago, in the spring," she answered.

He chuckled, and a knowing grin formed on his lips. "Right in the middle of the wet season in this area."

"I didn't know that at the time, but I certainly do now."

They stepped down off the sidewalk in between the *Bulletin* office and the fire station then returned to the sidewalk once more.

Mr. Watson stepped outside his store a little ahead of them and swept the walkway in front of his door. He nodded as they approached. Trevor tipped his hat and Anna smiled.

"Fine day for a walk," Mr. Watson said.

"It certainly is," Trevor replied.

"I really enjoyed that article about you and the Red Hawk, Mr. Fox," Mr. Watson said. He smiled at Anna. "And I see it didn't take long for you to find a companion. No one in town finer than our Miss Clairmont."

Anna placed her hand on her chest. "Aw, thank you, Mr. Watson. That is so kind of you."

Mr. Watson shrugged. "Just telling how I see it."

"And I would have to agree," Trevor said.

Anna dipped her head and averted her eyes. She couldn't help but smile though, at their high praise.

"And now we've gone and embarrassed her," Mr. Watson said. "You two enjoy your stroll this morning," he added in parting.

"Thank you," Trevor replied. "We will." He patted Anna's hand again and smiled as he looked down at her. "You might have only been here a little over a year, but you have made quite a name for yourself."

"The other merchants in town have been so kind, and I do make friends easily."

"You did a fine job of helping *me* feel comfortable." He guided her around a raised wooden plank. "I can see why others are so fond of you."

It was true. When she lived in New York, she'd remained forever in her sister's shadow. Out here, though, she could be herself and allow her natural personality to take center stage. Anna had never felt more free than when she had escaped the confines of being Maggie's younger sister.

"There's something familiar about you, though," Trevor continued. "From the moment we met, I had the feeling we'd known each other far longer."

Oh no! Anna stumbled at his confession but righted herself quickly. Had he remembered something? She'd better steer this conversation somewhere else. "Others have told me that as well. That might be part of the reason I ended up with Jacquie's here in Breckenridge," she replied. Good. Get back on track with the story she'd been sharing.

"Yes, you were saying you ran into trouble around the reservoir." He guided them past a few houses after leaving the business district and toward a small pond surrounded by little painted wooden fences and beautiful flowers.

Anna smiled at a pair of ducks dipping their heads beneath the water and giving themselves a bath. "Yes, and that's where I met Morning Fawn. The man driving the wagon had already established a bartering friendship with her camp, and she was coming to meet him. As he got us unstuck, she showed me some of the items she used to barter with. That's when the idea came to me about opening a shop."

"How fortunate that you found a place you could purchase."

"Yes, the previous owners had recently left town due to an illness in their family that required them to return home." She glanced up at him, his jaw set firm and his confident posture communicating a resolute determination to prosper no matter what. "Like you, I, too, needed a change from the life I used to lead. I hadn't yet decided what I would do, but I trusted God would guide me...and He did."

"Hmm," was all Trevor said in response.

They walked for several moments in comfortable silence. A pair of magpies flew in and landed on the fence, chirping and squawking at either each other or the ducks, Anna couldn't tell. The sun glinted off their shiny feathers, spotlighting the royal blue on their wings. They might have a penchant for being aggressive, but Anna loved their beauty. One took flight, its black head surrounded by a ring of white and its white-tipped wings spread wide. A moment later, its partner followed. Their effortless flying reminded her of the freedom she'd discovered by leaving her old life behind. As they rounded the other side of the pond, Trevor slowed their pace.

"So, you really believe God helps you and leads you to certain things?"

"Yes, I do," Anna answered without hesitation.

It wasn't a question she thought she'd ever hear from a man like Trevor, but one look at the serious expression on his face and the contemplative stance he took, staring out at nothing in particular, and Anna knew his inquiry was genuine. Maybe he left New York searching for more than he thought.

"Take the two of us, for instance," Anna continued. "Some might say our meeting was purely circumstantial, but I disagree. Neither one of us is from here, and we both traveled a long distance to get here. I don't believe that the article featuring you or the fact that you chose my shop to enter was a coincidence."

She'd questioned all of that herself over the past several days. One of the main reasons she'd decided to take her inheritance and leave New York was to escape the pain of rejection. But she felt none of that here, even with Trevor back in her life. Maybe what they'd both needed was a change of scenery.

Trevor freed her hand from his arm and stepped toward the fence. He rested his elbows on the top rail and leaned against it. Again, silence fell between them. Trucks and motorcars driving through town hummed and rumbled, and the occasional tinkling of a bicycle bell rang out. The man-made sounds mixed with those of nature, the various chirps, calls, and cadences of the hawks, owls, magpies, and woodpeckers.

"You definitely have given me a lot to think about, Miss Clairmont," Trevor finally said. He straightened and once again extended his elbow out to her, which she took. "I'd like to invite you to visit the ranch as soon as you can make yourself available."

"I'd like to come and see the ranch," Anna replied. "The miners here talk about the impressive outfit the Logans run, and I've had several meals featuring some of the beef that comes from the Red Hawk. It would be fun to see it all up close."

He led them back toward the business part of town. "Just name the day. It really is a remarkable place. You have to see it to believe it. And I look forward to showing it to you."

The enthusiasm in his voice matched the joy on his face. He looked like a little boy who had just been given his first piece of candy from the dry goods store.

Laughter bubbled up from within and escaped. "As long as you don't have any plans of making me clean up after the animals, it should be an enjoyable experience."

Trevor laughed as well. "I can promise that won't happen." He glanced down at her with a twinkle in his eye. "I can't say we won't be getting you up on a horse, though."

"We'll see about that."

They made their way back to her shop, where Trevor paused and turned to face her. He looked down at the sidewalk. "I...uh. . ." He whipped his hat off his head and fingered the rim, turning it around and around between his hands. "That is. . ."

"Is there something else you wanted to ask, Mr. Fox?"

"Tomorrow's Sunday, and well. . ." He stopped, took a deep breath, and made eye contact. "Would you mind if I joined you soon for Sunday services?"

"At church?" she blurted. Trevor Fox wanted to go with her to church? Now, that *was* a surprise.

"Yeah, that is, if you don't mind."

He had such trouble asking, and his last comment held such hope that she'd agree, how could she deny him?

"I wouldn't mind at all. When you're ready, you let me know. You might even find some answers to some of those questions you were asking earlier."

"Maybe." He gestured toward the front door of her shop. "Well, I've brought you full circle, and I enjoyed our little stroll. Thank you for joining me, Miss Clairmont."

Anna stepped toward her shop and placed her hand on the doorknob. "It was my pleasure, Mr. Fox."

"May I call you on you again?"

She looked over her shoulder and smiled then nodded. "I will be here."

"Good." He replaced his hat and tipped it with his thumb and forefinger before stepping off the sidewalk and crossing the street. She followed his departure, and a moment later, he turned to catch her watching him. He winked, and heat warmed her face. Ducking her head, she slipped inside her shop and out of view.

Trevor was far too charming for his own good.

Chapter 5

Two weeks. It had only been two weeks since she and Trevor had reconnected. They'd taken several walks together and shared a few meals at the Arlington Hotel. Each and every day they shared together made her realize one thing. She had never stopped loving him. And now, he sat beside her in church for the second week in a row, in the pew she chose each week. She almost wanted to ask someone to pinch her and see if this was real.

Anna shifted her attention to the front of the room and the ornate rose window above the altar. Both sides curved to a point at the top, and the circle in the middle glowed red-orange with a patterned mixture of blues in the center. The golden background behind the circle glowed with the illuminating sunlight. Below the window sat the altar, with two cushioned chairs on either side of the pulpit on the platform raised just one step above the rest of the room.

She couldn't help but think about the difference between this church and the one she had attended back in New York. This one was simple, with the focus on the congregation gathering to worship together. The other seemed to focus on appearances. It had four sections of pews and three long aisles leading to the front. This one had only two small sections and a single aisle down the middle. And the rest of the windows were made of basic glass, unlike the abundance of stained-glass paintings covering the windows of her old church, each one depicting a scene from the Bible and casting an ethereal light about the main room. The light here felt more warm and welcoming. Did she like one more than the other?

More importantly, what did Trevor think? Anna risked a glance sideways at her companion. He sat straight and tall on the pew next to her, his eyes and attention focused on the front of the room. He'd returned once again to the customary suit and tie she so often saw him wear back home. No cowboy hat and boots today. He'd met her at her shop door before stepping aside to showcase the beautiful Tin Lizzie he'd driven from the ranch. Although the walk wouldn't be far, he'd insisted upon driving her. He'd definitely gone out of his way to impress this morning.

A hush fell over those gathered as the soft piano and old organ played the opening notes to the first hymn they'd sing. Everyone stood to join together in song. Anna turned to offer her hymnal to Trevor only to see he had already flipped to the correct page and held out a book for her to share with him. During the first verse she didn't hear anything from him. He merely followed along in silence. Before the end of the second verse, though, a rich baritone joined in just slightly off-key, and her heart skipped a beat.

Was he familiar with the hymn or had he merely picked it up just now?

"Close your mouth, Miss Clairmont," Trevor leaned over and whispered. "You might catch flies."

Anna snapped her jaw shut. When had it fallen open? And how had she allowed Trevor to see her surprise? He must think she'd judged him and found him lacking if she assumed he wouldn't be familiar with any of the hymns. That wouldn't help at all in her attempt to share the Gospel with him. Of course, right now, she wondered if she even needed to.

At the conclusion of the final hymn, everyone took their seats, and Reverend Mason stood from one of the chairs to walk to his position behind the pulpit.

"A blessed day to be in the house of our Lord. Thank you all for coming to worship with us this morning." He opened his Bible then placed both hands on either side of the podium. "I'd like to begin today talking about the simplicity of faith, of trusting God with the big as well as the little things in our lives."

Anna had a difficult time focusing on the message with Trevor sitting right next to her. Everyone else gathered kept their eyes forward, paying rapt attention as the reverend presented the points of his talk. Anna wished she could do the same.

About midway through the sermon, Trevor reached over and covered her hand with his. She flinched then winced, sure he was going to yank back his hand. But instead, he held firm. Anna glanced over at him, and at first, he stared straight ahead. Then he looked down at her, and the corners of his mouth turned up just slightly in a soft smile. She returned the smile and tried to center her attention again on the sermon.

Trevor knew exactly what he was doing. She'd seen him do it time and time again with many other ladies. His confidence in his actions reminded Anna he was no stranger to the courting rituals. It might be a whole new world of experiences for her, but she accepted the attention of a rather well-versed and experienced guide.

◆•————•◆

Trevor placed a hand at the small of Anna's back and escorted her down the aisle toward the double doors at the back of church. The gauzy part of her dress covered the skirt underneath, giving it an ethereal quality, especially when the breeze from outside caught the material and sent it fluttering. He couldn't believe she'd actually let him keep his hand covering hers for the latter part of the sermon. He almost hadn't done anything for fear it was too soon. They'd only been out together a few times. It looked like his boldness had paid off, though.

"Thank you for coming today." The reverend greeted a couple in front of them first, shook their hands, and then turned a warm smile on Anna. "Another fine morning for worship, Miss Clairmont. I'm glad to see you've brought a friend with you today."

Anna returned the smile then turned toward Trevor. "Yes, this is Trevor Fox. He works out at the Red Hawk Ranch."

"Ah, yes." The reverend nodded. "I believe the Logans have visited a few times, if my memory serves me correctly. One of their ranch hands was fortunate enough to give my youngest granddaughter riding lessons last summer."

Trevor laughed and his shoulders shook. "Oh, yeah, that was Charlie. I heard the stories of that adventurous little gal. She must have fallen into the dirt at least a dozen times or more, but she wouldn't give up." He winked at the reverend. "Quite a lot of spunk in that one."

"Indeed," the reverend replied. "Takes after her father, a general in our great army."

"Guess it's a good thing Charlie let her keep at it until she mastered it, then." Trevor whistled. "I can only imagine what might've happened had the father felt the need to track Charlie down later."

"True, true." The reverend clapped Trevor on the shoulder. "So, will I be seeing you next week, then?"

"You just might," Trevor replied. Especially if he could again have such a charming companion by his side, sharing a hymnal. Who would've thought going to church and singing songs from a book could actually be enjoyable? If his friends back in New York could see him now. They'd never believe it.

"Well, you folks enjoy the rest of your Sunday," the reverend said in farewell as he prepared to greet the next people in line.

"So, what did you think?" Anna asked Trevor as soon as the two of them had moved away from the crowd and stood near a black wrought-iron fence about twenty feet from the main doors.

"I actually liked it," Trevor replied. "The reverend made a lot of good points. Things I never thought about before."

"Such as?" Anna asked.

"Well, like how much faith I already have in the everyday things in my life. Things like trusting an automobile is going to deliver me safely from one place to the next, or how a chair won't break when I sit on it. If I can trust things like that, it shouldn't be too difficult to trust God." Trevor shrugged. "Just hadn't ever heard it put that way."

Far too many people he knew were either overly pious with sour faces, or they treated him like some kind of street rat because he wasn't a regular churchgoer. If going to church meant he'd end up acting like any of them, he wanted no part of it. Anna wasn't anything like that, though. She wore her faith like a second skin. Comfortable, and always with her.

She smiled. "That's one of the reasons I love Reverend Mason. He has a way of taking what others complicate and making it sound so simple. Makes me wonder why I never thought of it before."

Trevor snapped his fingers. "Exactly! He made it easy to understand." He turned toward Anna and wrapped his hand around one of the black spikes at the top of the fence. "Everything else I've heard has made having faith seem like a long list of rules I'd have to follow." There were enough of those with his father's company in New York. He made a sweeping gesture back toward the church. "But this? This I could actually do."

The smile moved from her lips to her eyes. "Well, then, I'm glad you joined me this morning."

"I am as well." He glanced back over his shoulder at the unassuming building. "It's a nice little place."

"Not too long ago, it was both the church and the school here in town."

"Really?" He couldn't imagine all the children in town attending school in such a small space. "Oh, I guess the mining has picked up only in recent years, so there likely hadn't been much of a need for more before that."

Anna nodded. "Right before the Great War, funds from mining were used to build a rather impressive brick schoolhouse for all grades from kindergarten through the twelfth year." Her face brightened. "It's amazing. It even has an indoor swimming pool."

"Swimming inside? Now that *is* impressive."

"Nothing like that back in—" She stopped and looked away. "Back where I grew up."

Why did she hesitate to tell him where she had lived before? In all the conversations they'd shared over the past two weeks, she'd kept the specific details about her former life very vague. She'd mentioned an older sister and a brother, but never said their names. Something bothered her. He could see it in her eyes.

"So, what did they do with all the old classrooms?" He had to get them back to talking about positive things.

"Oh, they're now used for Sunday school for the children in town."

"I'll bet the church loves having all that extra room, especially with how many around here seem to love the way the reverend preaches."

Anna smiled. "Yes. There has been a lot of growth in recent years. It appears word is spreading."

Good! She was warming back up again. Now, how could he make this moment last longer? He didn't want to say good-bye just yet. A glance around them showed several families setting up for a picnic. That would be perfect! "Do you have plans for lunch?" he blurted out.

She looked surprised. "Lunch? No, I don't."

"What would you say to a picnic in the great outdoors? With me?" he added.

Anna narrowed her eyes, a bemused grin on her lips. "What did you have in mind?"

"Ohh, I thought it might be a good time for me to show you the ranch." He smiled. "Since I brought the Tin Lizzie, it wouldn't take long at all for us to get there." He reached for her hand and held it lightly. "You did promise you'd come for a visit."

She glanced down at their joined hands and swallowed. The slightest shiver made her fingers and hand tremble. Trevor fought hard to keep from smirking. Anna might be aloof when it came to revealing facts about her past, but she couldn't hide her reaction to him. He'd never worked this hard to woo any other ladies. What had begun as a farce for appearances only had become so much more. The challenge made it even more fun.

"Yes, I did," Anna finally said. "I suppose today is as good a day as any."

"Great!" Trevor raised her hand to his lips and kissed its back. "We can stop by Kistler's and have him prepare a quick lunch for us then be on our way."

Anna held his gaze for several moments, her blue eyes changing from a hint of gray to a lighter hue. She swallowed again and licked her lips. "I'd like that," she whispered.

Was she nervous, or excited? He couldn't tell. Surely he could find out more during their picnic.

Chapter 6

Trevor plopped down on the red-checkered cloth beside Anna, and she jumped in response.

"Sorry. I didn't mean to scare you."

She waved him off. "It's all right. My thoughts were elsewhere."

Her voice trembled a little. She wasn't comfortable. But why? He palmed their two tin cups of water in one hand and their lunch in the other as he assessed the secluded spot. The rear walls of one of the bunkhouses kept them hidden from view of the ranch, and the creek to the south afforded a natural barrier. None of the other cowboys would find them here. Maybe that's what bothered her? How alone they were?

"See? What did I tell you?" Trevor announced with forced pride. "This is the perfect spot."

Anna looked around them with a guarded expression. "It is out of the way. That's for certain." She hesitated a moment then nodded. "But it does appear to be a good choice. You were right when you said this ranch is amazing. It's gorgeous!"

"Yes, it is." He grinned. "Sure makes it hard to think of it as work when surrounded by all this."

She looked around. "How did you find this place?"

"Oh, um, I was out walking one day and stumbled upon it. Seemed like it would be a good place for an impromptu picnic."

Anna shifted her focus and regarded her skirts as if they held some special secret. "It does seem lovely."

Her voice was so soft he had to strain to hear her above the gurgling of the creek. It was time for a change of subject. He opened the basket and pulled out fried chicken, apples, and bread. "We didn't get a chance to discuss this earlier in the week. How has your work been going?"

Anna looked at him and smiled. "Quite well. And yours?"

He shrugged. "There haven't been any surprises or problems."

"I did have a situation a few days ago when Morning Fawn brought her latest wares to sell."

Finally. A topic that seemed to excite her. "Oh? What happened?"

"Well, she had some new fringed deerskin shirts, only this time, she brought one of the braves from her camp with her to model them for me."

Trevor raised one eyebrow. "Model? How did that go?"

She giggled. "It was clear he wasn't used to being inside a shop, especially not one with so many tables and displays. He kept bumping into things and trying not to knock over anything."

He could almost see where her story was headed, but he let her tell it.

"He was uncomfortable, but it wasn't a problem until he tripped over one of the baskets on the floor and grabbed one of the tables to regain his balance." Anna looked away as she recalled the details. "The only problem was, the table he grabbed held small pottery bowls filled with shells, beadwork pieces, and arrowheads, along with a selection of hand-carved flutes."

"Oh, no!" Trevor closed his eyes, as if doing that would prevent what he knew had happened.

"I lunged for the table, trying to keep the items from falling, but I was too late." A dimple showed in her left cheek when she pressed her lips together. "And not only that, but I also tripped. I ended up sitting in a heap on the floor with those pieces all around me and some of them clinging to my clothing." She sniggered. "It was quite a sight."

Trevor chuckled at the mental image he formed from her description. The ladies he normally found among his acquaintance would never have laughed about such a predicament. The mere idea of dirt usually sent them running off to change clothes. To imagine them enduring a debacle like that and taking it all in stride as Anna had done, well, it wouldn't happen.

"Did you ever get to see those new shirts on display?"

"Not in the least," she replied. "By the time we got everything cleaned up, Falcon Hunter couldn't leave my shop soon enough." She smiled and took a drink from her tin cup.

Trevor waggled his eyebrows. "Bet that brave will think twice before agreeing to anything Morning Fawn asks in the future."

Her lips tightened, preventing the water she'd just drunk from escaping.

He laughed and placed his hands in his lap as he attempted to school his expression into one of nonchalance. It was no use. "I'm sorry," he said through barely contained chuckles. "I do thank you, though, for sparing me the spray of your drink."

With a swallow and dainty clearing of her throat, Anna once again regained her composure. "You are most welcome," she replied, raising her cup again to her lips. "But I cannot guarantee that should a repeat occurrence take place, you will remain free from harm."

It took Trevor a moment to process what she'd just said. He narrowed his eyes at the playful underlying threat laced in her words. She spoke with such calm, her expression devoid of any mischief. He couldn't tell if she was flirting or serious. And she likely preferred it that way. Such a unique blend of sophistication and affability.

He reached for a piece of chicken. Holding it up for her perusal, he raised his eyebrows and grinned. "Well? What do you think?"

"About your sense of humor or the choice piece of chicken you've selected?" She took a bite of her apple, the corners of her lips turning up as she chewed.

"My—" He paused. Wait a minute. Had she just teased him about his sense of humor? He clenched his jaw and raised his chin a fraction of an inch. "The chicken, of course."

She swallowed and held the apple in front of her lips. "In that case, I approve." Anna pointed to the two drumsticks that remained. "You left me my favorite piece."

He leaned back on his elbows and regarded her through half-lidded eyes. "Well, you were the one to specifically ask for them. I enjoy them, too, but I wouldn't dream of taking food from a lady." Taking a bite of the much larger piece he held, he released an exaggerated groan. "Mmmm. It's the best chicken I've ever had."

Anna covered her mouth and giggled. "You'd better be careful about saying things like that. Wouldn't want the cook here at the ranch to find out. He or she might get jealous."

Trevor shook a finger in her direction. "That's not true. The cook here has nothing to worry about. But I haven't tasted his fried chicken yet."

Anna daintily set about unfolding her napkin and setting it in her lap. When she looked up at him again, she grinned. "Then you might want to reserve your judgment until you've had the chance to sample his chicken, too."

He reclined a bit and propped himself on one elbow. "I suppose you're right."

"What about you?" He took another bite of the chicken and swallowed. "How does this compare to *your* previous experiences?"

"Our cook didn't often make meals like this. They were far more involved." As soon as she answered, Anna gasped and covered her mouth.

He drew his eyebrows together. "Your cook?" But he thought she was part of the working class. Why would she have someone preparing meals for her?

She composed herself quickly and reached for one of the drumsticks. "The one at my former home," she replied.

"And where is that home?"

"Umm, not too far from here, but far enough."

There it was again. The evasive and nondescript answer. Perhaps there was something she didn't want to tell him. Painful memories, maybe? Or she might be ashamed of where she'd lived? "How have your parents gotten along with you gone for more than a year?"

Anna polished off the drumstick and set the bone aside. "Well, they have my older brother to help."

He pushed himself to a sitting position and leaned forward. Softening his voice, he tried to coax out a little more about her home life. Maybe it would give him more insight into her background. "But I get the feeling they don't exactly approve of your choice to leave."

A pained expression flitted across her face before she had the chance to hide it. "They would definitely prefer it if I had not traveled this far away, but they had no reason to make me stay, either." She looked away and plucked a dandelion gone to seed. "Besides, my sister was more their favorite anyway. She kept them plenty busy with all her affairs."

If only he could take away the hurt she was feeling and replace it with the carefree nonchalance she'd often shown. Then again, if he did that, he might not find out anything more about this young woman who'd suddenly become such an important part of his life.

"Have you told them you've settled quite nicely where you are?"

"Yes." She inhaled and puffed out her cheeks then blew on the white seeds of the weed. "And I even told them how happy I am."

Trevor reached out and covered the hand in her lap with his own, offering her a smile. "Well, if they care about you, as it seems they do, telling them you're happier away from them might not reassure them in the way you had hoped."

$$\bullet\!-\!\bullet\ \underline{\hspace{2cm}}\ \bullet\!-\!\bullet$$

Anna looked down at the hand covering hers, his tanned skin a stark contrast to her pale peach shade. Working on the ranch had certainly changed him. . .for the better. She gave him a wary look. "Mother did mention her concerns about that, especially way out here away from Denver or even Colorado Springs."

Actually, truth be told, Mother didn't just "mention her concerns" the first time Anna had called to let them know where she'd settled. Father hadn't been too pleased, either, but at least he had maintained a cool head about it all.

"And what about your father?" Trevor continued, as if he'd read her thoughts. "I'd think he'd want to keep his daughter safe, too."

"Yes. But he was more willing to trust me when I told him there was no cause for concern." She toyed with the idea of removing her hand from underneath his, but it felt so good to have his touch and reassurance.

"Any plans to ever return?"

She narrowed her eyes. "Why do you ask?"

Trevor leaned away and rested his forearms on his knees. She immediately felt the loss of warmth from his withdrawn hand, but his nearness still offered a great deal of comfort in its place. . .in spite of his obvious probing.

"It's not easy leaving everything you've ever known, especially when there's a bit of turmoil connected to your departure. You'll have to eventually make peace with it, somehow." He gave her a rueful grin. "I should know."

Anna ducked her chin. It was exactly what Morning Fawn had told her. "Oh. Yes. It has been bothering me lately." She had hoped her teasing remarks and smiles might cover up the inner turmoil. Obviously it hadn't. Trevor had seen right through her unsuccessful attempts. And now he wanted to know more.

She saw his hand before his fingers touched her chin and he raised her head to meet his gaze. "Hey," he said softly "you can't be expected to be blithe all the time. Life isn't that perfect."

He stroked the underside of her chin, and she quelled the shiver that started somewhere near the base of her spine. She got lost in the coffee-colored depths of his caring eyes.

"I have a feeling you won't allow this turmoil to go on for too long," he continued. "Your heart's far too big to allow unrest to cloud those beautiful blue eyes for long. You will find a way to triumph."

Anna wanted to pull away. She needed to put some distance between them, but his intent gaze held her captive. As his face came closer, her heart pounded faster. She'd dreamed of this moment for years, but nothing compared to experiencing the real thing.

As if of its own accord, her mouth parted and her eyes drifted closed. A second later, Trevor's lips touched hers, and her breath caught in her throat. She felt him shift as both of his hands moved to frame her face. The tender way his mouth caressed hers was almost her undoing. His kiss was so genuine, so honest. And she hadn't been either of those things with him. Anna couldn't bear it any longer, and she pulled back.

Trevor didn't move. She kept her eyes downcast, unable to meet his eyes and the questions she was sure she'd find there. He reached up and touched her cheek. It was then she felt the wetness under his thumb. When had she started crying?

"Anna." Trevor's raspy whisper cut straight to her heart. "Please let me in."

"I can't," she breathed. "Not yet." She braved a glance at his face.

The quick flash of pain at her initial response changed to one of hope. "I'll wait," he said. "Until then, we'll keep things as they are."

She didn't trust herself to speak, so she merely nodded. Oh, how she wished he could become something more than that. His concern for her warmed her heart. And the softness in his eyes all but wore down her resolve to keep parts of her life a secret. No. She dared not risk it. She walked on thin ice as it was.

If she didn't control the circumstances as much as possible, that thin layer would crack and she'd be pulled beneath the safe surface into the turbulent waters below. If the crashing jolt of reality coming face-to-face with the day-to-day world she'd created didn't ruin her, the possible betrayal on Trevor's face would.

"I best be getting you back to town." Trevor stood and dusted off his pants then retrieved his hat and slapped it on his head. He held out a hand to assist her. "You ready?"

She placed her hand in his and forced a smile. She could at least attempt to bring things back to where they were before. "Not exactly, but what other choice do we have?" Standing, she fluffed out the folds of her skirts.

Trevor bent to pick up the basket then straightened and gave her a wink. "I think I'll refrain from answering that, for now. Don't want to say or do something I might regret."

Wasn't *that* the truth! "Me, either," she mumbled.

"What was that?"

Anna cleared her throat. "Uh, nothing." He started walking, and she fell into step beside him. The least she could do was show her appreciation for the enjoyable thirty minutes they'd shared. "Thank you for inviting me to lunch. And for finding this little spot."

He stopped and turned toward her. "You're welcome. We should do it again."

He still wanted to spend time with her. That was a good sign. "Perhaps," she answered.

⁘

"Well, off I go." He touched two fingers to the brim of his hat and saluted. "Until next time."

Anna rushed inside and pushed the door to the shop closed behind her. She'd had such a good time with Trevor today. In fact, every time they were together, he managed to lift her spirits and make her forget the deception that shrouded their entire relationship. . .even if only for a little while. And his kiss! She touched her fingers to her lips, reliving each and every breathtaking moment. It was everything she'd imagined and more. But that was where she had to watch out. If she wasn't careful, the sincerity in those deep-brown eyes of his would be her undoing. She had to figure out a way to tell him the truth. They'd come too far for her to turn back now.

Chapter 7

Anna flattened her copy of the *Rocky Mountain News* out on the counter in front of her. The *Bulletin* provided all the local news and even a sampling of news from throughout the region, but the *News* and the *Denver Post* covered so much more. She was glad Mr. Evans carried all three in his pharmacy.

Of course, a more fanciful reason for wanting the *News* was the serial she'd discovered just two months ago. She couldn't stay away from it. *The Loves of Lady Arabella.* Far different than her somewhat solitary life—until recently, that is—the story of Arabella's many courtships helped Anna get lost for a brief time in someone else's life, fictional though it was.

She finished the latest installment and was about to turn the page when the page opposite the serial caught her eye. Anna froze. Her mouth went dry, and her heart pounded in her chest. No, no! Not yet. She wasn't ready. But that didn't seem to matter to the truth printed for all the world to see.

There, in incriminating black and white was her photo staring back at her. Just above that was a photo of Maggie with Graham Middleton, the successful railroad investor who had tried on three separate occasions to court Maggie, only to be dismissed. Anna read the announcement of their pending nuptials to take place by summer's end. Obviously, his persistence had paid off.

But why was her name and image included with the banns? And how had it reached a paper this far west? She skimmed the brief article. Mention was made of her standing in attendance with her sister once she returned from her travels abroad. Anna frowned. Travels abroad? Is that what Mother and Father were calling this new life of hers? They must have been the ones to get this message printed in the local papers. How else would the editors find this kind of story?

Oh, no! Did Trevor read the *News*? He was voracious with the *Wall Street Journal* and the *New York Times* back home. Did he also stay connected to the papers of the larger cities and regions, as she did?

Before she could ponder it further, the door to her shop opened, and there stood Trevor, holding a folded-up copy of the same paper spread out in front of her. At least she had her answer. By the hurt and anger blazing in his eyes, though, she wished she didn't.

"Why didn't you tell me?" His voice held a measure of contempt mixed with control. He took several slow steps toward her, each one feeling like a nail in the coffin burying her with her deception.

"Trevor, please, let me explain." Though she really had no right to expect him to.

"Oh, so *now* you're ready?" Thinly veiled anger laced every word as he stood in front of her, only the counter between them. "Tell me, Miss Clairmont, just how long were you going to wait before telling me the truth?" He narrowed his eyes, slapped down the paper he held, and rammed his finger at her likeness. "Or should I call you, Miss St. Claire?"

Anna had no words. She'd rehearsed her speech dozens of times over the past several weeks since he'd first walked back into her life. Never had she imagined this would be how Trevor found out. A dull ache formed at her temples, and her stomach twisted in knots. She opened her mouth then closed it. Still, no words came. She swallowed once, twice, three times, trying to restore moisture to her mouth and lips. She had to get something out, before he turned around and walked out of her life forever.

"I wanted to tell you yesterday," she finally managed, though her voice sounded hoarse, even to her. "But I couldn't."

"So instead you allowed me to believe you were someone you're not, all the while toying with my affections? From what I now remember, I would have expected more of you."

"That's not it at all!"

She could see she'd hurt him deeply. He tried to hide it behind his anger, but the pain was there in his eyes and in his face. And he had every right. Could she blame him? But he had to understand.

"I was scared," she blurted.

The anger dissipated one or two degrees. "Scared of me?"

"No," she replied. "Scared you'd reject me and walk away. . .like you did so many times before." Anna boldly reached out to touch his hand lying on the counter between them. "But after yesterday, I wasn't scared anymore. I was going to tell you the next time I saw you," she said softly.

Trevor tensed then clenched his hand into a fist and jerked it out from underneath hers. The anger returned. "I guess we'll never know now, will we?"

He snatched up his copy of the paper, spun around, and stormed toward the door.

"Trevor!" she called. "Please, don't go." She moved from behind the counter and toward him then stopped. "Not like this," she added, almost in a whisper.

He had his hand on the doorknob but let go at her words. His arm fell back to his side, and his head dropped to his chest.

Anna could imagine the inner battle that waged within him. She'd experienced it herself more than once, each time she would introduce a gentleman caller to Maggie. Maggie would turn on her flirtatious charm, and Anna would be forgotten. Betrayed more than once by her own sister.

As if he'd suddenly remembered how she'd hurt him, Trevor again grabbed the doorknob, only this time, he turned it and yanked it open. He'd just stepped over the threshold when what sounded like a small explosion vibrated through the walls and shook the ground.

Trevor glanced over his shoulder at her, and she started to move toward him. A shout came from down the street.

"Fire!"

Trevor jumped into action and took off running. Anna grabbed the door as it started to close and stepped out onto the sidewalk. She saw the other merchants racing down the street. A flurry of activity commenced near the firehouse across the way. Flames drew Anna's eyes to the Denver Hotel, not too far from where she stood. What in the world had happened? What was that explosion?

Black smoke curled into the sky as the fingers of the fire clawed at the windows above the ground floor. Screams for help rose above the crackle of the roaring fire and the shouts of the townspeople.

The hotel guests! Anna finally found momentum and an adrenaline rush. Some of them were bound to sustain burns in varying degrees before the volunteer firemen could get to them. She had tended to the wounds of many back in New York when she'd volunteered with one of the hospitals. Maybe she could help now.

She raced down the sidewalk, pausing only to weave her way through the throngs of townspeople gathered. Most stood back and allowed the firemen room to work, but as soon as Anna broke through to the front of the mass, she caught sight of a familiar sandy-haired cowboy grabbing coarse burlap blankets from a pile someone hastily dumped on the street. As she passed the various merchants, miners, and piles of supplies, only one thought crossed her mind.

Please, God, don't let it spread too far.

The firemen focused their efforts on the biggest flames, and the some of the men pitching in to help formed a water brigade to add to what the fire truck could offer. Trevor tossed blankets to other men, and they worked to squelch any errant flames attempting to spread to the neighboring buildings. As the fire was forced back, some of the firemen were able to enter the building.

"Use them to beat out any new burning from the sparks," he called, his commanding authority inciting action, as usual.

As the first victims were brought out of the hotel, Anna leaped into action. Right at the same time Trevor did. They ran into each other at the edge of the inferno.

"Someone help the victims over here!"

Anna and Trevor took a step at the same time. She looked up at him. "I volunteered at a hospital," she shouted above the noise.

He hesitated only a moment as he held her gaze. Then he snatched a pail of water from somewhere and grabbed her hand, pulling her with him toward where they were taking the burn victims.

"Here. You can use this to help," Trevor commanded, thrusting a wet cloth in her direction.

Anna nodded, and in silence, the two of them worked side by side until they'd tended to all those who sustained injuries. When the last spark was extinguished, all those gathered breathed a sigh of relief. Black soot and scorch marks now covered the entire front of the hotel and small areas of neighboring buildings in the immediate area. The sudden halt to the frantic pace almost seemed eerie.

Thanks to the quick work of all who came to help, no lives were lost. Those with more serious injuries were taken to the doctors' offices. As the flurry of activity settled and people returned to what they'd been doing, Anna risked a glance at Trevor. He sat back on his heels, gathering the soiled cloths from all around him and dumping them in a bucket.

Anna reached for a rag at the same time Trevor did, and their hands brushed against each other. She shivered and he froze. Then he finally looked her in the eyes again. This time, instead of anger, there was resignation. Anna didn't know what to make of that. Was it a good or a bad thing? Before she had time to guess, Trevor dipped one of the cloths in a nearby bucket of water and slowly brought it up to her face.

◆━ ・ ━◆

Tenderly, Trevor wiped the smudges from Anna's cheeks and forehead. She closed her eyes at his touch. Her chest rose and fell in rapid succession. She licked her lips then drew her lower lip between her teeth. He reached out with his other hand and tucked a few errant strands of hair behind her ear then ran his fingers under her long braid and drew it over her shoulder.

When he paused, Anna opened her eyes.

The time had come. The moment of reckoning hovered over his head like a cloud. They had to talk about this. They had to get everything out in the open.

God, please give me strength and the right words to say.

Oh, how easily that had come to him. And it was all because of the woman who sat in front of him. How could he have allowed his anger to get the better of him?

Without a word, he slowly stood and drew Anna up with him. Taking her hand in his, he led her down the nearest alley and out the other side to where there was a small courtyard with a variety of shrubs and flowering plants forming a perimeter around several tables, chairs, and benches. He guided her to one of the benches and took a seat next to her. Even with smudges still on her face, Anna was beautiful. How in the world had he missed seeing her all those years before?

With care and caution, he reached for her hands and held them in his own, resting them where their knees touched.

Anna lifted her head to look at him. A soft smile formed on her lips. "Trevor," she whispered.

Trevor freed one of his hands and reached up to touch two fingers to her lips. "No, not yet," he softly implored.

Anna closed her eyes for a moment. The soft sounds of her breathing accompanied the faint sounds from the cleanup crew near the fire. When her eyelids opened again, the same doubt, uncertainty, and fear he felt was reflected back at him.

"Trevor, I have something—"

"Shh." He cut her off and again touched two fingers to her lips then removed his hand. She stared at him with doelike innocence. "Let me go first."

An almost imperceptible nod followed his entreaty. All right. He had her undivided attention. Now what should he say?

"Anna, I have been repeating the moment I saw that article in my mind over

387

and over, along with how I confronted you just a little bit ago. And I owe you an apology." There, that wasn't such a bad start. "We both have our reasons for doing what we did. I was wrong for getting so angry with you. You deserve more than that." He implored her with his gaze and gave her hand a tender squeeze. "Can you ever forgive me?"

It hadn't come out the way he'd rehearsed it in his head, but it could still work. At least he hoped it would.

Anna's hand moved beneath his, and she turned her wrist to interlace their fingers. He glanced down at their joined hands then back at her face. Tenderness replaced the uncertainty of a moment before.

"Yes," she whispered. "I was also wrong," she continued, "for being dishonest and even resenting you a little for your rejection. . .even if you had no idea you'd done it. Can you forgive me?"

He didn't hesitate. "Yes. Of course I will." How could he deny her what she'd just given him?

The tension in Anna's fingers released, and her expression seemed much more at peace. As she started to close her eyes, Trevor tightened his hold on her wrist. He had to get this out now, or he might lose his nerve.

"There—there's one more thing. Anna, it took temporarily relocating more than halfway across the country to make me realize just how special you are to me. I'm a fool for not seeing it sooner." He sought her gaze and held it. "I do remember you from all those years ago, but I didn't see you for who you truly are. Maybe I wasn't ready. I don't know. I'm also not the same man I was then. What I do know now is I don't want to lose you again."

A sharp gasp followed his declaration. This was it. He had to say it now.

"Anna, I love you. I believe the first seeds were planted when we were first introduced. But it took me getting away from that life, gaining a new perspective. I had to see you in a completely different light to really *see* you." He raised his free hand and gently caressed her cheek. "You've opened my eyes to so many things now. Things that were shrouded by the demands of my job and the people I thought were important. I owe you a great deal of thanks for that."

Her lips moved, but no sound came out. Then she seemed to find her voice.

"Trevor. I love you, too."

This was going far better than he thought it would. He grinned and slid to one knee on the ground. "Then, will you marry me and rescue me from the endless Ferris wheel that was getting me nowhere before I met you?"

"Yes!" she said without hesitation.

Trevor rose and leaned over her to give her a quick peck on the mouth. He pulled back to look down into her face. Her blue eyes darkened, and she licked her lips again. She raised her chin ever so slightly, issuing him a silent invitation. Lowering his lips, he positioned himself for a better kiss this time.

When he finally pulled back, all the emotions he felt reflected back at him in the depth of her eyes. Never had he ever felt like this with any other woman. Returning to his seat on the bench beside her, Trevor gave her hands a squeeze.

Amusement danced in her eyes. "I guess my sister won't be the only one with banns posted in the paper."

He chuckled. "No, I guess not." He gave her a sly grin. "I suppose I should make plans to call my editor friend back in New York." Trevor raised her hand to his lips and kissed her knuckles, peering at her over the tops of them. "Your parents aren't the only ones who can get an announcement in multiple papers in various states."

She giggled. "I have a feeling you have even more tricks up your sleeve, and I look forward to discovering them as we plan our future together."

He shrugged. They could discuss the details of the wedding and their engagement another time. God had smiled down upon them and given them a second chance at love, in spite of their bumbled attempts to handle things themselves. Right now, they had the realization of their shared love, and their relationship had been restored. Everything else would have to wait.

Amber Stockton has been crafting and embellishing stories since childhood, when she was accused of having an overly active imagination and cited with talking entirely too much. Today she has honed those skills to become an award-winning author and speaker, working in an industry where she helps others become their best from the inside out. She lives with her husband and fellow author, Stuart Vaughn Stockton, in Colorado. They have a daughter and a son and a vivacious flat-coat retriever named Roxie. Her writing career began as a columnist for her high school and college newspapers. She is a member of American Christian Fiction Writers and Historical Romance Writers. Three of her novels have won annual reader's choice awards, and in 2009, she was voted #1 favorite new author for the Heartsong Presents book club. She has sold twenty-one (21) books so far and is represented by Tamela Murray of the Steve Laube Agency. Learn more about her at her web site: www.amberstockton.com

What the
Heart Sees

by Liz Tolsma

Dedication

To the ladies in the Hartford History Room at the Jack Russell Memorial Library in Hartford, Wisconsin, especially Shirley and Bev, for all the help you gave me in writing this book and for the good work you do in preserving the area's history so future generations might appreciate their home town.

Chapter 1

Do you see the hat Mrs. Ebert has on this morning?" Florence Davis slid across the slick pew in the church balcony and whispered in Miriam Bradford's ear. "It must be from the '20s. And that color. Is it orange or salmon?"

Miriam elbowed her friend. "Hush. With rationing, none of us has had a new Sunday hat in years. She must have remade it."

The soft strains of the organ filled the church as Mrs. Ulhein struck the first chords of the prelude. The reverberations of the instrument filled Miriam. Quiet descended on the congregation as they bowed their heads in a silent prayer of preparation.

Down below, the creaking of a door opening broke the worshipful silence, followed by the clomp of many feet. Miriam leaned over the railing. A line of men dressed in blue pants, blue shirts, and work boots entered and snaked their way down the aisle to the front two pews. Florence's mother, the pastor's wife, scooted over on the well-worn bench to make room for them.

"Those are some German POWs they're holding at the Schwartz." Florence's voice held a breathless quality.

Germans. Miriam's mouth went dry. A certain young man's face flashed in front of her eyes, cinema style. Hair the color of Coca-Cola. Eyes the color of the Alpine sky. A smile that gave new meaning to the phrase "swoon worthy". . . And the exhilaration of being in his airplane, away from the craziness on the earth below. He'd begun to teach her to fly. And she'd loved it.

She shook her head to dislodge the image from her brain and studied the group of men marching forward. An American soldier in his dress uniform brought up the rear, no weapon in his hands.

She couldn't make out anything more than the backs of their heads. Some light-haired, some darker. Some tall, some short. Some stockier than others. "Why are they here?"

Florence strained forward. "Going to church, of course. Some say they are barbarians. My father wants to evangelize them, so he obtained permission for them to attend."

"They aren't."

"Aren't what?"

"Barbarians."

"That's right. You spent that summer in Germany with your mom just before the war. I keep forgetting."

The organist swelled the instrument's volume.

"Some of them are very good people caught up in circumstances beyond their control."

The organ fell silent, and Pastor Davis took to the pulpit. Five years ago, she sat in a church in Germany, not much different from this one. A small group of devout believers gathered for Sunday worship, just as these Christians did.

That golden, glorious summer. The one that would live in her memory forever. She sighed. Heat rushed into her face. She struggled to follow the pastor's sermon. Not a word of it sunk into her brain.

What she wouldn't give to go back and experience that again. The adventure. The exhilaration. And. . . Thoughts best not meditated on in the Lord's house.

Before she knew it, the pastor pronounced the benediction and released the congregation. The line of prisoners stood and turned.

Her breath caught in her throat. Her heart ceased beating.

Oh applesauce, it couldn't be. Her mind had to be playing tricks. He couldn't be here. Impossible.

But she hadn't forgotten the square set of his chin, the heavy eyebrows, the slight widow's peak.

"Paul."

◆—————◆

Paul Albrecht rose with his fellow prisoners of war in the quaint brick church lined with stained-glass windows. Almost like home. But this was Hartford, Wisconsin, in America. Where Miriam lived. She'd left him her address after that one amazing summer and told him to write. Then the world went crazy.

He gazed at the folks gathered for worship. Was she here? Probably not. The town boasted a good number of churches. And the chance that she was still unmarried was none. Striking auburn hair, deep dimples, a ready laugh. She would have had many suitors. All that mattered was her happiness.

That's what he told himself. But if he chanced to see her with a ring gracing her finger and a child clinging to her skirts, it would cut more than a bullet to the chest.

A quick glance around. Women wearing small hats with netting gabbed at the end of one pew. A group of men huddled beside each other at the back of the sanctuary, their hands stuffed in their pockets. A gaggle of girls giggled in unison.

And every person in the place stared open-eyed at the group of German soldiers.

Like they were a bunch of convicts paraded through town.

He shivered.

"Look at those men. What a disgrace. That they could show their faces in the Lord's house." The gray-haired woman who spoke stood tight-lipped, her arms crossed in front of her ample bosom.

"My dear late husband lost a limb to them in the Great War." Another woman, this one blond, shook her head.

The first woman nodded. "We'll have to speak to Pastor Davis about letting them return. It's not right."

The group of men pushed Paul forward. He shuffled along, his concentration on the well-worn wood floor. Even if Miriam was here, she would want nothing to do with the likes of him. Time and circumstances turned them from sweethearts to enemies.

He moved under the balcony and toward the exit. He had so hoped. . .

But it wasn't meant to be.

He swallowed.

"Paul."

He almost missed the soft, incredulous word in the din of conversation around him. He jerked his attention upward, to where the voice originated. Nothing but a blur of green.

Her favorite color.

He must have imagined it.

He exited the sanctuary to the fellowship hall in the rear of the church. The crowd parted like the Red Sea for the POWs to pass. In front of him, the paneled wood door stood open, the fresh, crisp fall air rushing inside.

"Paul."

Nein, he had to be hearing things. He couldn't look. Perhaps if he didn't turn around, he wouldn't be disappointed. Wouldn't get that crushing feeling in his chest.

"Paul, wait."

He had to know. He turned.

And there she stood, her red hair falling in curls around her cheeks, a dimpled smile cresting over her face. As beautiful as he remembered every day of these past five years.

"Oh, Paul, it is you." She rushed forward, her green-and-white polka-dot dress swishing around her knees. About a meter before she reached him, she stopped short.

"Miriam?"

"What are you doing here?"

"The Americans captured me. When they said I would come to Wisconsin. . ."

"The opening of the camp has been the talk of the town. But of all the soldiers that could have come, it's you." She whipped a handkerchief from her pocket and dabbed her eyes.

In many ways, she was the girl he remembered. Vivacious, beautiful, charming. Still, she held back. She didn't approach any closer but fisted her hands at her sides.

The guard came alongside them. "Let's move out."

Miriam stepped backward. "I should be going. It was great to see you again."

"Miriam, wait."

She paused.

"You are fine?"

"Yes." She studied her tidy fingernails. "And you?"

"All in one piece. I got through with no injury."

"Praise the Lord. When you didn't write, I thought for sure. . ."

"I was pressed into duty and lost your address."

"You know each other?" The guard's blue eyes widened.

Paul nodded. *"Ja."* He wouldn't elaborate on how. That precious memory he kept tucked away for safekeeping.

"You look well." Her voice softened. "Wonderful, in fact."

"You do, too. How do things go for you?"

A sandy-haired young man sidled up to Miriam, drew her into a sideways hug, and claimed possession of her. "Who is this, dear?"

"Someone I once knew."

"A relative?"

"No." She didn't say more. Perhaps she didn't remember that blissful season they spent together. How could he have expected a woman like Miriam to keep an impossible promise to always love a man on the other side of the battle lines? He stepped backward. "It was nice to see you." He measured his tone. "Take care of yourself."

He marched ahead.

"Paul." She chased after him. The weight of the stares of everyone in the building bore down on him. "It's not like that."

He kept walking.

"Miriam, get away from those men."

"But, Daddy."

Another reason it would have been better if he had never seen Miriam Bradford again.

Chapter 2

Miriam fled the fellowship hall, half in pursuit of Paul, half in flight from her father and Arthur. By the time she struggled through the crowd gathered around the entrance to watch the prisoners leave, he was gone. The prisoners were on their way down the small town's brick-building lined street.

The crisp fall breeze cooled her heated cheeks. She breathed in and released the air little by little. But her hands shook like poplar leaves.

He was here.

"What on earth is going on?"

At Florence's question, Miriam spun around. "I saw him."

"Him? *The* him?"

"Yes."

"The man who stole your heart? I can see why." Florence batted her pale lashes. "He is handsome."

"I can't believe he's here. What are the chances?"

"Very slim. But not unheard of. Remember, I told you about my uncle Karl who showed up on my mother's cousin's farm a couple of months back."

Miriam turned to catch another glimpse of Paul. The line of men snaked around the corner and out of sight. She sighed. "I'm in shock. I don't know what to do or say."

"Are you going to go see him?" Florence almost squealed.

"At the Schwartz ballroom?"

"My father told me they have visiting hours every Sunday. You could spend some time with him."

"There's another complication." She gestured in Arthur's direction. He stood in the church's doorway, a scowl marring his ruddy, boylike features. "To my father, he might as well be my fiancé."

Arthur Powell joined them, doffed his black hat, and nodded at Florence. "Good day. Always nice to see you." He redirected his attention to Miriam. "Isn't it time to go? The show is over."

"Miriam knows Paul from her time in Germany."

She held herself back from elbowing Florence in the ribs.

"Just remember, he's the enemy now." Arthur finger-combed his greased-back red hair. "You'd do well to steer clear of them. I wouldn't want anything to happen to you. Come on, Miriam. I'm hungry for dinner. Good day, Florence." He placed his cap back on his head.

"Go ahead, Arthur. I'll catch up to you at home."

"I can wait."

"No, it'll be awhile. Florence and I have some things to discuss."

"If you insist." With a huff, Arthur sauntered away.

"I wish Daddy would stop inviting him over."

"Just tell him."

"Tell me what?"

Miriam jumped and clutched her chest. This time, her father stood behind her.

"Didn't you hear me earlier, Miriam? You raced out of church like a dog after a truck."

"That was Paul Albrecht. The man I met in Germany. You know about him."

"Your mother should never have encouraged such a relationship. She should never have gone to that God-forsaken country in the first place. The trip took her life."

The back of Miriam's throat burned.

"Let's get going home. We don't want to keep Arthur waiting. There's a fine young man."

A fine young man, indeed. Solid. Dependable. Boring. He could see no farther than the farm that enabled him to stay out of the military. She had bigger plans. But Daddy liked him. And encouraged him too much. She couldn't conjure up any excitement for him.

"Have a nice afternoon." Florence flashed Miriam a crooked grin and waved.

Miriam shot her a narrow-gaze look then climbed aboard the old farm wagon with Daddy. He clucked to the horses, and they plodded toward their own farm a couple of miles outside town. Several times throughout the trip, she opened her mouth to tell him to stop inviting Arthur to the house. But she couldn't form the words. He would be angry, and probably very disappointed. Like he was when he'd forbidden her from joining the WACs.

She had only relented because of his heart palpitations. The doctor said any upset might bring on a heart attack.

Situated among dried cornstalks, their white farmhouse appeared in the distance, a big red barn behind it. Quintessential Wisconsin. Nothing compared to the rows upon rows of ornamented stone buildings that crowded Germany's cities, or the quaint beam-and-plaster Alpine chalets.

Different. Unique. Exotic.

She inhaled and forced herself to speak. "Daddy—"

"I don't want to hear one word about that Nazi you spoke to this morning. Your mother may have been soft with you, but she's not here now. And I will not have my daughter involved with the likes of him."

Not wanting to cause Daddy any heart trouble, she shut her mouth. But she couldn't shut her heart.

◆—◆

The hum of voices swirled around Paul, and the aromatic sting of tanning chemicals tickled his nose as he wiped the sweat from his brow. While the work at W. B. Place

Tannery wasn't as grand or adventurous as flying a plane as he had in the Luftwaffe, it kept him and his fellow prisoners occupied. And the American government put most of the money he earned into a savings account. That would go toward getting his own plane after the war.

Before the war. After the war. The entire world defined time that way. But not him. Well, maybe he did, but he distinguished time as before Miriam and after Miriam. Before her, he'd been—how did the Americans say it—a lone ranger. On his motorcycle, on his own. After her, he dreamed of nothing more than having her ride behind him, gripping him around the middle. Or flying beside him.

He forced his attention to the job in front of him. His distant dream faded even more after Sunday. How could he have expected her to wait for him? Ever believed that her feelings for him wouldn't change, despite being on opposite sides of a worldwide conflict?

The whistle blew, indicating the end of their shift. In a short amount of time, their guards had them piled into the back of an old truck and drove them through the center of town on their way to the round ballroom containing their barracks. Paul pulled his coat tighter. Even early in the season, a cold wind blew. He studied the shiny storefront windows as they puttered along.

Werner Frank sat beside him. "You've been somber these past few days."

"Ja, I suppose I have been."

"Does it have anything to do with that beautiful redhead you chatted with after church on Sunday?"

"It might. Do we have to talk about it?"

"We do, when she has you so down."

Paul shrugged. "There's not much to say. I met her back home in '39. It was nothing more than a youthful crush."

"An infatuation wouldn't make you this glum."

"She has a new beau. That's the way it should be. Expecting her to wait until the war ends and all is forgiven between our countries would be foolish."

"But you did."

"What can I say? I'm foolish."

"Nein, you aren't. But in love, that you are."

"She has a new man in her life. And that's the end of that."

"Do you want it to be?"

As the truck's gears ground, Paul broke his gaze from the bungalow-style houses and turned to the dark-haired man beside him. "I'm surprised they didn't tap you for the SS. You would make an excellent interrogator. You're persistent enough." The truck halted for a mother and her large, unruly brood of little ones to cross the street.

"Paul."

That voice again. The one he couldn't forget, even if he wanted to. Which he didn't. He peered over his shoulder. Miriam hustled in their direction, her book bag bouncing on her hip, her unbuttoned green coat flapping in the wind. She had this half-restrained, half-exuberant way of moving. And speaking. And doing anything she did.

That's why he loved her.

He groaned and turned back.

"Paul." Within a second, she caught up with them, breathless.

His heart lurched. "Miriam, please, don't make this harder on either of us than it has to be."

She touched his arm. Even through his coat, her touch was soft and gentle. "It's not like that."

Soon enough, the truck would roll along. "When we met, we were young and naive. We never dreamed the world would become engulfed in war. But it did, and that's the way it is. Nothing will ever be the same."

"Maybe not."

He gave her a small smile. "You have your new boyfriend."

The young mother still occupied the middle of the street as one straggler bent to pick up something. "Come on, Willy. We have to hurry."

"My father wants me to marry the neighboring farmer so our property will stay in the family, but he's stuffy and boring."

"Isn't that as it should be?"

"I don't know."

"Besides, your father doesn't approve of me." His stomach dropped like a broken lift.

"He doesn't understand."

The woman and her children stepped up the curb, and the truck lurched forward. After a block or so, Paul turned around. Miriam stood in the same spot, her shoulders drooped.

Chapter 3

December 1944

Miriam pulled her mother's dishes decorated with bluebirds from the cabinet and set two of them on the scarred farmhouse table in the middle of the kitchen. Each day she performed this chore her heart squeezed a little. Mama should be here.

The wood floors squeaked as Daddy entered the room. The sweet tobacco smoke of his pipe announced his presence. "Put on another plate."

She narrowed her eyes and stared.

"Don't give me that look. Yes, Arthur is coming. I expect you to be nice and spend some time with him. If you would get to know him, you would see he's a fine young man. He'll get those silly notions of flying in an airplane out of your head."

If she heard once more about Arthur being a fine young man, she might scream. "We went to school together. I know him."

"Good." As if that settled everything. "I'll get the checkerboard set up." He left the kitchen.

She had to restrain herself from slamming the plate onto the table. Didn't he see? She could never spend evenings playing checkers in front of the fire. She placed the silverware beside each plate like Mama had taught her. "I wish you were here. You could talk to Daddy for me. Make him see what I've been trying to tell him."

She went to the stove and stirred the pot of stew. Not much meat to work with these days, but the starchy fragrance of potatoes and the sweet aroma of carrots filled the room. Her stomach rumbled.

"Ah, you're hungry."

She jumped and spun around, pressing her midsection. "Arthur. I didn't hear you come in."

Color flooded his pasty face until it almost matched that of his red hair. "Sorry. I didn't mean to startle you."

She tipped her head. "Everyone does these days. I don't know what's wrong with me."

He pulled out the bench at the table, sat, and leaned on the tabletop. "It's those Germans at the Schwartz. How unnerving to have them so close. You never know when one of them, or even a group of them, might escape and murder us in our sleep."

She covered her giggle with a cough. "You can't believe that. They're not dangerous."

"Not dangerous? They're the enemy."

"They don't have weapons."

"That wouldn't stop them. I've read the newspapers and seen the newsreels. They're

401

lethal and ruthless. And don't forget my brothers."

"I'm sorry." Charlie lay in a grave in France, and Fred languished in a German prison.

"Any one of them could have pulled the trigger that cost my brother his life."

"You don't know that. Not all of them are cold-blooded killers. I'm sure they wouldn't hold dangerous men here."

"Even so, you be careful. Nazis can't be trusted."

She could trust Paul. Couldn't she? A shiver raced through her. Yes, she could. He was a good man. Always very gentle with her. She stirred the stew. He wouldn't hurt anyone.

Arthur stood behind her. "He fought against us."

Had Arthur read her thoughts? "He couldn't control being drafted." She opened the oven and tapped the top of the bread. Hollow sounding. Perfect. She pulled out the loaf.

"Don't be so sure."

"Here." She handed him the stew pot. "Please put this on the table."

Throughout the meal, Daddy and Arthur chatted with each other, paying her little attention. Not until after evening devotions did Arthur speak to her. "Let me help with the dishes. We can get to our game faster."

The radio in the other room crackled to life as Daddy fiddled with the dial to find *The Inner Sanctum*, his favorite show. Much too scary for her. "Thanks, but I'm going to finish these and go upstairs. I have a pounding headache." Ever since he'd walked into the kitchen, her temples throbbed.

"You don't want to play one game?" A lost puppy couldn't match the sadness in his green eyes.

"Maybe another night."

"I'll dry." Arthur grabbed a dish towel, helped her finish, and then left. She tiptoed through the living room so she didn't disturb her father.

"Where's your beau?" He puffed on his pipe.

"He went home. I'm not feeling well. And he's not my beau."

"Because you don't encourage him. What's become of you?"

"Nothing. I don't see Arthur as my husband. He's so vanilla pudding when I want a chocolate éclair."

"I don't know what that means." Daddy rubbed his furrowed forehead. "But the next time Arthur comes over, you'll spend the evening with him."

The pounding behind her eyes intensified.

◆•————•◆

"Rise and shine. Everyone up."

At the guard's call, Paul rolled over on his bed and rubbed his eyes. He forced his lids to open. Around the spacious, circular room, bunks lined the walls. A large stage occupied one wall, a long bar another. Around him, men groaned and pulled themselves from under their warm blankets. Once home, he planned to sleep and sleep and never have anyone wake him again.

He jumped from the bunk and pulled on his pants and boots.

Beside him, Werner did the same thing. "Another day of the grind."

"Tanning hides is not what I envisioned myself doing. Glamorous, it is not."

"But a sight better than fighting."

Paul shrugged. "Part of me is glad to be safe, out of the fray. But that's not patriotic. And what about our countrymen, still spilling their blood for an unjust cause?"

"Therein lies the dilemma." Werner buttoned his shirt, and they crossed the hall to the dark-paneled dining room for breakfast. "God has a reason for each of us to be here right now."

A vision of Miriam, dimples in her cheeks, her auburn hair streaming behind her in the wind, flashed through Paul's mind. Was that the reason that the Lord brought him here, to this place, at this time? Her father's disapproving voice rumbled in his brain.

"Hey, Albrecht, when are we going to have another soccer match?" Jorgen Baum slapped Paul on the back as he walked by. The beefy man's strike stung Paul's shoulder.

"In this weather? It snowed last night." Had they really been here long enough for the seasons to turn?

"Prison making you soft?" Jorgen and a few of his comrades chortled.

"Fine. If you want a match in the snow, we can have one."

"Next weekend works for me. In the yard. Maybe the locals will come, and we can show them German superiority. Maybe even your pretty little girlfriend." Baum strode away.

Paul clenched his fists, but Werner shook his head. "A fight isn't worth it. Why did you agree to the match?"

"Captain Atkins asked me to join their team and keep an eye on them. Try to keep them in line."

"I hope you know what you're doing."

Paul's oatmeal settled like a lump in his stomach. Werner's words reverberated in his ears as they climbed aboard the old farm truck for the trip to the tannery.

The early-season snow transformed the landscape from brown monotony to white magic. The fluffy flakes reflected the sun, a dazzling display of light. Paul squinted against the brightness. He sat in the front seat and stared out the window. Even though it didn't boast the mountains of his hometown, this place wasn't bad. You could even call it pretty.

Up ahead, a woman trudged, bent against the wind, a red-and-blue scarf over her head, the hem of her green coat swinging as she walked a familiar walk. He couldn't keep away the smile that tugged at his lips.

They approached Miriam, and he rolled down his window.

The captain bumped his arm. "Close that. It's chilly."

"I want to say good morning."

"Is that your girl? The one I've heard about?"

"She's not my girl, but yes."

The captain blew the truck's horn, an old-fashioned *ah-ooga*.

Miriam turned, shielded her eyes, and walked at the same time. Before Paul greeted her, her feet slipped. With a wild flailing of her arms and legs, she thunked to the ground. "Ouch."

Paul grabbed the door handle, his throat tight.

Chapter 4

S top the truck." Paul grabbed the door handle.

The captain peered at him and scrunched his eyebrows together.

"We have to help her."

The guard pulled to the curb and slid to a halt. Paul jumped out and sprinted to where Miriam lay sprawled on the ground. "Are you hurt?"

Unshed tears sparkled in her leaf-green eyes. "My right ankle throbs."

He knelt beside her. "Let me look." He untied the laces of her black snow boot and tugged on it.

"Ah, ah, ah." She squirmed away from him.

"That much it hurts?"

She nodded.

"Let's go to the truck. It will be easier to see. And then you don't sit on the cold, wet ground."

"No, I'm fine."

Before she could object further, he swooped her into his arms.

Just like he had that long-ago summer.

"This is like time has stood still." She rested against his shoulder.

"Your feet got cold in the mountain brook."

"You carried me to the bank. And picked edelweiss."

"Leontopodium alpinum."

"You're still interested in botany."

He bent down to kiss her, much as he had done that memorable day.

"Albrecht, how is she?"

The captain's words snapped him back to attention. "She hurt her foot, sir." He set her on the truck's seat and slid off her boot. Ugly black-and-blue bruises colored her ankle. He twisted the foot from side to side.

"Ow, that hurts."

"Ja, but it's not broken."

She crossed her arms over her chest. "And you're a doctor now?"

"Nein, but I learned first aid in the military."

She grabbed her boot. As she slid it on, she sucked in her breath. "I have to get to school before I'm late."

"You aren't walking." Paul turned to his captain. "Can we take her there?"

"Load her in. I'll soothe the plant manager's ruffled feathers."

Paul crinkled his forehead, not understanding the idiom.

Miriam slid over on the seat so that the driver and Paul sandwiched her between them. "Thank you for the ride. And the medical attention."

He leaned over and whispered in her ear. "You don't have to be so formal. You weren't a minute ago."

She pulled a handkerchief from her book bag and dabbed her eyes. "Don't make this harder than it has to be."

He rubbed her arm. "I didn't mean to upset you."

"I'm in an impossible situation. Can't you see?"

Unfortunately, he did. "Is it you or your father?"

"He doesn't comprehend. My mother died a few weeks after we returned from Germany."

"*Liebchen*, I'm sorry. I didn't know."

"He blames her death on the trip. And on the country, and everyone who is German. He's afraid to lose me."

"Love doesn't fade away."

"I know."

His heart vaulted. Did that mean she still loved him? "Give him time."

The driver pulled up to the school. Outside, children swung on the swings and ran about in the fresh snow. Like children anywhere. Paul flung the door open then helped her out before turning to the captain. "Let me bring her in. I'll be right back."

"You owe me for this one, Albrecht."

He probably did. He held Miriam by the forearm as she hopped up the steps and into the building. Several teachers swarmed her as she limped down the hall with his help.

"What happened to you, dear?" The older woman with graying hair peered through her wire-rimmed glasses.

"It's nothing. I fell and twisted my ankle." She turned to him, her face crimson. "Thank you for your assistance. I'm in good hands now."

"I'm glad I could help. Have a good day." My, did he want to kiss her. But this wasn't the time or the place. Instead, he turned to leave.

Behind him, one of the teachers huffed. "Is he one of those Germans?"

He couldn't make out Miriam's answer.

But he didn't miss the woman's retort. "I'm surprised at you. I always thought you had better sense than that."

He grimaced.

◆—•———•—◆

"I'm surprised at you. I always thought you had better sense than that." Lucy Whimple crossed her arms over her ample bosom and huffed for the second time in as many minutes.

"Yes, dear." Betty Dorne peered at Miriam through her bangs. "Fraternizing with the enemy. What must your father think?"

Miriam drew in a steadying breath. She didn't need their disapproval on top of everything. "Paul isn't the enemy."

Lucy stepped back. "You said he was from the camp."

"He is. But he isn't the enemy. He got caught up in the war, drafted into the Luft-waffe. What else could he do but join?"

"There had to be other options."

Miriam hopped in the direction of her second-grade classroom. The women fol-lowed her. "What would you have had him do? If he didn't join, he would have been arrested and killed for being a deserter."

"Sometimes you need to stand up for your principles." Lucy opened the door to Miriam's classroom and switched on the lights.

Miriam bit her tongue to stop the sharp retort that sprang to her lips. "Thank you. I believe the bell is about to ring."

Betty shook her head. A frown marred her wrinkled features. "You'd be wise to stay away from that lot, if you know what's good for you."

Betty's warning rang in her head long after she left. The bell clanged and marked the beginning of a new school day. The children streamed in and deposited their snowy coats and boots in the hall before pouring into the classroom.

Tommy Gilbert stopped at her desk. His words whistled through the gaps in his teeth. "Miss Bradford, was that a German who came to school?"

She folded her hands. "Where did you hear that?"

"Didn't have to hear it. Me and Danny saw the truck. My pops told me about them. Told me to stay away from the camp's fence. But it's fun to see what they're doing."

"You'd best obey your father." The words slipped out of her mouth before the mean-ing of them struck her. She also had a father to obey.

The morning progressed with only occasional murmurings from the children about the German prisoner who brought Miss Bradford to school. When the bell dismissed the students for lunch recess, she all but slumped at her desk.

"Knock, knock." Florence stood at her door.

"Come in."

"I have papers to grade, but I thought I'd see you instead." She pulled one of the children's chairs to Miriam's desk at the back of the classroom and sat, her knees almost level with her chest. "Throughout the morning, I've heard whispers about you and a certain POW."

Miriam pinched the bridge of her nose and sucked in a deep breath. "I'm the talk of the town." She tried to laugh, but it came out more like a strangled squeak.

"Oh, sweetie, don't bawl. You'll only get me started."

This time, Miriam's laugh was genuine. "You're the most sympathetic friend a girl could have."

"Tell me all about it."

She shared her morning plight. "How is it that he keeps popping up in the right place at the right time?"

"Aren't you glad he is?"

"Yes. No."

"Which is it?"

"I don't know. When I see him, my hands sweat, and my heart beats a little faster. Isn't that crazy?"

"Sounds to me like a woman in love." Florence sighed.

Miriam twirled her red pen. "He's an amazing man. We had a summer together I will never forget. But I don't know if I'm in love with the man or the memory."

Florence leaned across the desk. "What do you mean?"

"It's been over five years since I've seen him. So many things have changed. We're at war with his country. I've lost my mother. Things aren't the same. Am I remembering that golden period of my life and wishing to recapture those days? Or is there more to our relationship?

"And what about Arthur? And my father. He's opposed to Paul. Won't even discuss him. I'm so confused. What should I do?"

Chapter 5

The wind burned Paul's cheeks as he and the rest of the soccer players cleared the snow from the field. They were crazy for being out here, but you could only play chess and cards for so long.

"Hey, Albrecht, hurry up. Let's get this game in before dark." Jorgen Baum ran down the field with his shovel, like a train plowing through a drift.

Paul pushed his own pile. He'd show Baum who was stronger and faster.

With both teams working, they soon had the brown, frozen turf exposed. Paul set the ball in the middle of the field, and the teams lined up opposite each other. Baum gave a shrill whistle, and his team's forward kicked the ball.

The ball careened in Paul's direction. He went to pass it to a teammate when Baum pushed him. *Umph.* His backside met the unforgiving ground. "Hey, ref, how about a foul?"

Fritz Drothe shook his head and crossed his arms. Not surprising, since he was Baum's bunkmate.

Paul jumped up and ran to guard his team's goal. The opposition's forward side-stepped a defender and shot. Goal.

The game continued until sweat rolled down Paul's back despite the chilly temperatures. After several falls, his backside ached. He'd have bruises for sure. Baum's team triumphed.

As Paul headed for the ballroom, the rest of Baum's team gathered in a circle, bent together. He ambled over, but they kept their voices low. From the camp's perimeter, a guard eyed the group.

Paul crept closer until he picked up their words.

"Where shall we go?"

"There are several taverns not too far away, by the railroad tracks."

"But what are we going to use for money? We can't buy drinks with the scrip we're given."

"I have a little pocket change." Paul could almost hear Baum's grin. "And we'll charm the ladies into buying us a beer or two."

"Won't they recognize our accents?"

Baum shrugged. "Who needs words?"

Paul pushed between two men and into the center of the ring. "What are you planning?"

"Nothing for you to concern yourself with." Baum spat the words between clenched teeth.

"But it is."

"You're spying for Captain Atkins. Getting cozy with that American. Just because you speak English doesn't mean you're superior. I suspect you're a Jew lover as well." Baum marched away.

Paul followed in his wake. "I'm not going to allow you to do this. Our captors treat us well. We're better off here than we were in the fighting. I've put on weight. We have had it good. Don't do anything to mess it up. You know about the jail cell under the cellar stairs."

"You worry too much. A little pansy captured in France without firing a single shot." Baum spat at Paul's feet.

Heat rose in Paul's chest. "How dare you?"

"You aren't truly a man."

"And how do you expect to get out of here? All of you missing will be noticed."

"That's where you come in." Baum sneered. "If anyone says anything, you tell them we're in the latrine. Bad food in the dining hall."

"And if I refuse?" Paul wiped a bead of sweat from his forehead.

"You don't want to know."

Even in the dimming light, Paul didn't miss the wicked gleam in Baum's narrow-eyed gaze. The group dispersed and headed to the barracks.

Paul didn't follow. He rubbed the back of his neck and wandered in circles around the property, the white pines, *Pinus strobus*, perfuming the air. Just like at home, in the forest, where he'd hike for hours to clear his head.

He peered at the sky, pink and purple and orange tingeing the streaky clouds. "God, what do I do?"

Should he snitch and turn the men in? His midsection tightened. Rumors flew through the camp that the men who comprised the team had been SS officers. They weren't supposed to be here, in the middle of a civilian population. If the stories proved true, though, they wouldn't hesitate to carry out their threats.

But was it right to have this knowledge and keep it to himself? "Lord, help me."

"Paul? Paul? Is that you?"

He had wandered near the fence and a clump of leafless lilac bushes, *Syringa vulgaris*. That's where the soft, feminine voice emanated from. "Miriam?"

The lilac bushes' branches stabbed and scratched Miriam as she approached the fence. Since her conversation with Florence last week, the thought that she was more in love with a memory than with a man tormented her. She couldn't erase the idea from her mind.

To be fair to Arthur, and her father, she had to know.

She popped through the bushes against the low snow fence surrounding the property. For the past several nights, she'd come, holding her breath, waiting in vain for Paul to appear.

A lone figure moved about the grounds, just his height and weight, hands in his pockets as usual. His almost jaunty walk gave him away. "Paul."

The shadow approached. "Miriam?" He stood in front of her, dirty and radiating heat.

"What have you been doing?"

"Playing a game of soccer. Why are you here? How is your ankle?"

"Fine. I was out for a walk when I wandered by."

"That's not true. Your voice lowers when you fib."

She deflated. "All right, I've been here four nights in a row, hoping to catch a glimpse of you."

He leaned over the fence. "What about your father? And Arthur?"

"Daddy thinks I'm upstairs in bed. But I had to know if there's anything left between us."

"I thought about you all the time. You kept me going."

Her breath caught in her throat. She choked back tears. "Are you in love with me? Or with a snapshot in your pocket?"

"You assume I keep your picture with me."

She drew back.

He reached for her. "I was only pulling your feet."

"You mean pulling my leg."

"Ja, your leg. Of course, I had your photo with me always."

"So which do you love?"

A long silence stretched in front of them. He rubbed his eyes and puffed out a breath. "I don't know. Years have gone by. I'm not the same man you met, not that carefree spirit. If you knew the things I saw. But I pray you never do."

She rubbed his thumb and spoke in an almost indiscernible whisper. "I can't imagine." What must he have endured? "Someday, maybe, you'll share that with me."

"All I know is every time I imagine my future, I see you in it."

Her heart rate increased, like it did when she flew, and a smile escaped. "I'm glad."

"Let's get to know each other. See if the future we dreamed of is possible."

"That would be great."

"Right now, I have a dilemma."

She straightened her shoulders. "Anything I can help with?"

"If you knew someone was going to do something wrong, should you reveal those plans, even if it puts you at risk?"

"That's a tough question. What's going on?"

"The soccer players are sneaking over the fence tonight to go into town. They've threatened me if I don't cooperate. And I believe they will follow through."

"I've heard of some of the men going out dancing and such. But they'll harm you if you tell?"

"The captain put me in charge of them, to keep them from trouble. They view me as a weakling, a snitch. Yes, they wouldn't hesitate to hurt me."

"Those who go out always come back, don't they?"

"Ja. They know how good they have it. They could be hungry and shot at. Or worse."

The tang of adventure tickled her tongue. A chance to spend some time with Paul out from under watching eyes. "I have a plan."

"Do I want to hear it?"

"Sure you do. We'll follow them. Watch from a distance. If they don't get into any mischief and come right back, what harm is it? If they do, you go to the captain."

He shook his head and blew out another breath. "I don't know."

Her heart already racing, she leaned closer. "Come on. It will be fun. Remember your sense of adventure. And we'll get to spend time together."

Chapter 6

Paul peered at Miriam, her face glowing in the waning moonlight. He glanced at the guard who scanned the prison's perimeter. Should he follow the men and make sure they didn't get into trouble? That would mean breaking the rules himself. Then again, it might be the best solution. He could keep watch on them without risking his well-being.

"So, are you going to do it?"

Miriam's whispered question stirred his blood. His pulse pounded in his ears. That rush of adrenaline that hadn't coursed through him since his capture. "The war has dimmed my sense of adventure."

"This isn't battle. It's detective work. Completely different."

A rustle in the bushes broke the stillness of the evening. The players were leaving. "Fine, let's go."

With a push on his chest, Miriam held him back. "Wait a minute. The guard is walking this way." She hunkered behind the *Syringa vulgaris*.

He strolled away from the fence, toward the barracks, whistling a tune. "Good evening, Corporal Whitlock."

The dark, curly haired soldier nodded. "Isn't it a bit chilly for a turn around the park?"

"The crowded building gets stuffy. Smoky, you know."

"Maybe you should join the men in the tents on the grounds."

The POWs' ranks had swelled over the weeks until no more room remained inside. The military pitched five tents that slept six men each. "I hear the heaters you installed keep them warm. Perhaps I should." Especially if he was going to be in the habit of sneaking out.

Both men continued on their ways. After several paces, Paul spun and waited until Corporal Whitlock turned in the opposite direction. With as much speed as he could muster without drawing attention to himself, he raced to Miriam and hopped the fence.

She muffled a cry. "Let's get going."

He took her by the hand, and they sprinted around the trees, headed toward town. He squeezed her fingers. "It's been a long time since I've held your hand. How soft it is."

She brushed against him as they slowed to a walk. "This is wonderful, to be together. Close, like we were."

Though the desire to kiss her tugged at him, he didn't give in to it. They had to rebuild their relationship first. And find out what his fellow prisoners were doing. Up ahead, several shadows raced down the street. "Come on, we can't lose them."

"They're turning the corner." Miriam pointed to her right.

A brisk walk of several minutes brought them to the heart of the small downtown. The five men slipped into one of the local drinking establishments.

Miriam tugged on him. "I can't go inside. My father would have my hide."

"That's fine." He didn't indulge in the libations they offered. "We can peer through the window. Sit outside and listen and make sure they aren't wreaking havoc."

Still holding hands, they tiptoed to the window and gazed inside. The prisoners, their long coats hiding the POW stamp on their clothes, dispersed among the young ladies at various tables. Not too long afterward, all five of them settled at a table with beers in their hands and wide grins on their faces.

Paul stepped away from the window. "Are you cold?"

"A little."

He pulled Miriam close and rubbed her arms. She still melded into him just right. "Tell me about your time during the conflict."

"There isn't much to say. I served in North Africa, and the Allies captured me in France."

"Is it as horrible as they say?"

He sucked in his breath. Scattered memories flitted through him. The ping of gunfire hitting their plane. The screams of dying men. And blood. So much blood. Everywhere. He shuddered. "It's worse. No amount of training can prepare you for battle. Men hating other men so much they would kill them. Hitler feeds in more troops because he's losing them at a terrific rate."

She kissed the top of his hand. A shiver raced through him. "I'm so sorry for you."

"But God was good. I haven't suffered a single wound, not even a scratch. And now, I'm here as a captive, safe. Away from the fracas. You Americans treat your prisoners well. I cannot complain."

"And I try not to. But teaching in a small school in a little town is going to drive me crazy. I want to be doing more for the war effort."

"Why aren't you?"

"I wanted to join the WACs, but Daddy wouldn't hear of it. I'm his precious little girl, a china doll he doesn't want shattered."

"Can you blame him?" He kissed her strawberry-scented hair. "When you love someone, you don't want to let them go." If only this moment would last forever.

She snuggled closer. "When you put it that way, I do understand. Every night, I've prayed for your safety."

"And I felt every one of those prayers."

"Good."

He pictured her smiling. "Do you want to fly again someday?"

"Do I ever." She broke away from him and spun in a circle. "Away from this misery, up in the sky, among the birds and the clouds. That's freedom. Like we had that summer. Cold, crisp air in the atmosphere. There is nothing better. And you never finished instructing me how to fly."

He chuckled. "Your sense of adventure is alive and well. Teaching school must be very boring. With your spirit, you deserve to be high in the clouds. Besides, I always loved how you look in a flight suit."

"I still have that leather jacket you gave me. I keep it hidden from Daddy. If he saw it, he would flip his wig. But it smells like you. Woodsy. Outdoors. Just a bit of fuel."

"The scents every woman wants made into perfume."

"Secretly I've been checking out library books about flying. So I'm ready for after the war. At some point, Daddy is going to have to let me go."

"When I get home, I think I might like to try farming. Perhaps raise goats or sheep."

She stepped backward. "Really? Can you see yourself doing that?"

"Sure. Feet on the ground. Dirt underneath my fingernails. That's my dream."

"Well, then. . ."

He pulled her close. "Of course not, you duck. I want to be in the cockpit. Maybe with you as my copilot."

"Applesauce. I thought you were serious. But it should be the other way around. I'll be the pilot, and you can be first mate."

From inside the tavern, glass shattered. Men shouted. Ladies screeched. Paul released Miriam and dashed to the window. His stomach dove. Baum stood in the middle of the room, hands fisted as a brawny man plowed toward him. Baum swiped at the man's head, sending him careening into a table, which tipped over.

Paul grasped Miriam by the wrist. "Let's go. I have to tell the captain." His heart pounded as fast as his feet as they flew over the frozen ground and back to the Schwartz. His mouth went dry as puffs of steamy air billowed in front of him.

They skidded to a halt in front of the fence. He pecked her on the cheek. "Thank you." Without pausing, he jumped the fence, ignored the guard calling after him, and raced through the entrance, through the dining hall, and to the captain's office. He pounded on the door.

"Come in, come in." Captain Atkins stood as Paul burst through the door. "What is it?"

Paul bent over, huffing and puffing to get enough air to speak. "Five of the men from the soccer team, Baum the leader, have left the premises. They're at a tavern not far away, and there is a fight. The men are in the middle of it."

Captain Atkins pushed past Paul. "Which one?"

"I don't know the name." Paul followed the captain into the darkened dining hall. "The one on the main corner of town."

"How do you know?"

Paul drew in a ragged breath. "I—"

"Never mind. We'll talk when I'm finished dealing with Baum and his gang." Captain Atkins rushed into the hall and called for some of the other guards to come with him. They streamed out the door. The place fell silent.

Paul leaned against the telephone booth situated between the ballroom's two large doors. His hands shook, his breathing ragged.

Why had he gone out? He'd gotten himself in a heap of trouble.

But was it worth it to spend a few minutes with Miriam? To dream again?

Chapter 7

Miriam stood in the shadows, light spilling from the circular ballroom, illuminating Paul as he sprinted toward the door. Her breath puffed in a haze around her. She'd been crazy to suggest they follow the team to the tavern. Paul was sure to be in a great deal of trouble.

Daddy would say she'd acted before she thought, like she was known to do. But Paul had been in an impossible situation. With the other men bent on mischief, there was no good outcome.

On the other hand, her heart pounded in a way it hadn't since they'd flown above the German countryside in Paul's plane. The thrill, the exhilaration she had missed returned. How refreshing. Arthur paled in comparison.

Arthur. Daddy. Oh applesauce, how was she going to explain her way out of this? If she hurried home, she might beat the town's gossips who would phone Daddy and tattle.

She loped to the farm, her ankle paining her the slightest bit. The snow crunched underneath her boots. Frost bit the tip of her nose. Inside her wool mittens, she curled her fingers together for warmth. Up ahead, lamplight shone from the kitchen window. Daddy wasn't in bed. She had to get inside. It wouldn't be long before Mrs. McKinnon called. Who needed a newspaper when you had that woman?

Miriam climbed the porch steps. One of the boards creaked underneath her feet. The storm door squeaked open. "Miriam, is that you?"

Christopher Columbus, he'd caught her. "Yes, Daddy."

"Get inside, right now."

She moved past him into the warmth of the kitchen. Arthur sat at the table caressing a cup of coffee. "Arthur, what a surprise."

He glanced up, his mouth down-turned. "There you are. I came to visit you and play a game of checkers. Imagine our surprise when we discovered you weren't home."

Daddy motioned for her to sit. "I didn't hear you leave. Where have you been?"

She unwrapped her scarf, hung up her coat, and sat. "For a walk." That wasn't lying. She had been walking.

"At night?" Daddy poured himself a cup of coffee but didn't offer her any. "And in this weather?"

"I had some thinking to do and needed a breath of fresh air."

Arthur passed her his mug. "Drink that. You'll be lucky if you don't catch your death of cold."

"I had my scarf and mittens. I'll be fine."

"Really, Miriam, sometimes I think the Lord didn't give you the sense He ga
cat." Daddy shook his head like always. "At least they curl up in the warm barn at nig

"Don't snap your cap. I'm an adult and responsible for my actions." The wc
slipped from her lips. They might come back to bite her.

Right on cue, the telephone on the wall beside her jangled. Daddy answere
"Hello, Mrs. McKinnon. Nice of you to call. What can I do for you?"

Arthur furrowed his brows and stared at her. She shrugged. If she acted like
didn't know what was going on, maybe they would never find out what she'd been u

"I see. Hmm. You don't say. I see. Very interesting. Thank you for calling." Da
hung up the receiver and turned to her. "That was Mrs. McKinnon."

"Oh, really? What did she want?" Miriam's palms sweated.

"Seems some of the POWs from the Schwartz escaped tonight."

Arthur gasped.

"They made their way to a tavern where someone recognized them. A fight broke o

"I knew they shouldn't bring such dangerous men into a town filled with innoc
women and children." Arthur scraped back his chair and stood. "I'm going to cont
the army in the morning and see what can be done about moving them somewhere e
The Arizona desert sounds good."

"Really, Arthur, you're making too much of a fuss about the entire incident. A
bad apples shouldn't ruin the entire lot," Miriam said.

Daddy crossed his arms. "How did you know it was just a few?"

"I'm assuming the entire camp didn't escape."

"And Mrs. McKinnon mentioned Paul Albrecht by name. Says he was someh
involved."

"Does she have a spy inside the Schwartz?"

"I don't know. But I'm curious about something."

She glanced at Arthur then returned her attention to her father. He was going
ask the question she dreaded.

"Did you have anything to do with this?"

"You aren't suggesting I was in that bar, are you?"

"I'd better not find out that you were." A vein bulged in Daddy's neck.

She hadn't meant to upset him. And surely didn't want to cause him a stroke.

Arthur paced the kitchen. "Where did you walk to tonight?"

"Is this the Hartford Inquisition?"

He leaned on the table, his face mere inches from hers. "Why won't you tell
where you went?"

She pushed her chair back, away from Arthur and his hot breath. "Fine. You w
the truth? I'll give it to you. Ready for it?"

Daddy glared at her. "The truth would be nice. And no more stalling."

"Yes, I was at the Schwartz tonight. I went so Paul and I could talk in private."

Arthur thumped to his seat. "About what?"

"Just a few things we needed to get clear. That's all. He shared with me that overheard some of the men were planning to break out and visit the tavern. They threatened his life if he told anyone, so we followed them instead. At the first sign of trouble, Paul went to the captain."

Daddy gripped the back of the chair. "You, you were. . .in a bar? With a German?" His eyes bulged.

She jumped up. "Sit down, Daddy, and take a deep breath. This stress isn't good for you."

"You should have thought of that before you went gallivanting all over town with the enemy."

Tears flooded her eyes. She tried to choke them back, to no avail. "Paul isn't the enemy. He's not dangerous. He's not going to hurt anyone. Why won't either of you see that?"

Arthur pushed her into the chair by her shoulders. He didn't let go but squeezed. "And why can't you see that he isn't any good? Look at the trouble he's in. He's not the man you think he is."

She wrenched herself from his grasp. "You don't know him, so don't presume to tell me what he's like."

"Have you forgotten so soon that the Germans killed one of my brothers on Normandy and that the other is being held somewhere deep in the Third Reich? And you want to defend them and what they've done? For all you know, your friend Paul is the one who pulled the trigger and ended my brother's life."

"That's a little far-fetched."

"It doesn't matter. The Germans are brutal, hard-hearted, calculating beasts. If you know what's good for you, you'll stay far away from Paul."

Miriam fled her seat to the kitchen doorway. She spun around to face her father. "And what would you have me do? Turn my back on my friend?" Her friend and maybe so much more.

Daddy finger-combed his thin, graying hair. "That is where the problem is, Miriam. In how you view these people. You see them as your friends because your mother was German. Because she took you over there and exposed you to them for an entire summer when you were young and vulnerable. They brainwashed you."

"That's not true. I got to see Paul's heart, not just his uniform. Who he is as a man. Isn't that what the Lord wants us to do? When Samuel anointed David as Israel's king, he told the people that man looks at the outward appearance but God looks at the heart. We're told not to judge."

"We have to make judgments about good and evil. About right and wrong. Don't get that confused. Don't forget which side Paul picked up arms for. Which side he killed for."

She shuddered and turned to head to the stairs. Heavy footsteps sounded behind her. "Miriam. Wait."

She spun around. "What do you want, Arthur?"

"The way you're talking about Paul is scaring me. You're defending him. But even more than that. I can't put my finger on it, but you're unsettling me. I thought we had an agreement."

She sighed as a pounding headache picked that moment to attack. "I don't reme
ber any agreement."

"That we would work toward marriage. But now Paul shows up, and you talk ab
no one and nothing but him. What's going on?"

She grasped the banister to steady her shaking knees. "I don't know. I truly d
know."

Chapter 8

The walls of the small office closed in on Paul. The wall clock *tick-tocked* away the minutes as he awaited the captain's return.

Paul rubbed his temples. He might have lost any chance he had to woo Miriam for a second time. For sure, the captain would transfer him to a more secure camp along with the rest of the rabble-rousers. And she would marry Arthur.

He paced across the room and back, a total of six steps. Over and over. Movie night went on in the main ballroom, occasional laughter punctuating the silence. After a while, the floors in the hallway creaked as men paraded to the basement to use the washroom before lights-out. Still no captain.

Paul sat in the wooden chair across from the captain's seat. How could he have been such a *Dummkopf*? What possessed him to follow them instead of reporting them? And yet, the thrill of the chase, the risk they took, enlivened him like nothing else had since his capture. He loved the excitement.

But it may not have been worth it if it cost him his last shot at happiness with Miriam. To see if they truly still loved each other.

He must have dozed, because before he knew it, the captain stood over him and shook him by the shoulder. "Albrecht, get up."

Paul sprang from the chair. "Sir."

"Well, well, well." Captain Atkins made a circuit around the room, his English slow and drawn out, different from Miriam's. "This is not what I would have expected of you."

"I'm sorry, sir."

"I want to know why."

Should he tell him about the threat? He would look weak. Like a complainer. "I heard of their plan and decided to watch them. When you put me in charge, you wanted me to do that, I thought."

"Keep an eye on them, yes. Help them escape, no."

"That part they did all on their own."

"You should have informed me."

"Yes, sir. I understand that now."

The captain heaved a sigh. "The men will be moved. Right now, I'm holding them in the cell downstairs."

Paul swallowed hard. "And what about me?"

"You've put me in a fine pickle. What am I supposed to do? The mayor is up in arms over this incident. The good people of this town won't be happy when they discover what

421

y'all have done. They'll want the camp shut down."

"Yes, sir. Though I'd very much like to stay."

"I figured as much. Does it have anything to do with a certain young lady you were spotted with tonight?"

"The decision not to tell you was mine. She had nothing to do with it."

"You met her before the war, didn't you?"

"Yes. We spent the summer of '39 together. I was shocked to find out I was being moved to her hometown."

"And she's the reason you don't want the camp to close."

"Among others, yes. You Americans treat your prisoners well. Much better than we treat ours."

"The Fritz Ritz is what y'all call it."

"Please, don't send me with Baum and his men. I've learned my lesson."

"But you've put me in an untenable situation. My supervisors will want to know what I did to handle this. If they find out one of the men went unpunished, I will be in serious trouble."

"Yes, sir." Paul slumped against the wall. "I'm sorry if what I did put you in a bumpy spot."

"Give me some time to think about it. You are dismissed."

Paul left the office and shut the door behind him. He crossed the hallway into the ballroom in almost total darkness and found his bunk.

"Quite the excitement, wasn't it?" Werner rolled over on his bed.

"Ja."

"I'm surprised you aren't locked up with the others."

"That may not last. The captain doesn't want to move me, but he may have no choice. The camp may even be forced to close."

"I'm sorry. I hope he takes your general record into account. He did put you in charge of those men for a reason."

"And I violated his trust." Paul yanked the sheets over his head.

"Why didn't you go to him?"

"They threatened me. Foolish, I know. But what else to do?"

"And Miriam went along with you."

"I can't let them send me somewhere else." Paul's windpipe tensed. "I can't lose her a second time."

The sweet and salty aroma of frying bacon awoke Miriam and called her downstairs. She pulled on her workaday green dress and ran a comb through her hair before descending to face her father. She strove to make her voice as bright as possible. "Good morning."

"Morning." Daddy flipped the bacon in the frying pan.

She poured herself a cup of coffee and bent over the stove. "Smells good. Do you want me to take over?"

"I can manage." No trace of emotion crossed his face.

A volcano of warmth built in her chest. "I'm sorry about last night."

"I'm disappointed. Lying and sneaking around isn't like you. That's Paul's bad influence. And the way you treated Arthur was uncalled for. He's a good man, and you spurn him. I won't stand for it."

The heat inside of her rose then erupted. She struggled to control her words. "For the thousandth time, I'm not interested in him. He may very well be a good man. In fact, I'm sure he is. But he's not for me. He's dull and boring. I want more out of my life than cooking and cleaning all day long. Whether anything happens between me and Paul, I won't marry Arthur. Please, stop inviting him over and encouraging him. He's going to wind up with a broken heart." She stomped out of the room.

"Miriam, come back. Miriam."

She pounded up the stairs to her room and slammed the door.

Daddy followed and knocked. "Young lady, you've gone too far."

She couldn't stem the tide of tears that streaked down her cheeks. "I'm sorry, Daddy. I shouldn't have stomped out of the room. But you can't make me marry him."

He entered. She turned her back to him. "Miriam, be reasonable."

"I would never be happy with him."

The bed bounced as he sat beside her. "You always were a stubborn girl. Couldn't sit still for the life of you. You gave Mama fits. She chased you until she was exhausted. One minute you'd be in the hayloft, the next by the creek, the next playing in the dirt."

"Being a farmer's wife wouldn't suit me."

"I've always wanted your happiness above everything else. Can't you trust that I know what is good for you?"

"But it's not Arthur."

"You don't even give him a chance."

She faced her father. Lines etched his face. His heart wasn't strong. How much longer would he be able to manage the farm on his own? He needed to slow down. Was she being selfish in not considering Arthur? Then he wouldn't have to worry about who would take over the farm when he couldn't work the land or care for the cows. But the farm was *his* life. Not hers. "Mama liked Paul. She saw him for who he was. Who he is."

"Your mother had a soft spot in her heart for you."

That old, familiar ache squeezed her chest. If Mama were here, she'd help Daddy to see reason. "She was a wise woman. If Paul wasn't a good man, she would never have allowed me to be with him."

"You know how I feel." Daddy stood and crossed his arms. "That's all I have to say about the matter. I don't want you seeing him or speaking to him."

"I'm not going to continue leading on Arthur. You're right. He's a good man and doesn't deserve to be strung along. He should have the chance to find someone who will love him like I never will." Miriam rose and brushed past her father. Once downstairs, she plucked her coat from the hook by the back door, slipped on her boots, and escaped into the frosty outdoors.

Arthur's farm abutted theirs. She pulled in a deep breath and trudged the quarter mile to the almost identical white farmhouse. When they'd been children, they had walked to and from school together. Most days he offered to carry her books. She never let him. In high school, he'd asked her to every dance. She turned him down every time. These days, he invited her to the cinema with him. They hadn't gone together once.

Why now did her heart pound in her ears and her hands tremble?

Chapter 9

Miriam stood on Arthur's front porch. Breaking his heart shouldn't be this hard. He was familiar and comfortable. Everything she didn't want. But the look on her father's face, the dejection and disappointment, haunted her. By rejecting Arthur, she was letting Daddy down.

Should she do this? She'd been so sure a few minutes ago. Determined to get her way. Should she sacrifice her happiness for her father's? Then again, a farm, a piece of property, was worth far less than a marriage. She wouldn't want to bring children into a loveless union.

No, it was better this way. In time, Daddy would forgive her. He loved her. He wanted her to be happy.

She opened the storm door and rapped on the inside one. Sure and firm. A minute later, Arthur stood in front of her. "Miriam, what a surprise to see you. Come in."

She stepped into the warm entryway.

"Take off your coat and stay. I can have a pot of coffee ready in a few minutes." Arthur's heavy brown work jacket hung on a hook on the wall, his three pairs of barn boots lined up in a perfect row on the floor beneath it.

She couldn't live in such order, such brownness. "I can't stay, but thank you."

"What brings you by?"

Her tongue stuck to the roof of her mouth as she parted her lips to speak. "This isn't easy for me to say."

"Are you sure you don't want to sit down?" He mussed his already wild red hair.

"No. I'm fine. Let me get the words out."

He nodded.

"Ever since we were little, you've been a good friend to me. A better friend than I deserve. I haven't always treated you the way I should have. I want you to be happy, with a woman who will love you fully, who will be happy at your side on the farm, who will give you a passel of children. Unfortunately, that woman isn't me. I love you, Arthur, but more like the brother I never had. I hope you understand."

His Adam's apple worked up and down. "For a while, ever since Paul showed up, I had a feeling this was coming." He leaned against the wall.

Her heart seized. "Believe me, this wasn't easy. You're a wonderful man. Sweet, caring, generous. You'll make some woman a terrific husband."

He touched her upper arm. "Thank you for your honesty. I have loved you ever since the third grade when you demanded that Willy Zimmerman give me back my lunch."

She chuckled at the memory. "You were skinny enough. I didn't want you to mis
meal. What he did wasn't right."

"You've always had this clear sense of justice."

"You aren't angry?"

"A little hurt. Very disappointed. I'll never love another woman the way I love yo

"Don't say that. Don't hold back your heart. That's not fair to you."

"Your father will be upset."

"He's not happy about my decision."

"Be careful." Arthur caressed her cheek. "You don't know what Paul is like. He ru
with a crowd of troublemakers. There are rumblings those men were part of the sec
police. A brutal lot who are doing who knows what to prisoners of war like my brot
Steer clear of him. Don't get involved."

"Thanks for the advice, but you don't know him the way I do."

"That was five years ago. People change. War has a way of doing that to a man."

"He's not like those others. And he wasn't part of the SS. He's happy he's here a
doesn't have to fight anymore."

"You've been warned." Arthur crossed to the door and opened it.

Guess that was the end of their conversation.

"Take care of yourself."

She stood on her tiptoes and pecked him on his rosy cheek. "Thank you for car
for me. Be happy." With that, she stepped into the chilly day. She'd tucked her Satur
shopping list into her pocket. Best to get that chore out of the way and get home to
a little cleaning and baking.

By the time she reached the grocer's, she had warmed through. Though Art
had been hurt, letting him down the way she had was for the best for both of them.
would come to see that in time. Her shoulders relaxed for the first time in weeks. Ma
even months or years.

The bell above the doorway jangled as she entered Heippe Cash Store. Most of
shoppers ignored the tinkling and carried on with their selections. Two or three glan
up. Mrs. Lundquist stared at her then turned to Mrs. McKinnon and whispered beh
her hand.

Since they stood near the canned goods and Miriam needed tomato soup, she sau
tered close to them.

Mrs. Lundquist fiddled with the multicolored scarf around her neck. "I'm surpri
to see you here, Miriam."

"Oh. Why?"

"After what happened last night. . ." Mrs. McKinnon shook her head.

"What happened last night?" Maybe that wasn't the right thing to say, but Miria
mind couldn't put together another coherent sentence.

"Really, dear." Mrs. Lundquist leaned closer, her voice a very loud whisper. "Ru
ning around with those sorts. Your mother may have been German, but your fat
doesn't approve. It's disrespectful to those of us who have lost loved ones in this terri
conflict." She dabbed the corner of her eye with a monogrammed handkerchief.

"I am sorry about your grandson."

"Two wars." Mrs. McKinnon grasped Miriam by the hands and held fast. "Those Germans have dragged us into two very costly, devastating wars. And to think you would taint yourself by associating with them."

Miriam glanced around the small market. Everyone stared at her. Her shoulders slumped even as her chest burned. "If you'll excuse me."

She fled the store without a single purchase.

◆————◆

Less than twenty-four hours after he had last found himself in Captain Atkins's office, Paul once again stood in front of the man's desk.

The captain motioned for Paul to sit. He lowered himself into the hard chair, his stomach twisting as it had the day he'd been called to the headmaster's office for an improper salute to the Führer. The captain fiddled with a pen, his fingers stained with ink. "I've been up most of the night pondering what to do to punish y'all and to keep the camp open."

"I'm sorry to have caused you such distress, sir."

"Not only you. They can't remain here. Come Monday, the other men involved will be shipped to a more secure facility."

"And me?" Paul's voice squeaked. He cleared his throat.

"You're another matter. You aren't former SS. That works in your favor. And you weren't part of the melee at the tavern. You did come to me with the information. Eventually. But not informing me right away will work against you. And leaving the property is also a black mark on your record."

Paul clenched the edge of the seat. "I'm not going elsewhere?"

"No. Don't think I didn't consider it, because it was an option. One that would have appeased those in town who aren't in favor of the camp. In the end, you did what you did because you thought it to be the right thing at the time. Mind you, it wasn't, but you didn't act out of malice. You've proven yourself in other situations to be trustworthy."

"Thank you, sir."

"There'll be consequences." The captain put down his pen and leaned forward. "You'll have extra KP duty for the next month. You'll oversee cleaning the latrine every evening as well. And you are to have no contact with anyone outside of the camp other than your employer. If I find you in violation, I will transfer you to a different facility immediately. Understand?"

Paul rubbed his hands on his pants. "I do, sir. Thank you. You will find me to be a perfect prisoner."

"I hope so, Albrecht. Now get to work. The kitchen staff needs help with lunch."

Paul left the room and entered the adjacent dining hall. The dark-paneled walls absorbed the light streaming through the windows. A cheery fire burned in the brick fireplace that dominated the outside wall, driving away the winter's chill.

He meandered past it into the kitchen, the hum of voices and clank of dishes reaching him.

The punishments weren't too bad. Kitchen duty didn't bother him. The latrine cleaning wouldn't be fun, but it had to be done.

But not to have contact with anyone on the outside? He doubled over, the breath knocked out of him. What about his relationship with Miriam?

Chapter 10

Miriam gathered the stack of papers she needed to grade that evening and stashed them into her book bag to bring home. When the parents came to pick up their children, not one of them said a word to her. Instead, all she got were sidelong glances and icy stares.

She knew why.

They had the same attitude as the women in the grocery store on Saturday. The same one the congregation had on Sunday. The same one they had on the day she hurt her ankle. She rubbed her aching neck. A good long bath and a bowl of warm chicken soup would do her wonders. If she hurried, she might be able to get home while Daddy still worked in the barn. That would give her a few minutes away from his disapproving look.

She stood and slung the bag over her shoulder. Mr. Norris, the principal, arrived at her classroom door and knocked. "Do you have a minute, Miss Bradford?" His double chin shook as he spoke. He drew a gold pocket watch from his red vest and checked the time.

There went any thoughts of avoiding Daddy. "Sure, what can I do for you?" Her stomach clenched.

She offered him her rolling desk chair and seated herself in one of the children's much smaller chairs.

He cleared his throat. "What I have to say isn't easy."

"You're firing me." Her voice squeaked.

"No, not at all. I'm sorry I gave you that impression."

She let out a breath she didn't know she'd been holding. "Thank you."

"But it has been a long day. Several of the parents came to voice their concerns."

"Concerns about me?"

"Yes. They're afraid, because of your association with the German prisoners and the trouble on Friday night, that you might be a bad influence on their children. That you might try to indoctrinate them with Nazi ideology."

Miriam almost toppled from the seat. "That's ludicrous."

"Is it?"

"I assure you it is. I was born and raised in this country, in this town, and love it as much as the next person. Just because I choose to view Germans as human beings doesn't mean I favor their dictator, because in many cases, they don't favor him, either."

"I'm glad. That still doesn't solve my problem."

"What problem is that?"

"Some of the parents don't trust you. They're afraid. Two have already asked to have their children transferred from your class to Miss Green's."

The room swirled in front of her. "Transferred?"

"I don't want to start a mass exodus from your tutelage, but I have a responsibility to keep the parents happy. I will honor their request. In addition, I'll monitor your classes full-time for the next week. After that, I will make unexpected visits throughout the day. And you can be sure your students will report anything you say that might be construed as sympathetic to the Germans. For your sake, I urge you to watch every word and stick to teaching the three R's. Nothing else." Mr. Norris hefted himself from behind her desk and glanced at his watch again.

"Thank you." The words pushed past the lump in her throat.

"For what?"

"For not firing me."

"I hope my trust in you isn't misplaced."

"It won't be. I promise I'll watch what I say."

"And I would advise you to stop seeing that young man."

She nodded. But her throat closed.

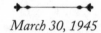

March 30, 1945

"Come on, Miriam, cheer up. You've been down in the dumps for months. You didn't even come with the gang to see *A Tree Grows in Brooklyn* last weekend."

Miriam reclined against Florence's flowered couch and sipped her chamomile tea. The herbal, earthy fragrance warmed her chilled spirit. "I wasn't in the mood."

"You haven't been in the mood for weeks upon weeks. What's going on?"

"How can I show my face in town after what happened at the grocery store?" She placed her cup on the coffee table, the taste all of a sudden bitter.

"That happened back in December."

"Everyone stares at me whenever I'm around. I see it. I feel it. They think they're doing it on the sly, but I know."

"So what?"

The back of her throat burned. "It's hard enough to teach. Mr. Norris is in and out of my room. It's distracting to the kids. What ones are left in the class."

"It isn't that bad. Only a few moved."

"What would I do without you? You always see the lemonade as mostly sweet."

"But you're still moping."

"Because I haven't heard from Paul since that night." She bit her lip to stem the flow of tears that threatened to fall. "Every day, the truck that takes him to the tannery passes me as I walk to school. Every day, I glimpse him through the window. The tiniest of glimpses. Just a flash of his head. But he never turns to look at me."

"Maybe it isn't him."

"No, it is."

"At least he's still around. They didn't send him to a different camp like the other men."

"But the war is almost over. The Allies will reach Berlin within a few weeks. And then what will happen to him? He'll return to Germany, and I'll never see him again. Maybe it's for the best. I don't want to hurt Daddy."

Florence chuckled. "You're the only person in the entire world who is sad about the end of the war."

A weight pressed on her chest.

"We should come up with a plan. Some way that will get you two the opportunity to talk to each other. Then together, you can figure out how to convince your father Paul is the man for you."

Miriam sat forward, a little bit of lightness returning. "A plan? Like what?"

"Well, my dad told me he went to see Captain Atkins earlier this week."

"Why?"

"As you know, he's been holding services there every Sunday afternoon for the prisoners because some of the members of the congregation didn't like worshipping with those heathens."

"You don't have to tell me who. I can guess."

"Anyway, because it's Holy Week, he thought it would be good for the prisoners to be allowed to celebrate Good Friday and Easter in a proper church building. Not that you can't worship God anywhere, but it's fitting to be in the Lord's house for the holidays."

"The men are coming to church today? And on Sunday?"

A grin brightened Florence's round face. "Yes, they are."

"What if Paul isn't among them?"

"What happened to your optimistic outlook?"

"Mr. Norris and several of the parents squashed it."

"Well, it's high time you regained it. Chances are good he'll be there. For the first time in a while, you'll see him, and not through a truck's window."

"But I can't talk to him. Mr. Norris would sack me for sure, and Daddy would flip his wig."

Florence jiggled her leg. "Then we'll have to be sneakier."

"Sneakiness gets me in trouble."

"I'll make sure it doesn't. Now help me think how we might pull this off."

They sat in silence and sipped their tea while the grandfather clock in the corner ticked away the minutes. The Westminster chimes struck eleven. In sixty minutes, the Good Friday service would start. Miriam snapped her fingers. "I've got it."

＊•————•＊

Paul filed into the church with a good number of the other prisoners. What a treat to be allowed to join the rest of the congregation for Good Friday and Easter services.

And an opportunity to see Miriam. He'd begged the captain to allow him to come. He had to promise not to speak to anyone until Atkins gave permission. After almost four months, the captain still maintained a tight hold on him. Not that Paul blamed him.

And there she was, this time in the back row instead of the balcony. With her auburn hair, he couldn't mistake her. She glanced at him and flashed him a brief smile. He could all but hear the angel chorus.

Though he put his effort into concentrating on the pastor's message, he couldn't keep his attention from straying to Miriam on the other side of the aisle. She didn't peer his way but kept her focus on the front of the church. Didn't she feel the same way? Perhaps she thought he was ignoring her on purpose. Or she was angry with him for what happened with their spying mission.

Before he knew it, the congregation rose, sang "O Sacred Head, Now Wounded," and the service ended. Befitting the somber occasion of Christ's death, the members filed out of the sanctuary without speaking. The captain brought the prisoners to their feet and led them in a line toward the door.

A bouncy, curly headed blond scampered beside the group. Paul swallowed and stared straight ahead. If only Miriam would come his way.

The young woman touched his hand. She wriggled her fingers, and a piece of paper passed between them. Maybe, just maybe, from Miriam? Or containing news about her?

Couldn't the captain walk any faster? Paul's stomach fluttered, and his hands trembled.

Please, Lord, don't let it be bad news.

Chapter 11

"Please, Daddy, listen to reason." Miriam wrung her dishrag over the sink, pulling it tighter than necessary. "With all the young men gone to war, there aren't enough hands to help with planting. I'm worried you'll work yourself too hard. I've seen you grabbing your chest several times in the past few days. You should go to the camp and hire a few to work the fields. It will never get done on time otherwise."

Daddy thumped his coffee cup on the table. "You know how I feel about those men. And one in particular. You'd better not be up to anything."

"I'm not." Other than the note Florence passed him last Friday, she hadn't had any contact with Paul all winter. Even though what she felt for him wasn't the leftover glow from one perfect summer. It was real. True love. She could never commit to anyone else because she'd already given her heart to Paul.

Arthur thumped his cup next to Daddy's. He didn't press her anymore, but he continued to be a constant fixture in their home. "In this case, I have to agree with Miriam."

She gasped and spun around. "Really?"

"You make a valid point. I'm having a hard time finding field hands." A cloud crossed his face. He and his brothers had worked together. It must be hard for him to run the farm on his own. "Even if we pool our men and work together, we won't get the crops in the ground in a timely fashion. Why should we worry about this when we have an abundance of men at our fingertips, ready to go? Men who are physically fit and able to work."

Daddy scratched the back of his head. "I don't know. What about those who got in the fight at the tavern?"

"They were sent to a different camp." Arthur shrugged. "They shouldn't have been here in the first place. Since then, there haven't been problems with the prisoners."

"Look at you, Daddy." Miriam sat beside him and rubbed his back. "You're exhausted trying to do this on your own. And it's only the beginning of the season. What are you going to be like by harvest? Don't be too proud to ask for help. Even Arthur can't do it alone."

Daddy scrubbed his stubble-covered face. "All right. If you two stop pestering me, I'll go tomorrow and hire several of them. What would I do without you, Miriam?"

Miriam kissed him on the cheek and sent a smile Arthur's way, even though her chest tightened. Daddy needed her more than she realized. "You won't be sorry. You'll see they aren't evil."

He glanced at her, his eyebrows raised, his mouth pursed.

She hurried to allay his suspicion. "And it will be a weight off your shoulders. You'll be grateful you did this."

What if everything fell into place with Paul? Her father depended on her. Could she leave him? She had to take care of him.

◆•————•◆

Paul paced in front of the captain's desk in the small office. "I want to get out of the tannery and work in the fields."

"Why now? You didn't express interest last fall."

"Things have changed. I spent all winter cooped up inside. With spring knocking on the door, I want to get out. Get some fresh air."

"I'm not sure." The captain cracked his knuckles.

"You told me not to talk with the townspeople. I've kept to my word. If I work in the fields, I would have to speak to the farmer and maybe his family." Paul's heart thumped in his chest. The family part is why he stood in the captain's office. "The troublemakers are gone. I've paid for my crime."

The captain sat silent for the longest time. Then he gave two small, slow nods. "You've proved yourself. The farmers are begging for workers. Though I hate to pull you from what you've been doing, getting the crops in the ground is most important. You may go."

Paul fought back the urge to whoop out loud. "Thank you, sir. I appreciate this."

Instead of preparing for the day at W. B. Place, Paul joined the crowd at the gate waiting to be hired by local farmers. Just as Miriam instructed Paul in the message her friend slipped him, he hung back until her father arrived. Here was an opportunity to spend more time with her and to try to convince her father he was the man for her.

He had to make up for his mistake with the soccer team. Had to convince Miriam that he truly loved her more than anything. And show her father he was an honorable and reputable man. One worthy of his only daughter.

Several area farmers came and claimed most of the men at the fence. They climbed aboard the trucks and motored out of town to the surrounding farms.

Would Miriam and her father show up? Maybe she hadn't been able to talk him into hiring hands from the camp. Maybe he was so opposed to the prisoners, and to Paul, that he refused to listen to her.

He was almost ready to head back to the ballroom for a day of staring at the ceiling when another truck chugged into the park. Sitting on the back of the pickup, outfitted in a bright yellow dress with green flowers, her sun-reddened hair tied back with a bandanna, was Miriam. Was it possible for a man's chest to burst open?

With as much nonchalance as possible, he sauntered to the gate, his coat in the ballroom, the sleeves of his blue POW shirt rolled up to show off his strength. Anything to get Mr. Bradford to hire him.

Mr. Bradford, Miriam, and Arthur spilled from the truck and made their way to the fence. After a brief chat with the guard, they picked fieldworkers. Men almost filled the back of the truck when Miriam pointed to him. He crept closer.

Her father shook his head.

"What do you mean, no?" Miriam stuck out her lower lip.

Heat rose within Paul. Oh, to taste those lips again.

"I mean that he's a bad influence on you. My answer is no."

"He can hear you. And understand English."

"All the better."

"Daddy, he's a hard worker. And a trusted man in this camp."

"That's not what I hear."

With his Adam's apple lodged in his windpipe, Paul stepped forward. "I'd like to work for you, sir."

Mr. Bradford straightened and stepped backward.

"Please, give me the chance to show you what Miriam knows to be true. I'm an honorable man. I made a mistake. If I could go back and live that evening over, I would change what I did. My actions, I am not proud of. But I have learned my lesson."

The older man wiped his hands on his overalls. With a cap on his head and a pipe in his mouth, he truly played the part of an American farmer.

"Daddy, please. You'll see I'm right."

Mr. Bradford stared at Arthur. "What do you think?"

"This is one decision I'd rather be left out of." The man clamped his jaw shut.

Miriam's father huffed. "You can come, but only on a trial basis. If I so much as catch a whiff of anything unseemly around you, it will be the last time I will ever allow you on my property or anywhere near my daughter. I will be sure your captain hears about it. He'll have you on the next train bound for a true prison."

Paul nodded and released a pent-up breath. "Thank you, sir. You won't be sorry."

"I'd better not be." He turned to his daughter. "You'll ride up front with me. Arthur can sit in the back with the other men."

Paul shot Miriam a soft glance and a small smile. Her belief in him meant everything. He scrambled aboard and settled himself in the bed of the truck beside Arthur.

"You're the man who lured my Miriam away from me." Arthur sized Paul up and down.

"Pardon me?"

"She loves you. Hasn't stopped talking about you since the minute she came back from Germany. You've stolen her heart."

Paul couldn't keep the grin from his face. "Thank you."

"You'd better not cause her any hurt. I don't know what it's going to take for you to win her father's favor, but you have a long hill to climb."

The expression was unfamiliar to Paul, but he understood the meaning. He had much hard work in front of him to make a good impression on Mr. Bradford. And with the war in Germany possibly only weeks from its end, he didn't have time on his side.

Chapter 12

Miriam loaded the large coffeepot into her childhood little red wagon. All morning, she'd been searching for an excuse to see Paul, to speak to him even a little. And a coffee break was the perfect solution. She grabbed the still-warm cinnamon coffee cake from the counter. She'd used a month's worth of sugar coupons to make it, but the splurge was worth getting to spend time with him.

Once she had everything in the wagon, she set off for the near field where the men labored to till the soil. *"Kaffee."*

They stopped their work and stared at her. The half-dozen or so men ranged in size from big to small and in age from young to much older. She continued to use her somewhat limited German. "And I have coffee cake. Come and eat while it is warm."

They dropped what they were doing and rushed to her side. She poured the coffee into Mama's everyday cups and sliced the cake.

Paul waited until the others sat in the soft dirt and consumed their snack. "Thank you for doing this." He gestured wide, including the fields and the other men. As he took the plate from her, their fingers touched.

She tingled from head to toe and commanded her knees to hold her upright. "It took some doing. Daddy wasn't keen on the idea, but Arthur is the one who talked him into it."

"That's the one who wants to marry you."

"Oh, so much has happened since we last spoke. I went to Arthur and told him I could never be his wife. He was hurt, of course, but he understands."

"Does your father?" He gazed at her with such an intensity she quivered.

She set the coffee in the wagon and then peered over the fields, just greening with the first warm days of the year. "I've tried everything I can to make him see reason. To show him not all Germans are bad." She turned to him. "Especially you."

He stroked her cheek, and she almost melted. "Do you know how I've missed you? I would have sent you letters, but the captain took away the privilege as part of my punishment."

"Daddy would have torn them up anyway." Her throat constricted. No, she couldn't cry.

Paul rubbed her upper arms. "Don't be upset, liebchen. We will find a way to be together."

"I can't leave my father. Not without his blessing." She stepped out of his reach. "He lost my mother. He can't lose me. And his health isn't the best."

"That's what this is about, isn't it? He can't let go of you. Arthur was safe, because he was your neighbor. You weren't going anywhere. In fact, your father would probably continue to take meals with you. Maybe even live with you."

"Yes, but I told you that I broke things off with Arthur."

"But has your father?"

Miriam gave a slow shake of her head. "Are you saying he needs to break up with Arthur?"

"In a way, maybe. Let go of the notion of you marrying and living on the next farm. That is what you want, isn't it?"

"I don't want to marry Arthur. That much I know."

He held her by the hand and stroked her thumb. Little shivers ran up and down her spine. She couldn't think with a clear head when he did such things.

"You got me through some very tough times during the war."

"Like what?"

"Like the days I spent flying over the desert in Africa, the Allies shooting at us. Bullets pierced the fuselage. One of them, I felt the wind of it slice the air beside my cheek. Or the day after the Allied invasion of France."

"We call that D-day. I listened to the radio all that day, thinking of you. Of what might be happening to you."

He closed his eyes, and his grip on her hand tightened. "Such carnage, you will never know. I hope you never experience anything like that. I flew support. I still see the bodies."

She touched the top of his hand. "That's all over now."

"Shot down, waiting for the Allies to determine my fate, if I would live or die, all I could think about was you. You and the Lord. If I would ever see you again, so I could tell you how much I love you."

"Paul, I—"

"Miriam, what on earth are you doing?" Daddy's voice in her left ear sent her shooting into the air.

◆━━━━◆

"Daddy, I can explain." Miriam's voice shook.

"No." A fire burned in Paul's chest. "I will. She did nothing wrong, sir. She brought the men a snack and a drink."

The older man narrowed his eyes, crinkles fanning from the corners of them. "Get back to the house, Miriam."

"Sir, she—"

"I said, get back to the house." Mr. Bradford's voice was as icy as the Alpine peaks in January.

Miriam grabbed the wagon's handle and bumped away so fast, the coffee urn threatened to overturn.

Her father turned to Paul. "I would thank you to stay away from my daughter. I already regret hiring you. I don't have to keep you."

Paul wiped his sweaty brow. "I've been working harder than any of the men. You've seen me. You know it. What is it you have against me? What don't you like about me?"

"Your ideology. And your desire to steal my daughter from me."

If Mr. Bradford hadn't been wearing that frown as proudly as any dandy wore his zoot suit, Paul might have laughed. "I'm no Nazi."

"Miriam told me you belonged to the Hitler-Jugend."

"The government required every boy my age to join. I had no choice. But my parents never bought into Hitler or his fanatic ideals. And neither have I."

"You fought for him."

"Again, not by my own choice."

Mr. Bradford harrumphed.

"And I don't have plans to steal your daughter. I love her. What I want is to have her by my side every day for the rest of our lives. We've lost so much time already. This war stole years from us that we could have had."

"And where would you take her?"

"Wherever she wanted to go."

"Back to Germany, no doubt."

"We haven't discussed that. But Germany will be a desolate land for many years."

"That country ripped my wife from me. She was sick when she came back and died soon afterward. I refuse to let it claim another loved one." Mr. Bradford spun on his heel and marched away.

Paul worked hard the rest of the morning. Once the bell rang for lunch and he washed up, only one seat remained at the large farm table. Next to Mr. Bradford. Two spots down from Miriam. If only he'd been faster. He sat, and Miriam's father said grace.

His fellow prisoners chattered, but he couldn't concentrate on their conversations. Miriam sent him sideways glances every minute or so.

"What do you plan to do when the Allies claim victory?"

Paul worked to swallow the bite of pot roast in his mouth so he could answer Mr. Bradford's unexpected question. "I'd like to become a pilot for a commercial carrier."

"So, you'll be all over the place. You won't even have a home."

"No, sir, every pilot is based somewhere."

"Just think of it, Daddy." Miriam spoke to her father but stared at Paul, little lights in her eyes. "Getting to travel all over the world, seeing new places, meeting new people."

"Getting diseases and dying."

Miriam's voice softened. "Mama didn't die because she went to Germany."

"The war broke her heart." A tear shimmered in the corner of Mr. Bradford's pale blue eyes. "I will not allow you to steal her from me."

What would it take to convince him Paul would do right by her?

Chapter 13

P aul wiped the sweat from his forehead, probably smearing dirt over it as he did. He leaned against the plow and took a long, slow drink of the water Miriam brought.

"Sorry it's not lemonade."

The way her green eyes shimmered, how her hair glowed copper in the sunlight, how her dimples brightened her smile. He almost crushed the glass in his hand to keep from reaching over and taking her in his arms. Then an idea struck.

He pulled her behind the group gathered at the toy wagon, into a spot where her father wouldn't see them. "This is torture. I have to kiss you. Avert your eyes, men."

The group of his fellow prisoners guffawed but turned their backs to Paul and Miriam. He drew her into an embrace. She fit just right into his hold, her head nestled under his chin. Nothing had changed. "You're beautiful." He bent to kiss her.

"He's coming. Her father."

He jerked upright and stepped back with a groan. "Nein. Why now?"

She wormed her way through the group around the wagon and faced her father.

"Haven't you been out here long enough?" Mr. Bradford scanned the crowd. He must be searching for Paul. Checking on his daughter, for sure.

"I want to make sure the men have had all they need to drink. You don't want them fainting, do you?"

"You have lunch to prepare."

"The stew is simmering on the stove, and the bread is in the oven." She tipped her head to one side and peered at her father, her face as innocent as an angel's.

"Well—"

"Okay, men, let's get back to work." Paul clapped his hands, and the crew jumped into action. They placed their empty glasses and crumb-covered plates into the wagon and scattered to work the plows.

Mr. Bradford grunted as Miriam grabbed the wagon's handle. With a quick backward glance and a wink that Paul almost missed, she strode to the house.

"You would do well to stop ogling my daughter and keep the men working. A little more labor and a lot less lollygagging would go a long way." Mr. Bradford took one step toward the barn.

"Could I have a word with you?"

He didn't turn around. "If this is about Miriam, I'm not interested. I've said my piece."

Paul slapped his thighs. What more could he do? Maybe he and Miriam would have to elope. Or perhaps the Lord didn't want them together. Could that be why He had separated them for so long? Paul's heart constricted. *No, Lord, don't let that be the case.*

Miriam's father made his way over the just-tilled field. He stumbled once but righted himself. He stumbled a second time. This time he went down.

And didn't get up.

A chill raced through Paul. For half a second, he froze. Planes exploding in a burst of light. Men falling like shooting stars.

He couldn't do anything then.

But he could now.

"Mr. Bradford! Mr. Bradford!" Paul raced across the field, the heavy clay clods weighing down his shoes. He might as well have been lifting rocks. His lungs burned, but he wouldn't stop.

At last, he reached Miriam's father. All color had surged from his face. "My leg. Oh, my leg. The pain." He sucked in a breath.

Paul turned his attention to the man's leg. Instead of being straight, it twisted into an odd angle. Paul's stomach rolled.

A few of the other men reached them. "What happened?"

Paul grasped Mr. Bradford by the hand. "I think he broke his leg. Run to the house. Have Miriam ring for the doctor." One man shot off.

The two who were left stood beside Paul. "What should we do?" The more muscular of them rubbed his hands.

"We have to get Mr. Bradford out of the field. He's not going to be able to walk, and the wagon would be too jarring. See if you can find anything to make a stretcher from. And be fast." Paul's comrades sped away.

"How are you doing, Mr. Bradford?"

"I've never had pain like this before. It's terrible."

"Just relax. Soon the doctor will come. And the other men will have a stretcher. I know it hurts. One summer, when I was sixteen, I broke my leg. Such a silly thing, really. When you are young, you are invincible, you think. But riding my bike off the stable roof into a hay pile wasn't a good idea."

"Keep talking. It helps me to forget about the discomfort."

Here was Paul's chance. He had Mr. Bradford's undivided attention. "You must have done some crazy things when you were a boy, no?"

"Everyone did."

"But my leg, it healed. That was an important summer for me."

Mr. Bradford bit his lip.

Paul squeezed his hand harder.

"How so?"

"That was the first year it was compulsory for us to join the Hitler-Jugend. All that summer, instead of being involved in the movement, instead of going to camp with them, I laid in my bedroom. My mother spent many hours with me to keep me company. My friends were away.

"A good woman is my mother. Instead of hearing about Hitler, how wonderful he was and how awful everyone else was, my mother filled my head with lovely things. She taught me much about Jesus and how He lived His life. How He treated all kinds of people with love and tenderness."

"What is that verse?"

"In the Bible?"

"Yes. About Jews and Greeks."

" 'There is neither Jew nor Greek, there is neither bond nor free, there is neither male nor female: for ye are all one in Christ Jesus.' "

"And you believe that?"

"With all my heart. I only fight for Germany because it is where I was born. Where I am a citizen. I was required to go to war for her. But that doesn't mean I hold to what Hitler teaches."

Miriam raced across the plowed field, her hair coming loose from its pins, streaming behind her. She arrived breathless beside her father. "Daddy, what happened?"

He shifted positions and grimaced. Paul shed his jacket, rolled it up, and placed it under Mr. Bradford's head. "He broke his leg walking across the field."

She brushed a lock of her father's hair, the same color as hers, out of his eyes. "I've phoned Dr. Hamilton. He'll be here as soon as he can. Thank the Lord he wasn't out on a call."

Her father grasped her by the elbow. "You're a good girl."

The two men Paul sent after a stretcher hustled back. "We found this tarp, a couple of pieces of lumber, and these tacks. Will that work?" The leaner man, Hans, opened his hand in which he held several brass nails.

"We'll have to wrap the tarp around the lumber several times so it will support his weight."

"It's a good thing you are as thin as you are, Daddy." Miriam wiped a tear from her ruddy cheek.

Paul brushed her chin. "Don't worry. Once we have him to the house, the doctor will take care of him. Please, don't cry."

But the tears rushed down her face. "I don't want anything to happen to him."

Paul worked with Hans and Friedrich to build the stretcher. Once satisfied it would hold Mr. Bradford, they set about transferring him. "Hold on. This will hurt." Paul nodded to the others. "One, two, three."

Mr. Bradford cried out in pain as they moved him. Miriam gasped. "Please, don't hurt him."

"That's the worst." Paul motioned to Hans and Friedrich. "Let's go."

The rough terrain proved to make for difficult going, but they returned to the house as the doctor pulled up in his black Model A. The middle-aged man, well built and graying at the temples, stepped out and took over command. "Get him inside to the downstairs bedroom." His nurse, not much older than Miriam, also exited the vehicle. The doctor gave orders for the equipment he would need and disappeared inside, the woman following him.

Paul assisted Hans and Friedrich in getting Mr. Bradford situated in the wrought-iron bed. The three of them slipped from the room and left the doctor and his nurse to their work.

Miriam hustled about the kitchen, pulling her bread from the oven and dishing out bowls of stew though it wasn't even eleven o'clock in the morning. Paul moved to her side and pulled the ladle from her. "Stop it. You are worried, but he will be fine. The doctor will make sure of that."

She nestled against him and flooded his shirt with her tears. "But what will happen to him from here? What if he can't farm anymore?"

The question lingered in the air as Paul held her close, his own heart thrumming against his ribs.

Chapter 14

Miriam slunk into her father's room after Dr. Hamilton left, the shades pulled against the middle-of-the-afternoon sun. Her father lay in the big bed he once shared with her mother, sunk into the old mattress, Mama's red-and-green wedding ring quilt tucked to his chin. His eyes fluttered open when she scraped the old kitchen chair across the scarred wood floor to sit beside him.

"Guess I stirred the pot today."

Miriam laughed. "I see you broke your leg but not your funny bone. Do you have much pain?"

"The doctor gave me something. Don't worry. I'll be up and around in no time."

"I didn't say you wouldn't be."

"But that look on your face. Like you're afraid."

Her stomach quivered. Her father wasn't a young man anymore. Lines crisscrossed his face. For many years, her parents thought they couldn't have children. She surprised them when they had about given up hope. "I don't like seeing you in bed."

"Being here has given me time to think about my life."

She clutched her chest. "You talk like you're dying."

"Maybe not today or tomorrow, but the years are creeping up. I can't run the farm anymore. And you aren't interested in having it."

She opened her mouth to speak.

"I've accepted that. My father wanted me to have this farm. Pushed it on me, really. I wanted to be an auto mechanic."

"I never knew that."

"To please him, I put that dream to rest. And I tried to do the same to you, afraid I would lose you. But look at what happened. There are dangers on a farm as well as anywhere else in the world."

Miriam bit back tears. "I'll always be your little girl."

He patted her hand. "Yes, you will. And wherever you go, you'll come visit me, won't you? Tell me stories about the big world out there?"

"Maybe you can come with me."

"I'm too old. It's time to sell the farm to Arthur and move into town where I can enjoy my retirement."

"That sounds like a good plan." He was giving her the freedom she'd craved. But not what she wanted even more than liberty.

"And about Paul."

443

She jerked upright, her pulse thundering in her ears. "What about him?"

"Do you love him?"

"More than anything in the world."

"That is how it should be. I've been wrong about many things. Even though I haven't been kind, he stayed with me today, took care of me, and talked to me to help keep my mind from the pain. He's a good person. If he would do that for a crotchety old man, how much more will he do for the woman he loves?"

Her breath caught in her throat. "You're giving us your blessing?"

"If God gave you a second chance, who am I to stand in His way?"

"Thank you, Daddy, from the bottom of my heart." She kissed his forehead. "Thank you."

◆—————◆

May 7, 1945

Miriam tinkered in the kitchen, slicing bread and slathering it with the last of the strawberry jam she'd put up the previous spring. In another hour or so, she'd bring it to the hardworking men for their morning snack.

In the living room, Daddy relaxed in his chair, the aroma of his pipe drifting into the kitchen. Though fog dimmed her view, somewhere out there Paul worked. She'd probably find him in the barn today, with the drizzle ruining the warm spring temperatures.

She hummed along to the Andrews sisters as they sang "Don't Sit under the Apple Tree" on the radio. She glanced at her watch. Almost time for the nine o'clock news.

"We bring you a special news bulletin."

She perked up, hustled to the living room, and turned up the volume on the little Bakelite set. ". . .the unconditional surrender of Germany."

Could it be? Was it real? She sank to her knees and wept. Daddy reached over, smoothed her hair as tears streamed down his cheeks. "It's over. Praise the Lord, it's over."

"I have to tell Paul."

"Go, then." A smile crossed her father's face.

She raced out the door, not caring that the rain had intensified. As light as a feather, she flew over the farmyard and entered the barn. The cows lowed and swished their tails as if the world hadn't changed. "Paul? Are you in here?"

He stepped from the tack room, a harness in his hand. "I thought I would mend this for you."

"It's over. Germany has agreed to an unconditional surrender. No more fighting in Europe."

He dropped the harness, ran to her, and swooped her into his arms. Round and round he swung her. "Thank You, Lord, thank You."

"I'm getting dizzy." She couldn't help but giggle.

He placed her on the ground and stared at her, his eyes intense. He leaned forward. She licked her lips, trembling from head to toe. Then, as gentle as the spring rain, he kissed her. She drew him closer, and the kiss deepened. For several moments she couldn't breathe. He stepped back, and the air whooshed into her lungs. She lost her balance.

He caught her. "I love you, Miriam. Will you marry me?"

"Marry you?"

"Together, we will travel the world, raise a family, live a life of adventure."

Good thing he still supported her. "I love you, Paul, and would love nothing more than to be your wife."

Once more, she drew him to herself and kissed him. This time, for keeps.

Epilogue

May 1948

The quiet organ music floated under the door of the pastor's church study and helped steady Miriam. Florence laced flowers into her hair. Or attempted to. "Hold still so I can do this."

"I can't wait. I get to marry Paul today."

"You've waited this long. Surely you can hold on another few minutes."

"Three years since he proposed. Nine years since we first met. Who would have believed it would take so long?"

"You had a war to contend with first."

"And governments that move far too slowly." Paul didn't return to Germany for seven months after the surrender, and it took forever to get the paperwork and clearances he needed to return to the States. But here he was. She turned to her best friend. "I'm going to be his wife."

"Not until you quit moving so I can get this veil on right." Florence fussed for a while more before she stepped back. "There. Perfect."

"Thank you for everything. For being there and supporting us when no one else did."

"That's because I love you."

Daddy knocked on the door and entered. "Are you ready to go?"

They nodded. Florence grabbed her flowers and stepped out to march down the aisle.

With a swipe of his handkerchief across his eyes, Daddy offered Miriam his elbow. "You are the most beautiful bride ever."

"Mama would have objected to that."

"No, she wouldn't have, because you are. Now, let's finally get you married."

Daddy had to restrain her from running down the aisle to her most handsome groom. Paul wore a dark suit that complemented his fair complexion, his hair slicked back, a wide grin across his face. When she reached him, he grasped her by the hand, his fingers warm.

The day passed in a blur. The pastor pronounced them husband and wife, she ate cake and drank punch, and their guests showered them with rice. They ran outside the church hand in hand. Paul helped her into the car, stuffing the train of her white gown into the black Ford coupe. "I have a surprise for you, Mrs. Albrecht."

"That sounds wonderful. Both the name and the surprise."

He slid into the driver's seat, and they roared away. He grasped her hand and kissed it. "This has been the best day of my life."

"And of mine. To think that the Lord gave us such a second chance. All of the waiting was worth it."

"Worth every moment."

A little while later, they pulled up to a hangar at a small airfield. "Why are we here?"

"You'll see." He helped her from the car and led her across the tarmac to a private plane.

She bounced along beside him. "Is it what I think it is?"

"We are not driving to California. We are flying there. Just the two of us."

She squealed. "I love it. A lifetime of adventure with you." And right there, in the middle of the airfield, she kissed her new husband.

Liz Tolsma is a popular speaker and an editor and the owner of Write Direction E‹
ing. An almost-native Wisconsinite, she resides in a quiet corner of the state with
husband and their two daughters. Her son proudly serves as a U.S. Marine. They ado‹
ed all of their children internationally, and one has special needs. When she gets a ›
spare minutes, she enjoys reading, relaxing on the front porch, walking, working in ›
large perennial garden, and camping with her family.